神風

KaMi KaZe

5

士貴智志

SHIKI SATOSHI

Kami-Kaze Volume 5
Created by Satoshi Shiki

Translation - Ray Yoshimoto
English Adaptation - Luis Reyes
Retouch and Lettering - Star Print Brokers
Production Artist - Jessica R. Yurasek
Graphic Designer - Louis Csontos

Editor - Tim Beedle
Digital Imaging Manager - Chris Buford
Pre-Production Supervisor - Erika Terriquez
Art Director - Anne Marie Horne
Production Manager - Elisabeth Brizzi
Managing Editor - Vy Nguyen
VP of Production - Ron Klamert
Editor-in-Chief - Rob Tokar
Publisher - Mike Kiley
President and C.O.O. - John Parker
C.E.O. and Chief Creative Officer - Stuart Levy

A  Manga

TOKYOPOP and 🌑 are trademarks or registered trademarks of TOKYOPOP Inc.

TOKYOPOP Inc.
5900 Wilshire Blvd. Suite 2000
Los Angeles, CA 90036

E-mail: info@TOKYOPOP.com
Come visit us online at www.TOKYOPOP.com

ISBN: 978-1-59532-928-8

First TOKYOPOP printing: June 2007
10 9 8 7 6 5 4 3 2 1
Printed in the USA

KAMI·KAZE™

Volume 5

By Satoshi Shiki

HAMBURG // LONDON // LOS ANGELES // TOKYO

KAMI·KAZE ™

Imprisoned for a thousand years, the Eighty-Eight beasts seek resurrection from their world so that they can unleash their wrath upon present-day Japan, aided by a race of young elemental warriors known as the Kegai no Tami. Mikogami Misao and Ishigami Kamuro, two Kegai no Tami who have not forgotten the race's initial purpose of saving mankind from the beasts, are all that stand in their way. It is the blood of the five Kegai no Tami that is necessary to free the Eighty-Eight beasts from their capacity, and already the blood of three Kegai no Tami warriors has spilled, unlocking three of the powerful "torii" gates that imprison the beasts. With two gates remaining, the Gate of Water and the Gate of Sky, it would seem as if the destruction of the human race is now only a matter of time.

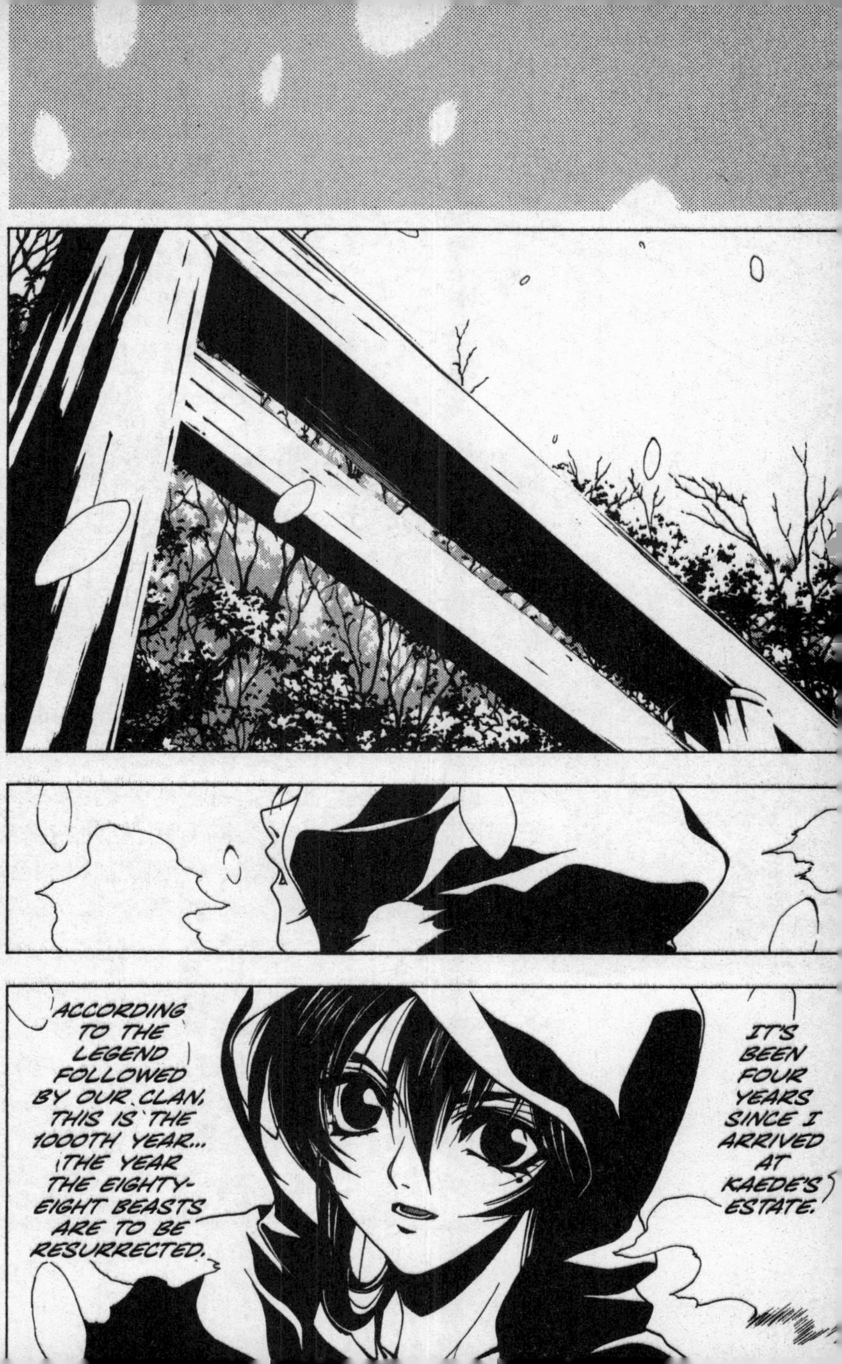
IT'S BEEN FOUR YEARS SINCE I ARRIVED AT KAEDE'S ESTATE.
ACCORDING TO THE LEGEND FOLLOWED BY OUR CLAN, THIS IS THE 1000TH YEAR... THE YEAR THE EIGHTY-EIGHT BEASTS ARE TO BE RESURRECTED.

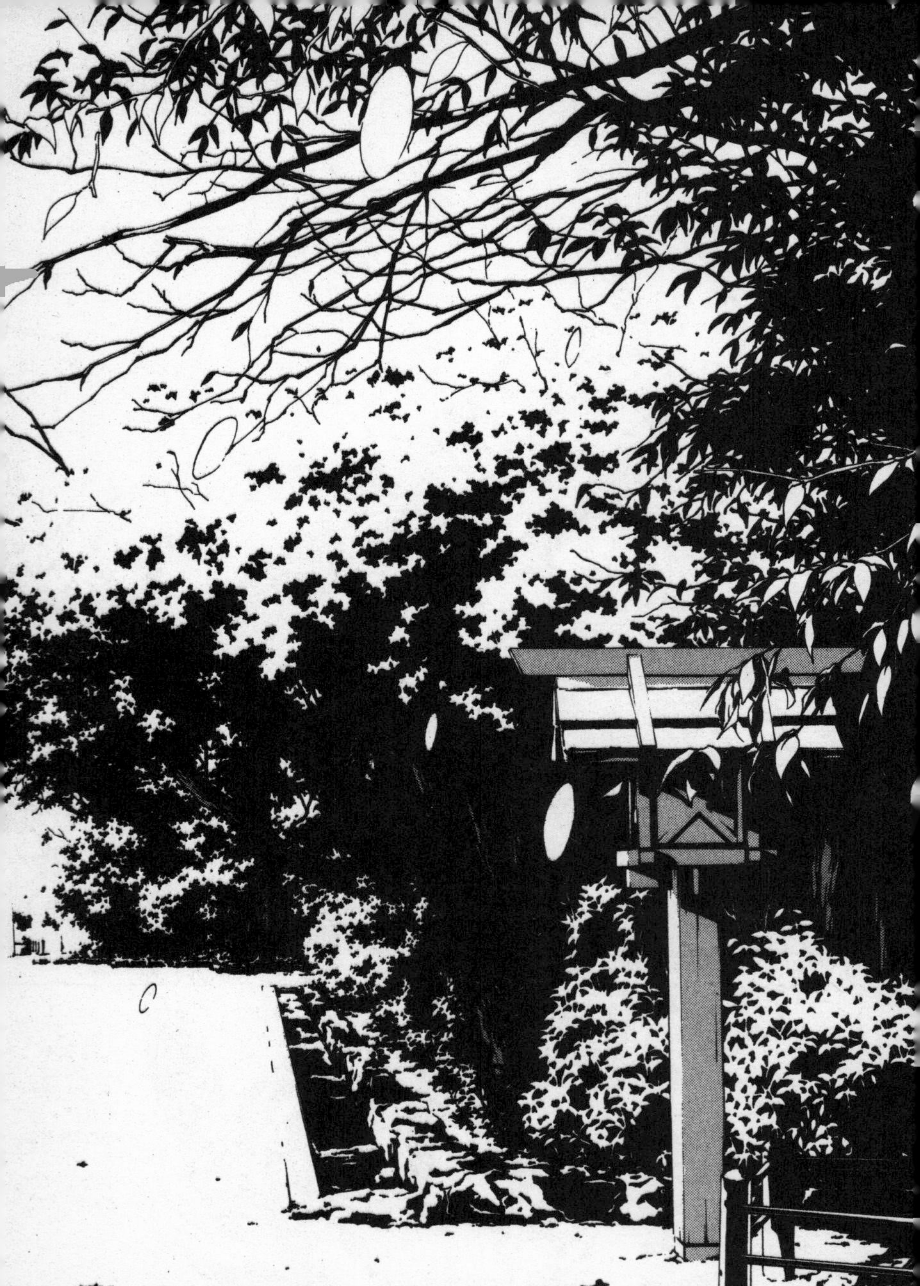

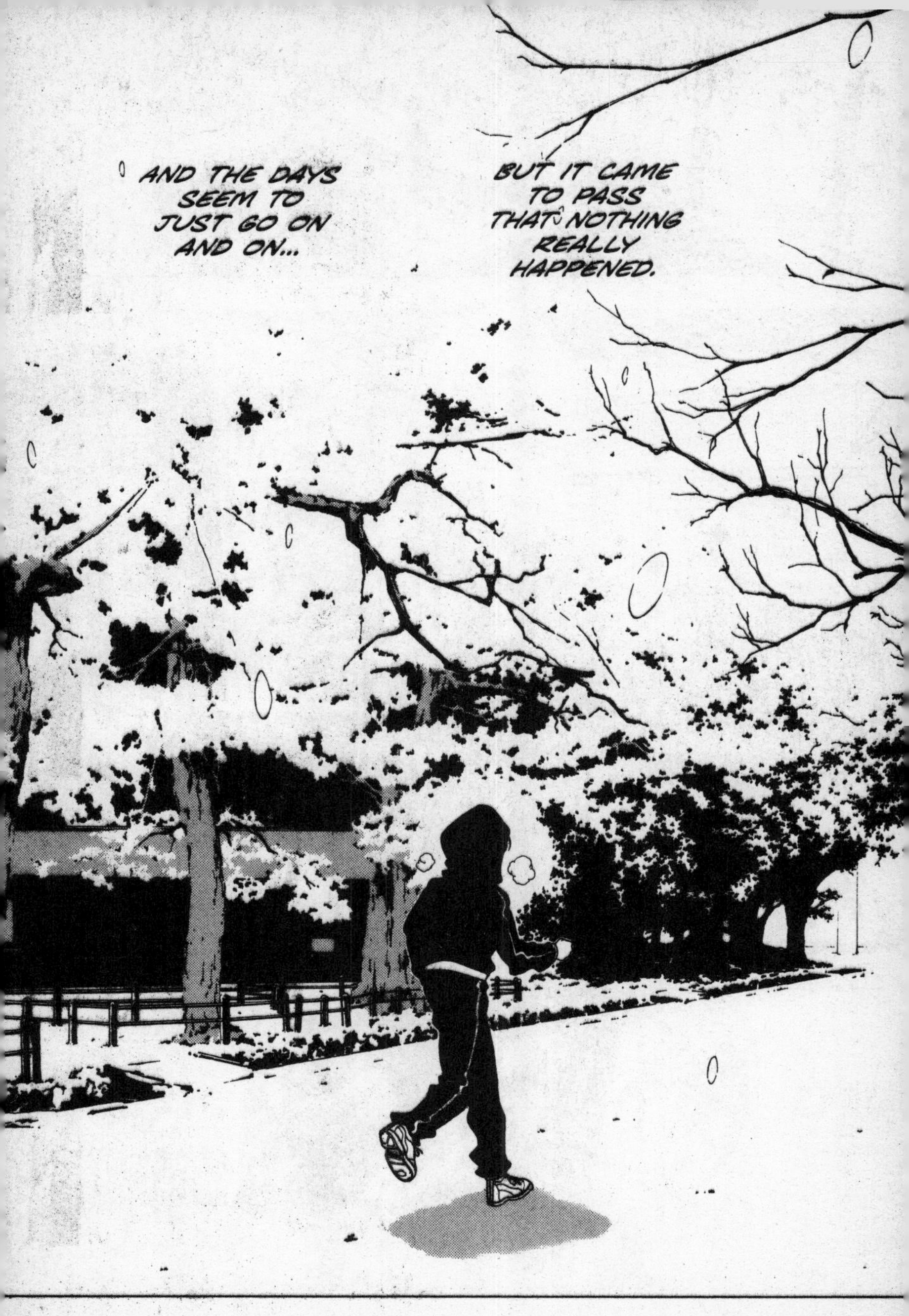
BUT IT CAME TO PASS THAT NOTHING REALLY HAPPENED.
AND THE DAYS SEEM TO JUST GO ON AND ON...

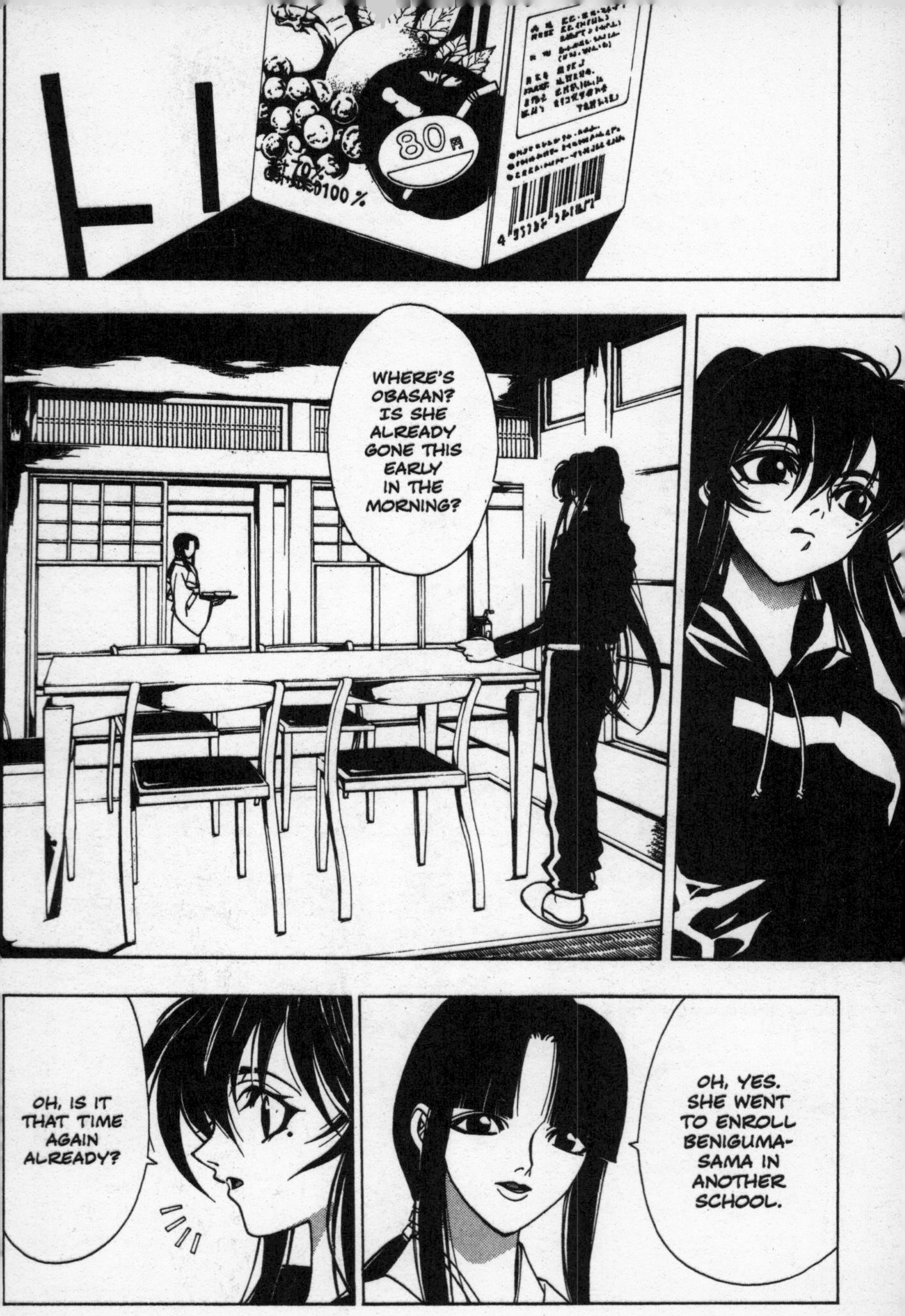
80円
WHERE'S OBASAN? IS SHE ALREADY GONE THIS EARLY IN THE MORNING?
OH, YES. SHE WENT TO ENROLL BENIGUMA-SAMA IN ANOTHER SCHOOL.
OH, IS IT THAT TIME AGAIN ALREADY?

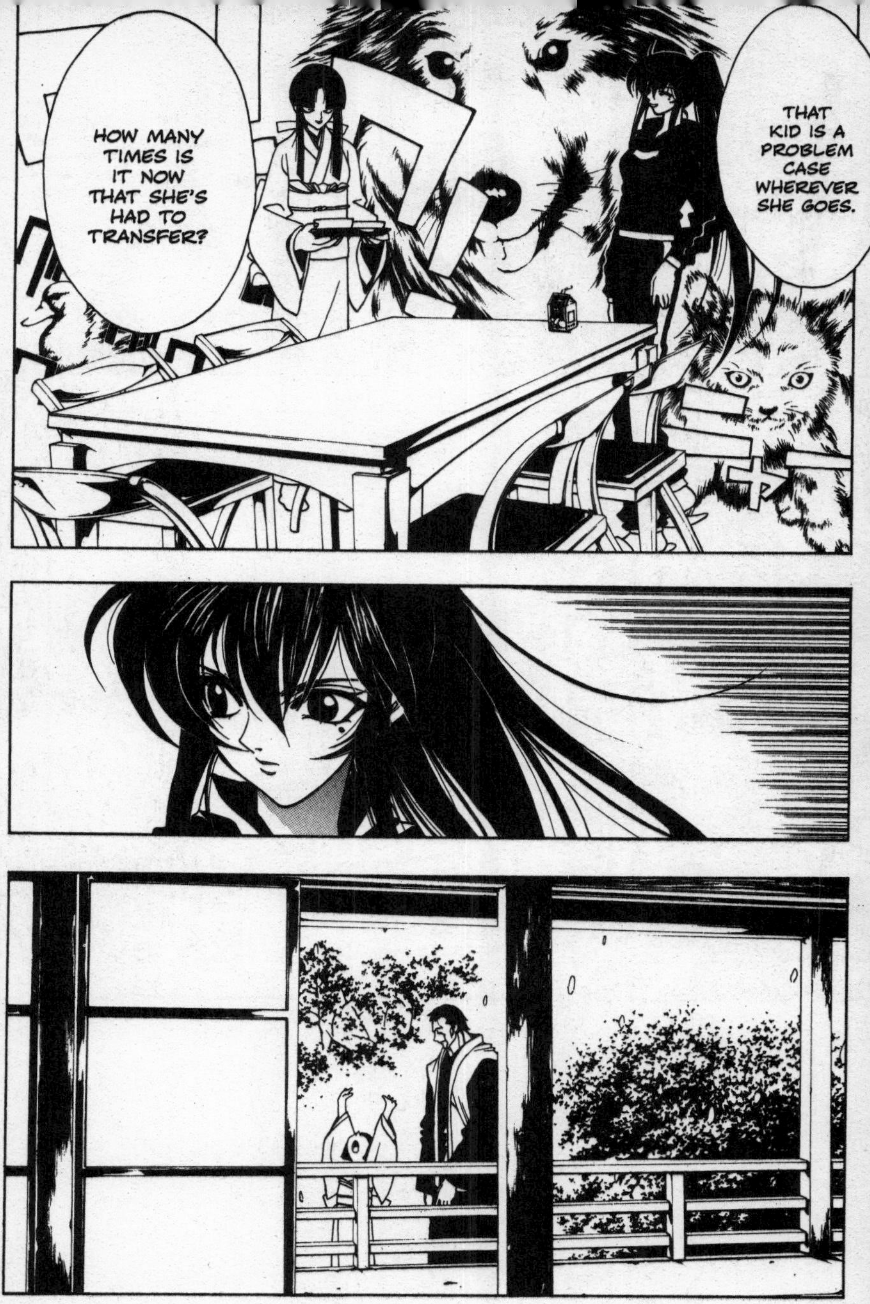
THAT KID IS A PROBLEM CASE WHEREVER SHE GOES.
HOW MANY TIMES IS IT NOW THAT SHE'S HAD TO TRANSFER?

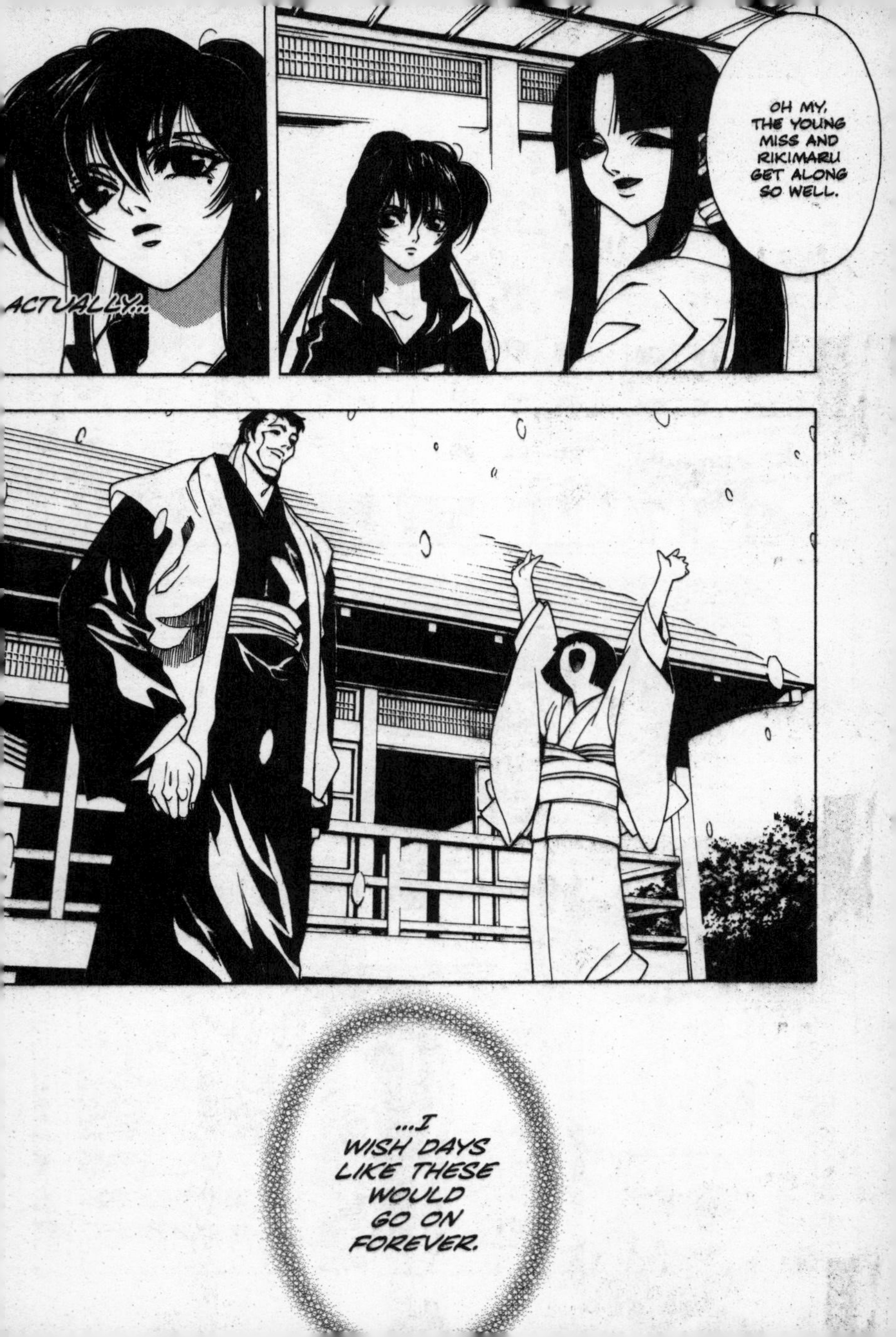
OH MY, THE YOUNG MISS AND RIKIMARU GET ALONG SO WELL.
ACTUALLY...
...I WISH DAYS LIKE THESE WOULD GO ON FOREVER.

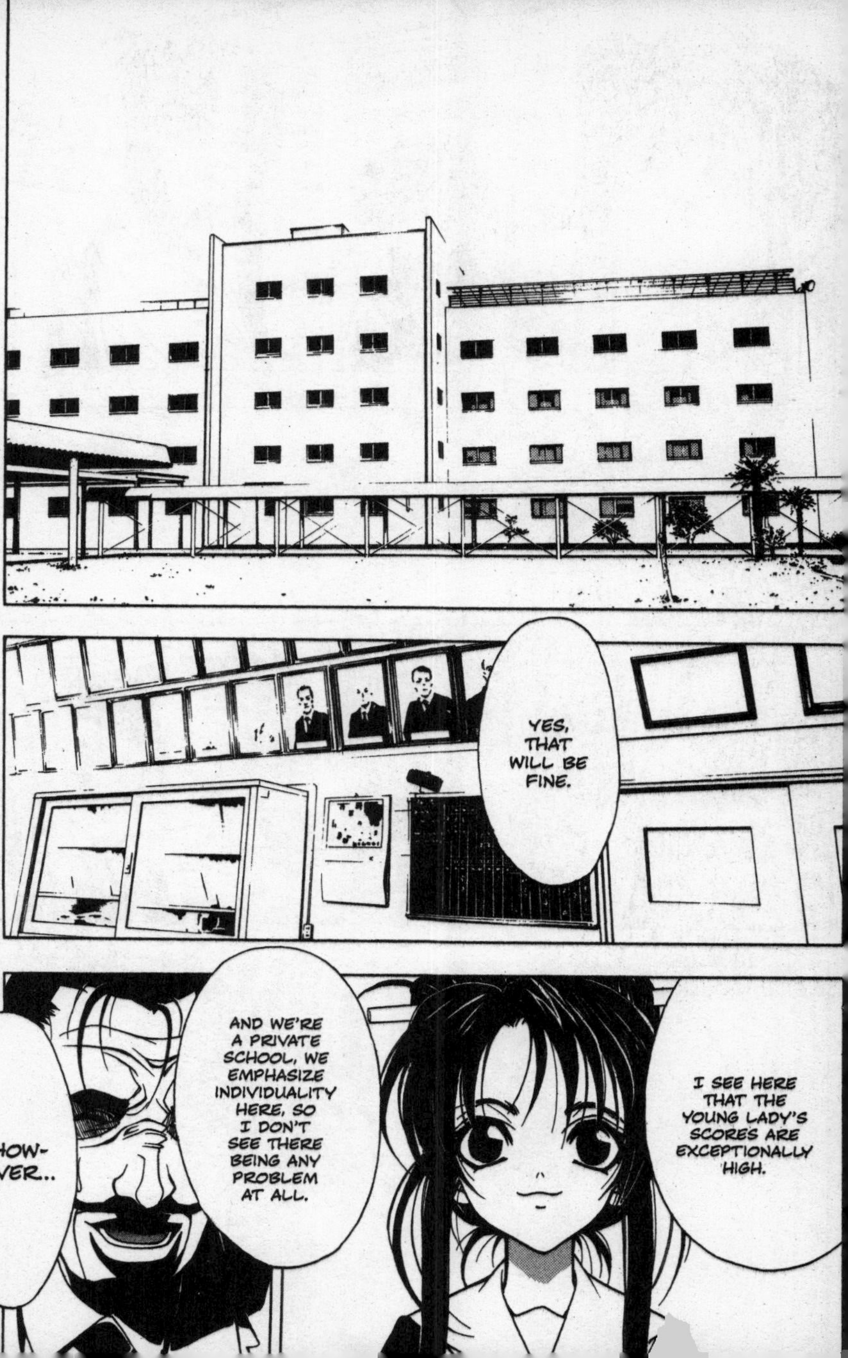
YES, THAT WILL BE FINE.
I SEE HERE THAT THE YOUNG LADY'S SCORES ARE EXCEPTIONALLY HIGH.
AND WE'RE A PRIVATE SCHOOL, WE EMPHASIZE INDIVIDUALITY HERE, SO I DON'T SEE THERE BEING ANY PROBLEM AT ALL.
HOW-EVER...

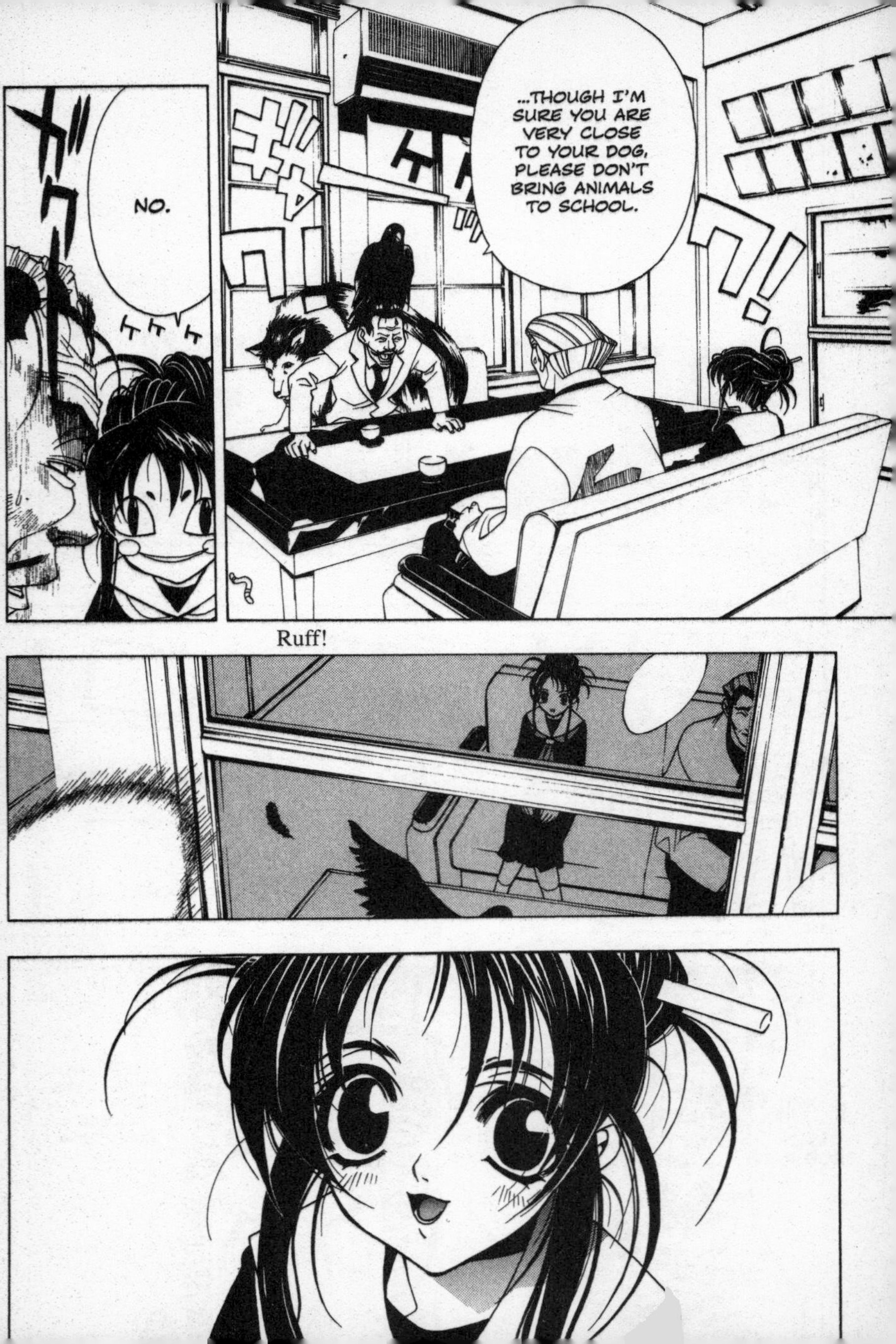
...THOUGH I'M SURE YOU ARE VERY CLOSE TO YOUR DOG, PLEASE DON'T BRING ANIMALS TO SCHOOL.
NO.
Ruff!

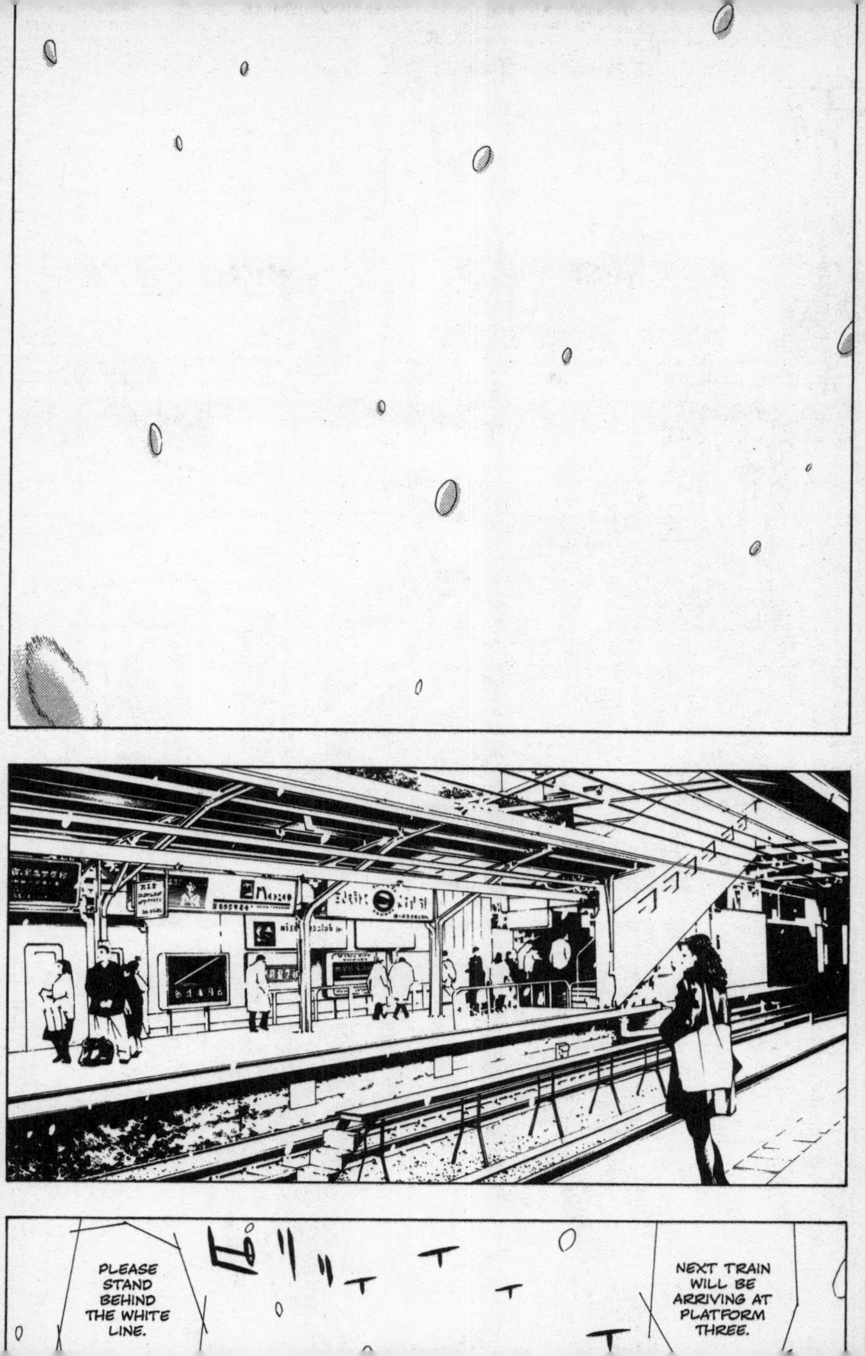
NEXT TRAIN WILL BE ARRIVING AT PLATFORM THREE.
PLEASE STAND BEHIND THE WHITE LINE.

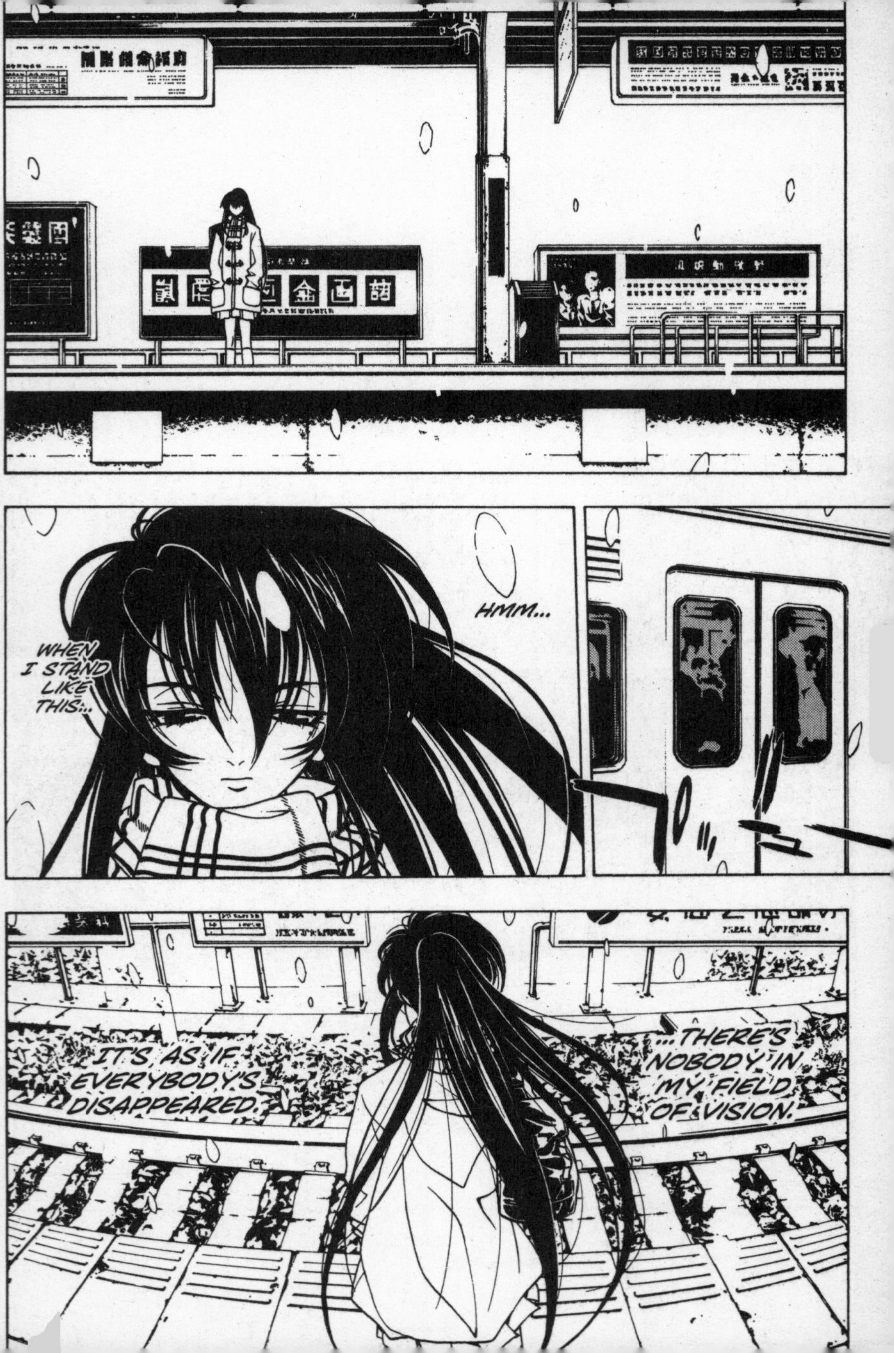
HMM...
WHEN I STAND LIKE THIS...
...THERE'S NOBODY IN MY FIELD OF VISION.
IT'S AS IF EVERYBODY'S DISAPPEARED.

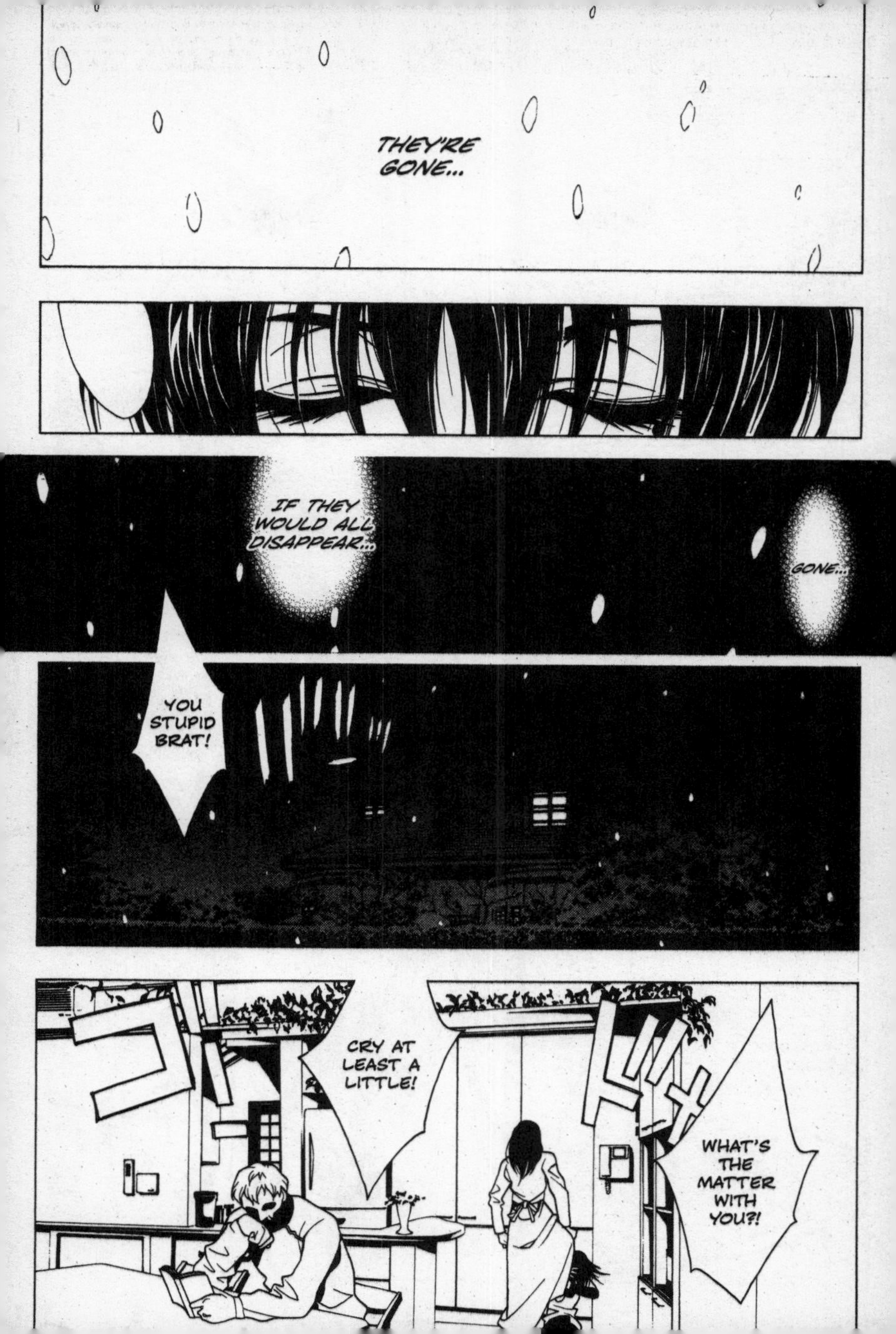
THEY'RE GONE...
GONE...
IF THEY WOULD ALL DISAPPEAR...
YOU STUPID BRAT!
WHAT'S THE MATTER WITH YOU?!
CRY AT LEAST A LITTLE!

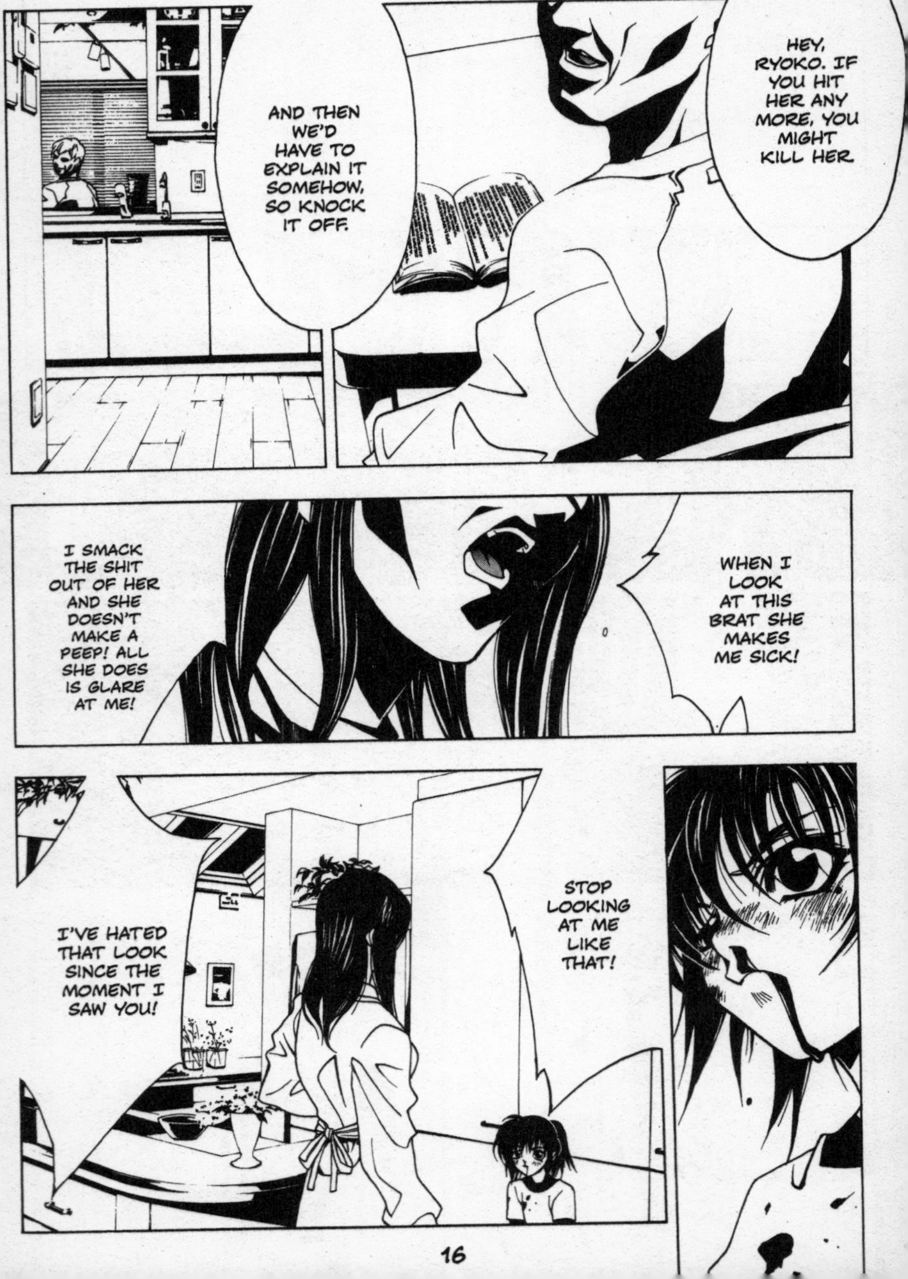
HEY, RYOKO. IF YOU HIT HER ANY MORE, YOU MIGHT KILL HER
AND THEN WE'D HAVE TO EXPLAIN IT SOMEHOW, SO KNOCK IT OFF.
WHEN I LOOK AT THIS BRAT SHE MAKES ME SICK!
I SMACK THE SHIT OUT OF HER AND SHE DOESN'T MAKE A PEEP! ALL SHE DOES IS GLARE AT ME!
STOP LOOKING AT ME LIKE THAT!
I'VE HATED THAT LOOK SINCE THE MOMENT I SAW YOU!

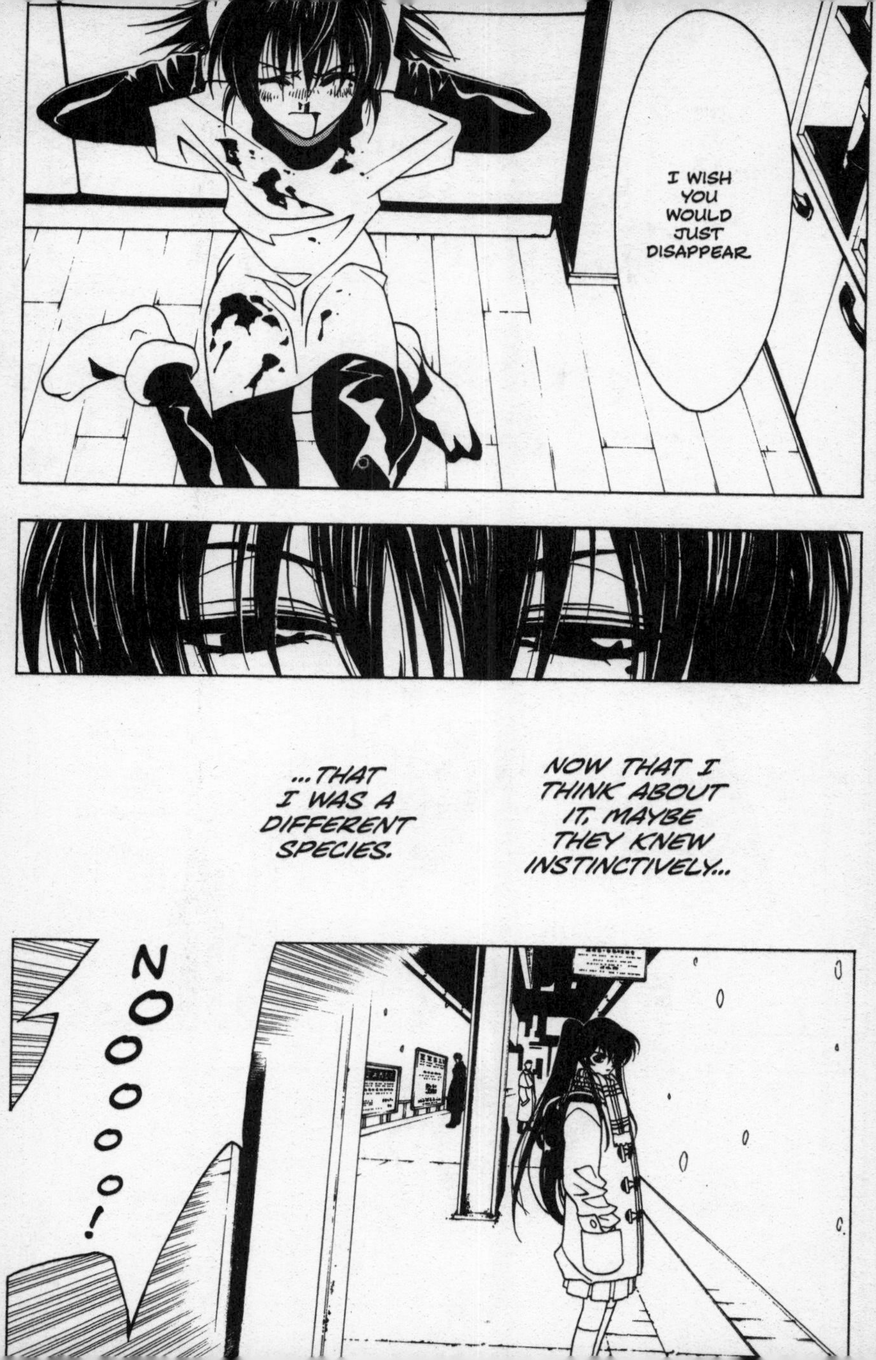
I WISH YOU WOULD JUST DISAPPEAR
NOW THAT I THINK ABOUT IT, MAYBE THEY KNEW INSTINCTIVELY...
...THAT I WAS A DIFFERENT SPECIES.
NOOOOOO!

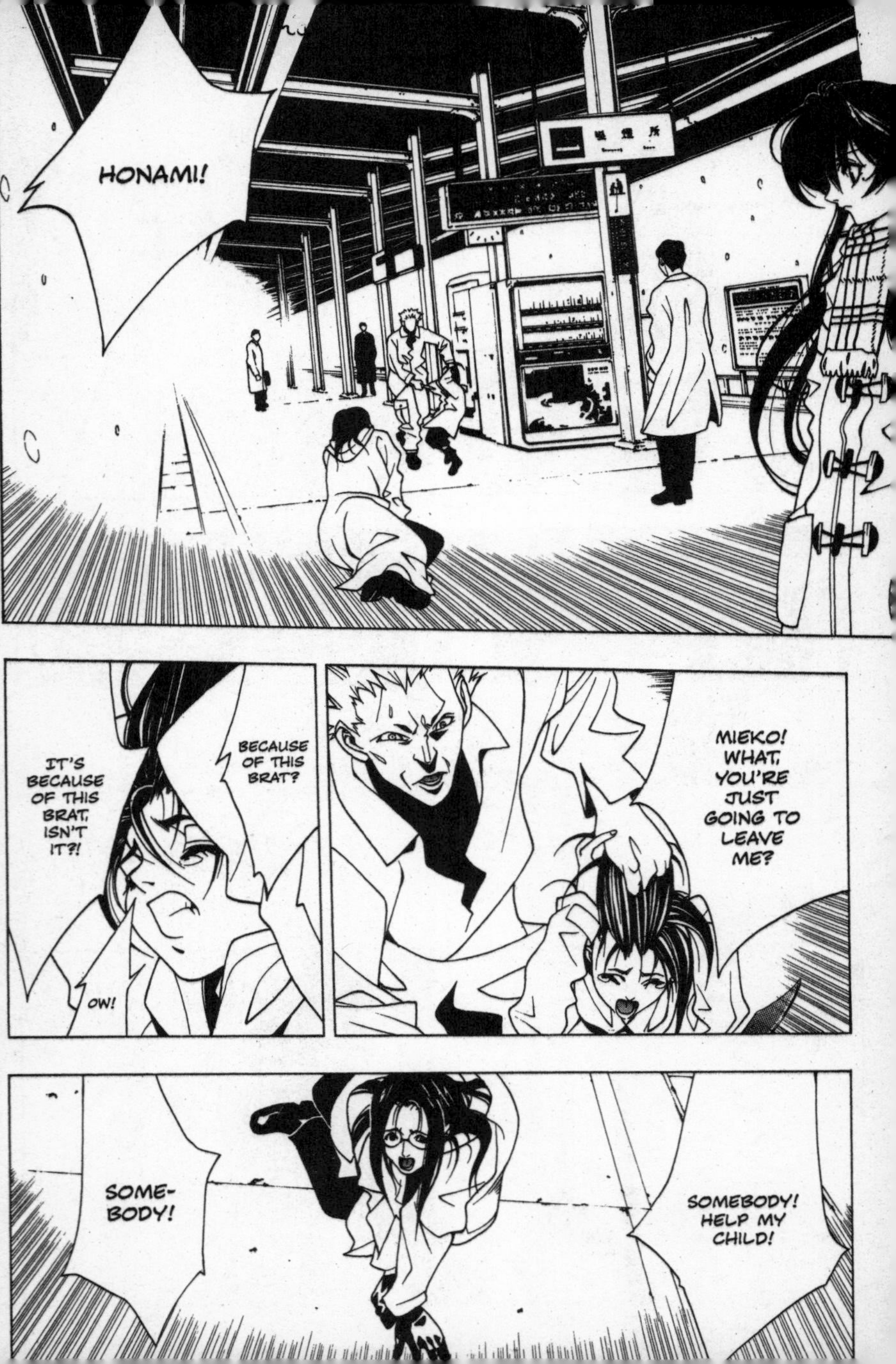
HONAMI!
MIEKO! WHAT, YOU'RE JUST GOING TO LEAVE ME?
BECAUSE OF THIS BRAT?
IT'S BECAUSE OF THIS BRAT, ISN'T IT?!
OW!
SOMEBODY! HELP MY CHILD!
SOME-BODY!

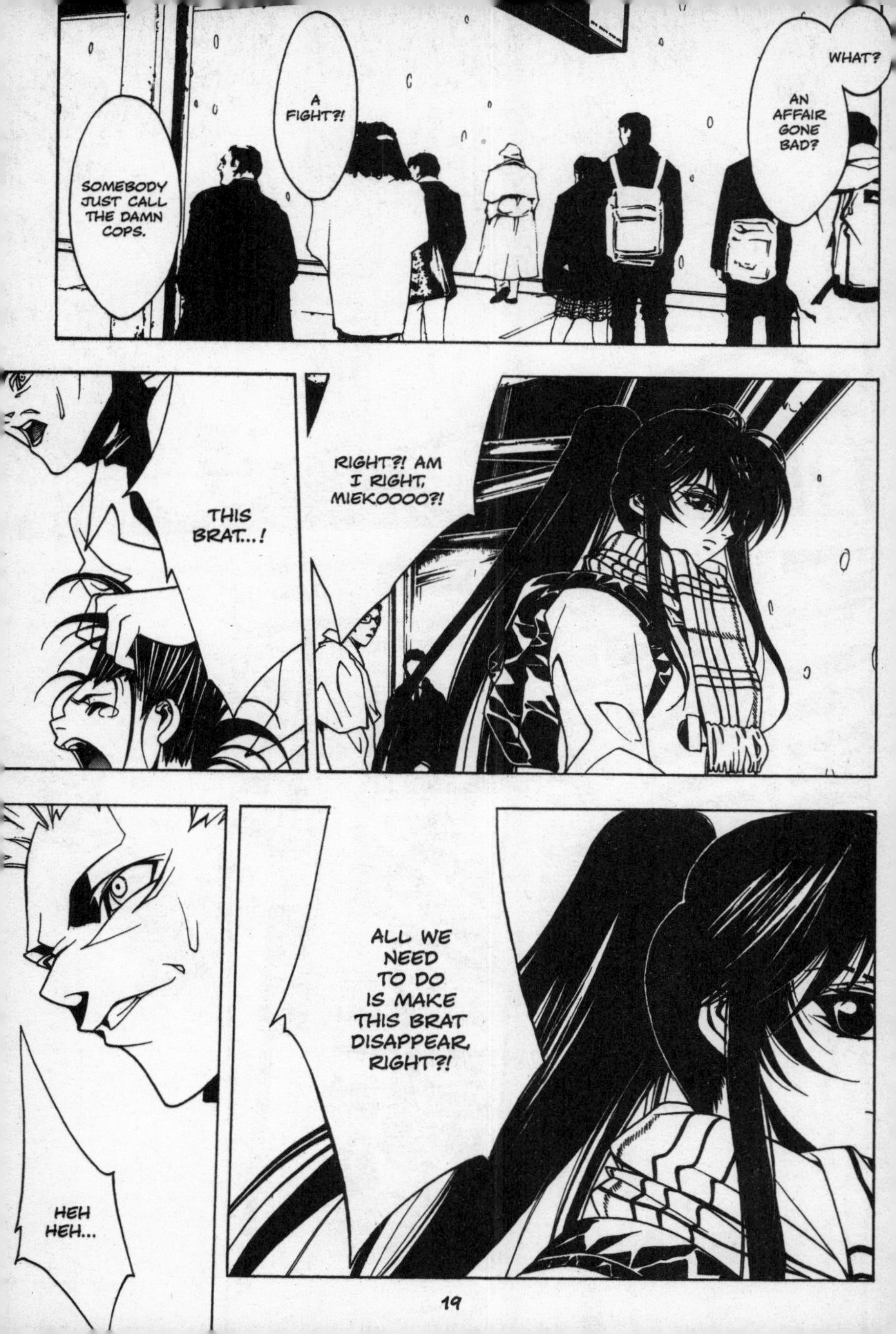
WHAT?
AN AFFAIR GONE BAD?
A FIGHT?!
SOMEBODY JUST CALL THE DAMN COPS.
RIGHT?! AM I RIGHT, MIEKOOOO?!
THIS BRAT...!
ALL WE NEED TO DO IS MAKE THIS BRAT DISAPPEAR, RIGHT?!
HEH HEH...

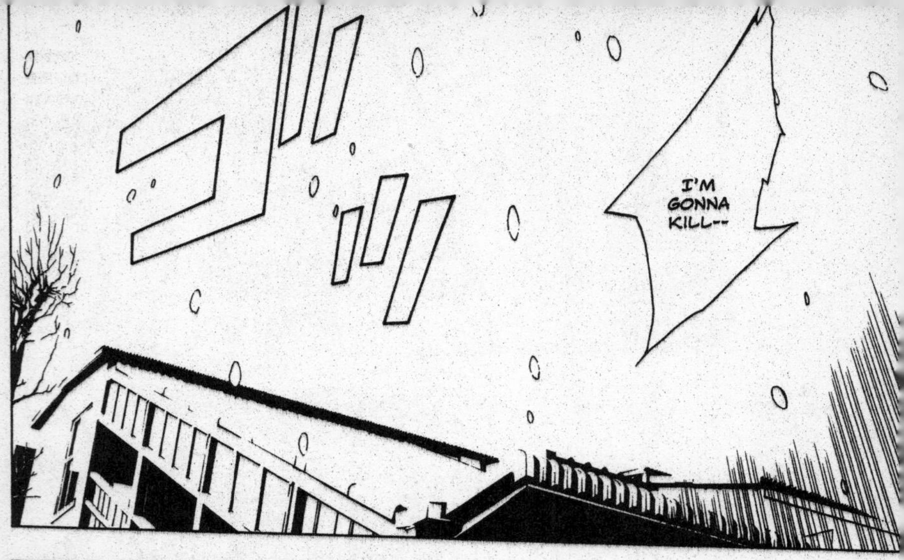
I'M GONNA KILL--

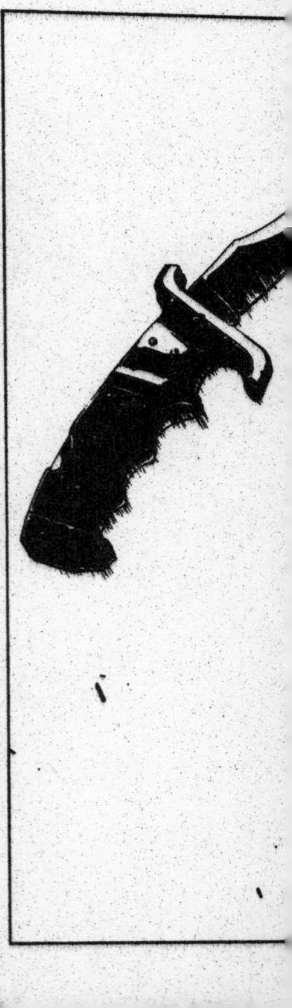

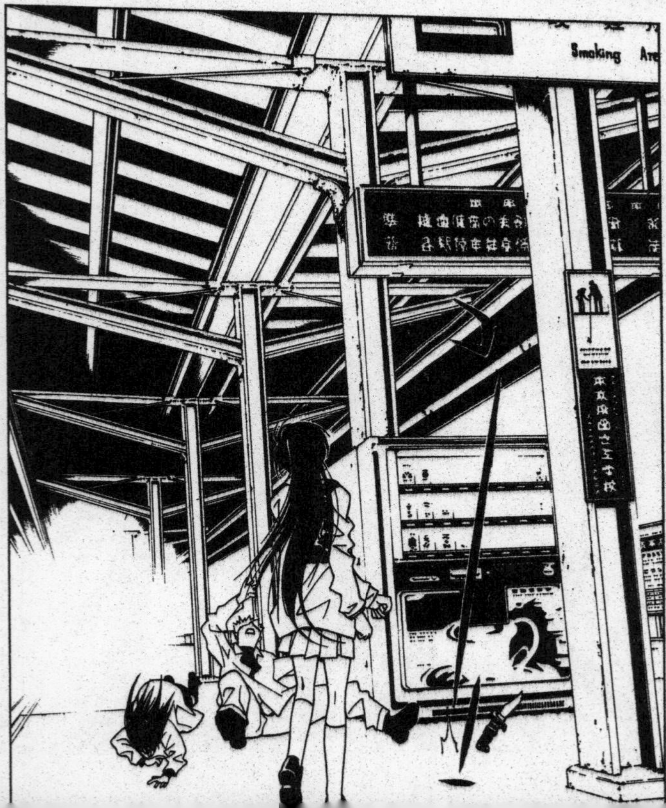
Smoking Are

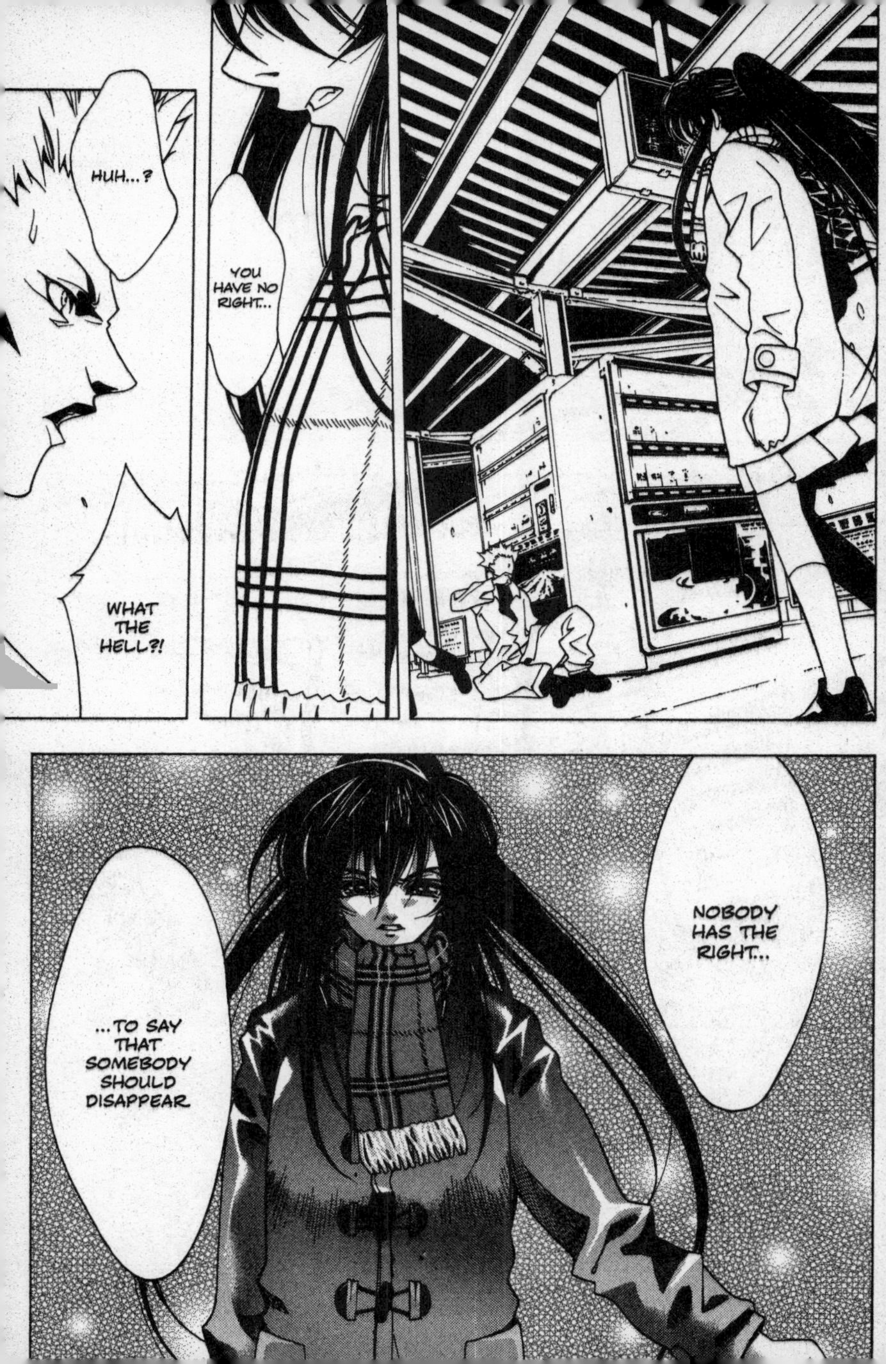
YOU HAVE NO RIGHT...
HUH...?
WHAT THE HELL?!
NOBODY HAS THE RIGHT...
...TO SAY THAT SOMEBODY SHOULD DISAPPEAR

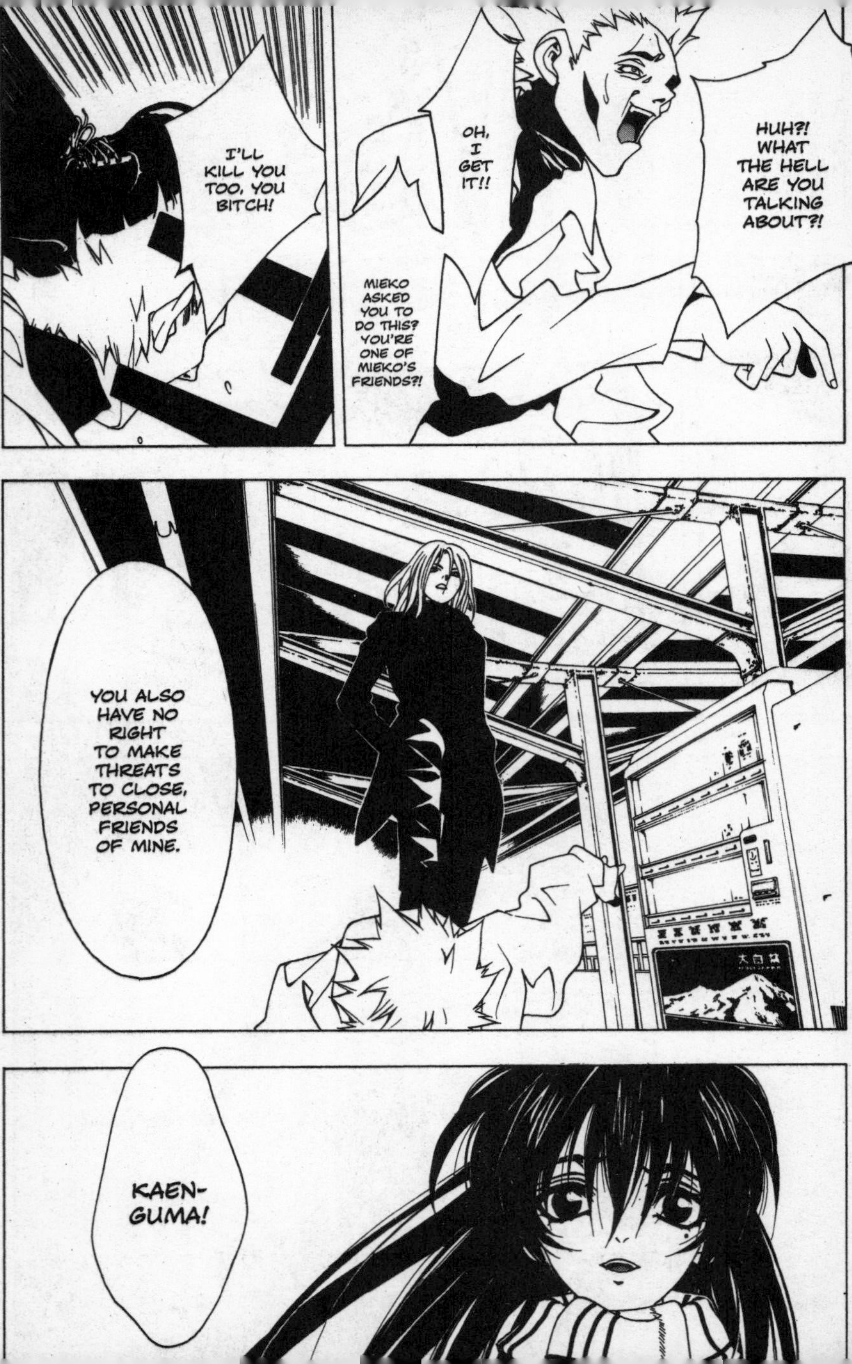
HUH?! WHAT THE HELL ARE YOU TALKING ABOUT?!
OH, I GET IT!!
MIEKO ASKED YOU TO DO THIS? YOU'RE ONE OF MIEKO'S FRIENDS?!
I'LL KILL YOU TOO, YOU BITCH!
YOU ALSO HAVE NO RIGHT TO MAKE THREATS TO CLOSE, PERSONAL FRIENDS OF MINE.
KAEN-GUMA!

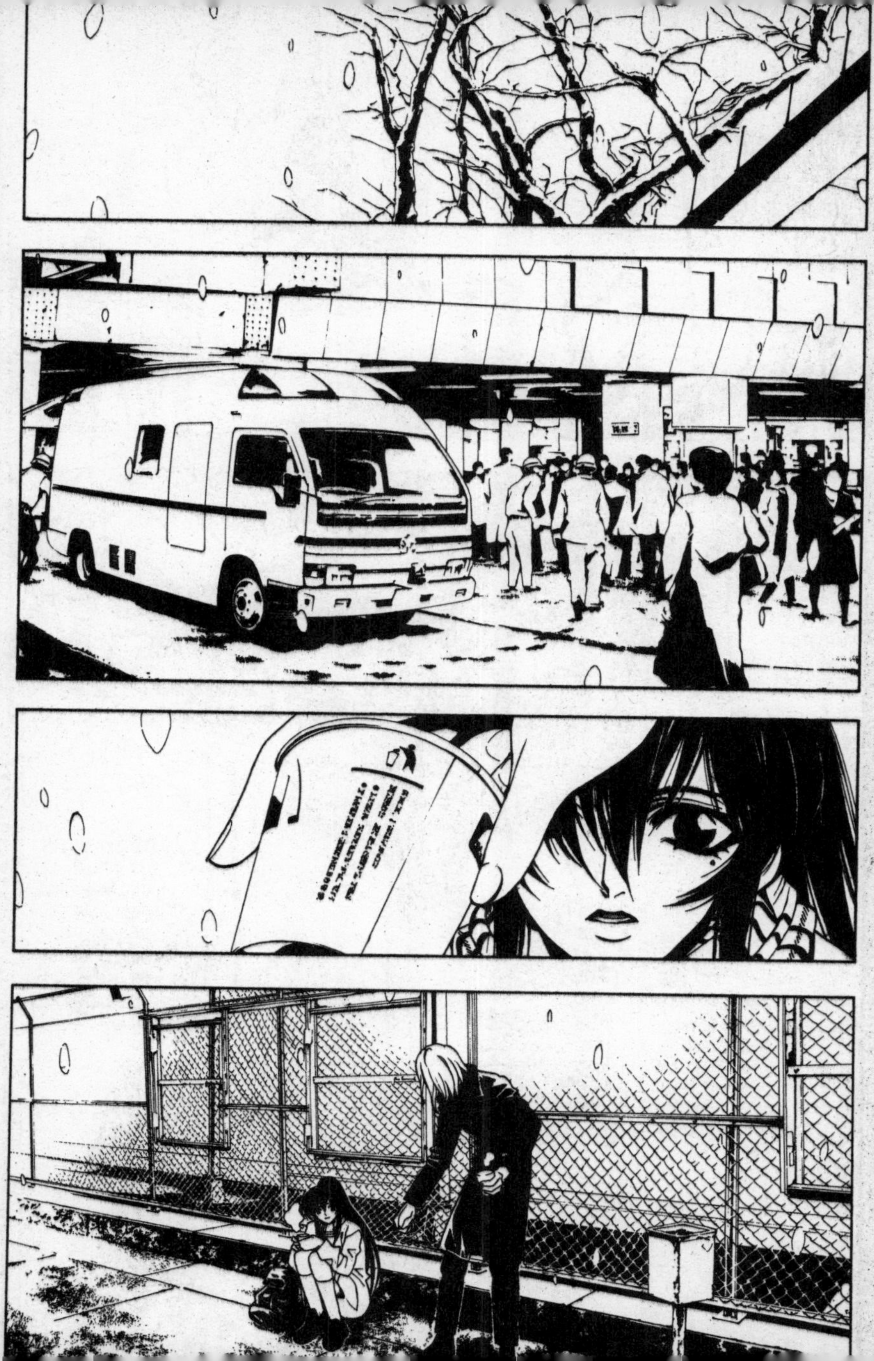

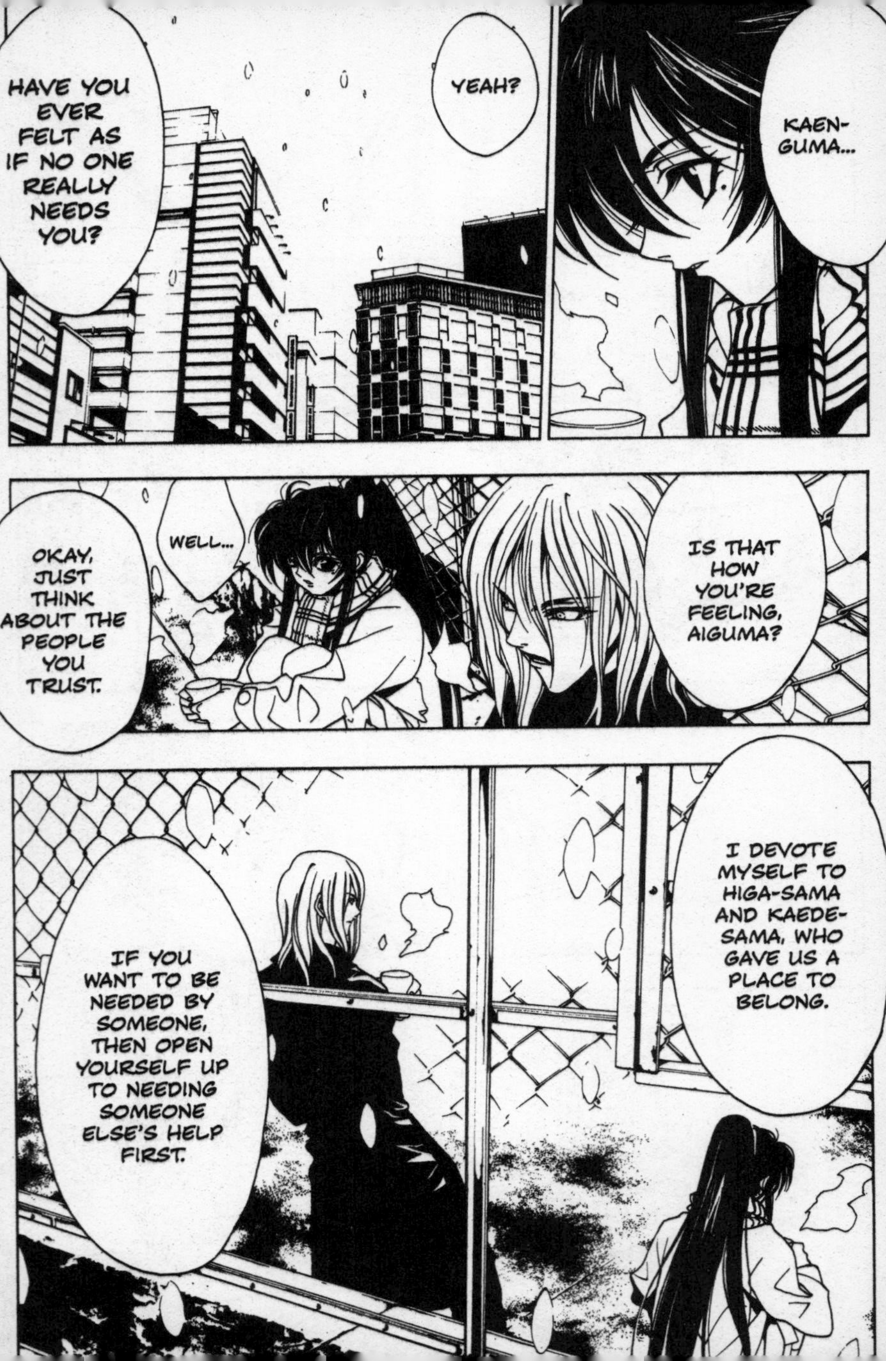
KAEN-GUMA...
YEAH?
HAVE YOU EVER FELT AS IF NO ONE REALLY NEEDS YOU?
IS THAT HOW YOU'RE FEELING, AIGUMA?
WELL...
OKAY, JUST THINK ABOUT THE PEOPLE YOU TRUST.
I DEVOTE MYSELF TO HIGA-SAMA AND KAEDE-SAMA, WHO GAVE US A PLACE TO BELONG.
IF YOU WANT TO BE NEEDED BY SOMEONE, THEN OPEN YOURSELF UP TO NEEDING SOMEONE ELSE'S HELP FIRST.

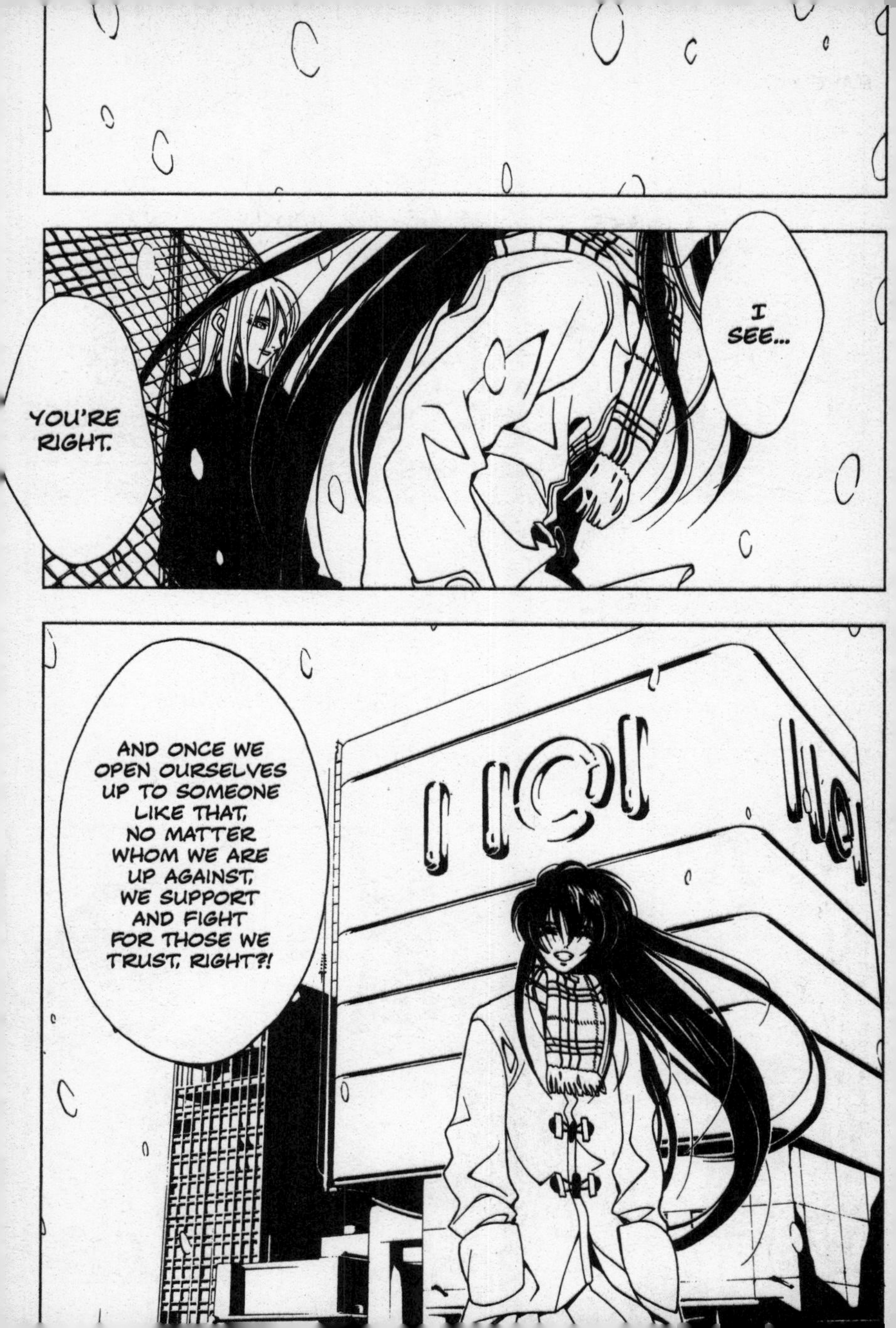
I SEE...
YOU'RE RIGHT.
AND ONCE WE OPEN OURSELVES UP TO SOMEONE LIKE THAT, NO MATTER WHOM WE ARE UP AGAINST, WE SUPPORT AND FIGHT FOR THOSE WE TRUST, RIGHT?!

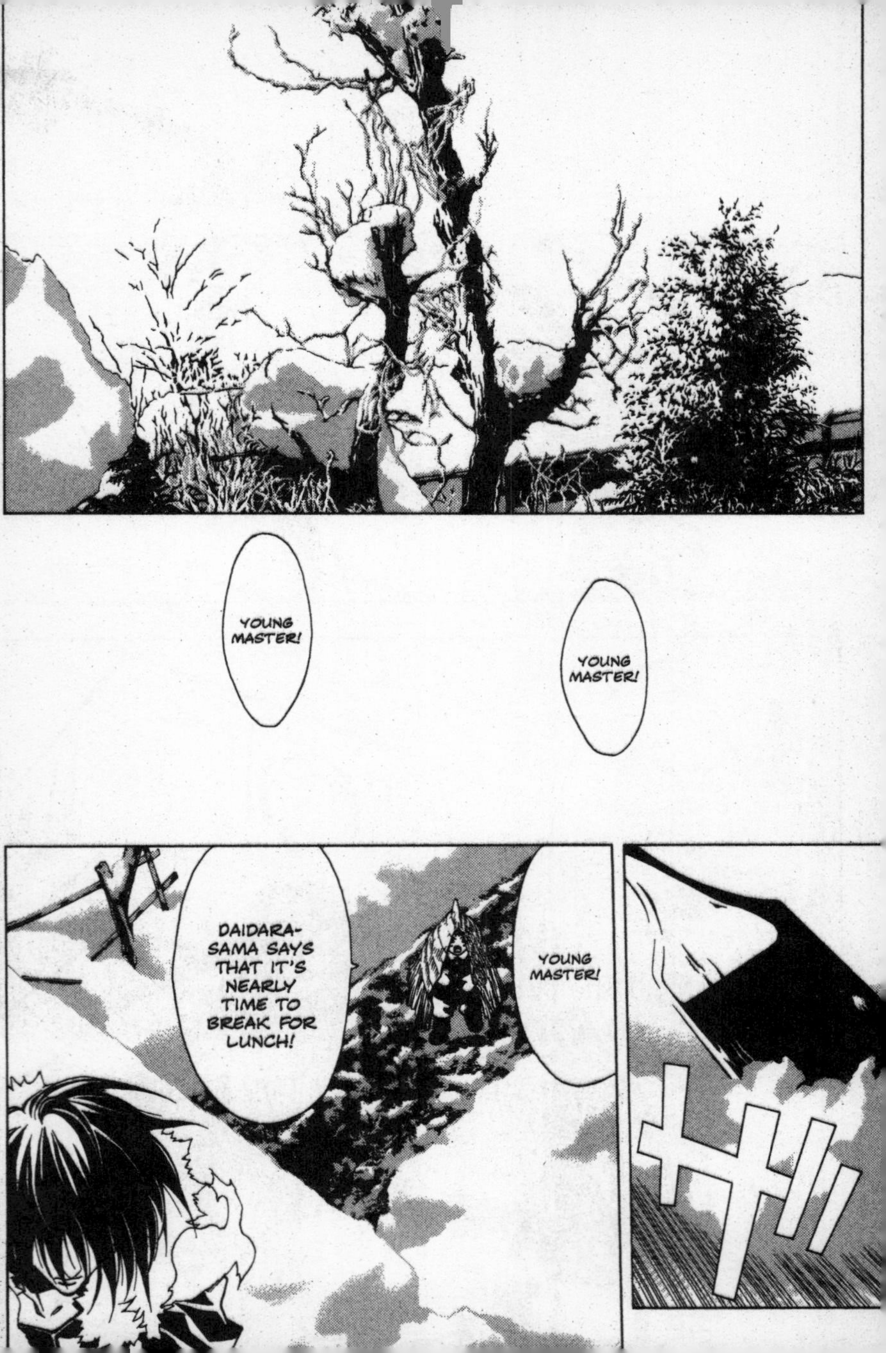
YOUNG MASTER!
YOUNG MASTER!
YOUNG MASTER!
DAIDARA-SAMA SAYS THAT IT'S NEARLY TIME TO BREAK FOR LUNCH!

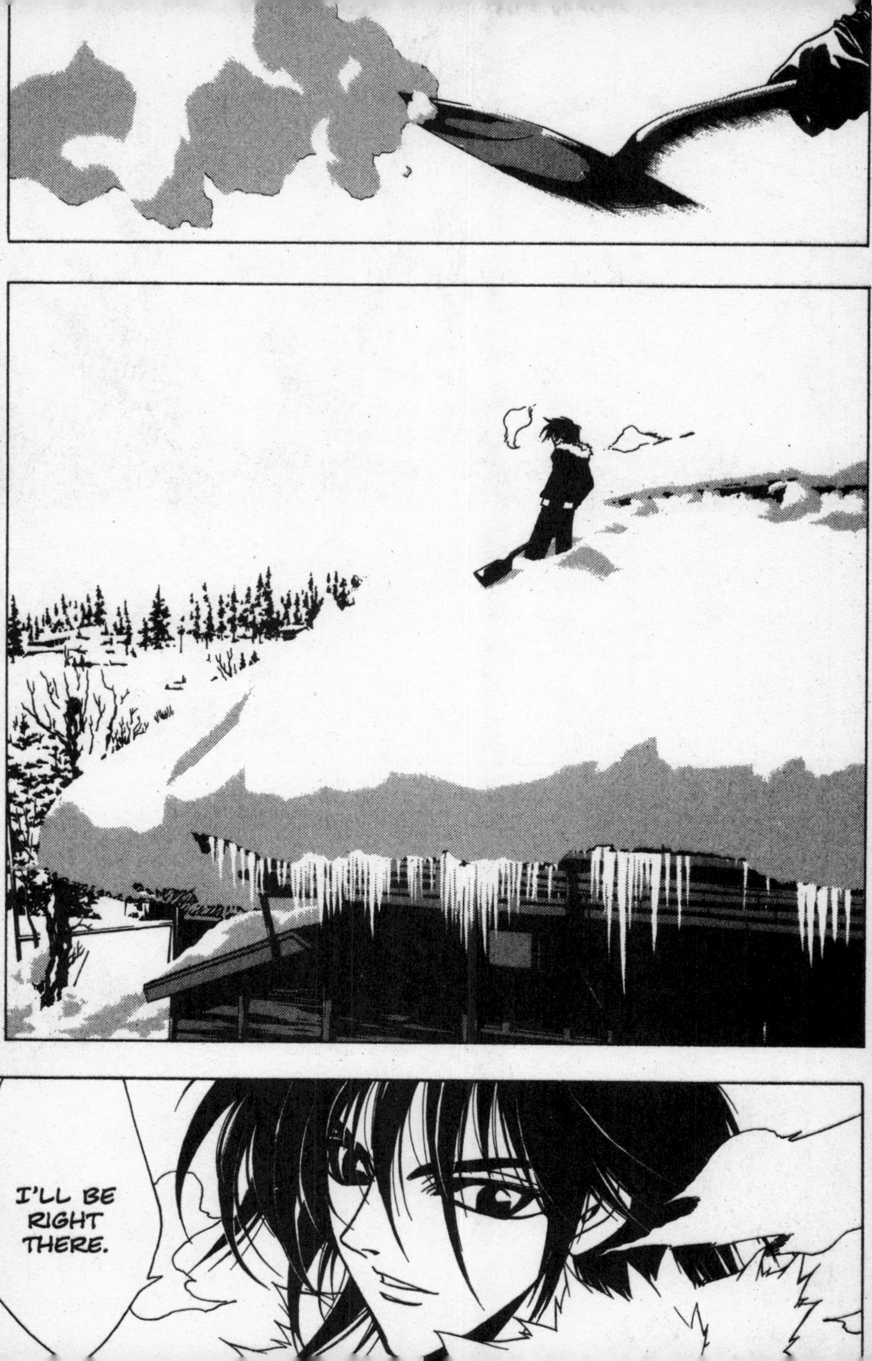
I'LL BE RIGHT THERE.

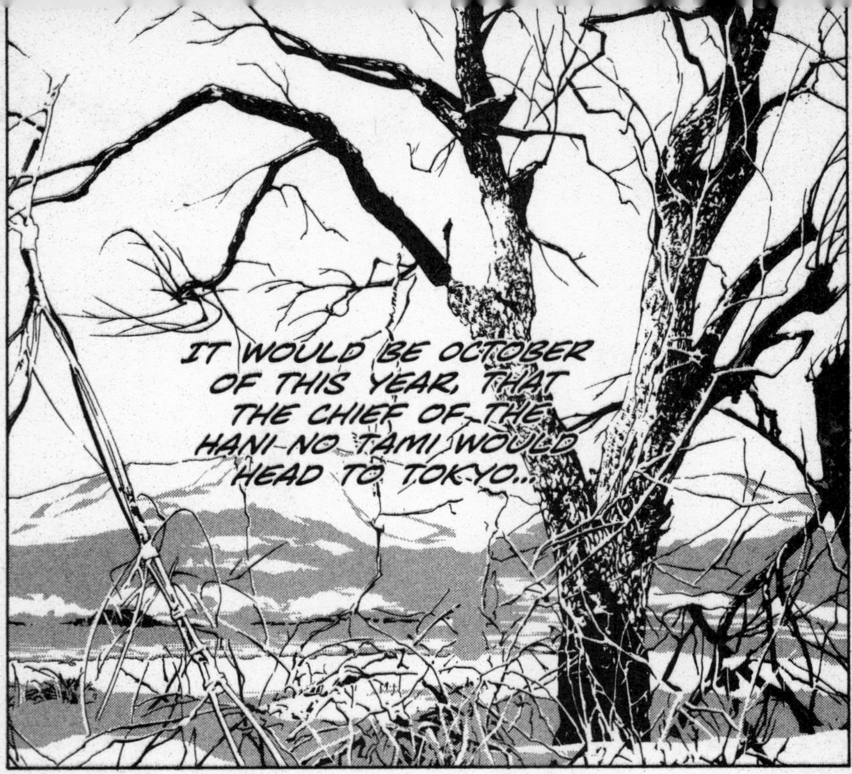
IT WOULD BE OCTOBER OF THIS YEAR, THAT THE CHIEF OF THE HANI-NO TAMI WOULD HEAD TO TOKYO...

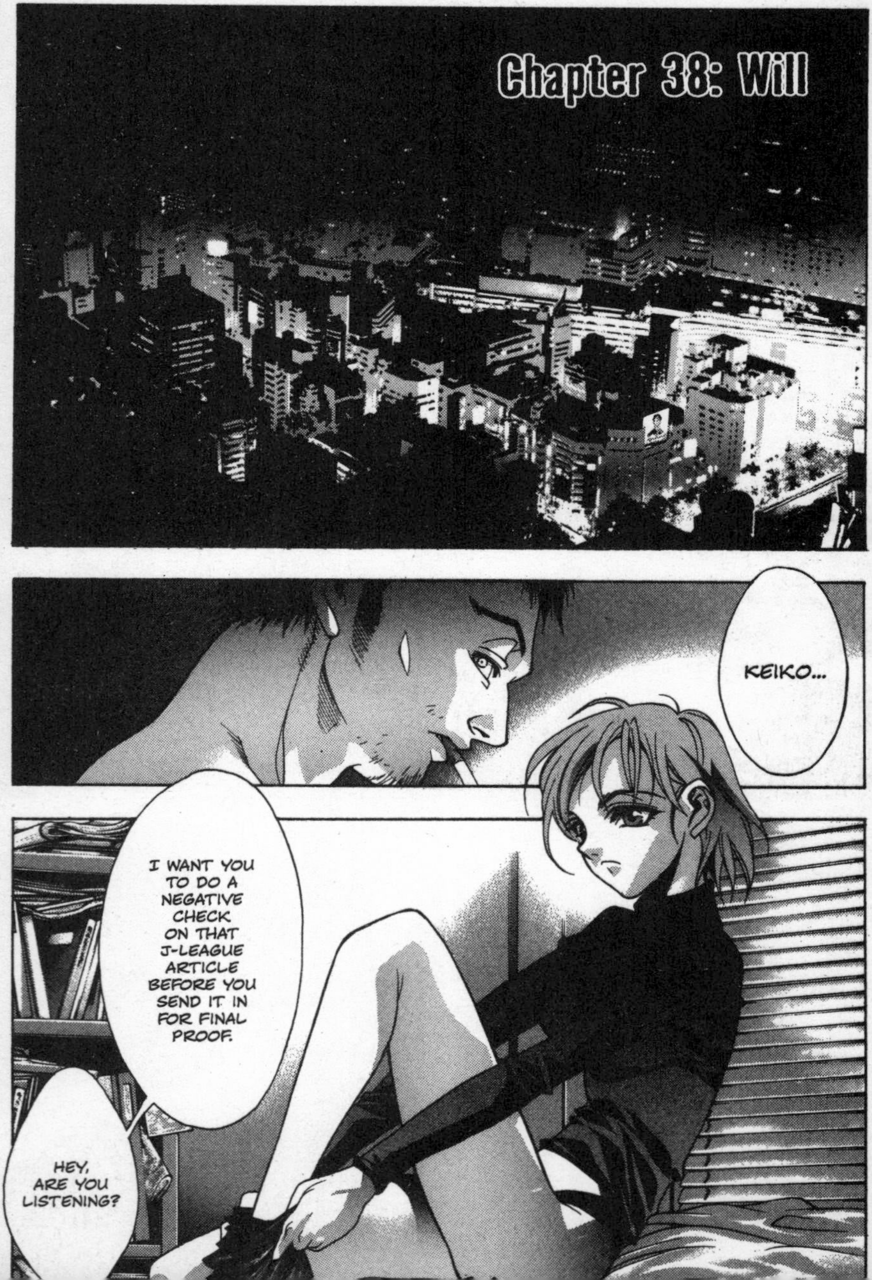
Chapter 38: Will
KEIKO...
I WANT YOU TO DO A NEGATIVE CHECK ON THAT J-LEAGUE ARTICLE BEFORE YOU SEND IT IN FOR FINAL PROOF.
HEY, ARE YOU LISTENING?

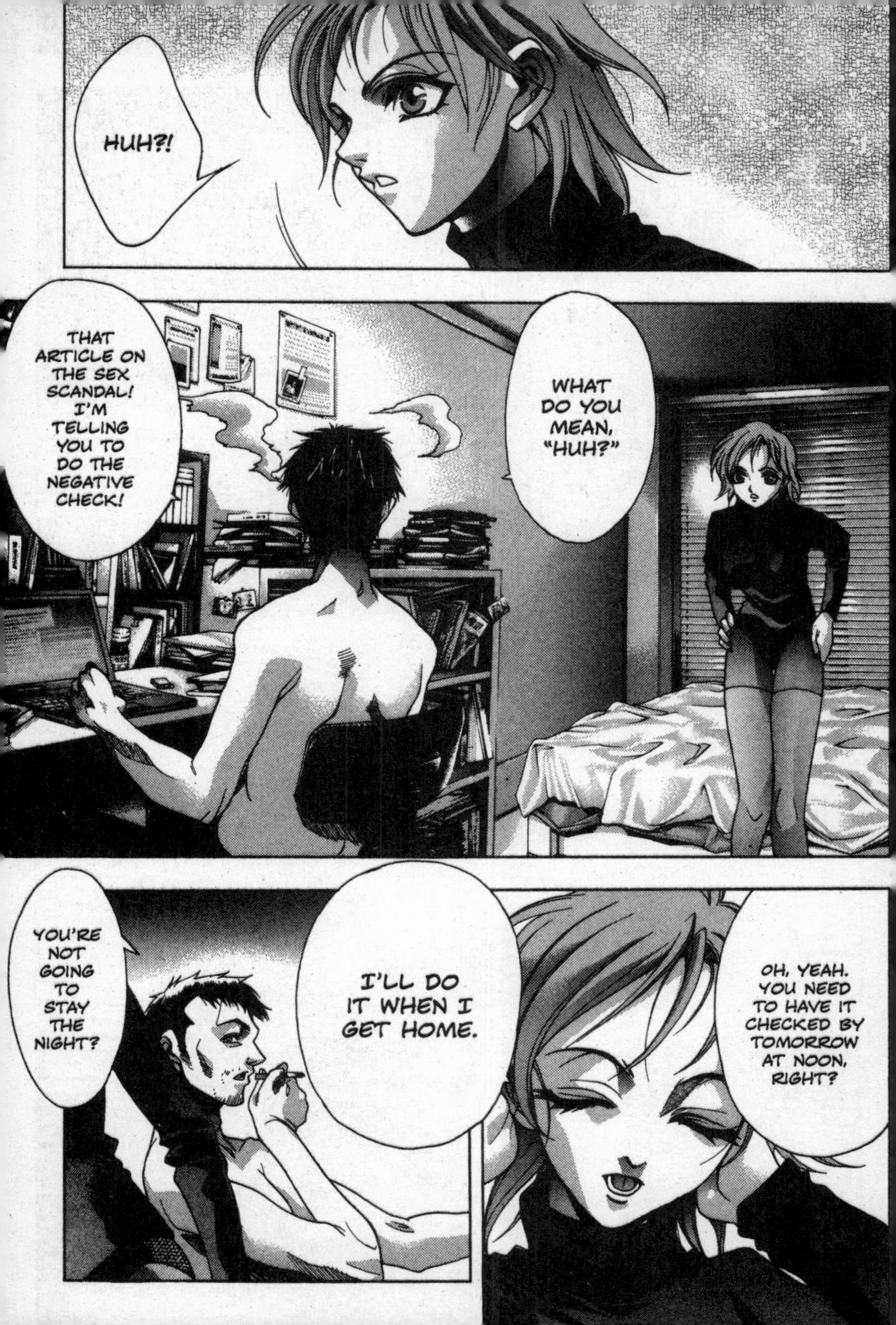
HUH?!
WHAT DO YOU MEAN, "HUH?"
THAT ARTICLE ON THE SEX SCANDAL! I'M TELLING YOU TO DO THE NEGATIVE CHECK!
OH, YEAH. YOU NEED TO HAVE IT CHECKED BY TOMORROW AT NOON, RIGHT?
I'LL DO IT WHEN I GET HOME.
YOU'RE NOT GOING TO STAY THE NIGHT?

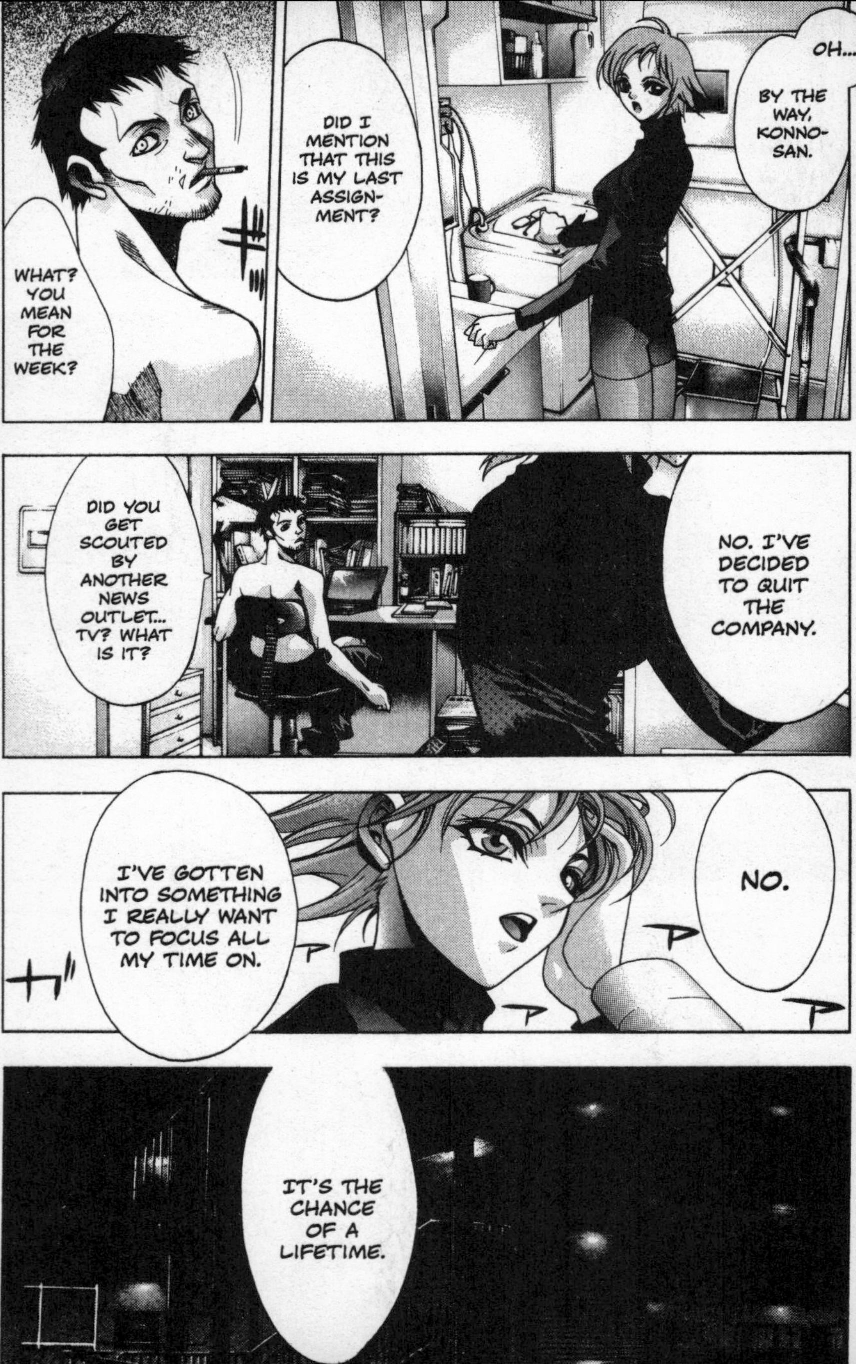
OH...
BY THE WAY, KONNO-SAN.
DID I MENTION THAT THIS IS MY LAST ASSIGNMENT?
WHAT? YOU MEAN FOR THE WEEK?
NO. I'VE DECIDED TO QUIT THE COMPANY.
DID YOU GET SCOUTED BY ANOTHER NEWS OUTLET... TV? WHAT IS IT?
NO.
I'VE GOTTEN INTO SOMETHING I REALLY WANT TO FOCUS ALL MY TIME ON.
IT'S THE CHANCE OF A LIFETIME.

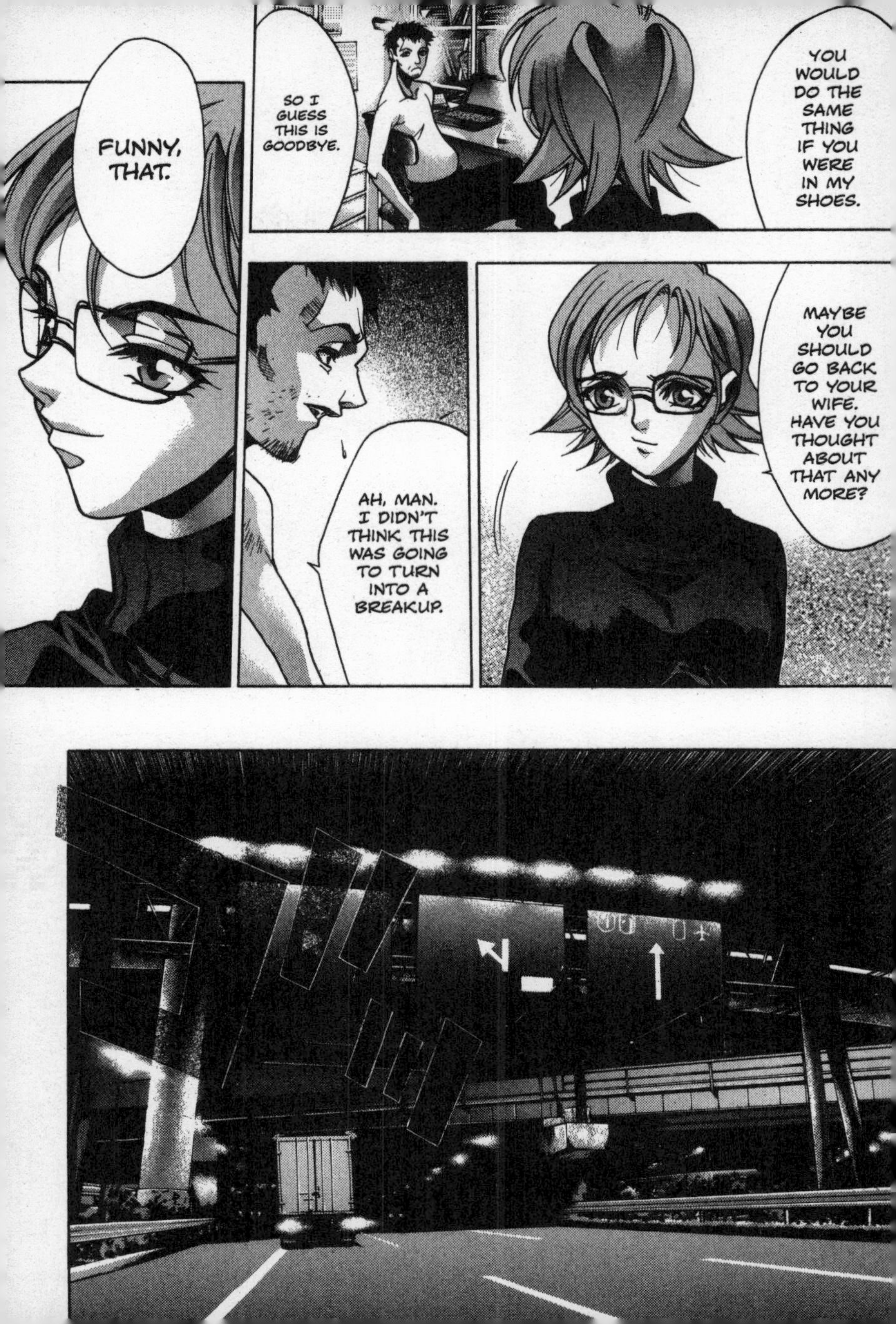
YOU WOULD DO THE SAME THING IF YOU WERE IN MY SHOES.
SO I GUESS THIS IS GOODBYE.
MAYBE YOU SHOULD GO BACK TO YOUR WIFE. HAVE YOU THOUGHT ABOUT THAT ANY MORE?
AH, MAN. I DIDN'T THINK THIS WAS GOING TO TURN INTO A BREAKUP.
FUNNY, THAT.

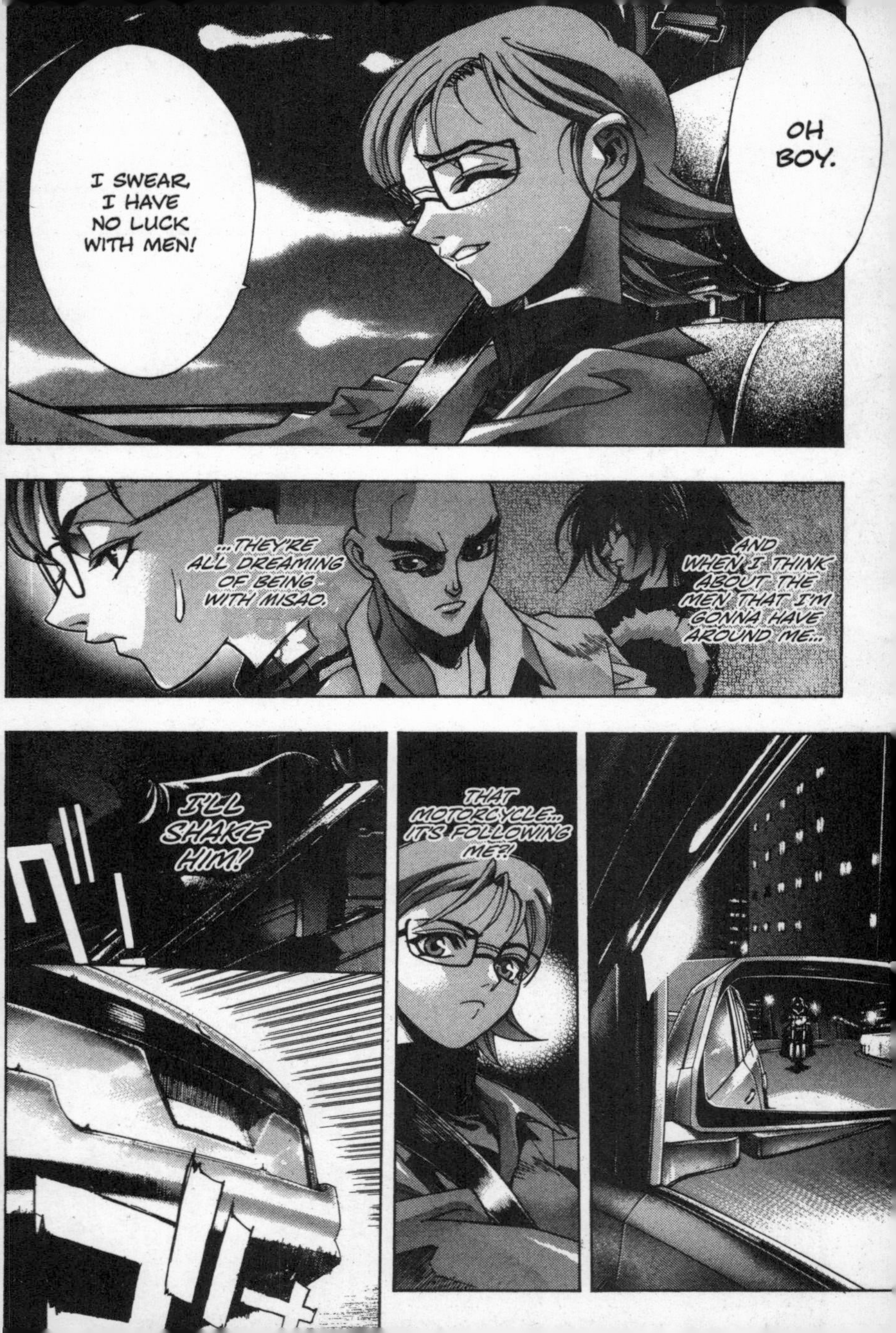
OH BOY.
I SWEAR, I HAVE NO LUCK WITH MEN!
AND WHEN I THINK ABOUT THE MEN THAT I'M GONNA HAVE AROUND ME...
...THEY'RE ALL DREAMING OF BEING WITH MISAO.
THAT MOTORCYCLE... IT'S FOLLOWING ME?!
I'LL SHAKE HIM!

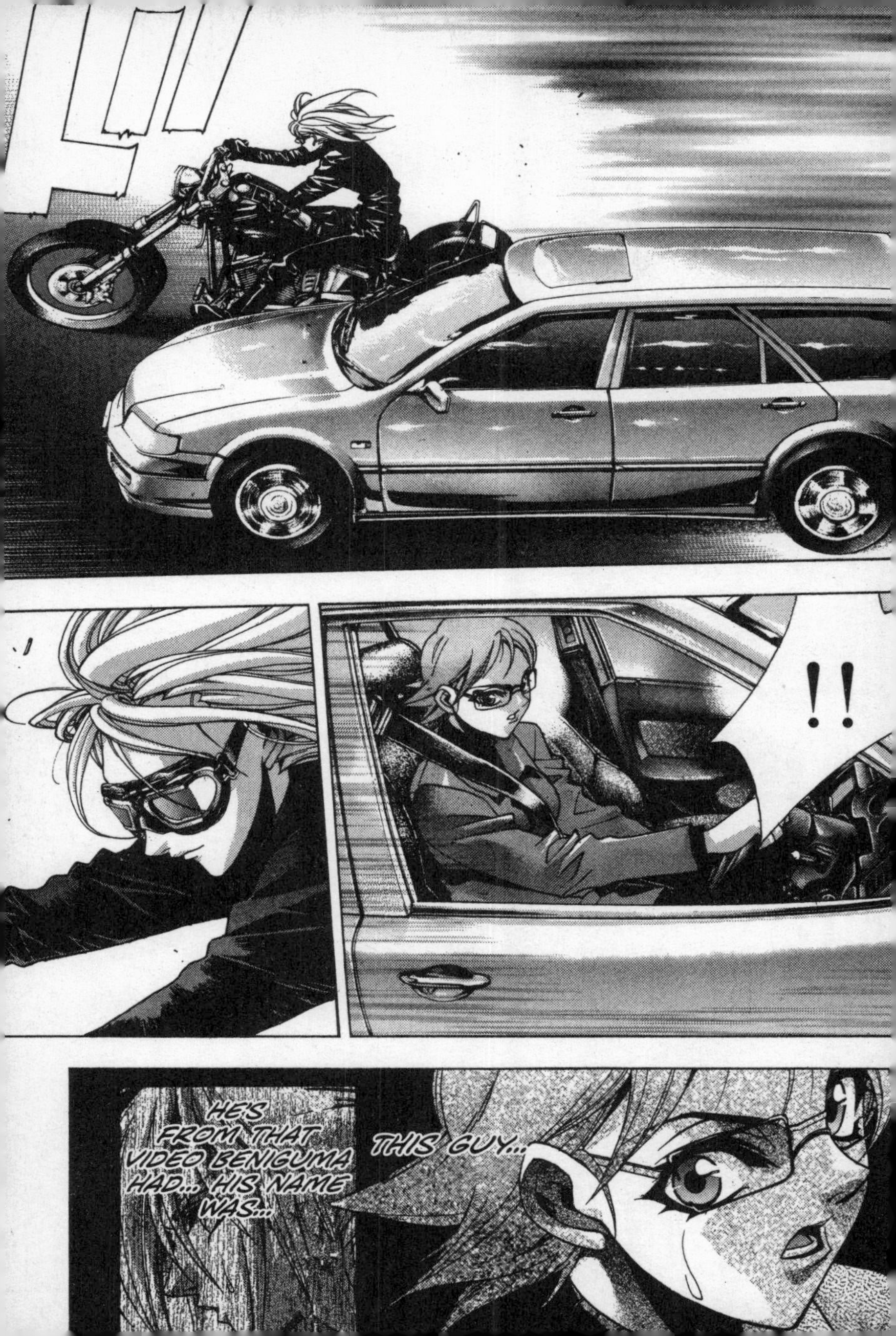
!!
THIS GUY...
HE'S FROM THAT VIDEO BENIGUMA HAD... HIS NAME WAS...

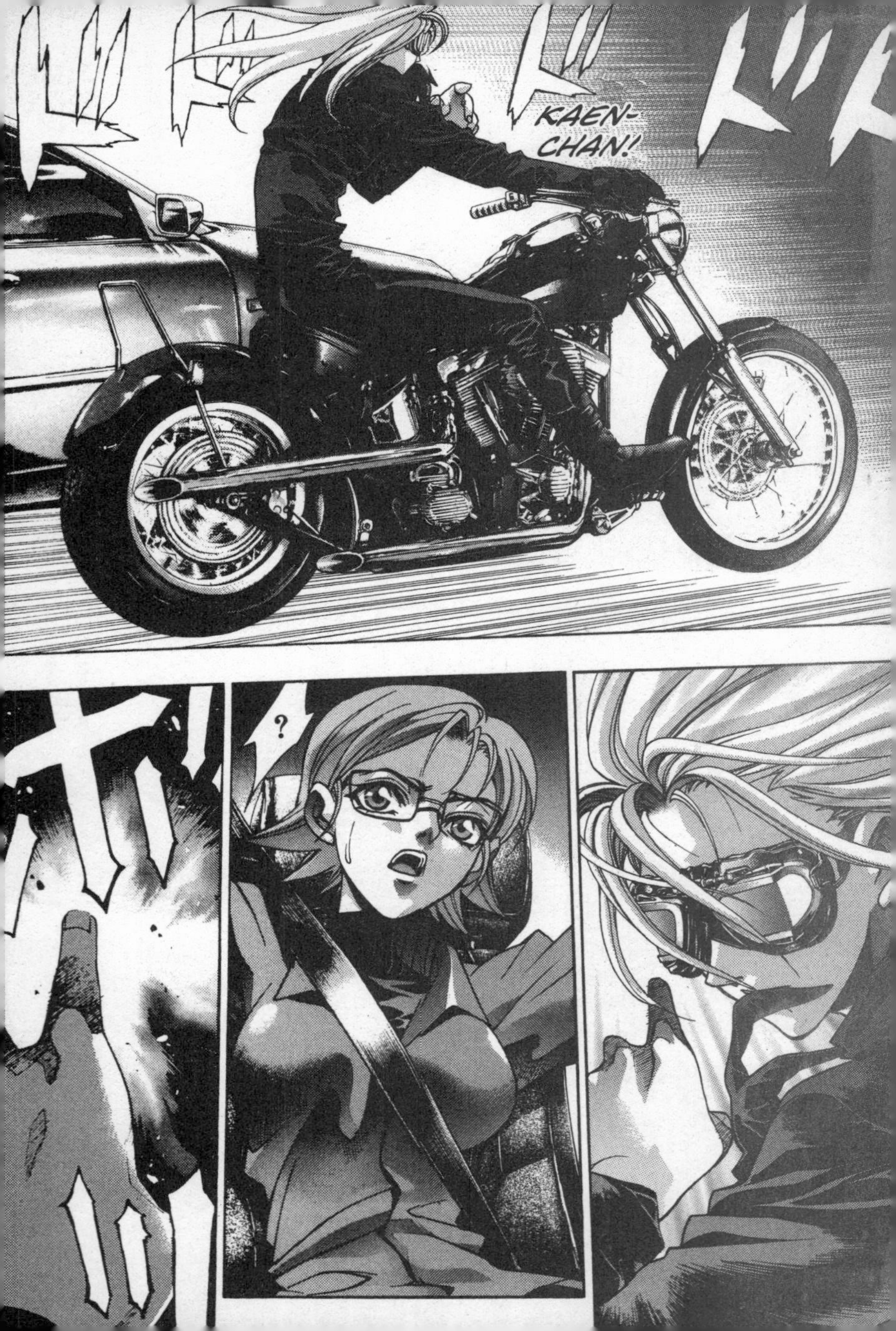
KAEN-CHAN!!
?

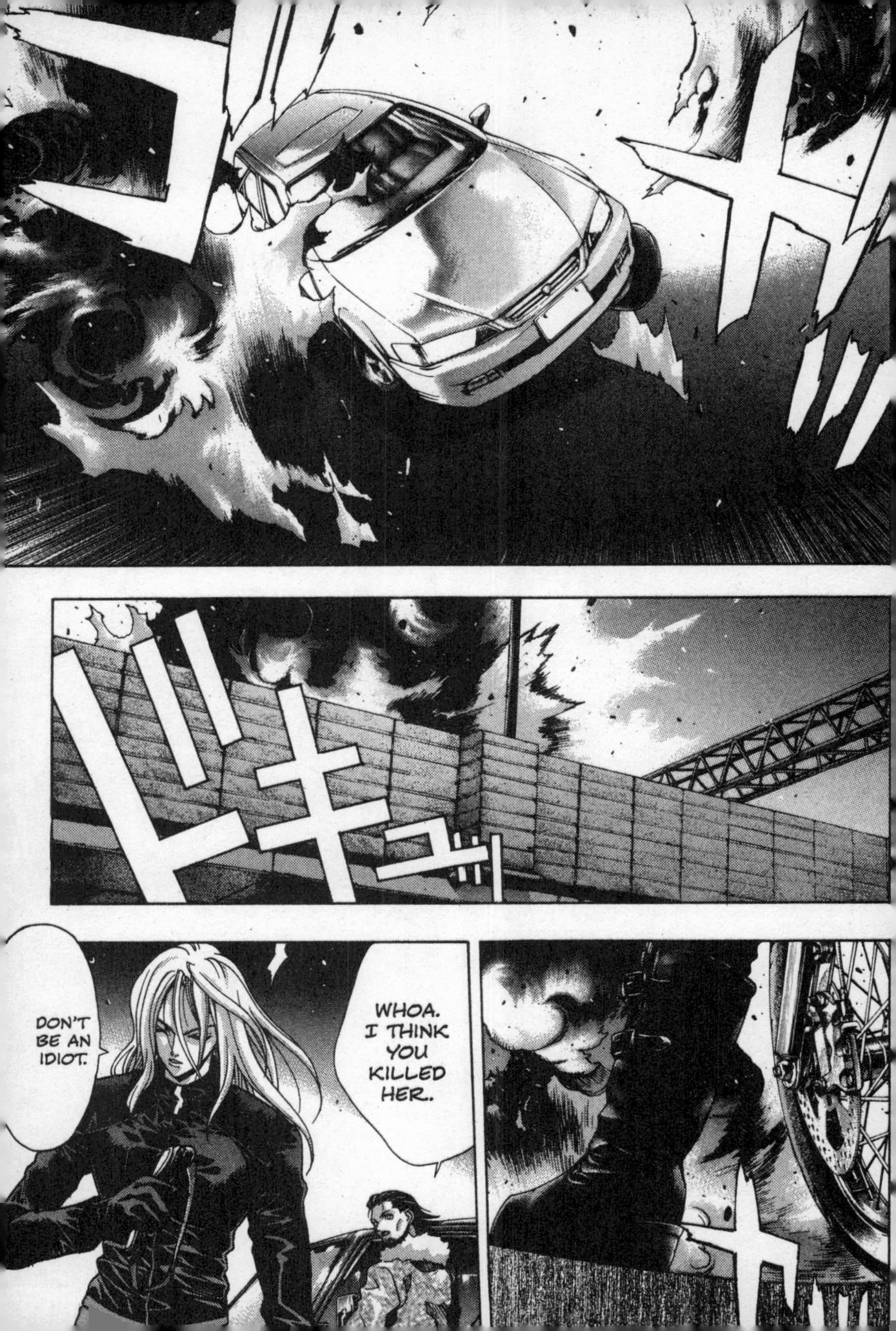
WHOA. I THINK YOU KILLED HER..
DON'T BE AN IDIOT.

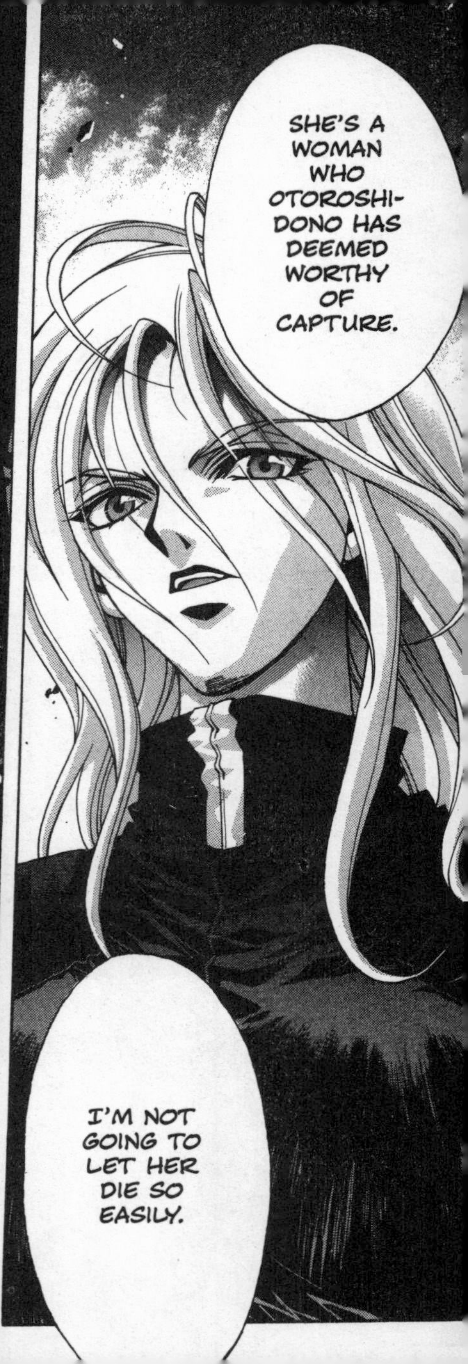
SHE'S A WOMAN WHO OTOROSHI-DONO HAS DEEMED WORTHY OF CAPTURE.
I'M NOT GOING TO LET HER DIE SO EASILY.
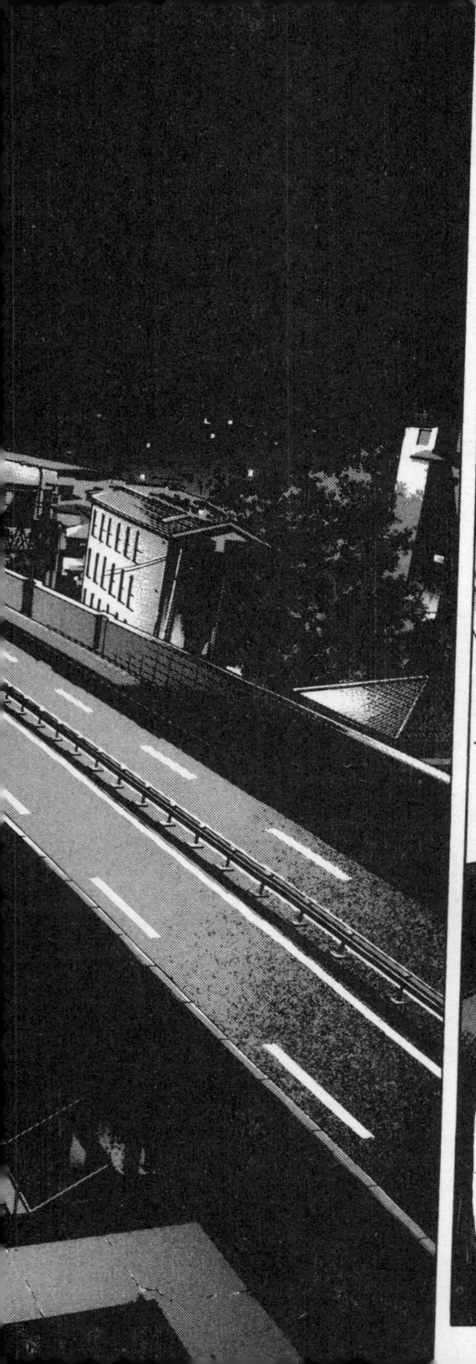

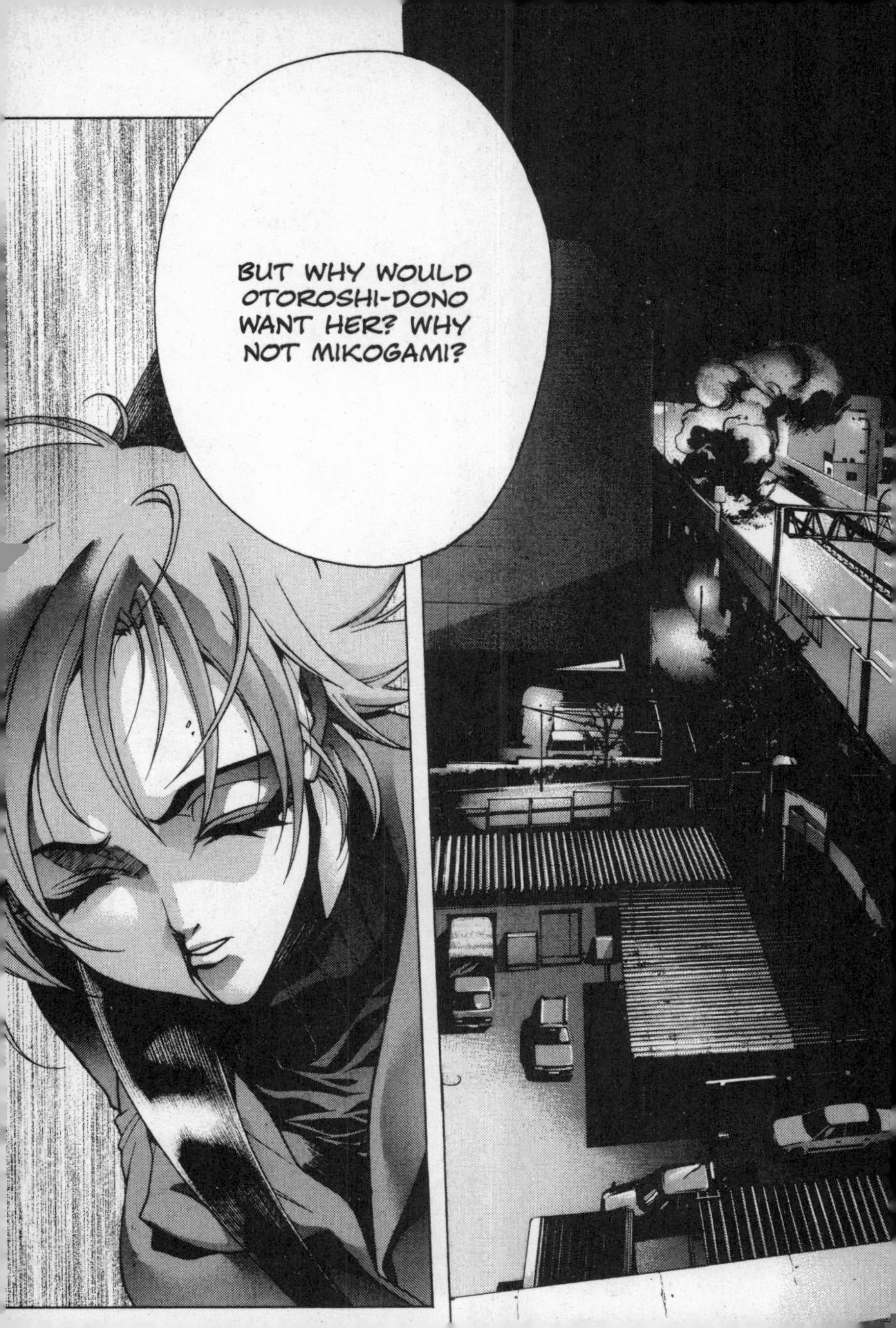
BUT WHY WOULD OTOROSHI-DONO WANT HER? WHY NOT MIKOGAMI?

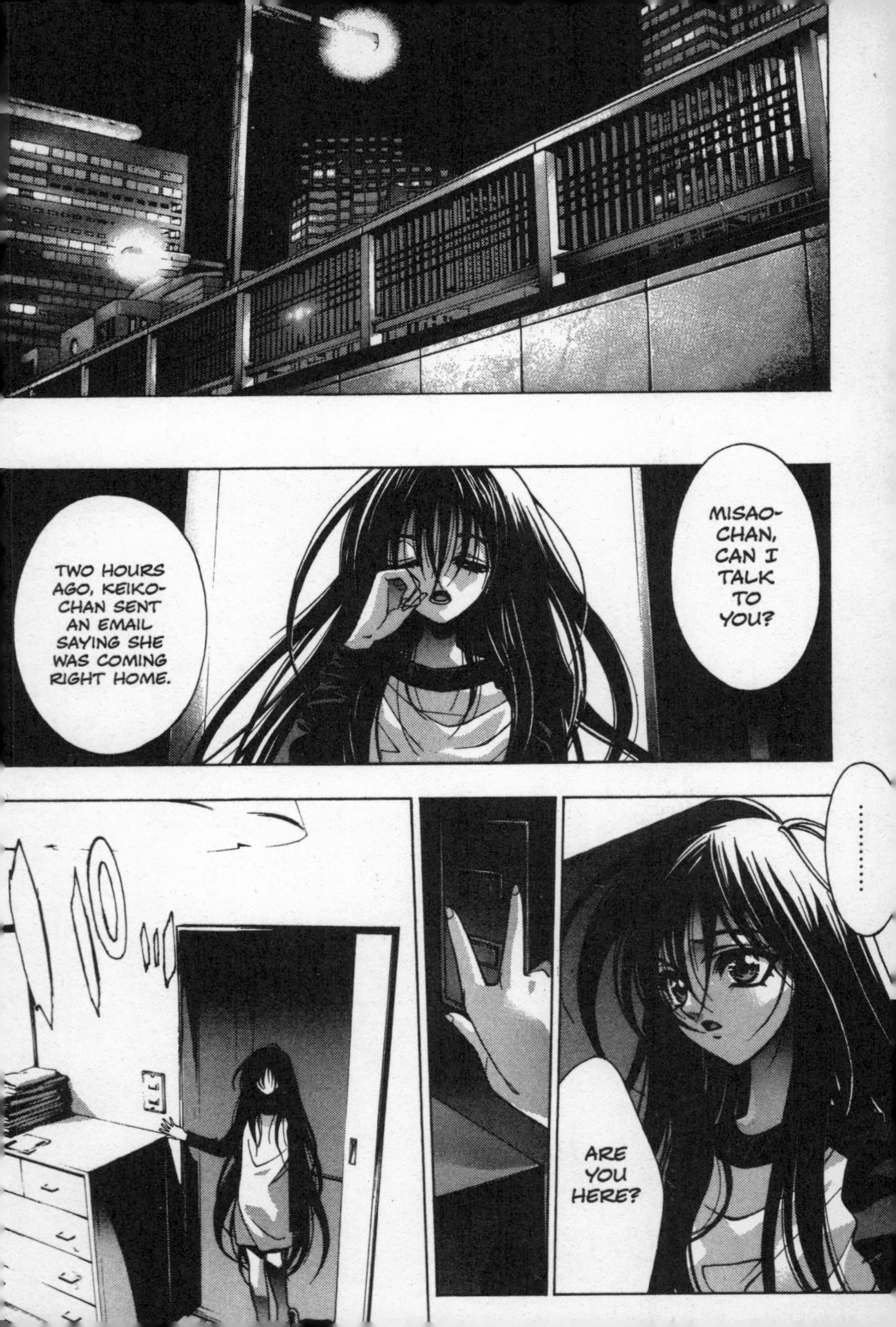
MISAO-CHAN, CAN I TALK TO YOU?
TWO HOURS AGO, KEIKO-CHAN SENT AN EMAIL SAYING SHE WAS COMING RIGHT HOME.
......
ARE YOU HERE?

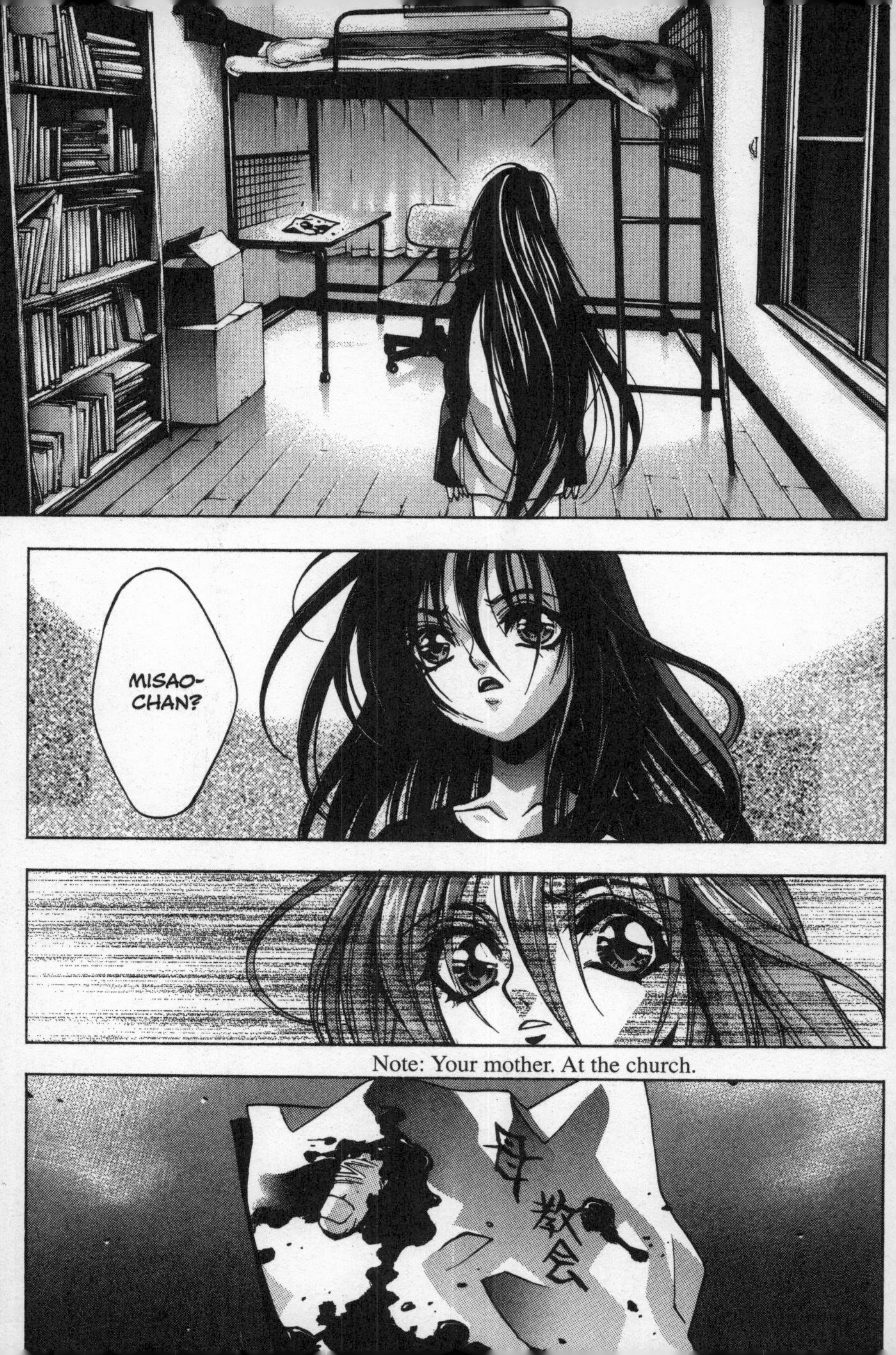
MISAO-CHAN?
母
教会
Note: Your mother. At the church.

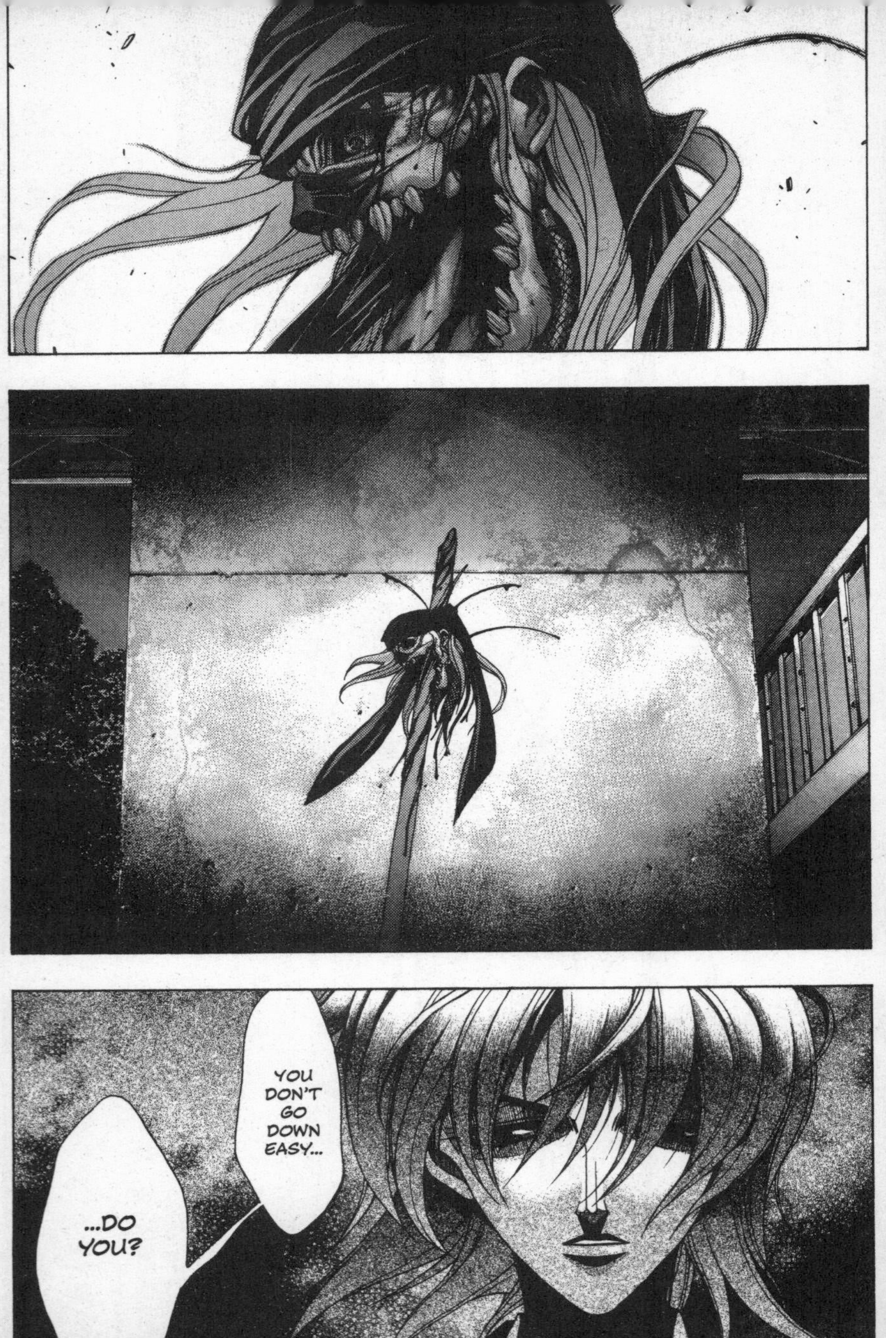
YOU DON'T GO DOWN EASY...
...DO YOU?

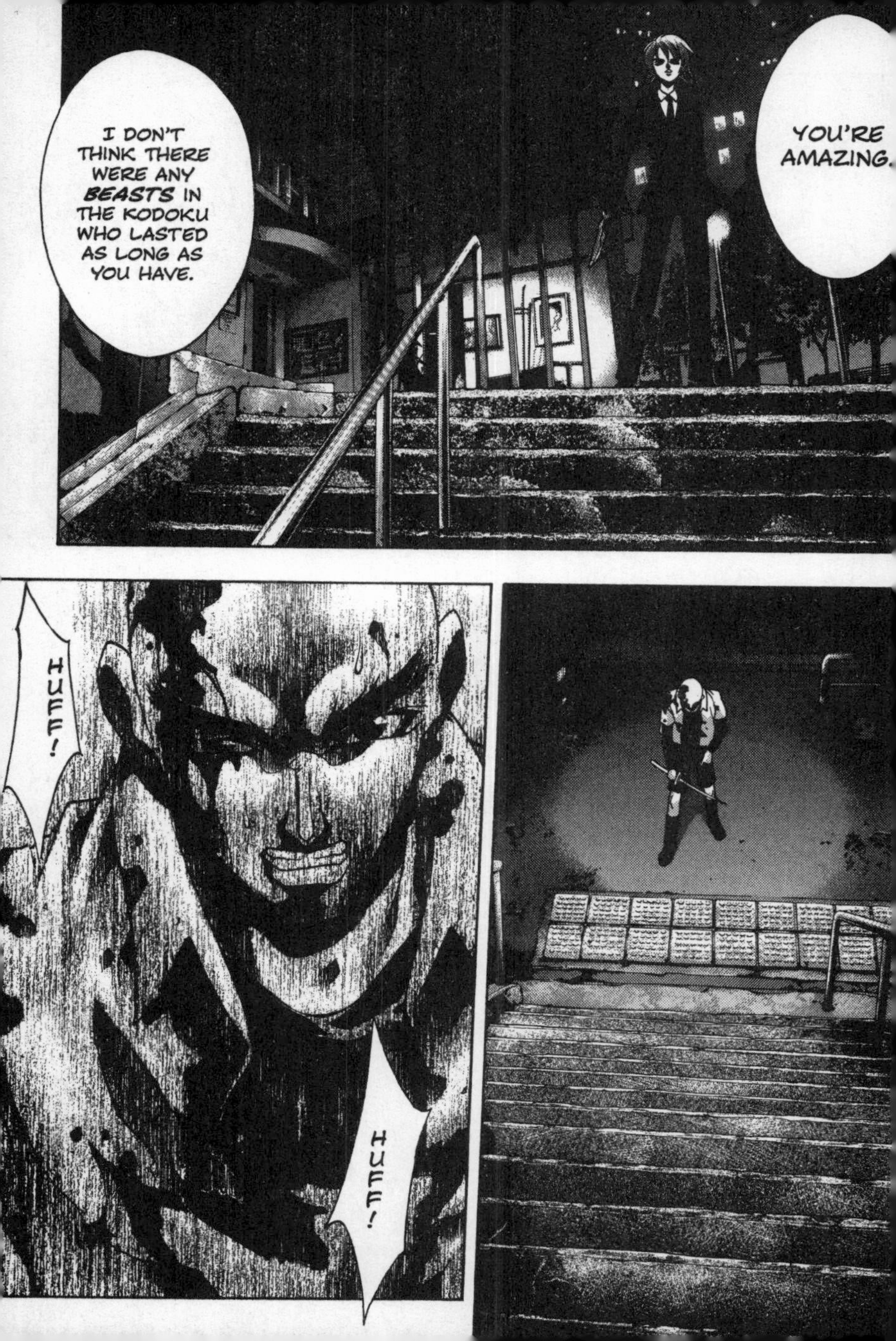
YOU'RE AMAZING.
I DON'T THINK THERE WERE ANY BEASTS IN THE KODOKU WHO LASTED AS LONG AS YOU HAVE.
HUFF!
HUFF!

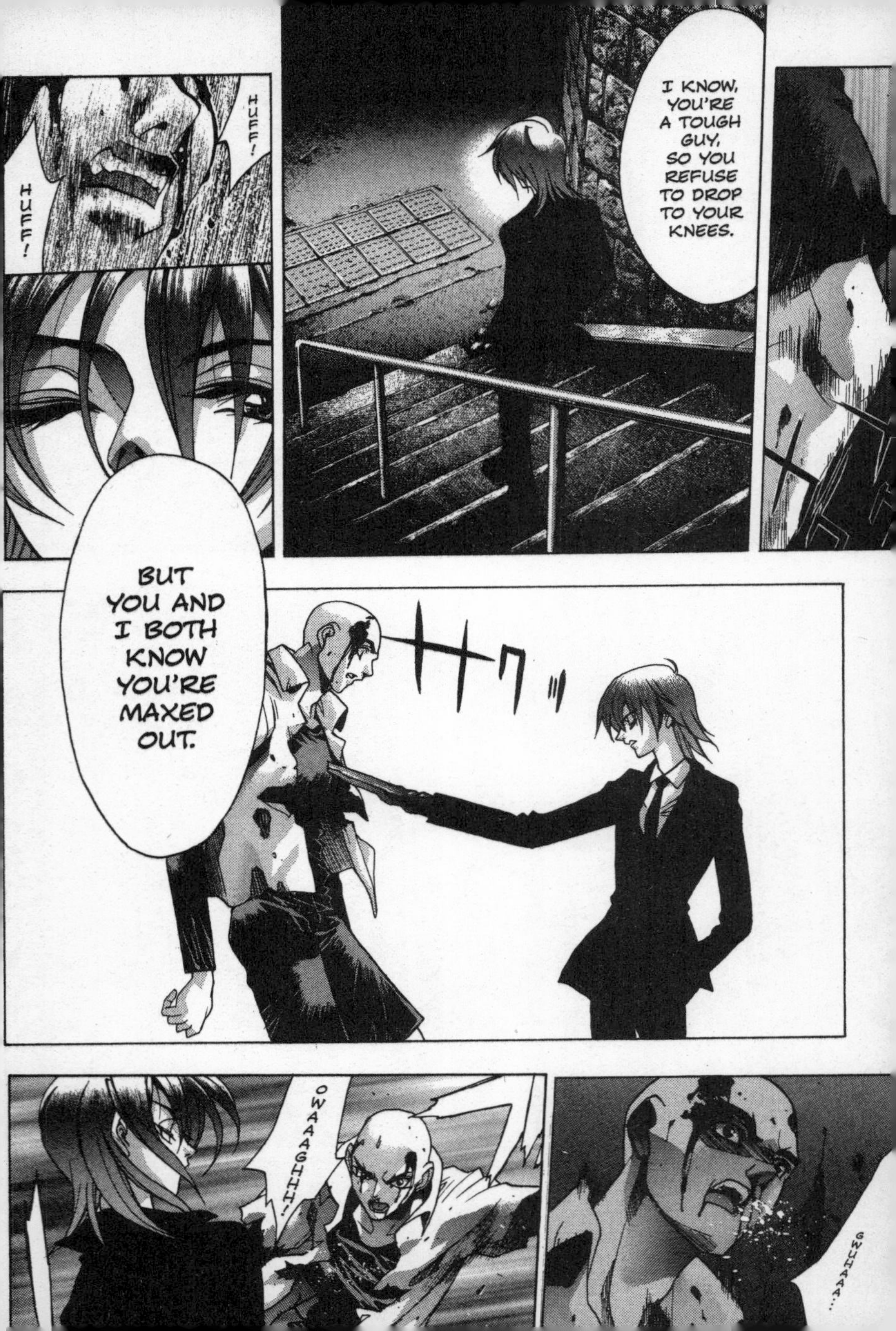
I KNOW, YOU'RE A TOUGH GUY, SO YOU REFUSE TO DROP TO YOUR KNEES.
HUFF!
HUFF!
BUT YOU AND I BOTH KNOW YOU'RE MAXED OUT.
GWUHAAA...
OWAAAAGHHH!

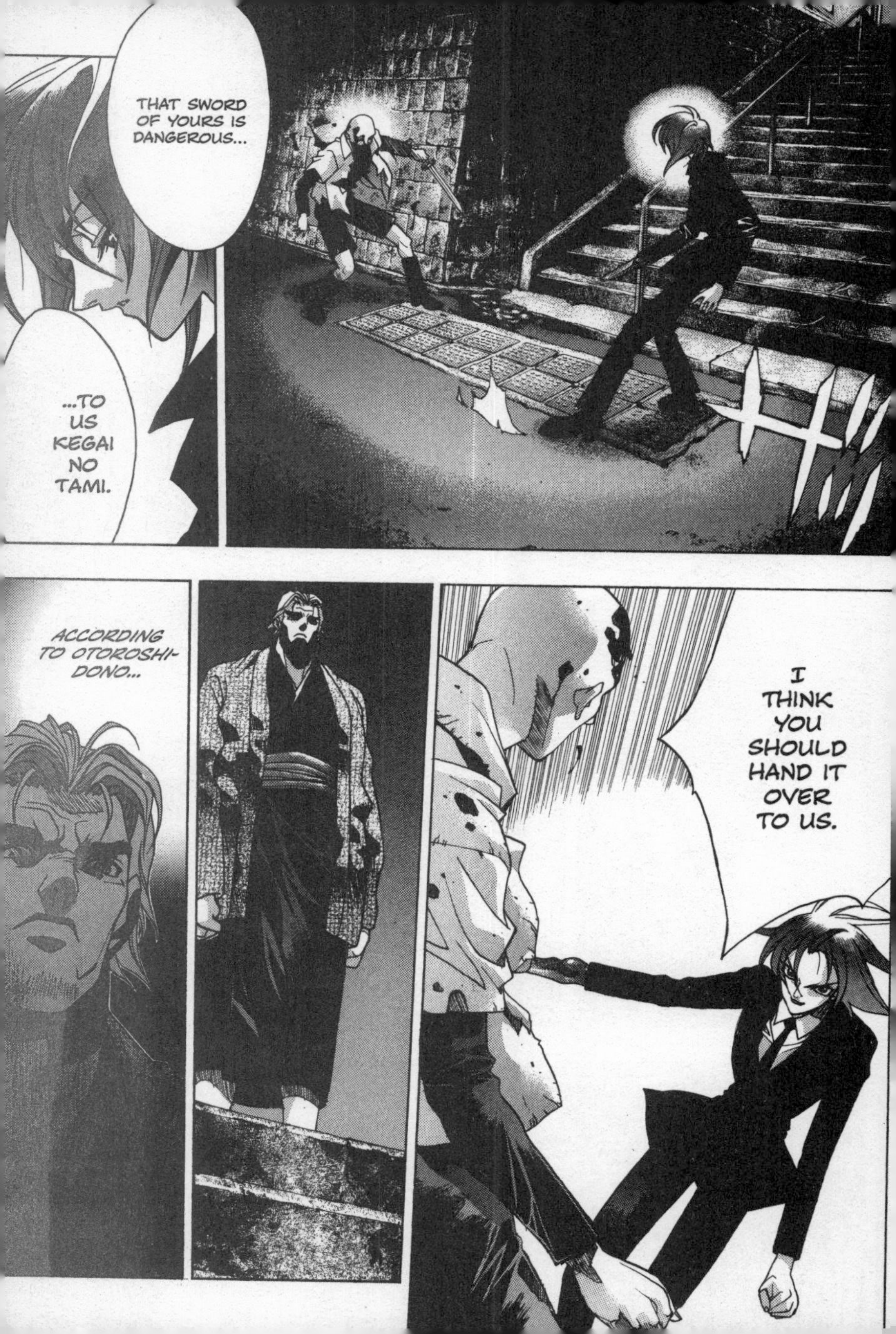
THAT SWORD OF YOURS IS DANGEROUS...
...TO US KEGAI NO TAMI.
I THINK YOU SHOULD HAND IT OVER TO US.
ACCORDING TO OTOROSHI-DONO...

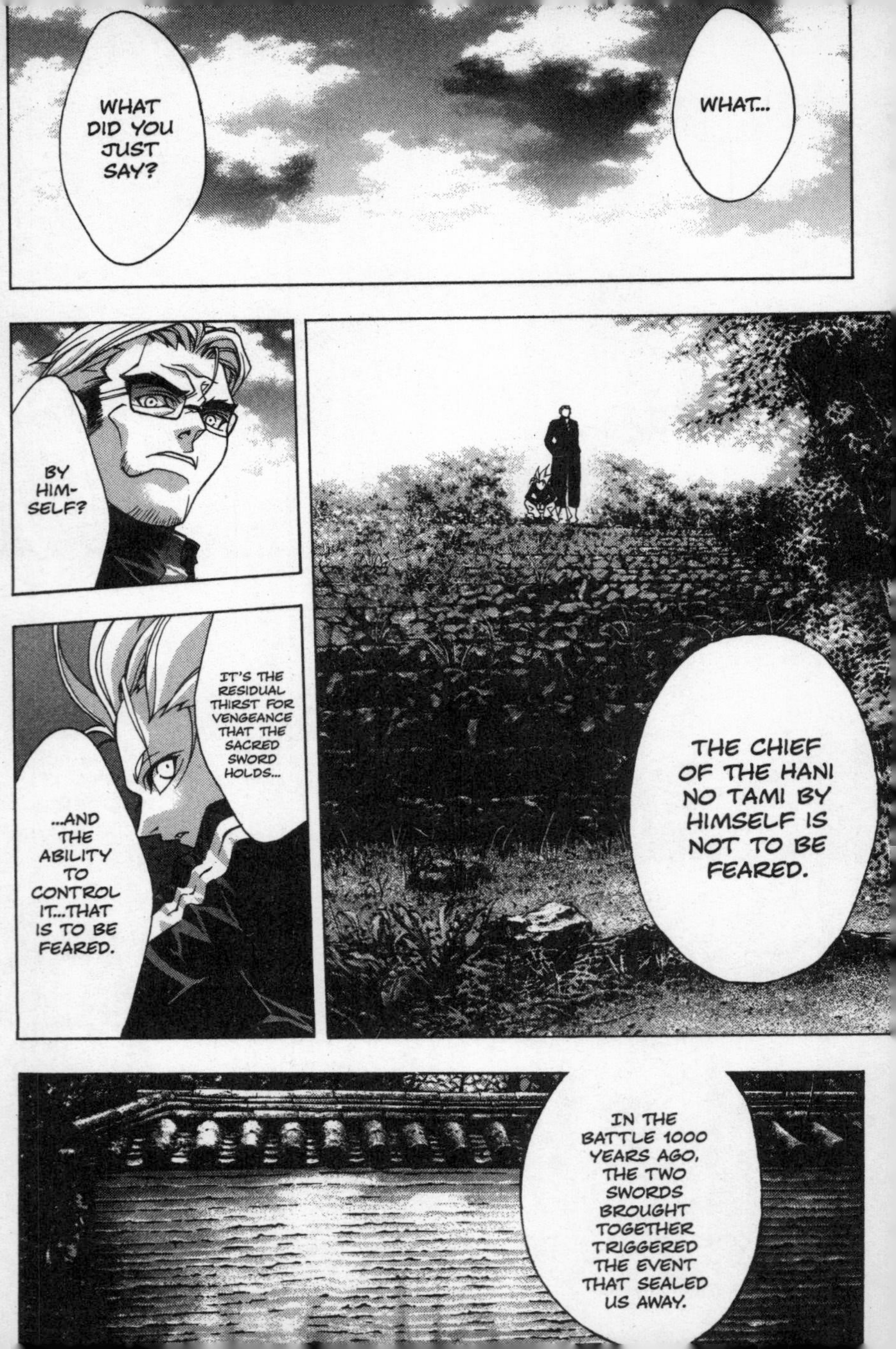
WHAT...
WHAT DID YOU JUST SAY?
THE CHIEF OF THE HANI NO TAMI BY HIMSELF IS NOT TO BE FEARED.
BY HIM-SELF?
IT'S THE RESIDUAL THIRST FOR VENGEANCE THAT THE SACRED SWORD HOLDS...
...AND THE ABILITY TO CONTROL IT...THAT IS TO BE FEARED.
IN THE BATTLE 1000 YEARS AGO, THE TWO SWORDS BROUGHT TOGETHER TRIGGERED THE EVENT THAT SEALED US AWAY.

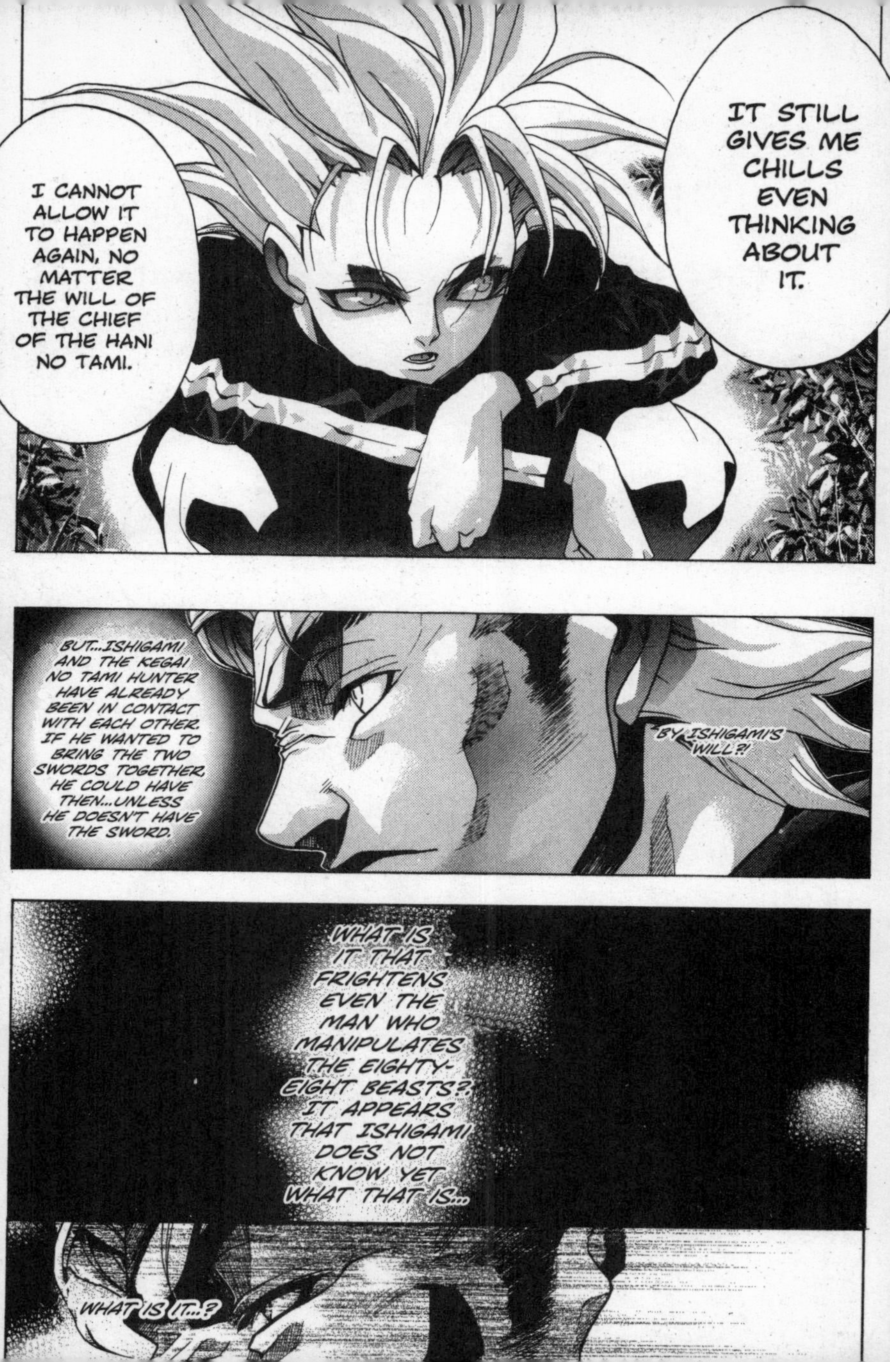
IT STILL GIVES ME CHILLS EVEN THINKING ABOUT IT.
I CANNOT ALLOW IT TO HAPPEN AGAIN, NO MATTER THE WILL OF THE CHIEF OF THE HANI NO TAMI.
BY ISHIGAMI'S WILL?!
BUT...ISHIGAMI AND THE KEGAI NO TAMI HUNTER HAVE ALREADY BEEN IN CONTACT WITH EACH OTHER. IF HE WANTED TO BRING THE TWO SWORDS TOGETHER, HE COULD HAVE THEN...UNLESS HE DOESN'T HAVE THE SWORD.
WHAT IS IT THAT FRIGHTENS EVEN THE MAN WHO MANIPULATES THE EIGHTY-EIGHT BEASTS?! IT APPEARS THAT ISHIGAMI DOES NOT KNOW YET WHAT THAT IS...
WHAT IS IT...?

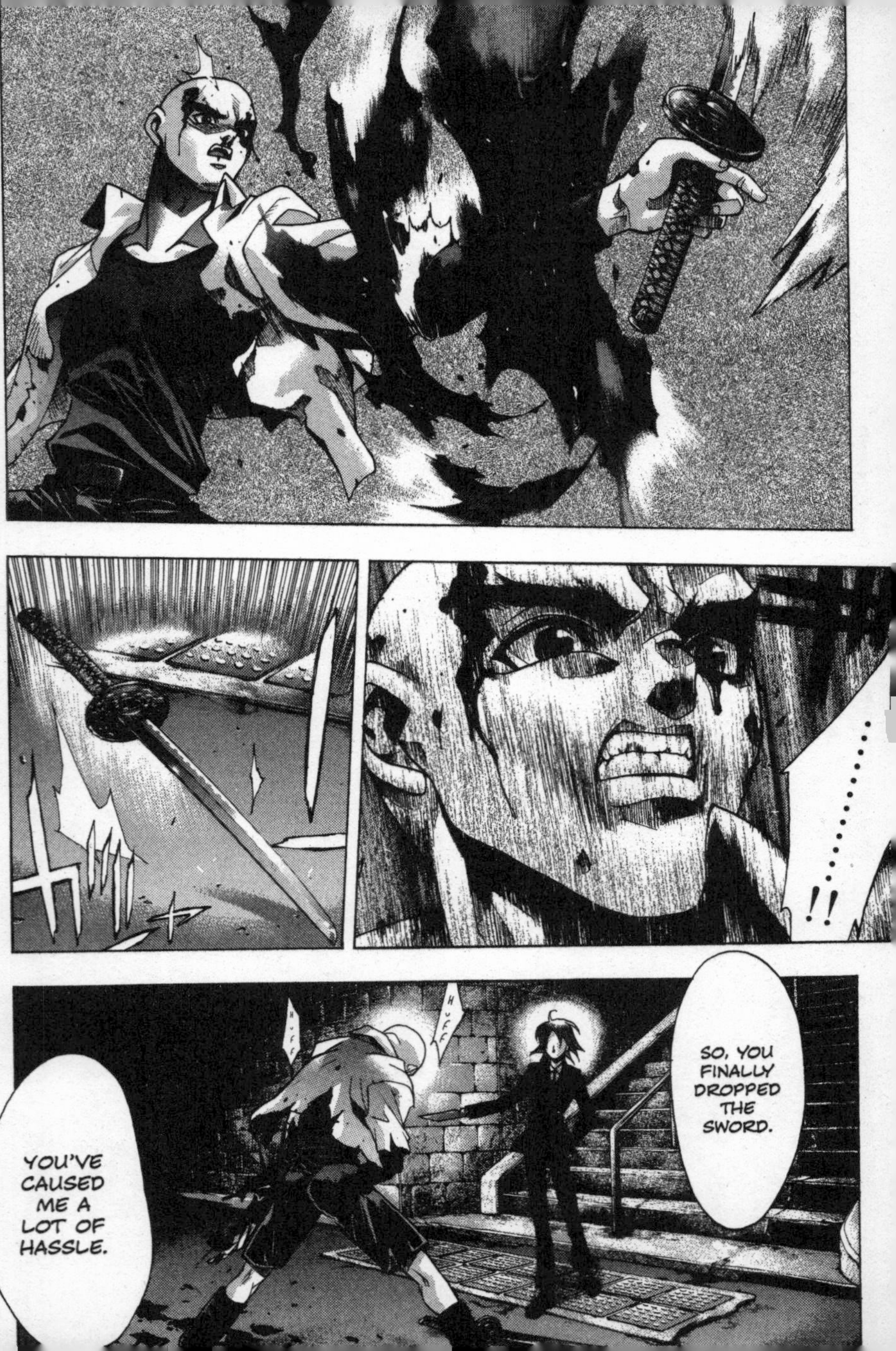
......
!!
SO, YOU FINALLY DROPPED THE SWORD.
HUFF
HUFF
YOU'VE CAUSED ME A LOT OF HASSLE.

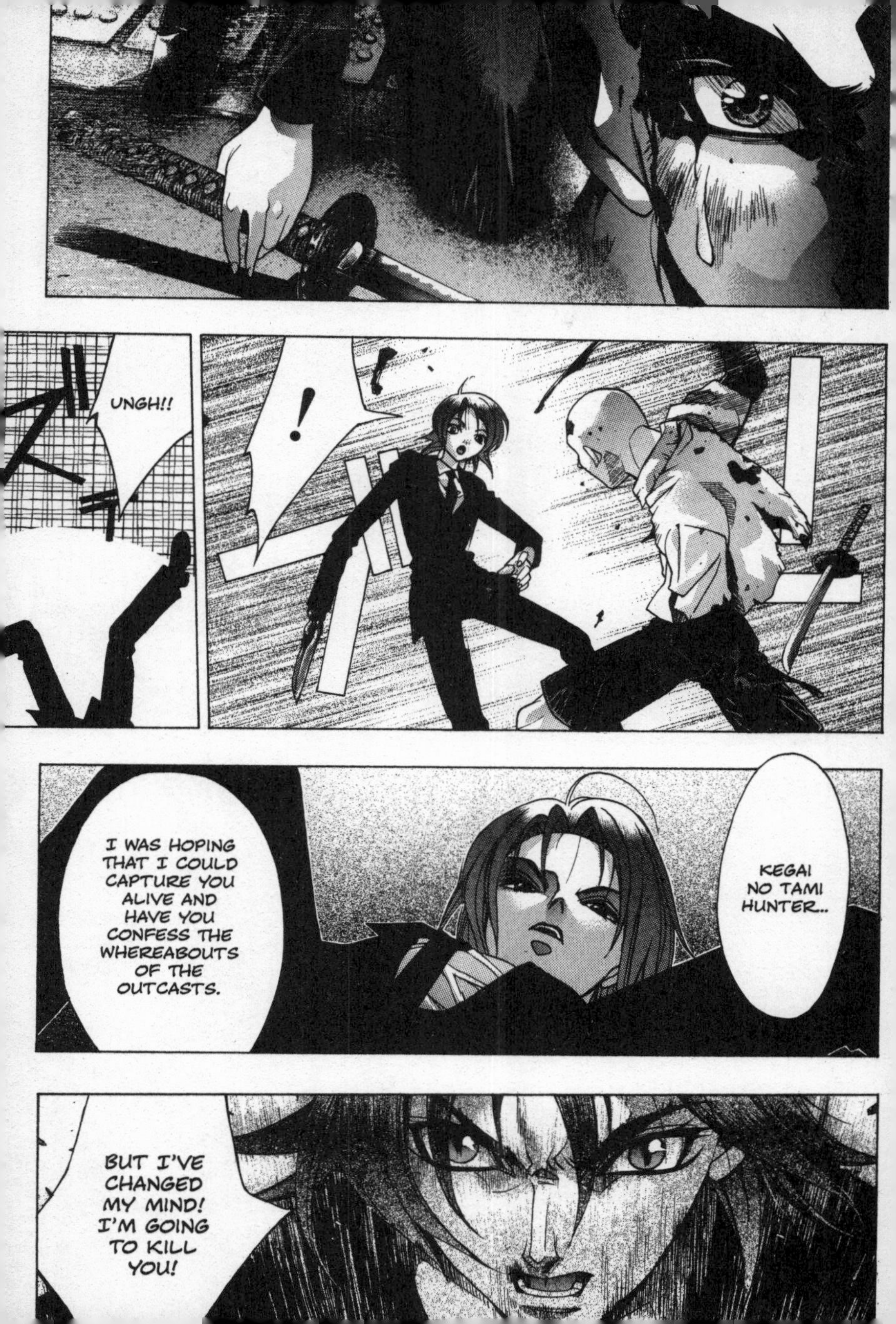
!
UNGH!!
KEGAI NO TAMI HUNTER...
I WAS HOPING THAT I COULD CAPTURE YOU ALIVE AND HAVE YOU CONFESS THE WHEREABOUTS OF THE OUTCASTS.
BUT I'VE CHANGED MY MIND! I'M GOING TO KILL YOU!

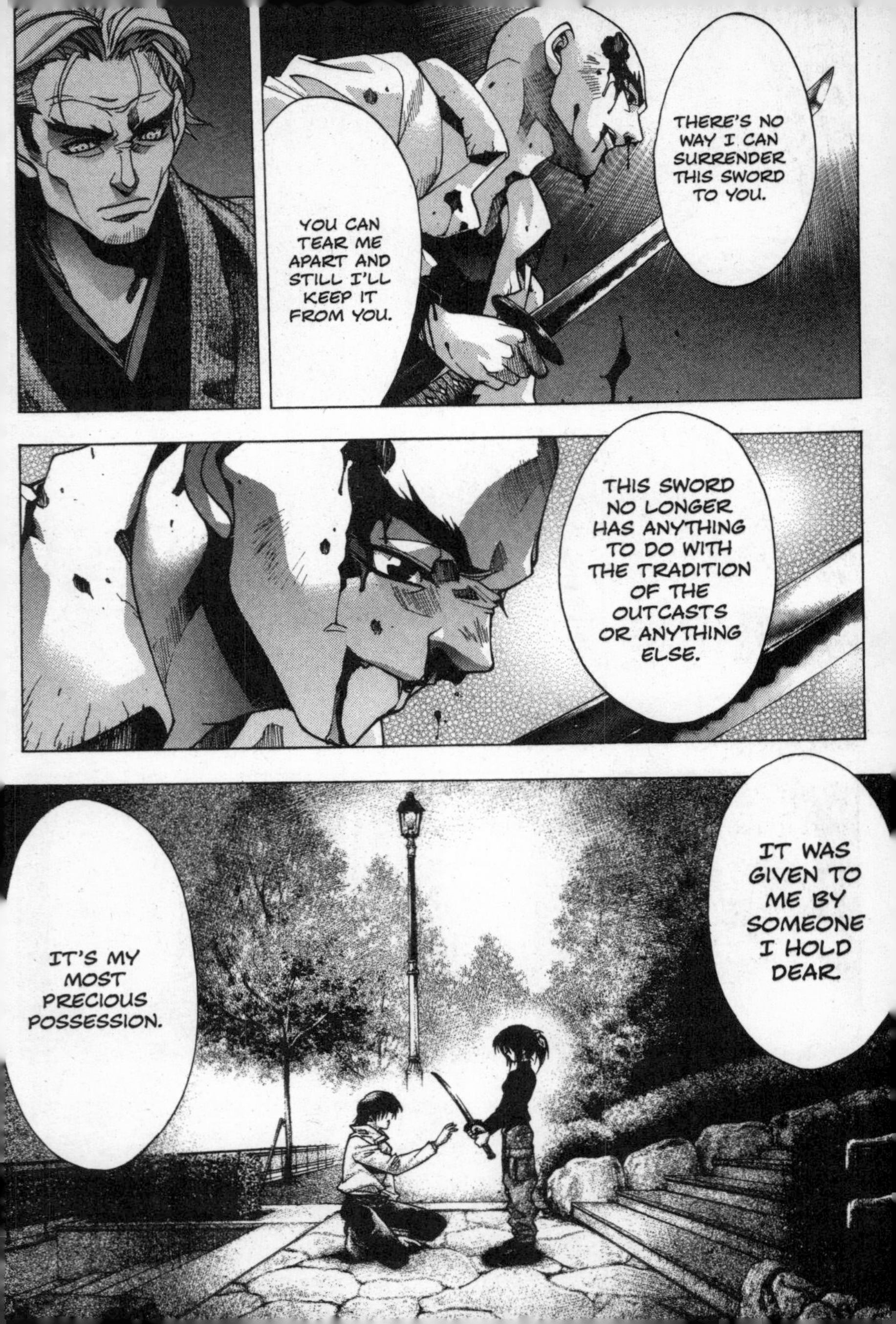
THERE'S NO WAY I CAN SURRENDER THIS SWORD TO YOU.
YOU CAN TEAR ME APART AND STILL I'LL KEEP IT FROM YOU.
THIS SWORD NO LONGER HAS ANYTHING TO DO WITH THE TRADITION OF THE OUTCASTS OR ANYTHING ELSE.
IT WAS GIVEN TO ME BY SOMEONE I HOLD DEAR.
IT'S MY MOST PRECIOUS POSSESSION.

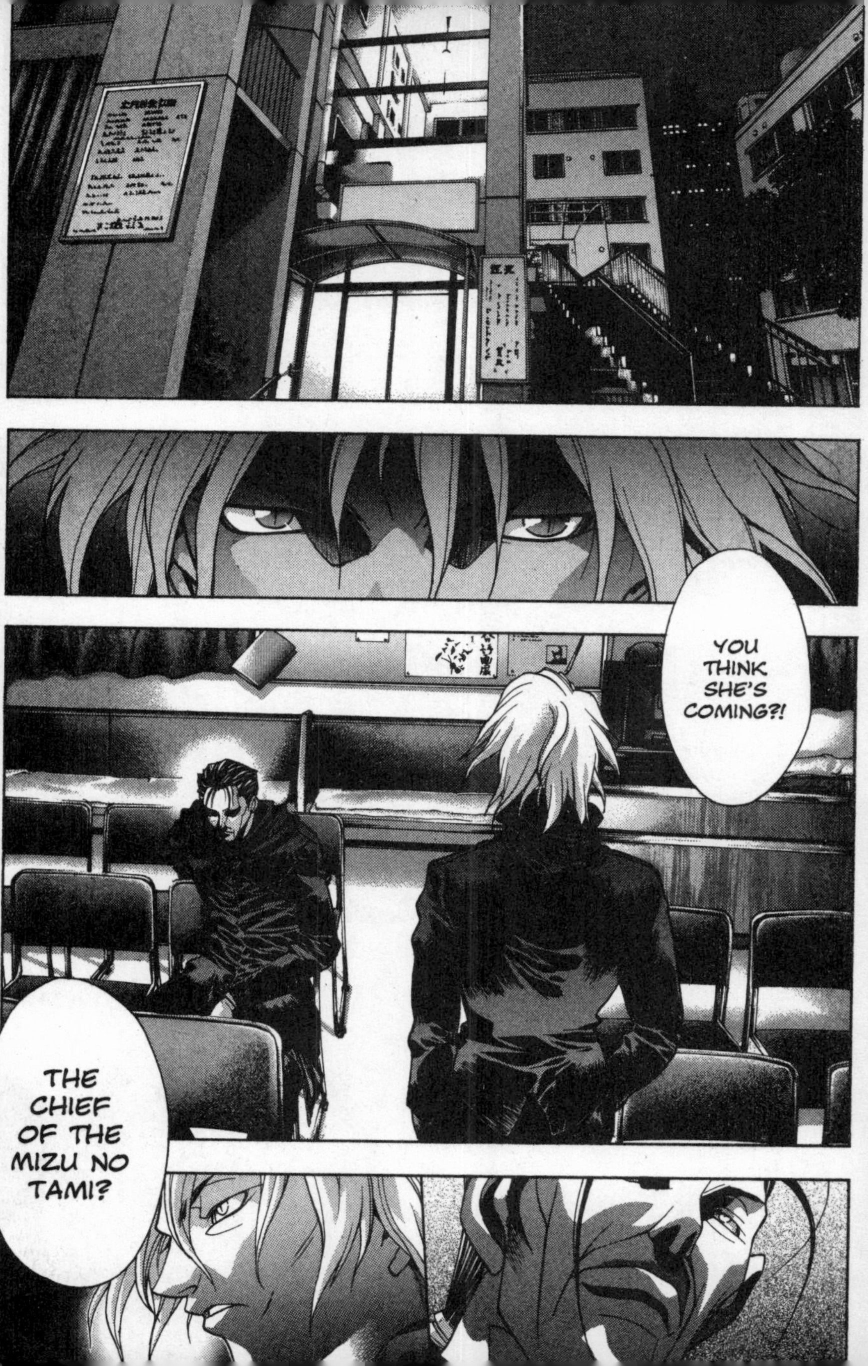
YOU THINK SHE'S COMING?!
THE CHIEF OF THE MIZU NO TAMI?

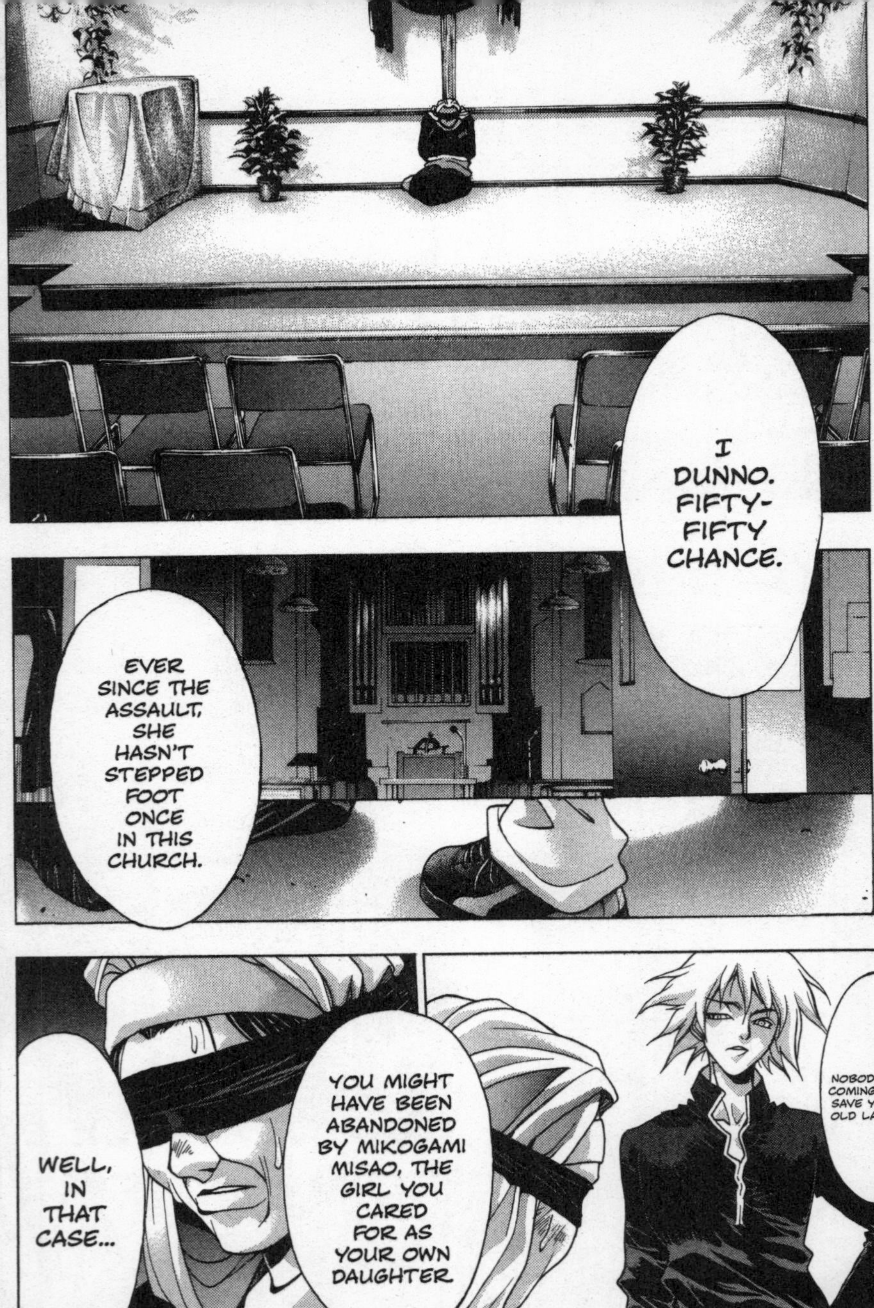

I DUNNO. FIFTY-FIFTY CHANCE.
EVER SINCE THE ASSAULT, SHE HASN'T STEPPED FOOT ONCE IN THIS CHURCH.
NOBODY'S COMING TO SAVE YOU, OLD LADY.
YOU MIGHT HAVE BEEN ABANDONED BY MIKOGAMI MISAO, THE GIRL YOU CARED FOR AS YOUR OWN DAUGHTER
WELL, IN THAT CASE...

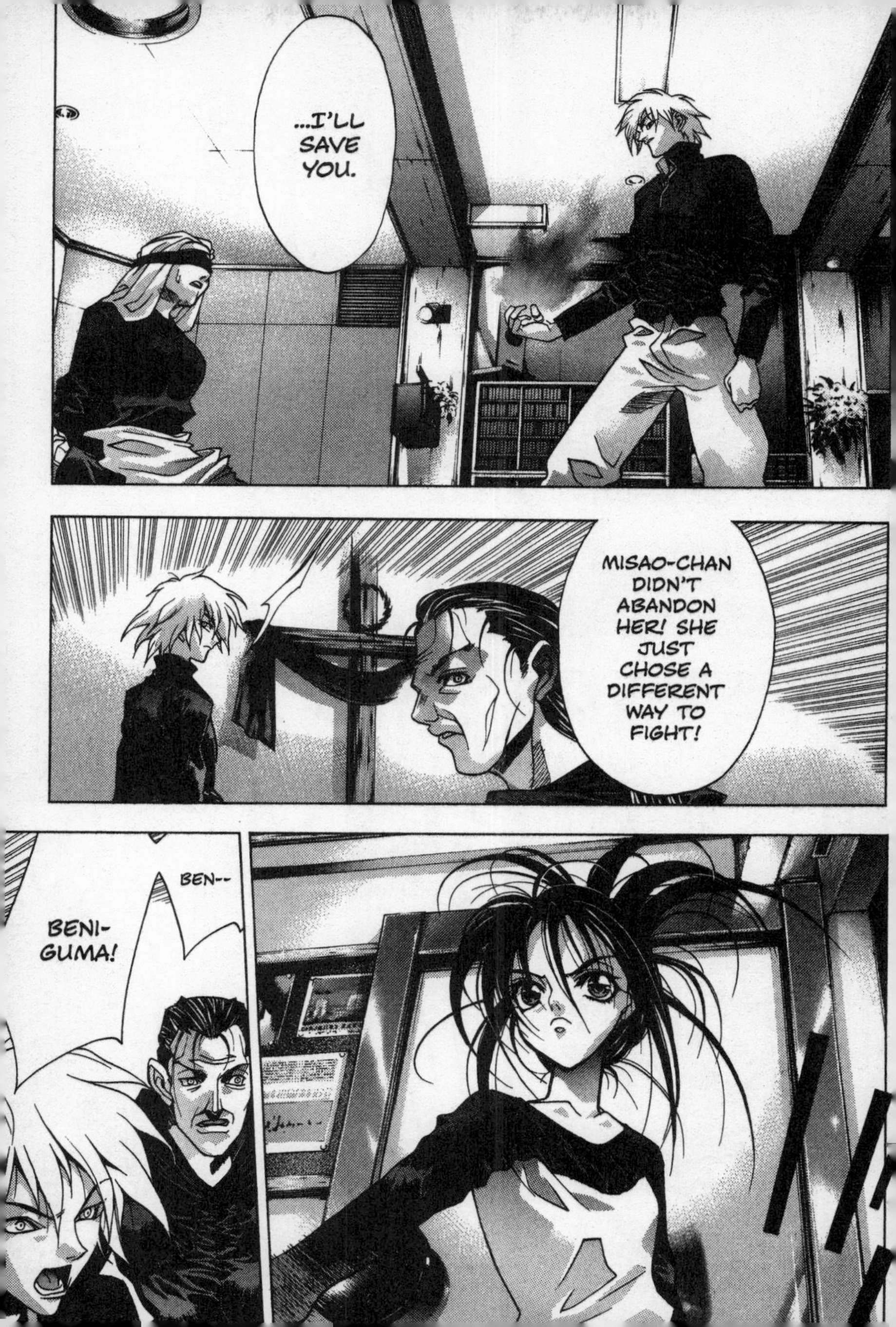
...I'LL SAVE YOU.
MISAO-CHAN DIDN'T ABANDON HER! SHE JUST CHOSE A DIFFERENT WAY TO FIGHT!
BEN--
BENI-GUMA!

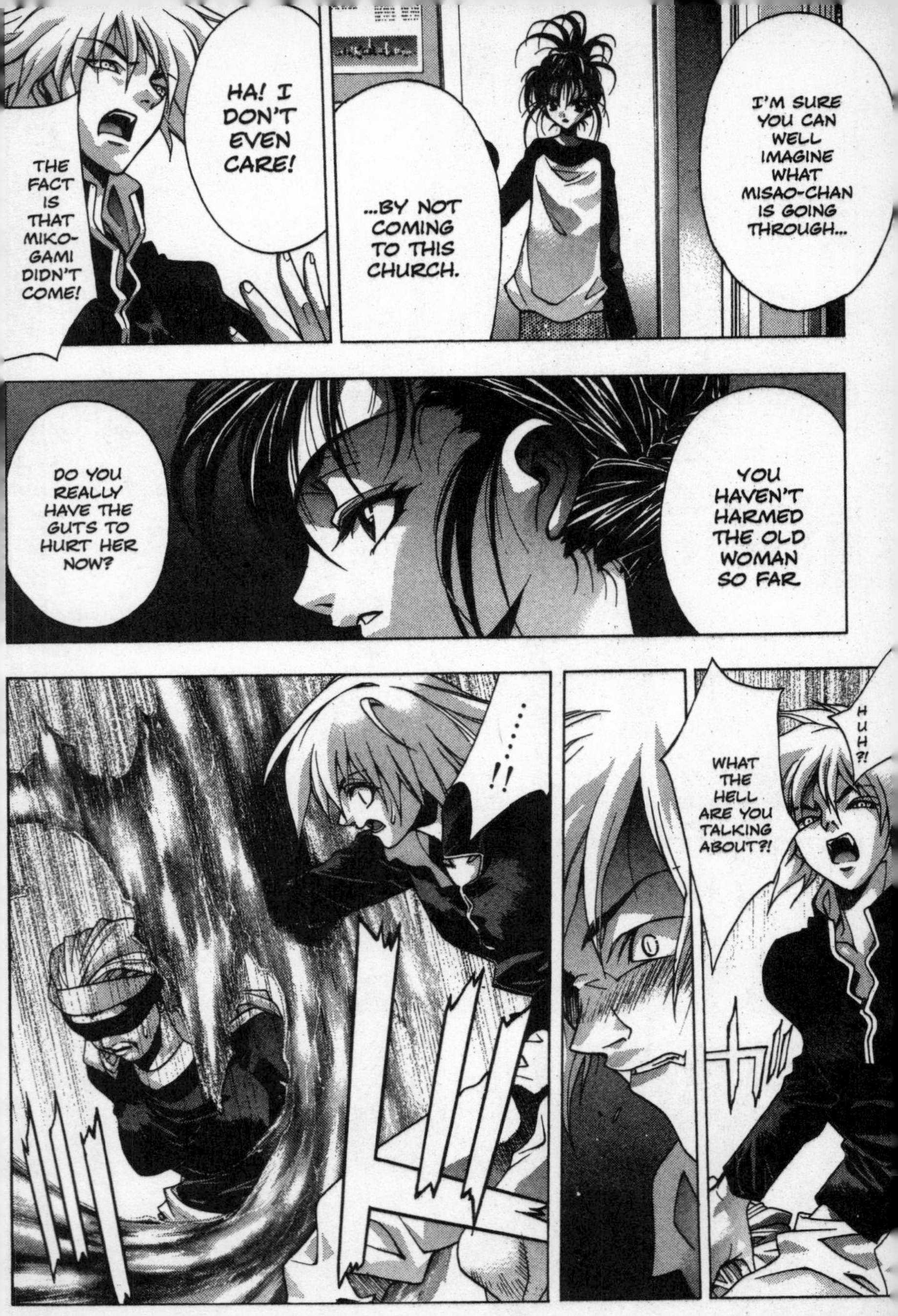
I'M SURE YOU CAN WELL IMAGINE WHAT MISAO-CHAN IS GOING THROUGH...
...BY NOT COMING TO THIS CHURCH.
HA! I DON'T EVEN CARE!
THE FACT IS THAT MIKO-GAMI DIDN'T COME!
YOU HAVEN'T HARMED THE OLD WOMAN SO FAR
DO YOU REALLY HAVE THE GUTS TO HURT HER NOW?
HUH?!
WHAT THE HELL ARE YOU TALKING ABOUT?!
......!!

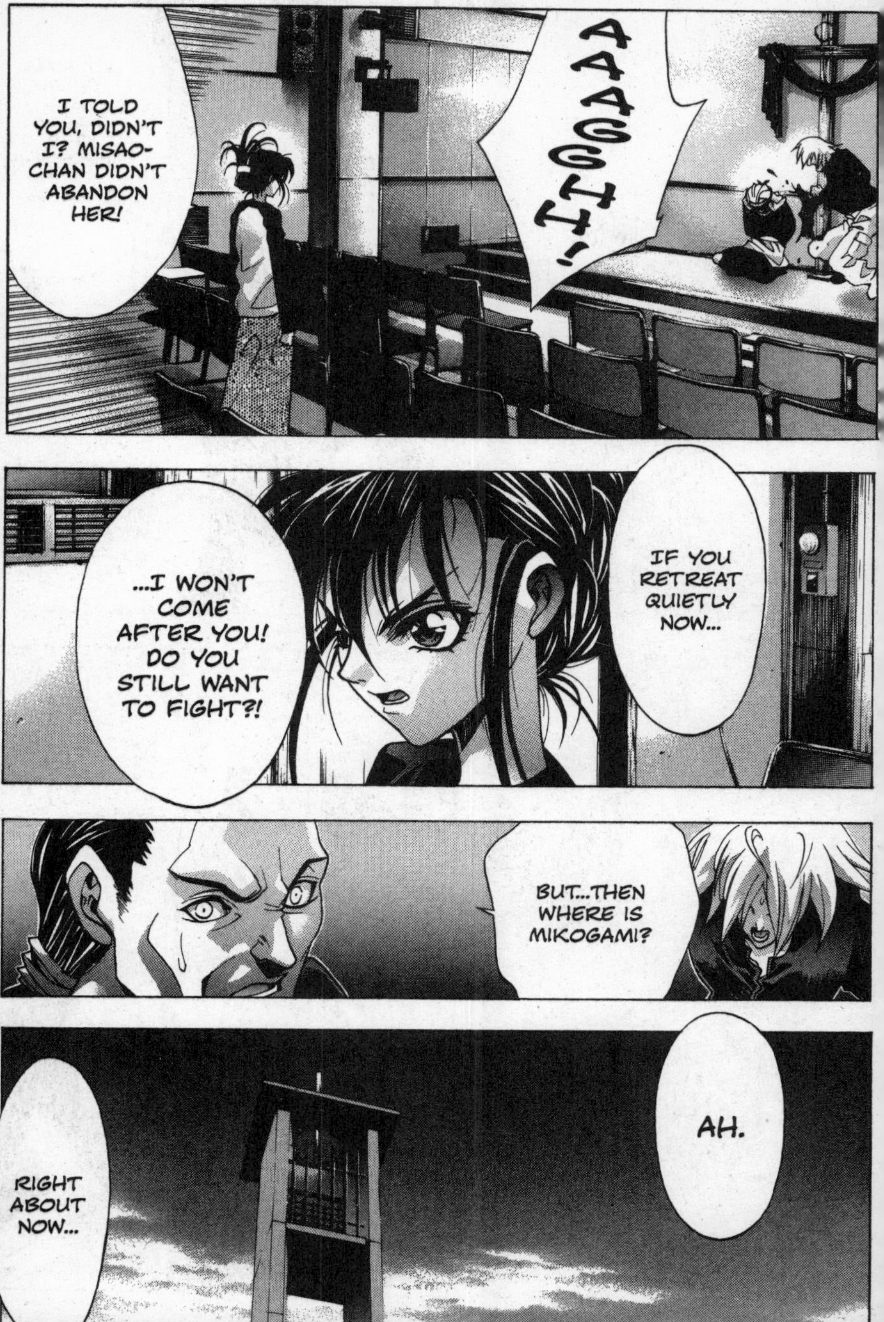
AAAGGHH!
I TOLD YOU, DIDN'T I? MISAO-CHAN DIDN'T ABANDON HER!
IF YOU RETREAT QUIETLY NOW...
...I WON'T COME AFTER YOU! DO YOU STILL WANT TO FIGHT?!
BUT...THEN WHERE IS MIKOGAMI?
AH.
RIGHT ABOUT NOW...

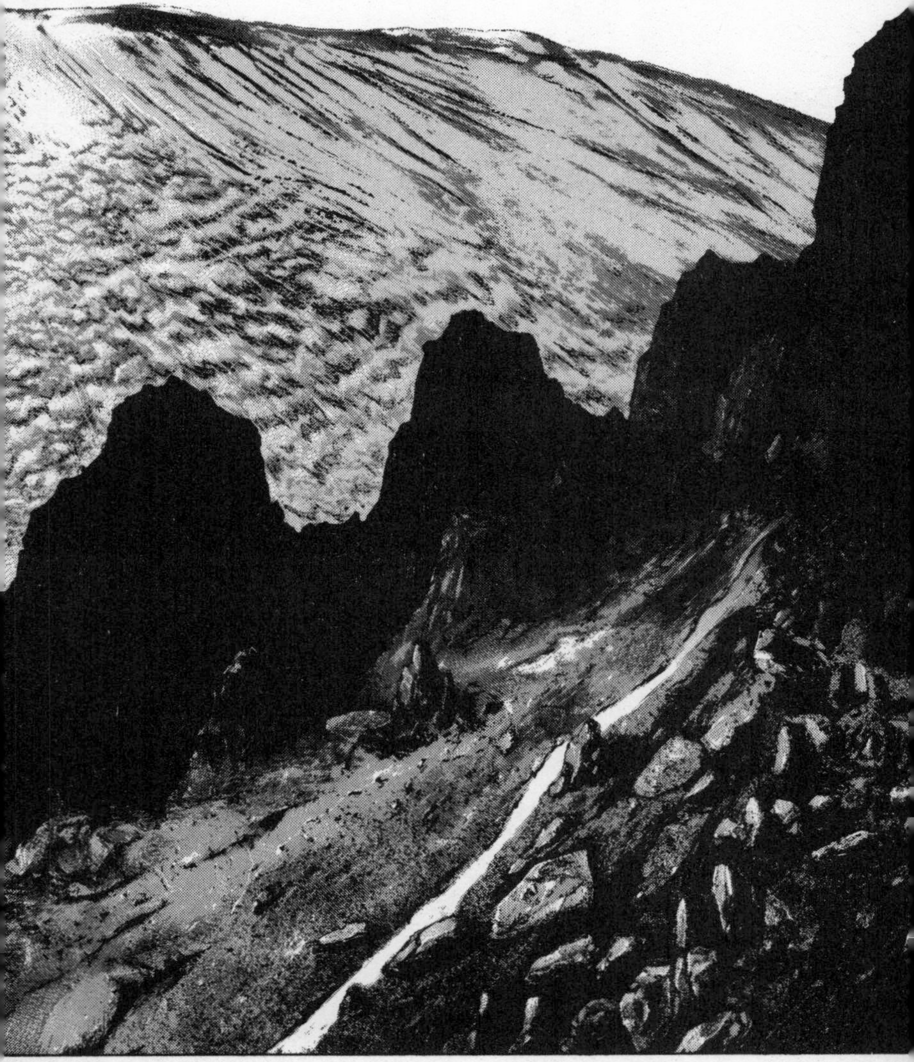

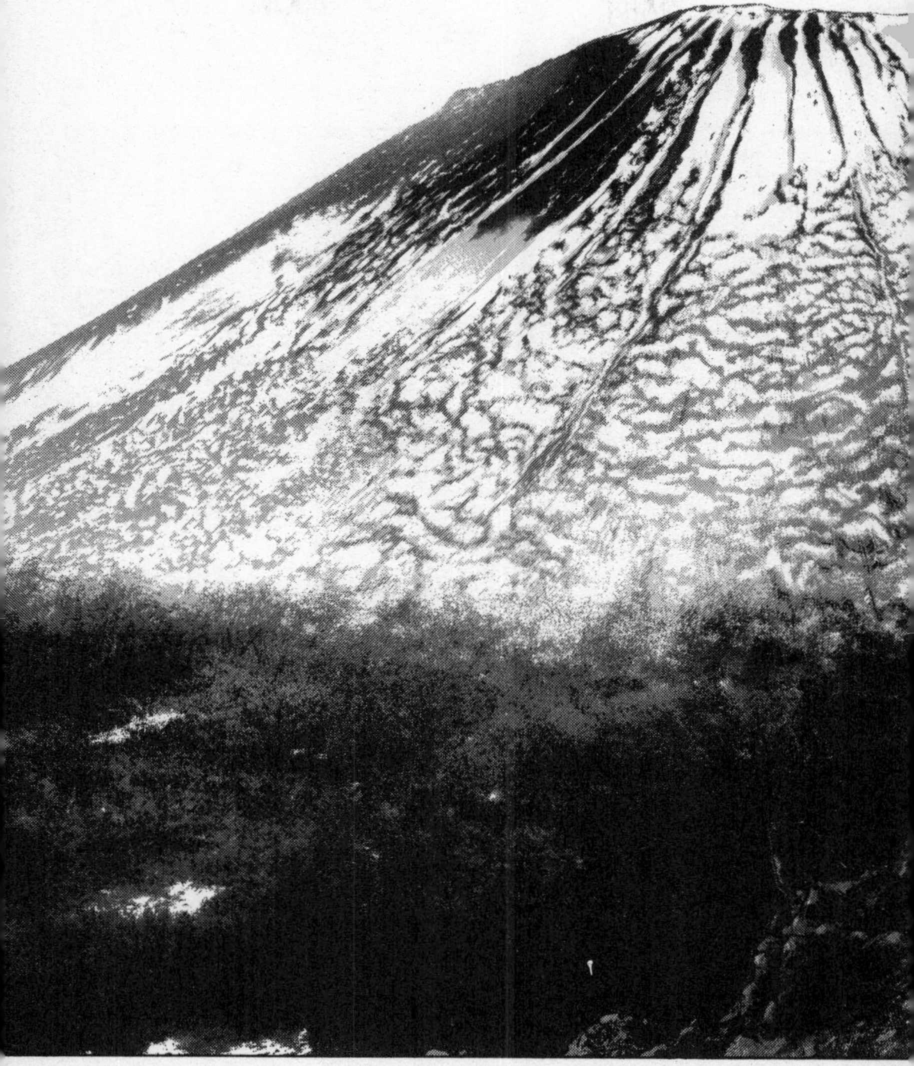

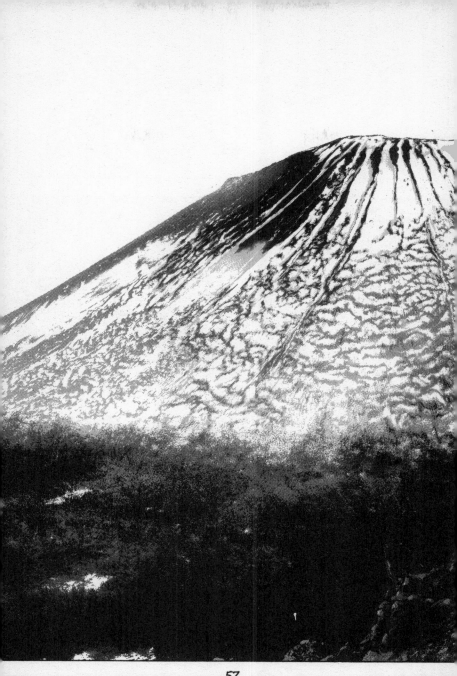

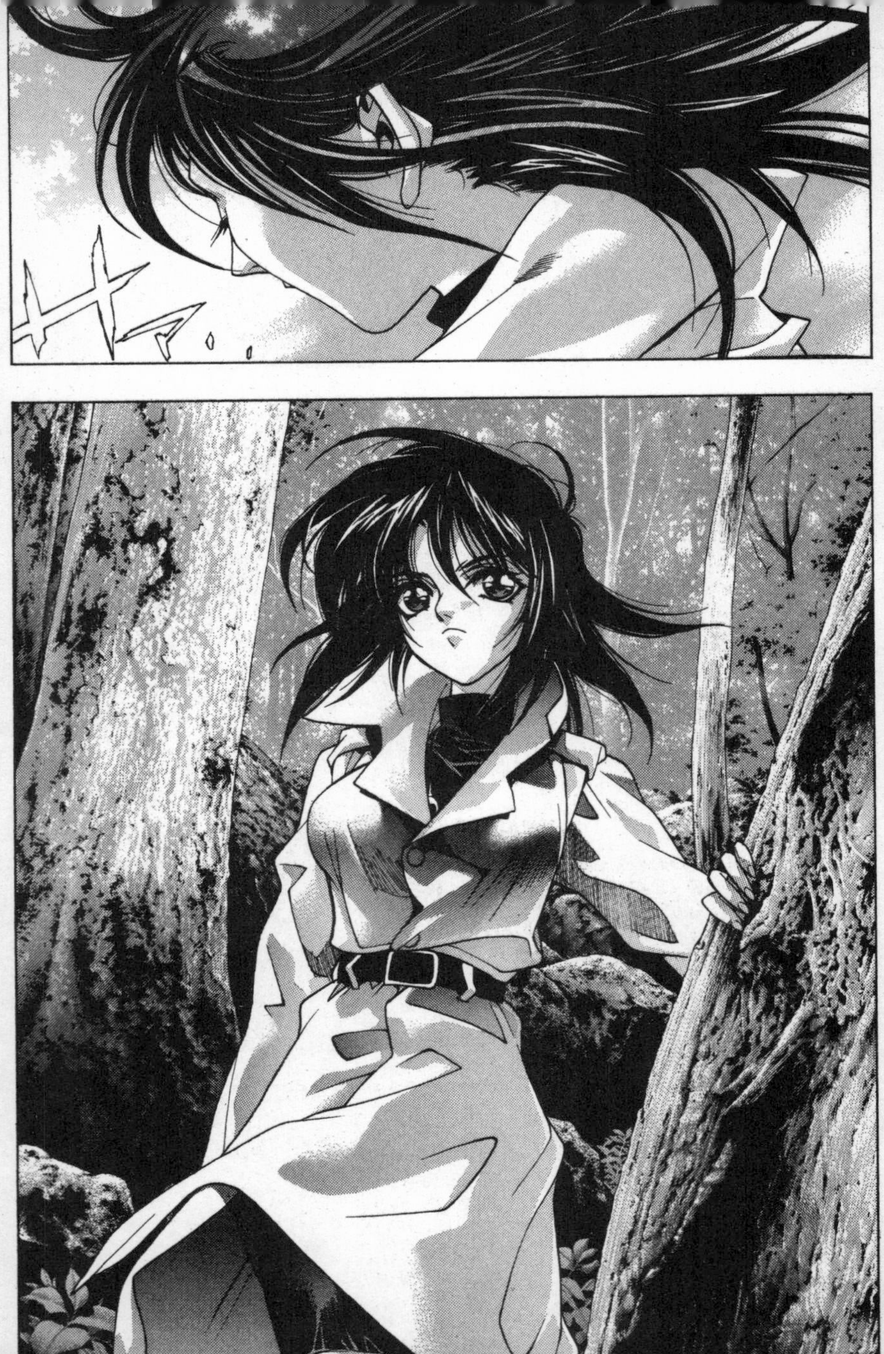
ハァ…

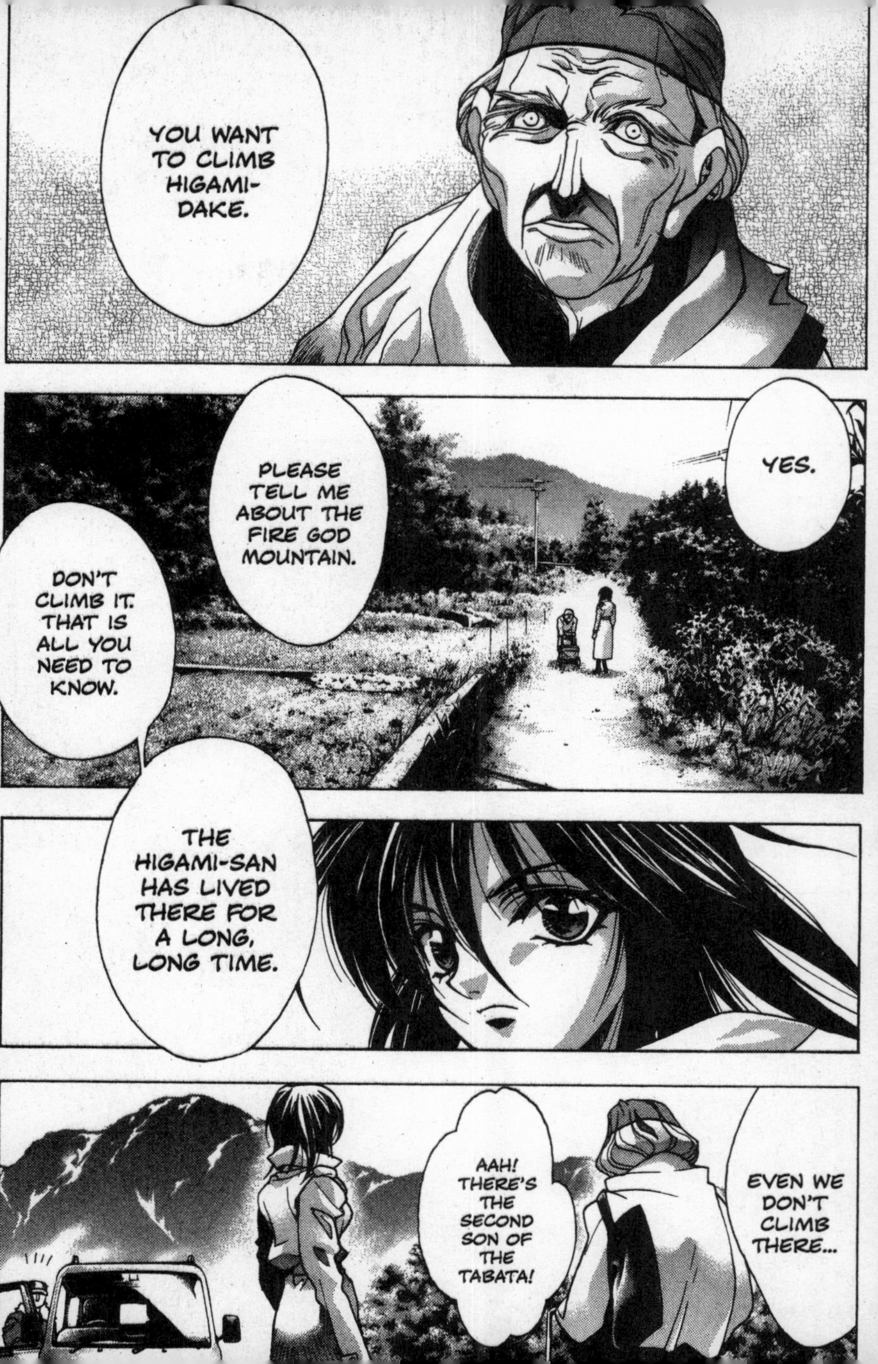
YOU WANT TO CLIMB HIGAMI-DAKE.
YES.
PLEASE TELL ME ABOUT THE FIRE GOD MOUNTAIN.
DON'T CLIMB IT. THAT IS ALL YOU NEED TO KNOW.
THE HIGAMI-SAN HAS LIVED THERE FOR A LONG, LONG TIME.
EVEN WE DON'T CLIMB THERE...
AAH! THERE'S THE SECOND SON OF THE TABATA!

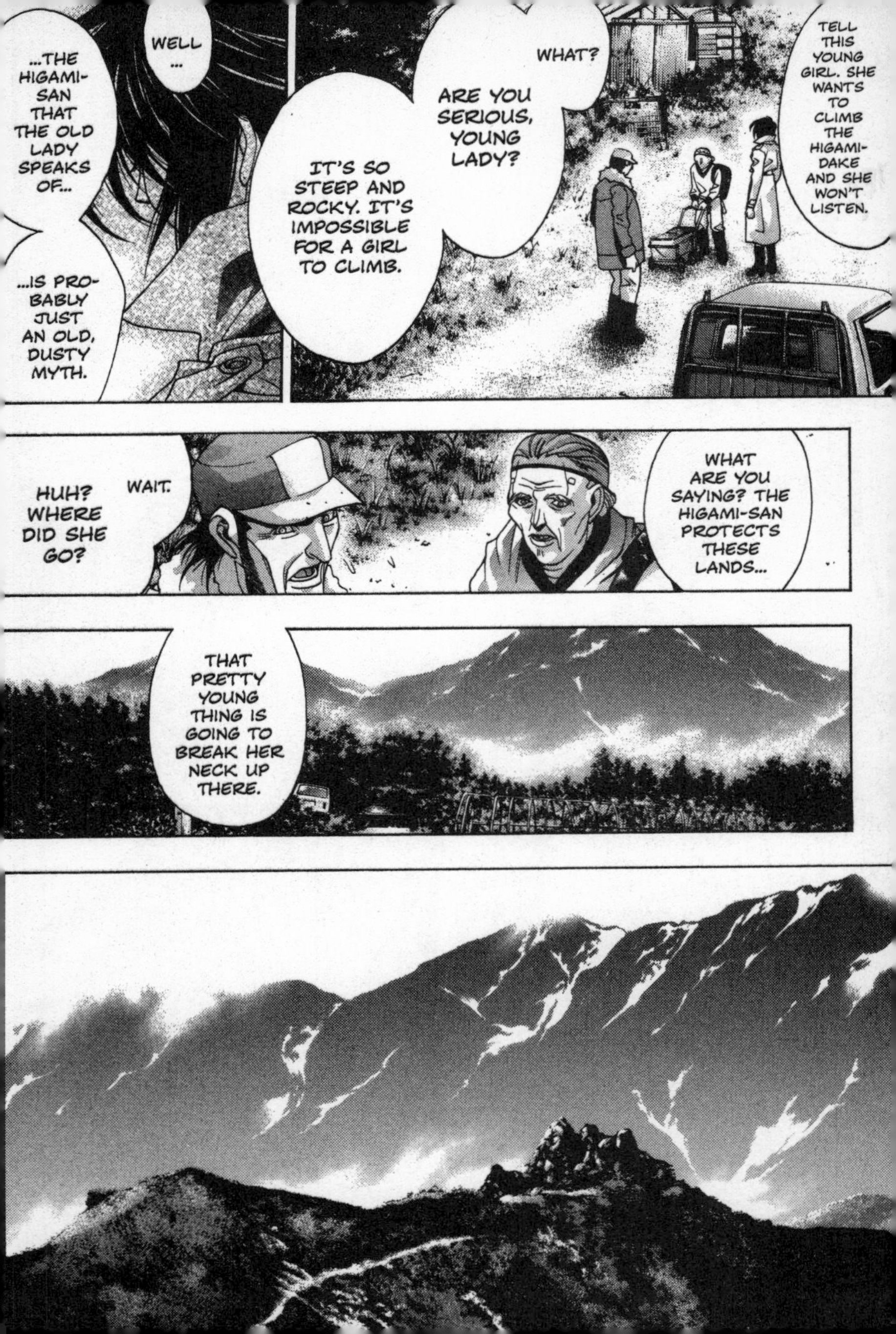
TELL THIS YOUNG GIRL. SHE WANTS TO CLIMB THE HIGAMI-DAKE AND SHE WON'T LISTEN.
WHAT?
ARE YOU SERIOUS, YOUNG LADY?
IT'S SO STEEP AND ROCKY. IT'S IMPOSSIBLE FOR A GIRL TO CLIMB.
WELL ...
...THE HIGAMI-SAN THAT THE OLD LADY SPEAKS OF...
...IS PROBABLY JUST AN OLD, DUSTY MYTH.
WHAT ARE YOU SAYING? THE HIGAMI-SAN PROTECTS THESE LANDS...
WAIT.
HUH? WHERE DID SHE GO?
THAT PRETTY YOUNG THING IS GOING TO BREAK HER NECK UP THERE.

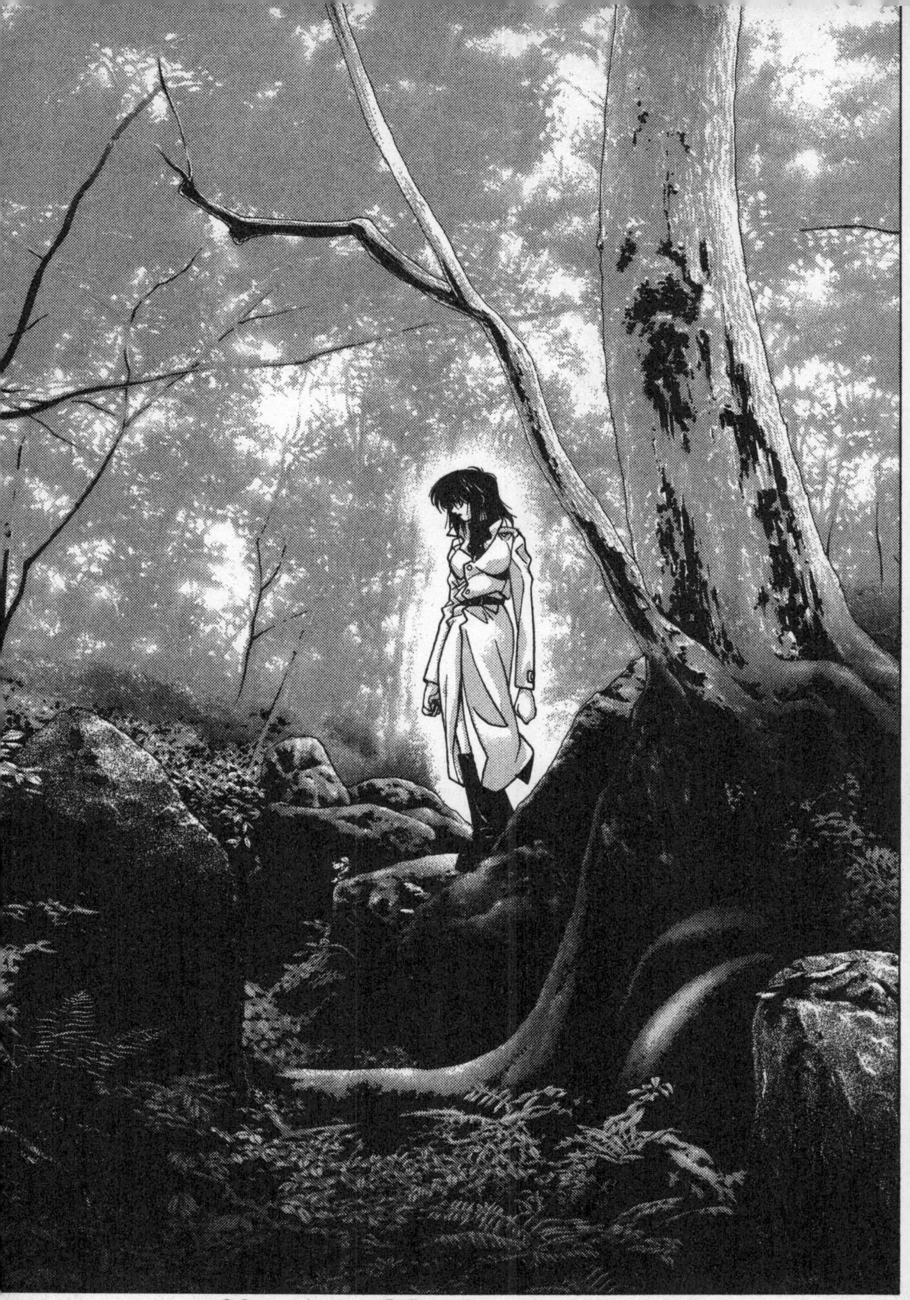

Chapter 39: Face Forward

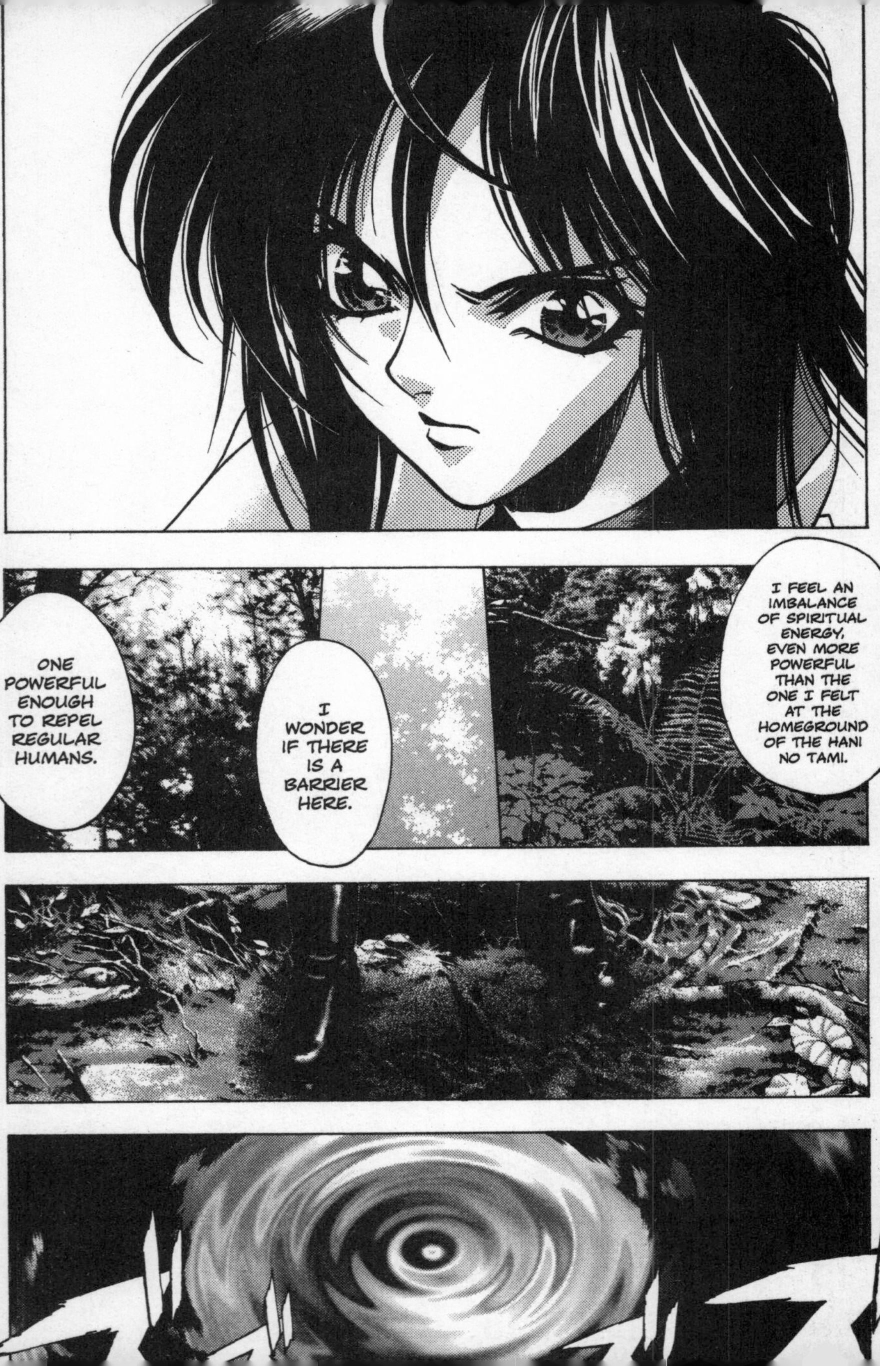
I FEEL AN IMBALANCE OF SPIRITUAL ENERGY, EVEN MORE POWERFUL THAN THE ONE I FELT AT THE HOMEGROUND OF THE HANI NO TAMI.
I WONDER IF THERE IS A BARRIER HERE.
ONE POWERFUL ENOUGH TO REPEL REGULAR HUMANS.

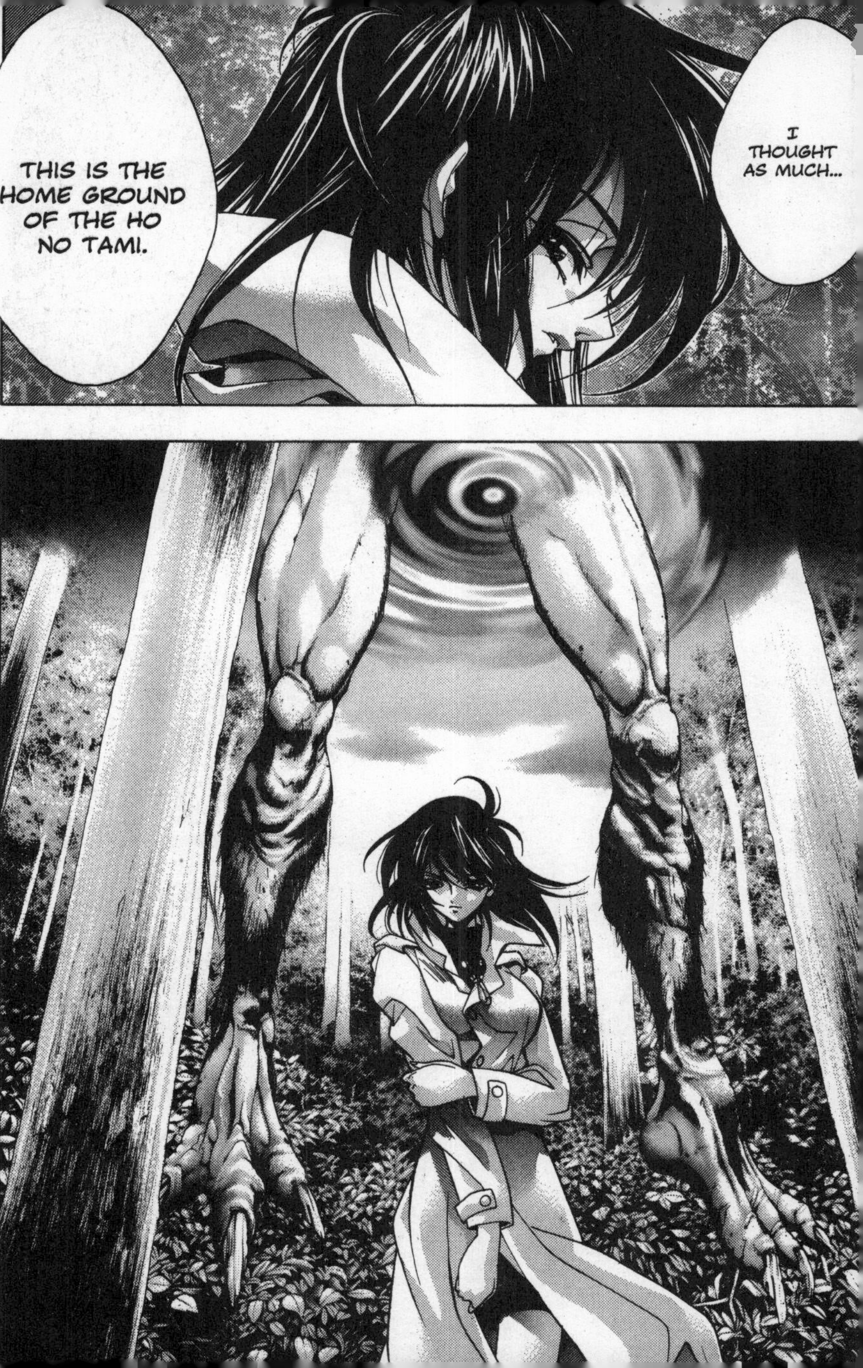
I THOUGHT AS MUCH...
THIS IS THE HOME GROUND OF THE HO NO TAMI.

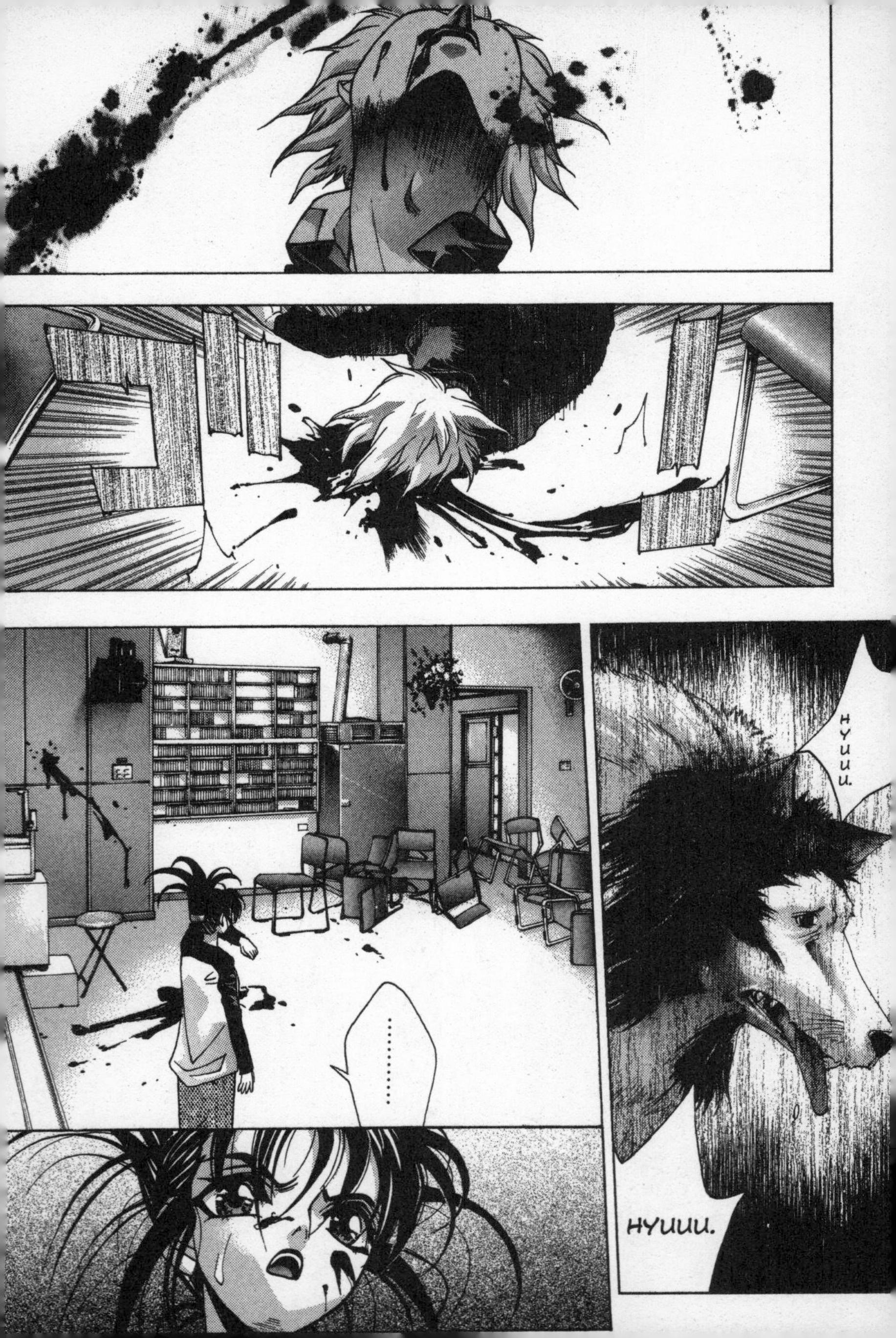
HYUUU.
HYUUU.
......

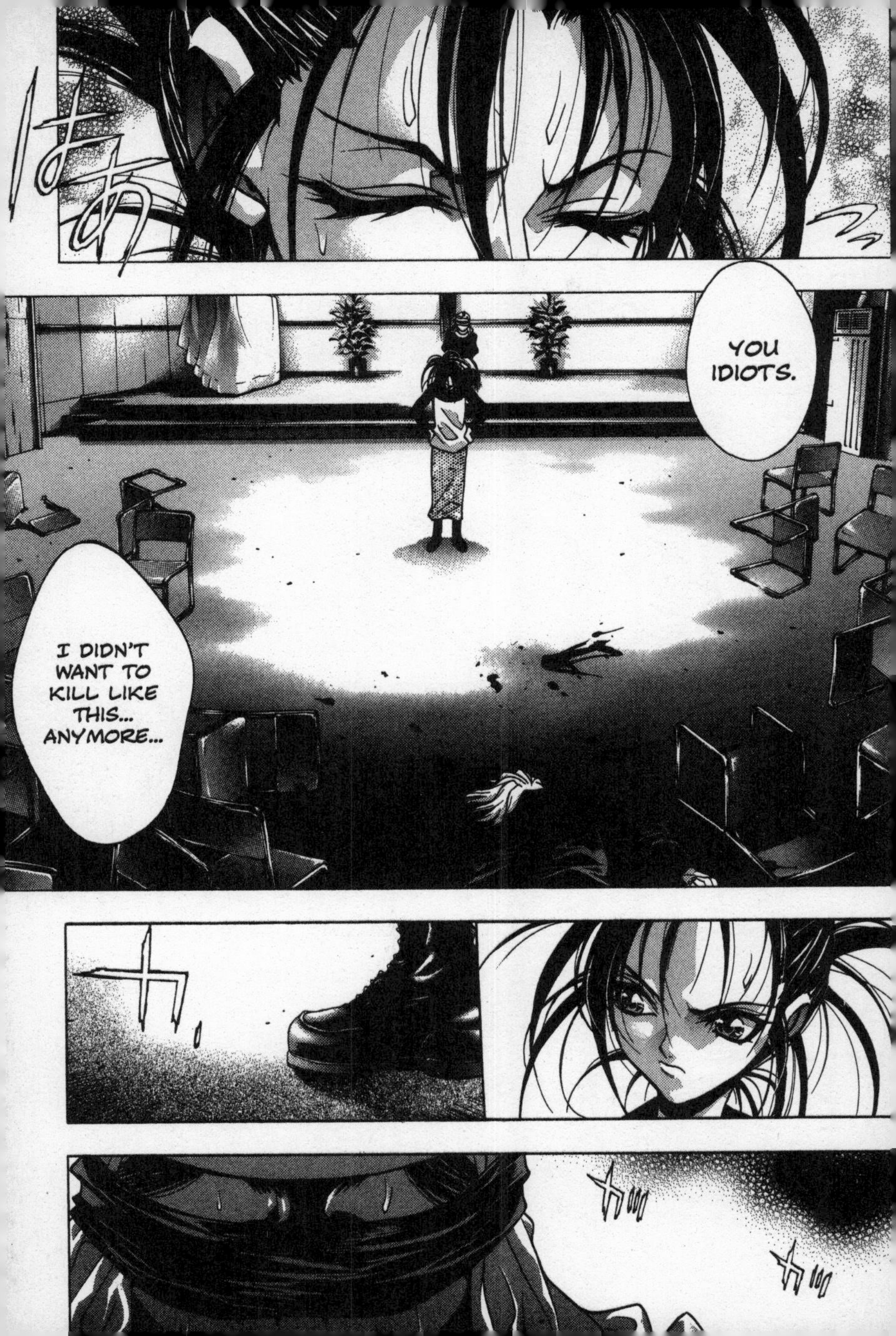
YOU IDIOTS.
I DIDN'T WANT TO KILL LIKE THIS... ANYMORE...

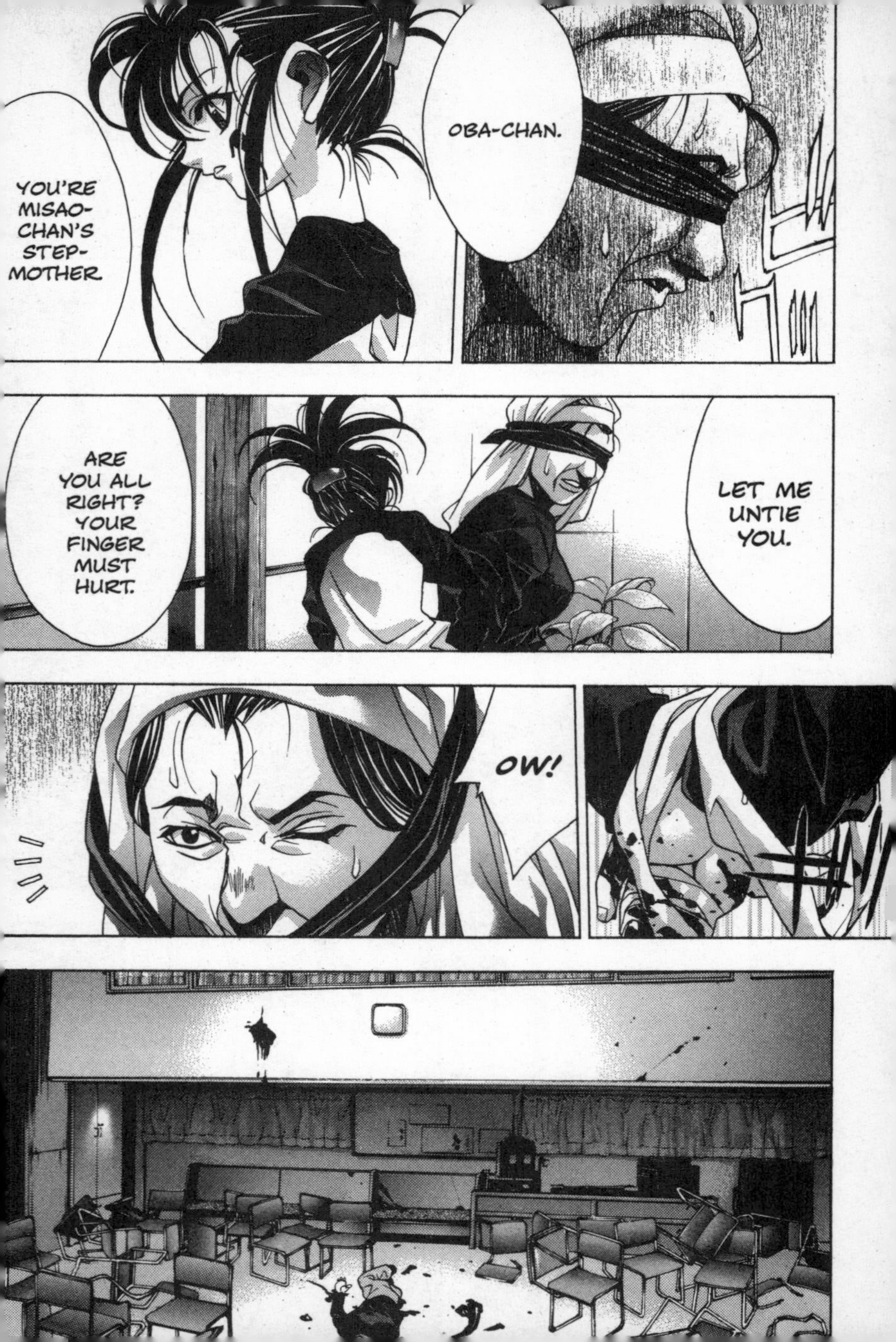
OBA-CHAN.
YOU'RE MISAO-CHAN'S STEP-MOTHER.
LET ME UNTIE YOU.
ARE YOU ALL RIGHT? YOUR FINGER MUST HURT.
OW!

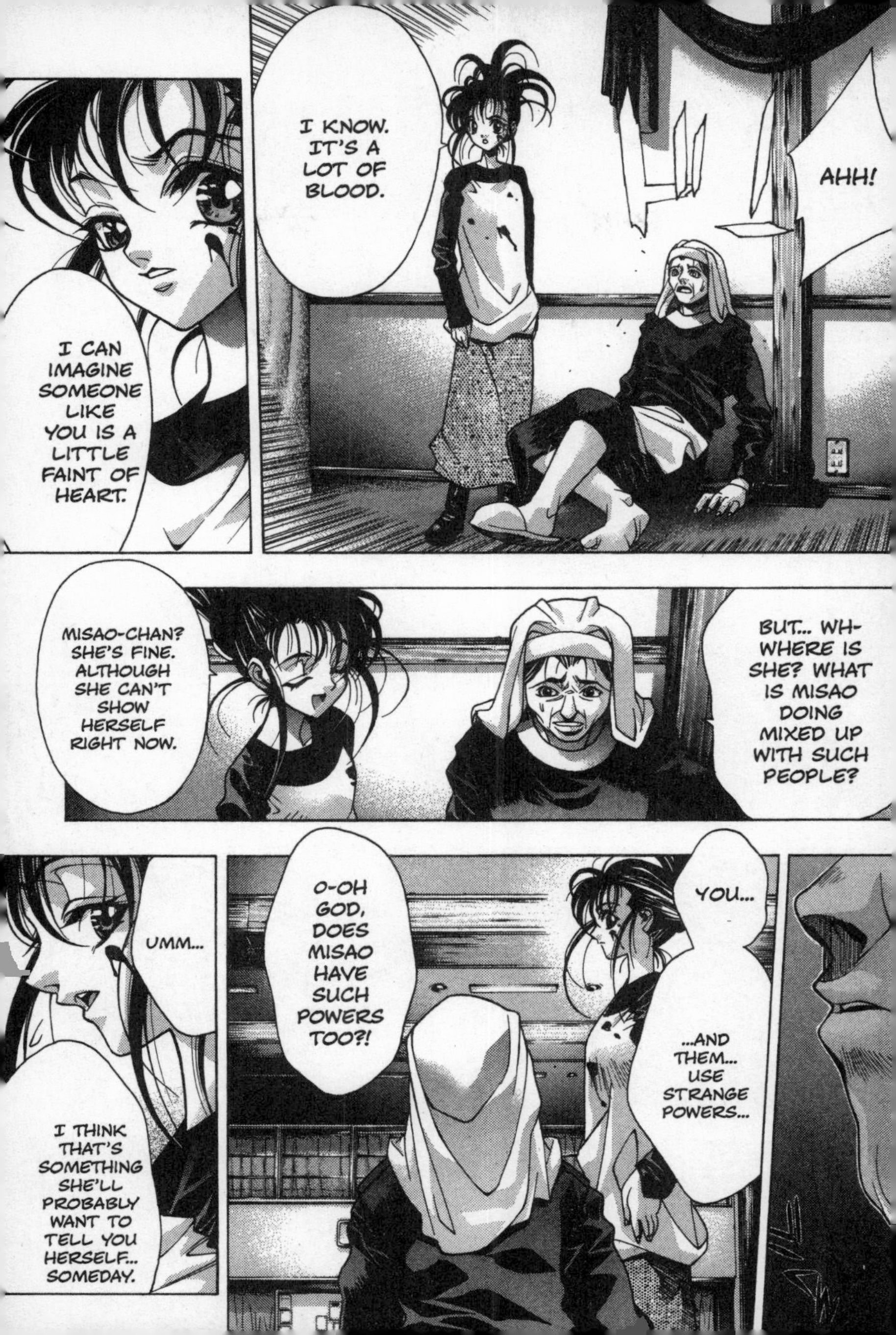
AHH!
I KNOW. IT'S A LOT OF BLOOD.
I CAN IMAGINE SOMEONE LIKE YOU IS A LITTLE FAINT OF HEART.
BUT... WH-WHERE IS SHE? WHAT IS MISAO DOING MIXED UP WITH SUCH PEOPLE?
MISAO-CHAN? SHE'S FINE. ALTHOUGH SHE CAN'T SHOW HERSELF RIGHT NOW.
YOU...
...AND THEM... USE STRANGE POWERS...
O-OH GOD, DOES MISAO HAVE SUCH POWERS TOO?!
UMM...
I THINK THAT'S SOMETHING SHE'LL PROBABLY WANT TO TELL YOU HERSELF... SOMEDAY.

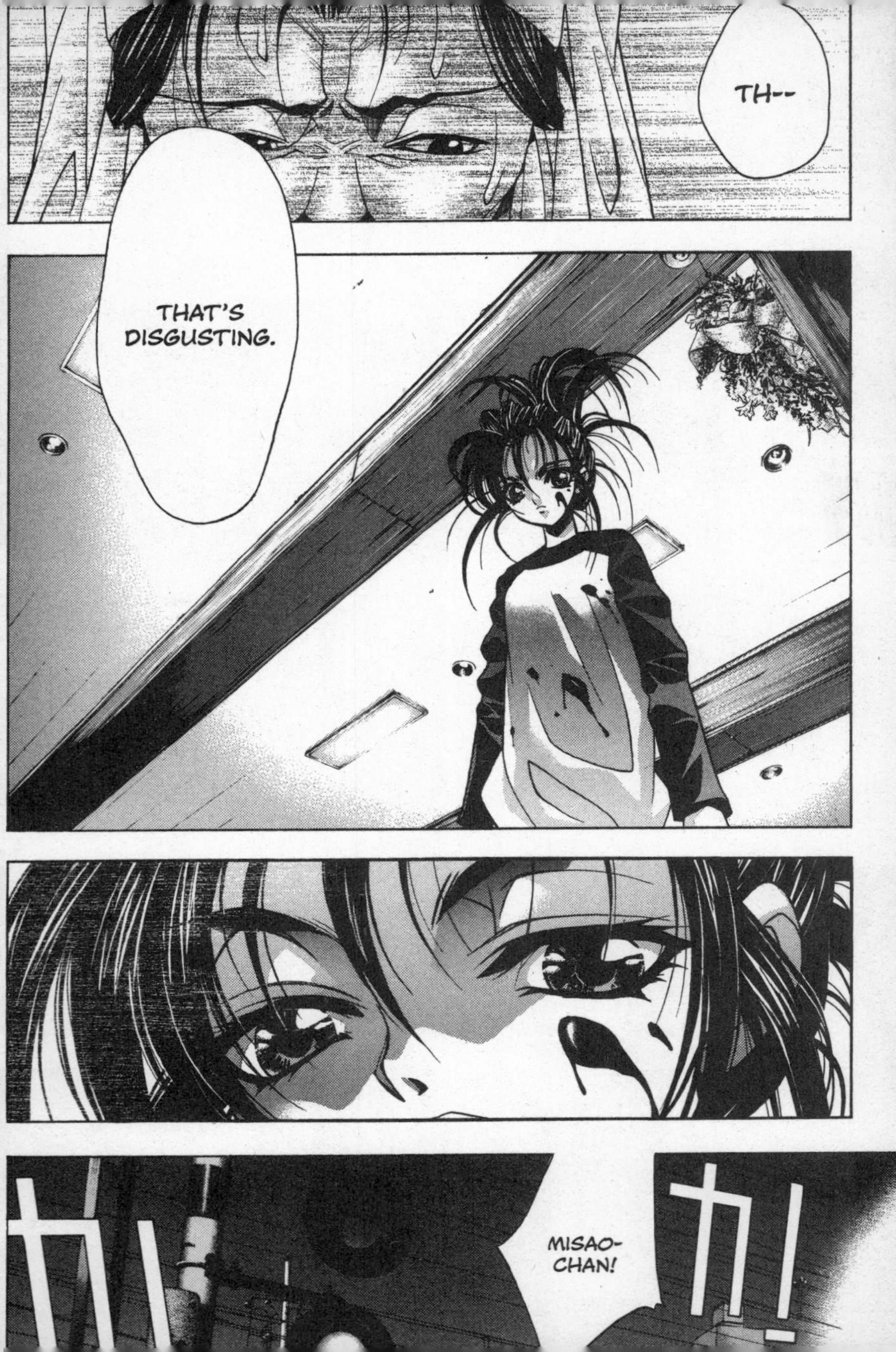
TH--
THAT'S DISGUSTING.
MISAO-CHAN!

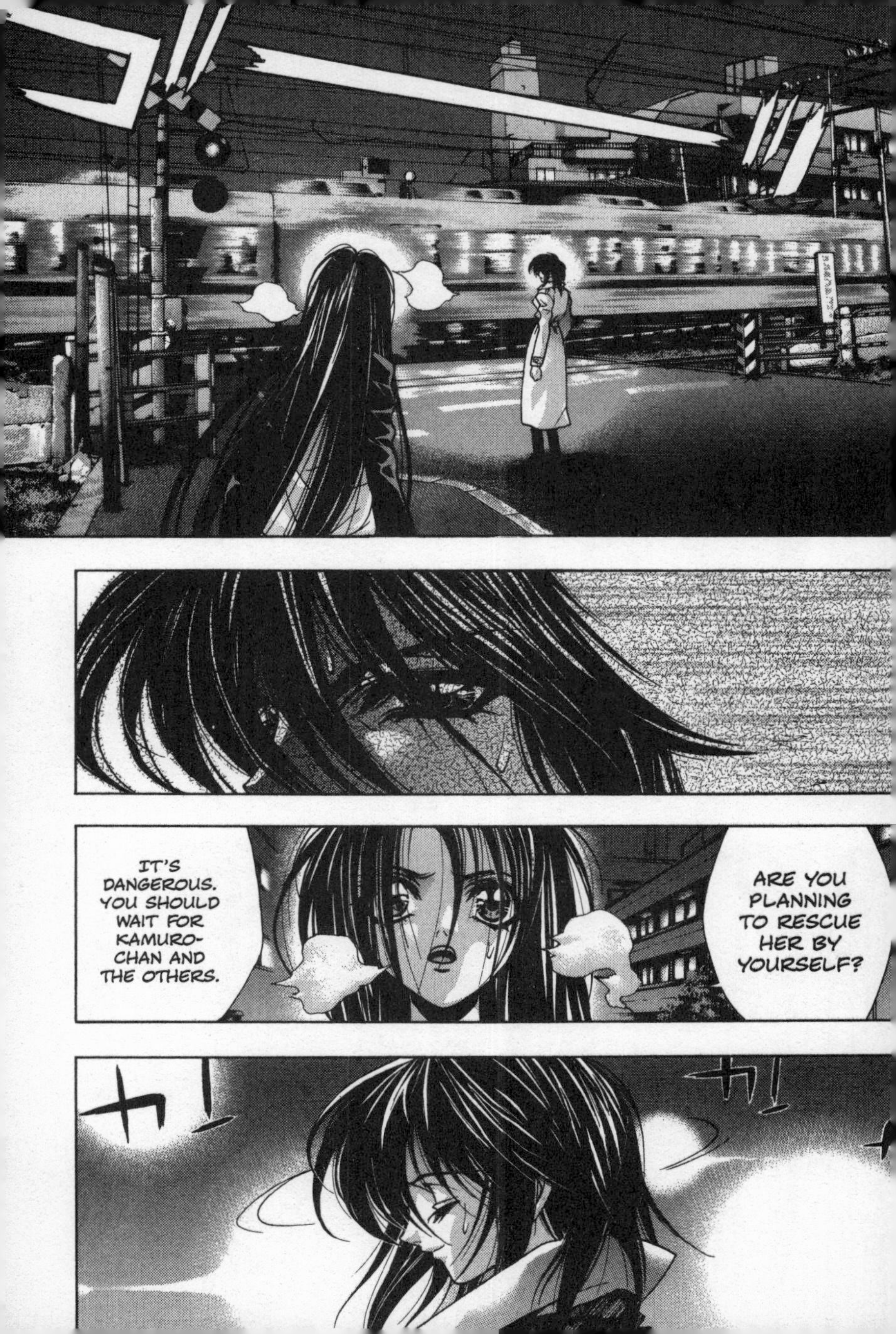
ARE YOU PLANNING TO RESCUE HER BY YOURSELF?
IT'S DANGEROUS. YOU SHOULD WAIT FOR KAMURO-CHAN AND THE OTHERS.

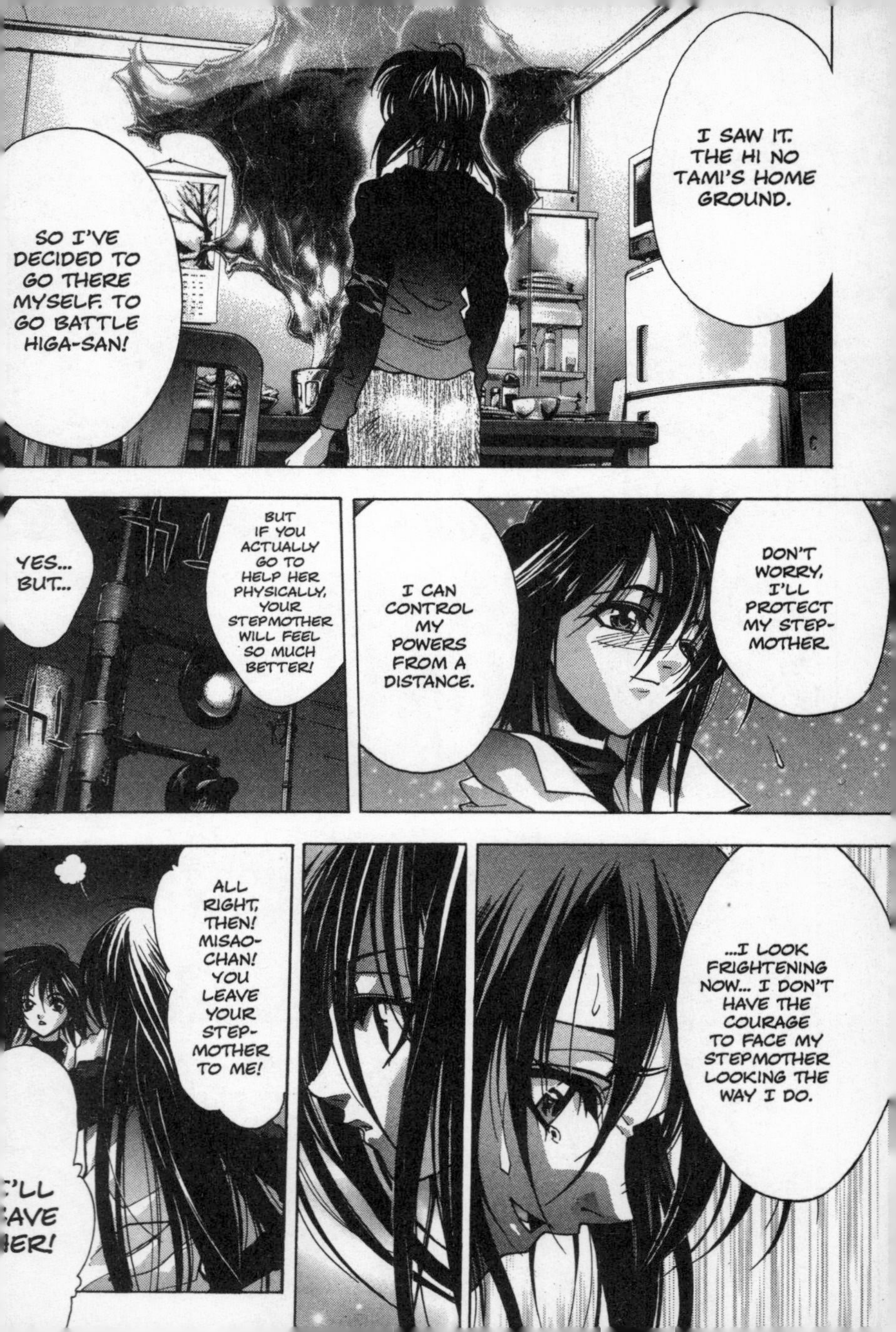
I SAW IT. THE HI NO TAMI'S HOME GROUND.
SO I'VE DECIDED TO GO THERE MYSELF. TO GO BATTLE HIGA-SAN!
DON'T WORRY, I'LL PROTECT MY STEP-MOTHER
I CAN CONTROL MY POWERS FROM A DISTANCE.
BUT IF YOU ACTUALLY GO TO HELP HER PHYSICALLY, YOUR STEPMOTHER WILL FEEL SO MUCH BETTER!
YES... BUT...
...I LOOK FRIGHTENING NOW... I DON'T HAVE THE COURAGE TO FACE MY STEPMOTHER LOOKING THE WAY I DO.
ALL RIGHT, THEN! MISAO-CHAN! YOU LEAVE YOUR STEP-MOTHER TO ME!
'LL AVE ER!

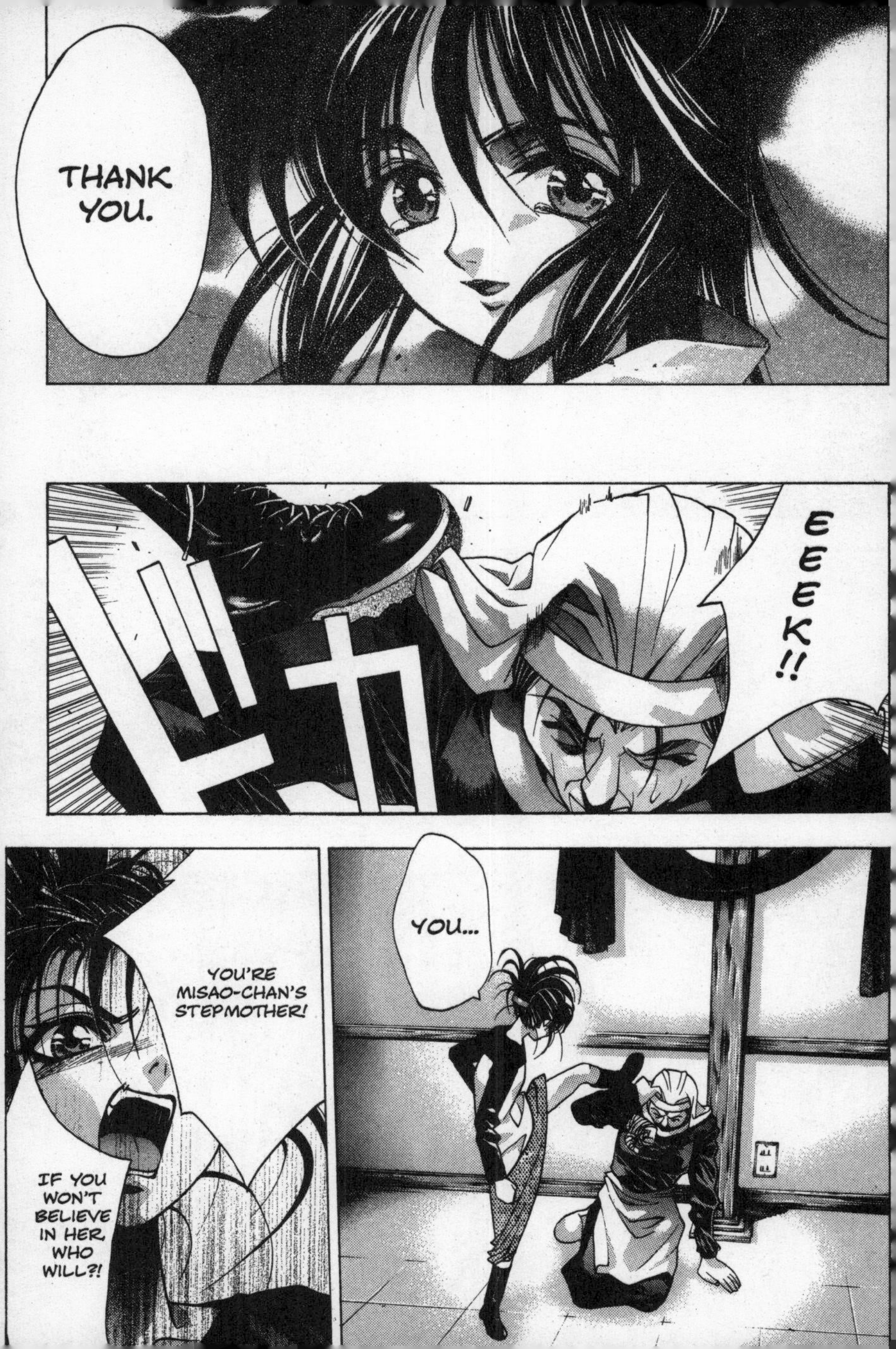
THANK YOU.
EEEK!!
ドカ
YOU...
YOU'RE MISAO-CHAN'S STEPMOTHER!
IF YOU WON'T BELIEVE IN HER WHO WILL?!

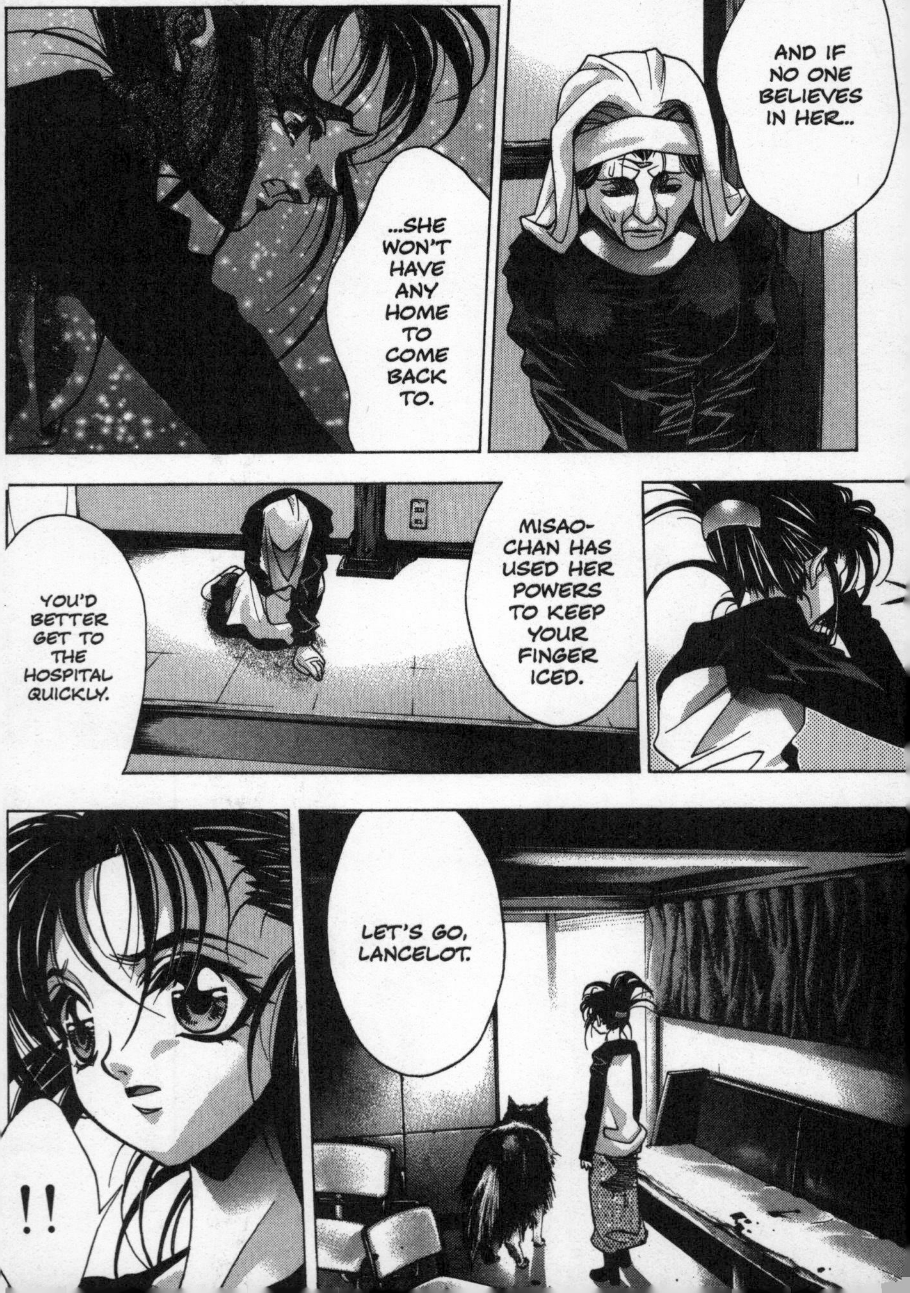
AND IF NO ONE BELIEVES IN HER...
...SHE WON'T HAVE ANY HOME TO COME BACK TO.
MISAO-CHAN HAS USED HER POWERS TO KEEP YOUR FINGER ICED.
YOU'D BETTER GET TO THE HOSPITAL QUICKLY.
LET'S GO, LANCELOT.
!!

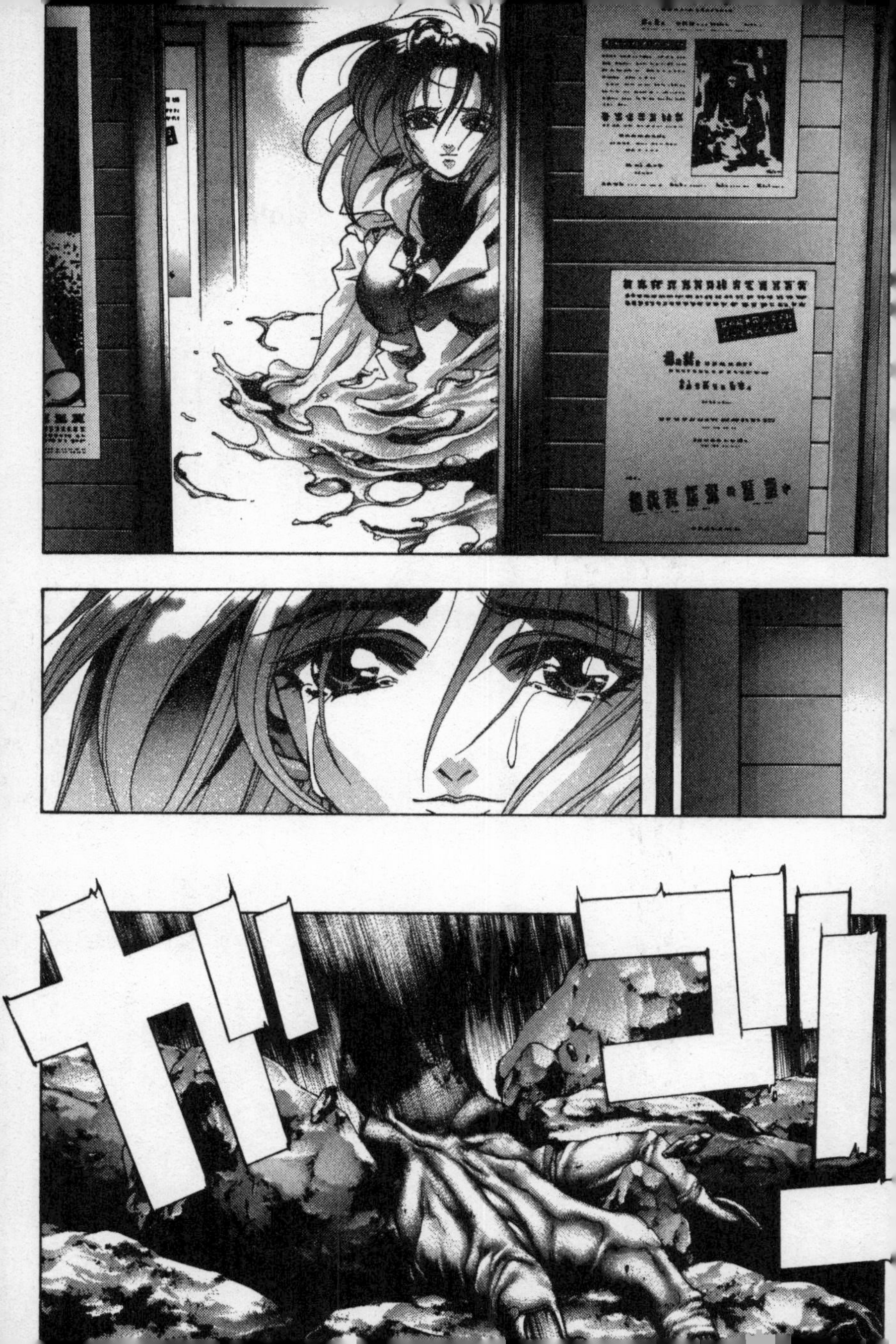
ガゴー

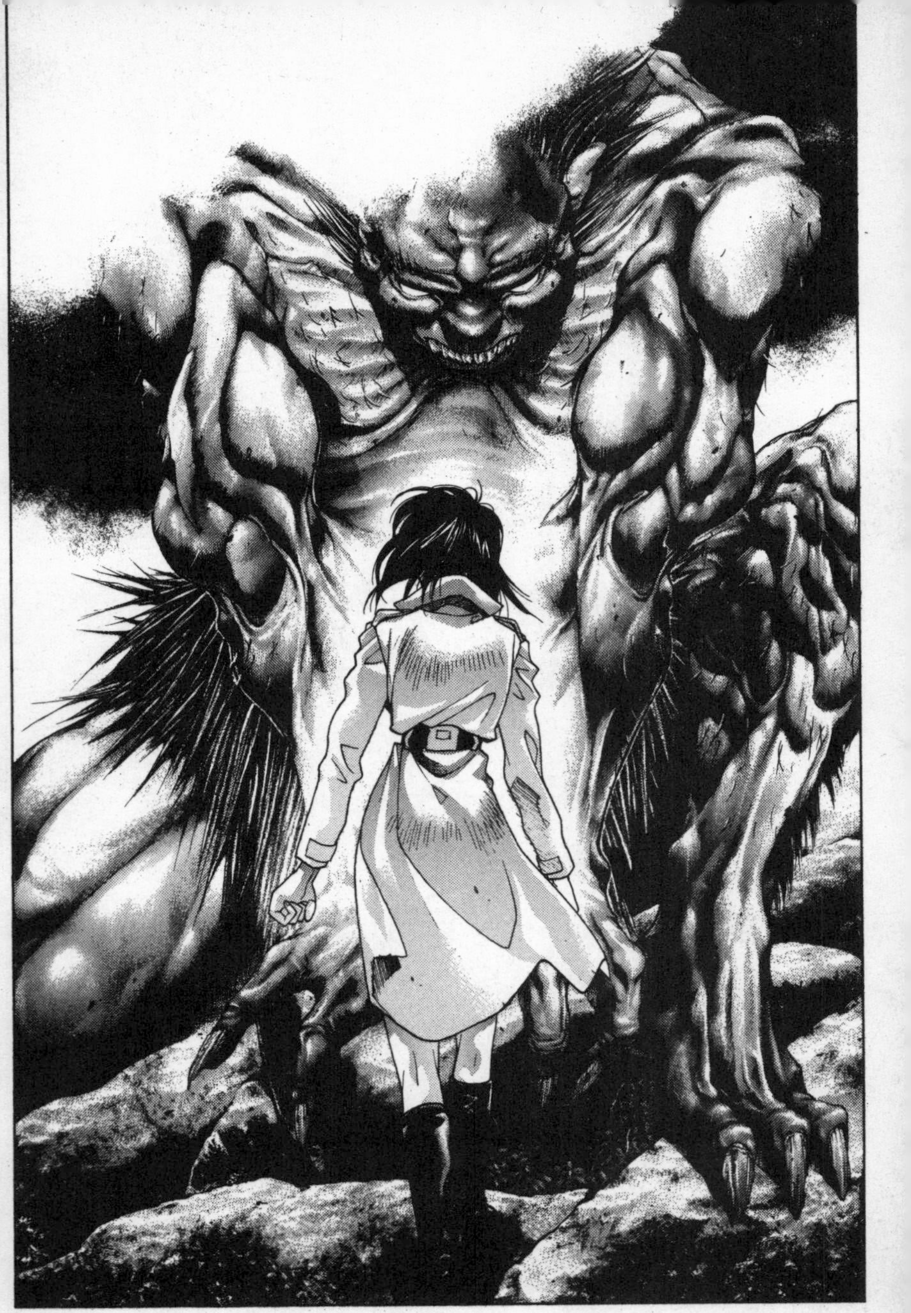

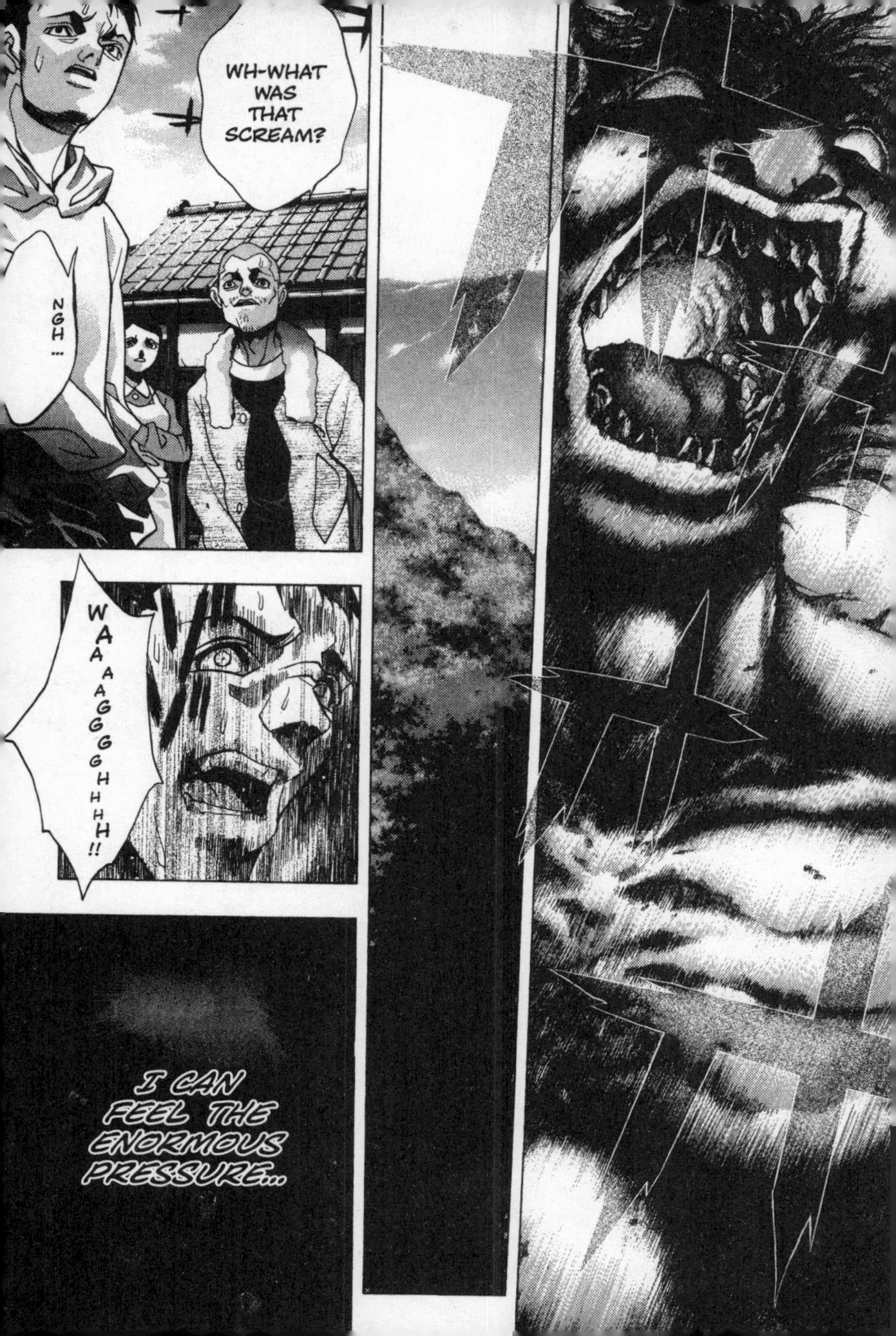
WH-WHAT WAS THAT SCREAM?
NGH...
WAAAAGGGGHHHH!!
I CAN FEEL THE ENORMOUS PRESSURE...

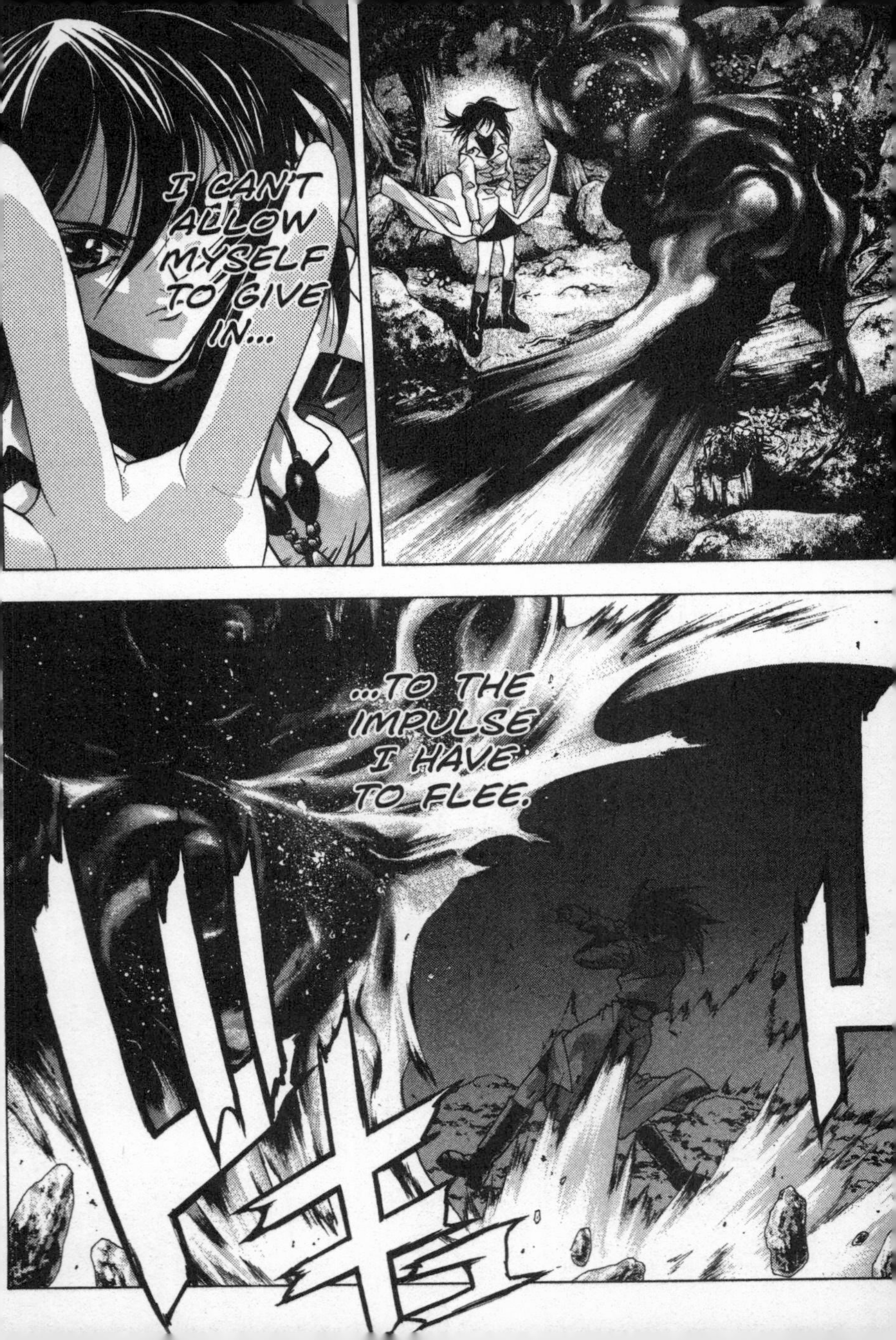
I CAN'T ALLOW MYSELF TO GIVE IN...
...TO THE IMPULSE I HAVE TO FLEE.

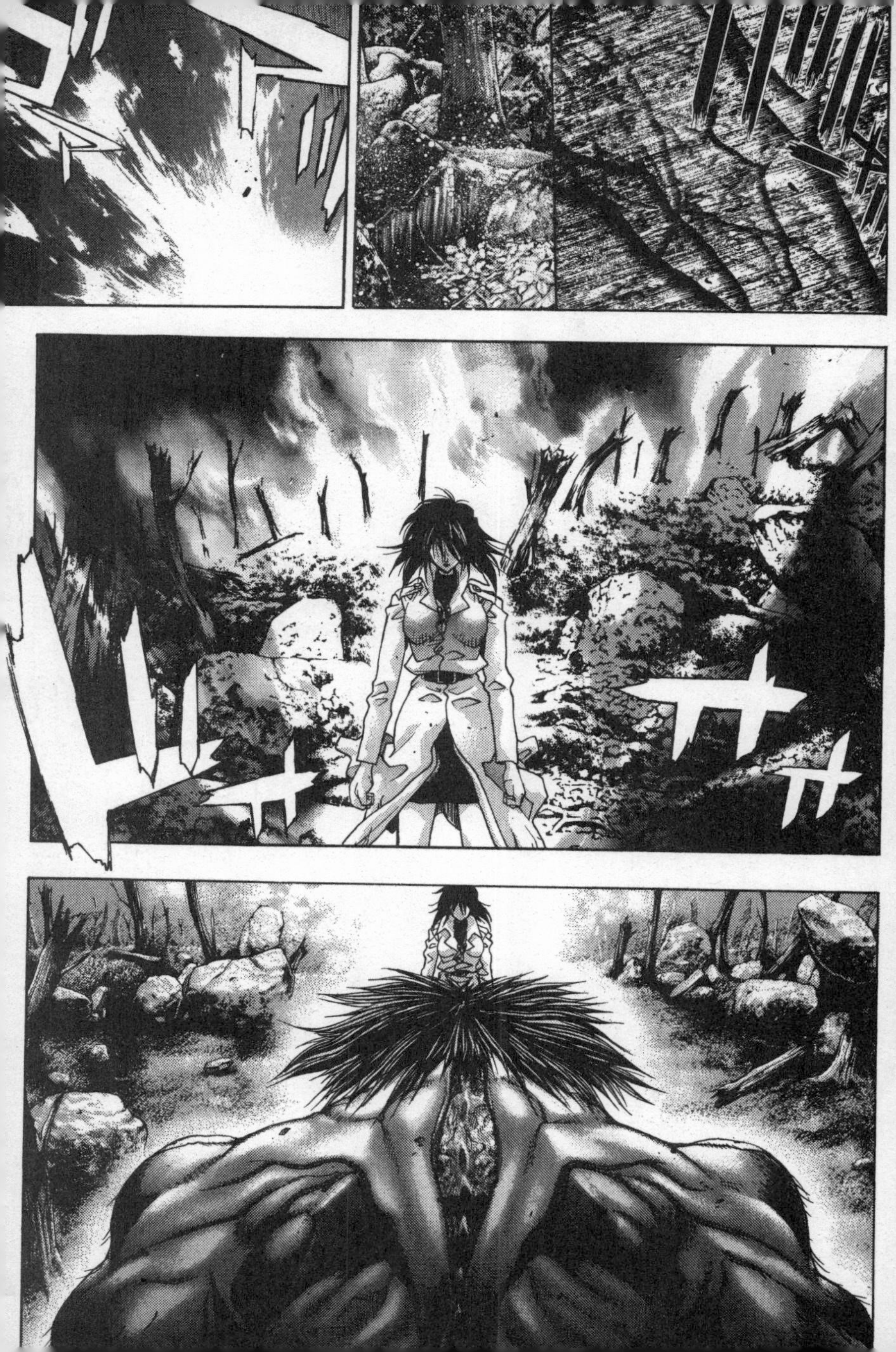

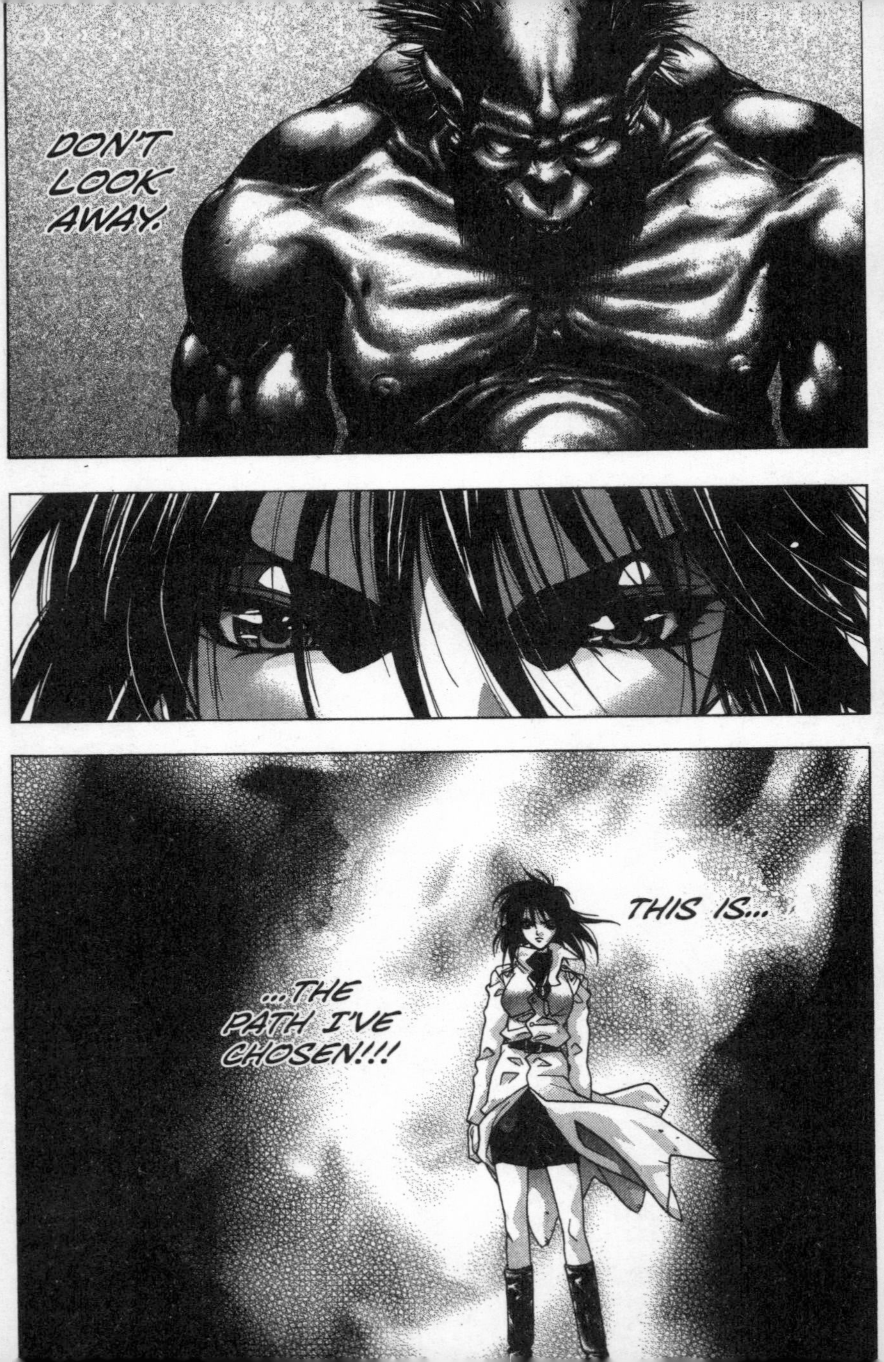
DON'T LOOK AWAY.
THIS IS...
...THE PATH I'VE CHOSEN!!!

I'M NOT AFRAID!!!

HUFF!

HUFF!!

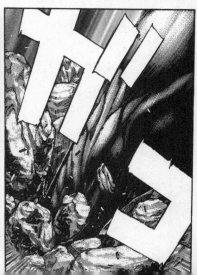

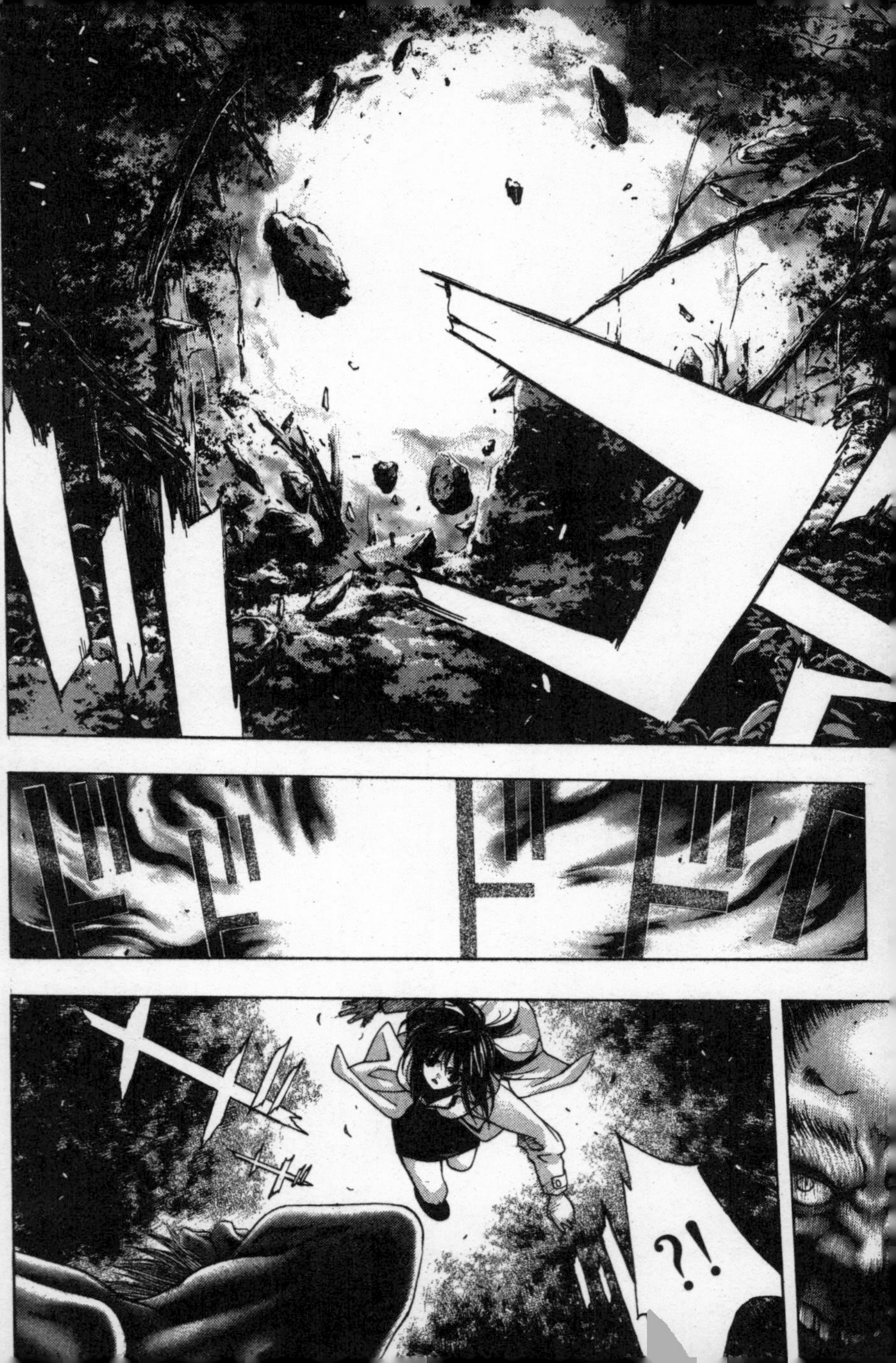
?!

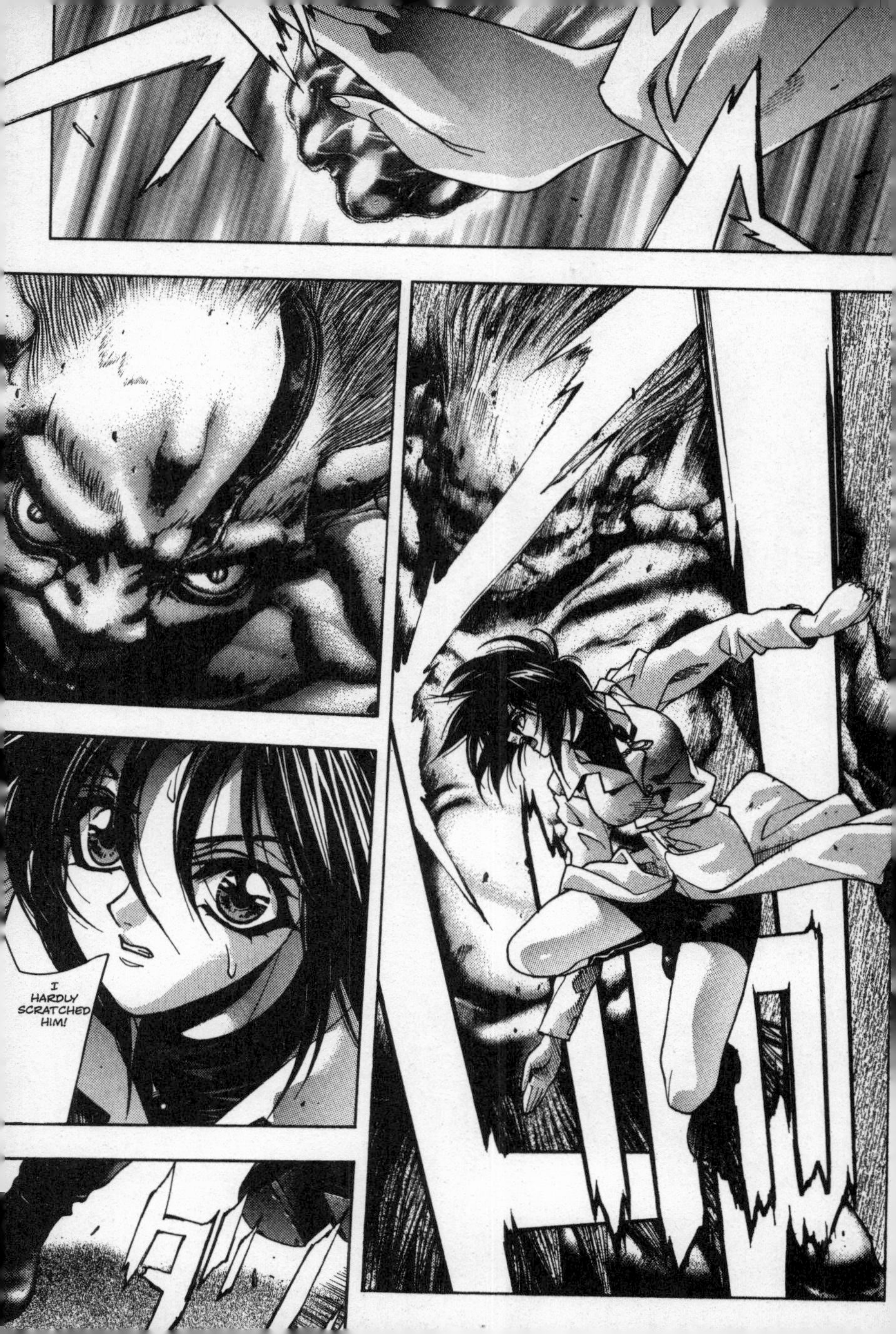
I HARDLY SCRATCHED HIM!

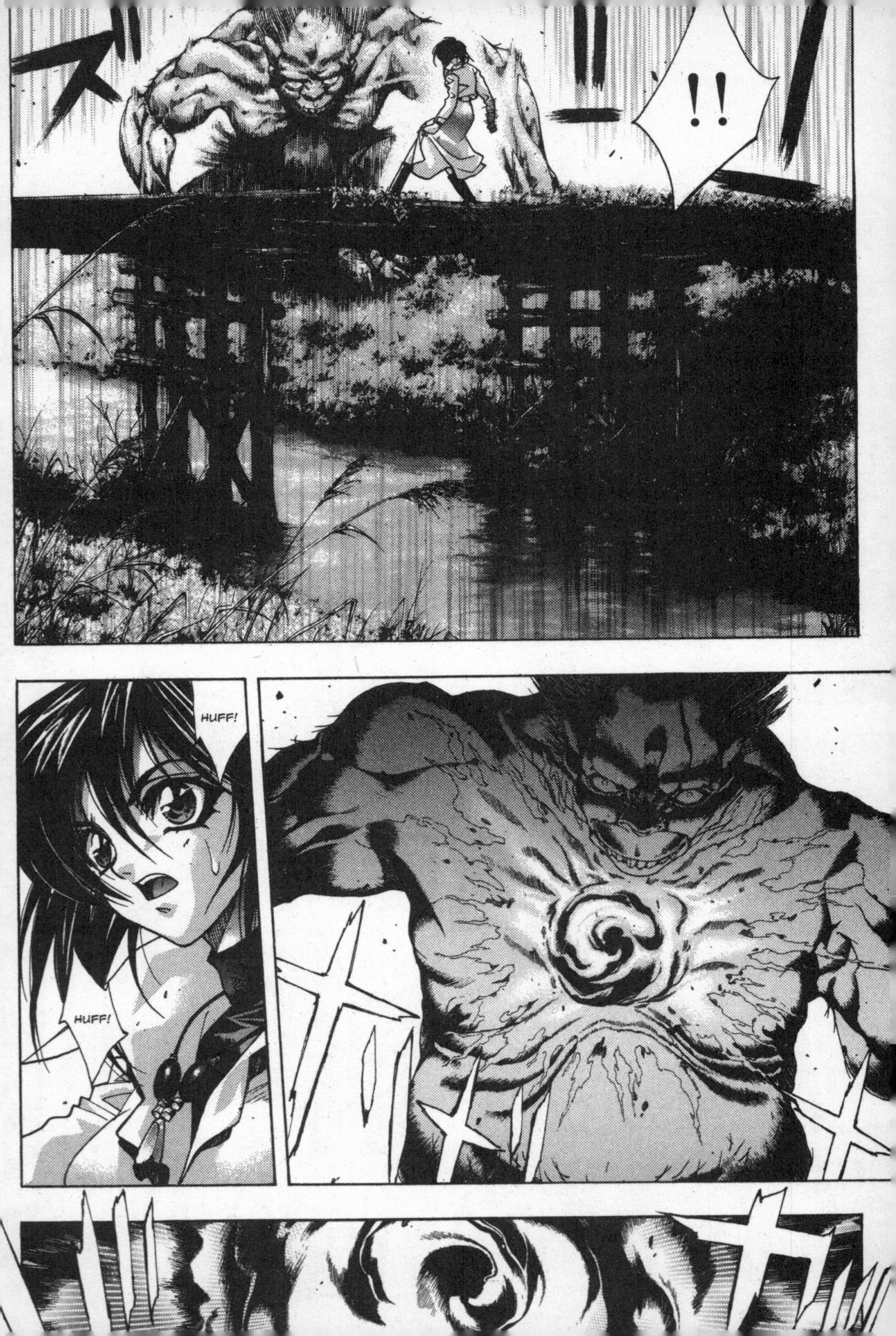
!!
HUFF!
HUFF!

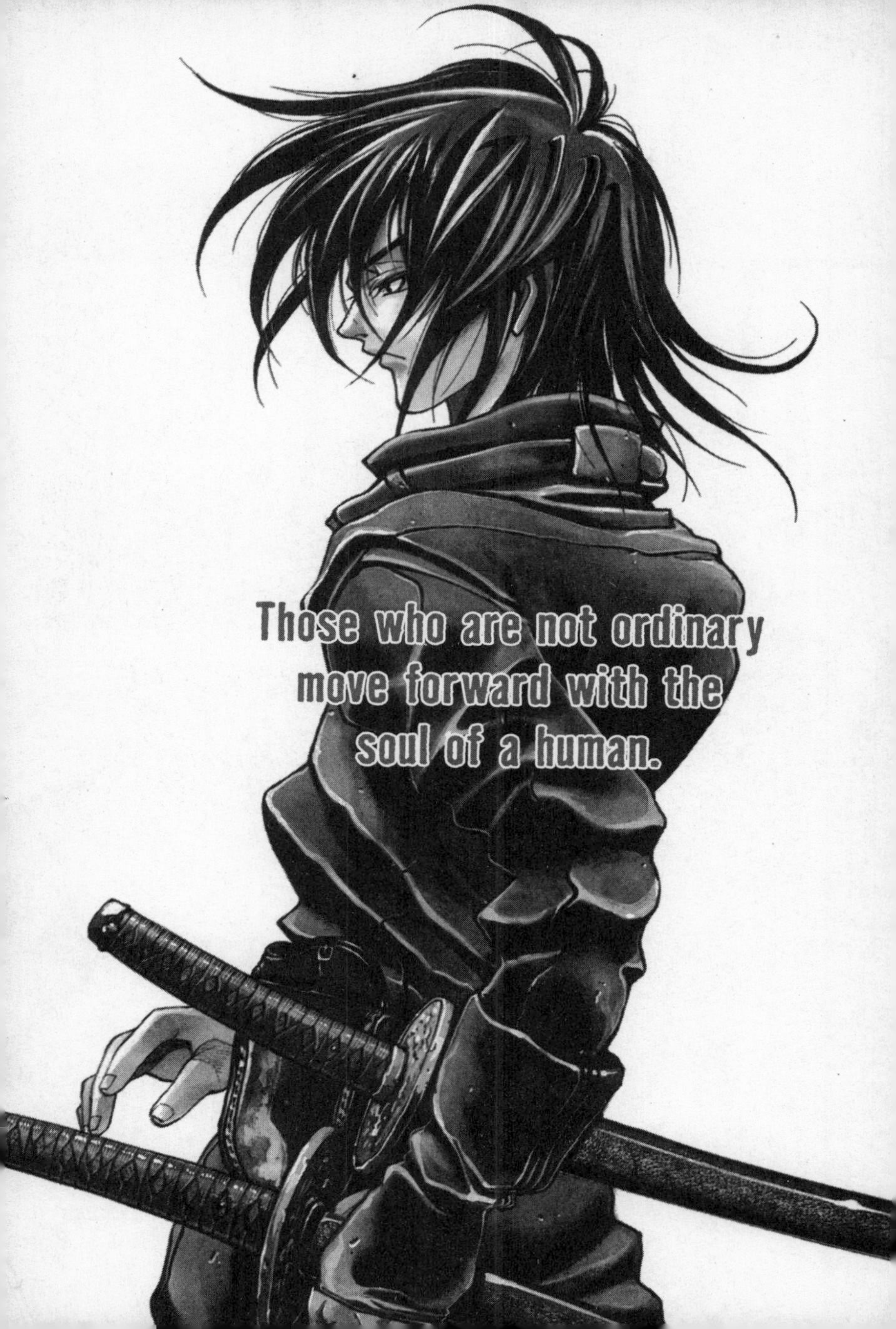
Those who are not ordinary
move forward with the
soul of a human.

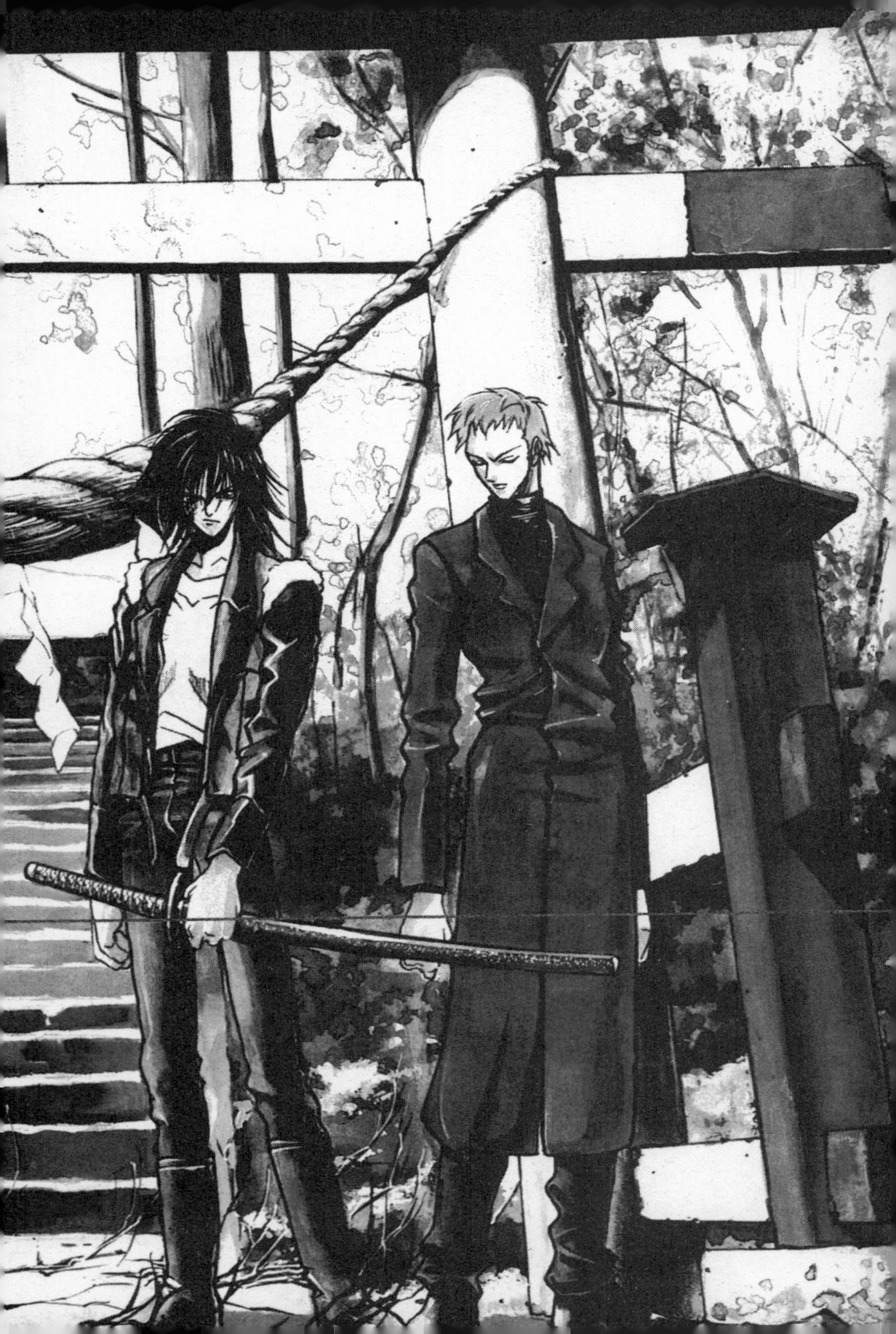

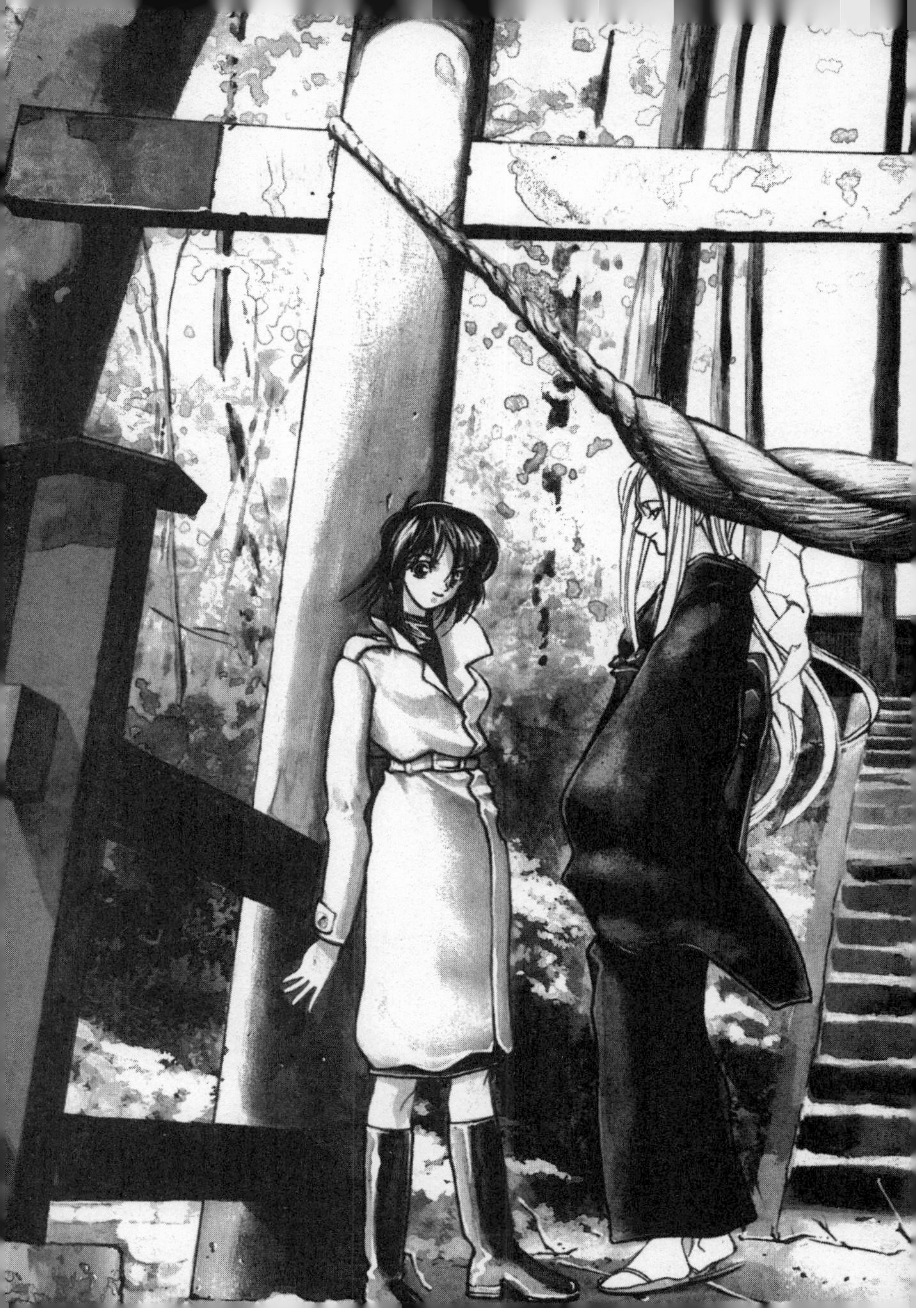

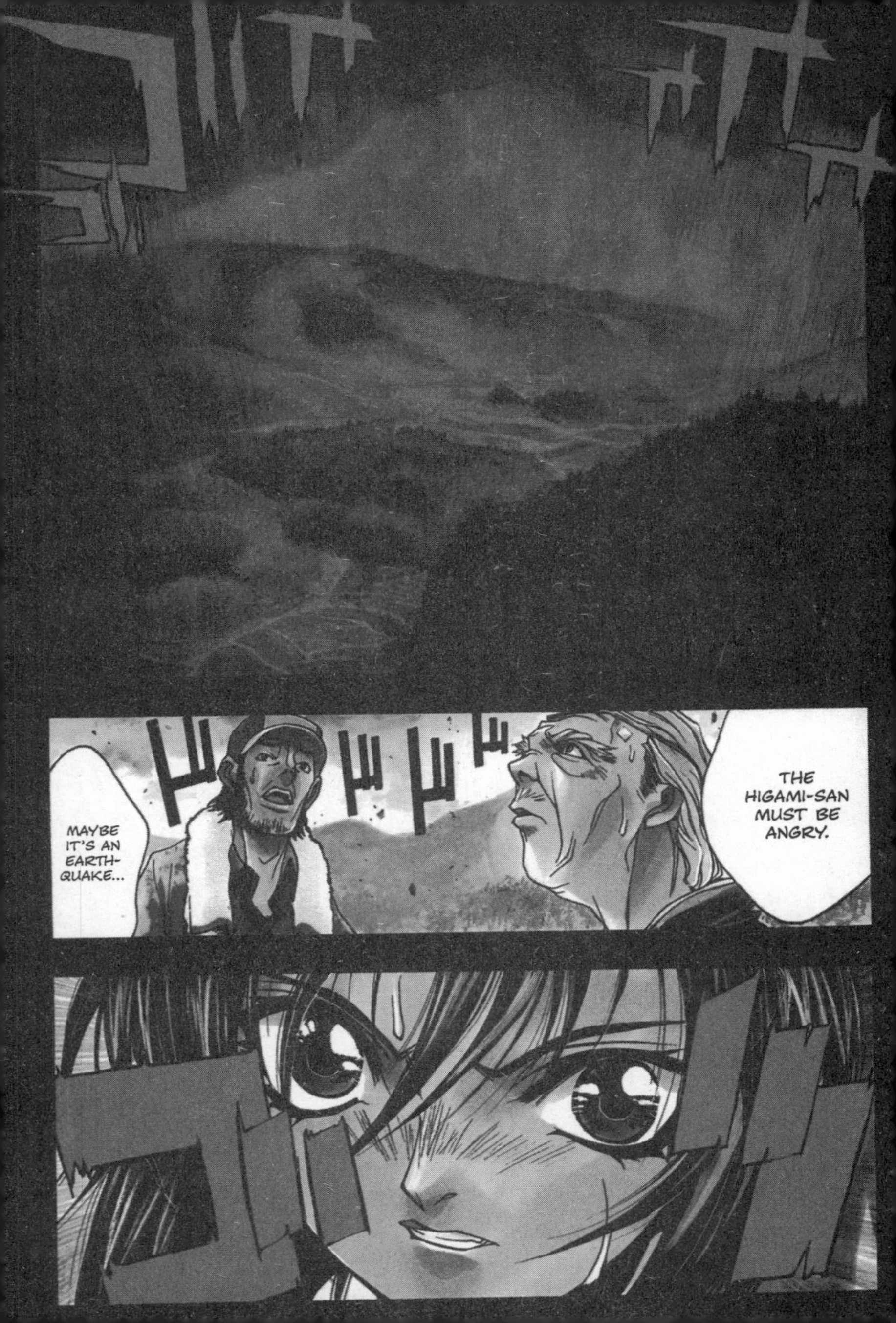
THE HIGAMI-SAN MUST BE ANGRY.
MAYBE IT'S AN EARTH-QUAKE...

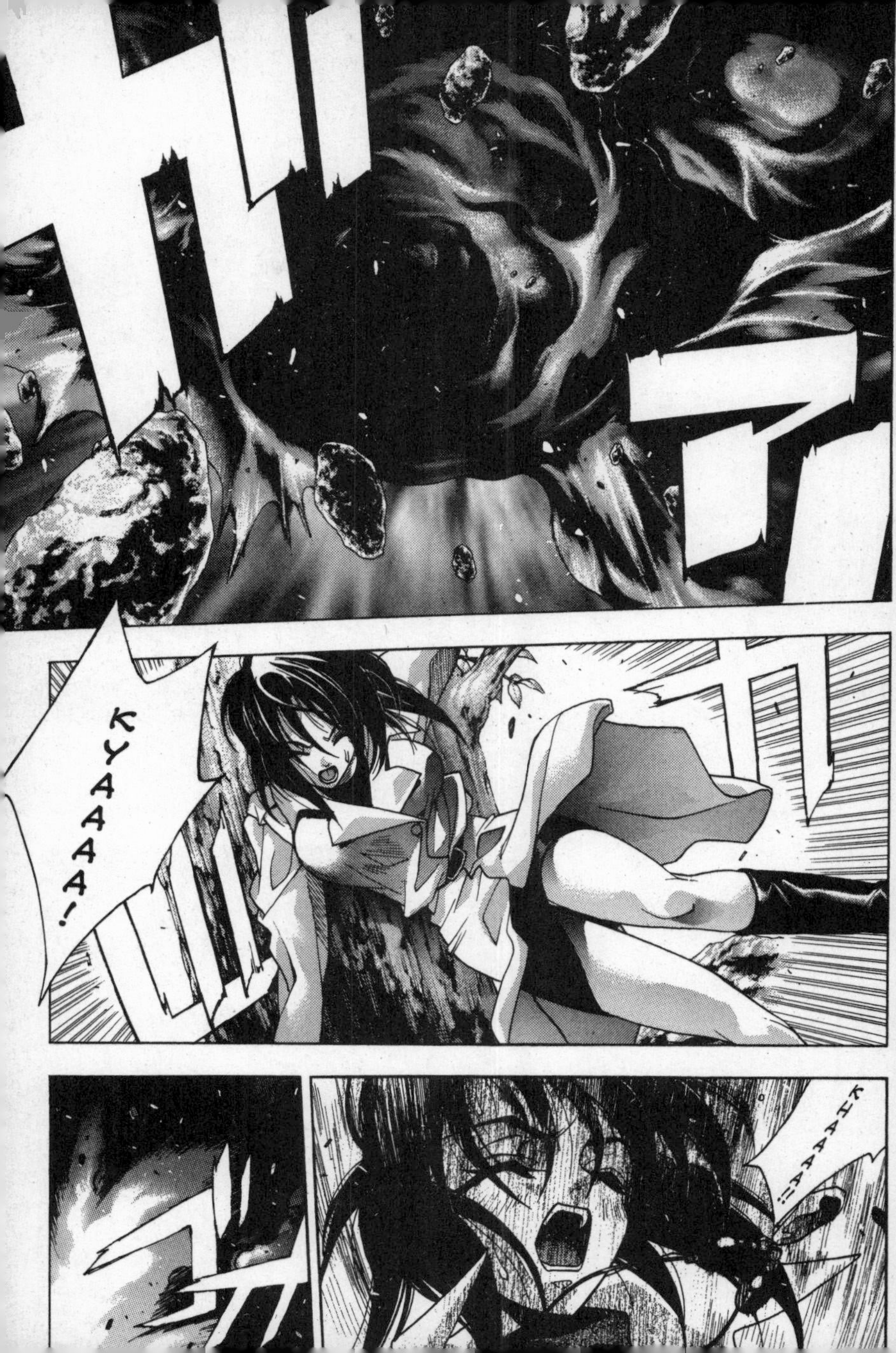
KYAAAAA!
KHAAAA!!

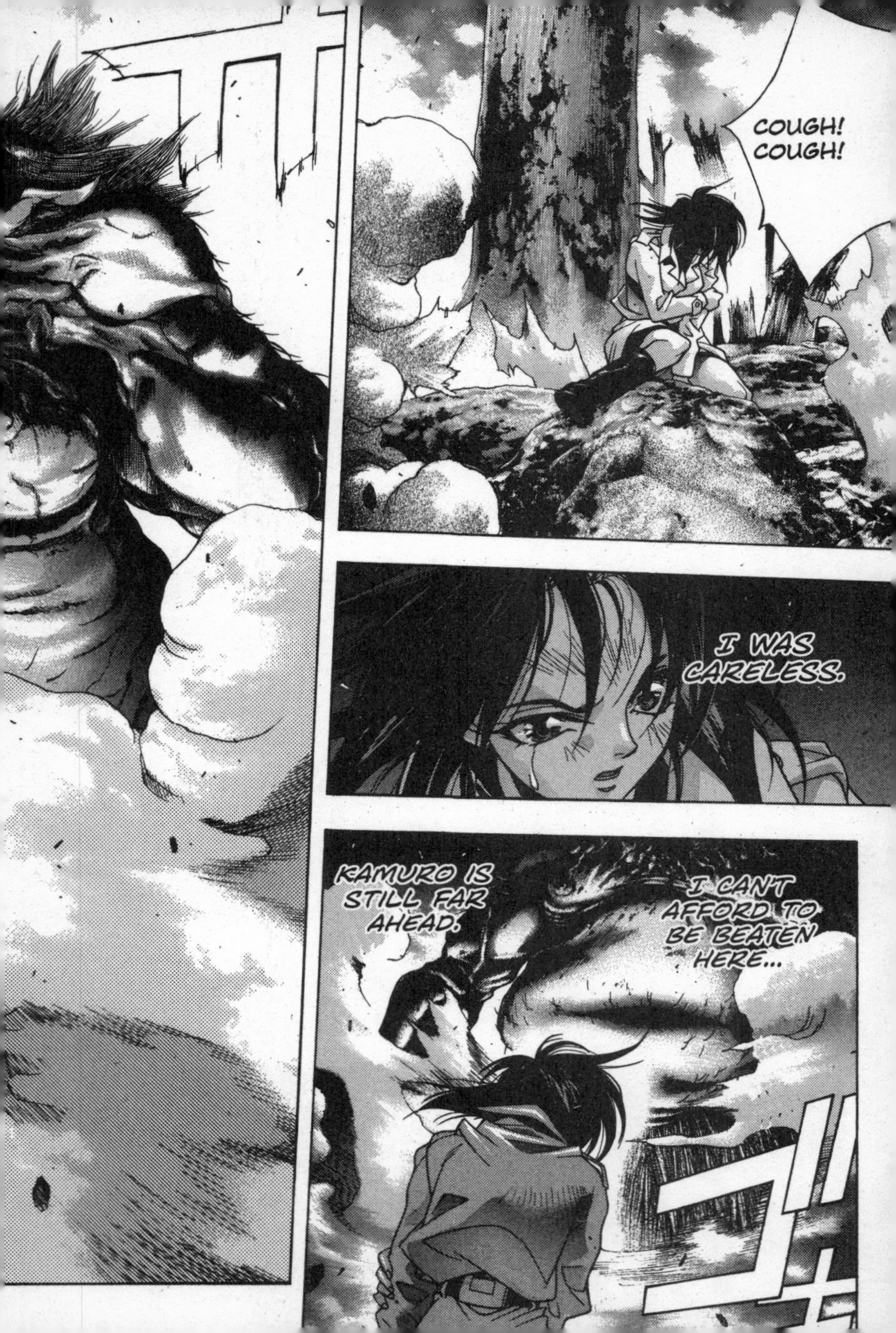
COUGH! COUGH!
I WAS CARELESS.
KAMURO IS STILL FAR AHEAD.
I CAN'T AFFORD TO BE BEATEN HERE...

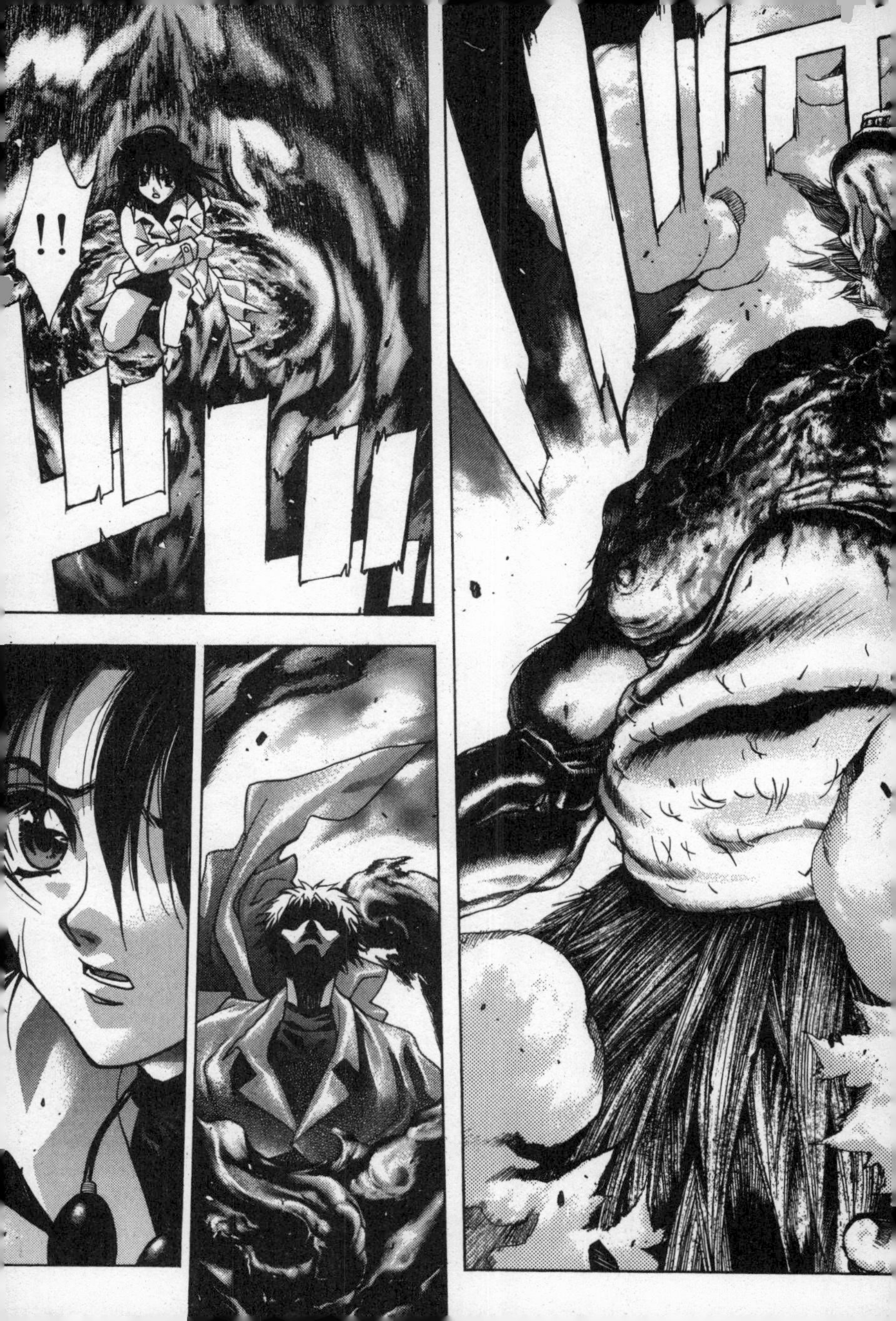
!!

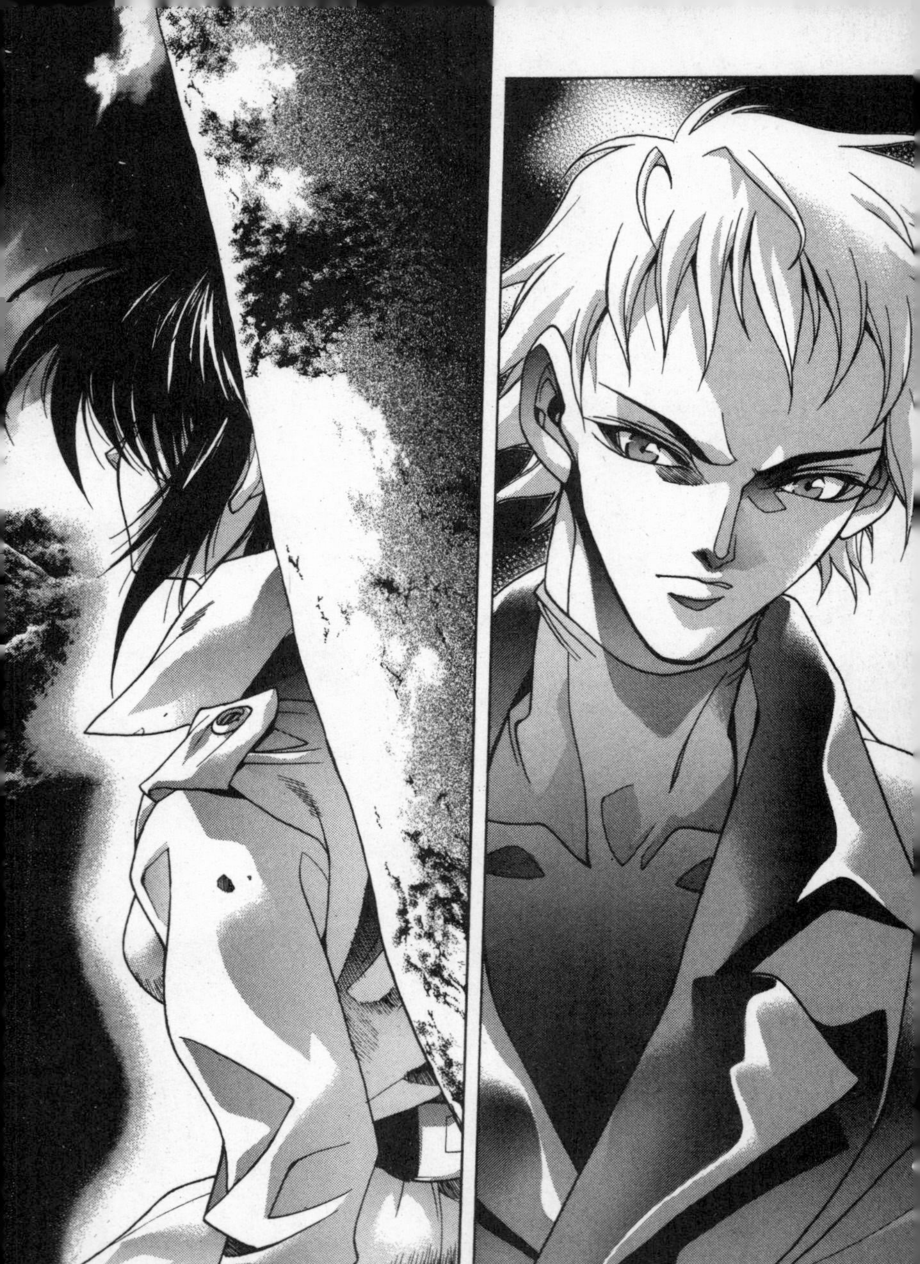

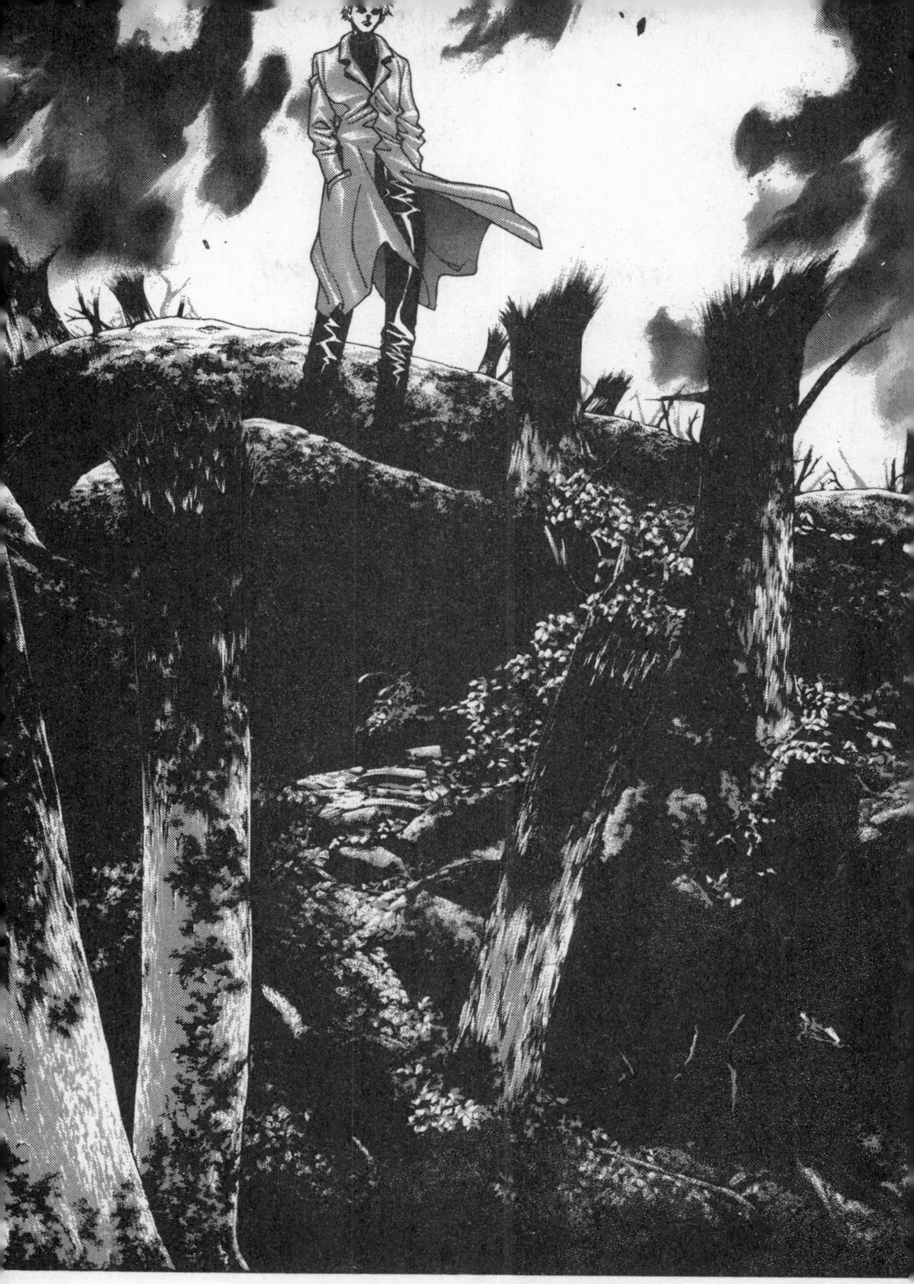

Chapter 40: Higami

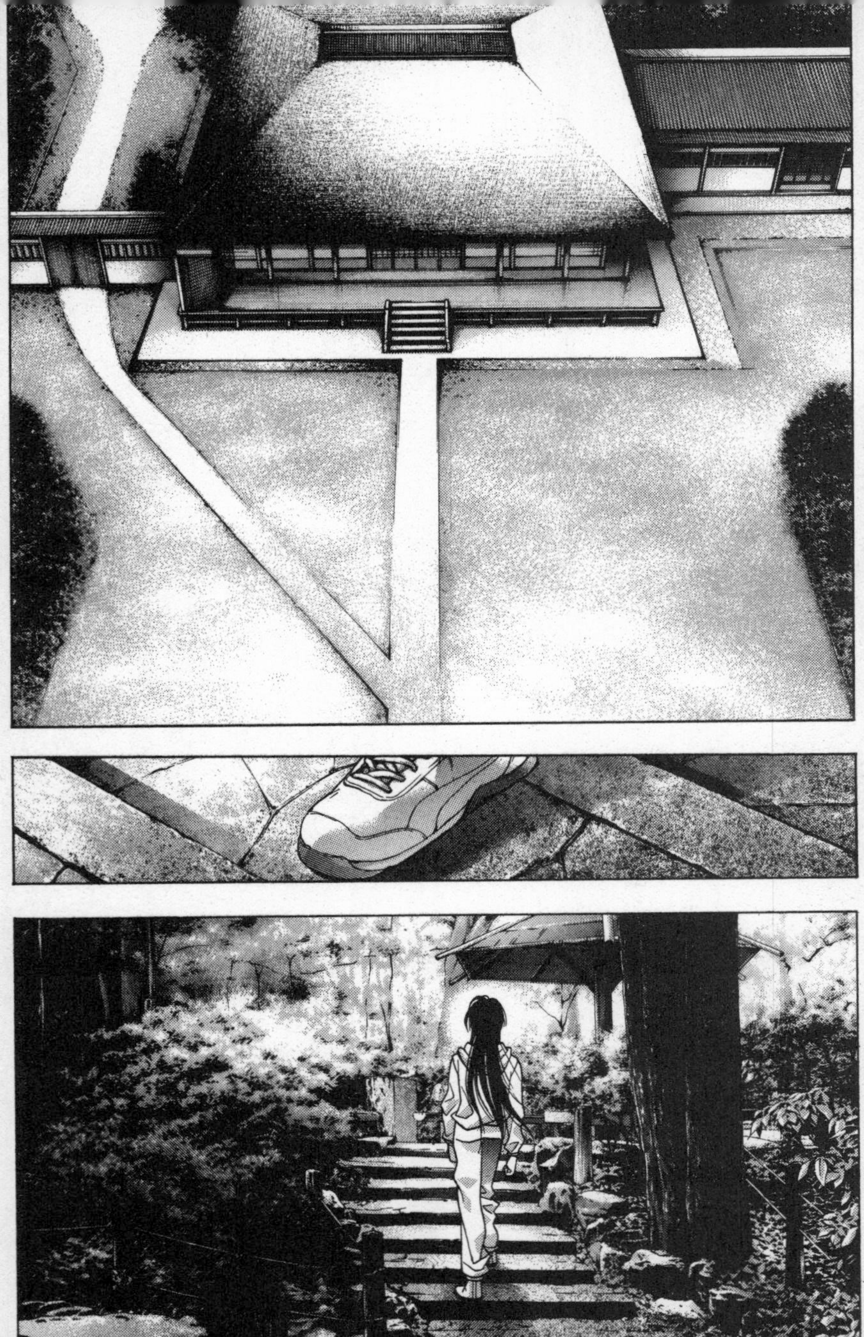

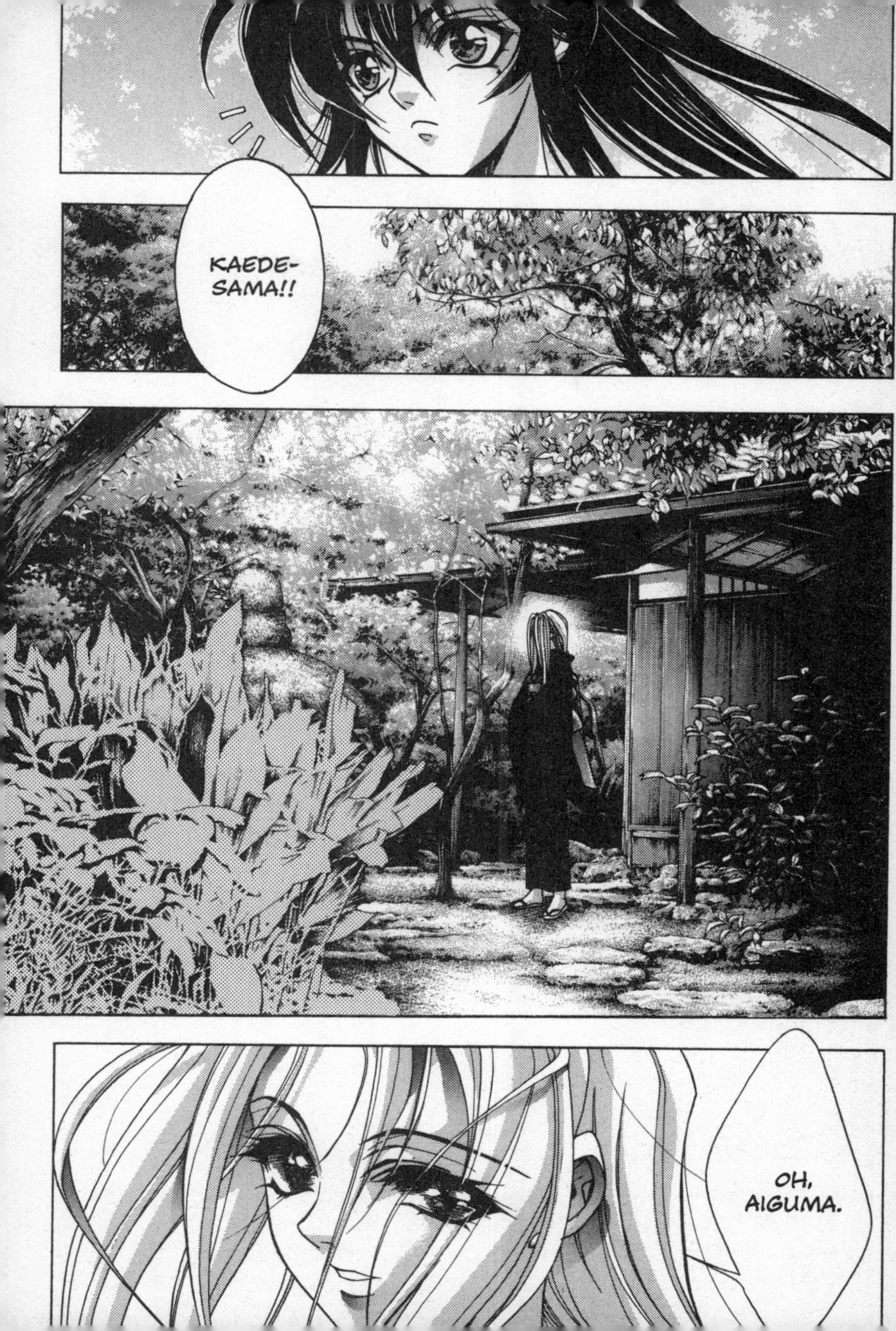
KAEDE-SAMA!!
OH, AIGUMA.

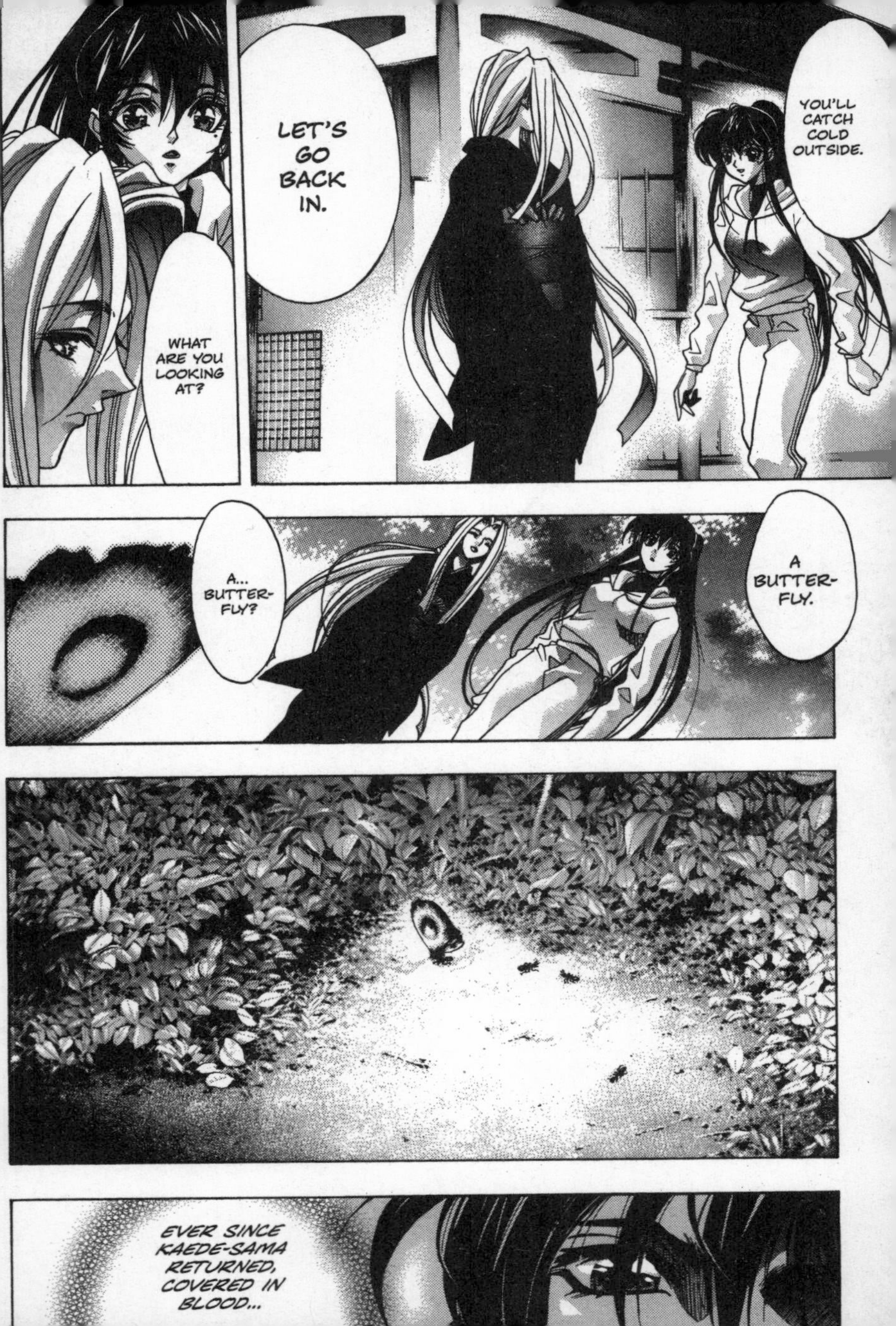
YOU'LL CATCH COLD OUTSIDE.
LET'S GO BACK IN.
WHAT ARE YOU LOOKING AT?
A BUTTER-FLY.
A... BUTTER-FLY?
EVER SINCE KAEDE-SAMA RETURNED, COVERED IN BLOOD...

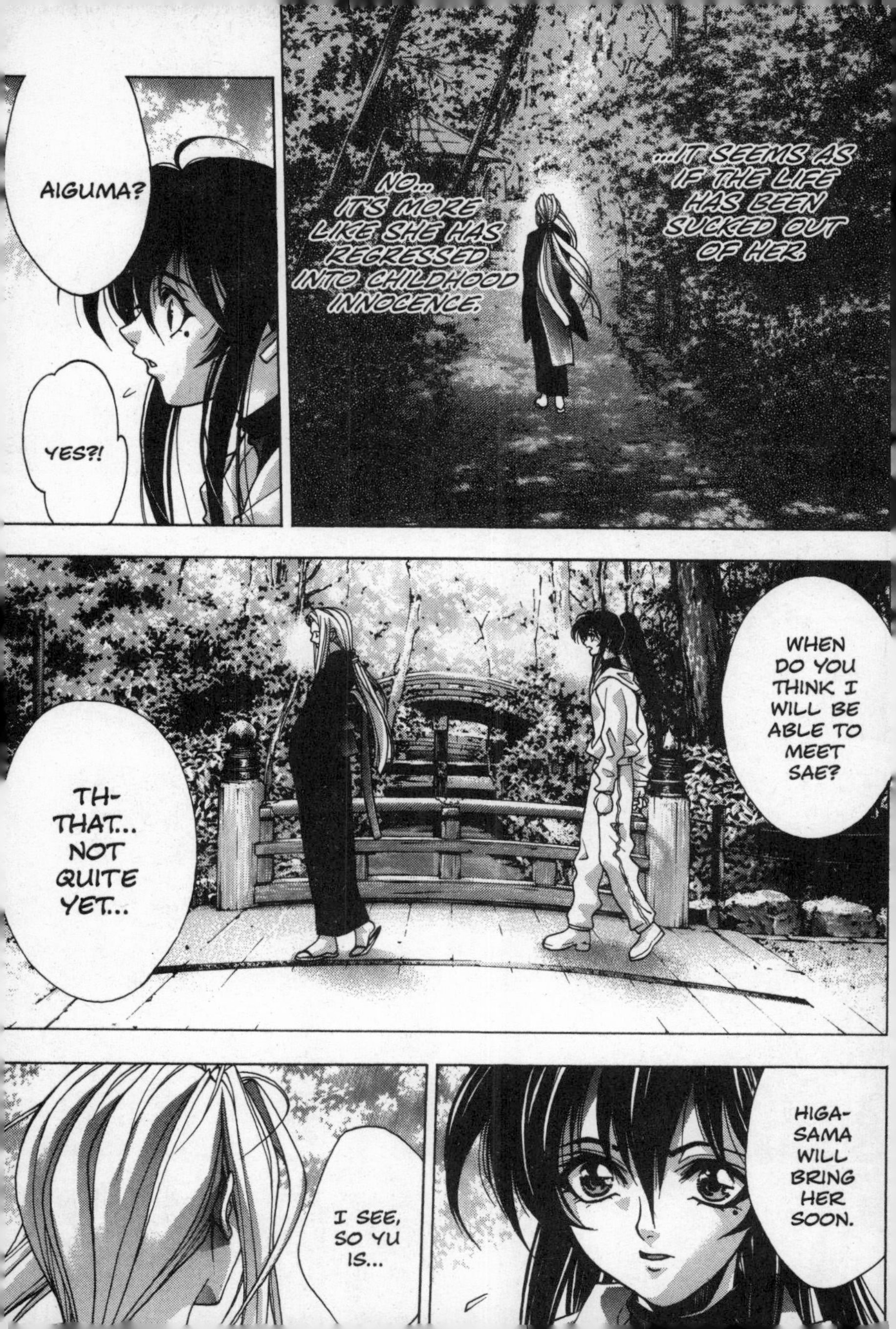
...IT SEEMS AS IF THE LIFE HAS BEEN SUCKED OUT OF HER.
NO... IT'S MORE LIKE SHE HAS REGRESSED INTO CHILDHOOD INNOCENCE.
AIGUMA?
YES?!
WHEN DO YOU THINK I WILL BE ABLE TO MEET SAE?
TH-THAT... NOT QUITE YET...
HIGA-SAMA WILL BRING HER SOON.
I SEE, SO YU IS...

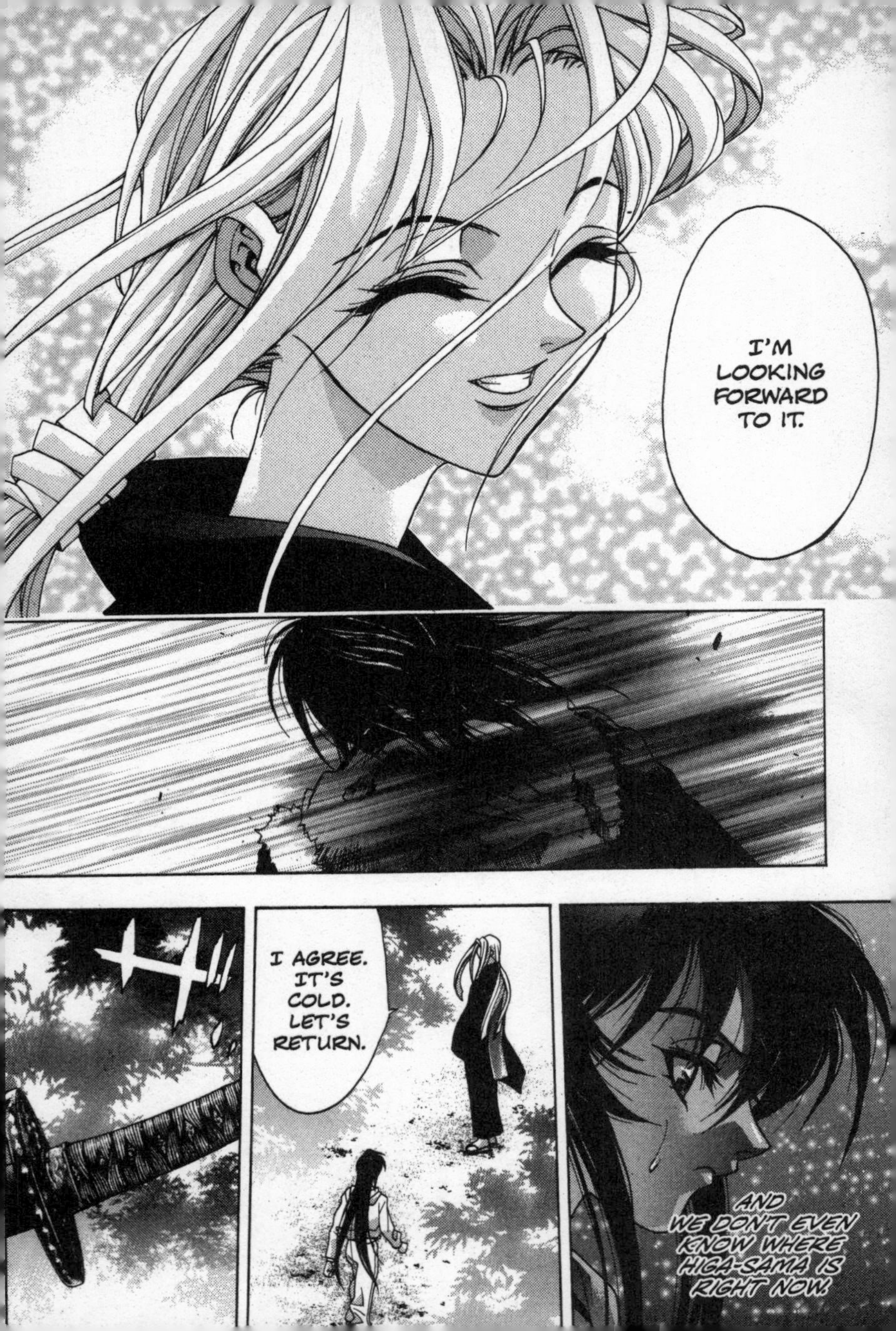
I'M LOOKING FORWARD TO IT.
AND WE DON'T EVEN KNOW WHERE HIGA-SAMA IS RIGHT NOW.
I AGREE. IT'S COLD. LET'S RETURN.

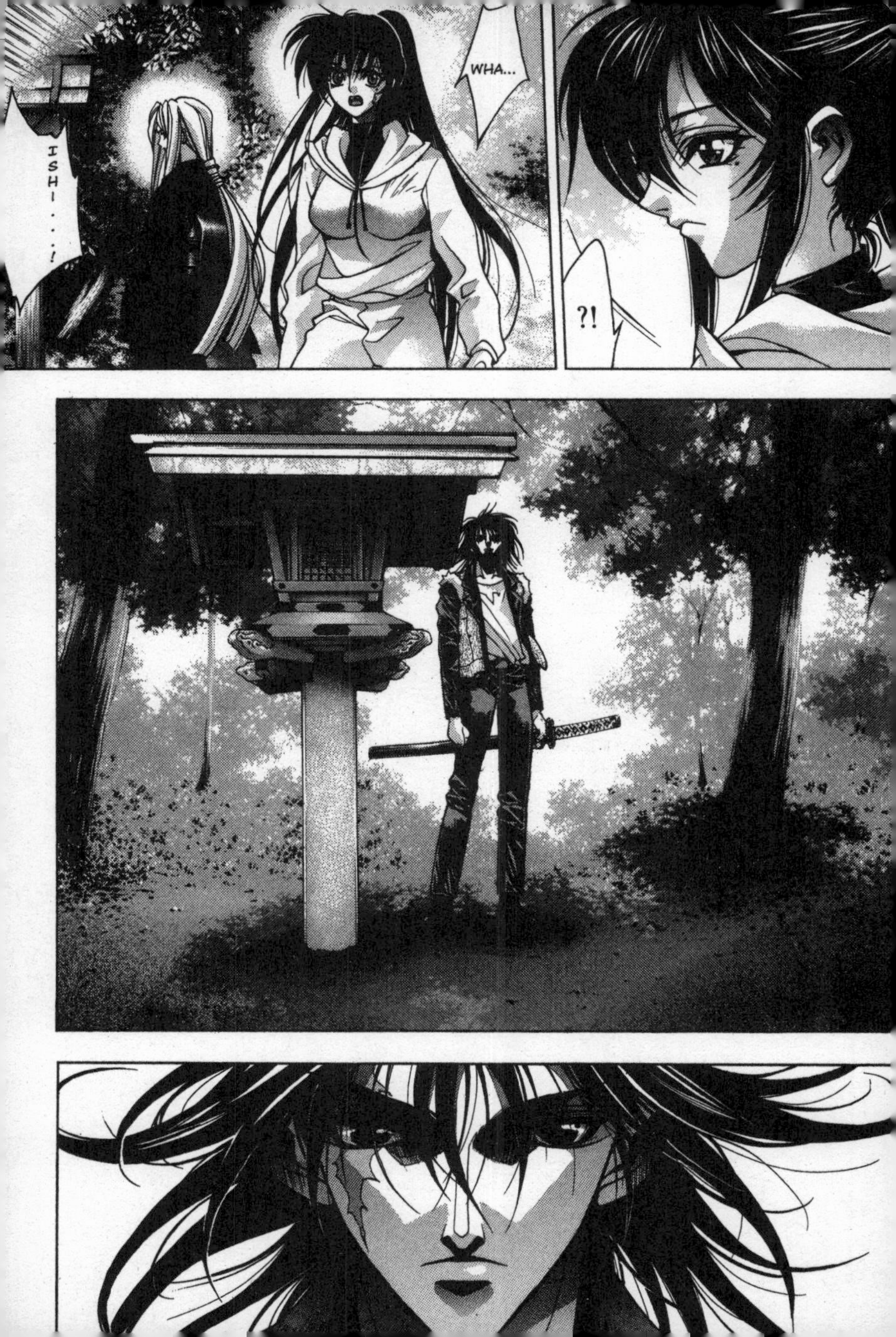
?!
WHA...
ISHI...!

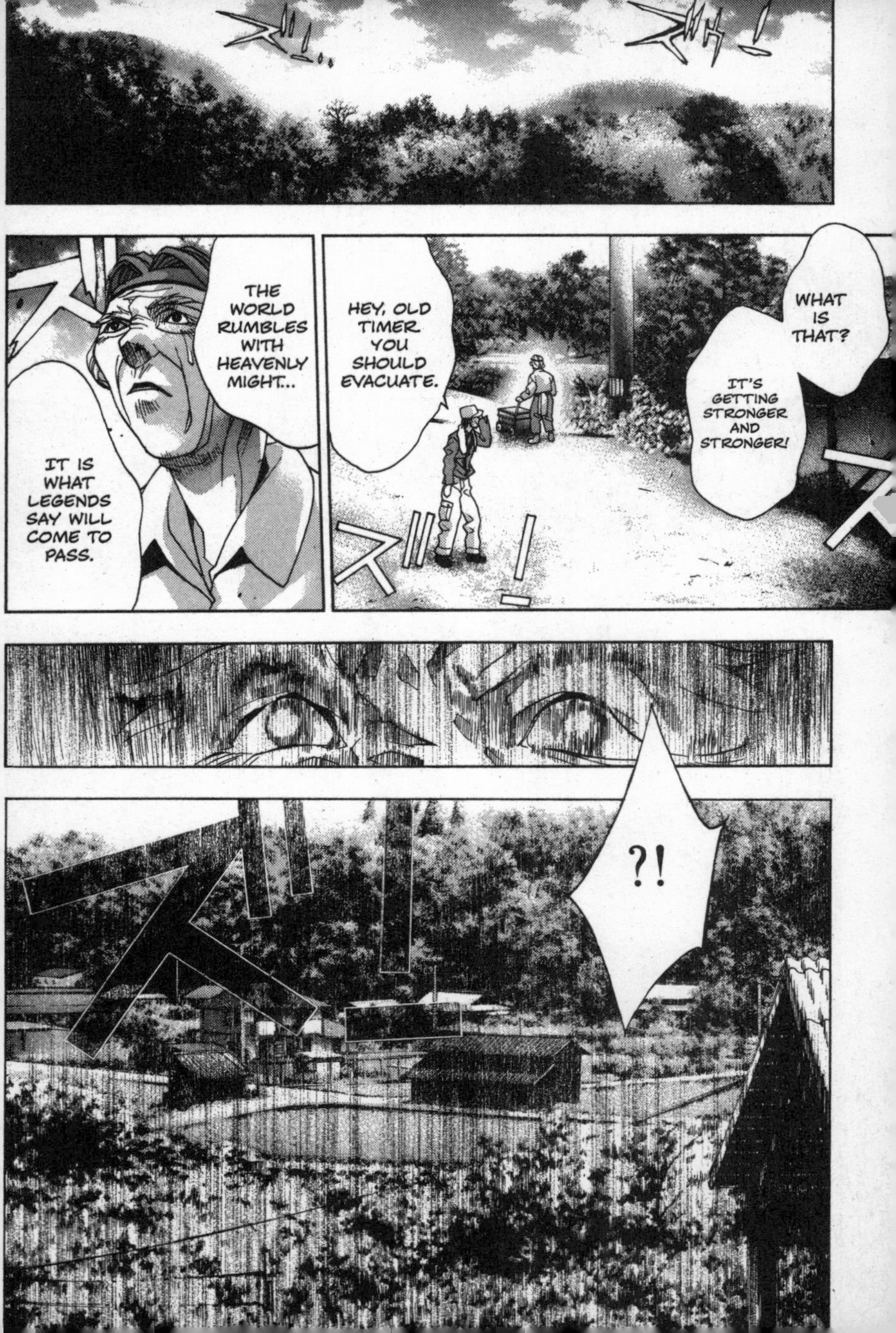
WHAT IS THAT?
IT'S GETTING STRONGER AND STRONGER!
HEY, OLD TIMER YOU SHOULD EVACUATE.
THE WORLD RUMBLES WITH HEAVENLY MIGHT...
IT IS WHAT LEGENDS SAY WILL COME TO PASS.
?!

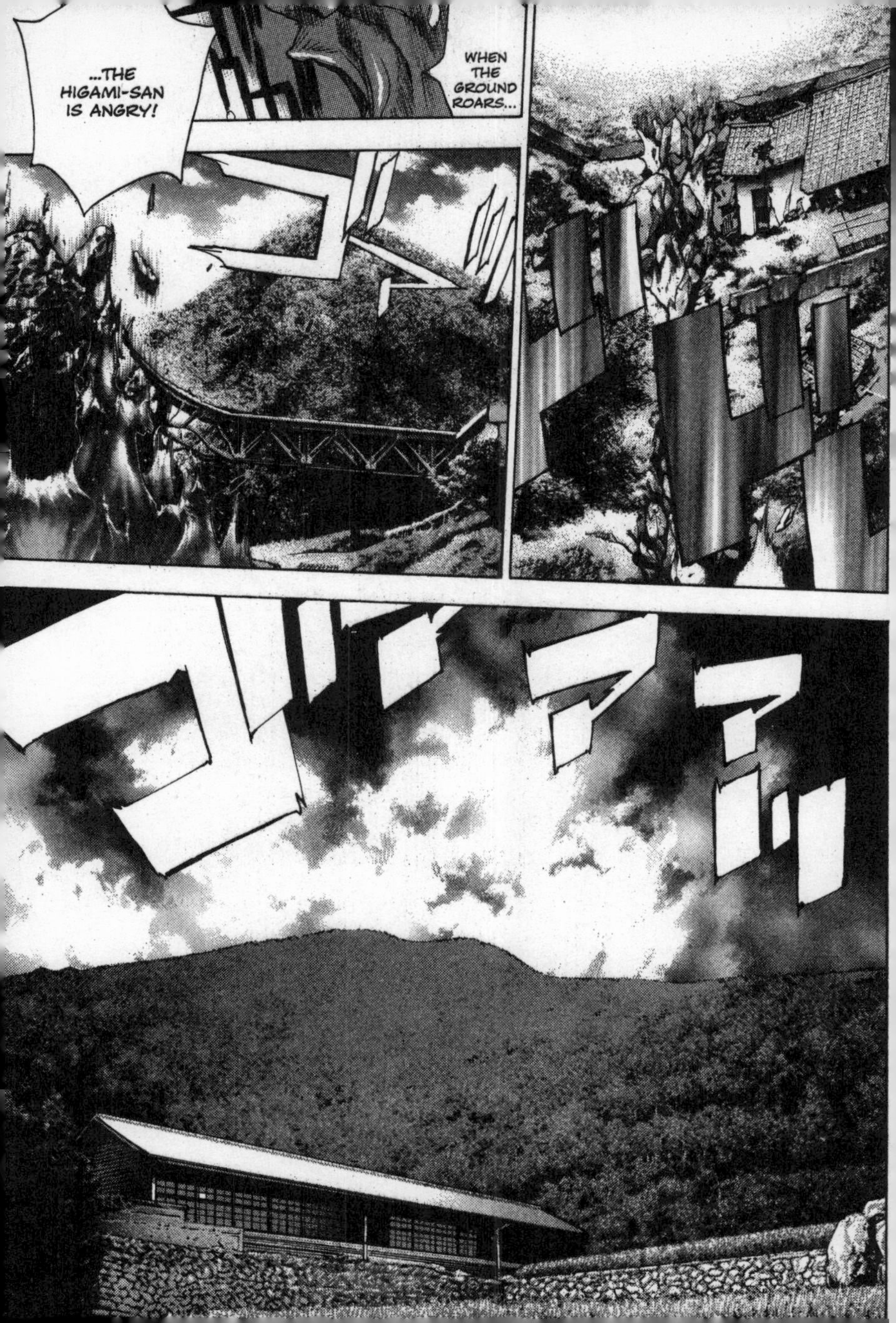
WHEN THE GROUND ROARS...
...THE HIGAMI-SAN IS ANGRY!

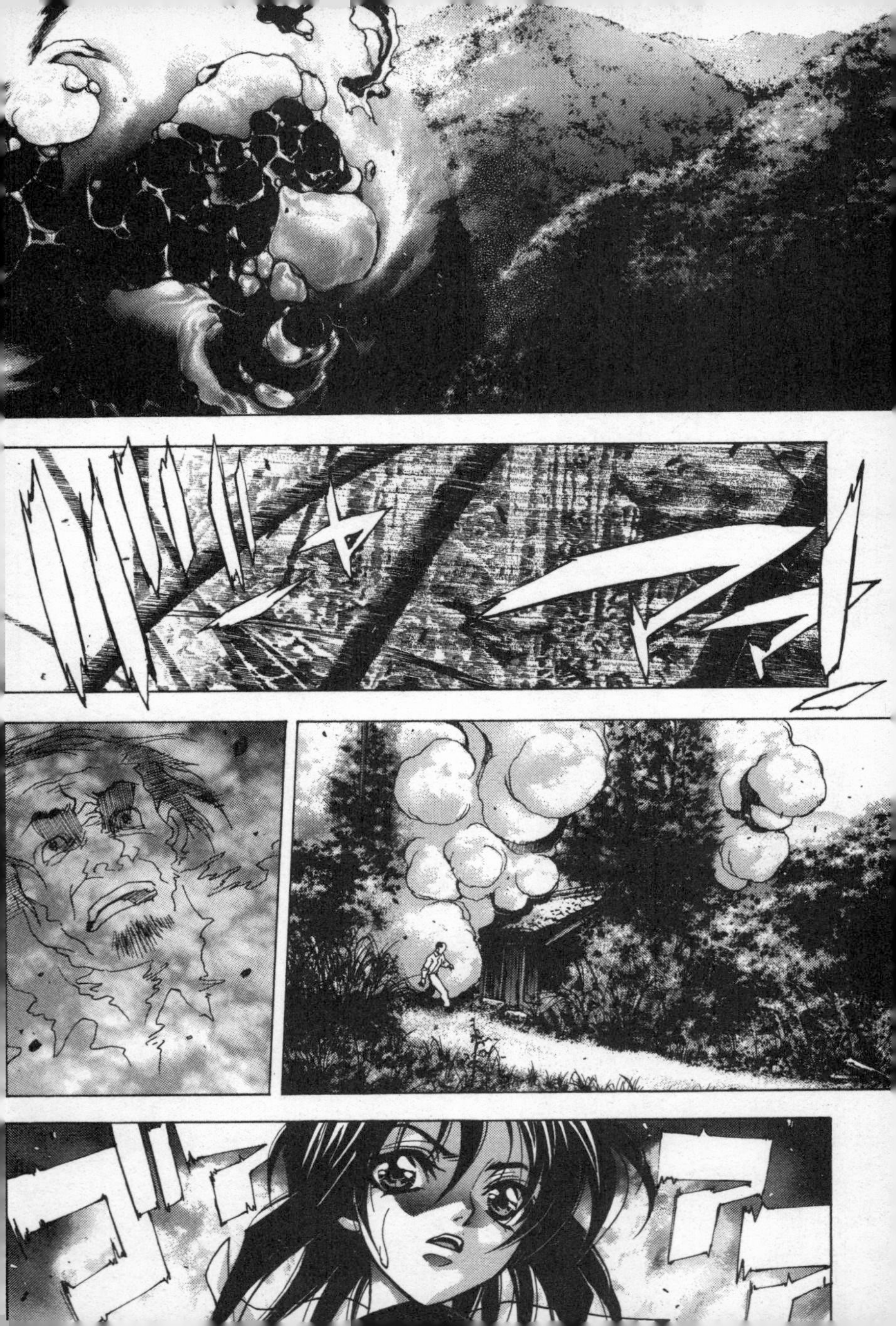

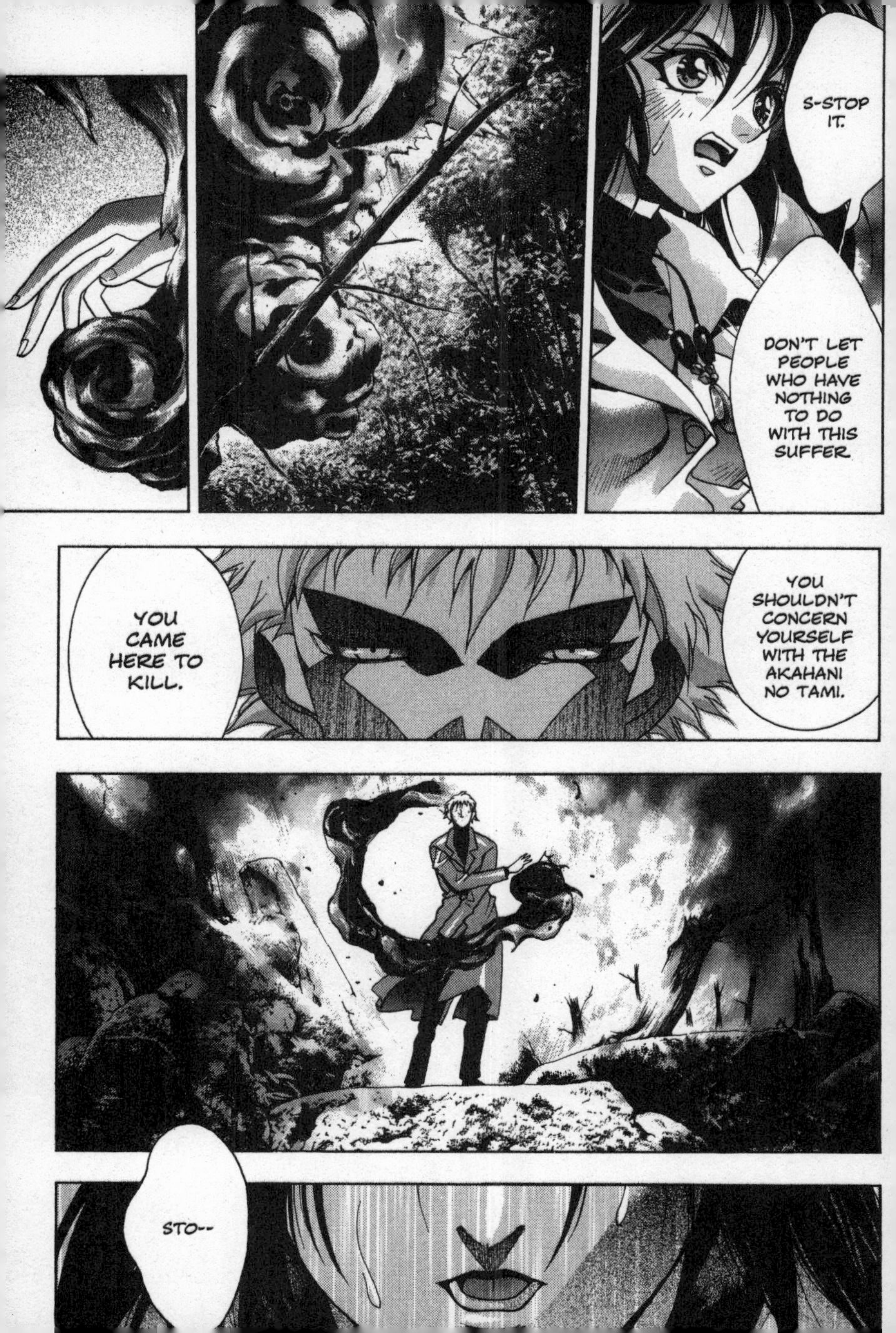
S-STOP IT.
DON'T LET PEOPLE WHO HAVE NOTHING TO DO WITH THIS SUFFER.
YOU SHOULDN'T CONCERN YOURSELF WITH THE AKAHANI NO TAMI.
YOU CAME HERE TO KILL.
STO--

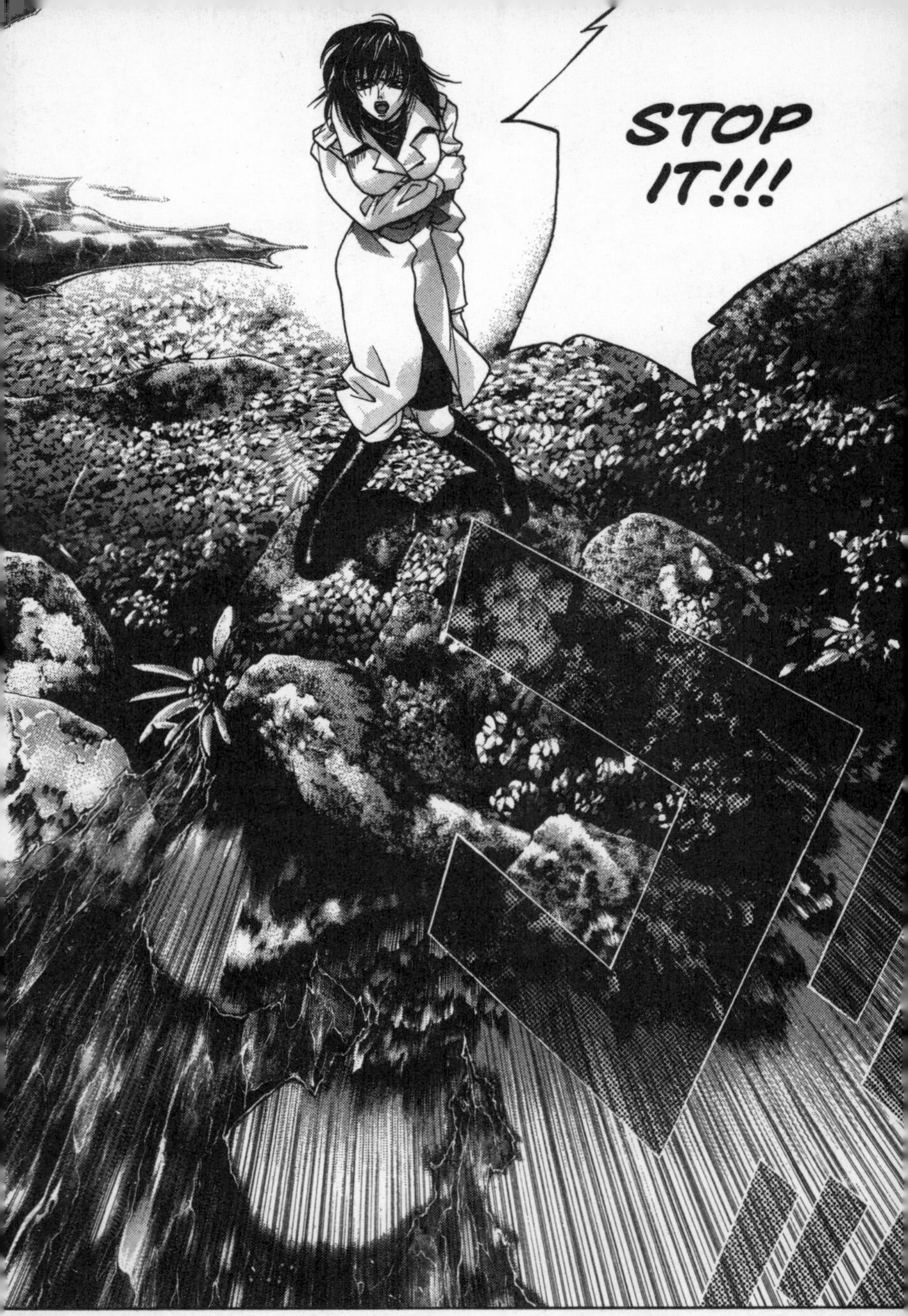
STOP IT!!!

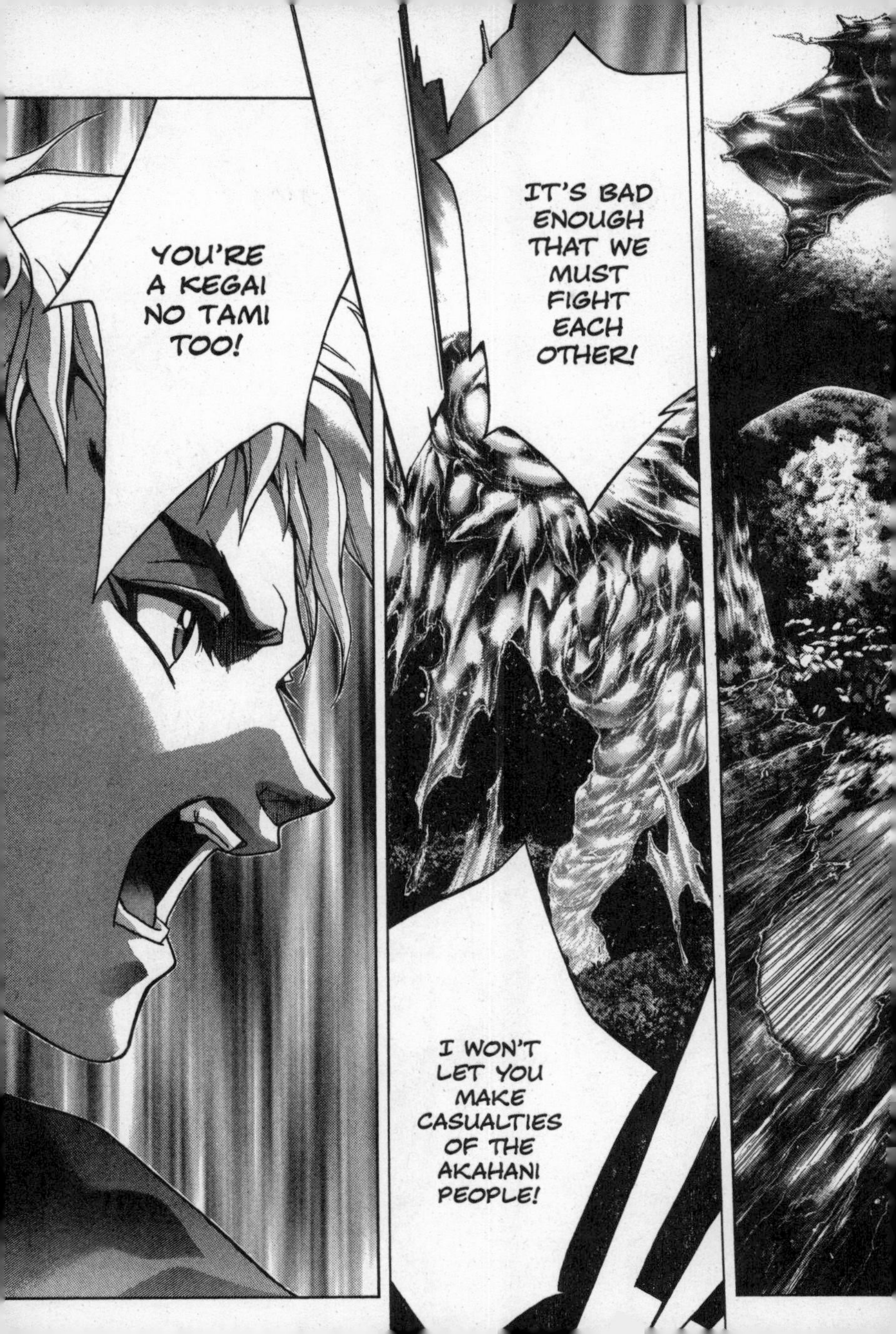
IT'S BAD ENOUGH THAT WE MUST FIGHT EACH OTHER!
I WON'T LET YOU MAKE CASUALTIES OF THE AKAHANI PEOPLE!
YOU'RE A KEGAI NO TAMI TOO!

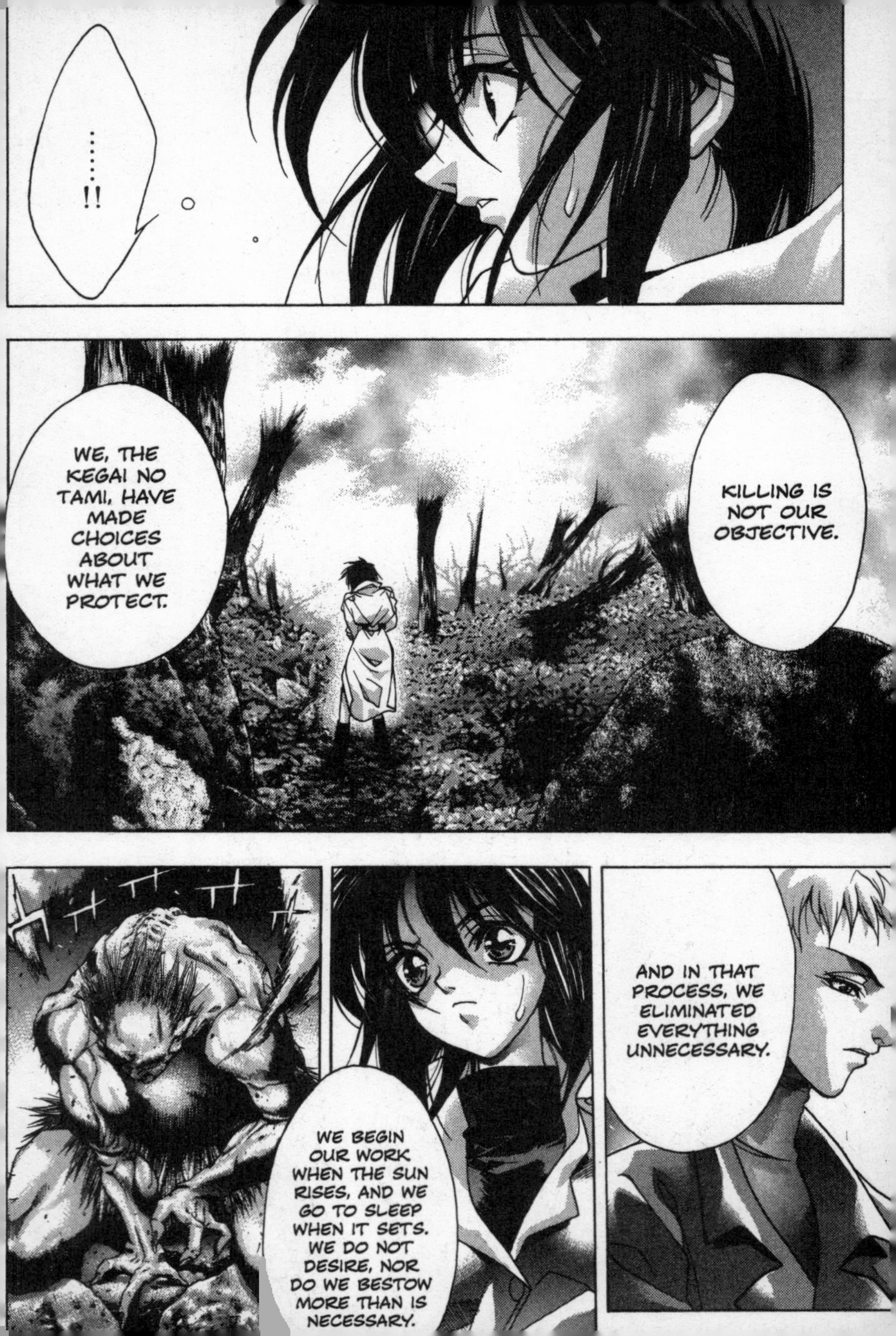
......!!
KILLING IS NOT OUR OBJECTIVE.
WE, THE KEGAI NO TAMI, HAVE MADE CHOICES ABOUT WHAT WE PROTECT.
AND IN THAT PROCESS, WE ELIMINATED EVERYTHING UNNECESSARY.
WE BEGIN OUR WORK WHEN THE SUN RISES, AND WE GO TO SLEEP WHEN IT SETS. WE DO NOT DESIRE, NOR DO WE BESTOW MORE THAN IS NECESSARY.

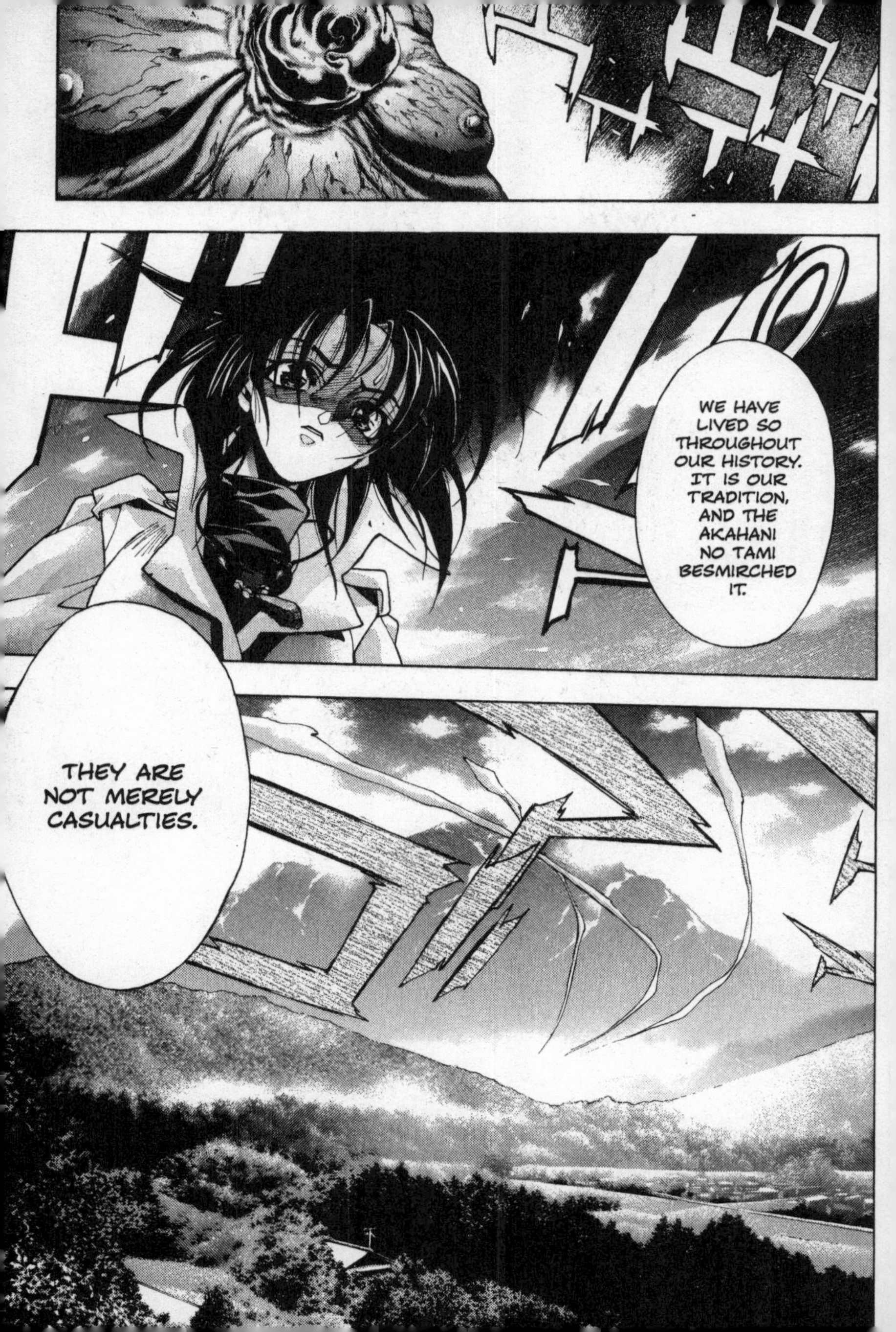
WE HAVE LIVED SO THROUGHOUT OUR HISTORY. IT IS OUR TRADITION, AND THE AKAHANI NO TAMI BESMIRCHED IT.
THEY ARE NOT MERELY CASUALTIES.

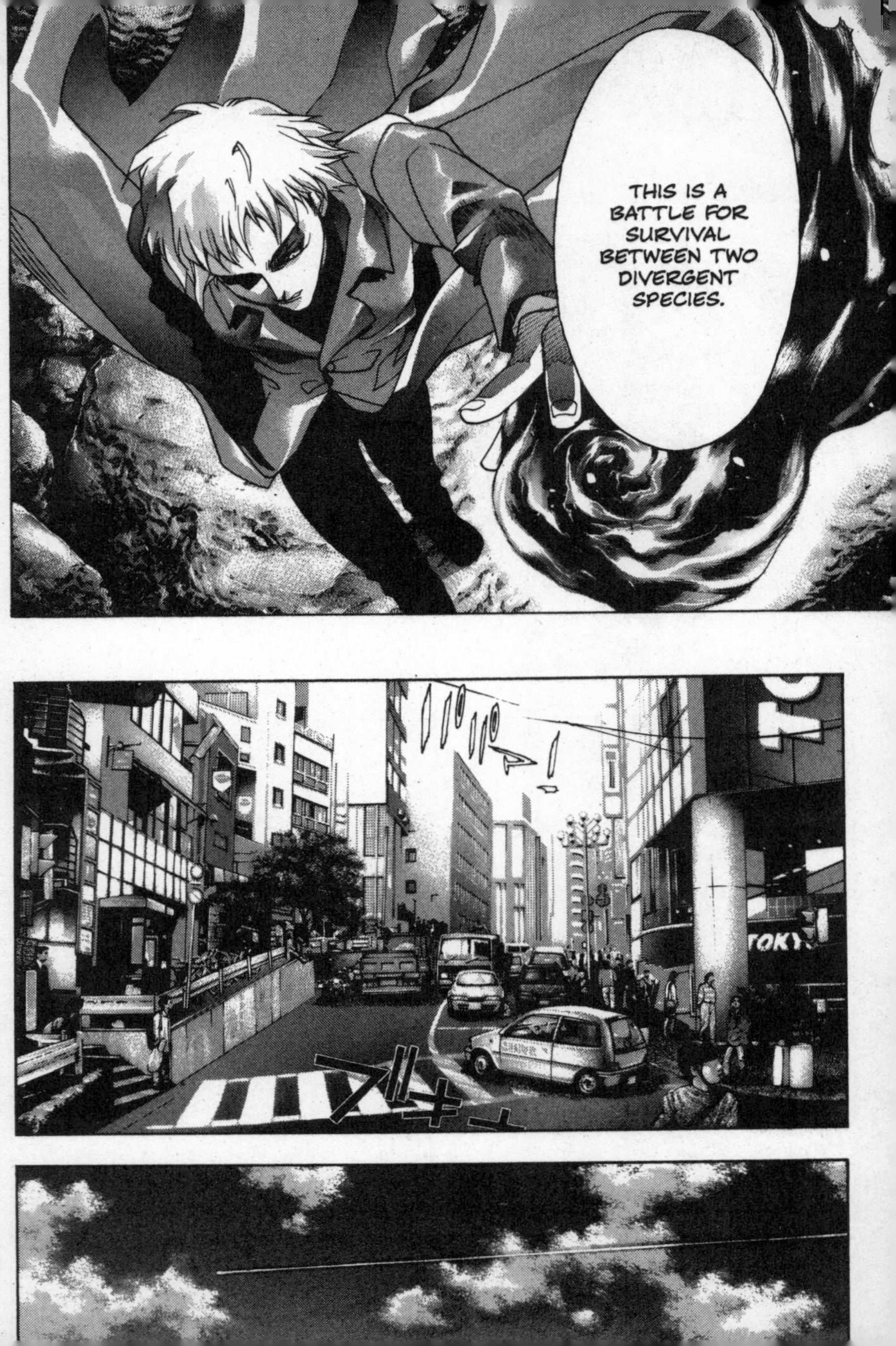
THIS IS A BATTLE FOR SURVIVAL BETWEEN TWO DIVERGENT SPECIES.

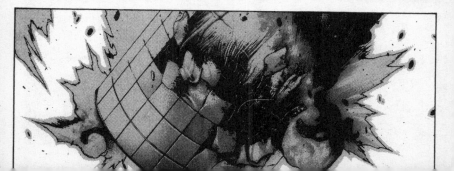

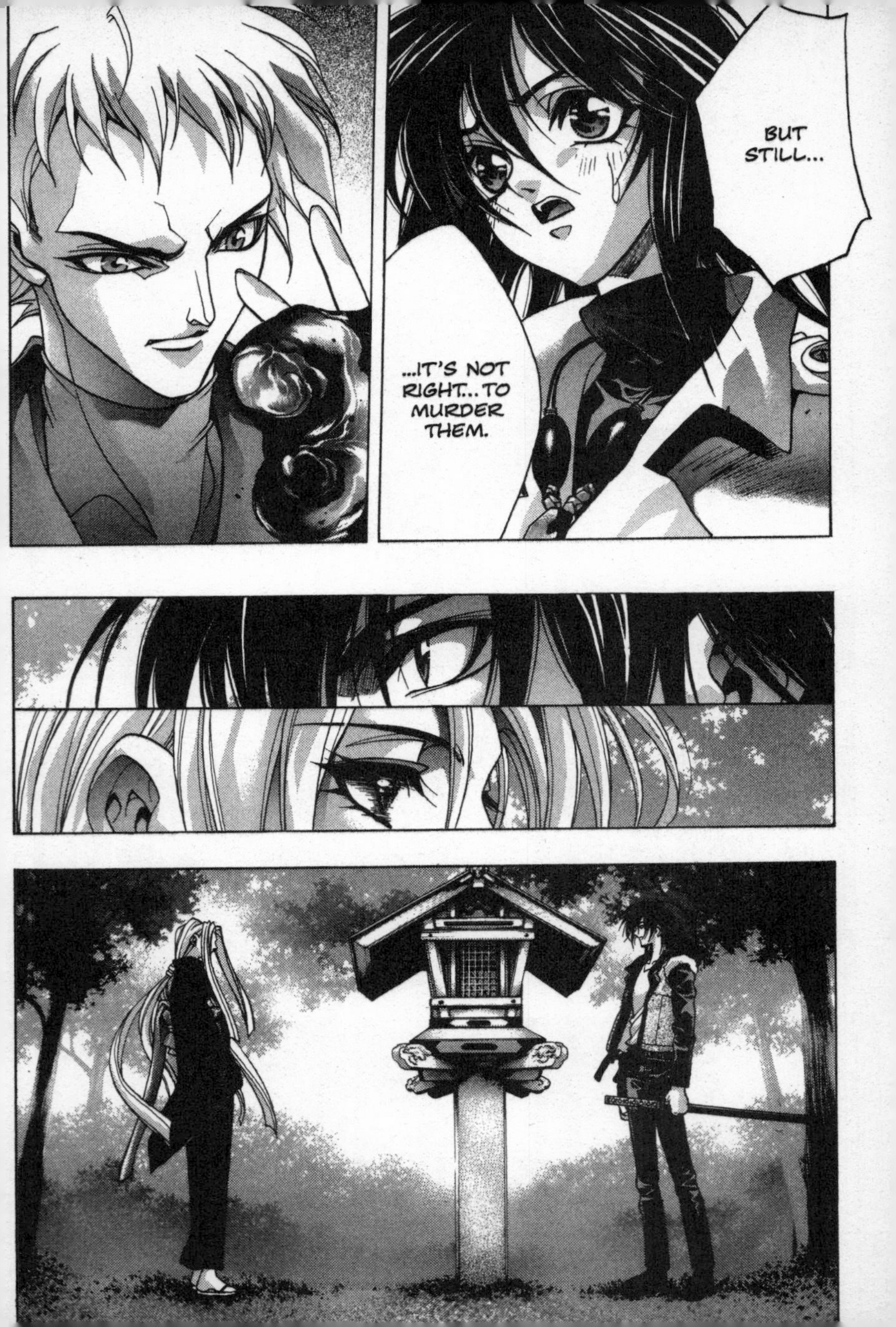
BUT STILL...
...IT'S NOT RIGHT... TO MURDER THEM.

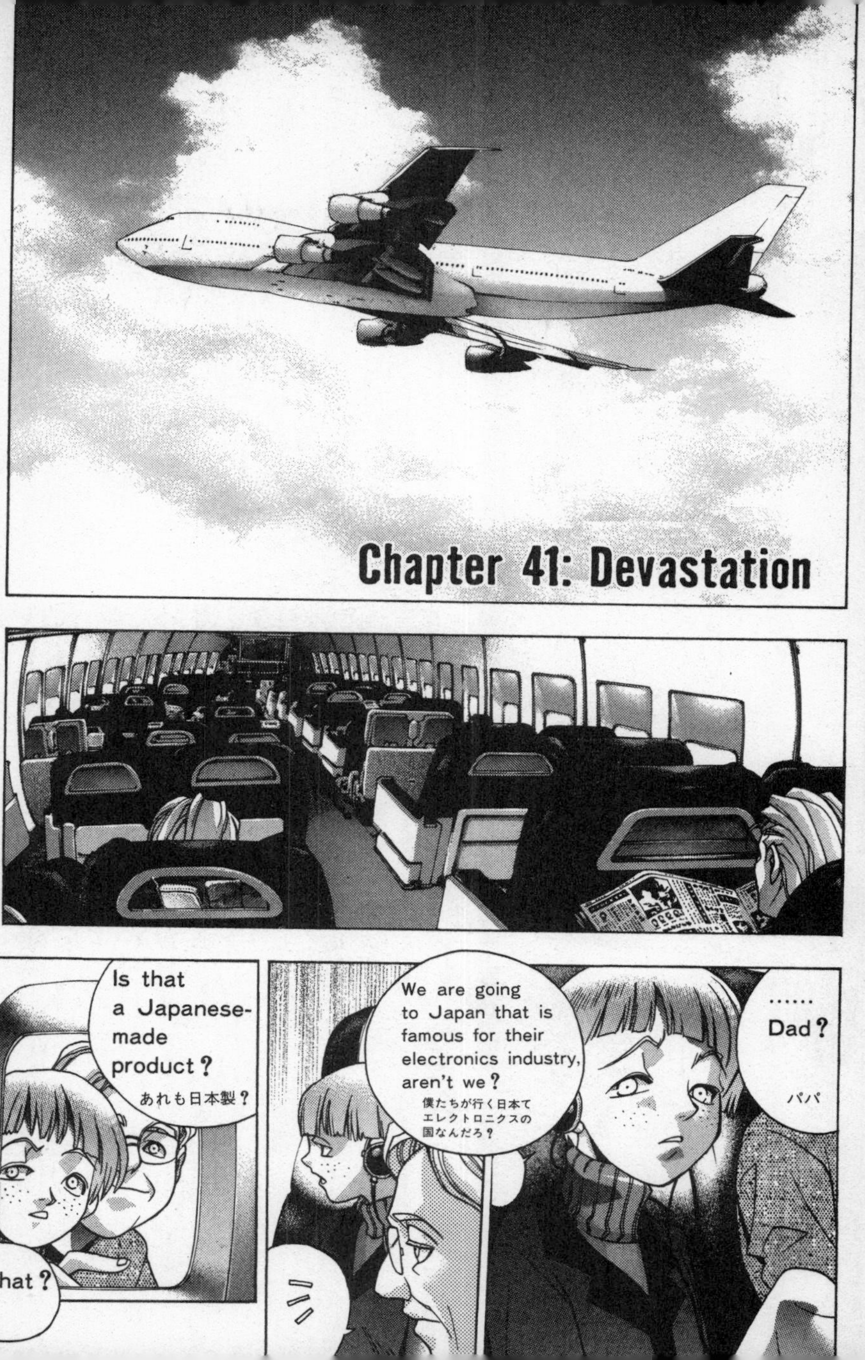
Chapter 41: Devastation
...... Dad?
パパ
We are going to Japan that is famous for their electronics industry, aren't we?
僕たちが行く日本て エレクトロニクスの 国なんだろ？
Is that a Japanese-made product?
あれも日本製？
What?

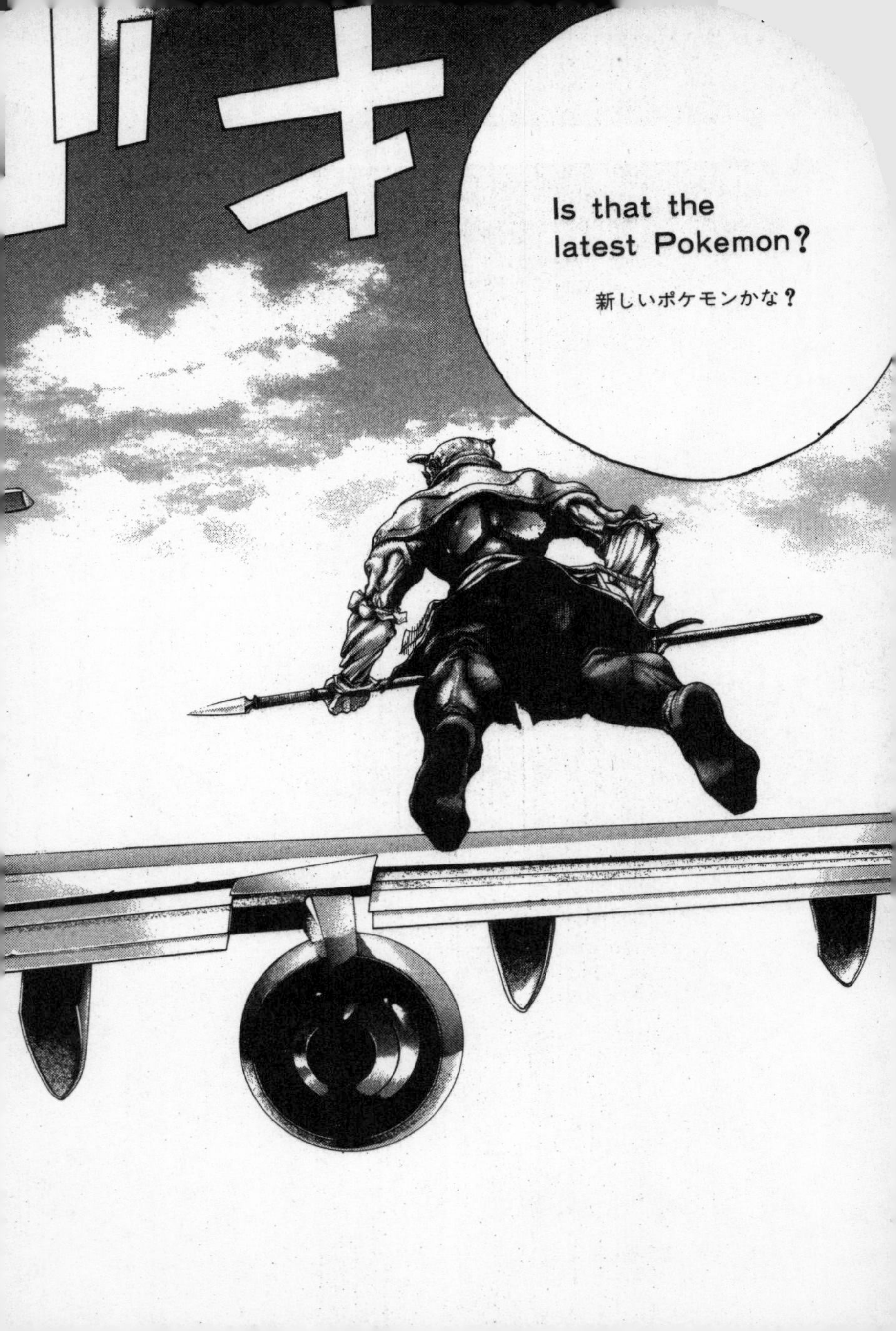
Is that the latest Pokemon?
新しいポケモンかな？

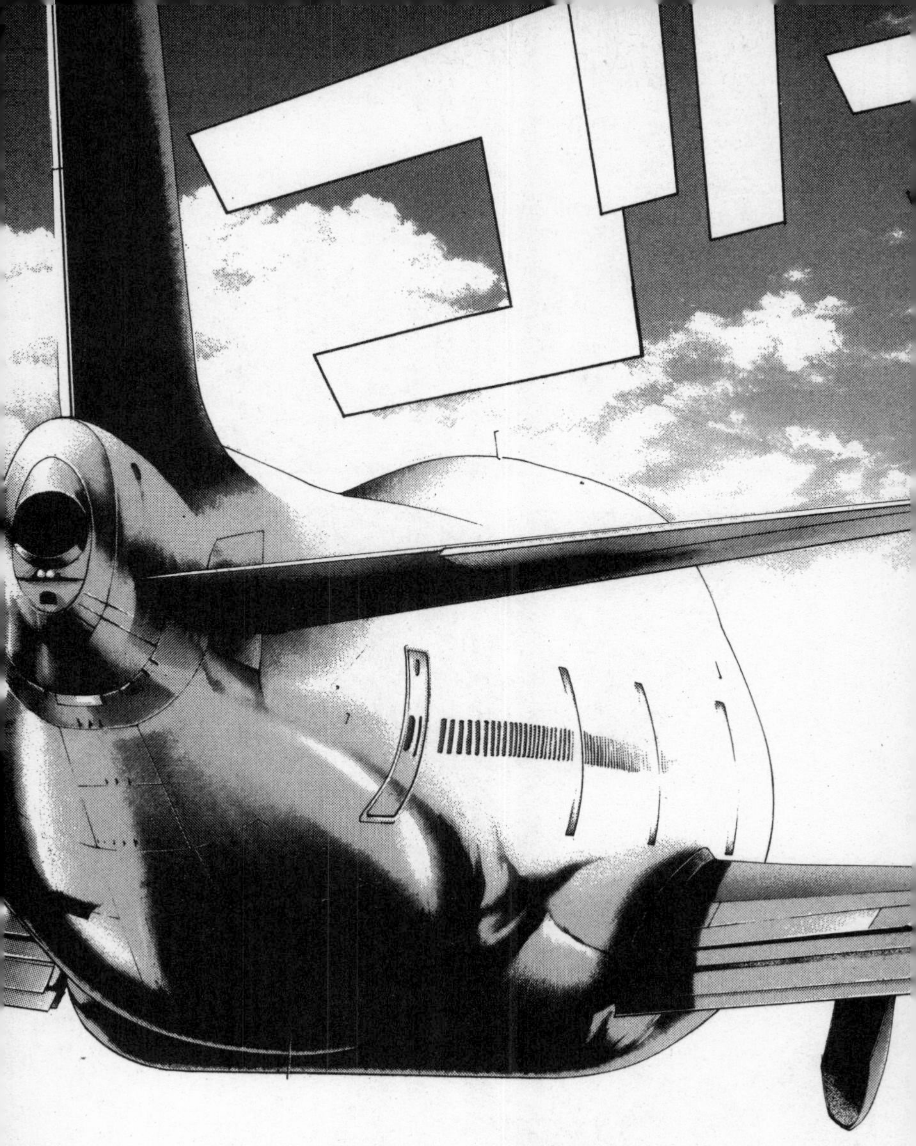
ゴ

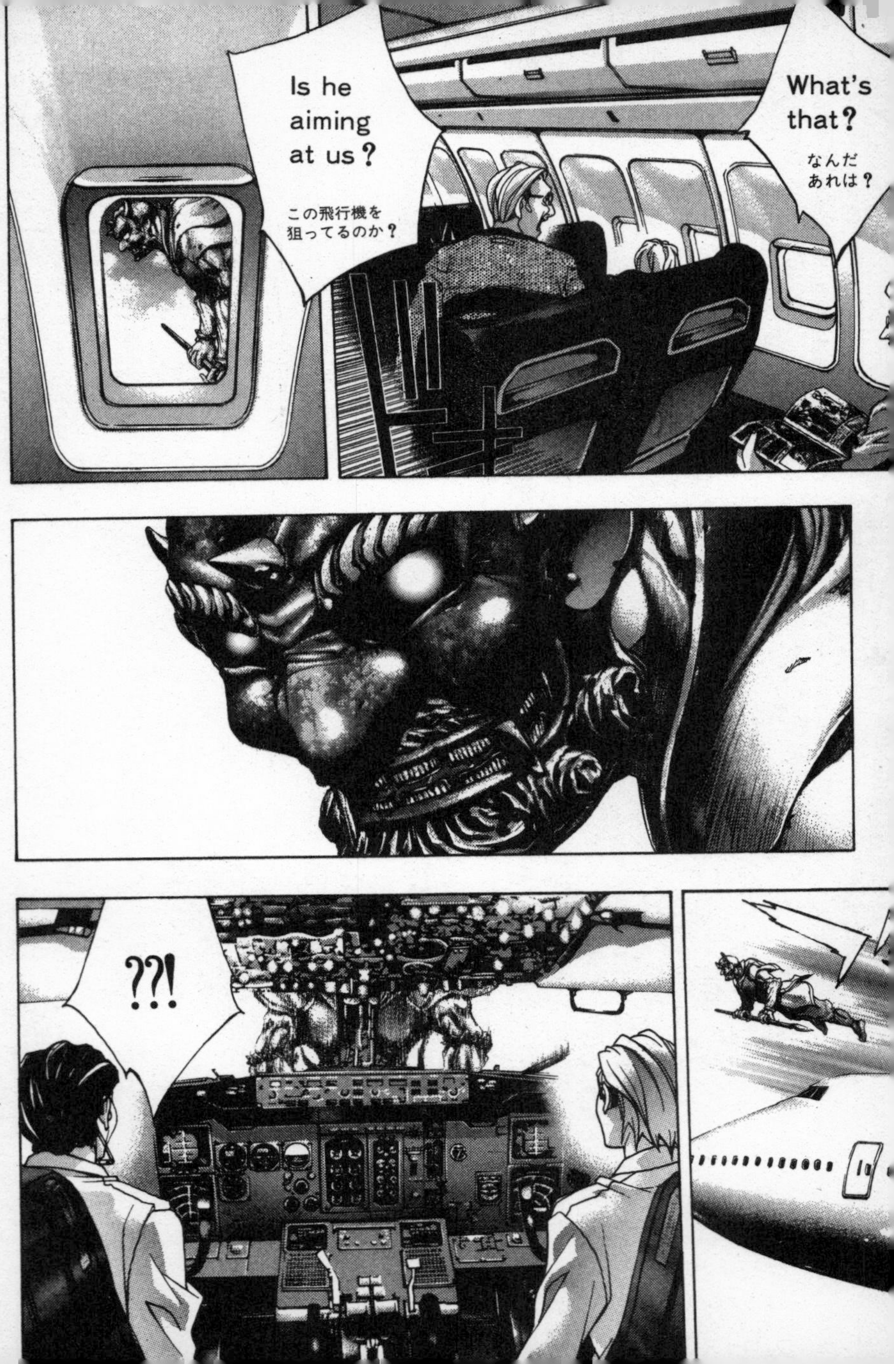
What's that?
なんだ あれは？
Is he aiming at us?
この飛行機を狙ってるのか？
??!

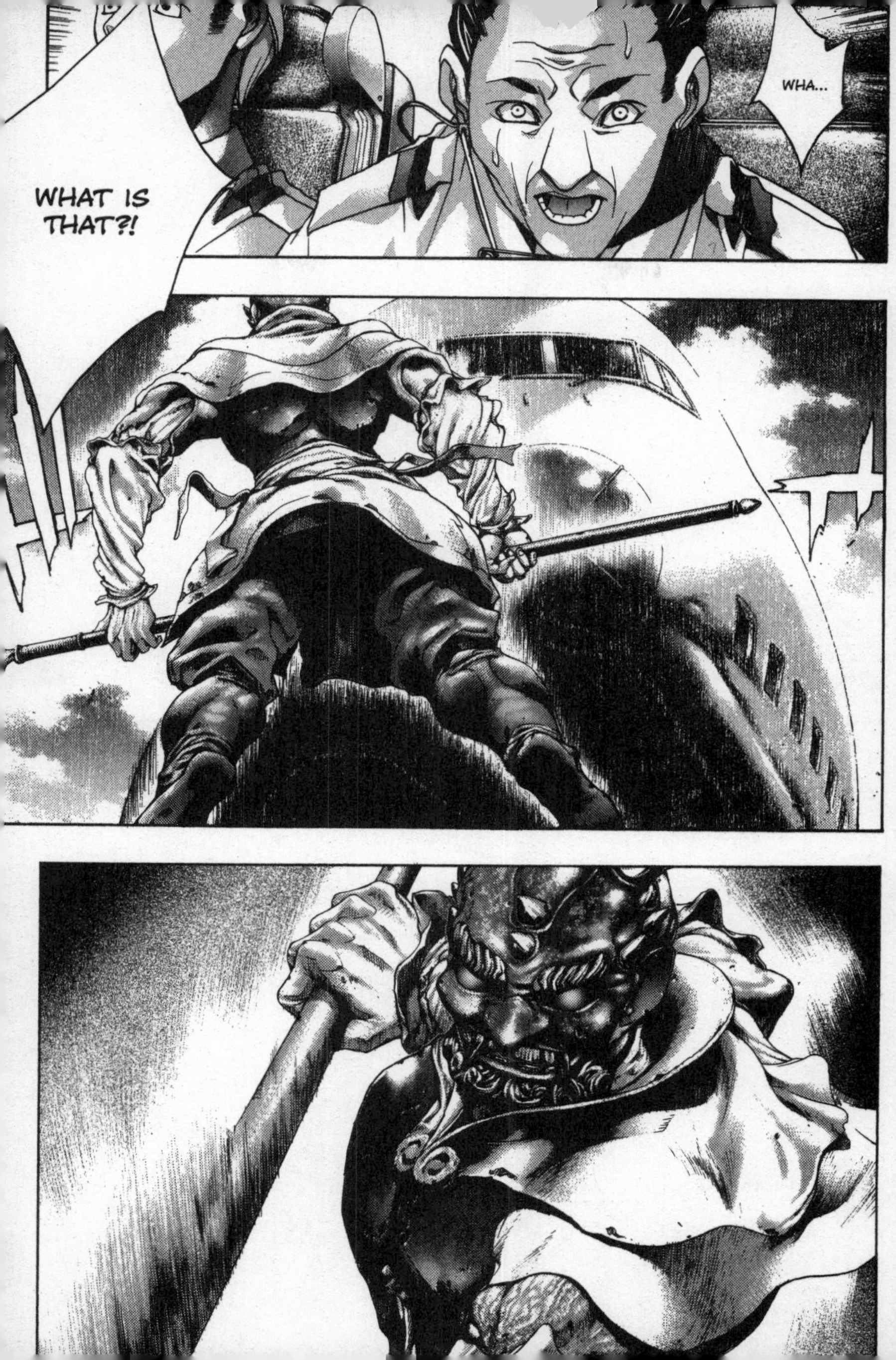
WHA...
WHAT IS THAT?!

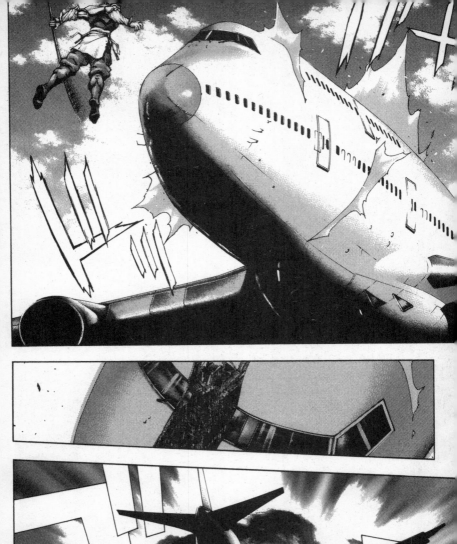

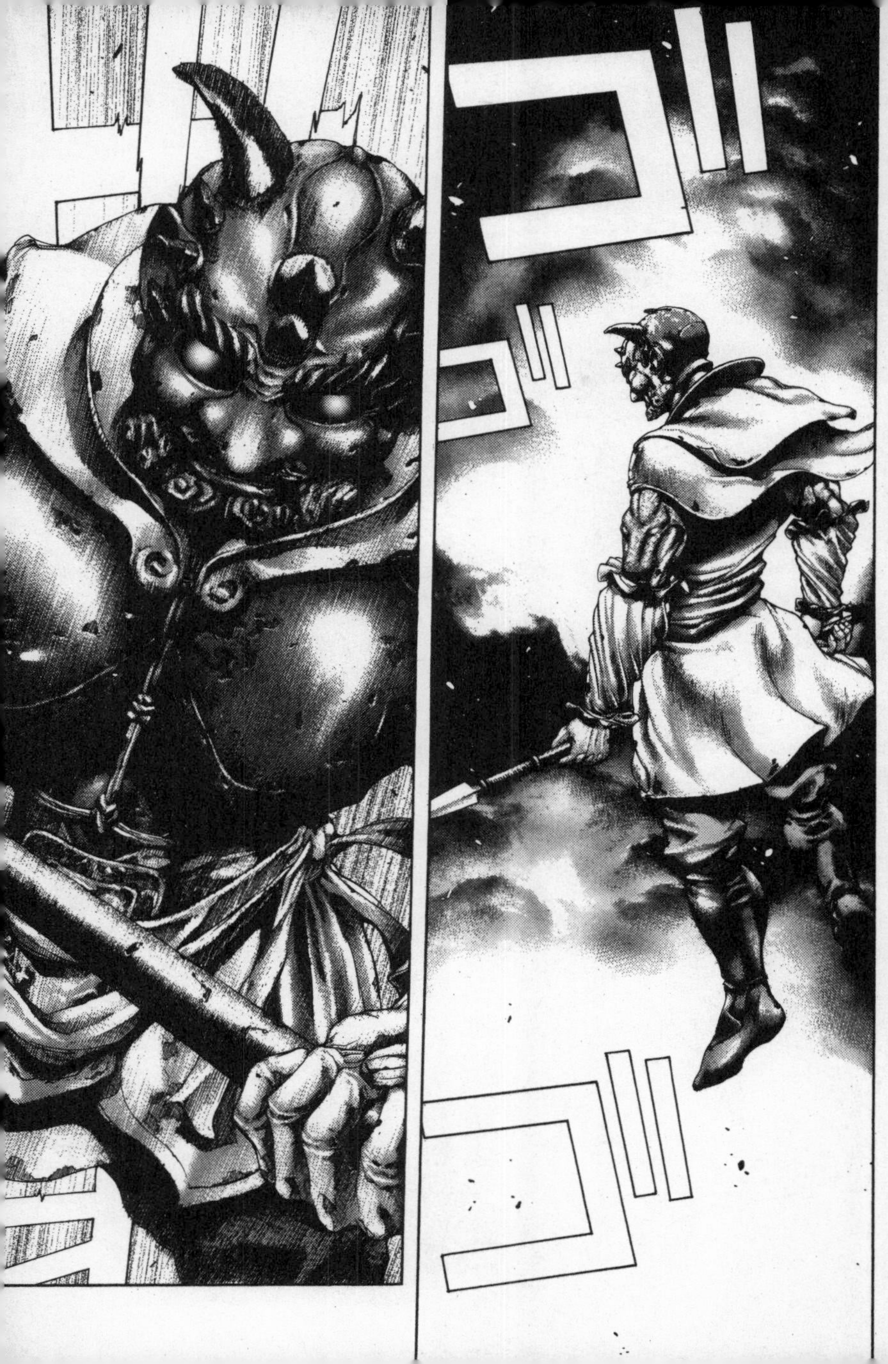
ゴ
ゴ
ゴ

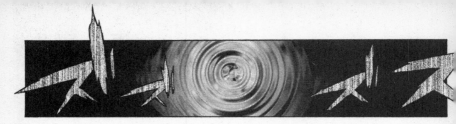

IT'S STILL NOT ENOUGH. SHOW ME THE FIRE OF YOUR HATE.

YOU BEASTS, WHO WERE IMPRISONED IN THE KODOKU NO TSUBO...

...I PREPARED THE HEART OF THE CHIEF OF THE KEGAI NO TAMI JUST FOR YOU.

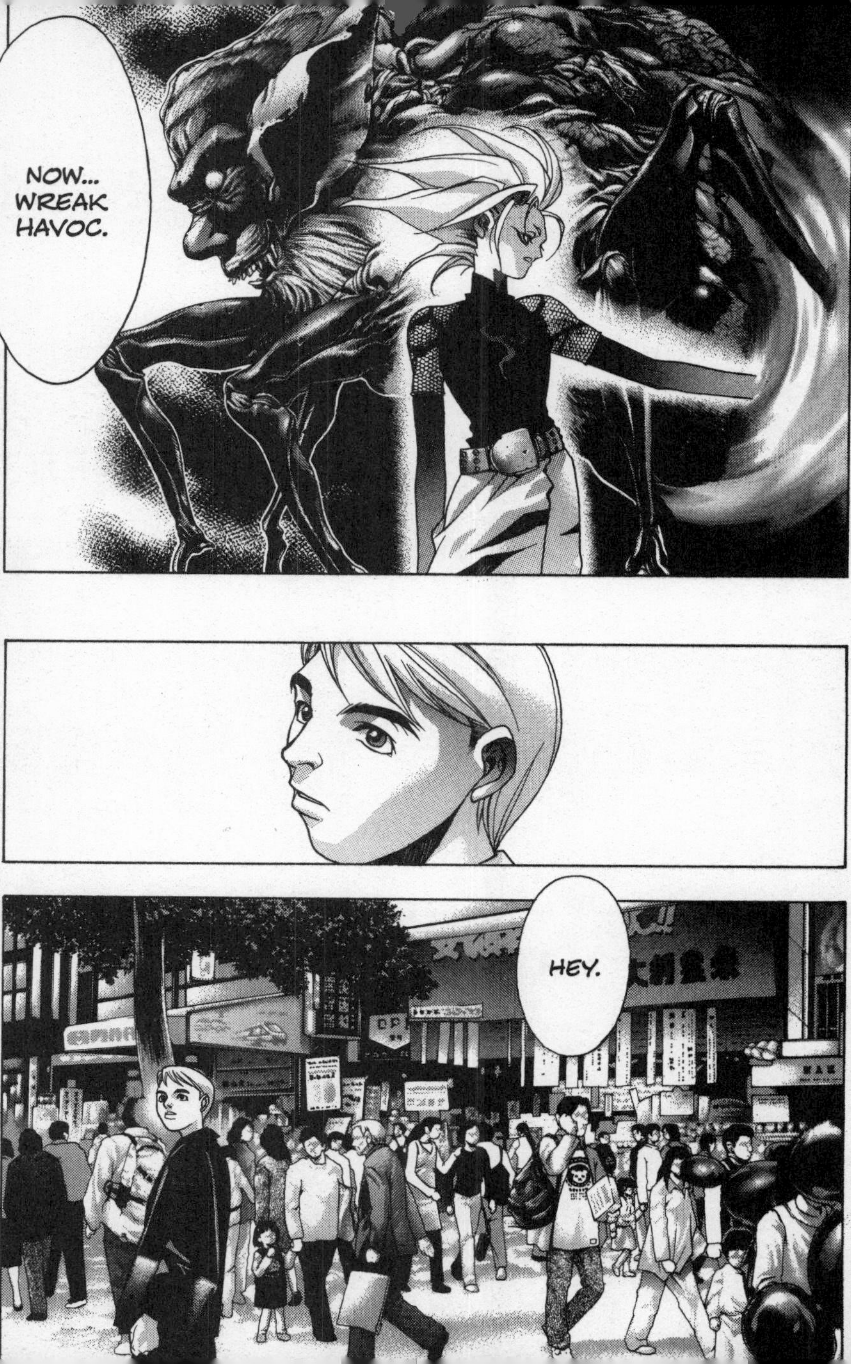
NOW... WREAK HAVOC.
HEY.

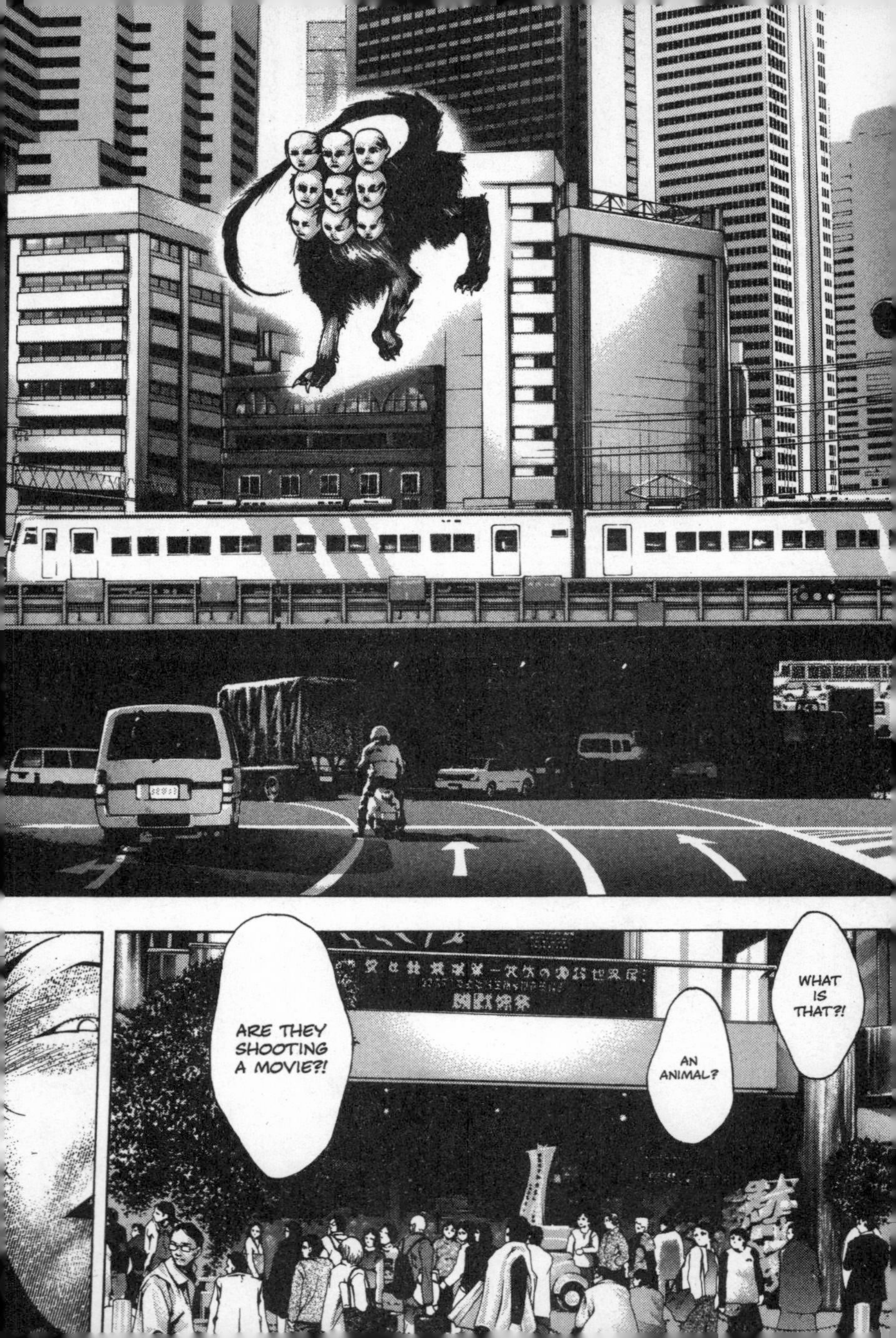
WHAT IS THAT?!
AN ANIMAL?
ARE THEY SHOOTING A MOVIE?!

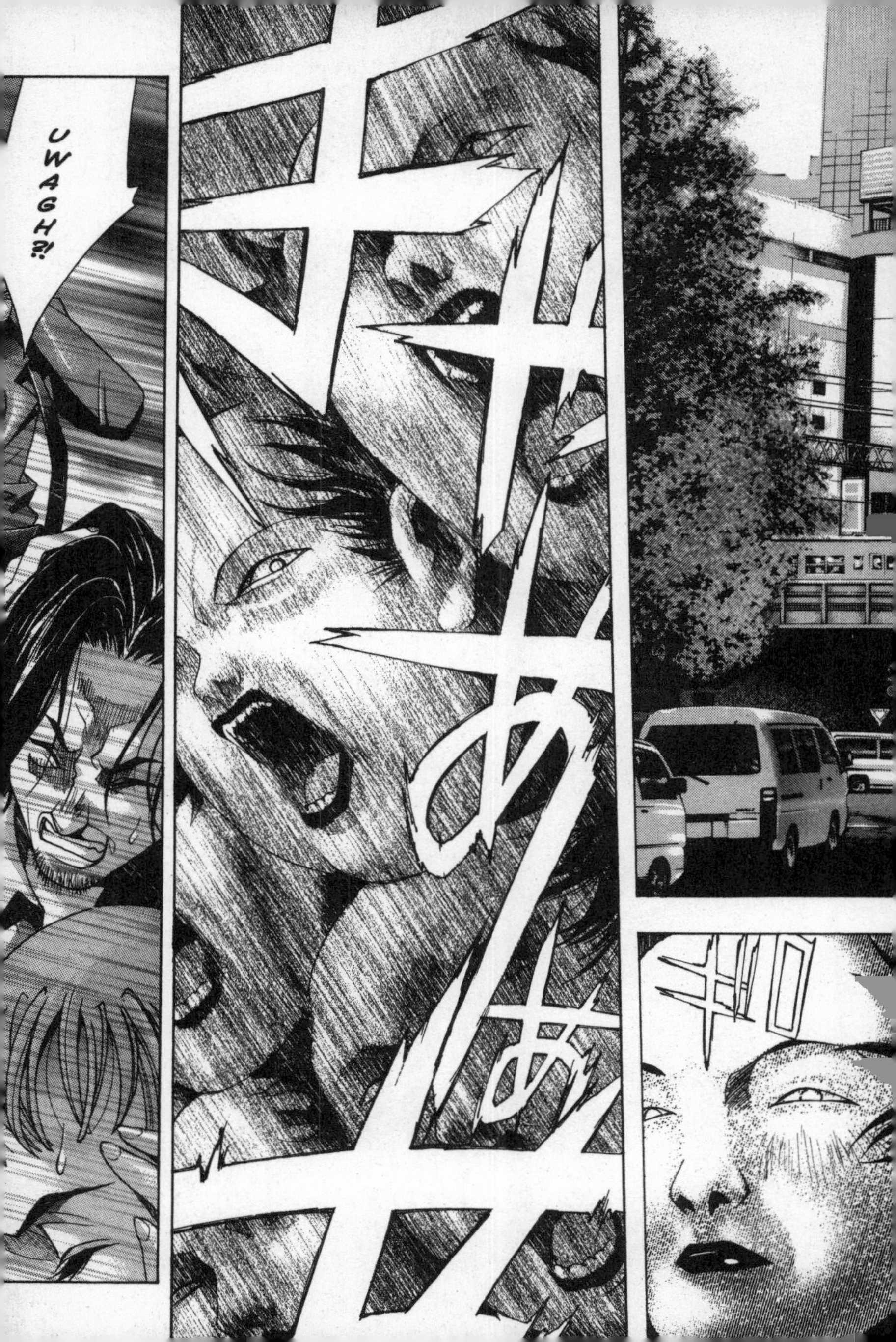
UWAGH?!

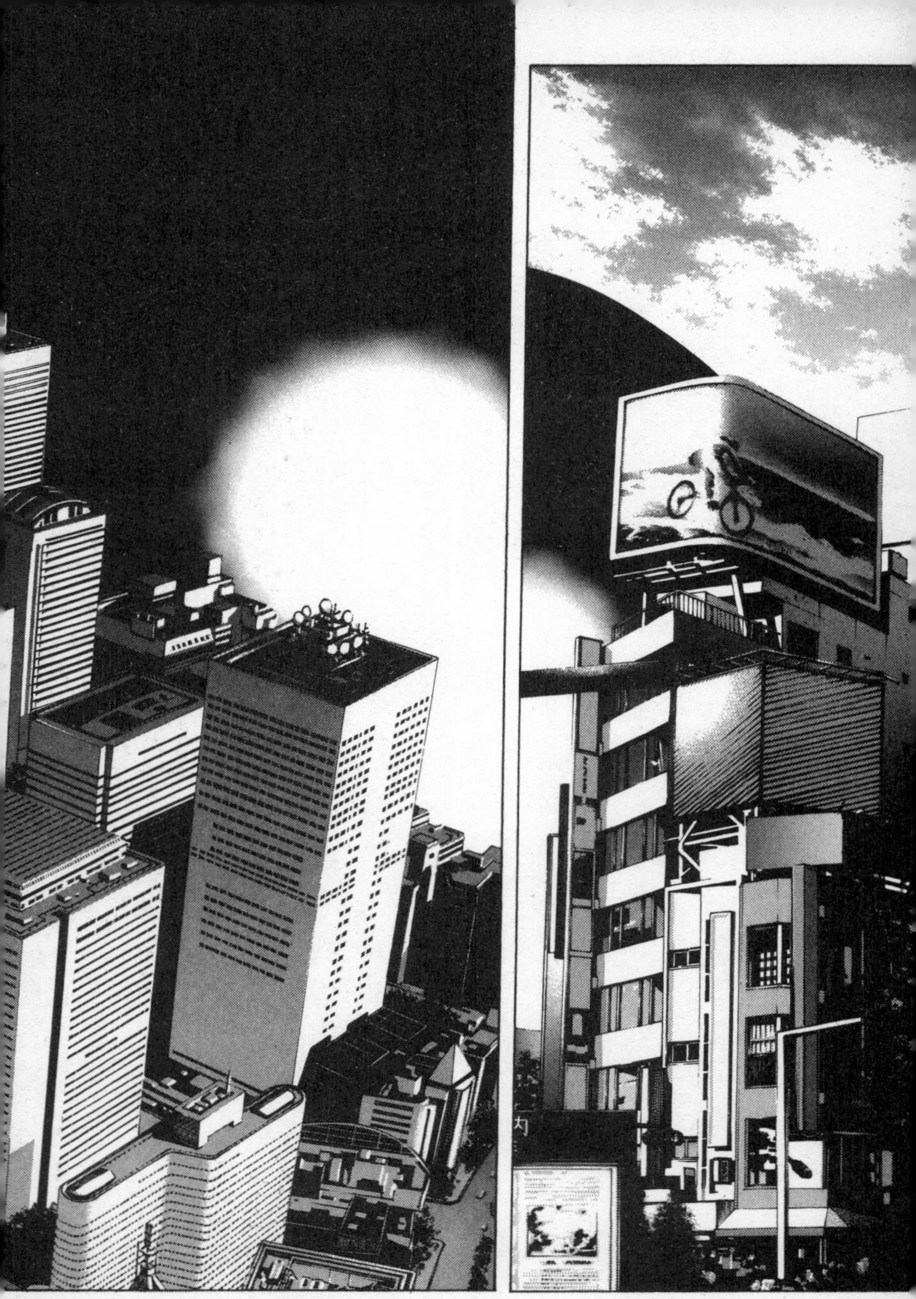

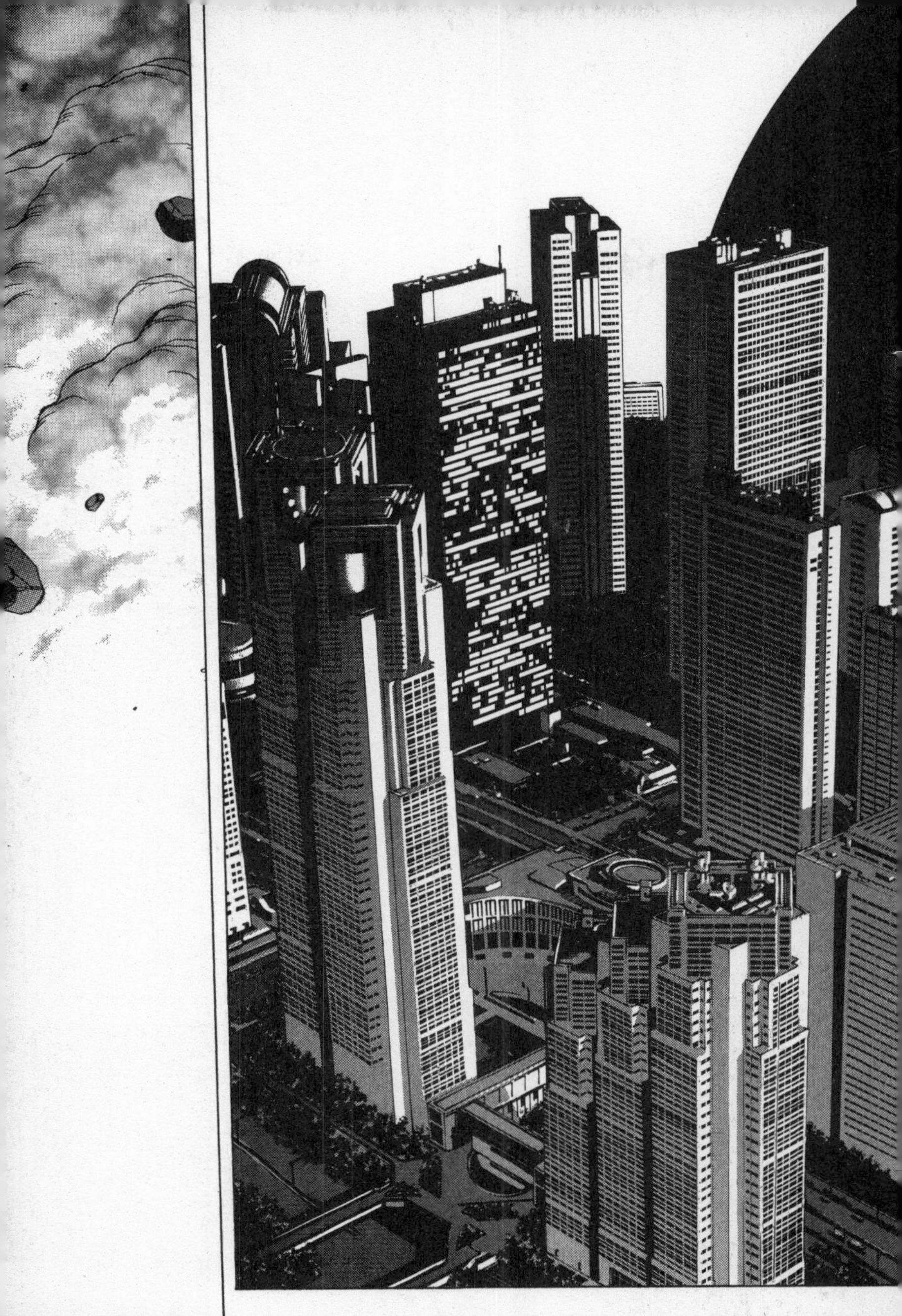

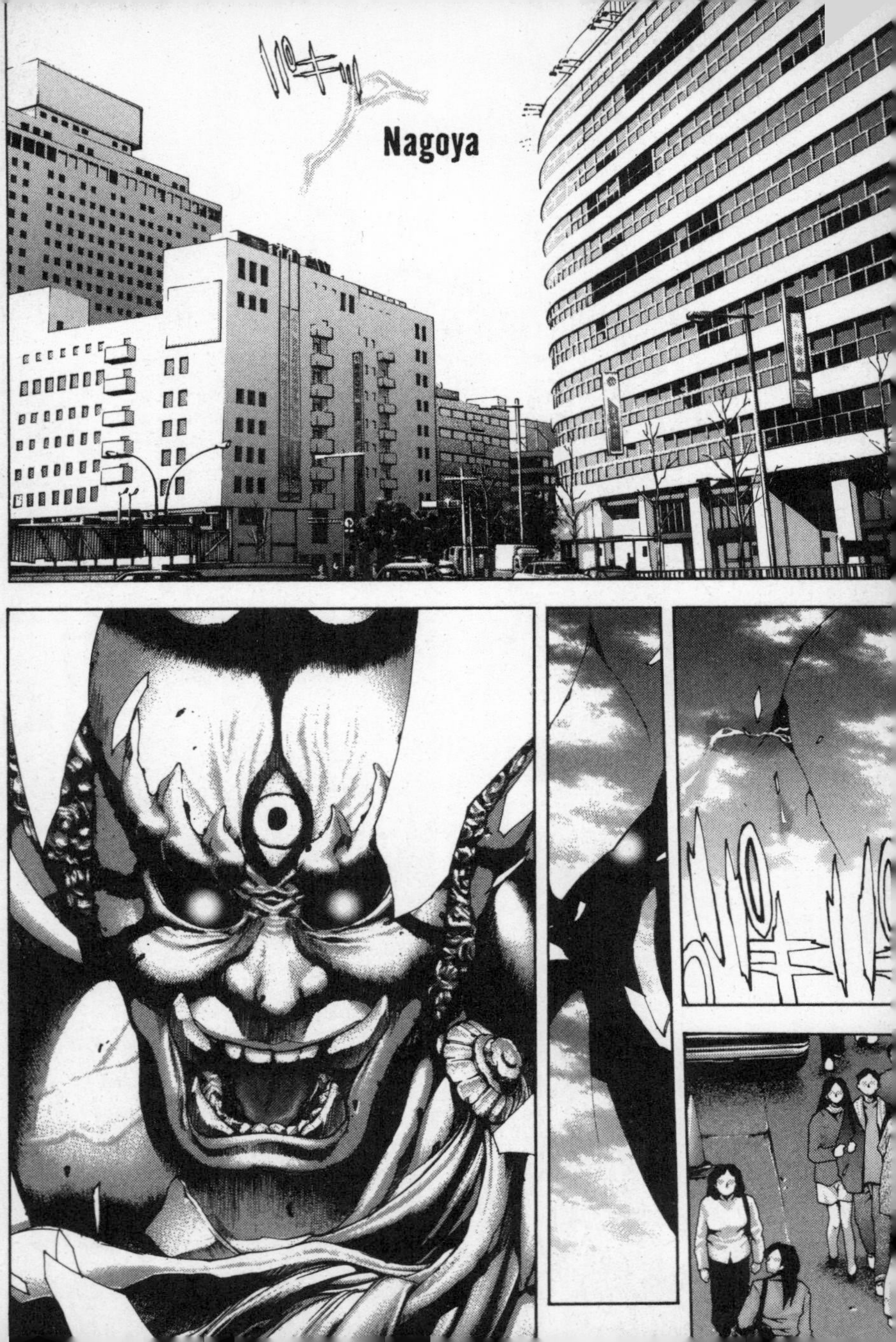
Nagoya

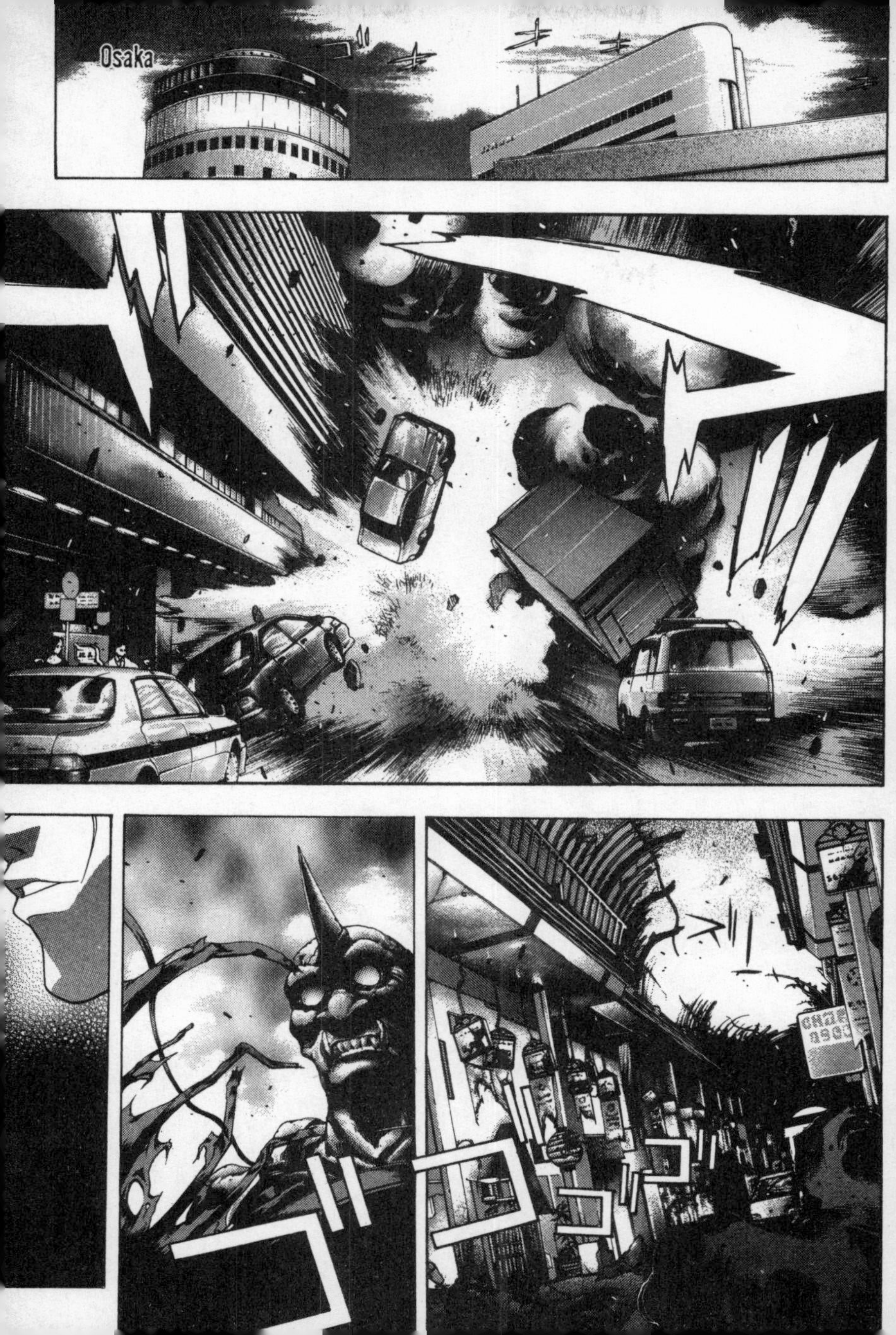
Osaka

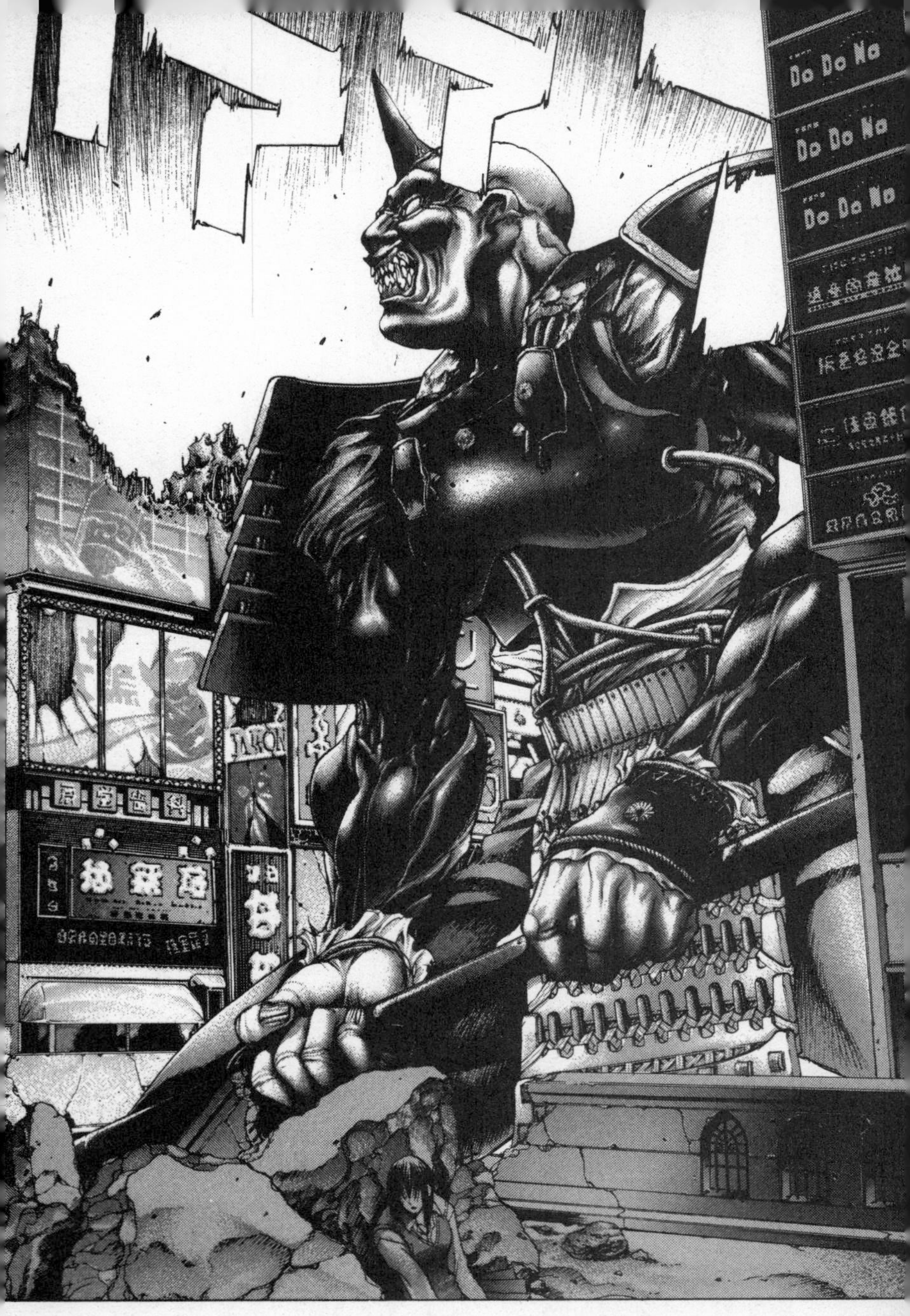
Do Do Na
Do Do Na
Do Do Na

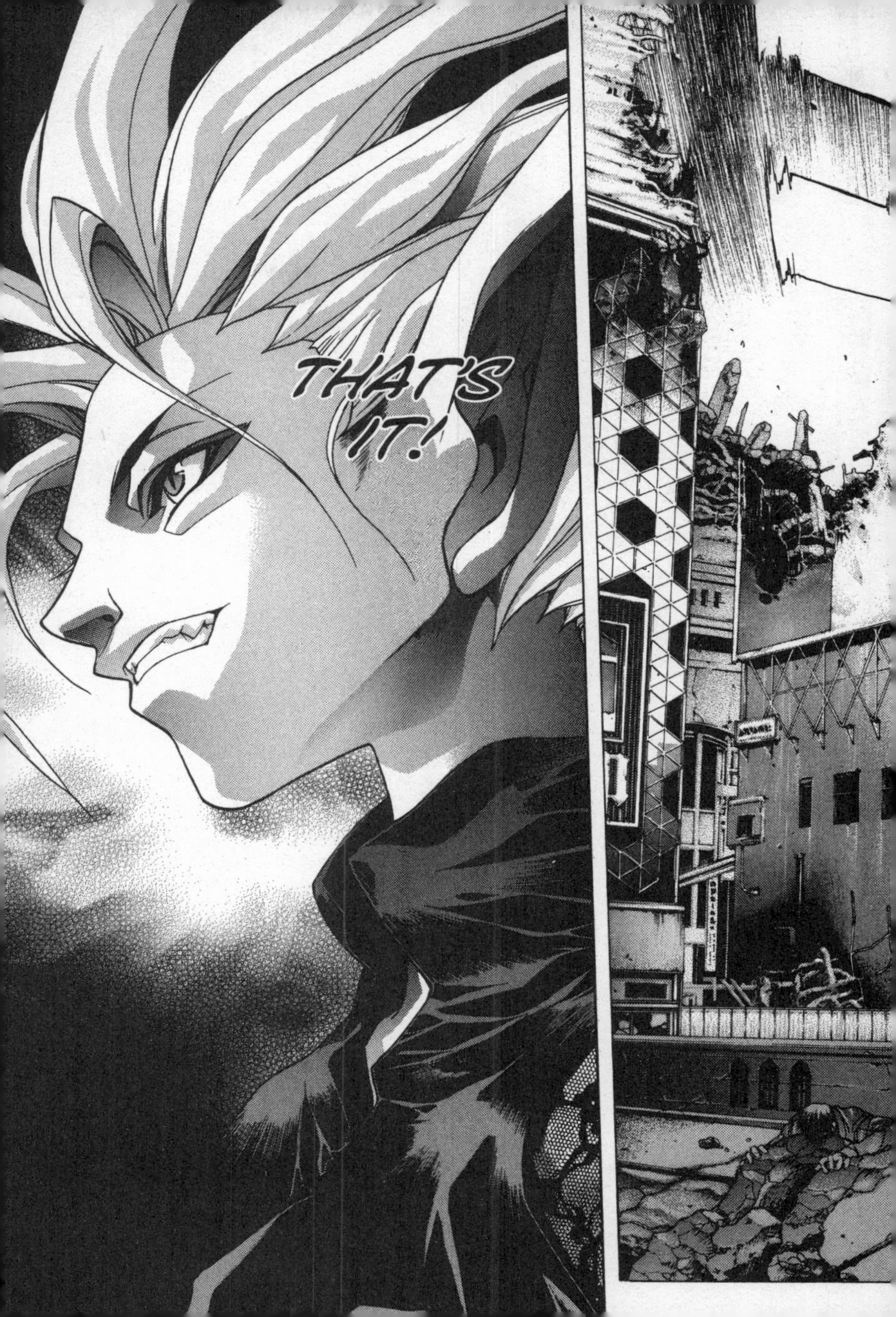
THAT'S IT!

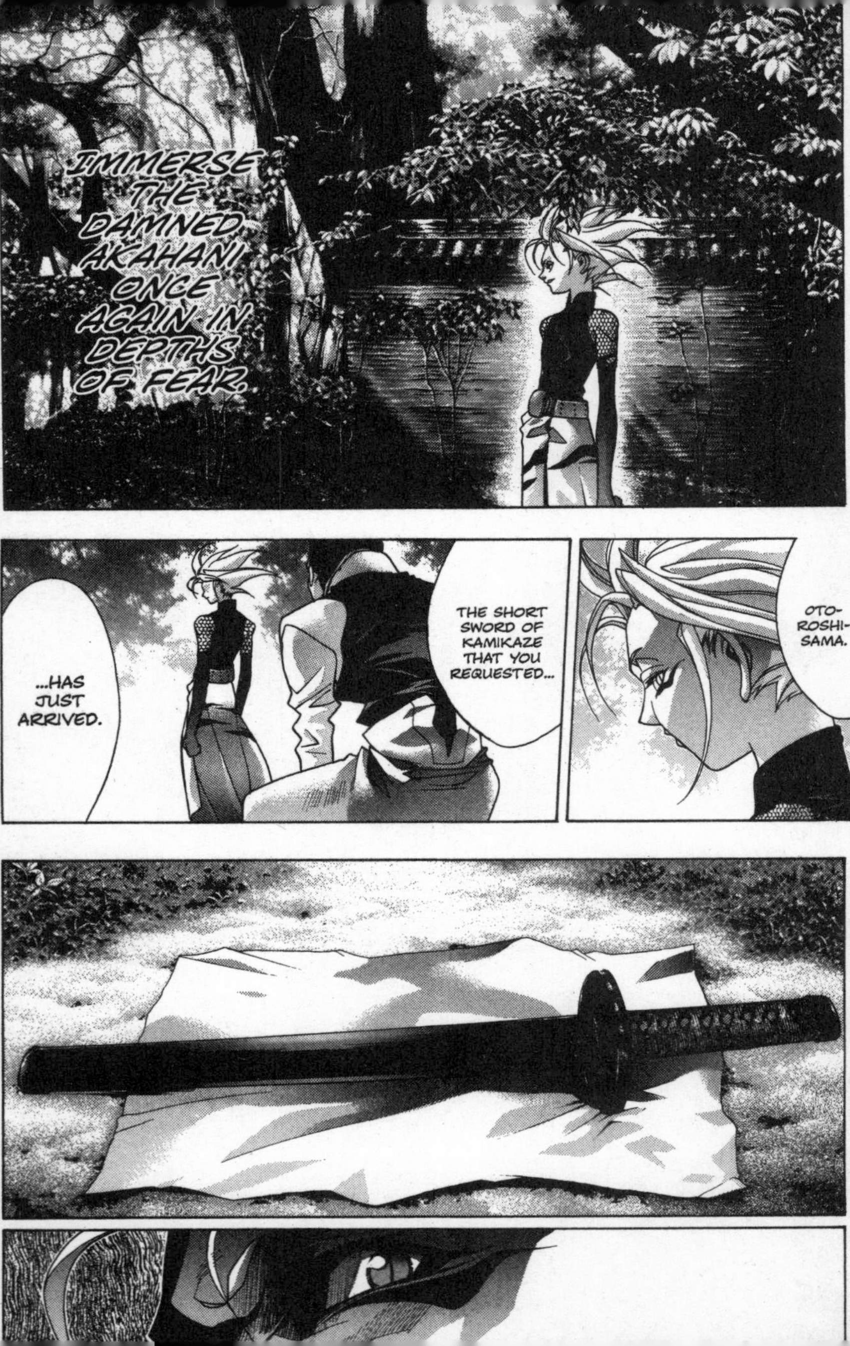
IMMERSE THE DAMNED AKAHANI ONCE AGAIN IN DEPTHS OF FEAR.
OTO-ROSHI-SAMA.
THE SHORT SWORD OF KAMIKAZE THAT YOU REQUESTED...
...HAS JUST ARRIVED.

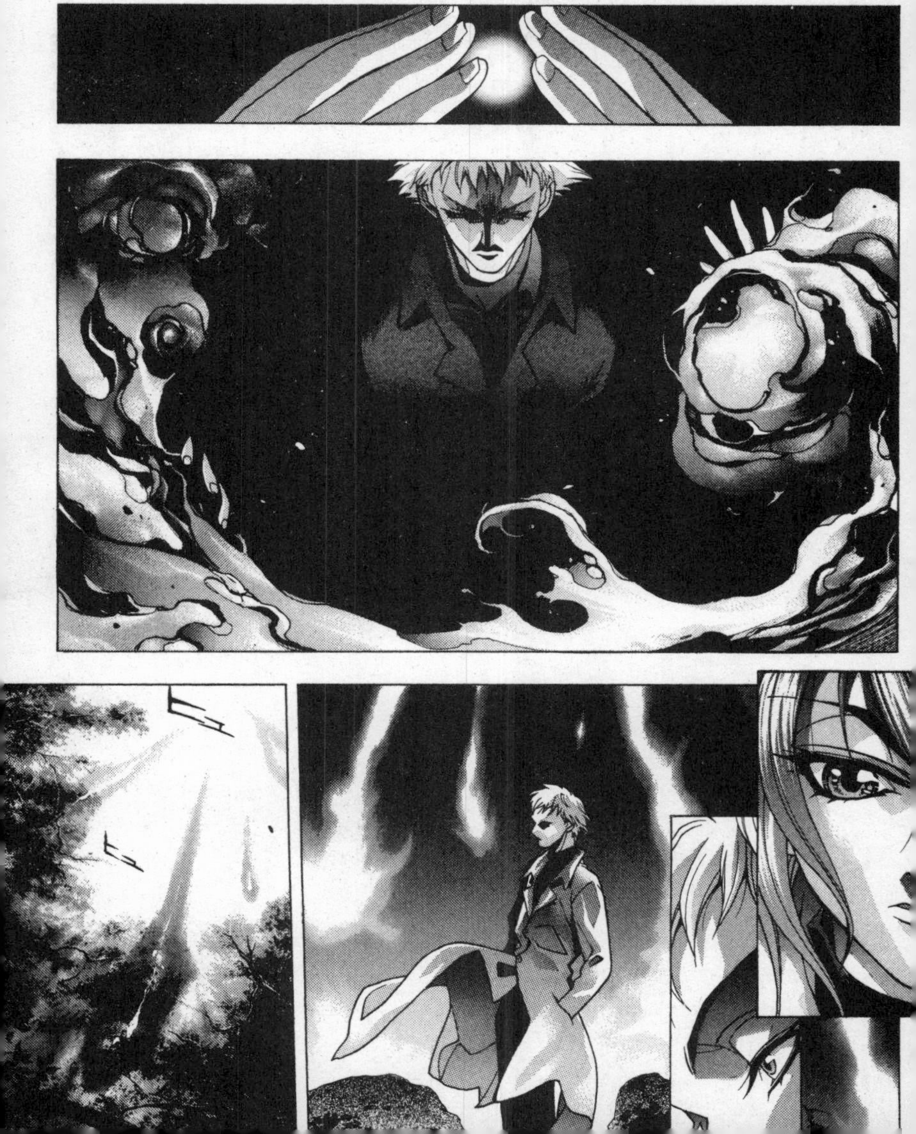

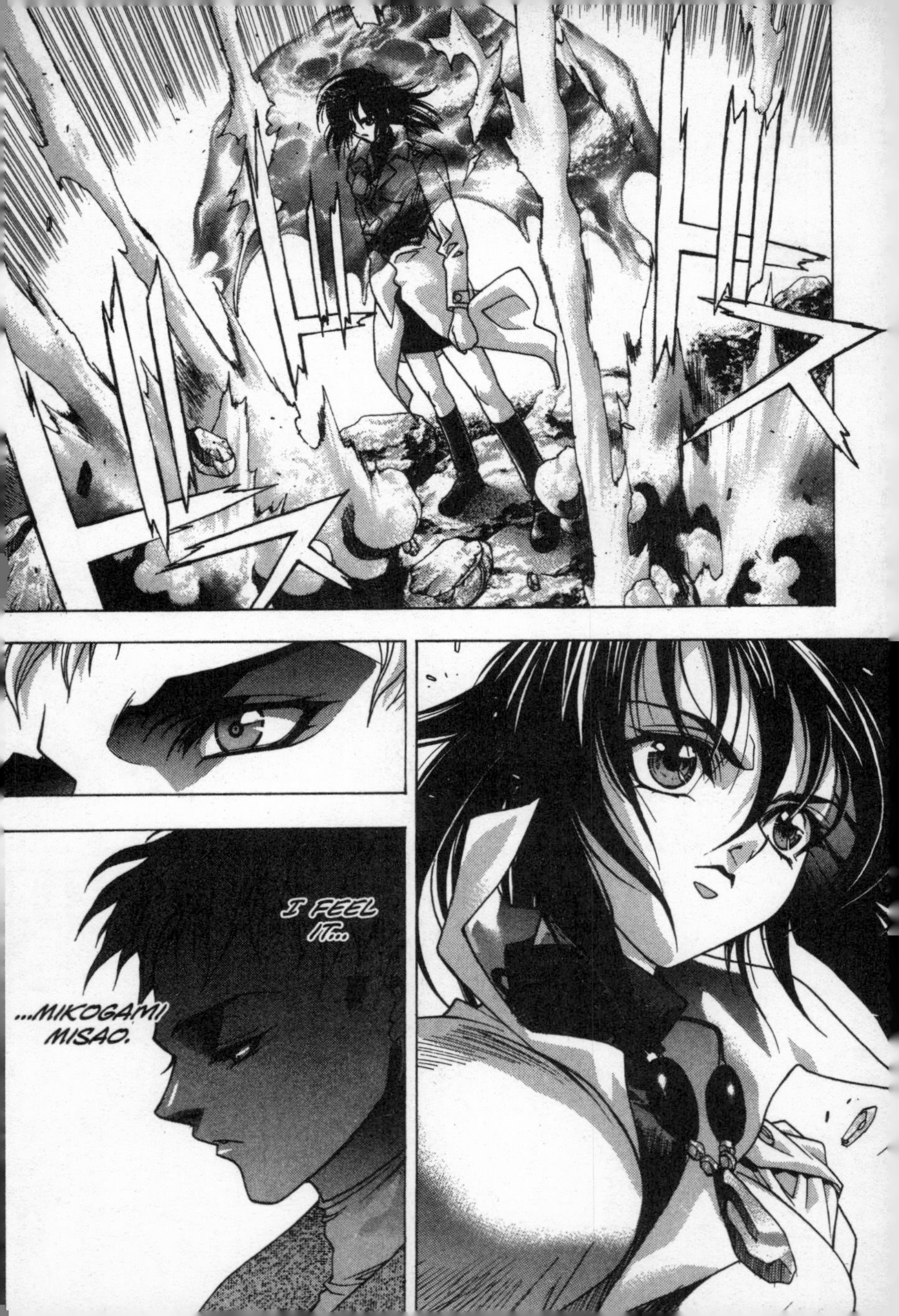
I FEEL IT...
...MIKOGAMI MISAO.

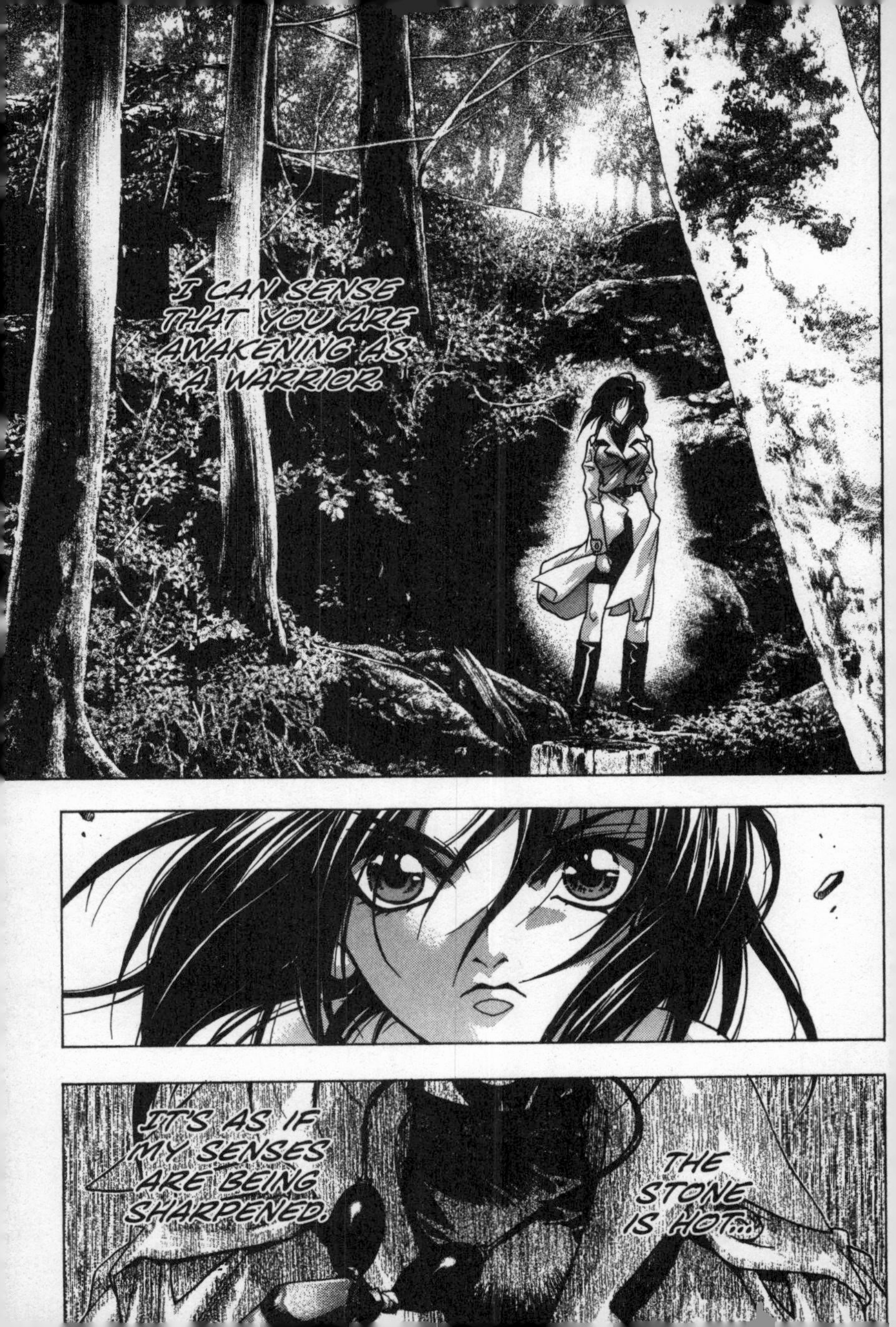
I CAN SENSE THAT YOU ARE AWAKENING AS A WARRIOR.
THE STONE IS HOT...
IT'S AS IF MY SENSES ARE BEING SHARPENED.

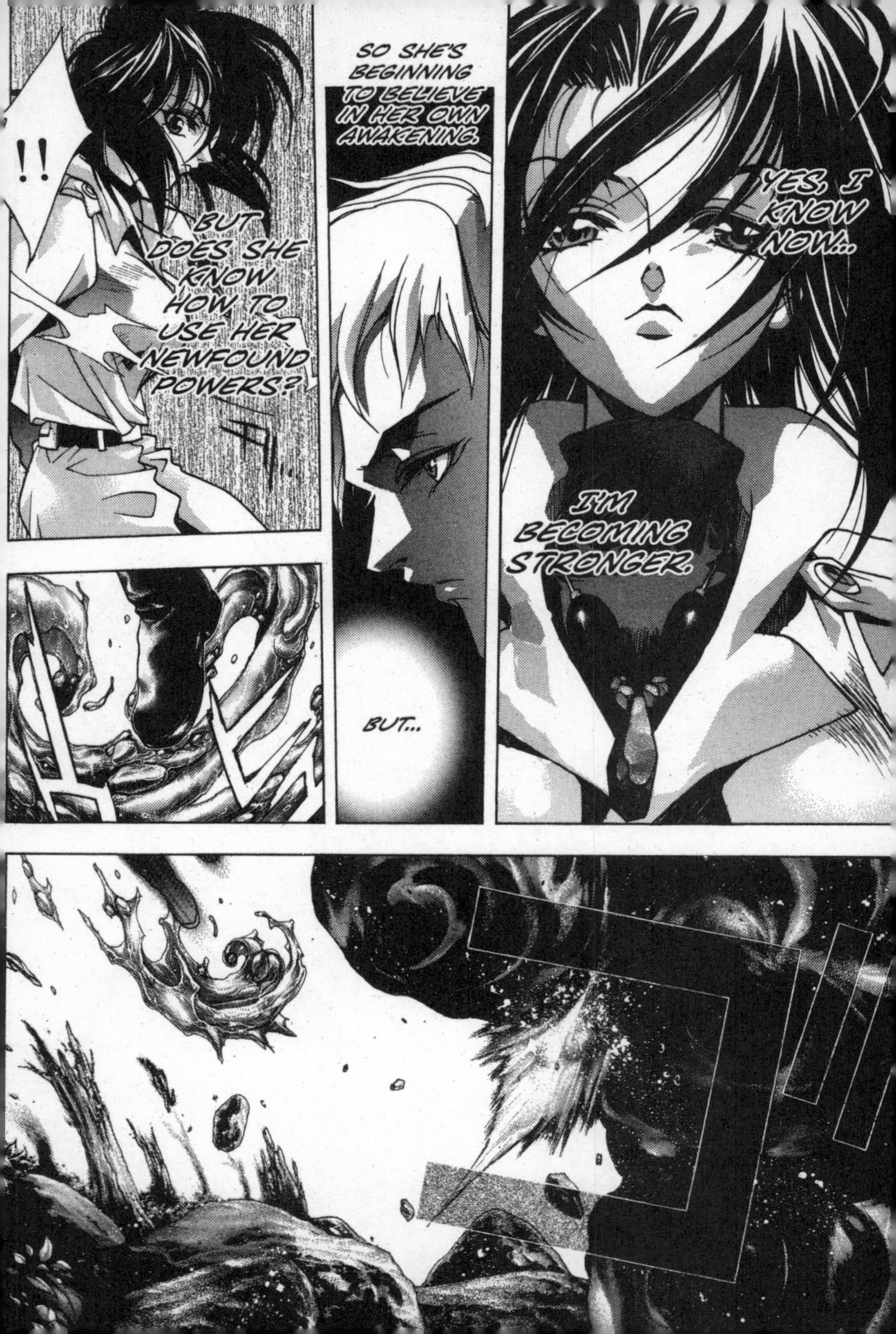
YES, I KNOW NOW...
I'M BECOMING STRONGER.
SO SHE'S BEGINNING TO BELIEVE IN HER OWN AWAKENING.
BUT...
!!
BUT DOES SHE KNOW HOW TO USE HER NEWFOUND POWERS?

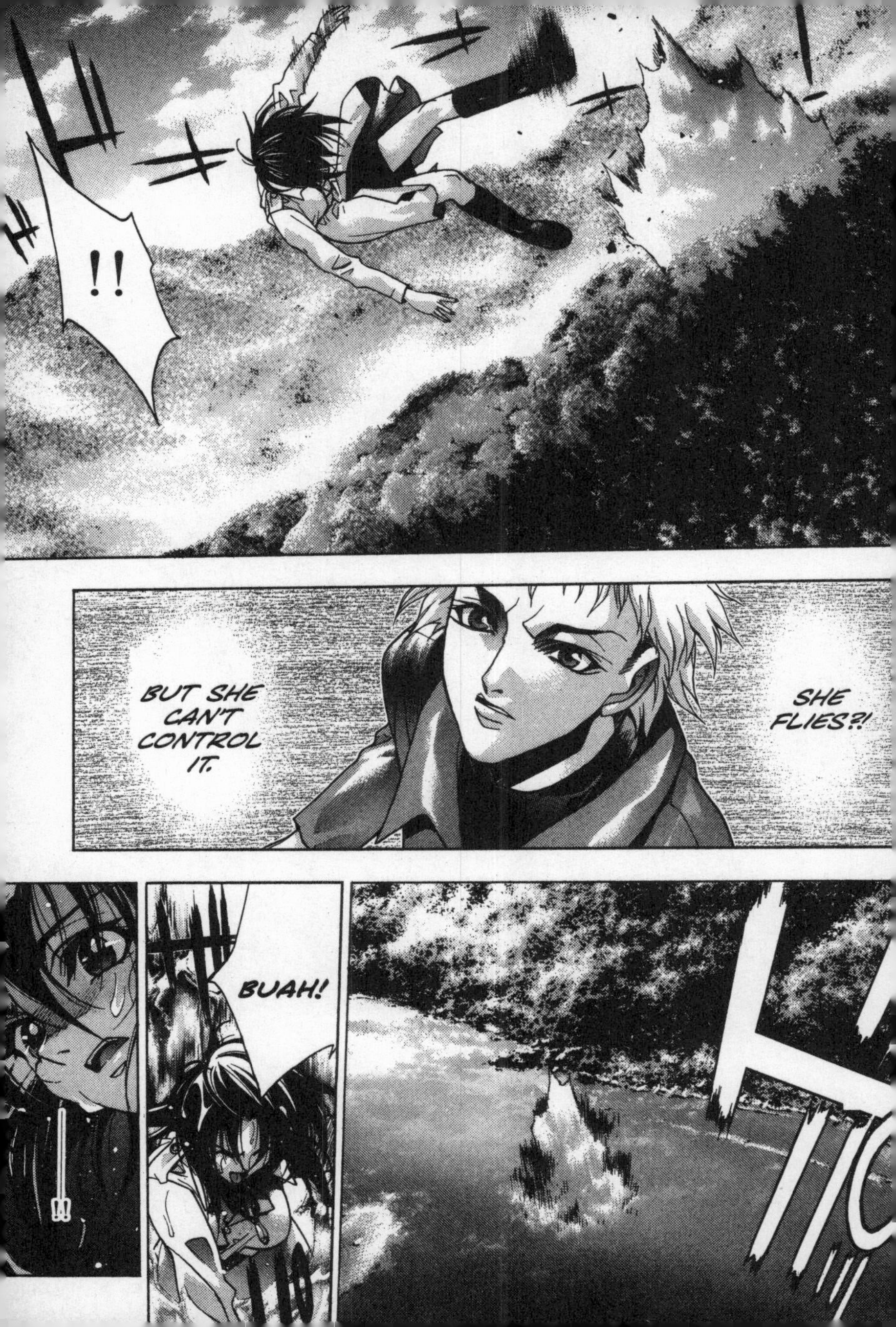
!!
SHE FLIES?!
BUT SHE CAN'T CONTROL IT.
BUAH!

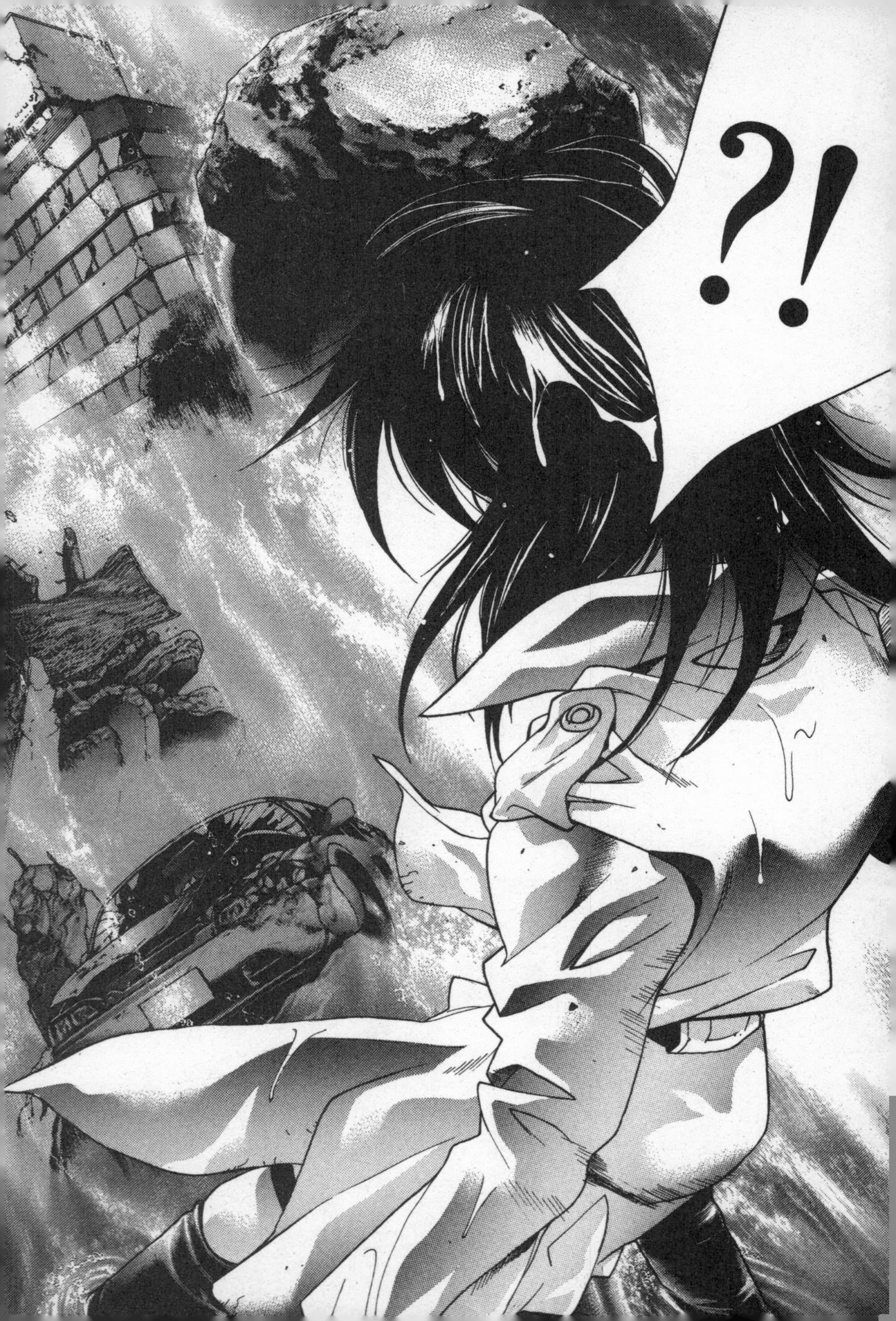
?!

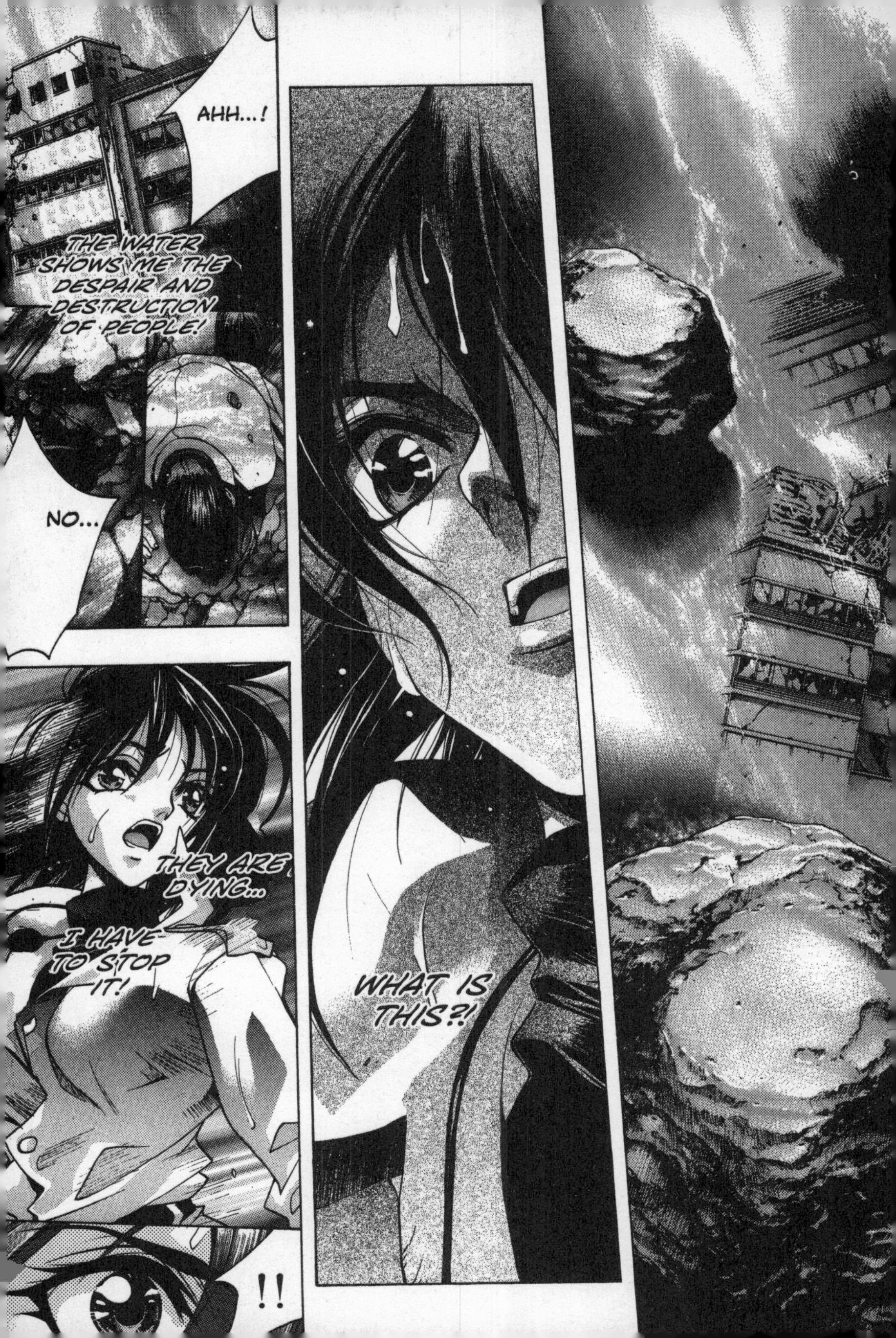
WHAT IS THIS?!
AHH...!
THE WATER SHOWS ME THE DESPAIR AND DESTRUCTION OF PEOPLE!
NO...
THEY ARE DYING...
I HAVE TO STOP IT!
!!

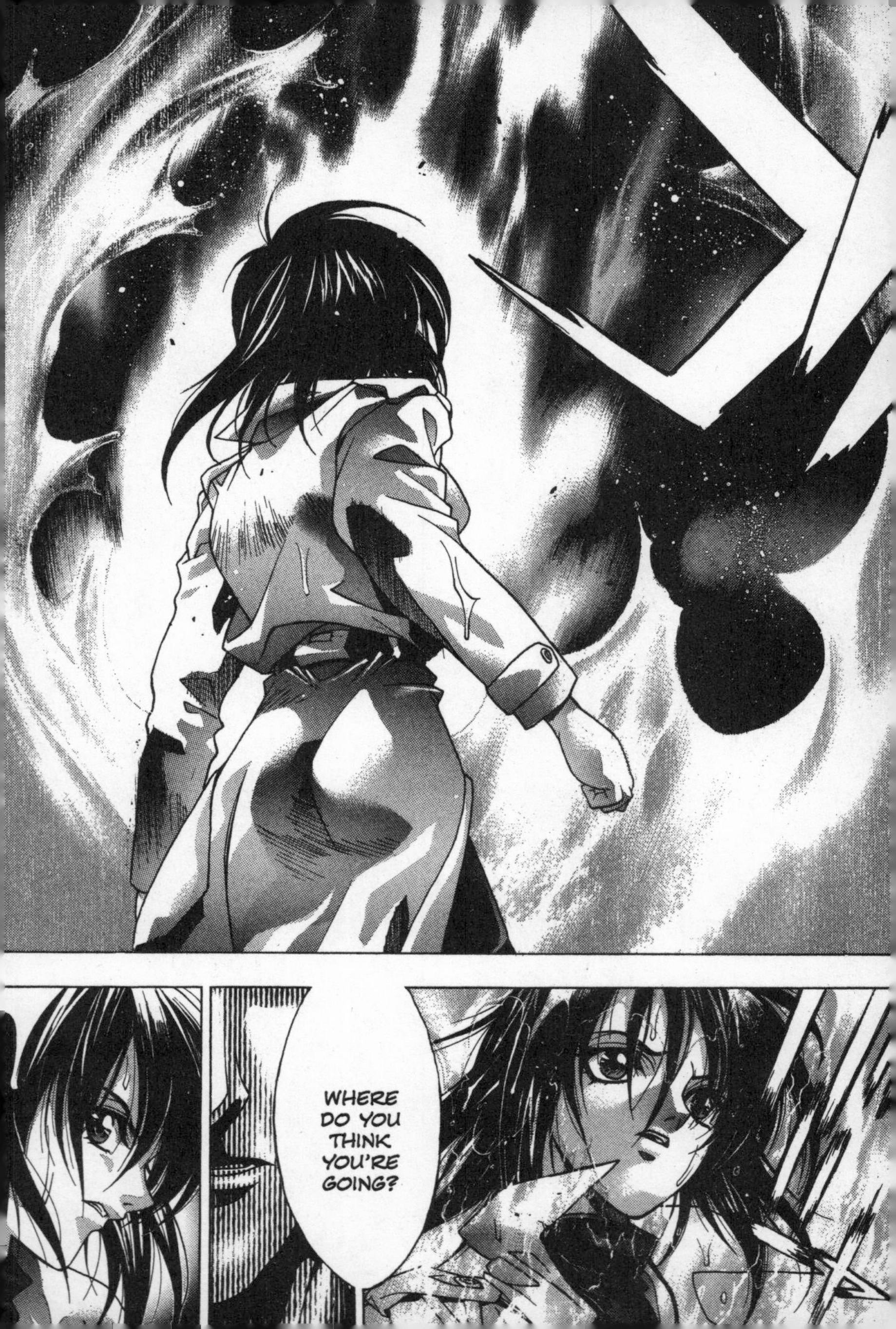
WHERE DO YOU THINK YOU'RE GOING?

YOU CAN'T LEAVE THIS LAND UNTIL YOU DEFEAT ME.

HIGA!

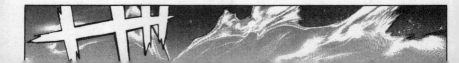

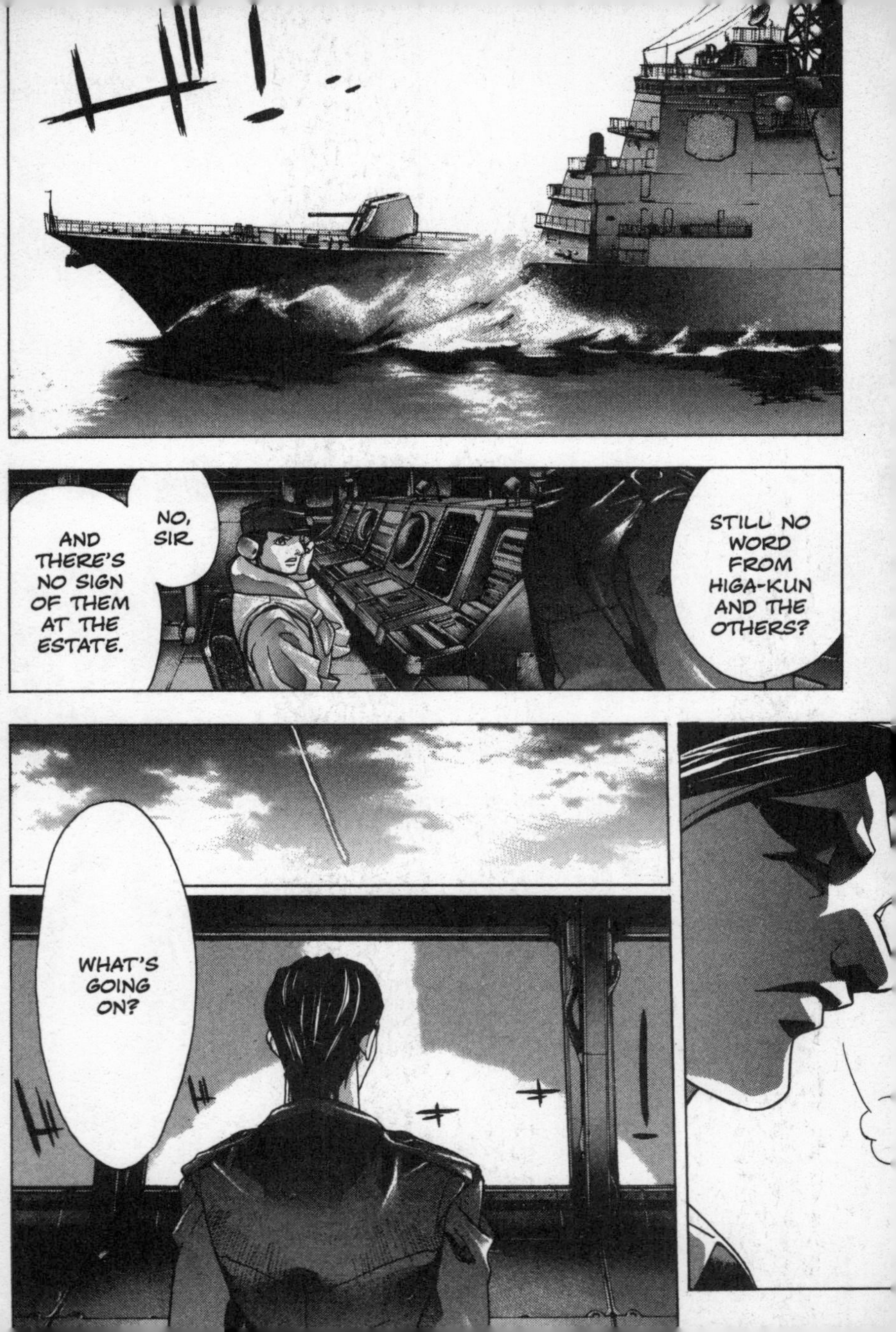
STILL NO WORD FROM HIGA-KUN AND THE OTHERS?
NO, SIR
AND THERE'S NO SIGN OF THEM AT THE ESTATE.
WHAT'S GOING ON?

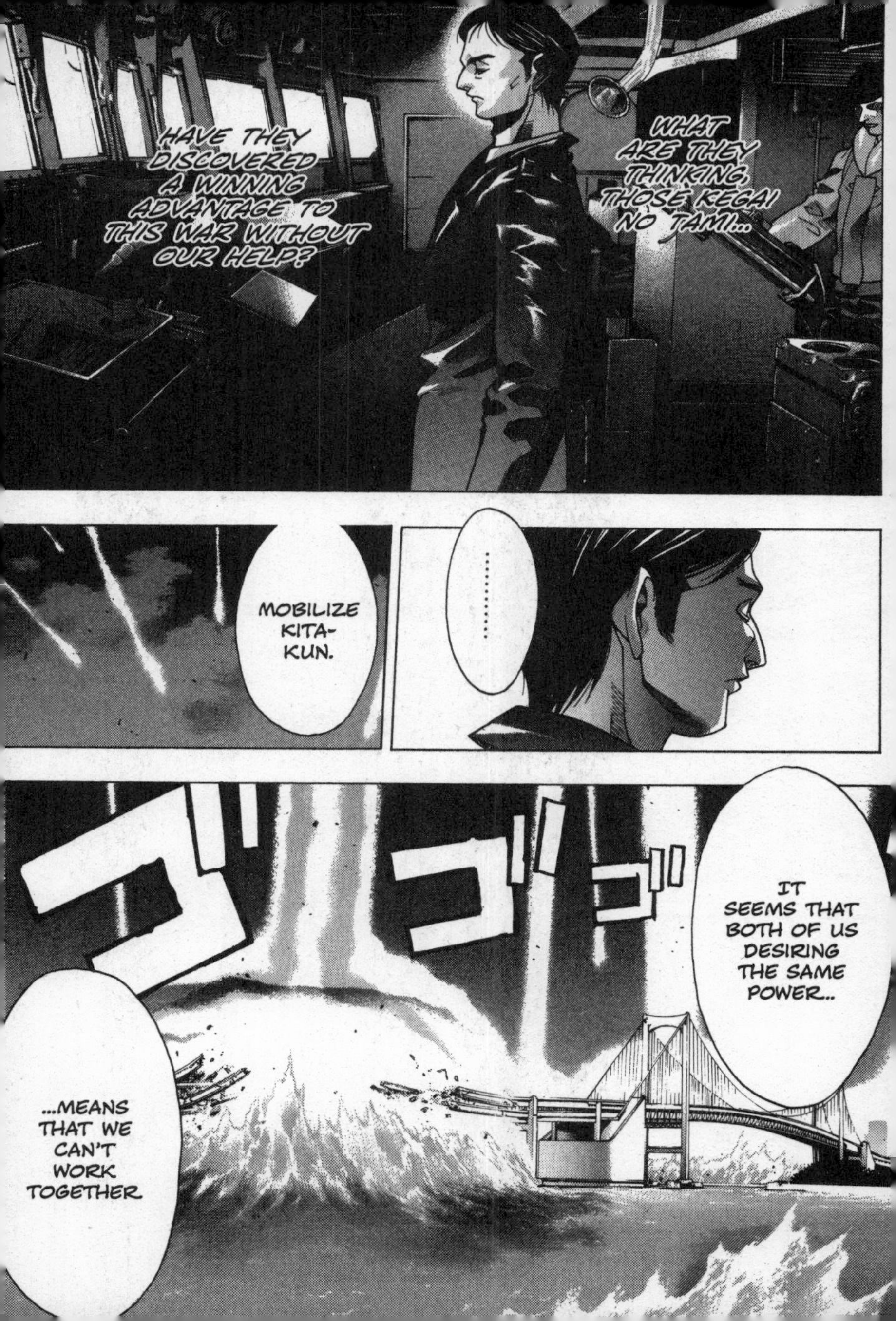
WHAT ARE THEY THINKING, THOSE KEGAI NO TAMI...
HAVE THEY DISCOVERED A WINNING ADVANTAGE TO THIS WAR WITHOUT OUR HELP?
......
MOBILIZE KITA-KUN.
IT SEEMS THAT BOTH OF US DESIRING THE SAME POWER...
...MEANS THAT WE CAN'T WORK TOGETHER

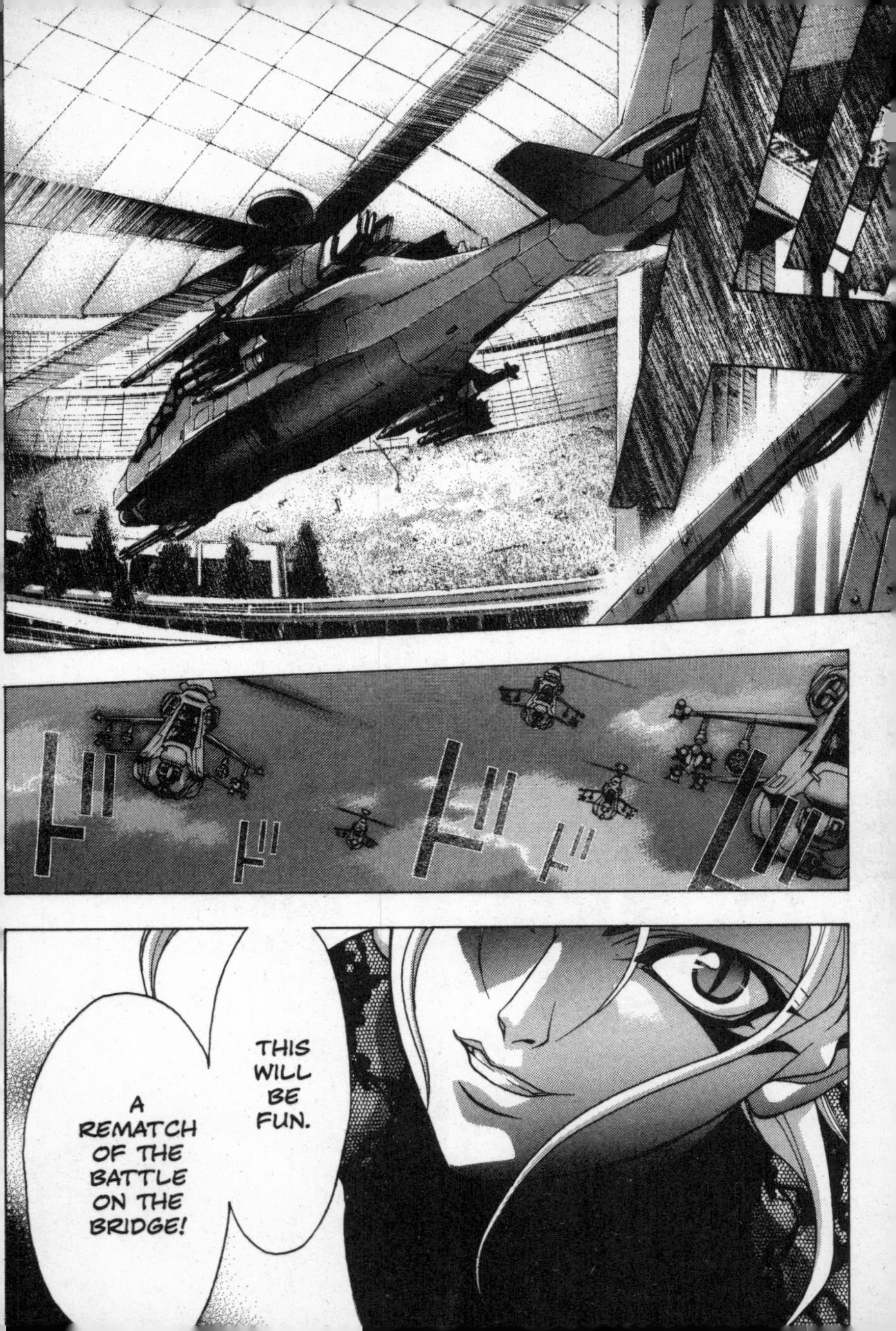
THIS WILL BE FUN.
A REMATCH OF THE BATTLE ON THE BRIDGE!

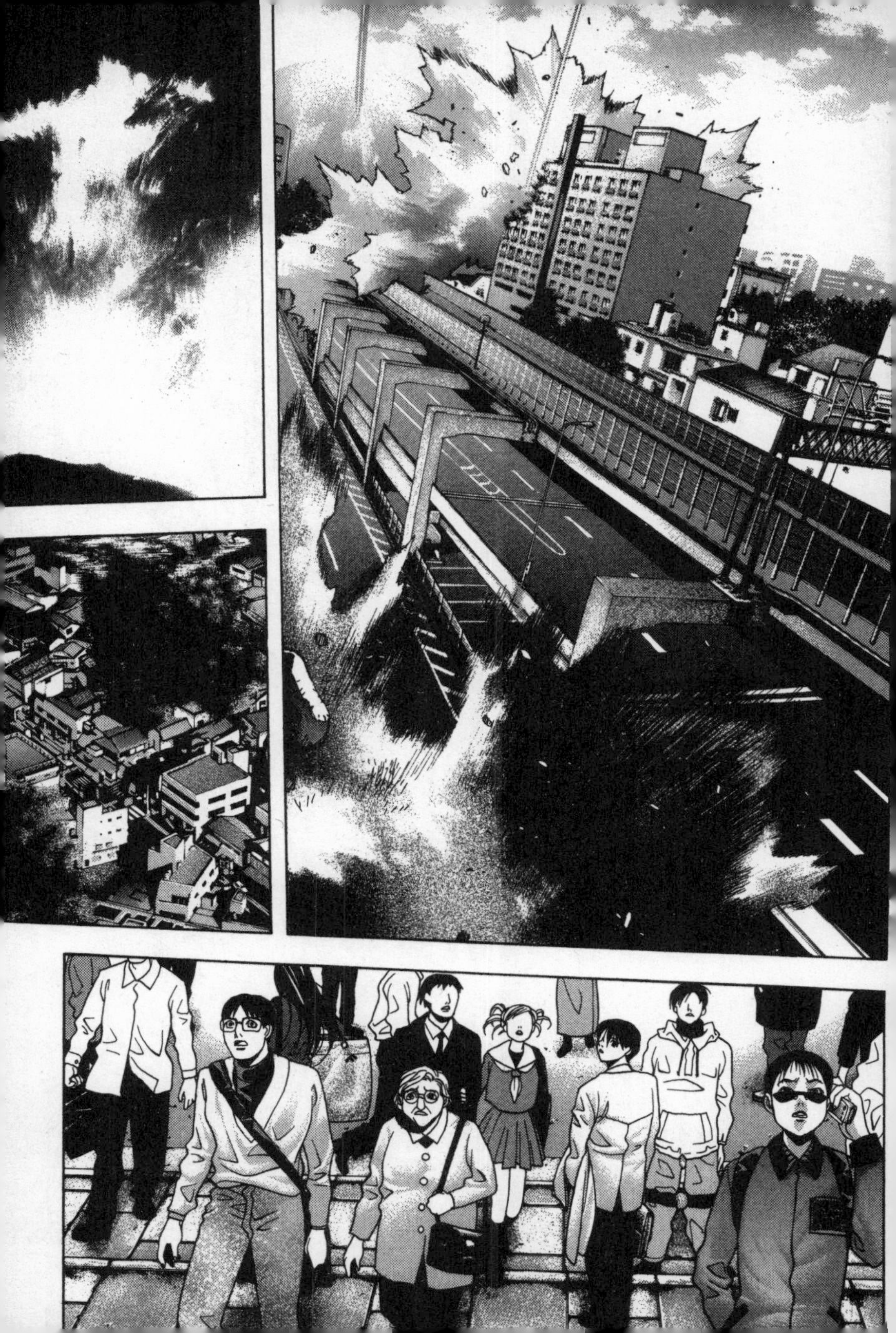

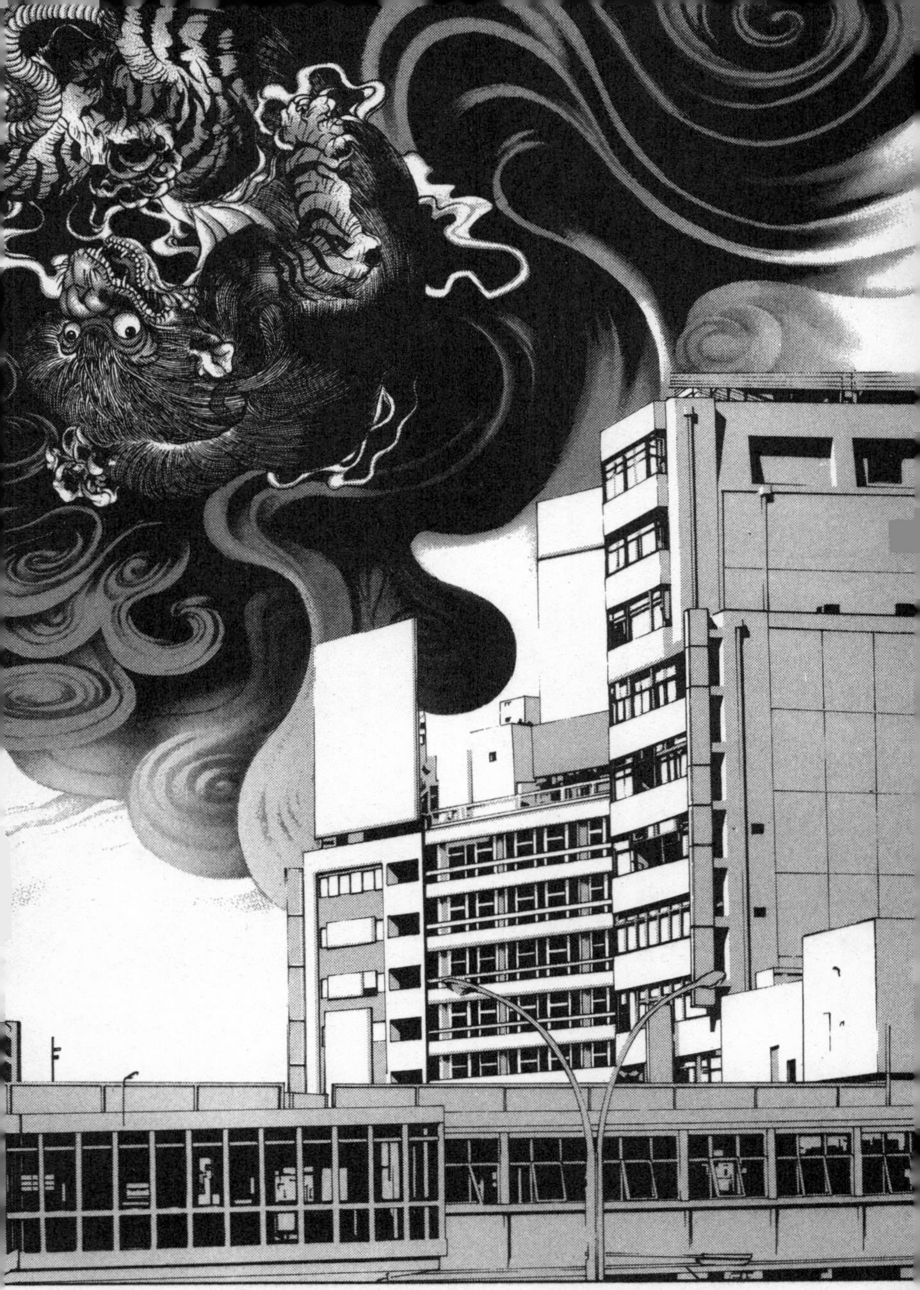

Chapter 42: Princess Bishagatsuku

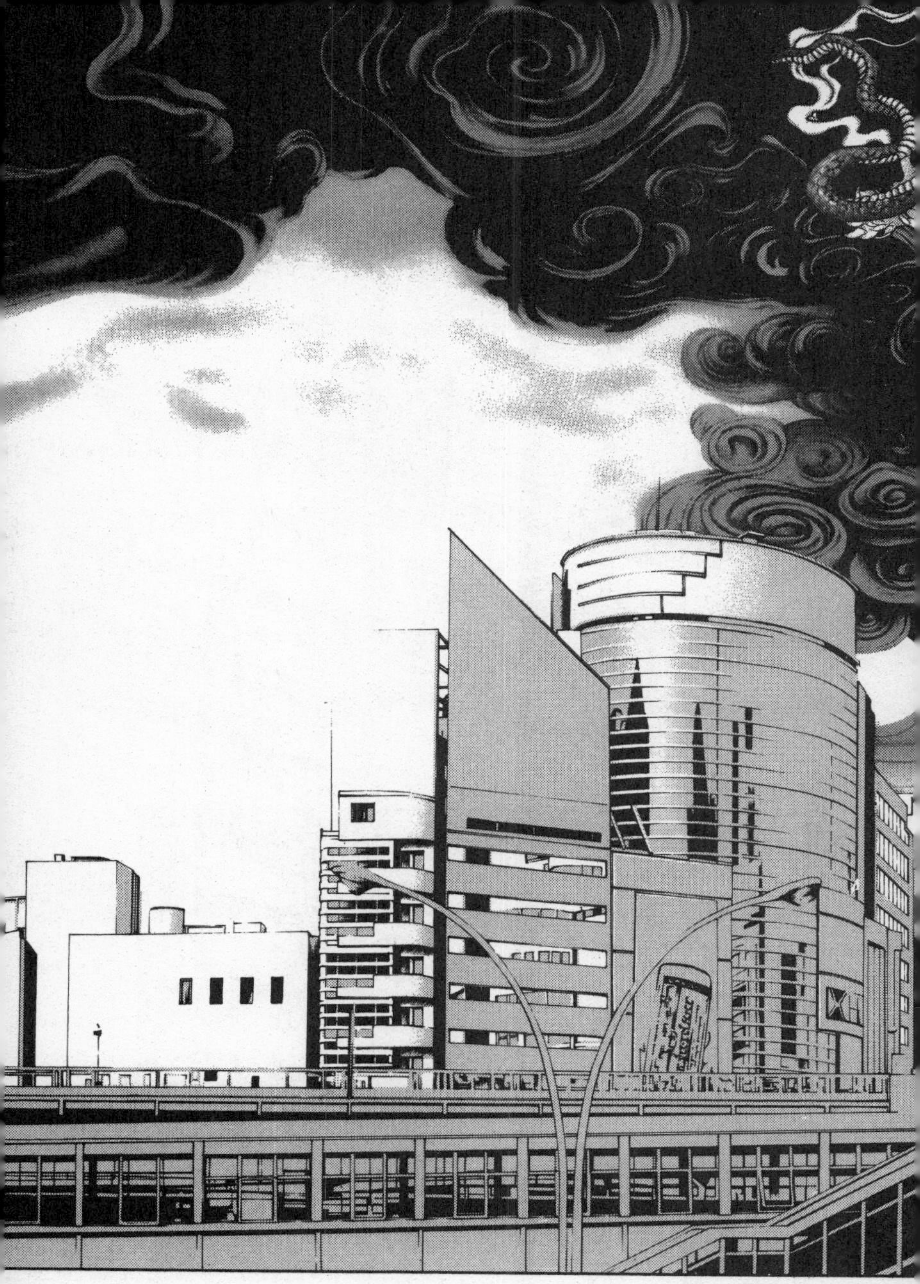

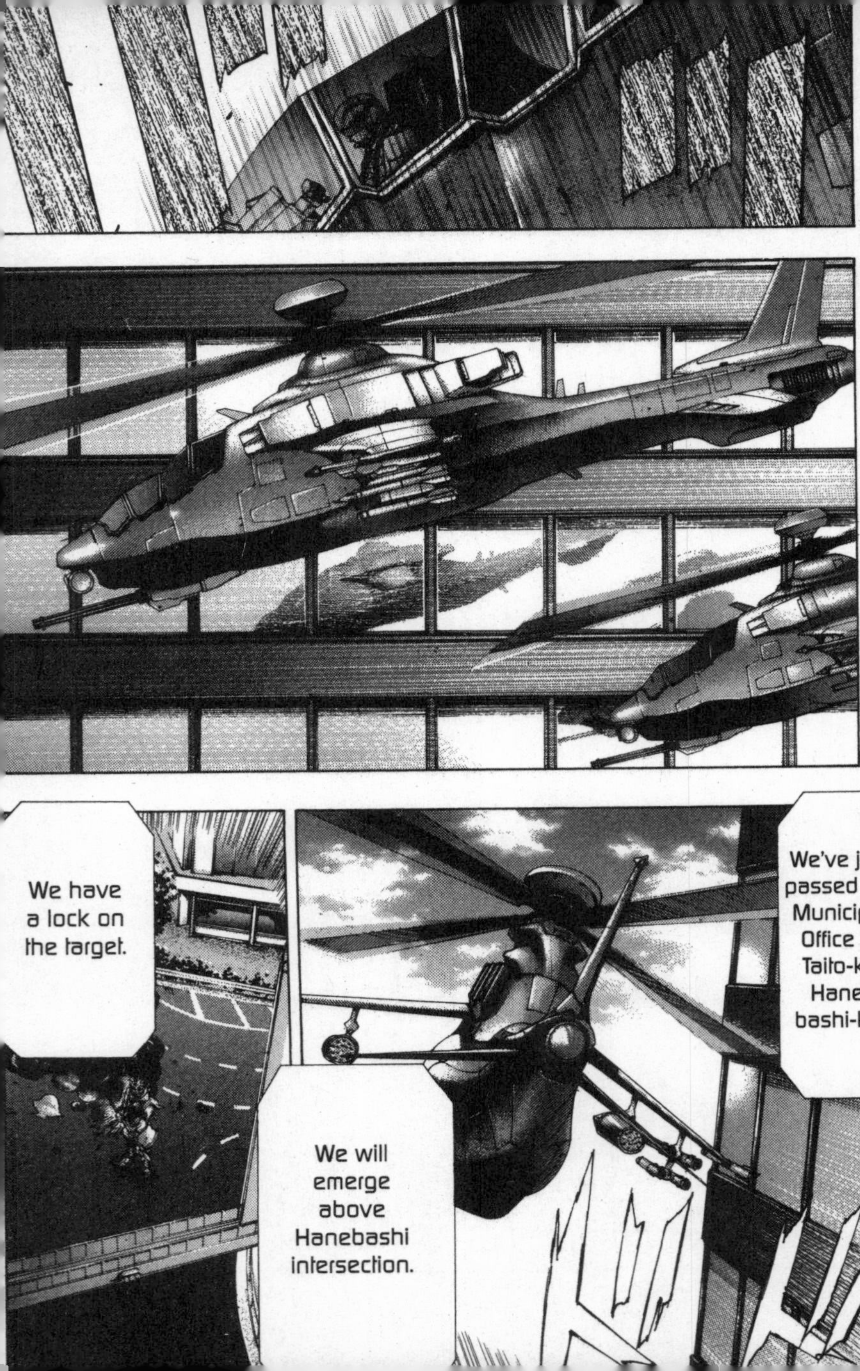
We've just passed the Municipal Office of Taito-ku Hane-bashi-ku!
We will emerge above Hanebashi intersection.
We have a lock on the target.

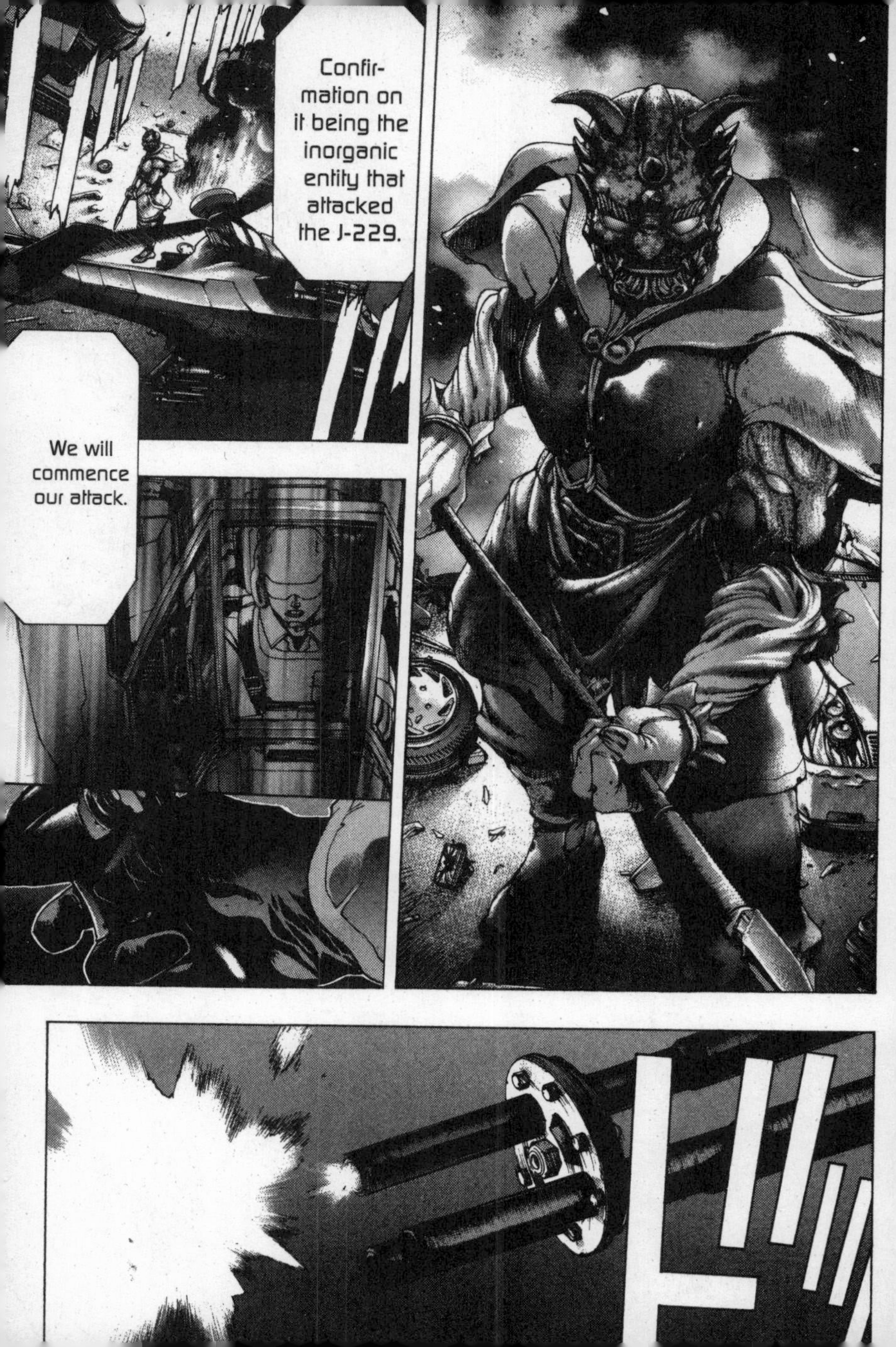
Confir-mation on it being the inorganic entity that attacked the J-229.
We will commence our attack.

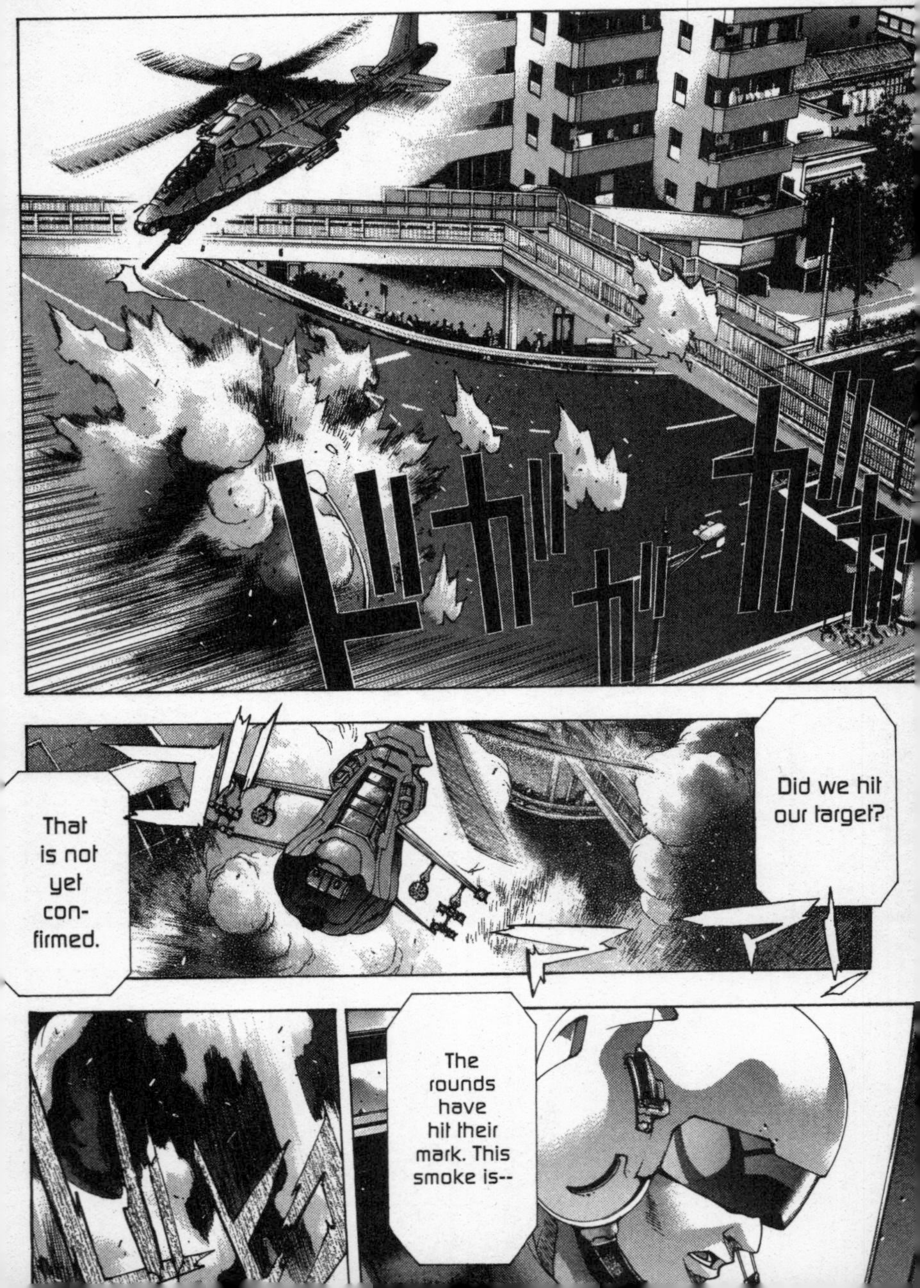
Did we hit our target?
That is not yet con- firmed.
The rounds have hit their mark. This smoke is--

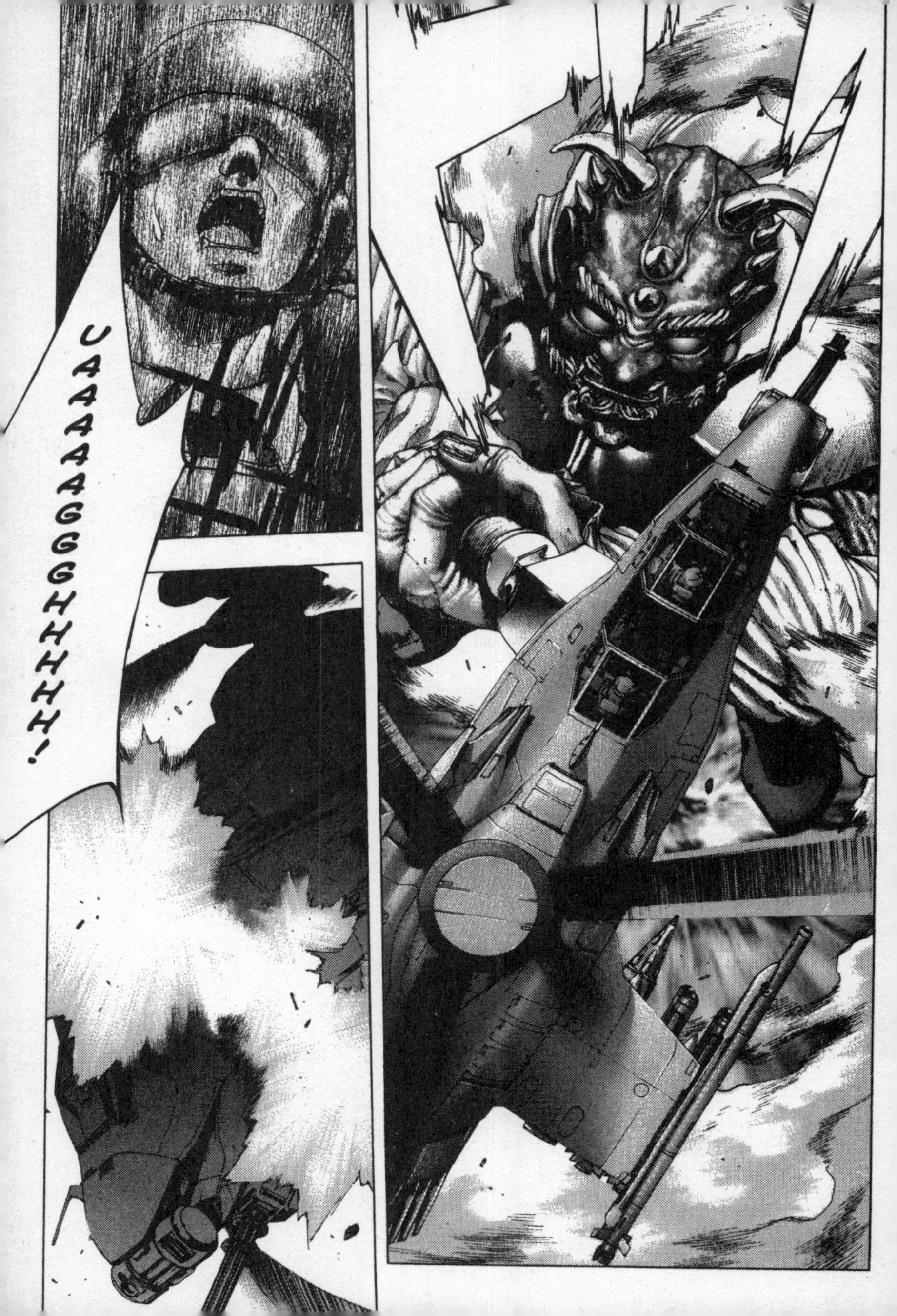
UAAAAAAGGGHHHHHH!

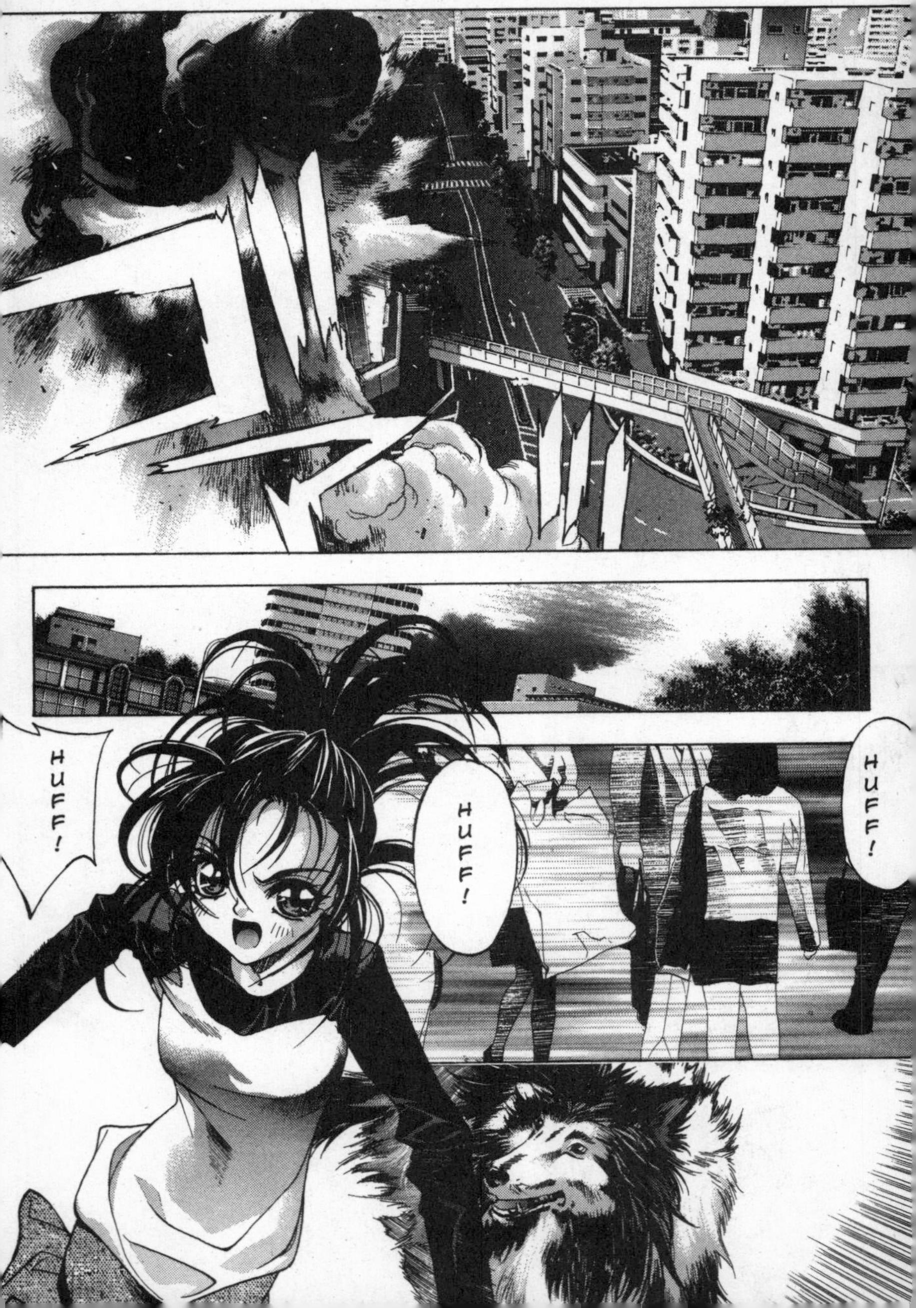
HUFF!
HUFF!
HUFF!

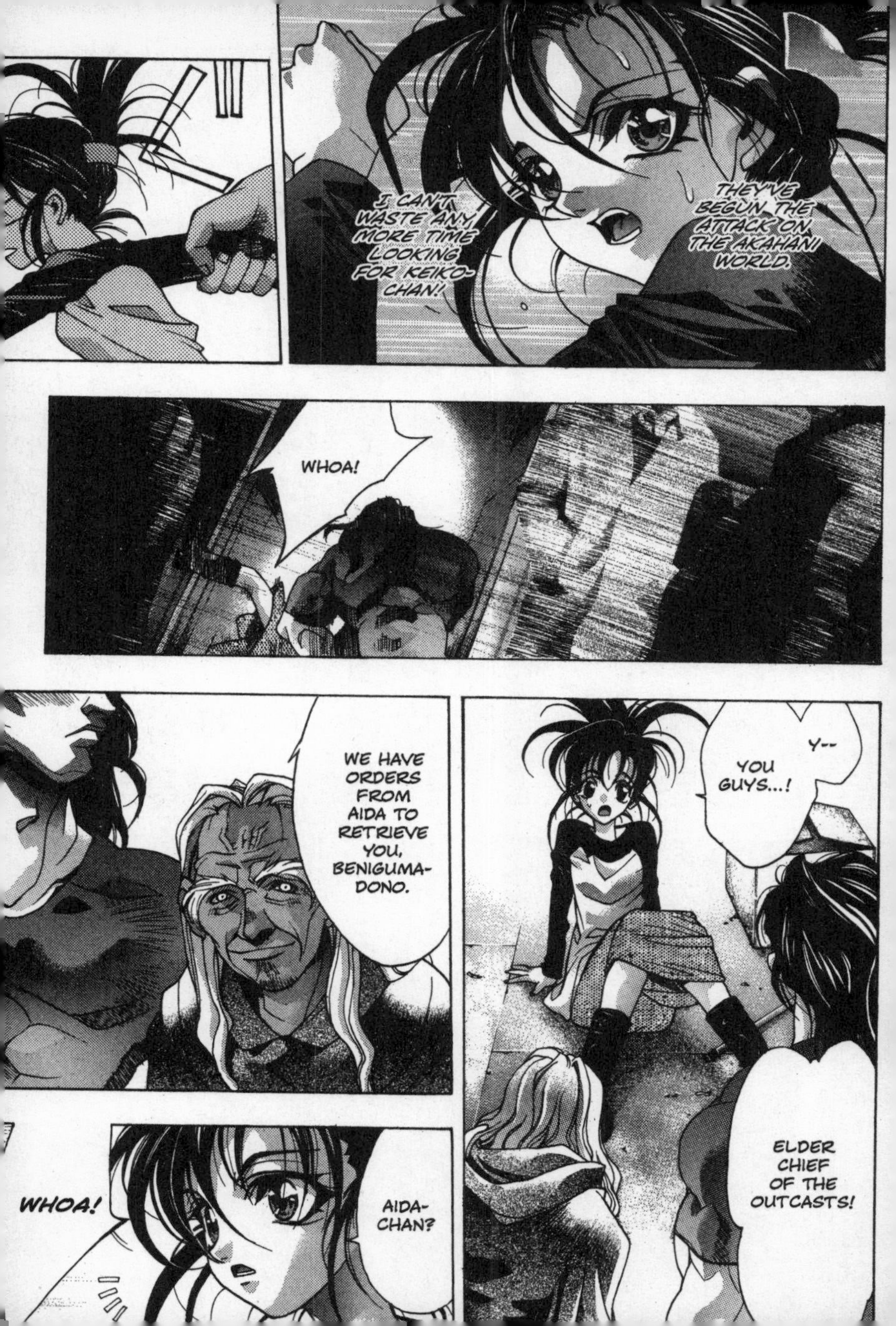
THEY'VE BEGUN THE ATTACK ON THE AKAHANI WORLD.
I CAN'T WASTE ANY MORE TIME LOOKING FOR KEIKO-CHAN!
WHOA!
Y-- YOU GUYS...!
ELDER CHIEF OF THE OUTCASTS!
WE HAVE ORDERS FROM AIDA TO RETRIEVE YOU, BENIGUMA-DONO.
AIDA-CHAN?
WHOA!

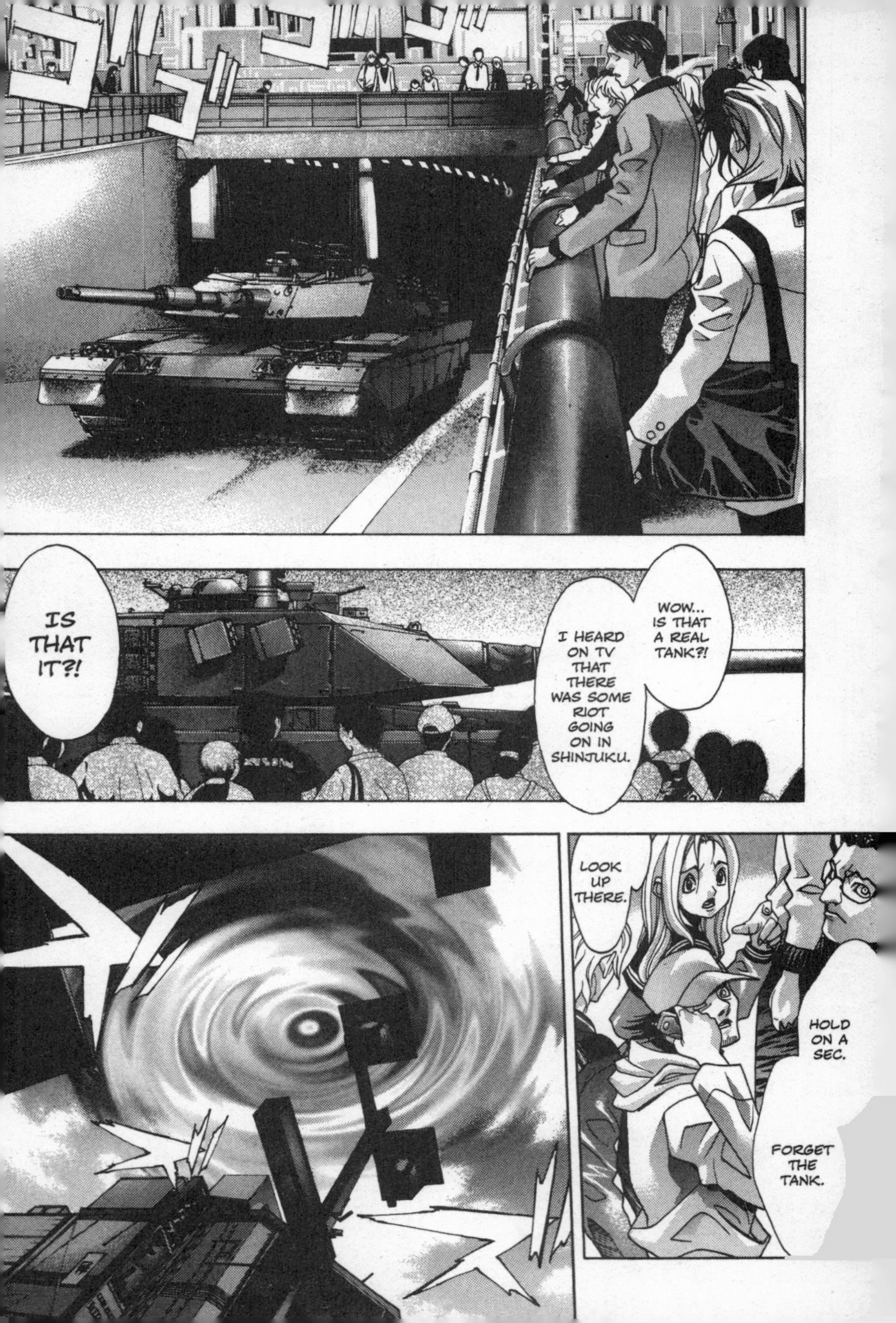
WOW... IS THAT A REAL TANK?!
I HEARD ON TV THAT THERE WAS SOME RIOT GOING ON IN SHINJUKU.
IS THAT IT?!
LOOK UP THERE.
HOLD ON A SEC.
FORGET THE TANK.

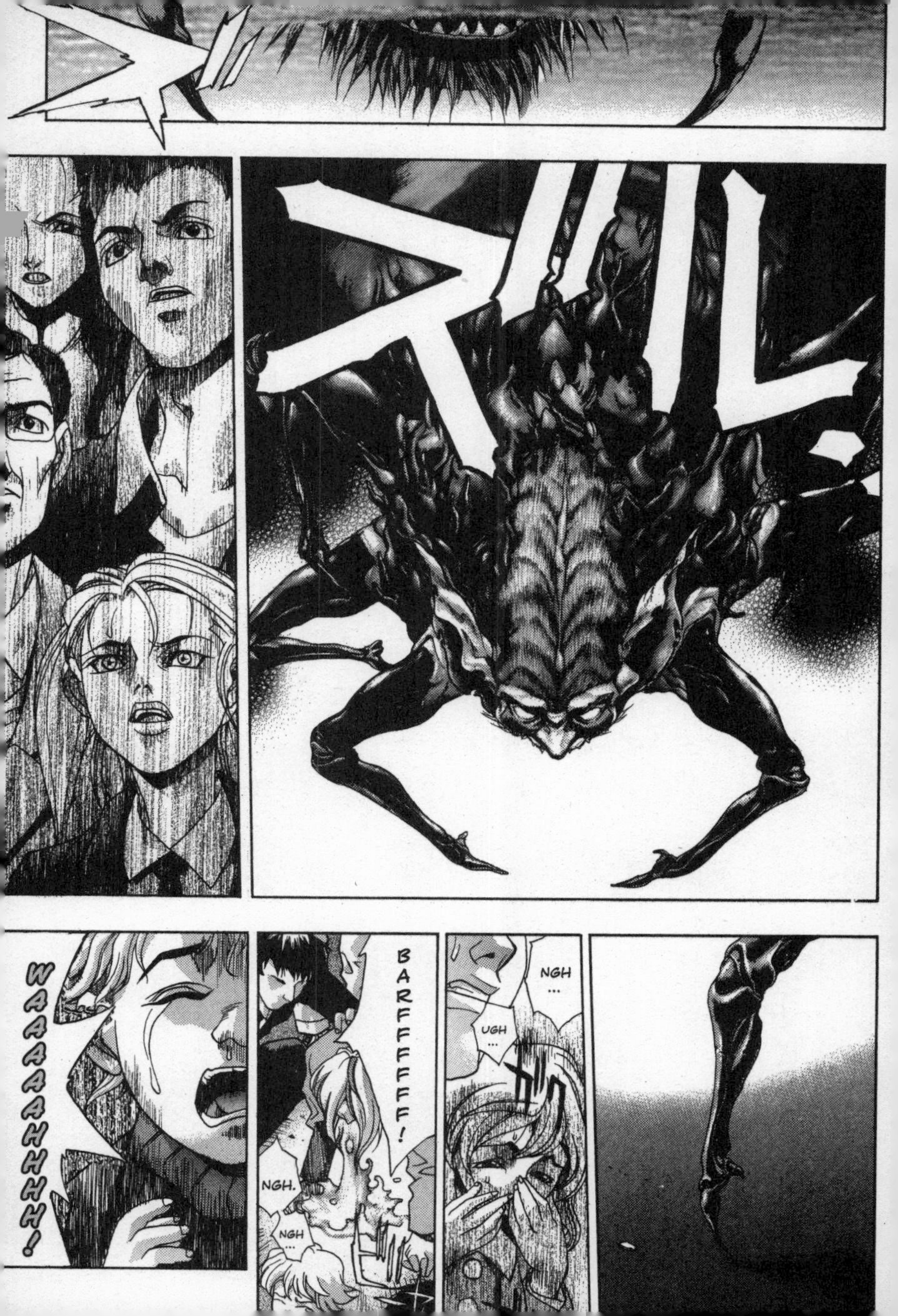
NGH ...
UGH ...
BARFFFFFF!
NGH.
NGH ...
WAAAAAHHHH!

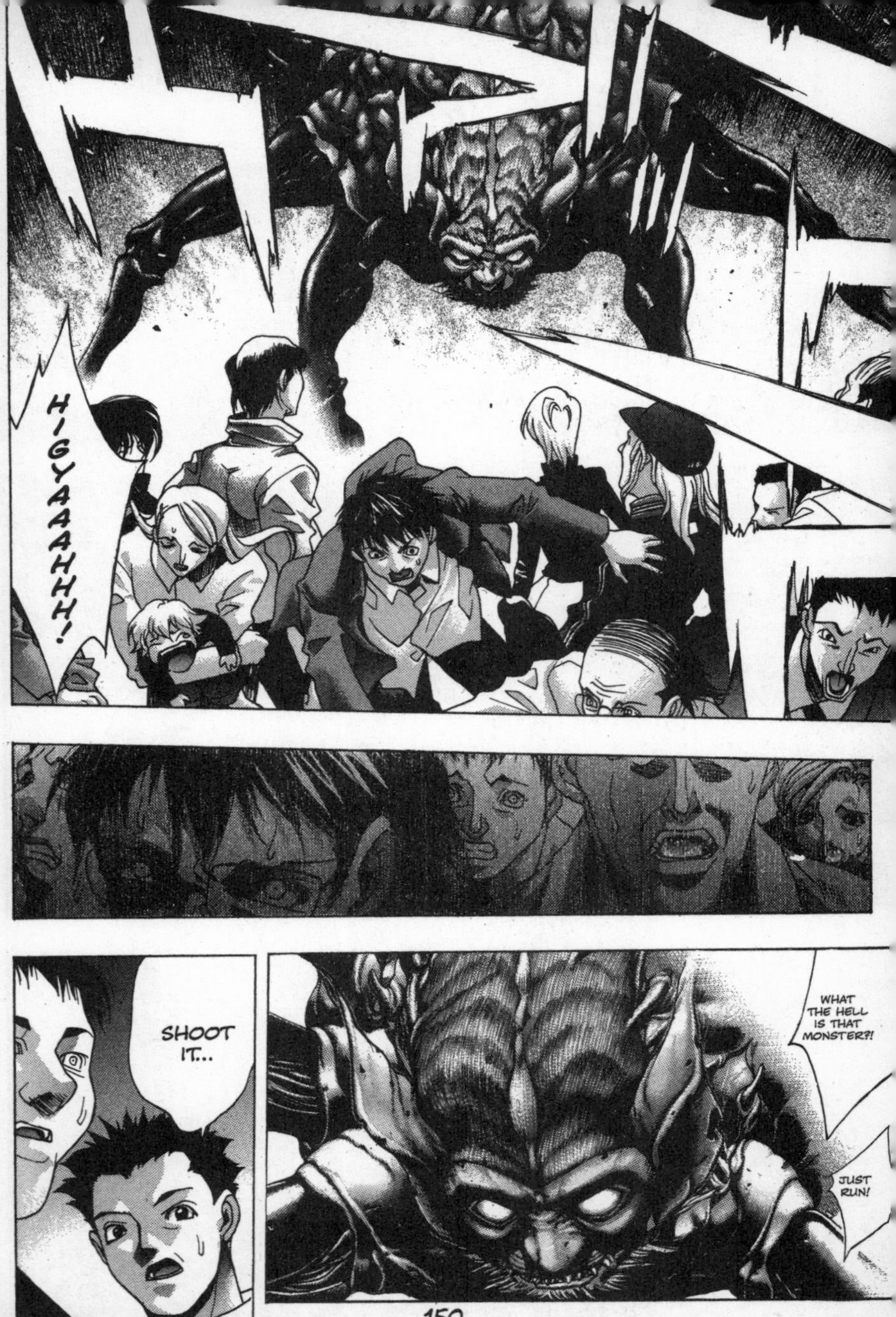
HIGYAAAAHHH!
WHAT THE HELL IS THAT MONSTER?!
JUST RUN!
SHOOT IT...

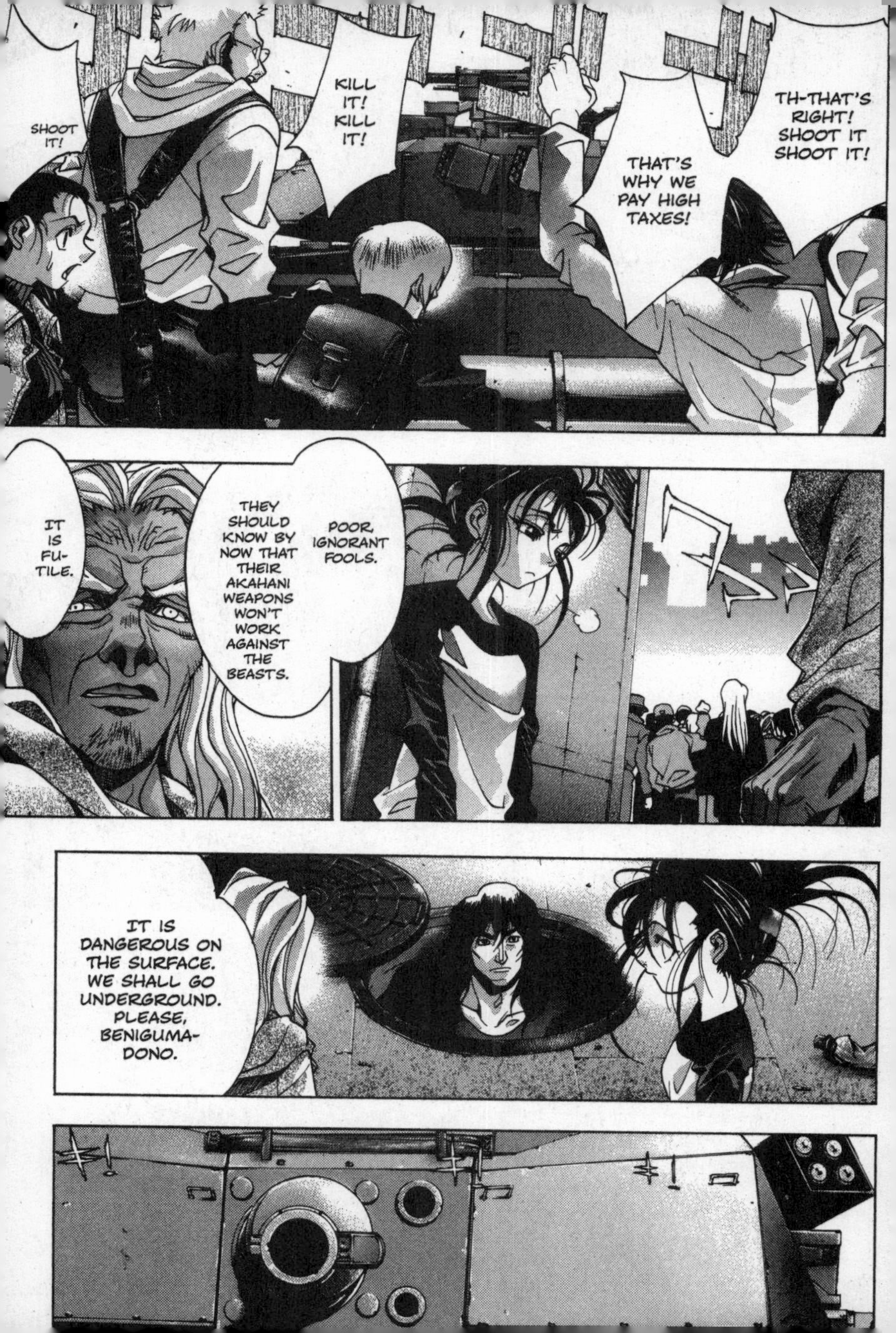
TH-THAT'S RIGHT! SHOOT IT SHOOT IT!
THAT'S WHY WE PAY HIGH TAXES!
KILL IT! KILL IT!
SHOOT IT!
POOR, IGNORANT FOOLS.
THEY SHOULD KNOW BY NOW THAT THEIR AKAHANI WEAPONS WON'T WORK AGAINST THE BEASTS.
IT IS FU-TILE.
IT IS DANGEROUS ON THE SURFACE. WE SHALL GO UNDERGROUND. PLEASE, BENIGUMA-DONO.

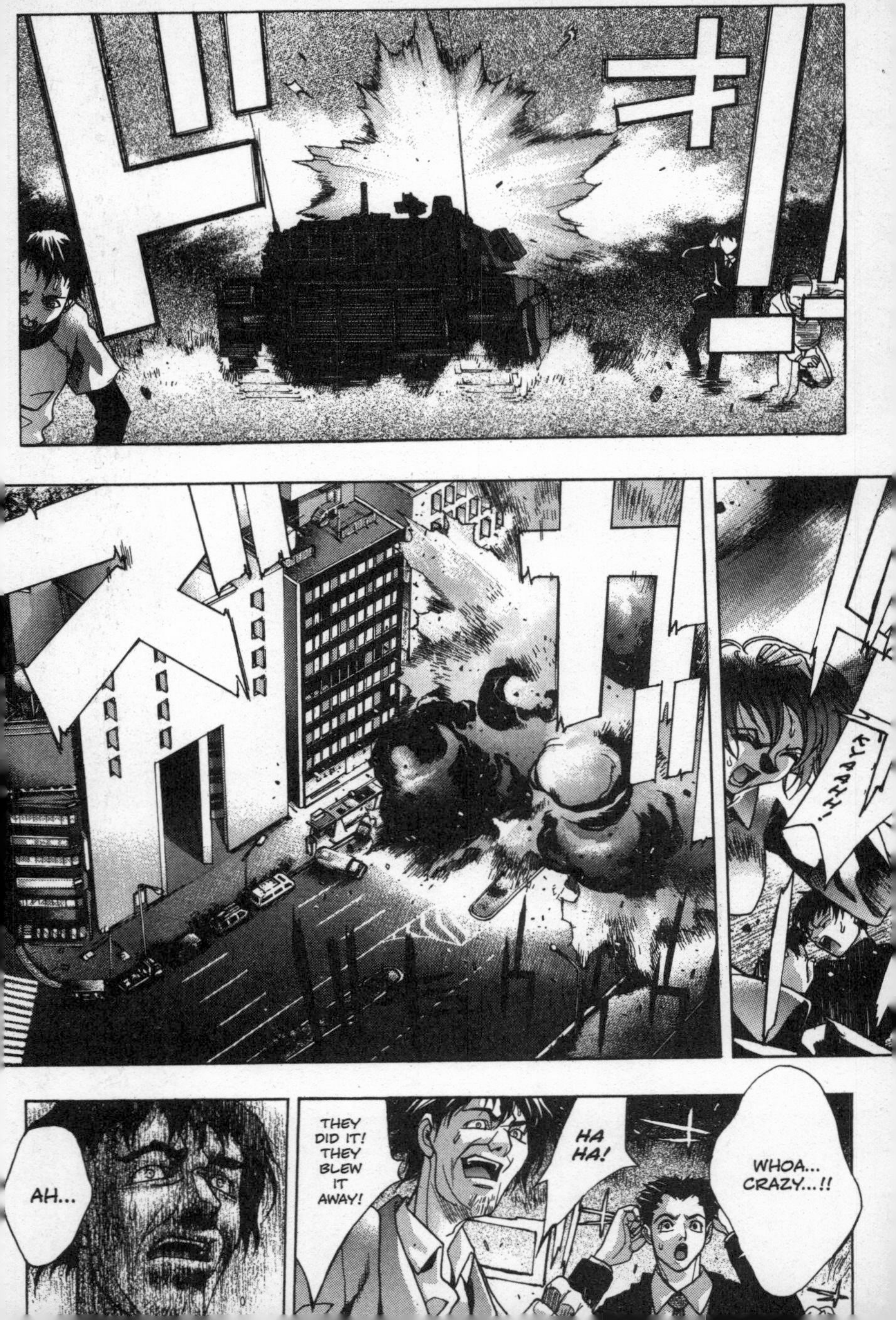
KYAAHH!
WHOA... CRAZY...!!
HA HA!
THEY DID IT! THEY BLEW IT AWAY!
AH...

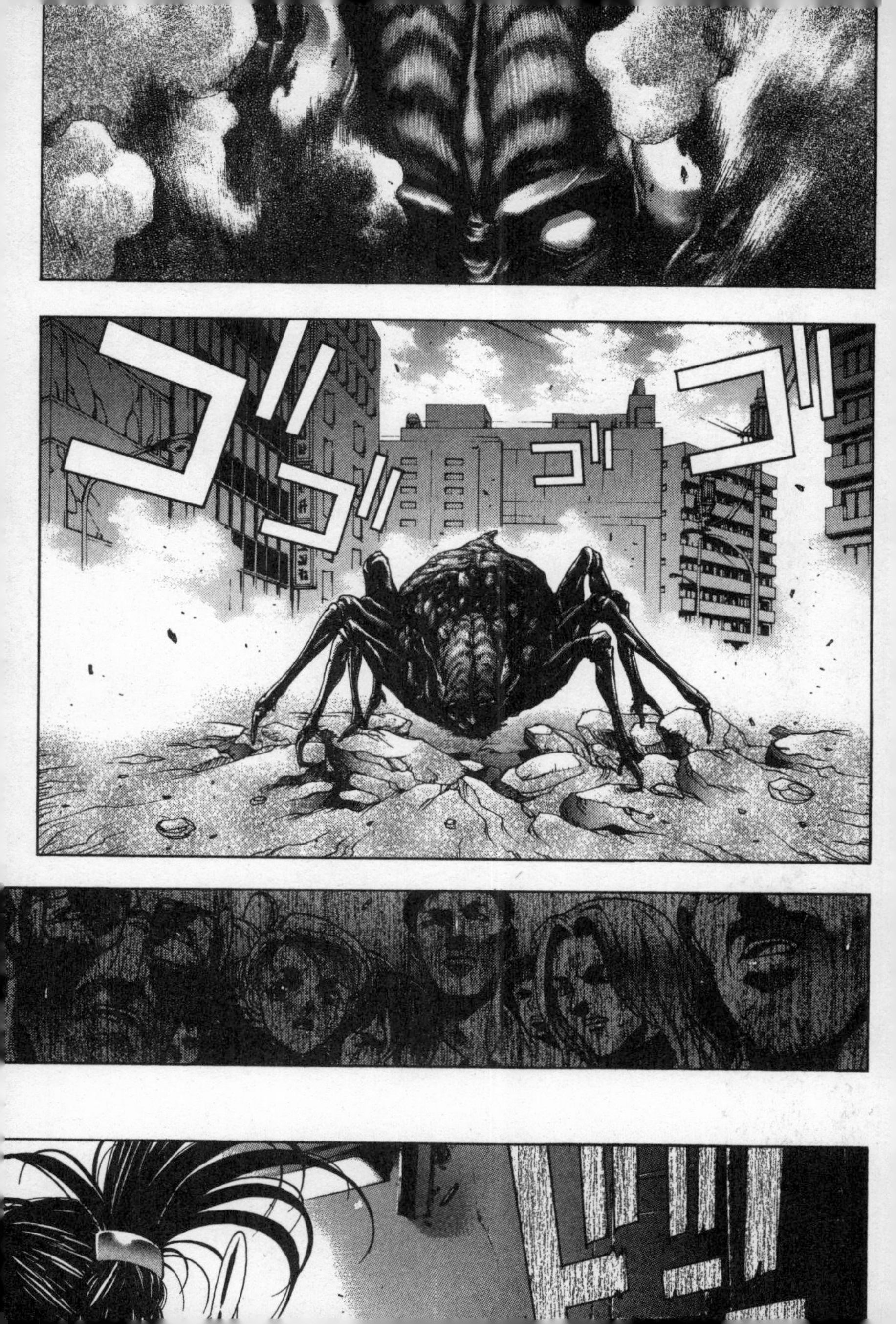
ゴゴゴゴ

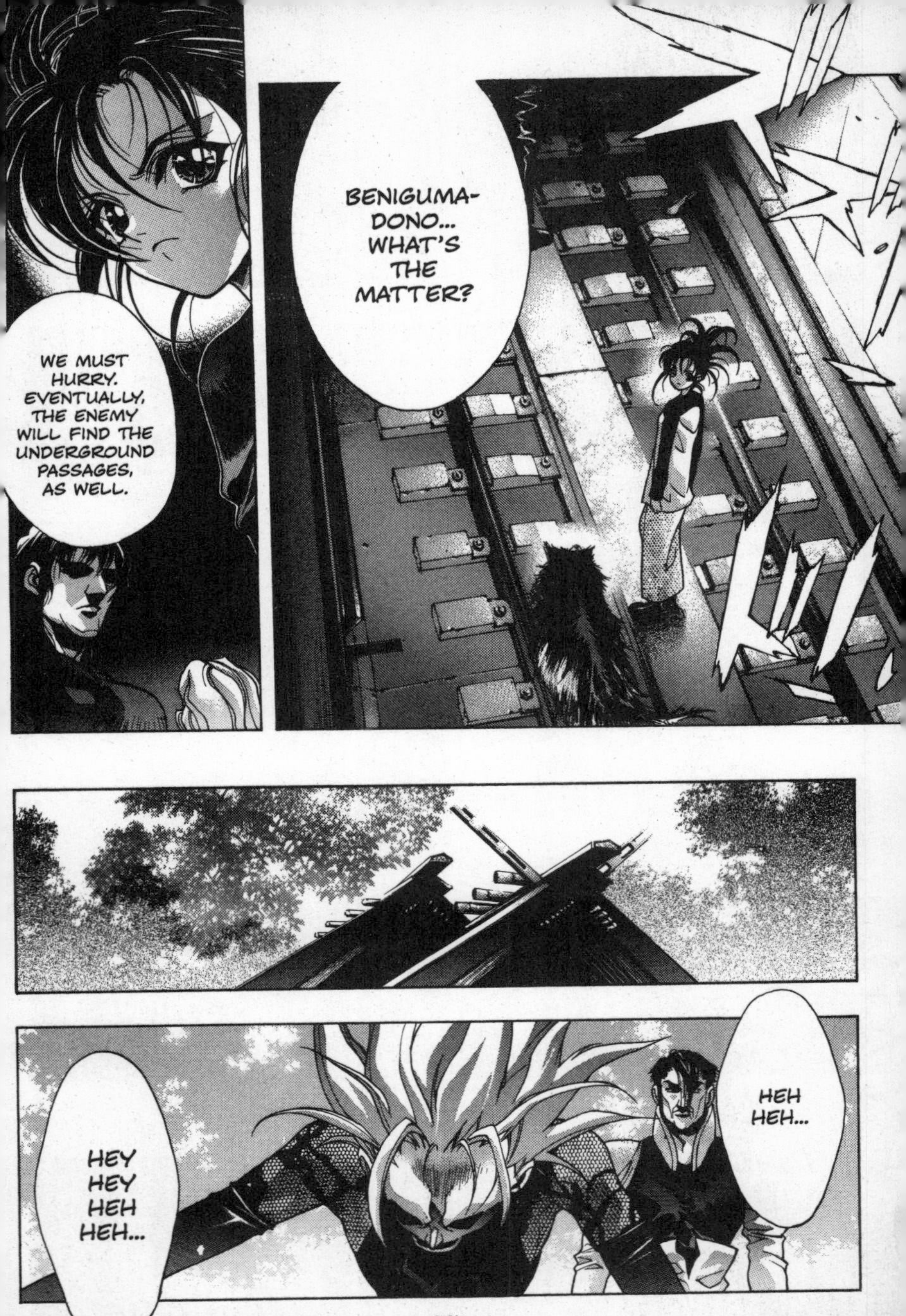
BENIGUMA-DONO... WHAT'S THE MATTER?
WE MUST HURRY. EVENTUALLY, THE ENEMY WILL FIND THE UNDERGROUND PASSAGES, AS WELL.
HEH HEH...
HEY HEY HEH HEH...

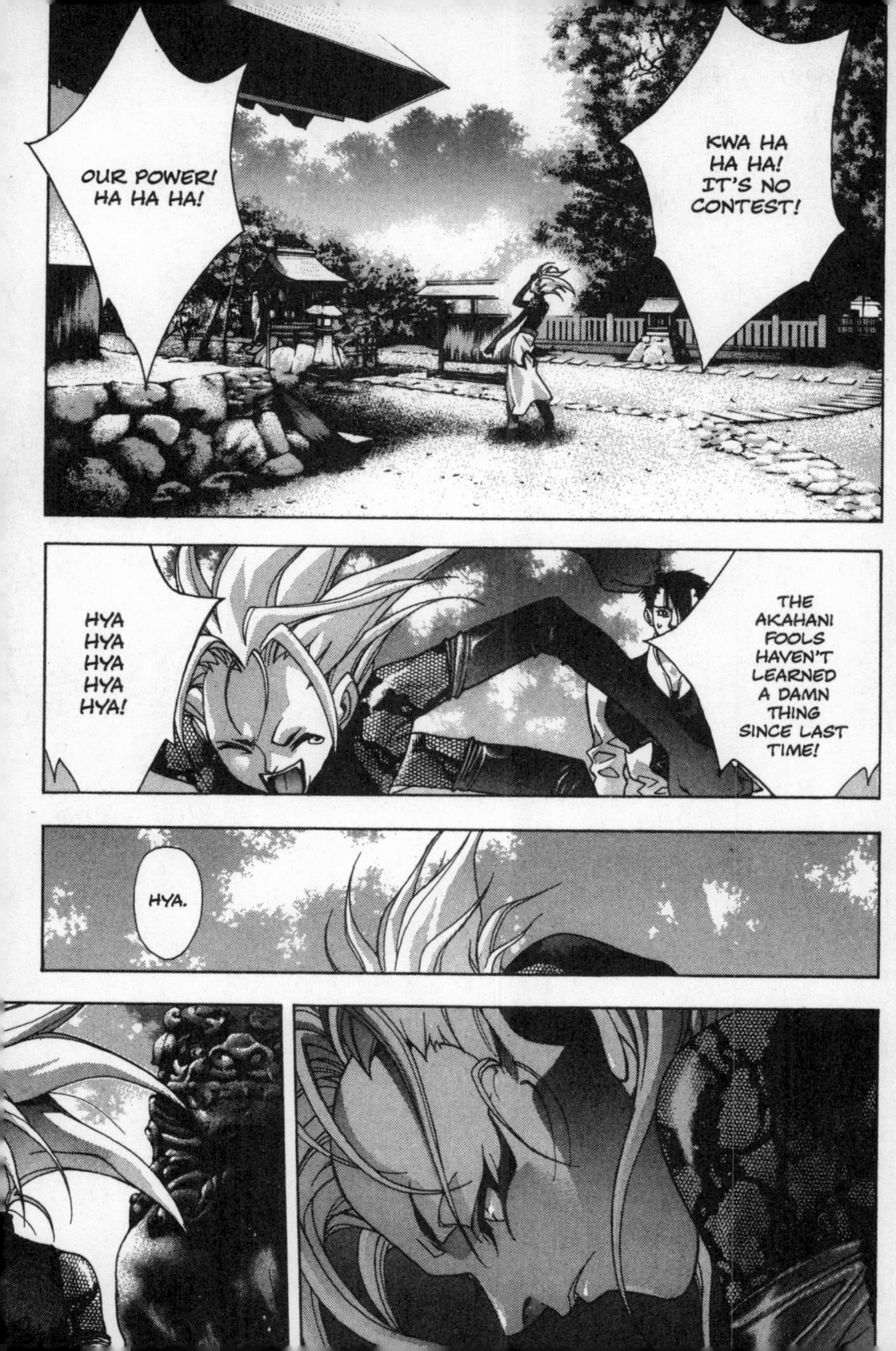
KWA HA HA HA! IT'S NO CONTEST!
OUR POWER! HA HA HA!
THE AKAHANI FOOLS HAVEN'T LEARNED A DAMN THING SINCE LAST TIME!
HYA HYA HYA HYA HYA!
HYA.

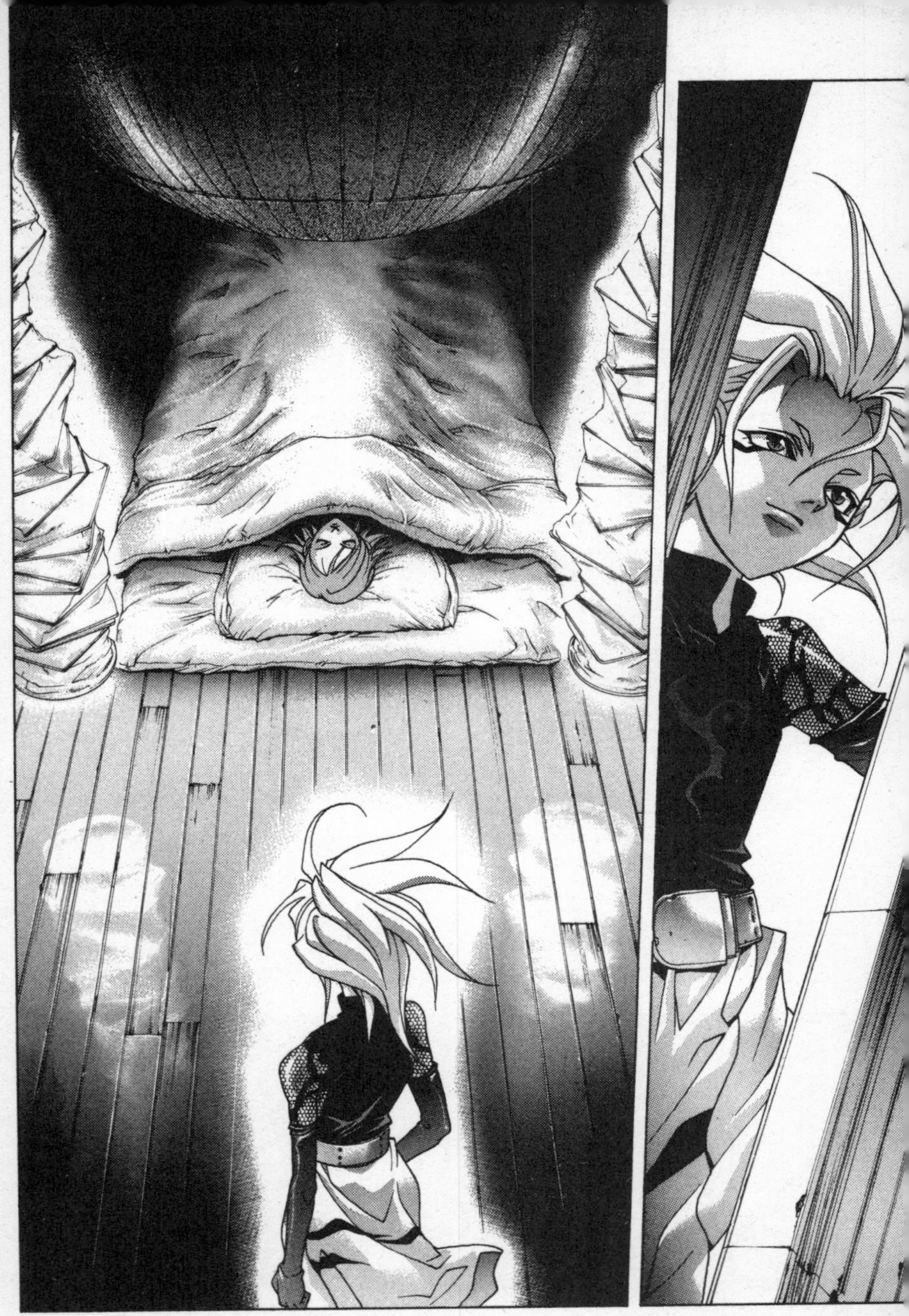

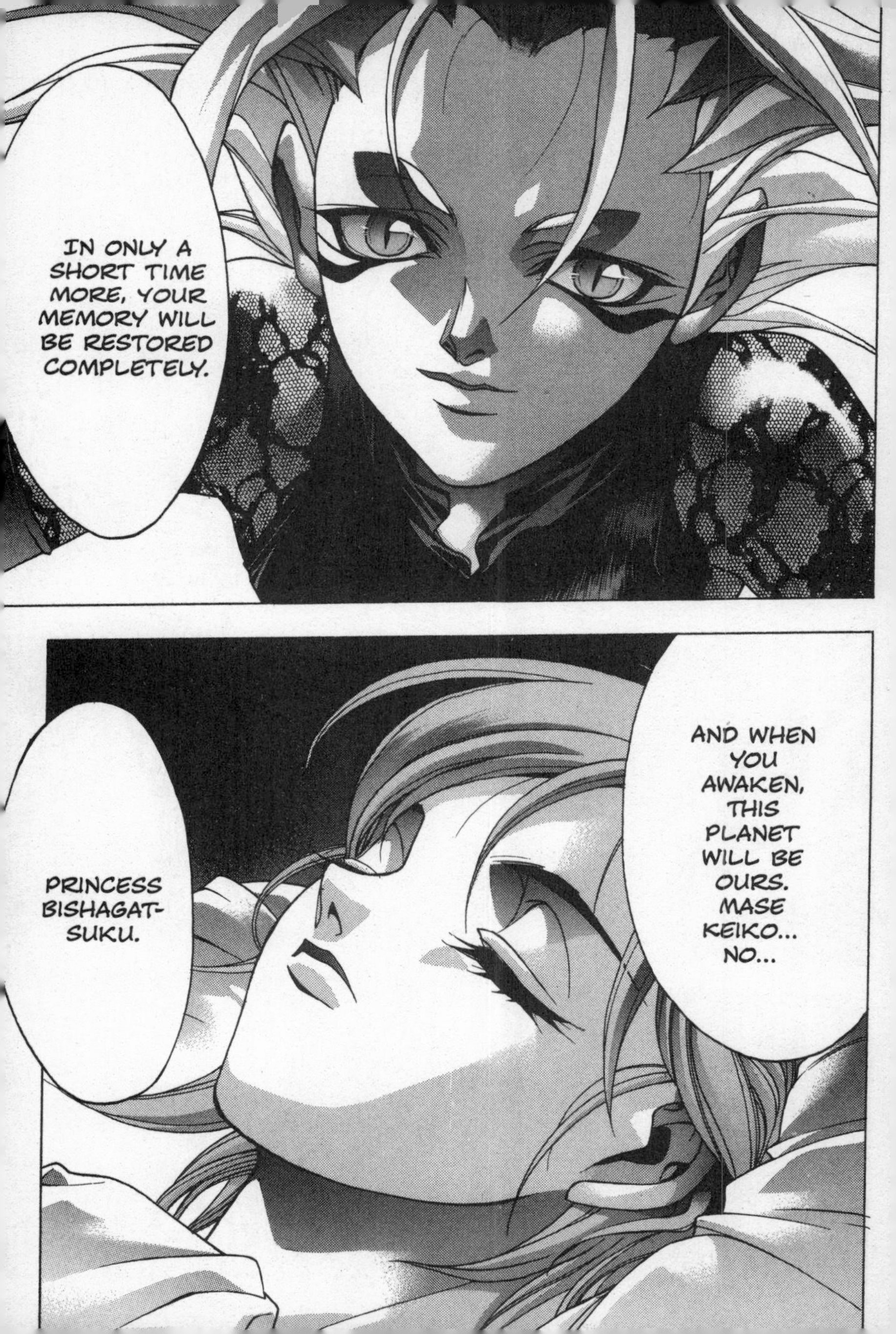
IN ONLY A SHORT TIME MORE, YOUR MEMORY WILL BE RESTORED COMPLETELY.
AND WHEN YOU AWAKEN, THIS PLANET WILL BE OURS. MASE KEIKO... NO...
PRINCESS BISHAGAT-SUKU.

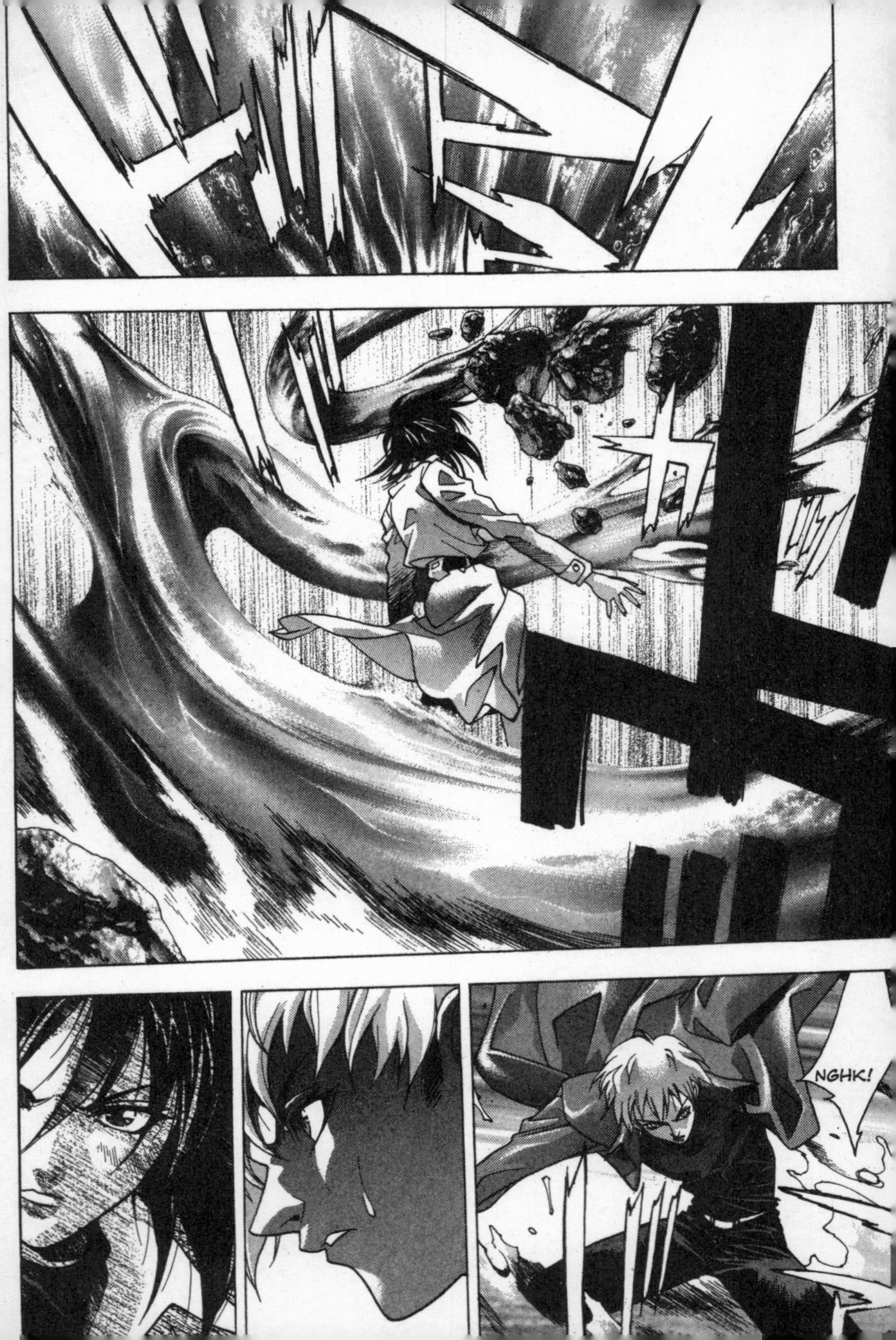
NGHK!

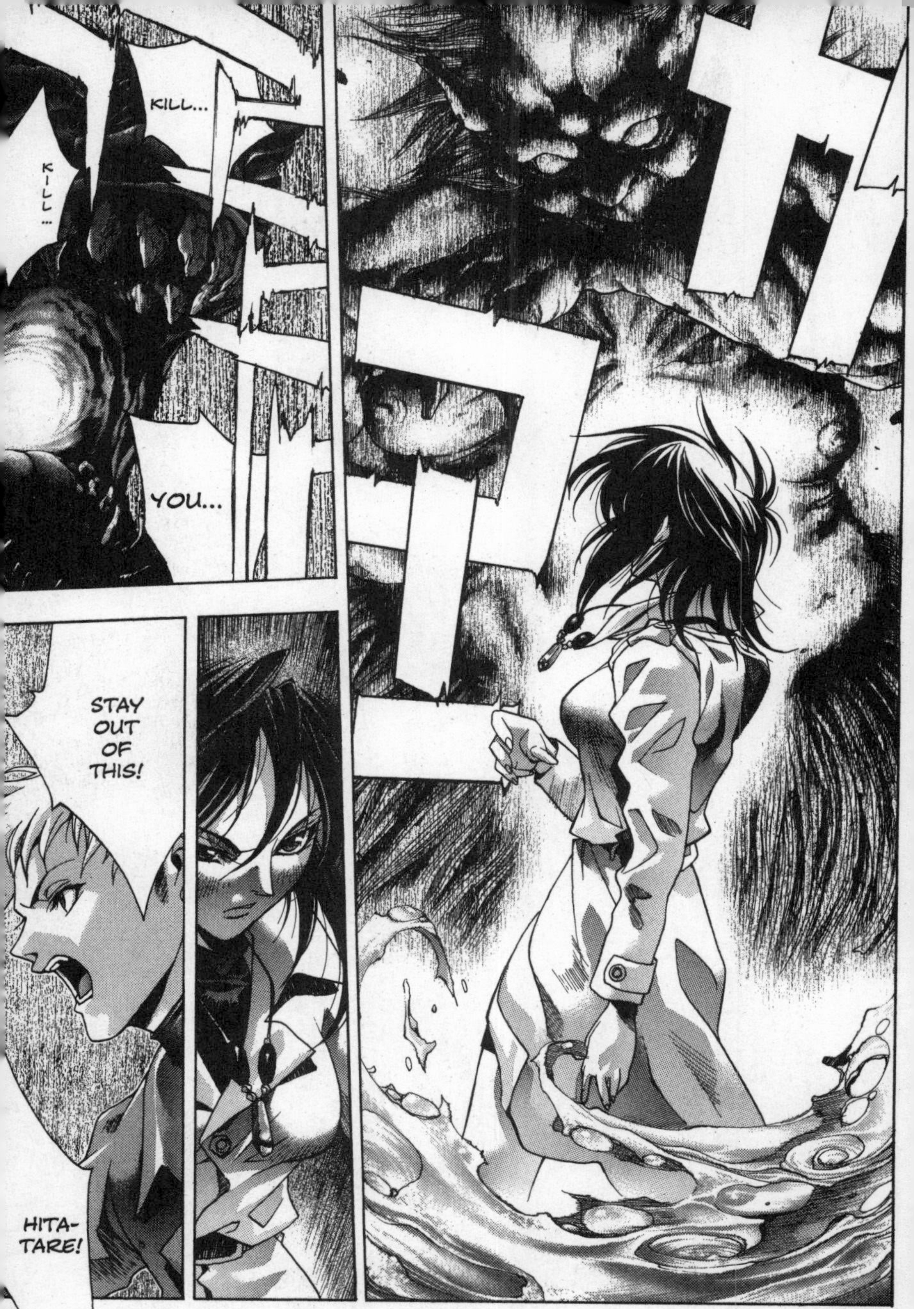
KILL...
KILL...
YOU...
STAY OUT OF THIS!
HITA-TARE!

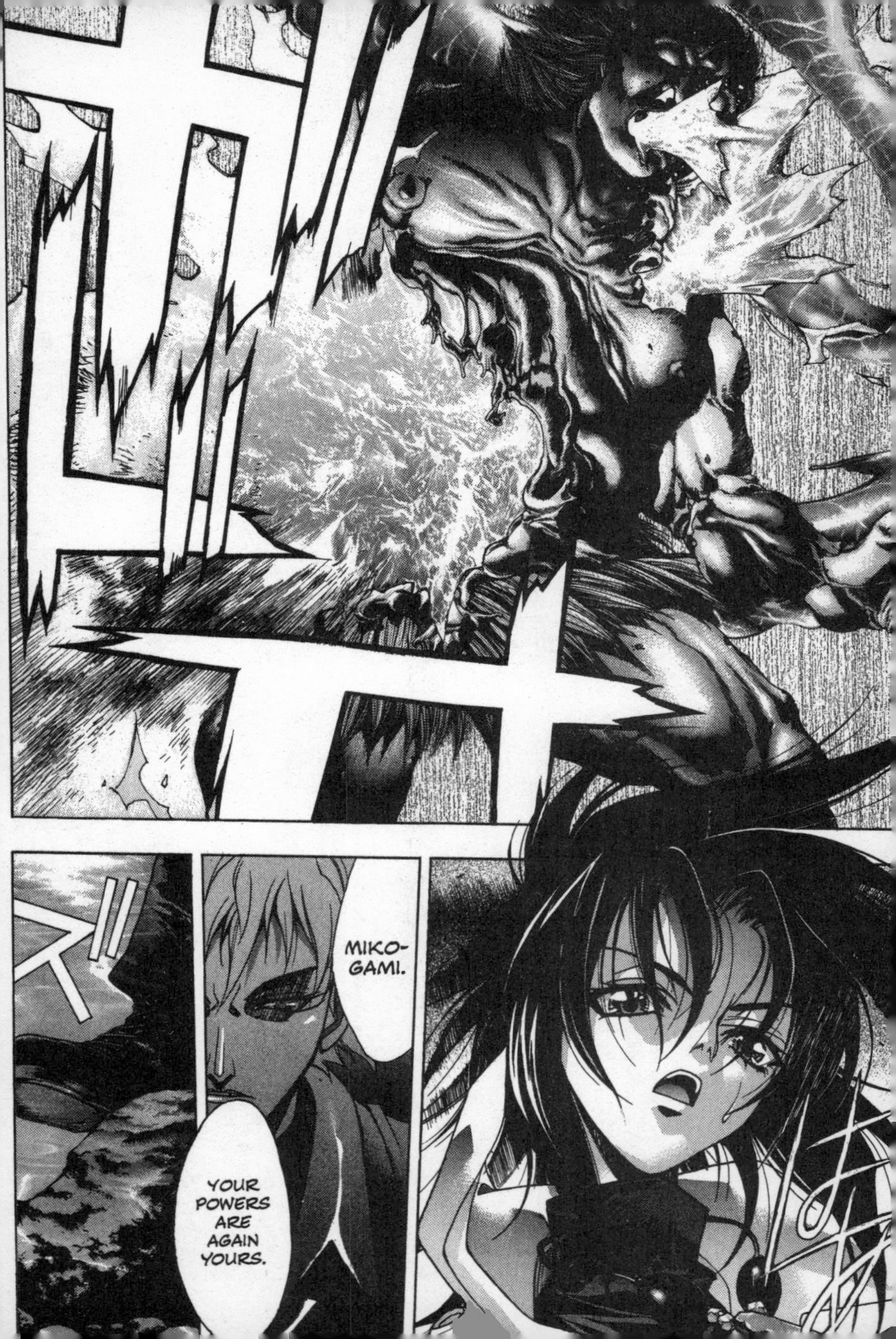
MIKO-GAMI.
YOUR POWERS ARE AGAIN YOURS.

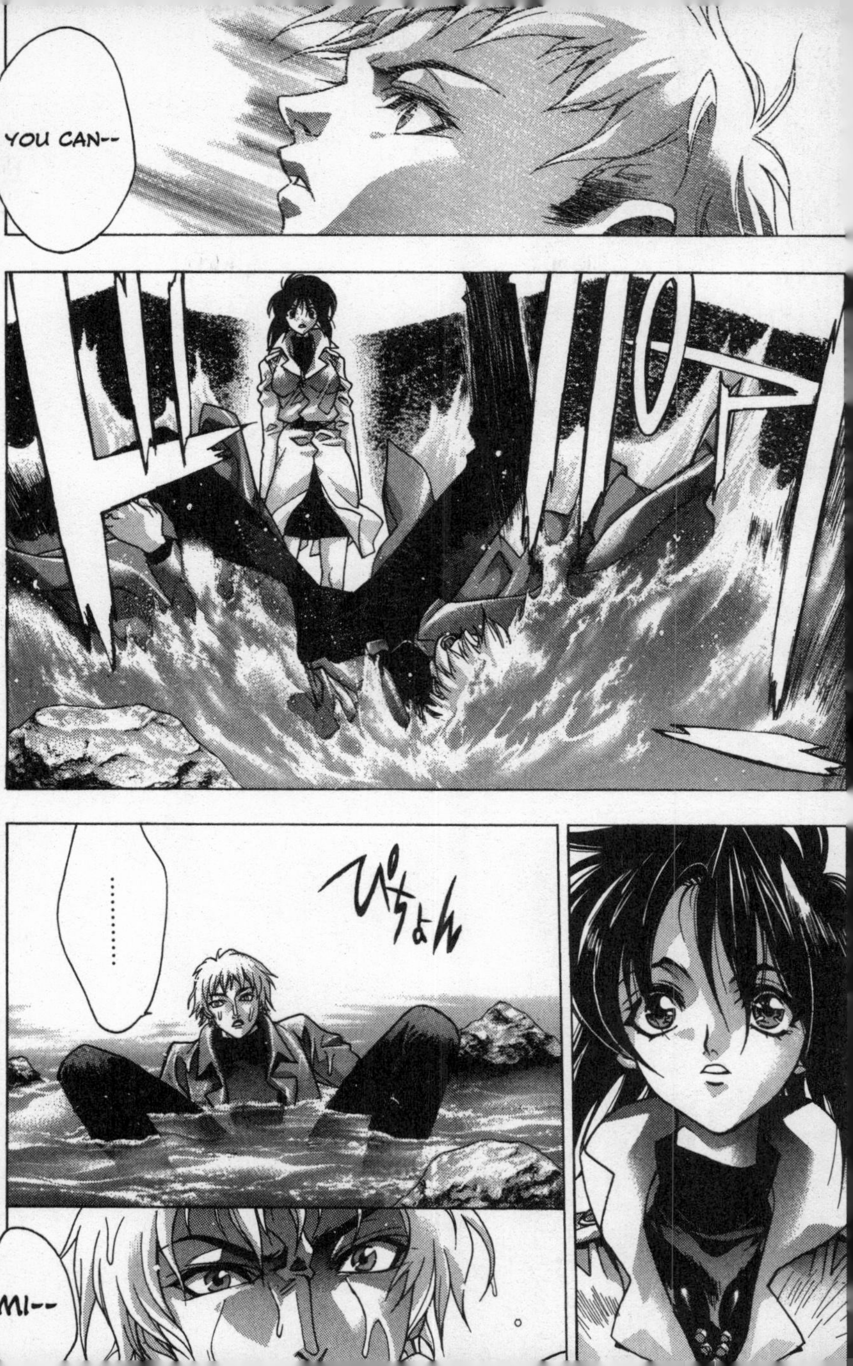
YOU CAN--
......
ぴちょん
MI--

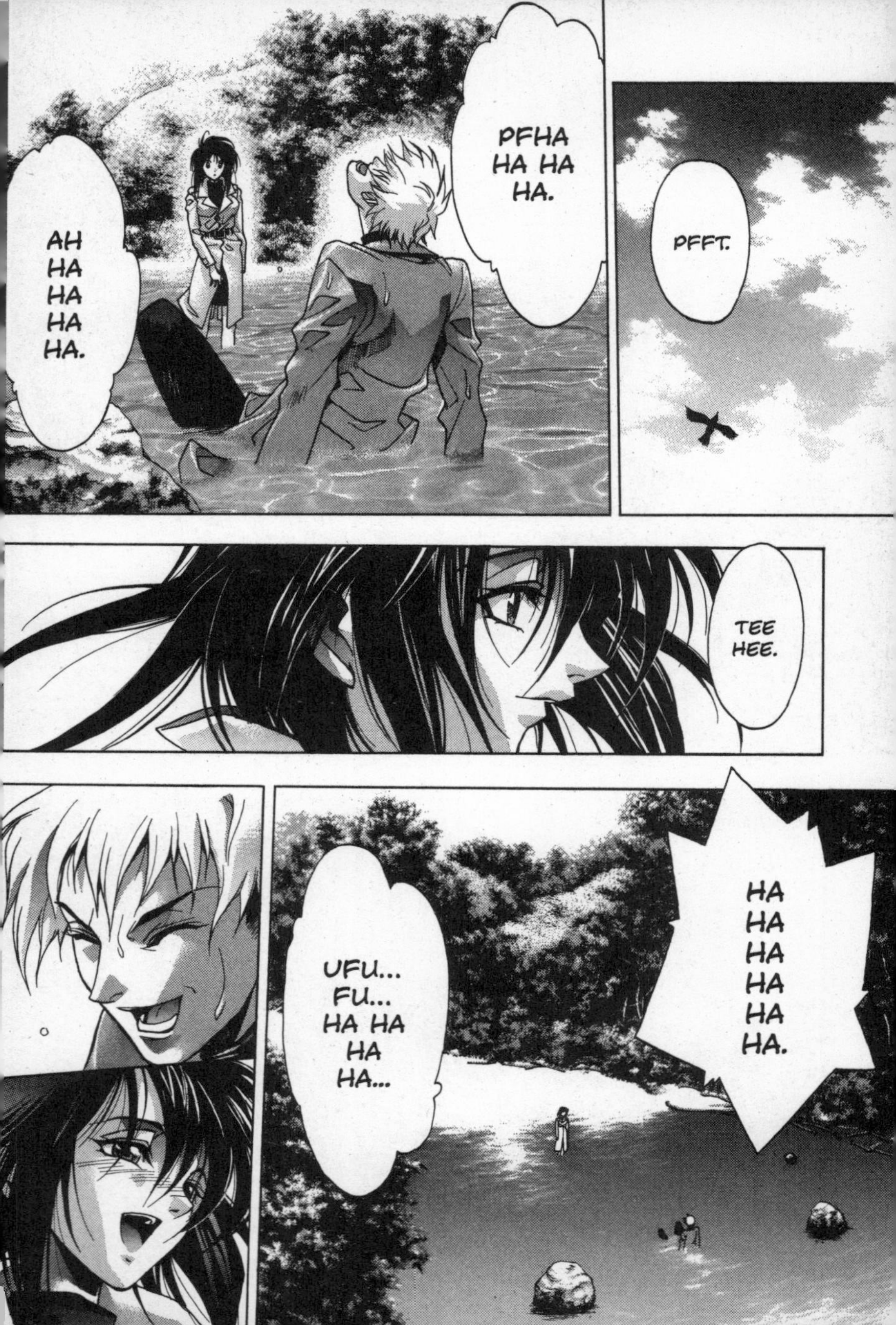
PFFT.
PFHA HA HA HA.
AH HA HA HA HA.
TEE HEE.
HA HA HA HA HA HA.
UFU... FU... HA HA HA HA...

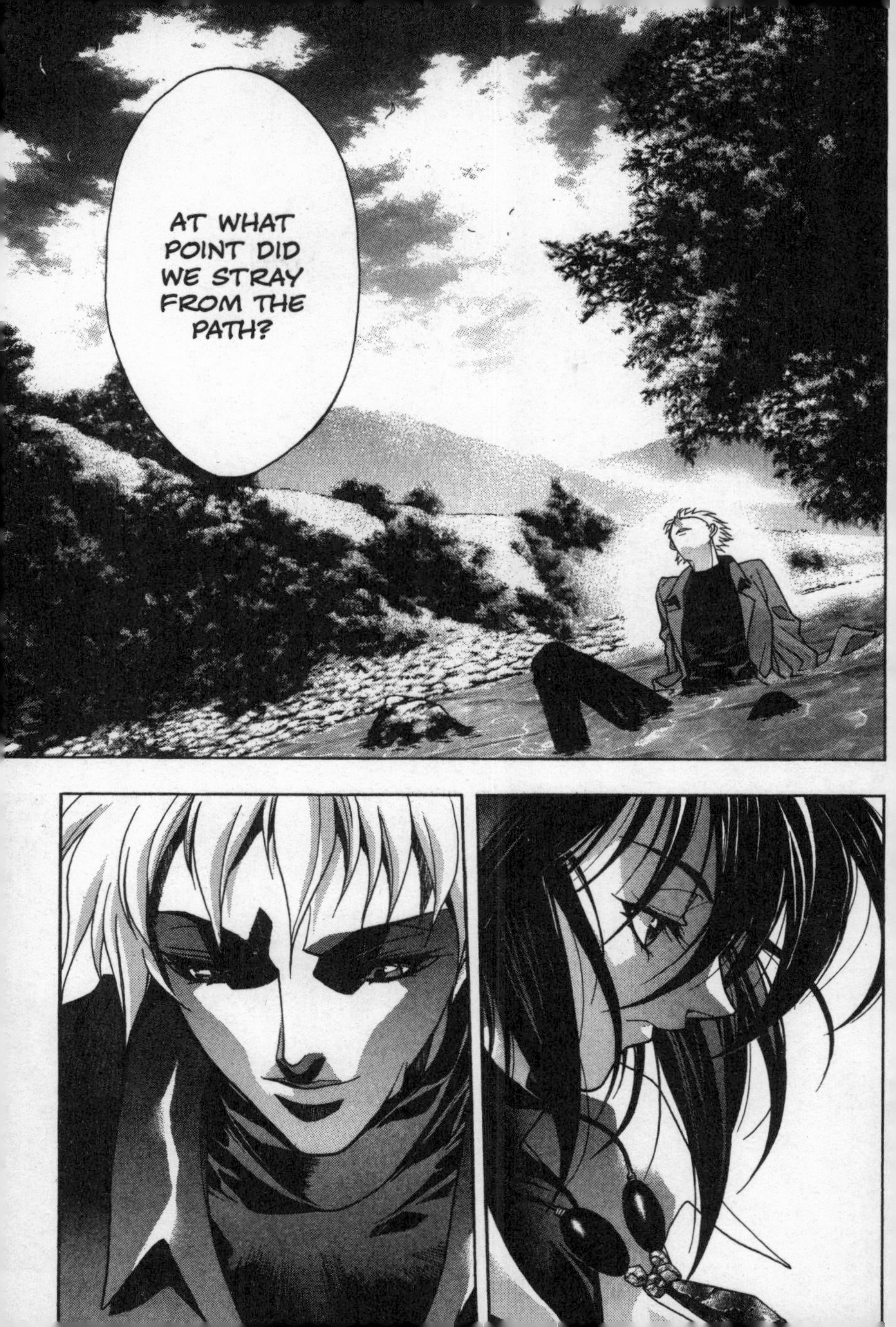
AT WHAT POINT DID WE STRAY FROM THE PATH?

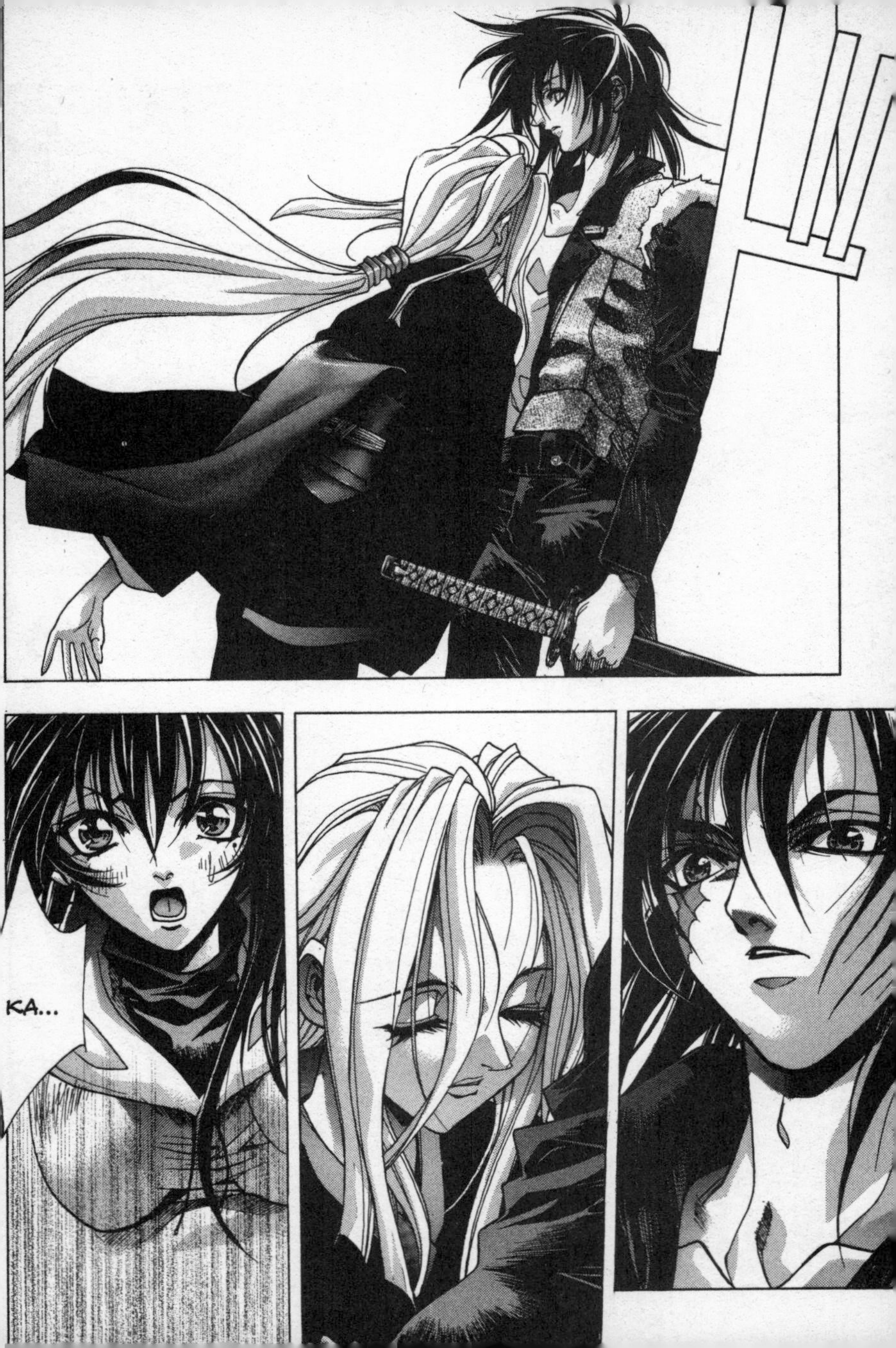
KA...

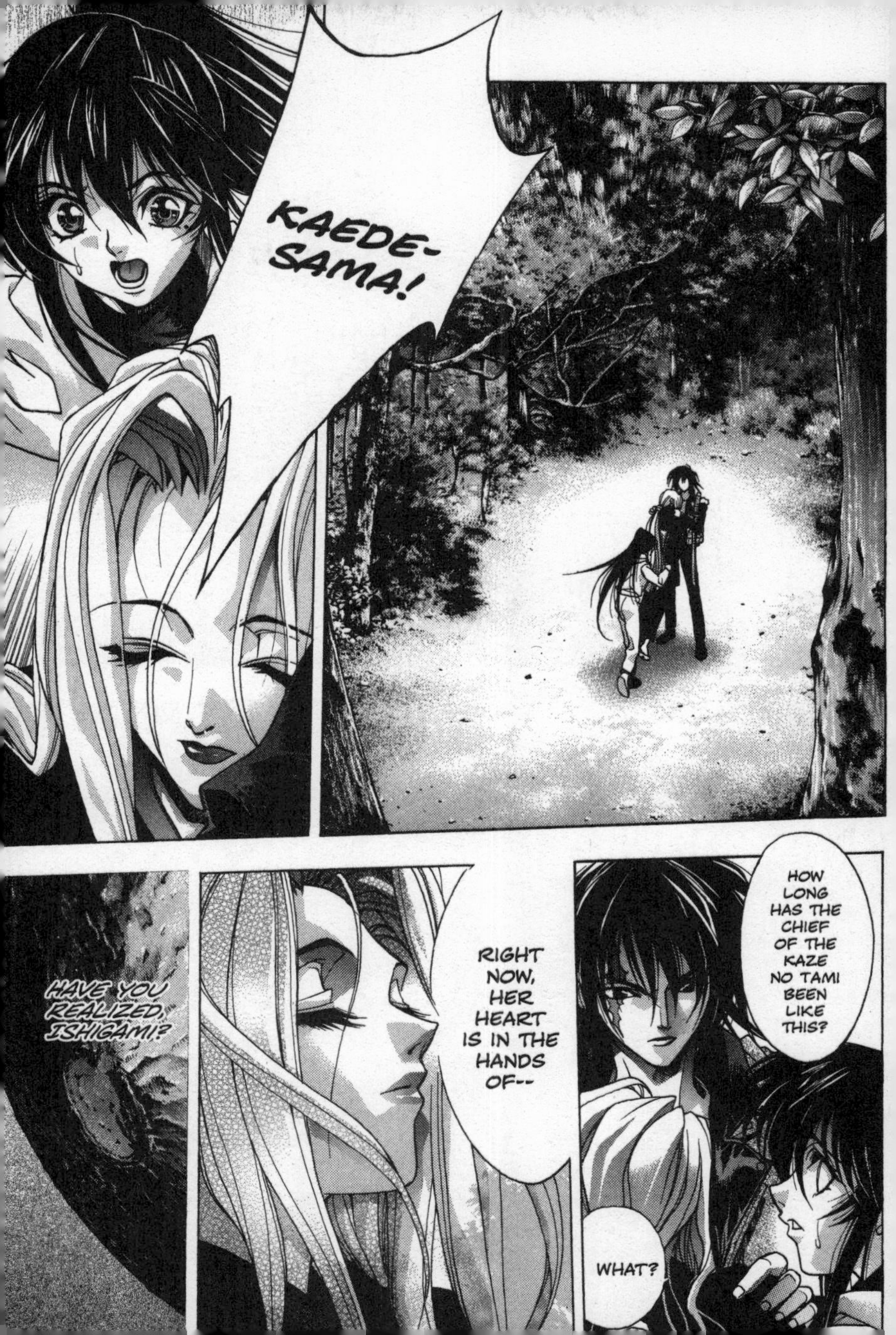
KAEDE-SAMA!
HOW LONG HAS THE CHIEF OF THE KAZE NO TAMI BEEN LIKE THIS?
WHAT?
RIGHT NOW, HER HEART IS IN THE HANDS OF--
HAVE YOU REALIZED, ISHIGAMI?

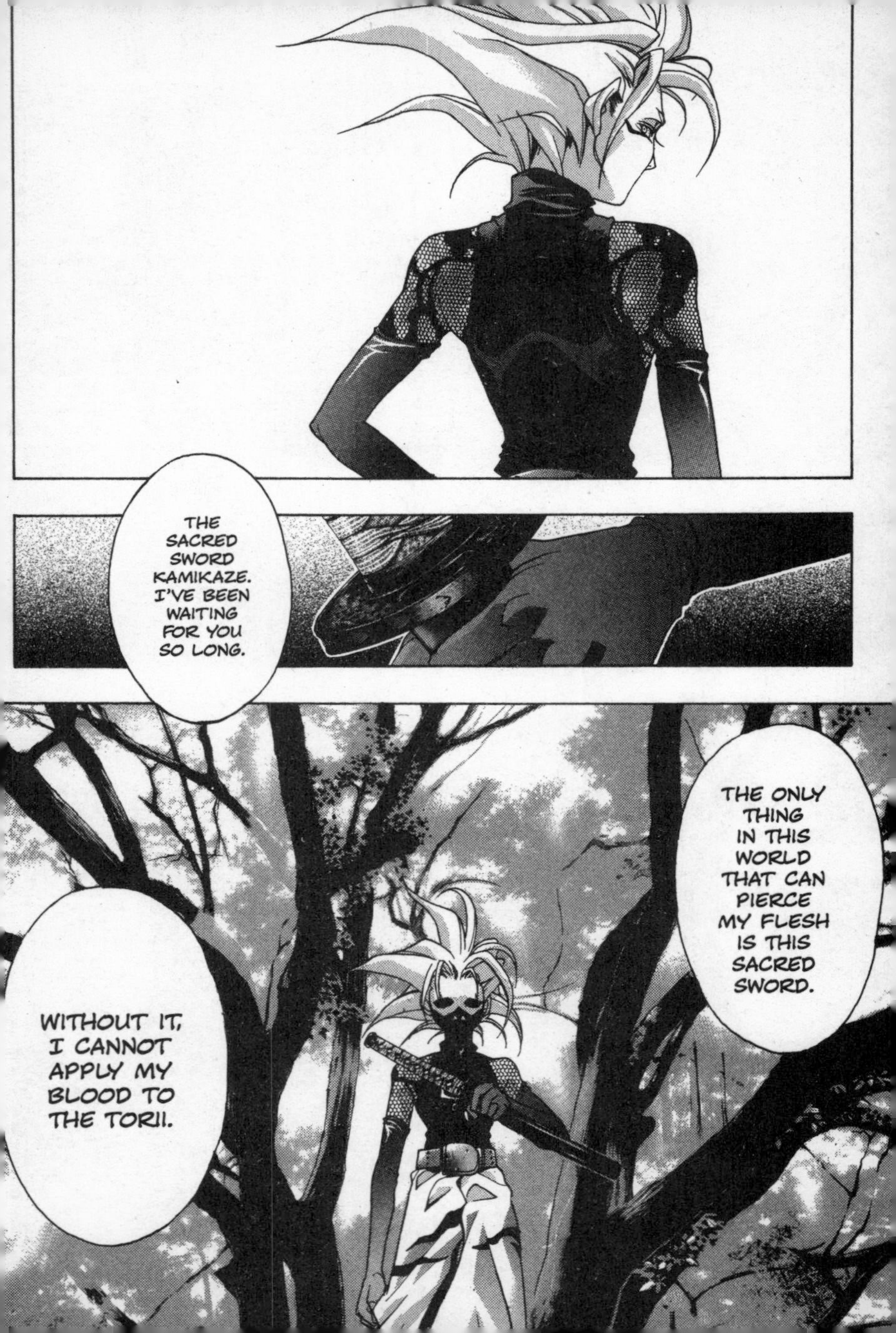
THE SACRED SWORD KAMIKAZE. I'VE BEEN WAITING FOR YOU SO LONG.
THE ONLY THING IN THIS WORLD THAT CAN PIERCE MY FLESH IS THIS SACRED SWORD.
WITHOUT IT, I CANNOT APPLY MY BLOOD TO THE TORII.

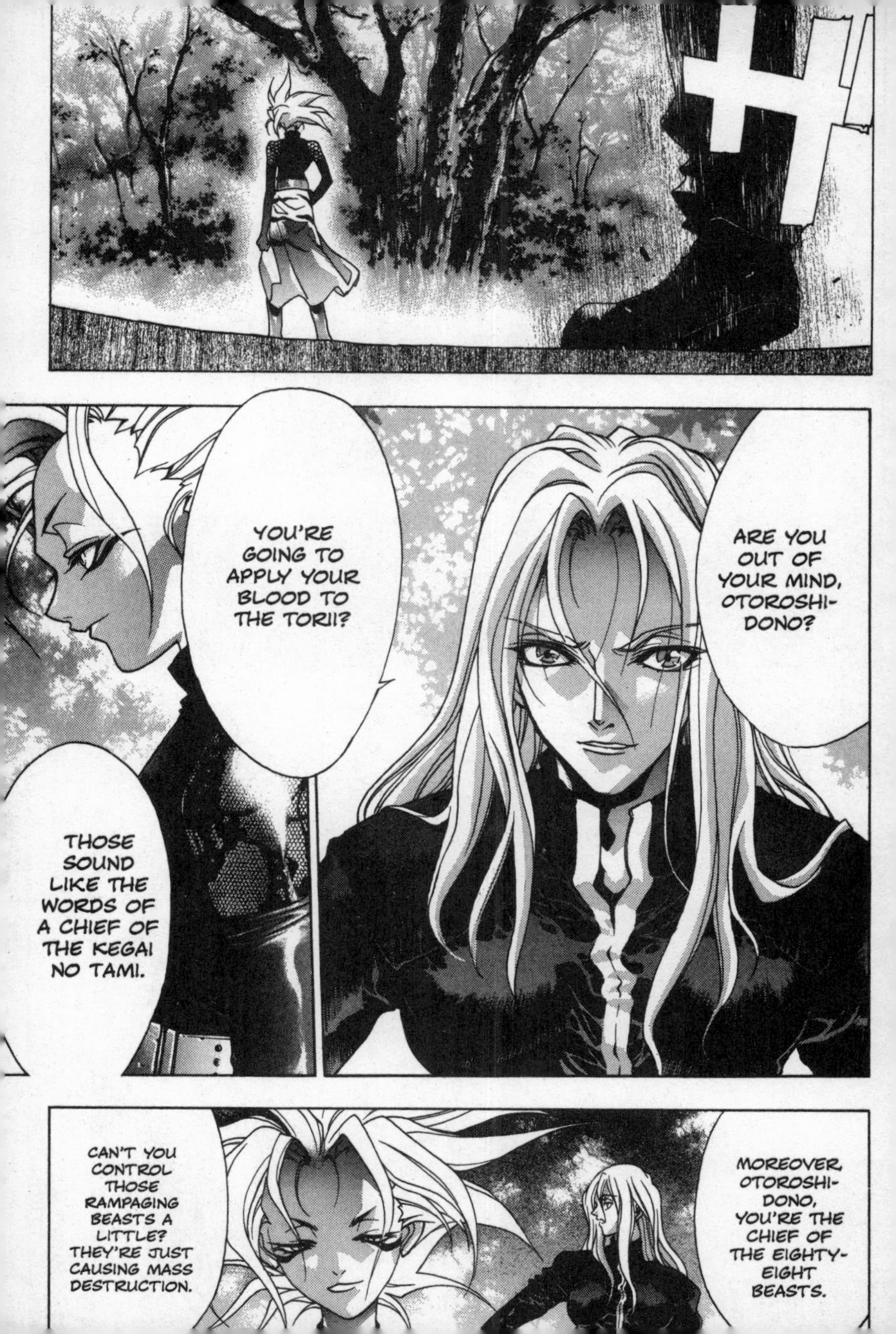
ARE YOU OUT OF YOUR MIND, OTOROSHI-DONO?
YOU'RE GOING TO APPLY YOUR BLOOD TO THE TORII?
THOSE SOUND LIKE THE WORDS OF A CHIEF OF THE KEGAI NO TAMI.
MOREOVER, OTOROSHI-DONO, YOU'RE THE CHIEF OF THE EIGHTY-EIGHT BEASTS.
CAN'T YOU CONTROL THOSE RAMPAGING BEASTS A LITTLE? THEY'RE JUST CAUSING MASS DESTRUCTION.

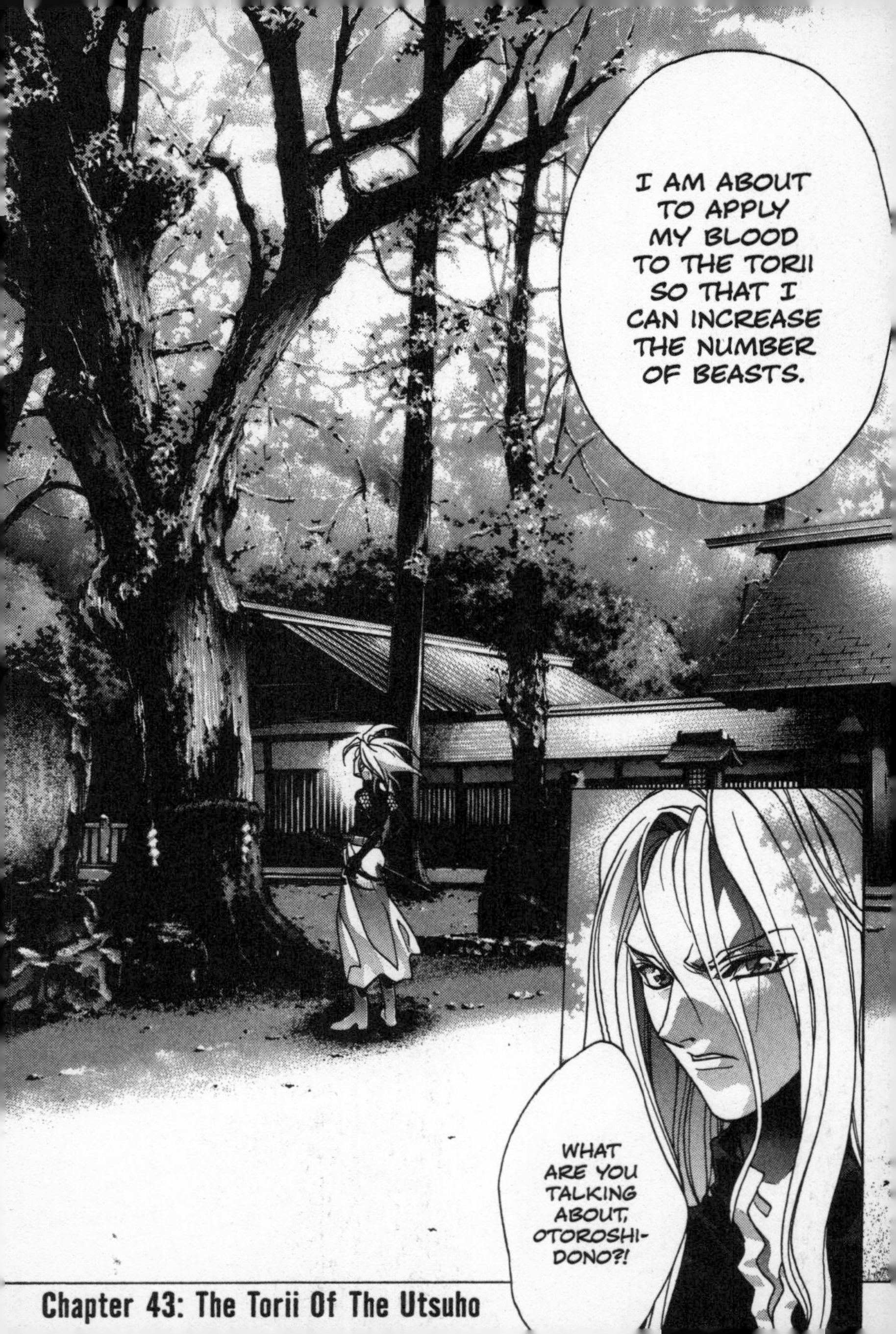
I AM ABOUT TO APPLY MY BLOOD TO THE TORII SO THAT I CAN INCREASE THE NUMBER OF BEASTS.
WHAT ARE YOU TALKING ABOUT, OTOROSHI-DONO?!

Chapter 43: The Torii Of The Utsuho

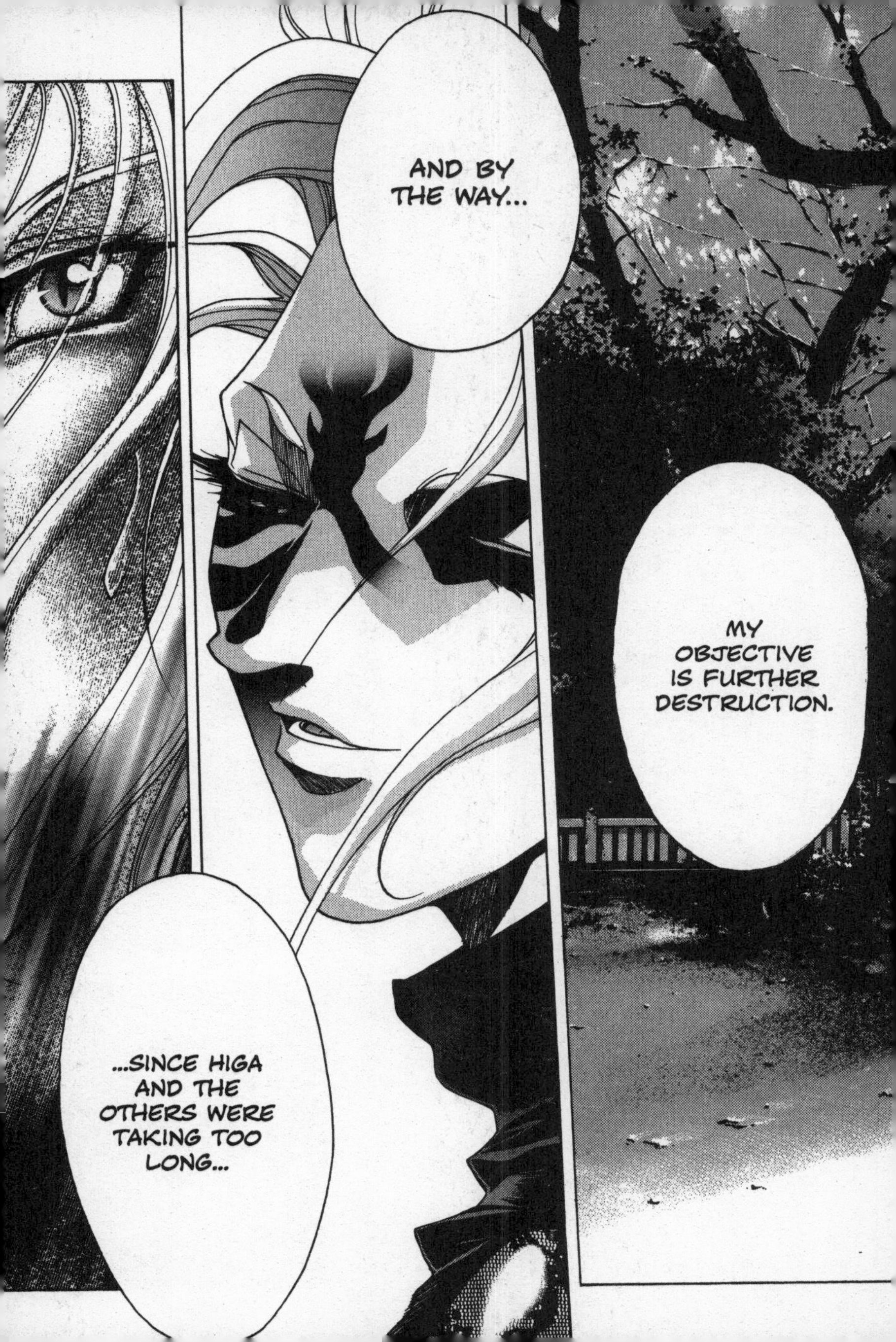
AND BY THE WAY...
MY OBJECTIVE IS FURTHER DESTRUCTION.
...SINCE HIGA AND THE OTHERS WERE TAKING TOO LONG...

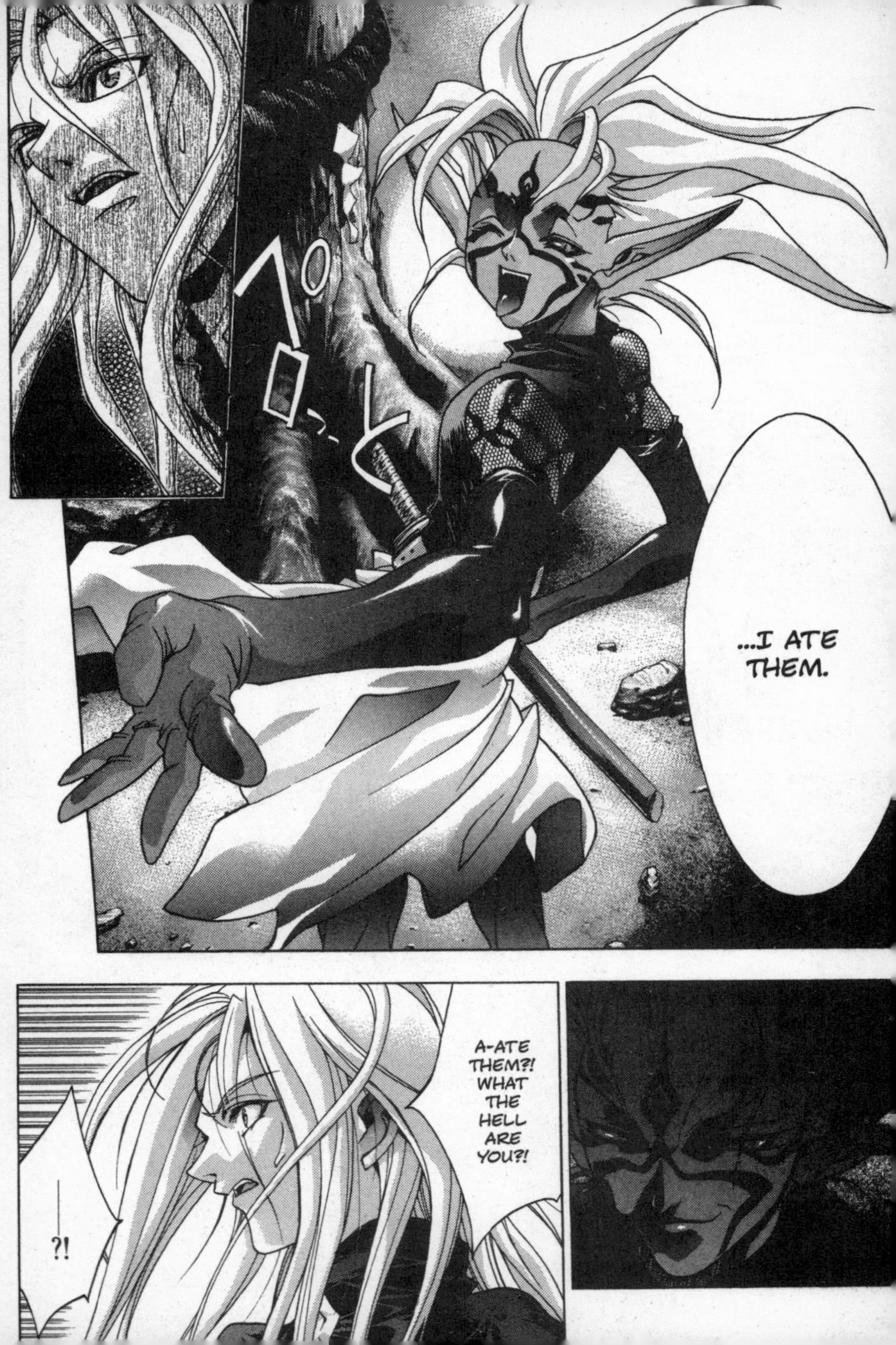
...I ATE THEM.
A-ATE THEM?! WHAT THE HELL ARE YOU?!
—?!

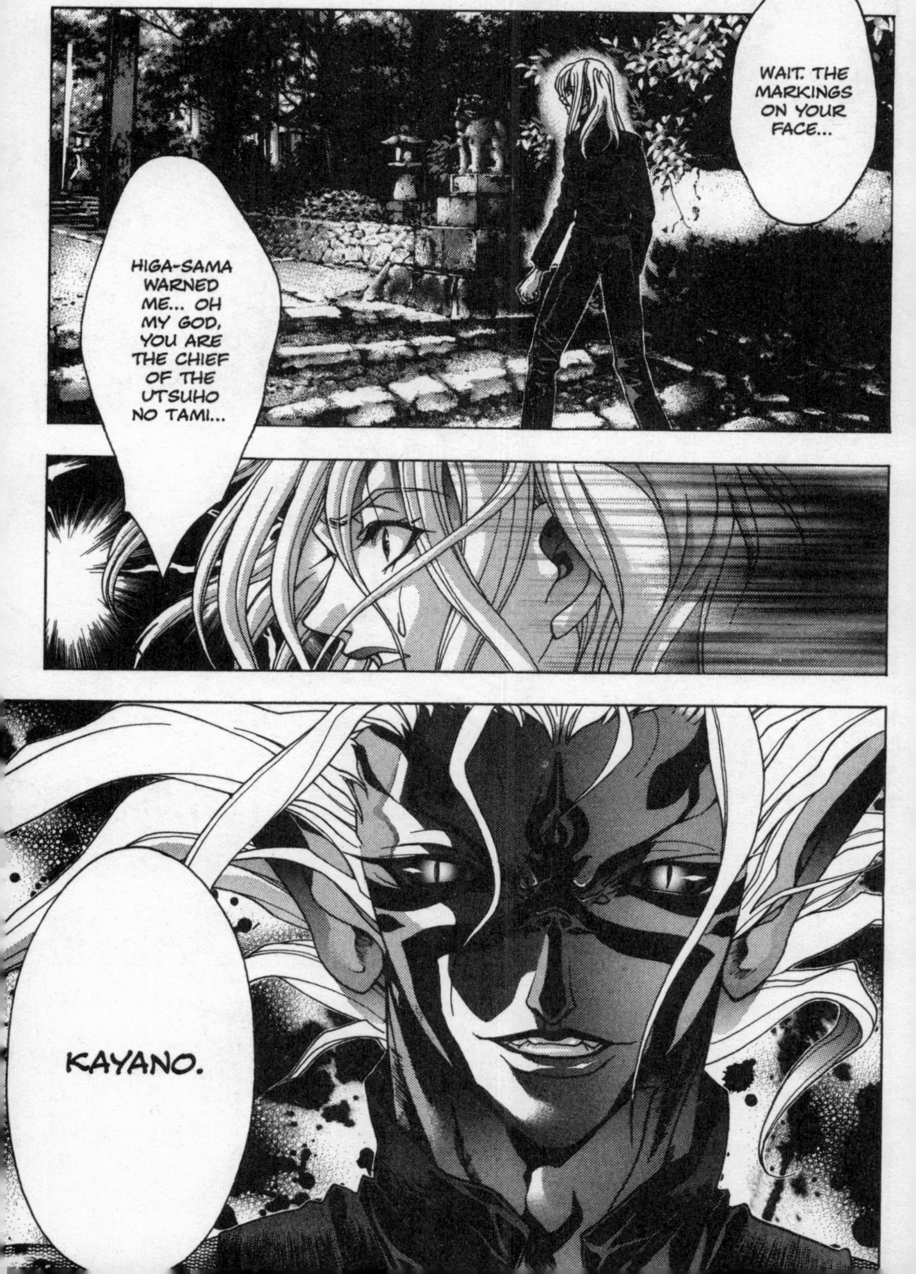
WAIT. THE MARKINGS ON YOUR FACE...
HIGA-SAMA WARNED ME... OH MY GOD, YOU ARE THE CHIEF OF THE UTSUHO NO TAMI...
KAYANO.

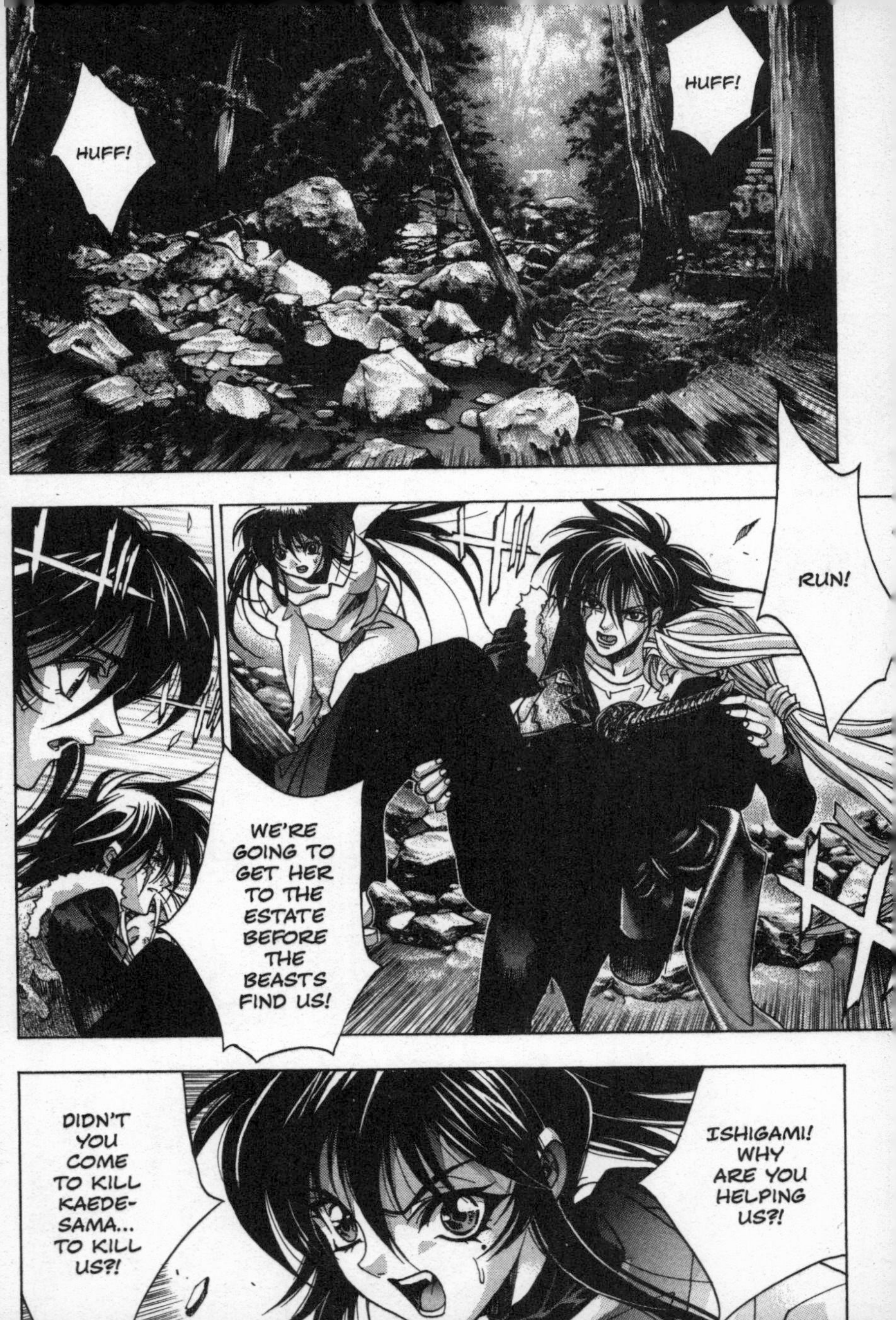
HUFF!
HUFF!
RUN!
WE'RE GOING TO GET HER TO THE ESTATE BEFORE THE BEASTS FIND US!
ISHIGAMI! WHY ARE YOU HELPING US?!
DIDN'T YOU COME TO KILL KAEDE-SAMA... TO KILL US?!

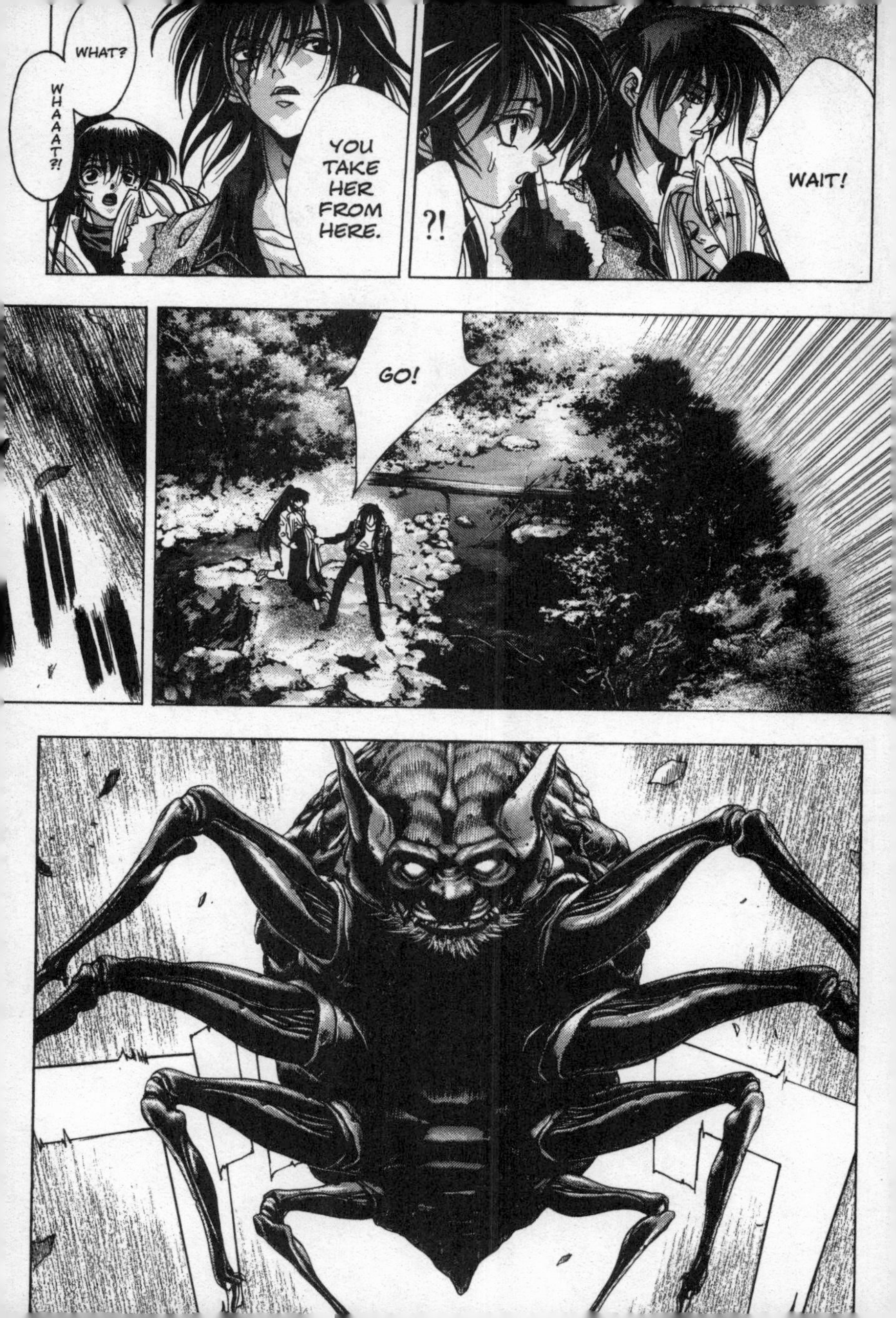
WAIT!
?!
YOU TAKE HER FROM HERE.
WHAT?
WHAAAT?!
GO!

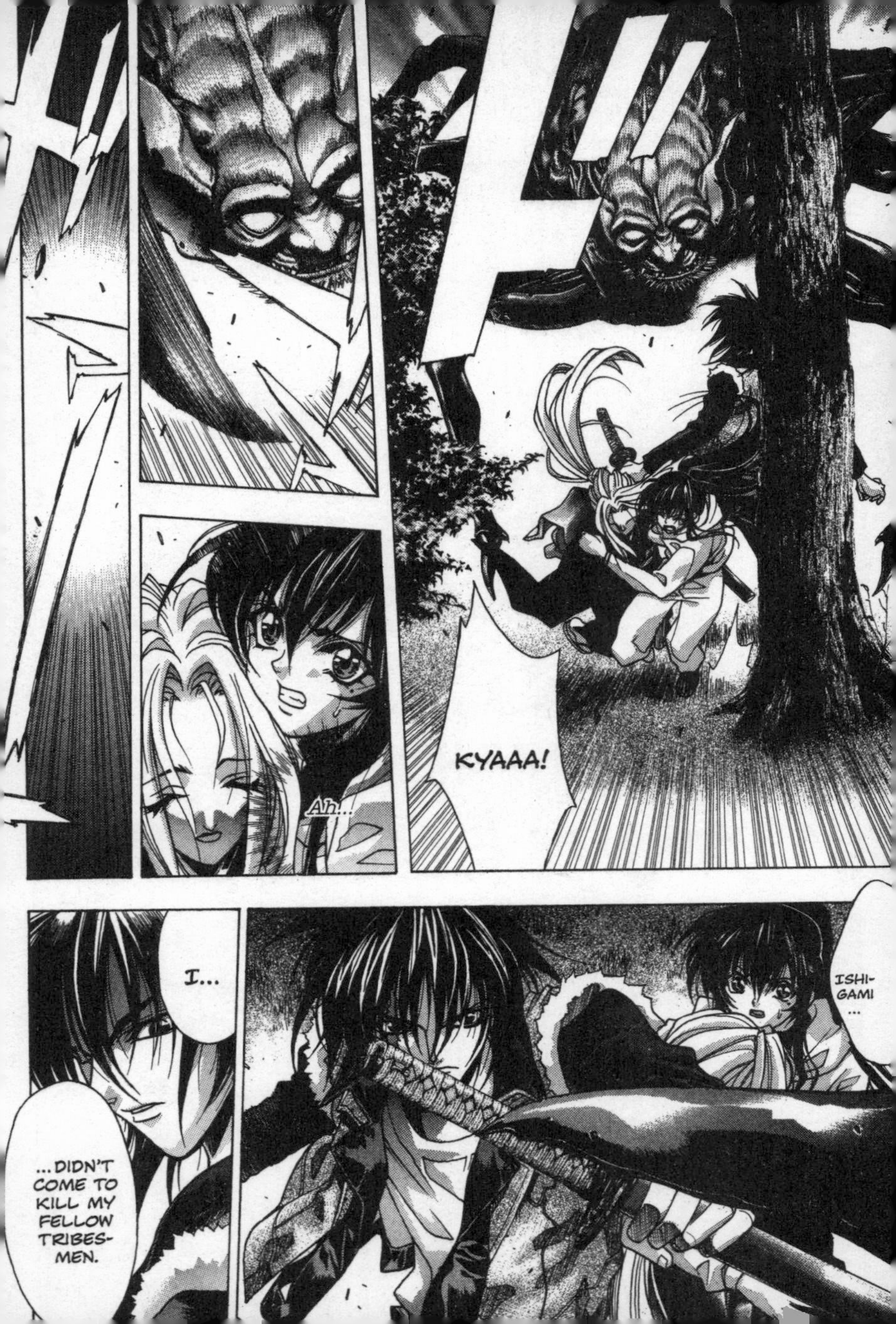
KYAAA!
Ah...
ISHI-GAMI ...
I...
...DIDN'T COME TO KILL MY FELLOW TRIBES-MEN.

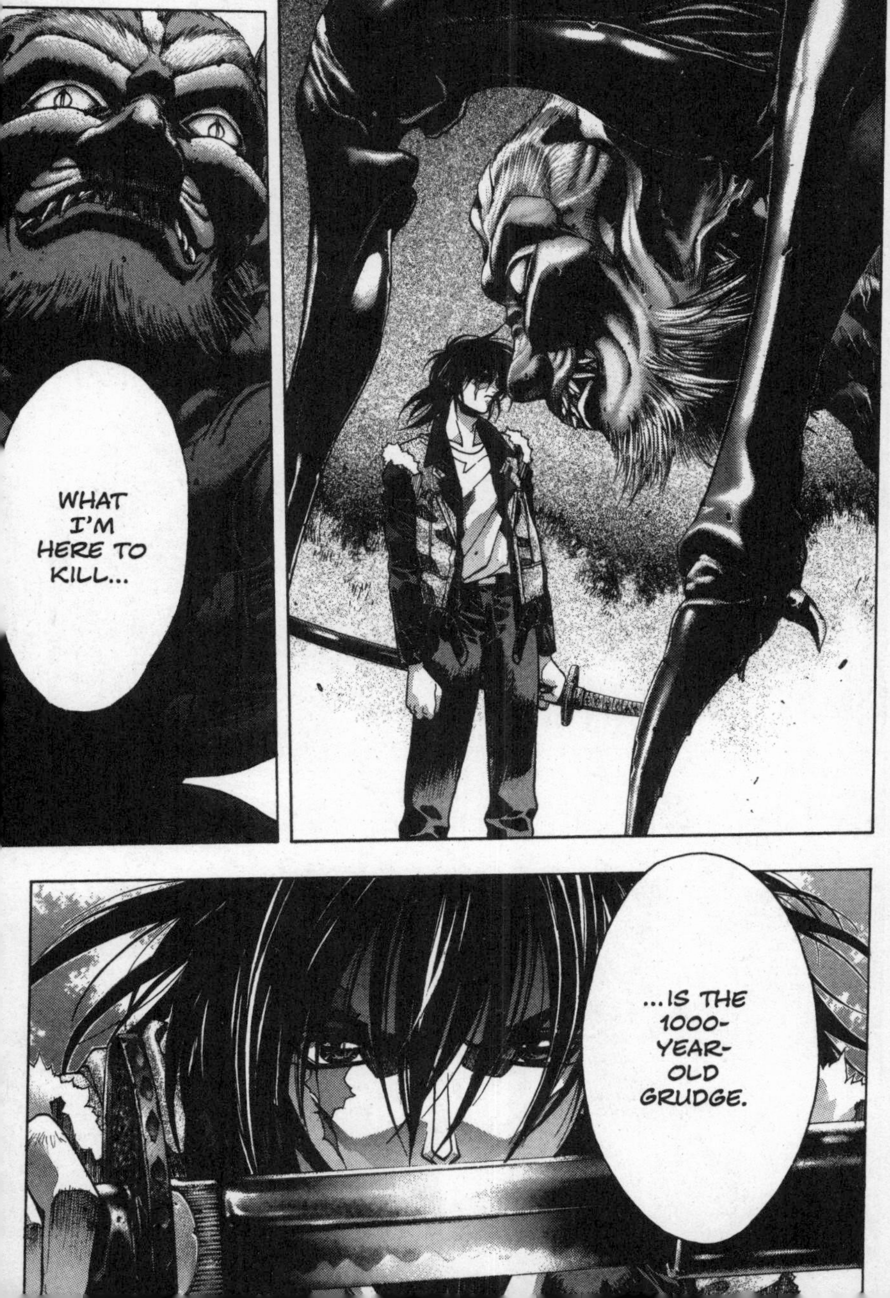
WHAT I'M HERE TO KILL...
...IS THE 1000-YEAR-OLD GRUDGE.

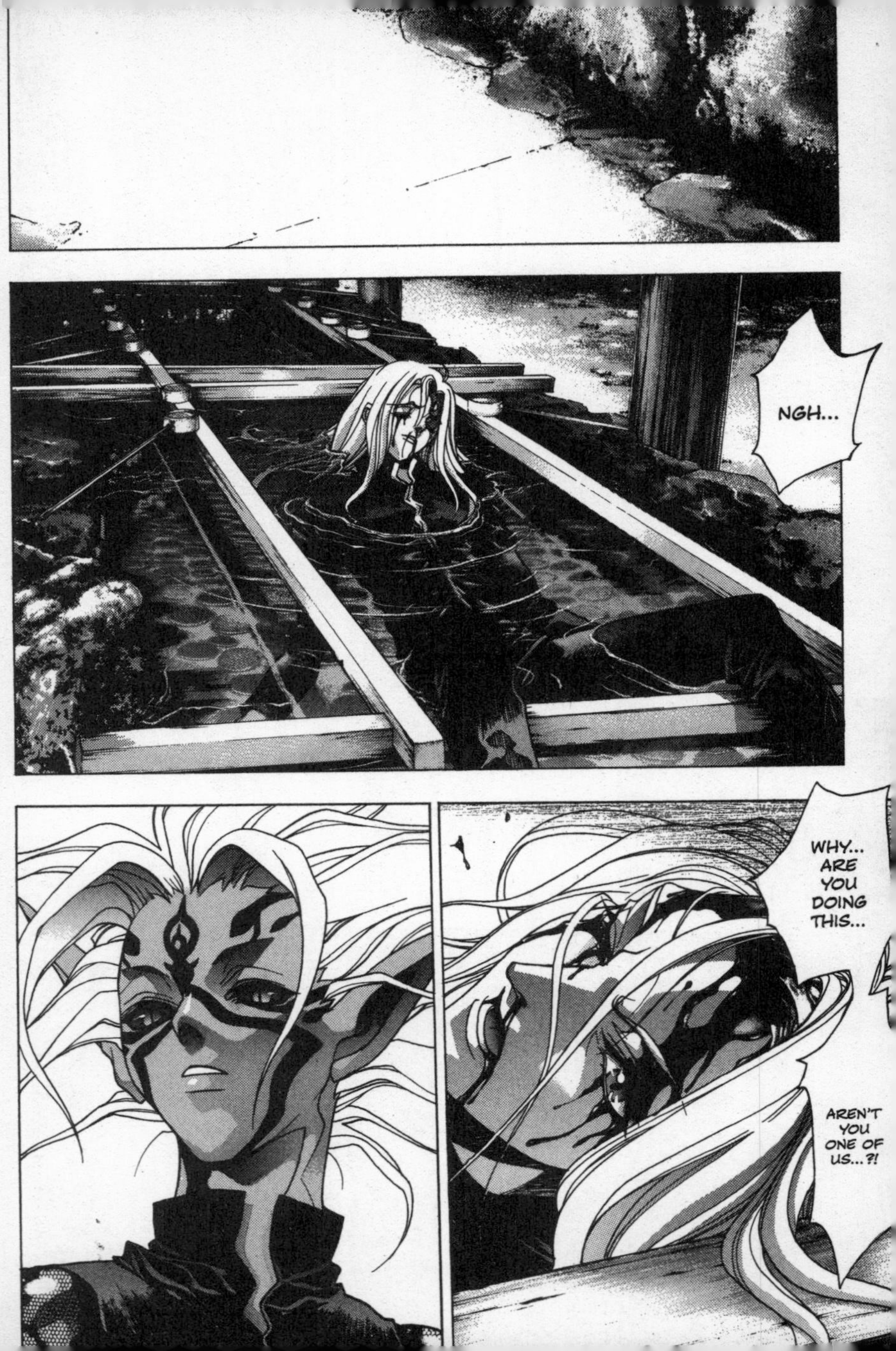
NGH...
WHY... ARE YOU DOING THIS...
AREN'T YOU ONE OF US...?!

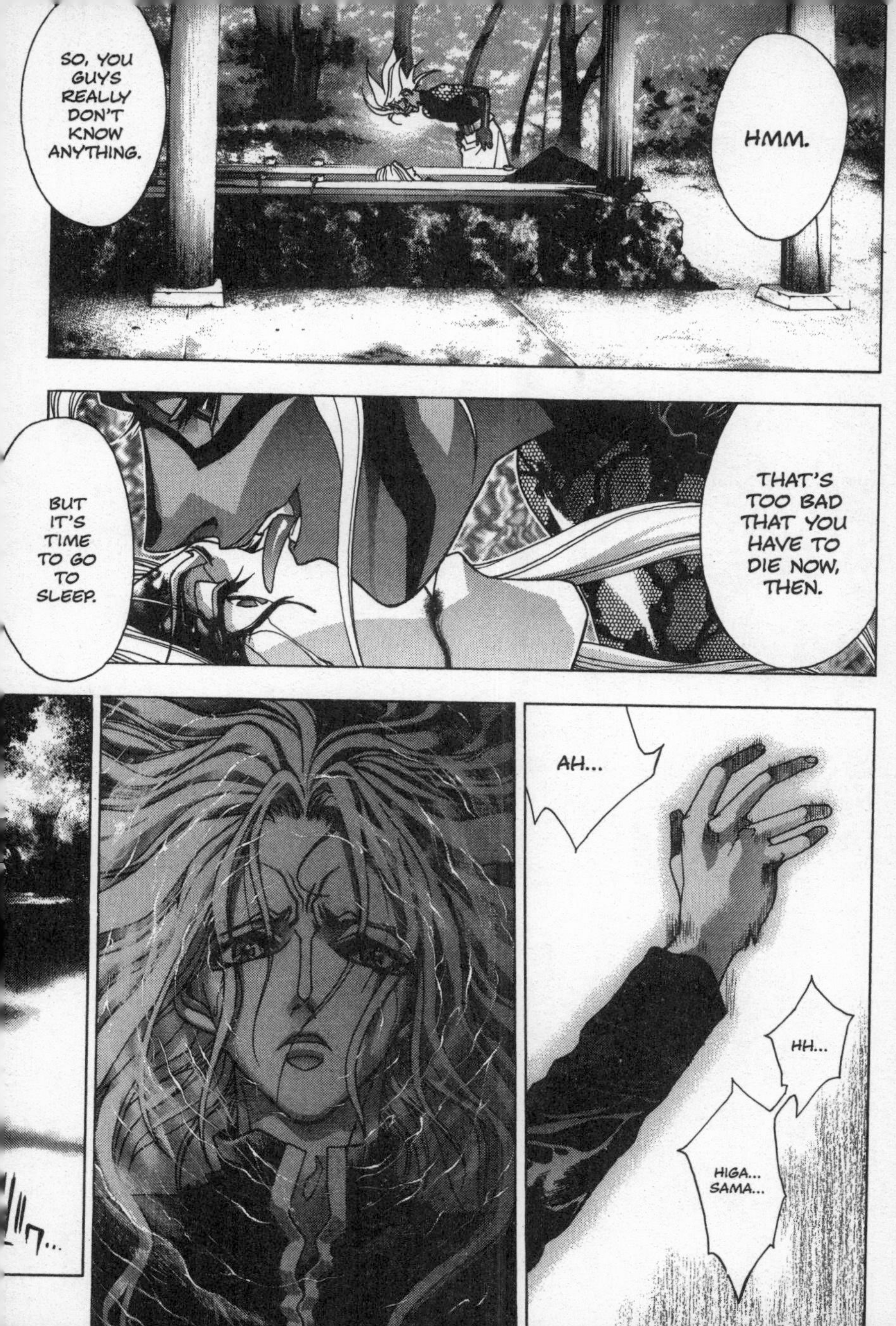
HMM.
SO, YOU GUYS REALLY DON'T KNOW ANYTHING.
THAT'S TOO BAD THAT YOU HAVE TO DIE NOW, THEN.
BUT IT'S TIME TO GO TO SLEEP.
AH...
HH...
HIGA... SAMA...

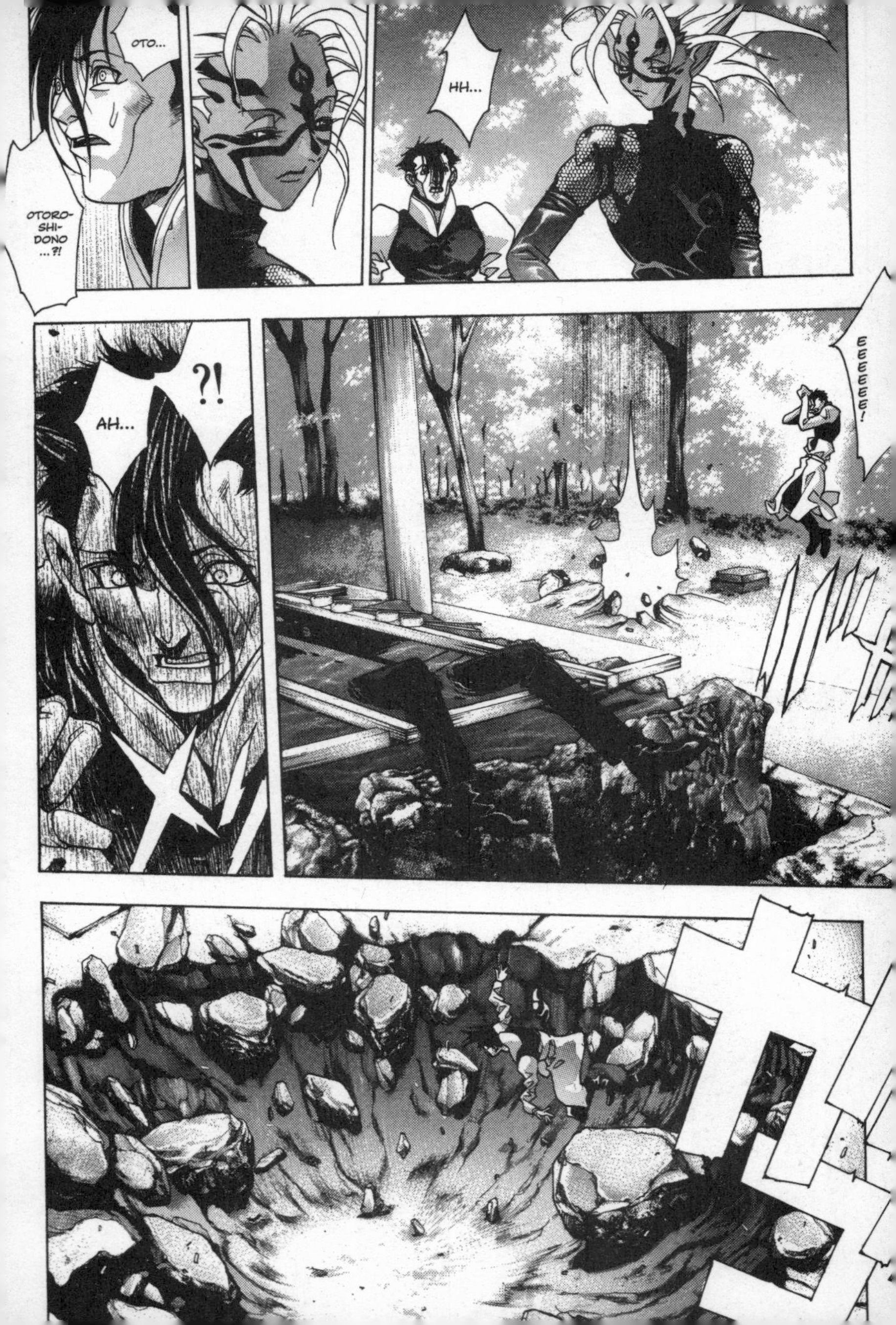
HH...
OTO...
OTORO-SHI-DONO ...?!
EEEEEE!
?!
AH...

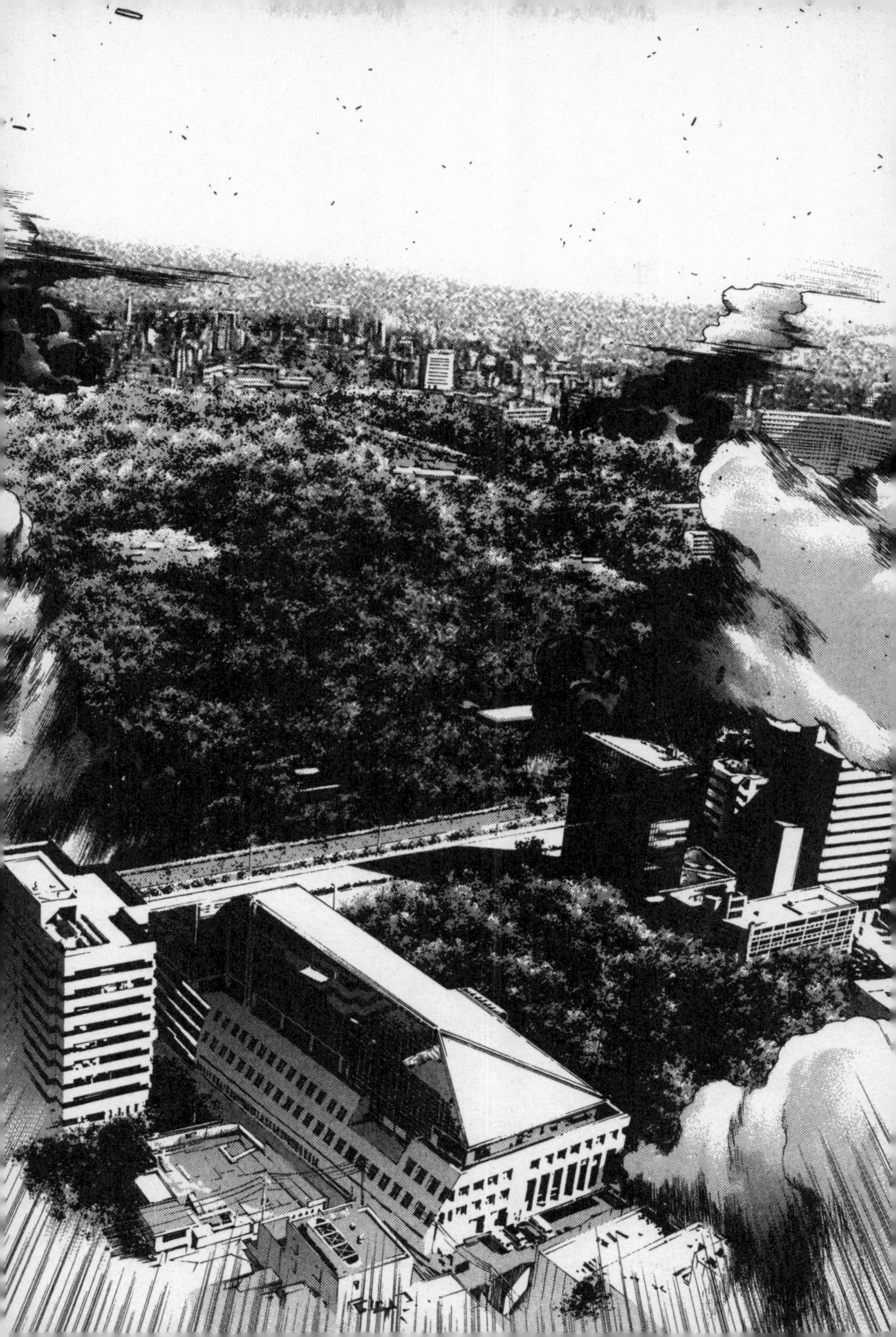

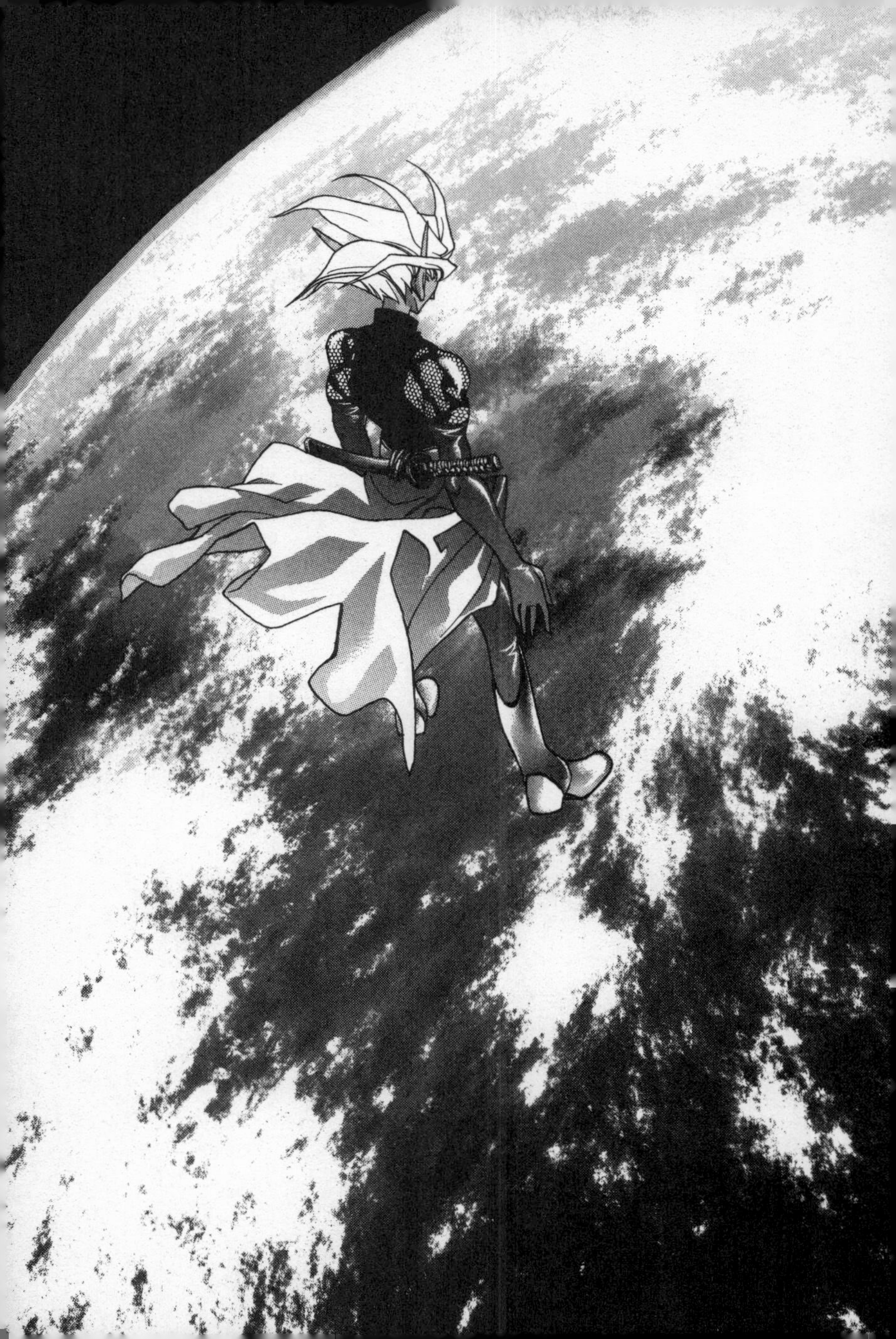

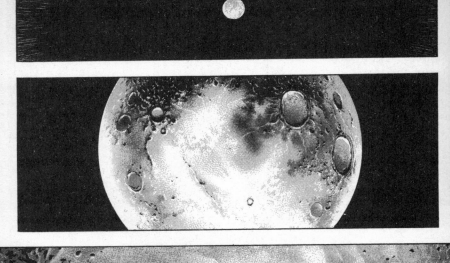

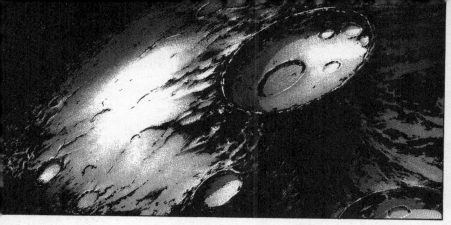

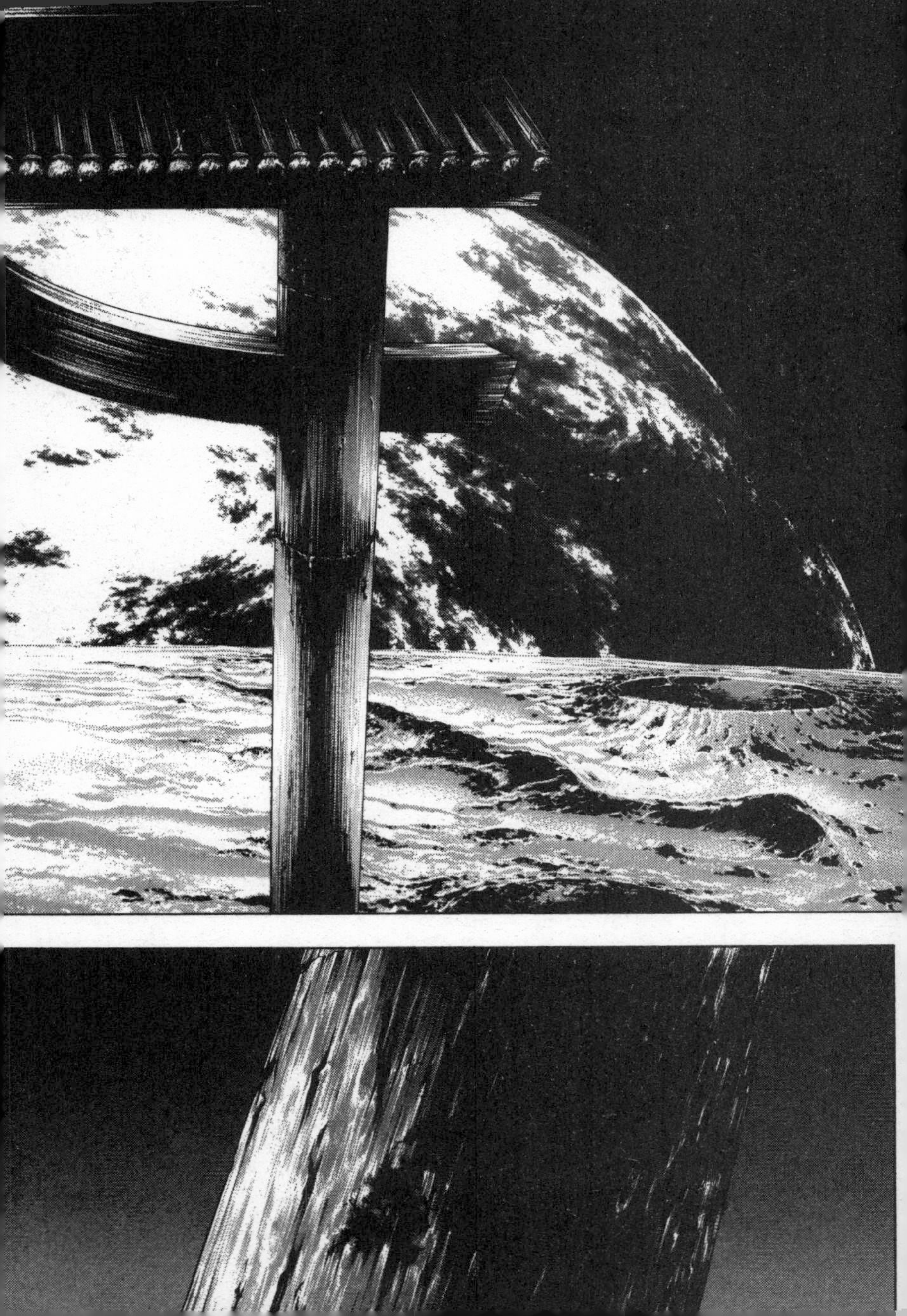

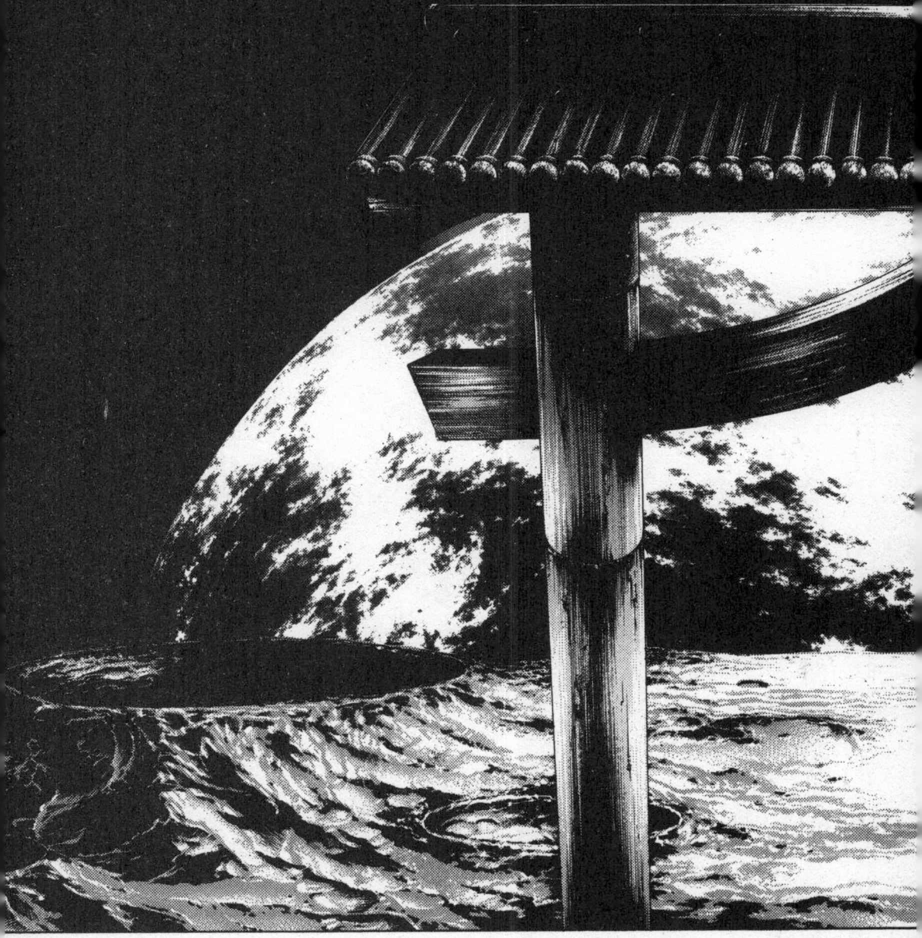
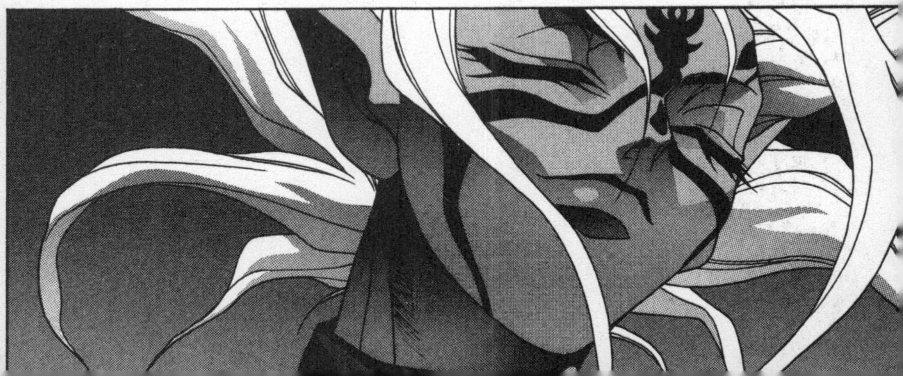

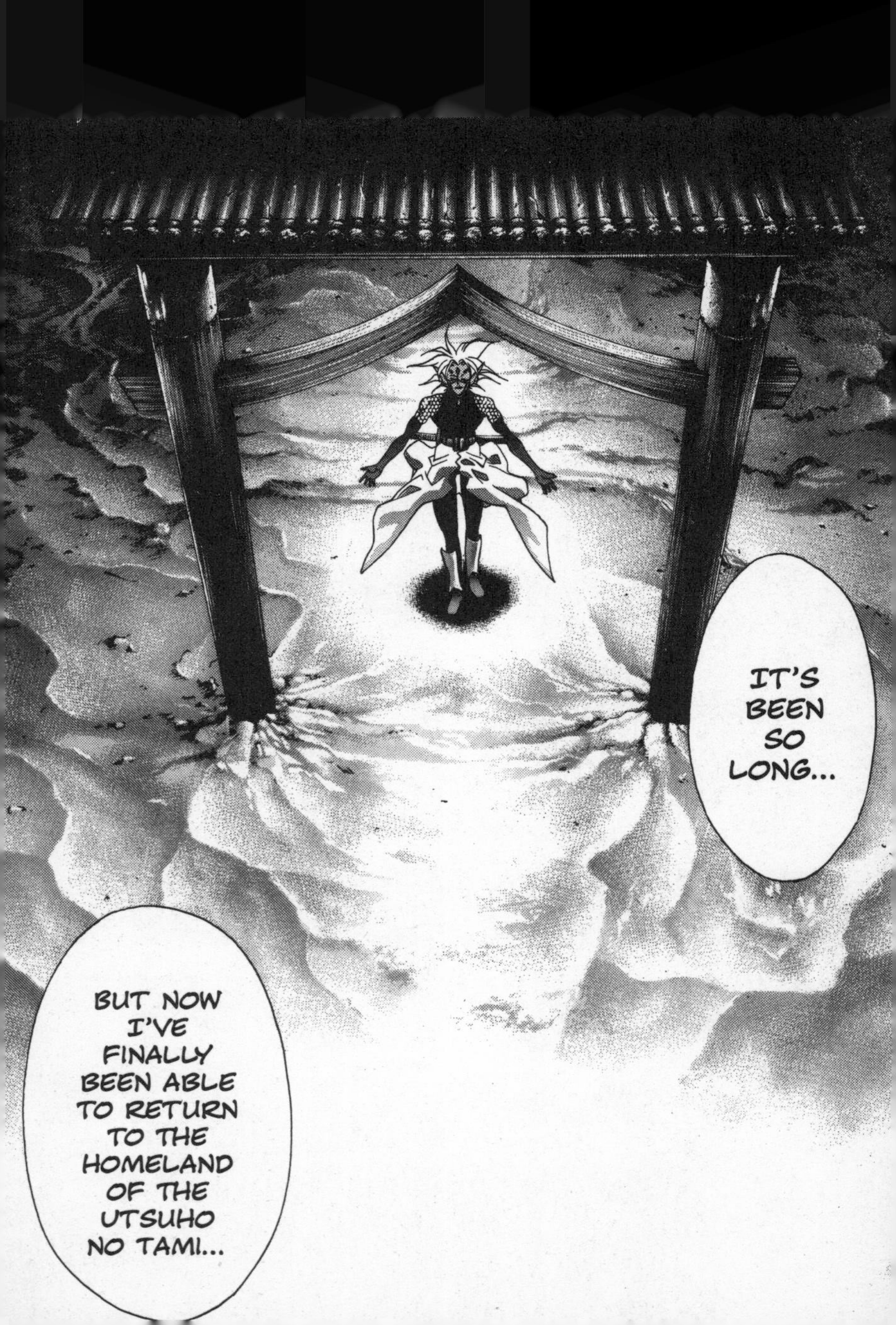
IT'S BEEN SO LONG...
BUT NOW I'VE FINALLY BEEN ABLE TO RETURN TO THE HOMELAND OF THE UTSUHO NO TAMI...

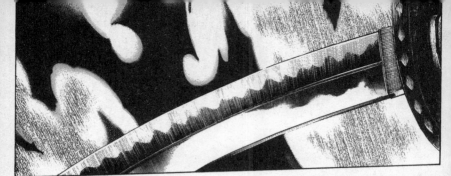

HA
HA...

AH
HA
HA
HA
HA!

HA
HA
HA
HA!

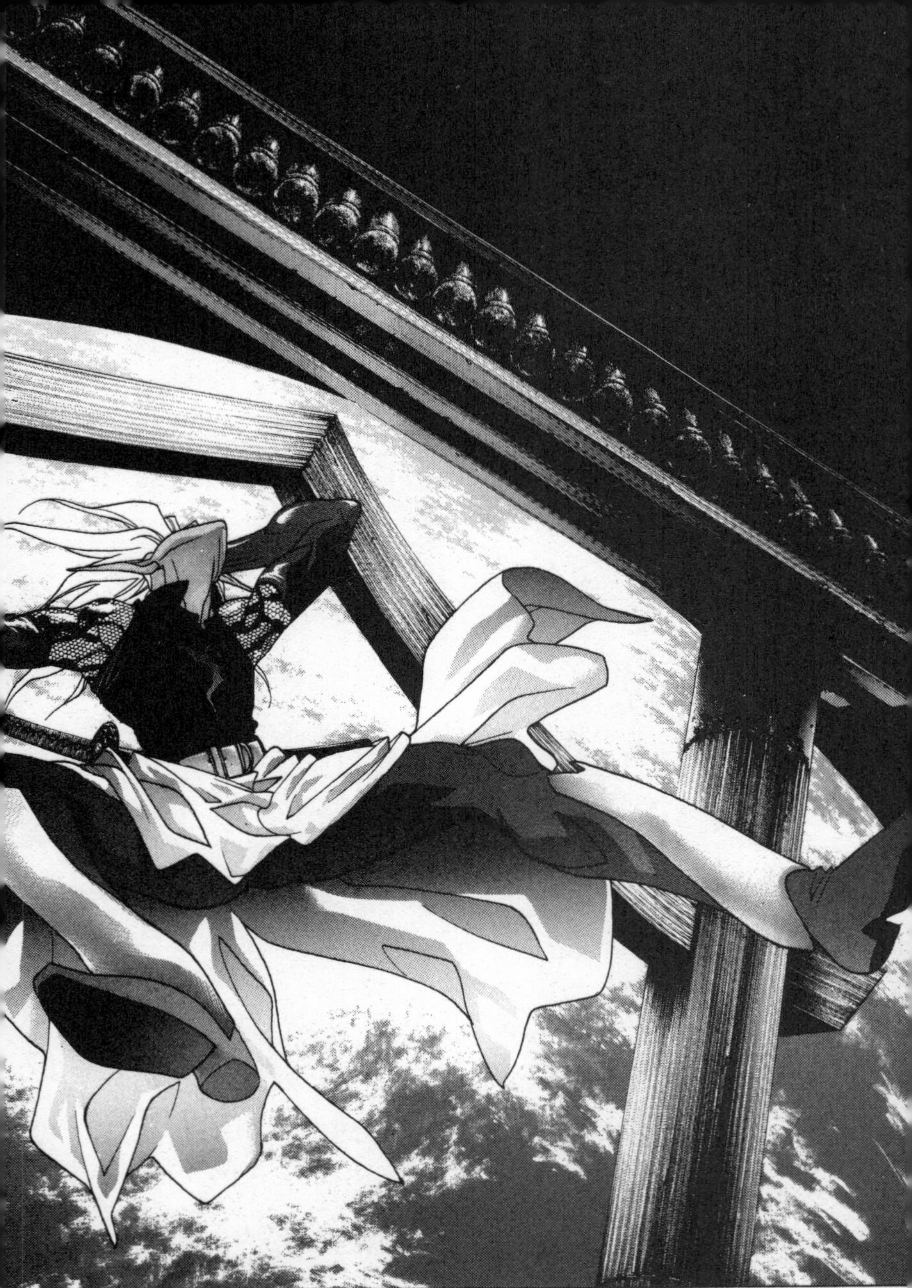

Chapter 44: An Apparition

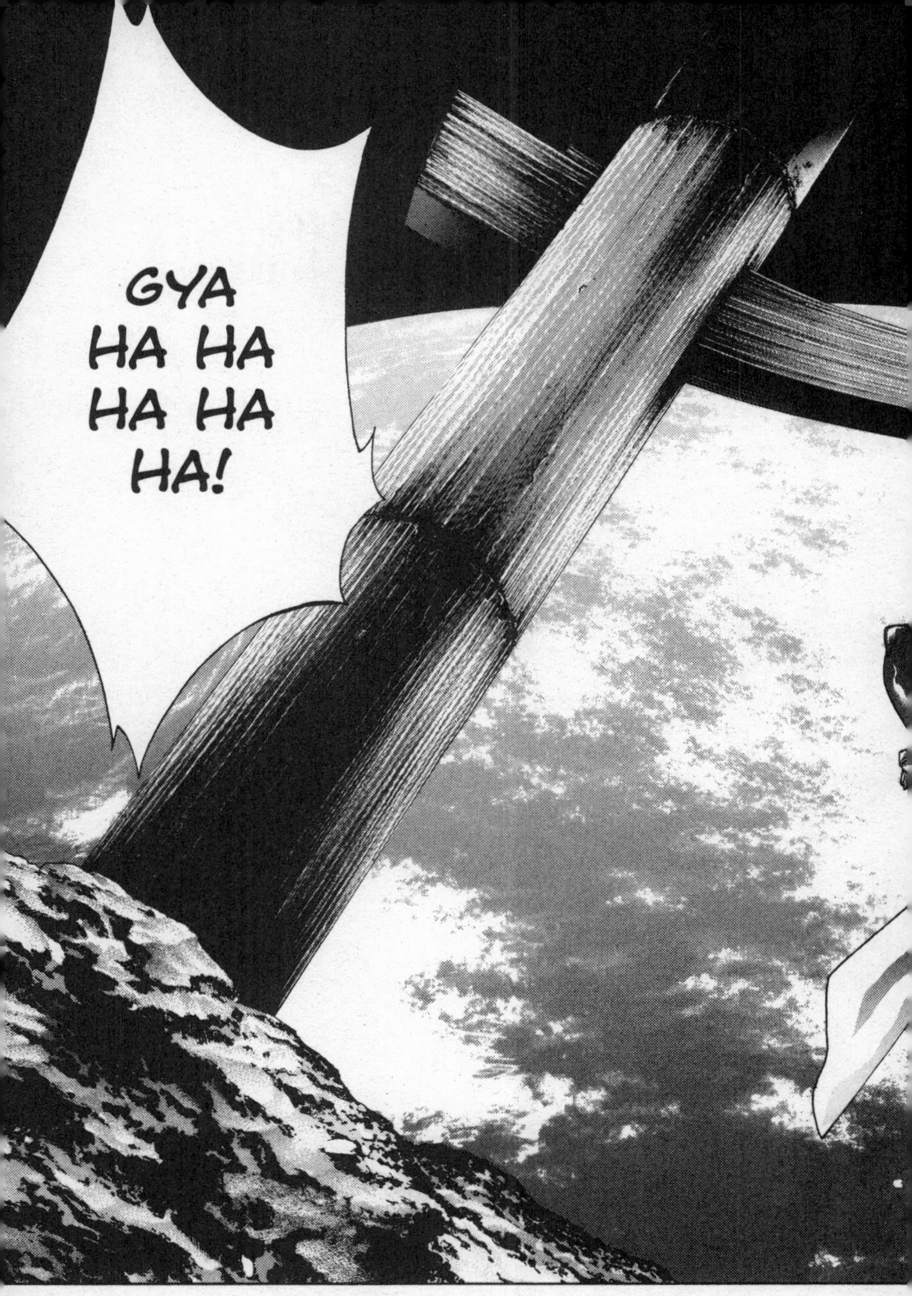
GYA HA HA HA HA HA!

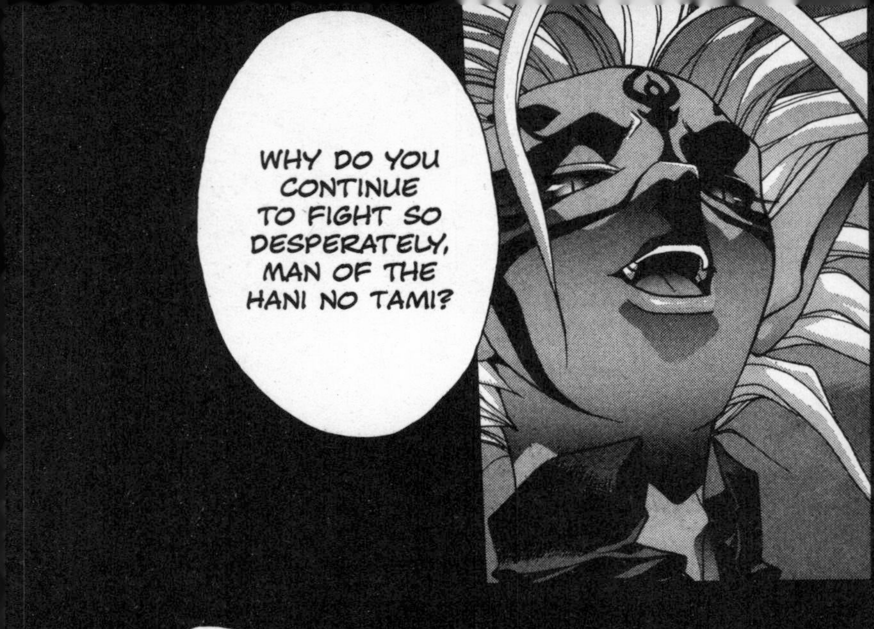
WHY DO YOU CONTINUE TO FIGHT SO DESPERATELY, MAN OF THE HANI NO TAMI?

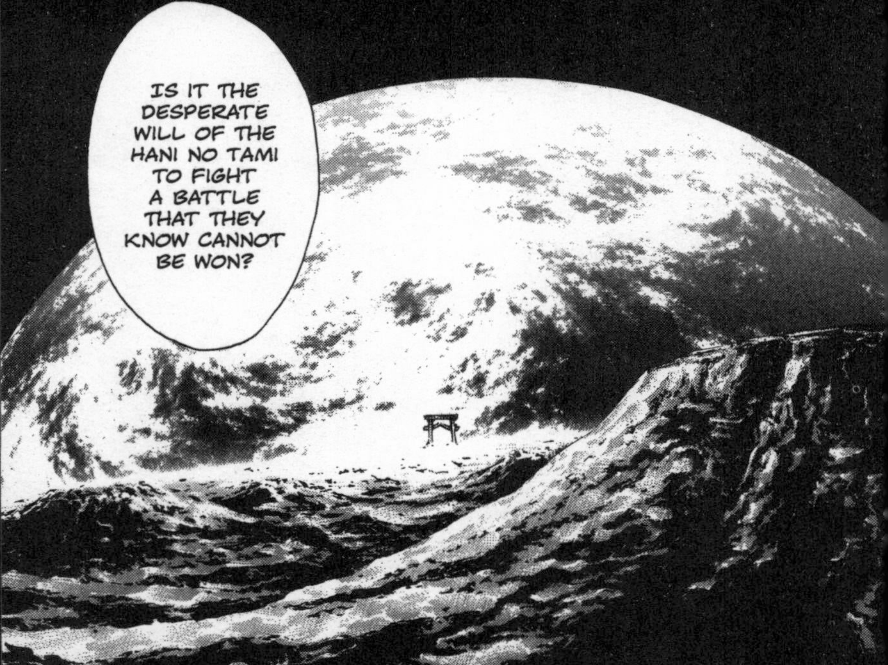
IS IT THE DESPERATE WILL OF THE HANI NO TAMI TO FIGHT A BATTLE THAT THEY KNOW CANNOT BE WON?

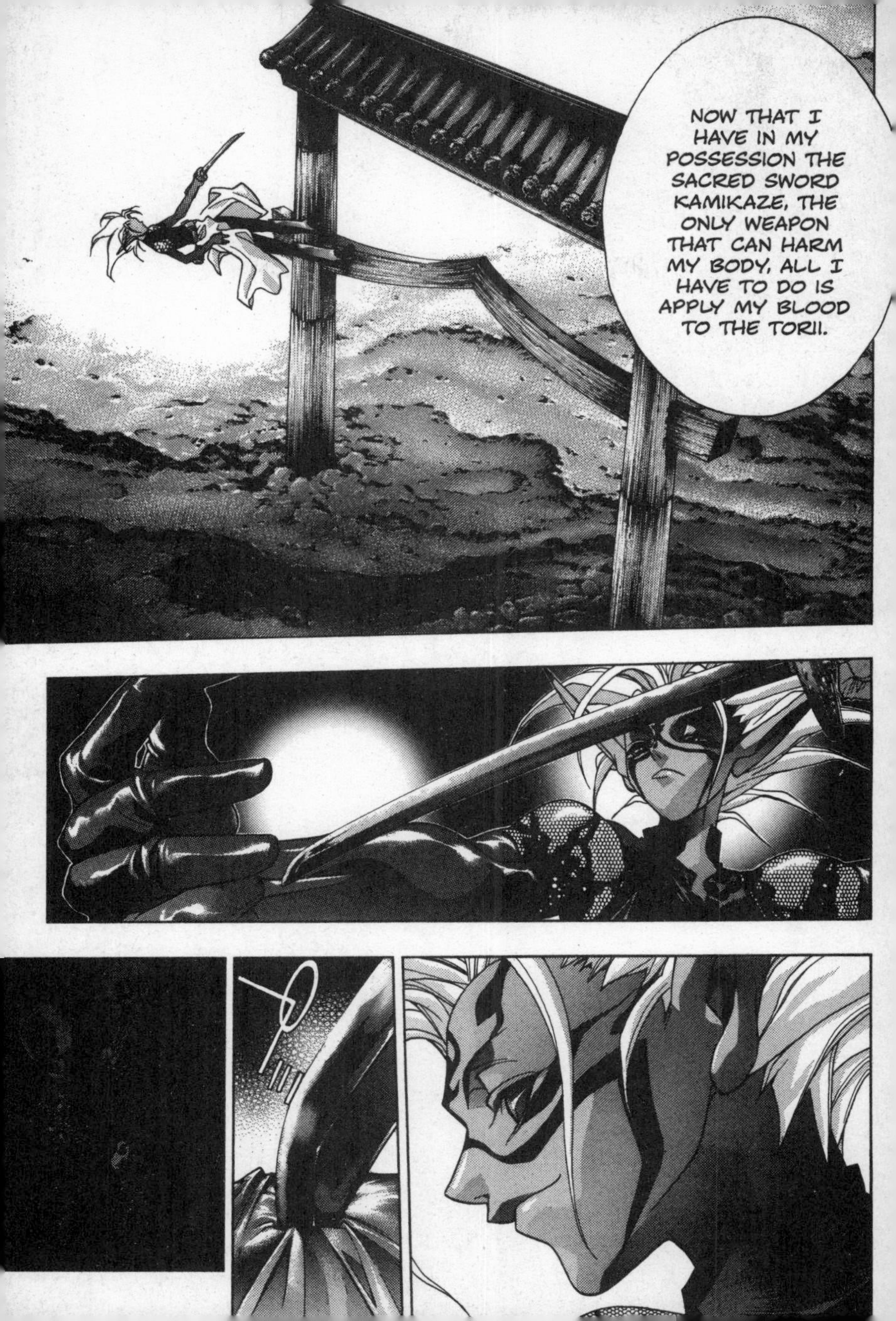
NOW THAT I HAVE IN MY POSSESSION THE SACRED SWORD KAMIKAZE, THE ONLY WEAPON THAT CAN HARM MY BODY, ALL I HAVE TO DO IS APPLY MY BLOOD TO THE TORII.

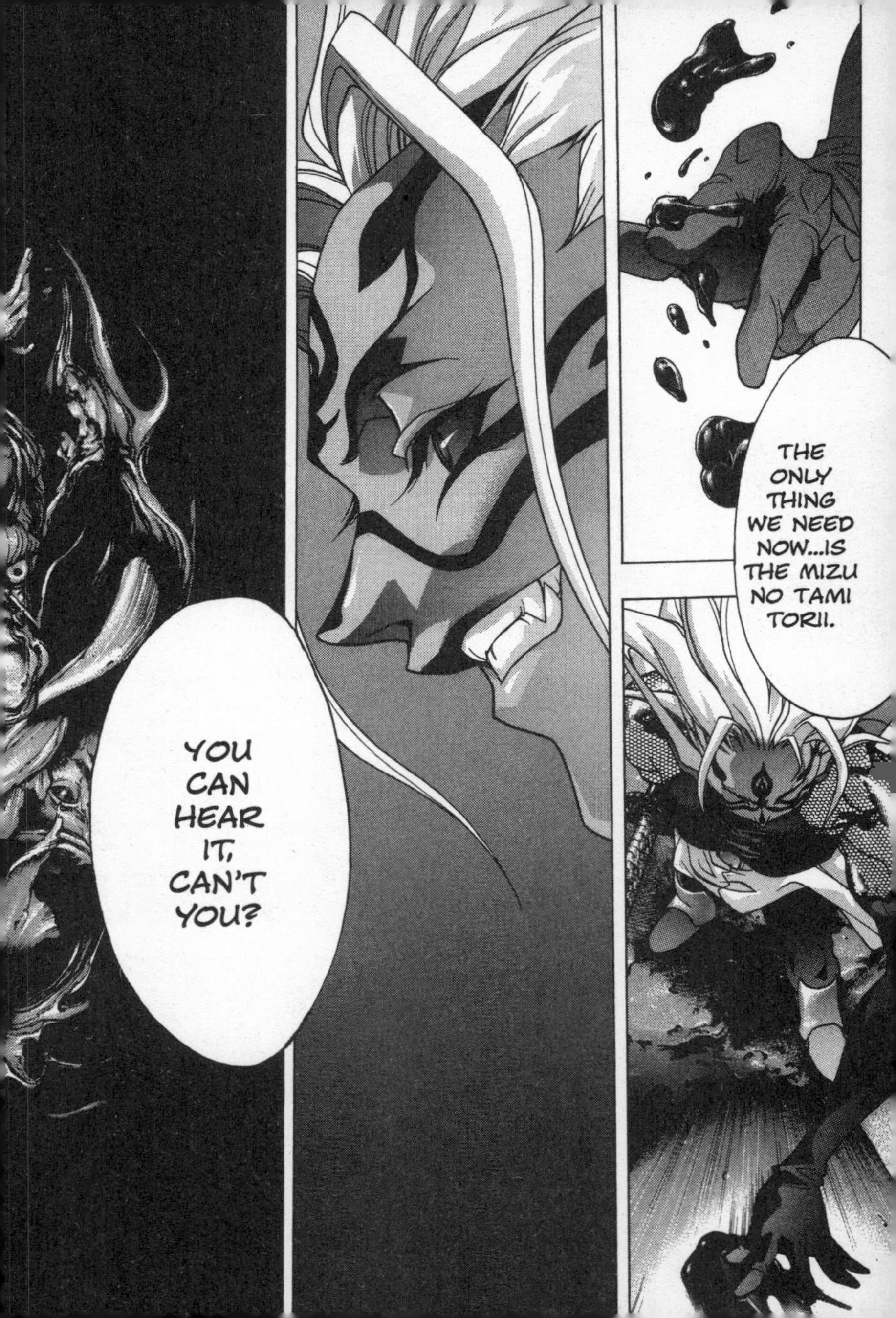
THE ONLY THING WE NEED NOW...IS THE MIZU NO TAMI TORII.
YOU CAN HEAR IT, CAN'T YOU?

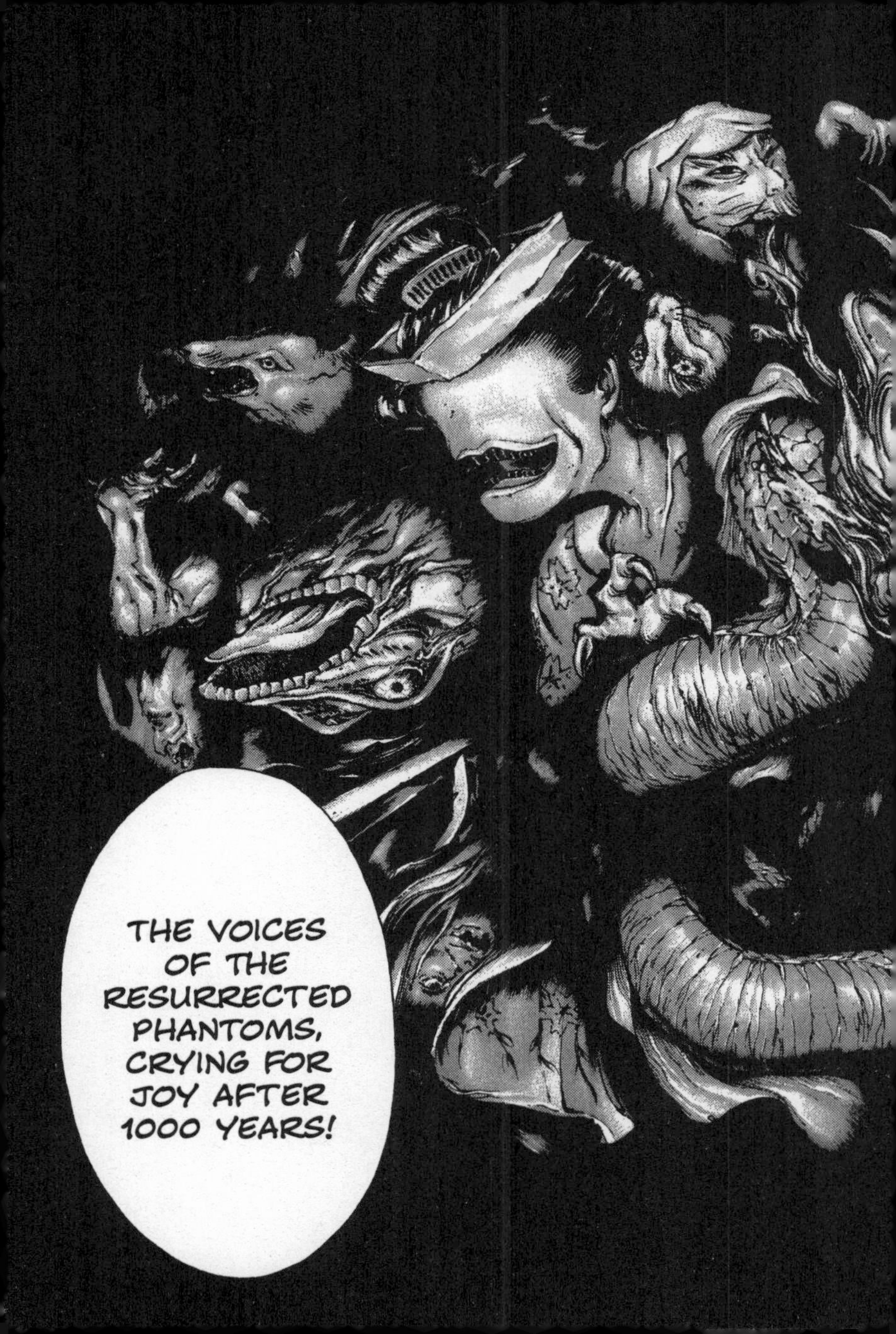
THE VOICES OF THE RESURRECTED PHANTOMS, CRYING FOR JOY AFTER 1000 YEARS!

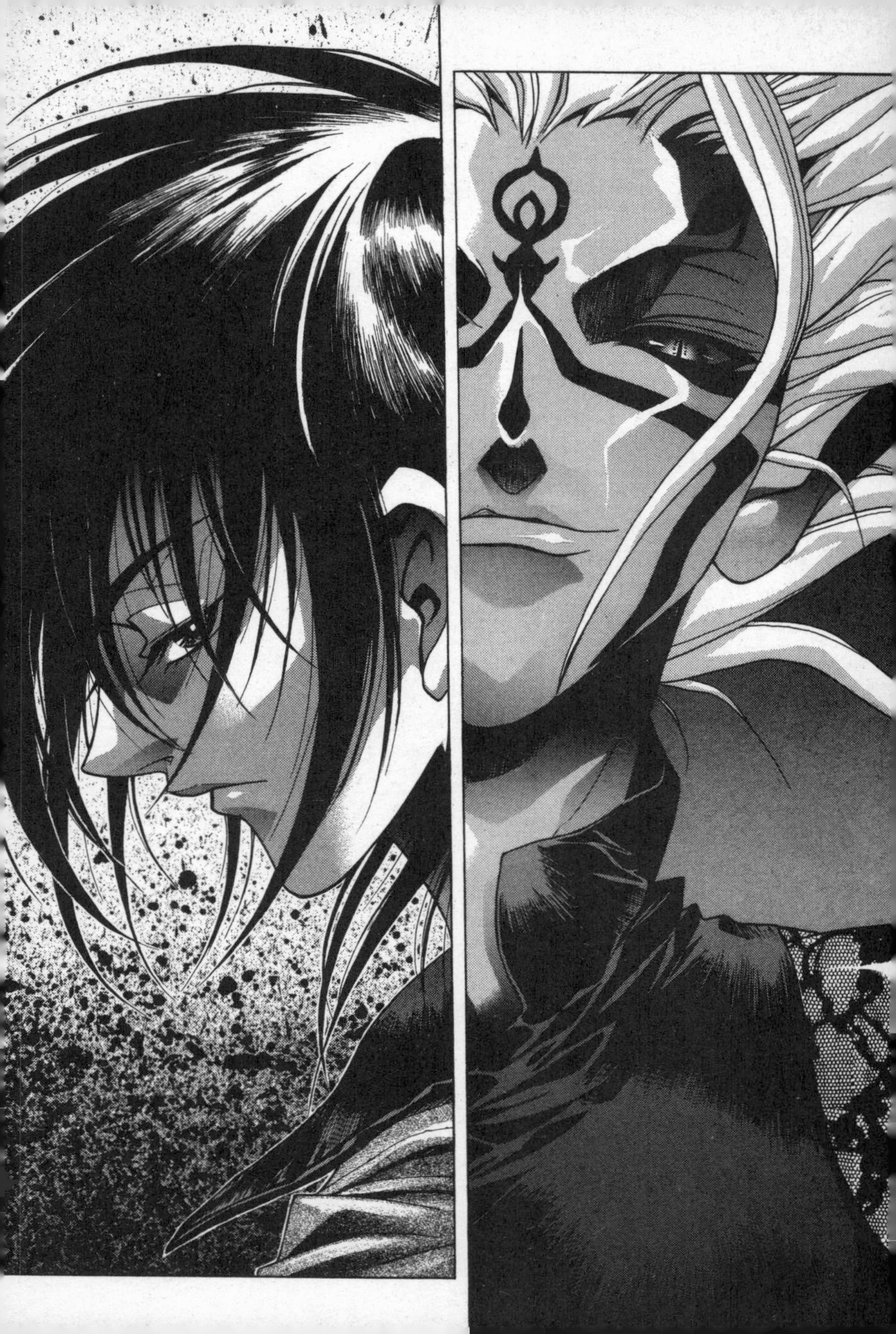

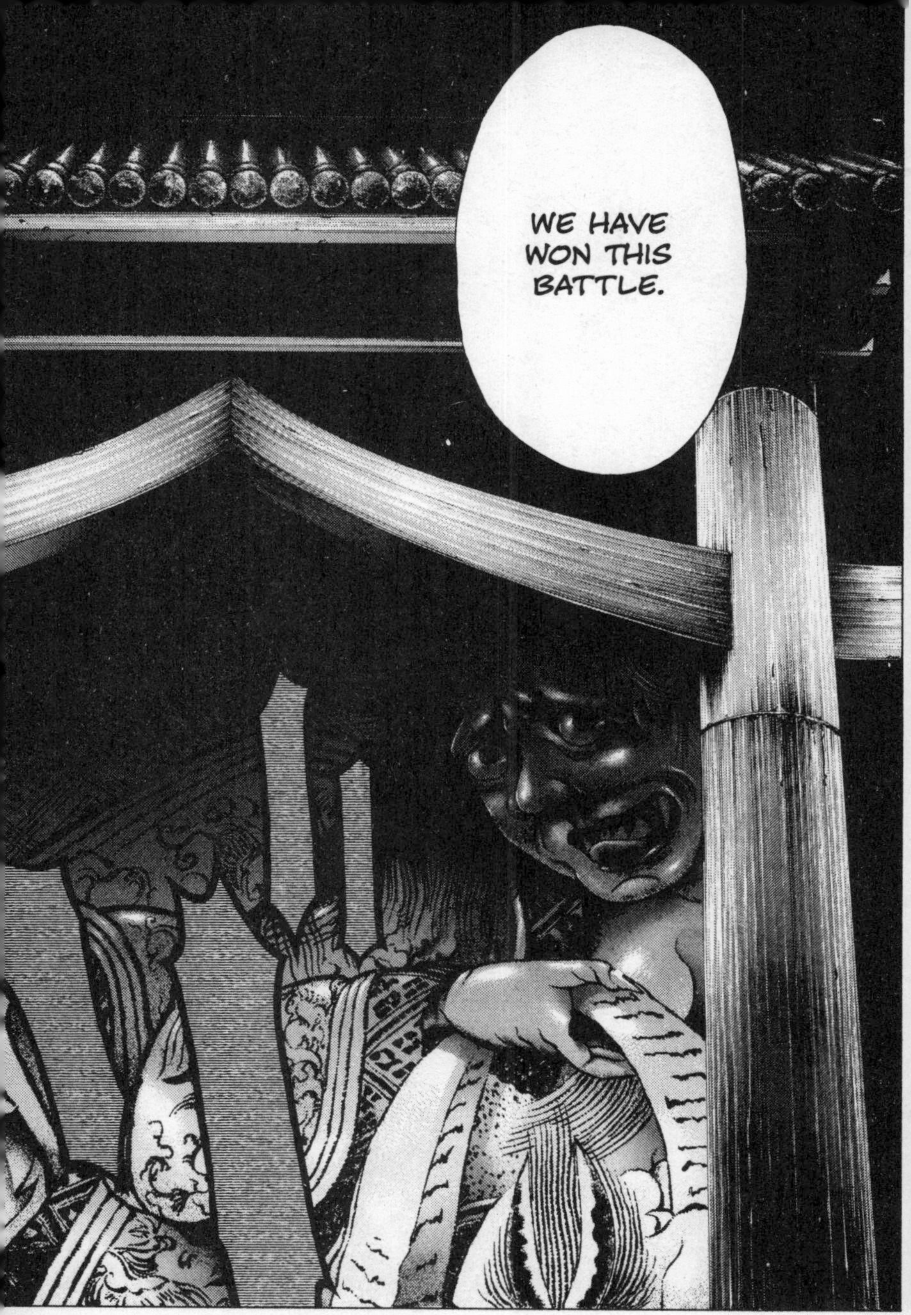
WE HAVE WON THIS BATTLE.

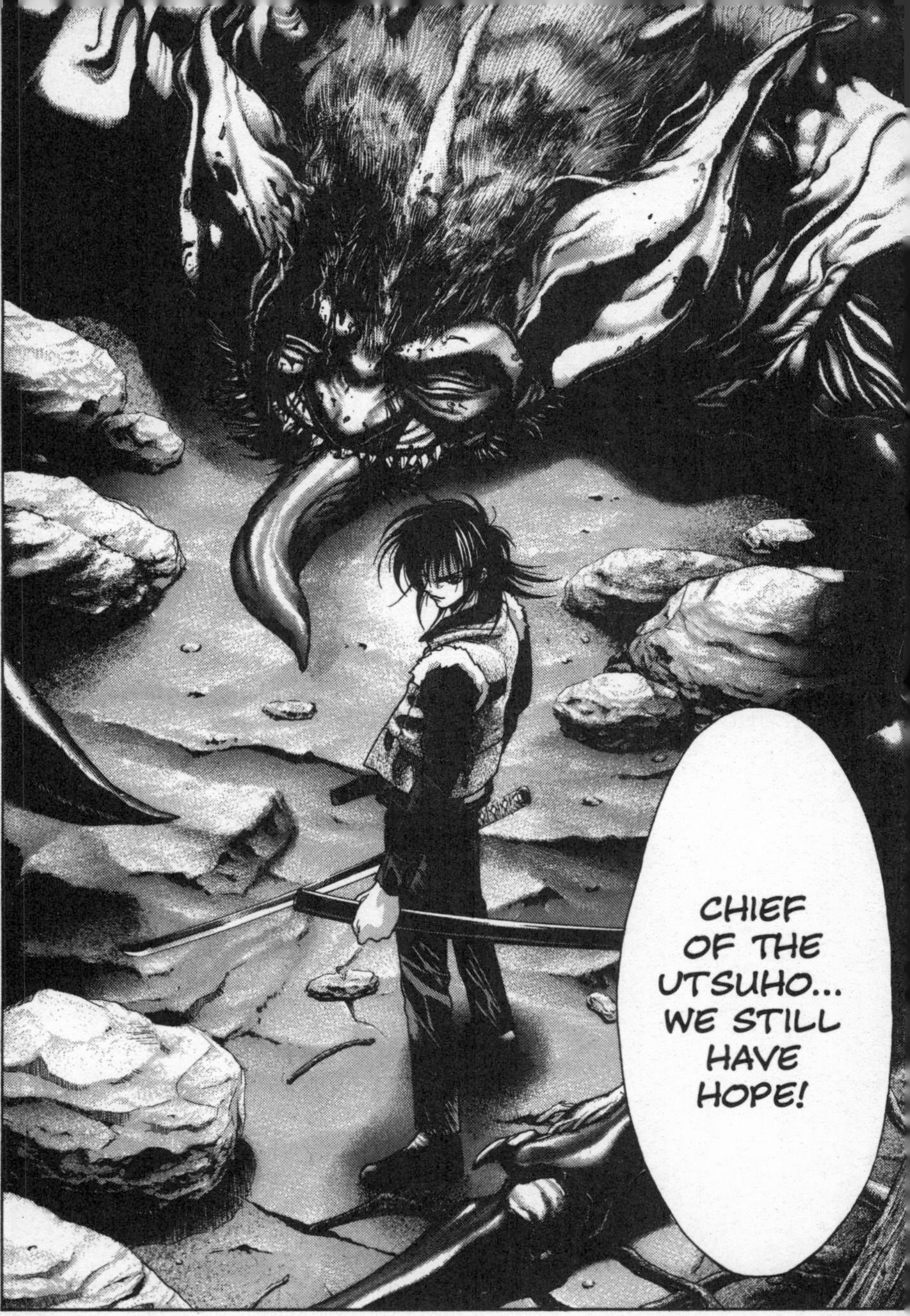
CHIEF OF THE UTSUHO... WE STILL HAVE HOPE!

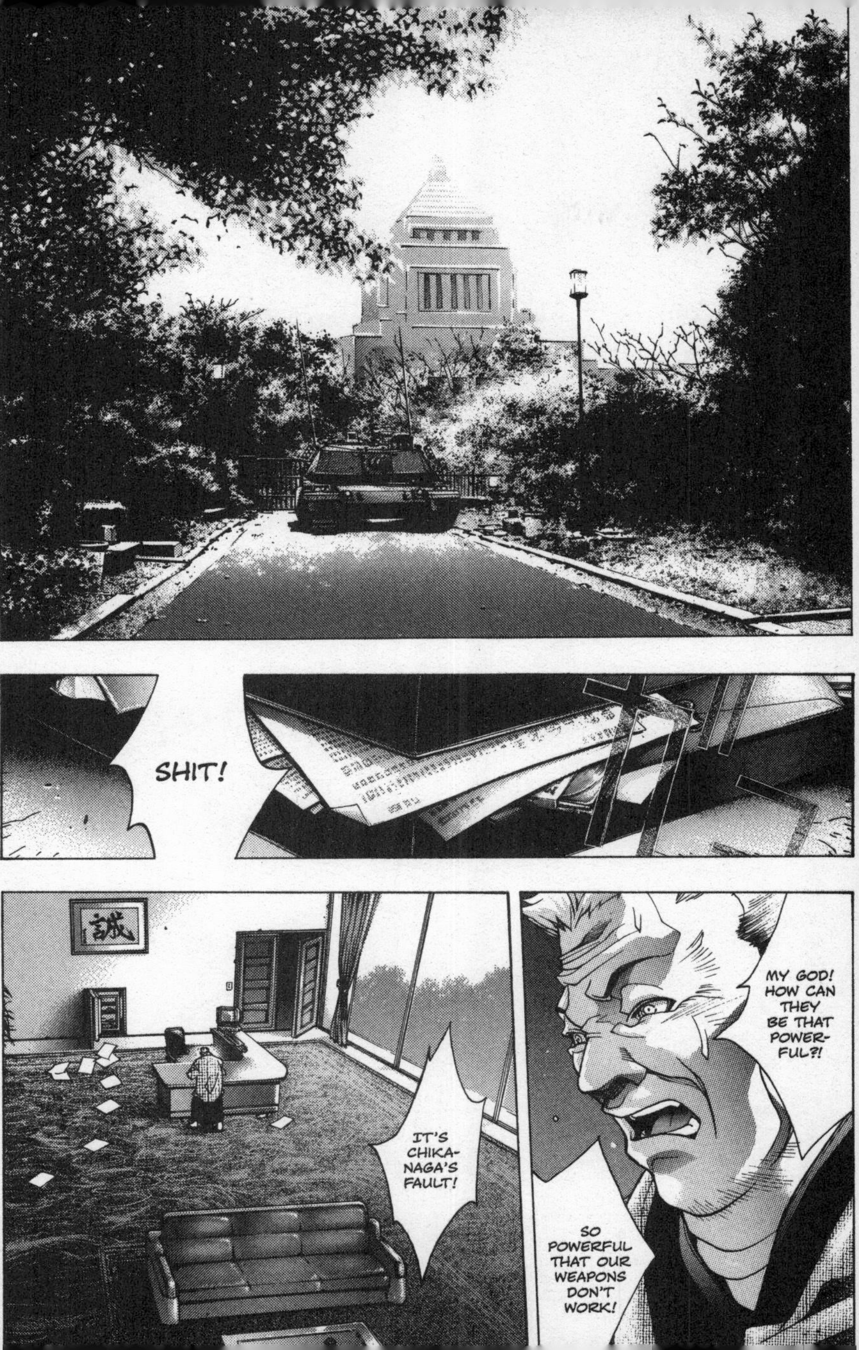
SHIT!
MY GOD! HOW CAN THEY BE THAT POWER-FUL?!
SO POWERFUL THAT OUR WEAPONS DON'T WORK!
IT'S CHIKA-NAGA'S FAULT!

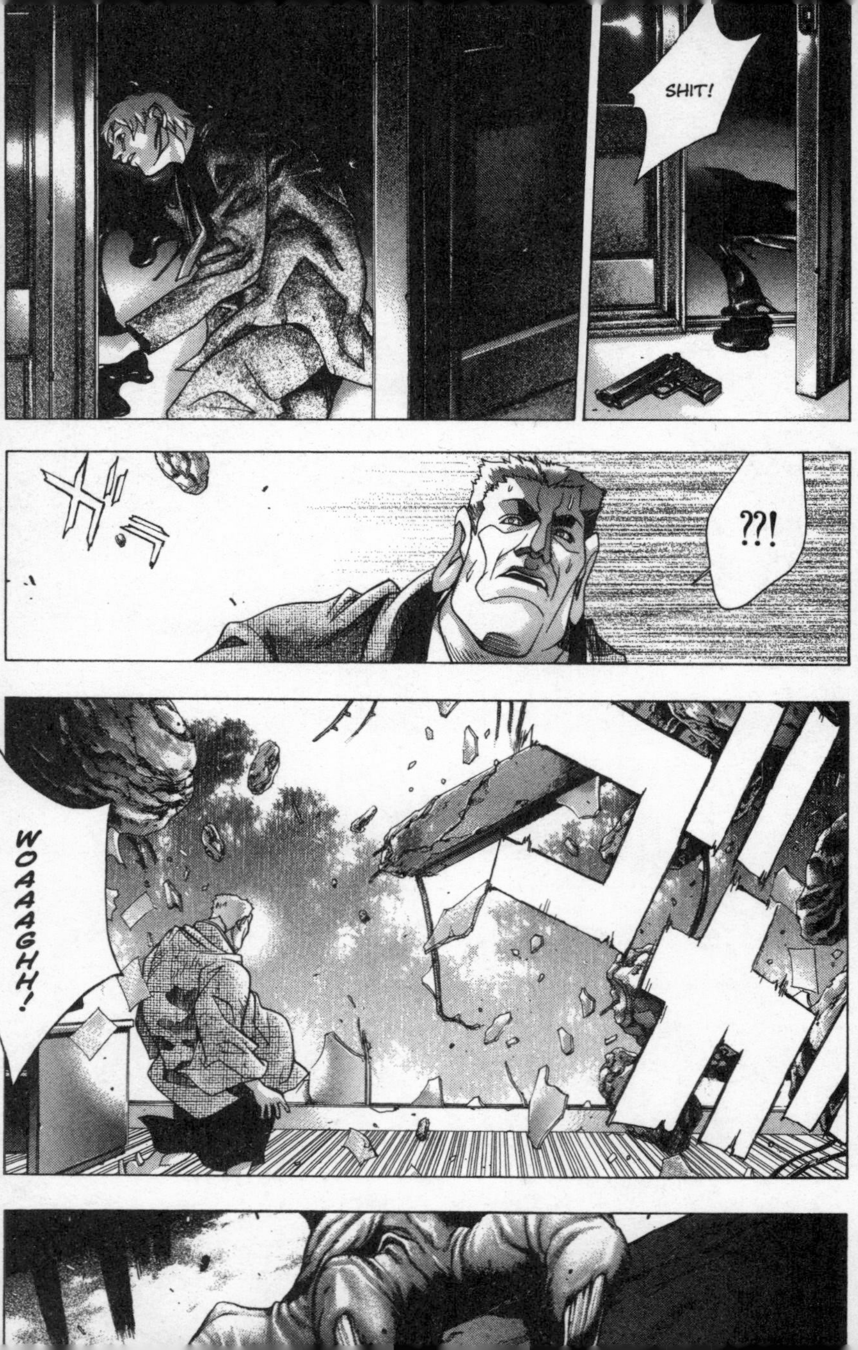
SHIT!
??!
WOAAAAGH!

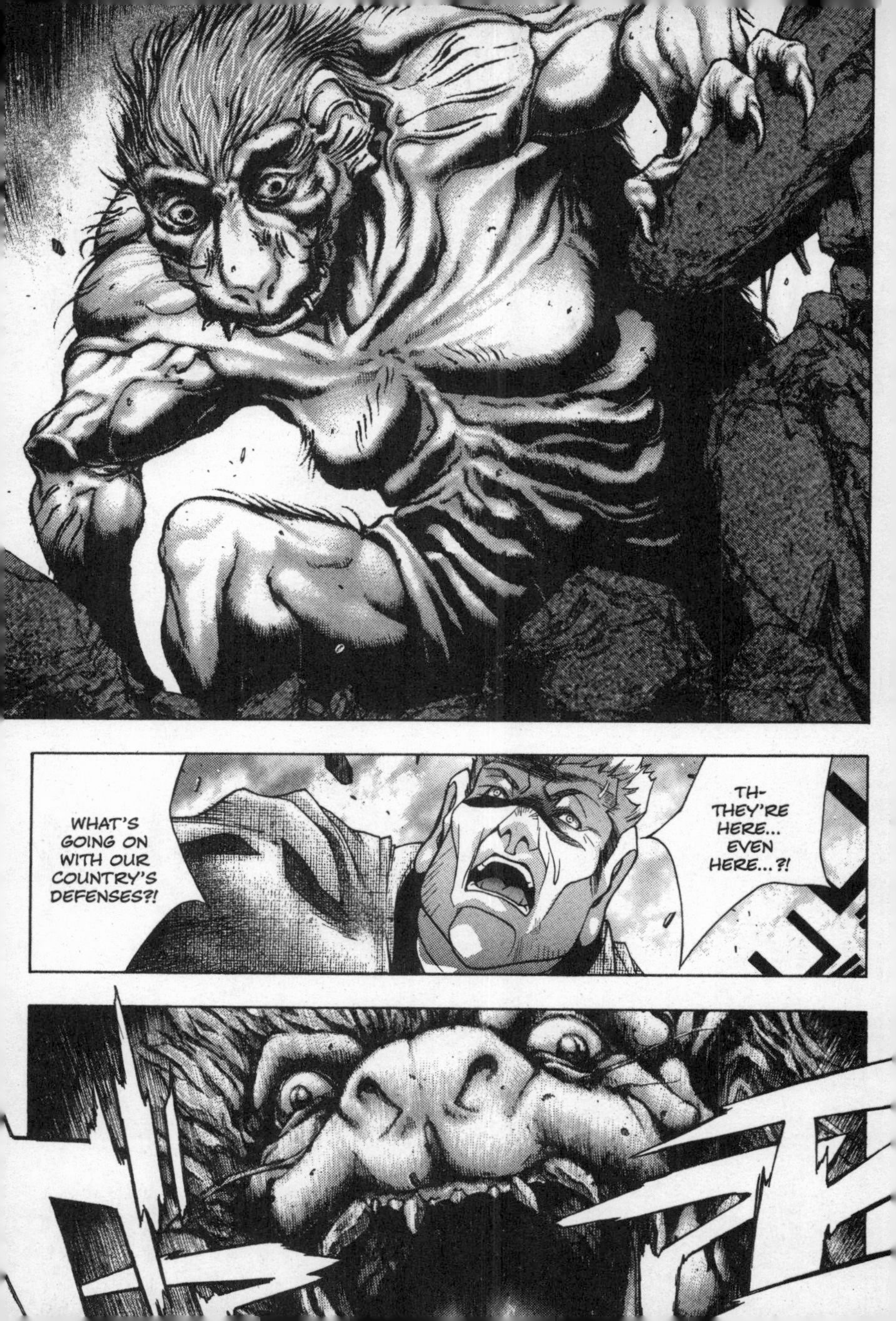
TH- THEY'RE HERE... EVEN HERE...?!
WHAT'S GOING ON WITH OUR COUNTRY'S DEFENSES?!

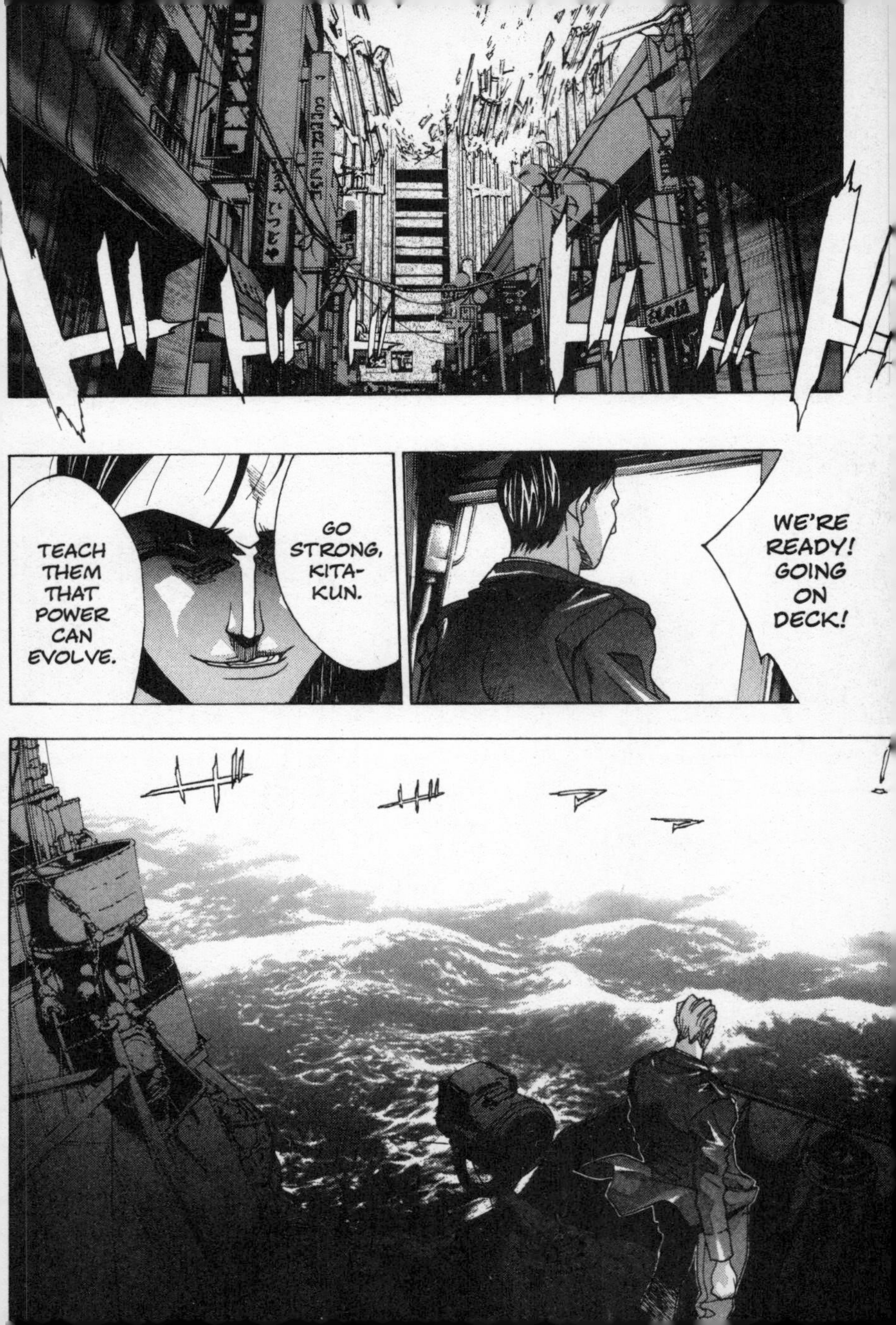
WE'RE READY! GOING ON DECK!
GO STRONG, KITA-KUN.
TEACH THEM THAT POWER CAN EVOLVE.

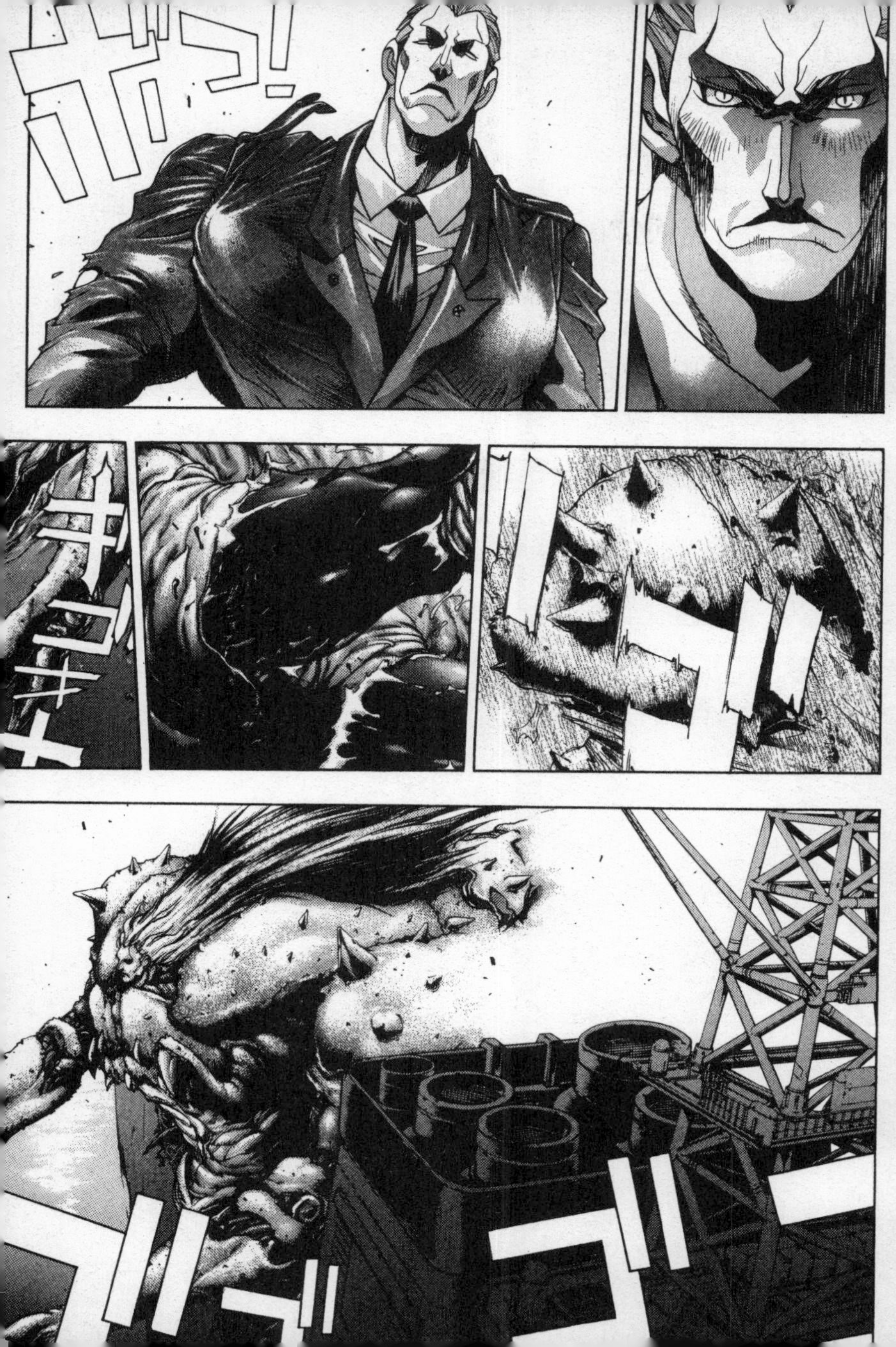

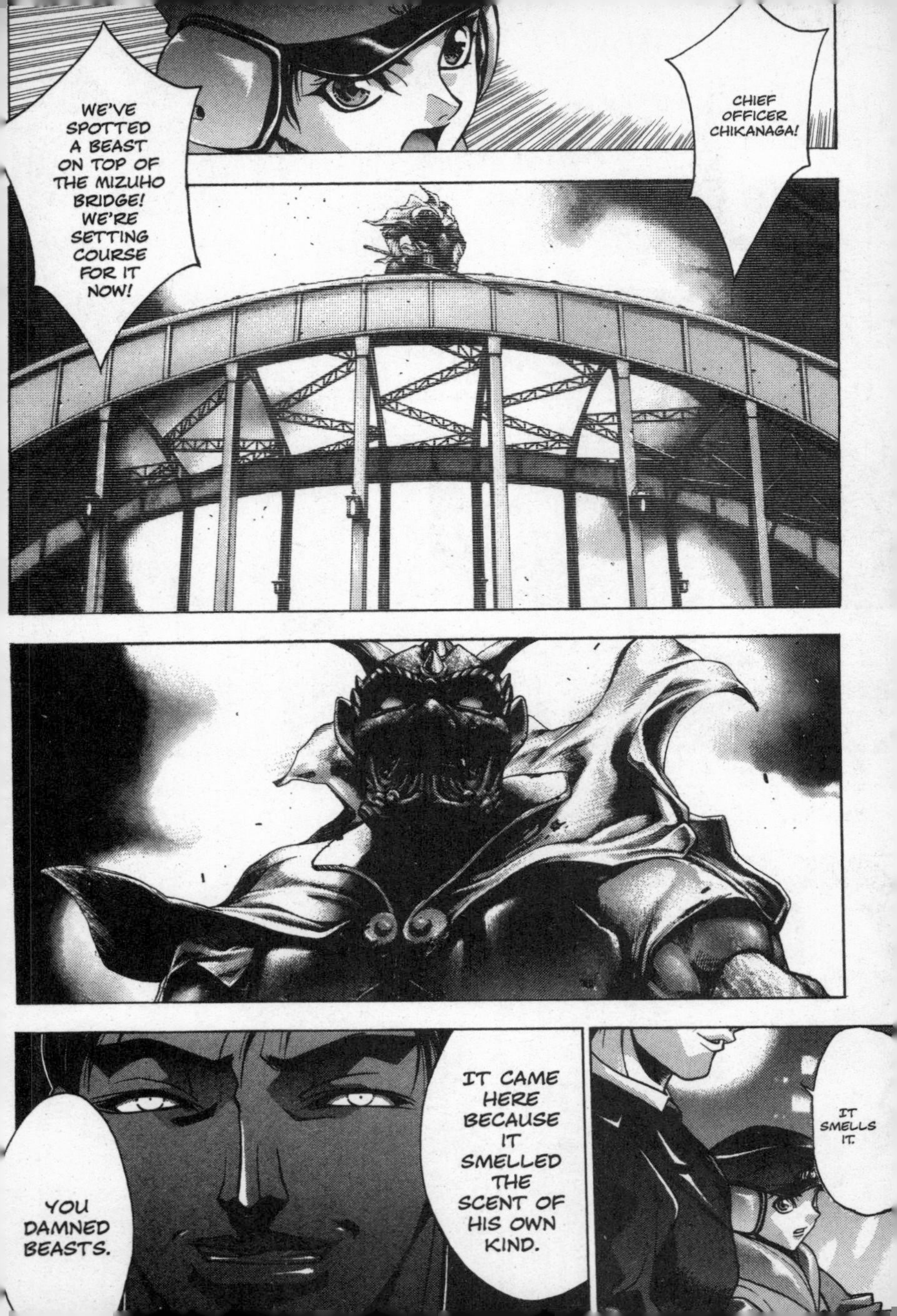
CHIEF OFFICER CHIKANAGA!
WE'VE SPOTTED A BEAST ON TOP OF THE MIZUHO BRIDGE! WE'RE SETTING COURSE FOR IT NOW!
IT SMELLS IT.
IT CAME HERE BECAUSE IT SMELLED THE SCENT OF HIS OWN KIND.
YOU DAMNED BEASTS.

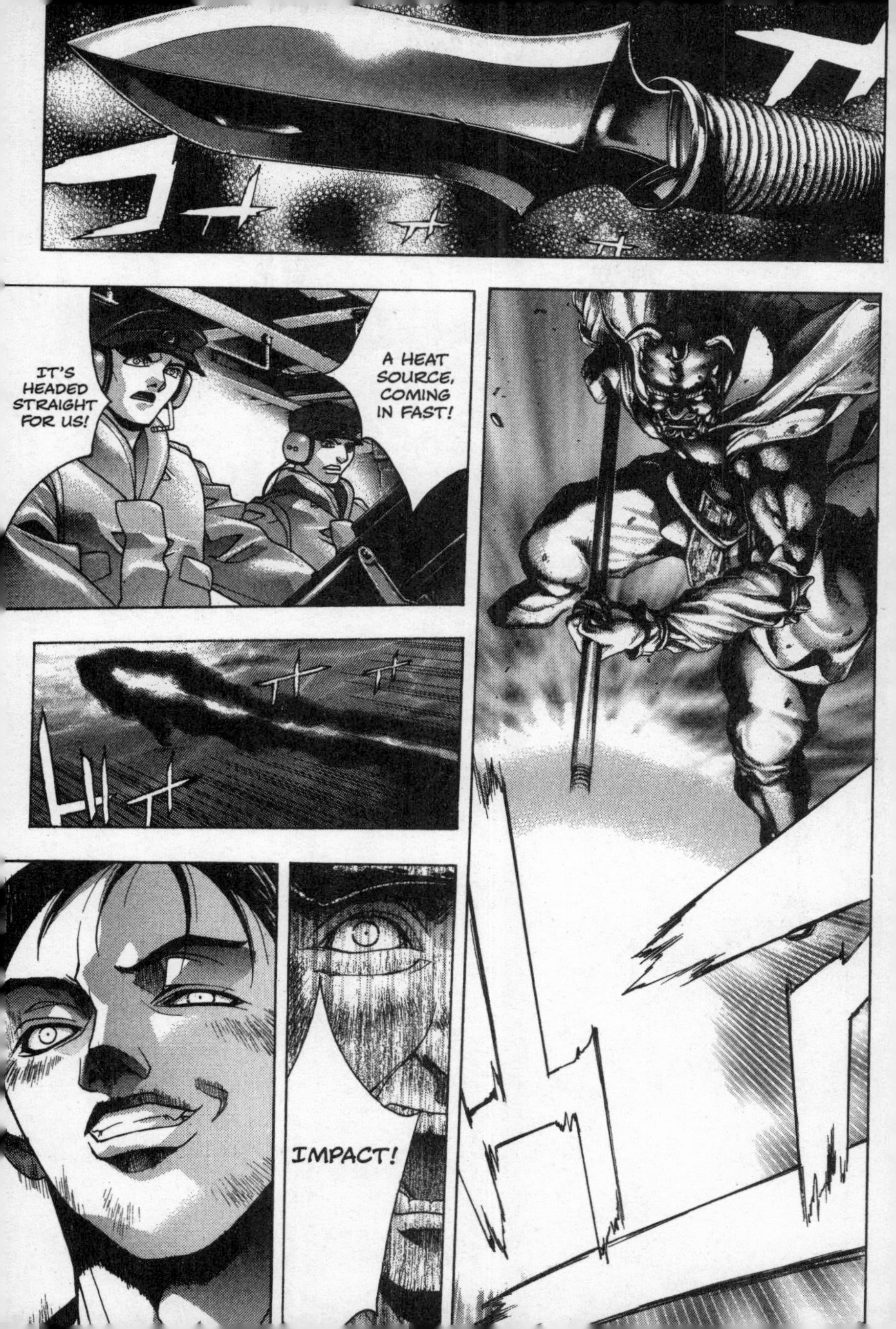
A HEAT SOURCE, COMING IN FAST!
IT'S HEADED STRAIGHT FOR US!
IMPACT!

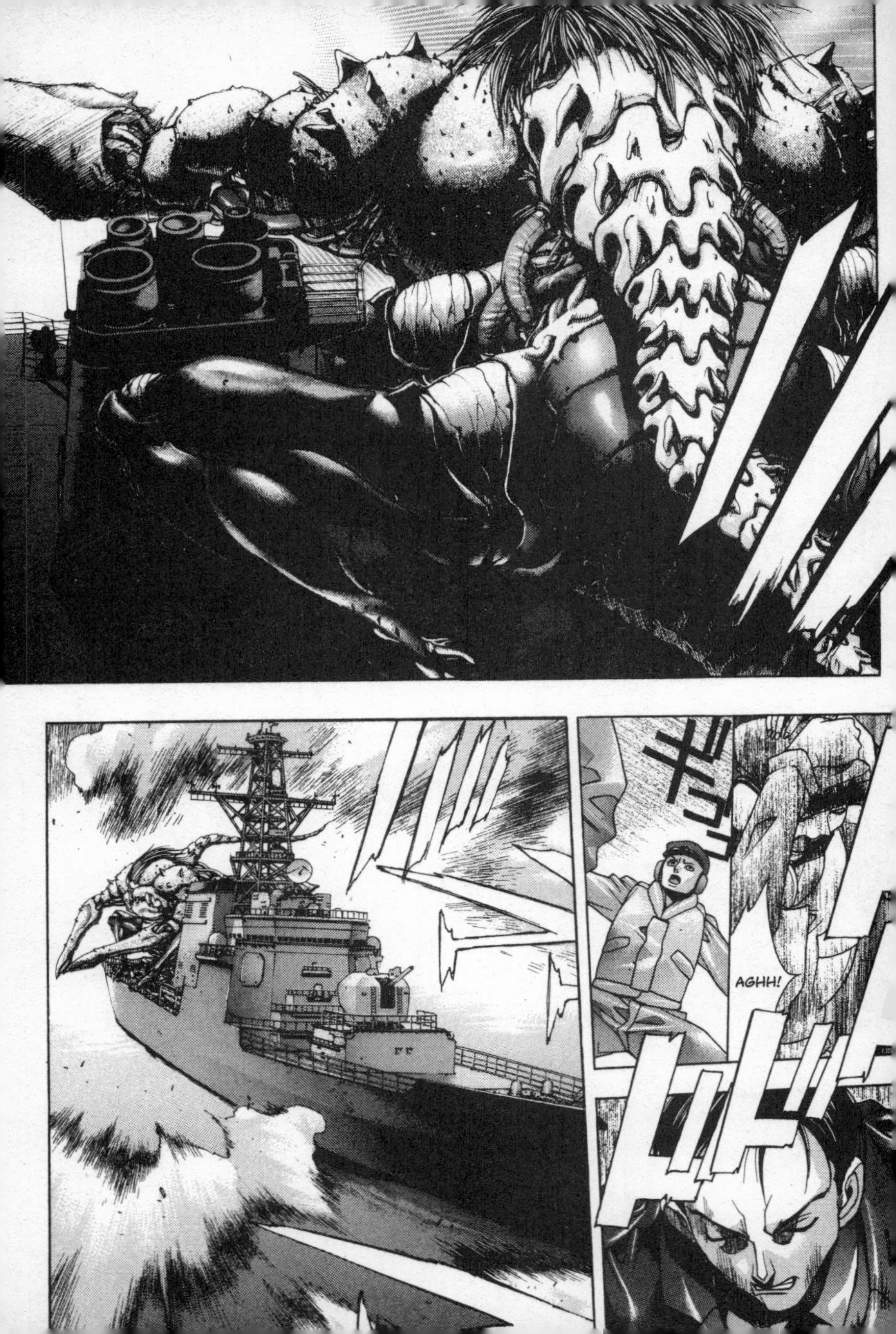
AGHH!

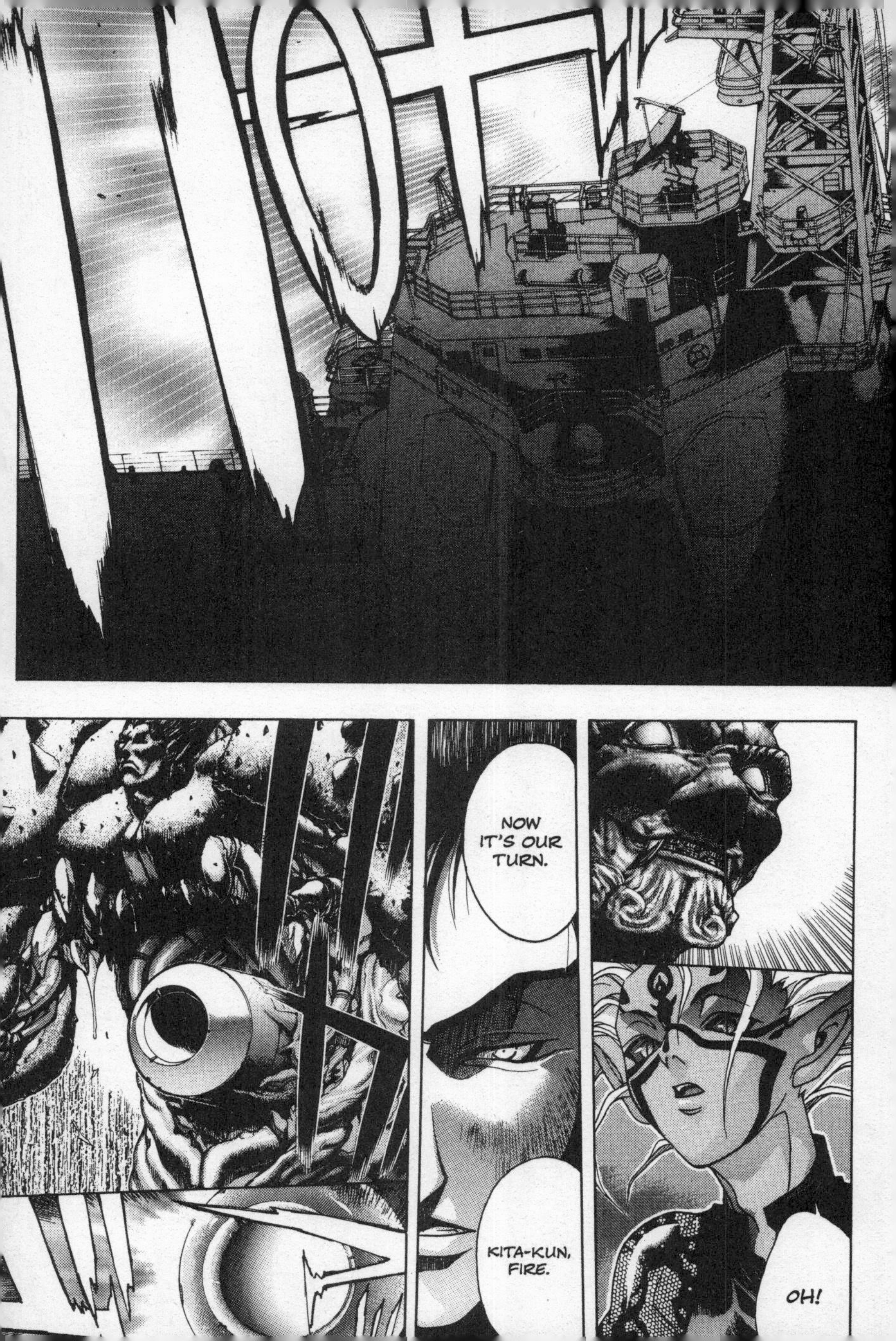
OH!
NOW IT'S OUR TURN.
KITA-KUN, FIRE.

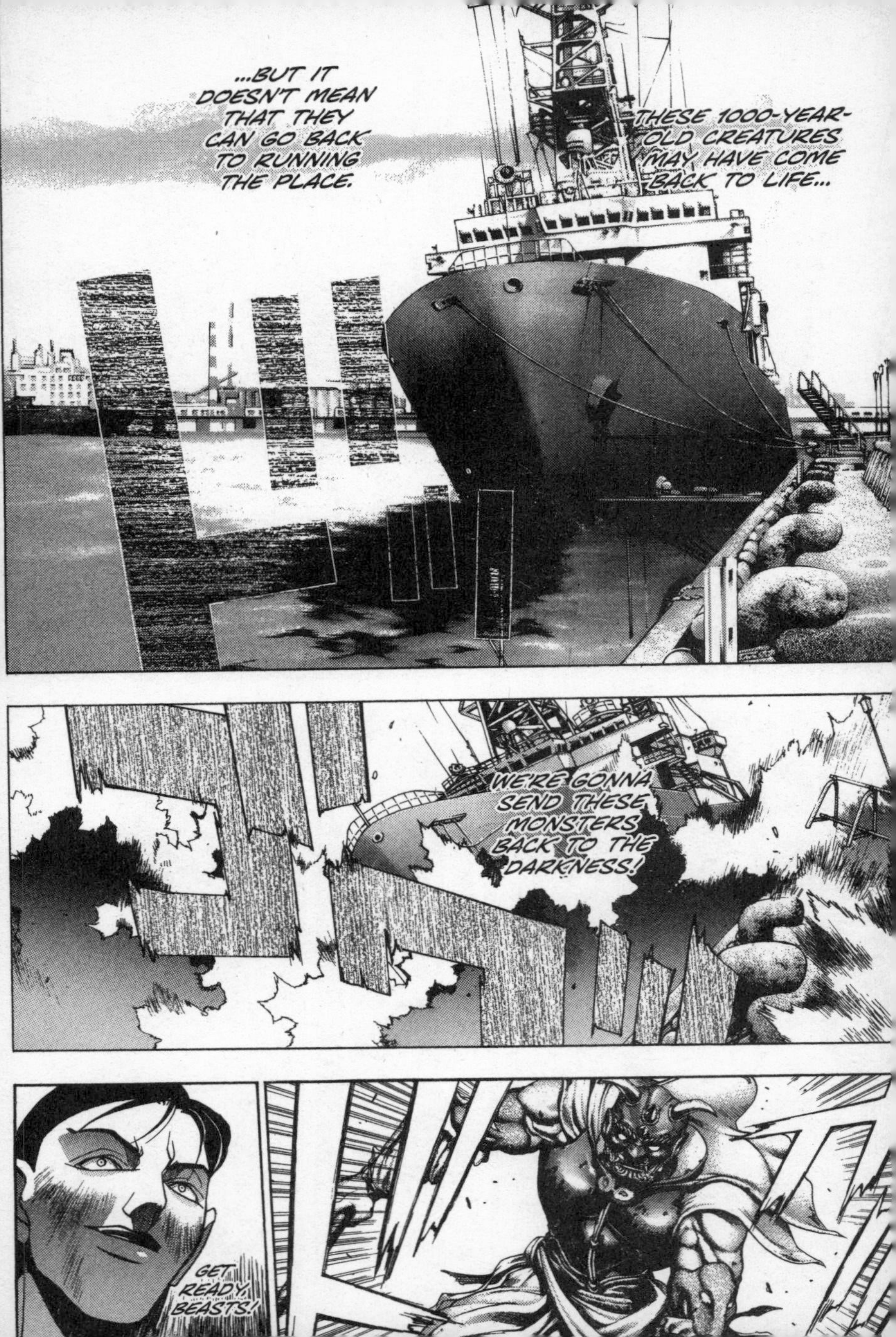
THESE 1000-YEAR-OLD CREATURES MAY HAVE COME BACK TO LIFE...
...BUT IT DOESN'T MEAN THAT THEY CAN GO BACK TO RUNNING THE PLACE.
WE'RE GONNA SEND THESE MONSTERS BACK TO THE DARKNESS!
GET READY, BEASTS!

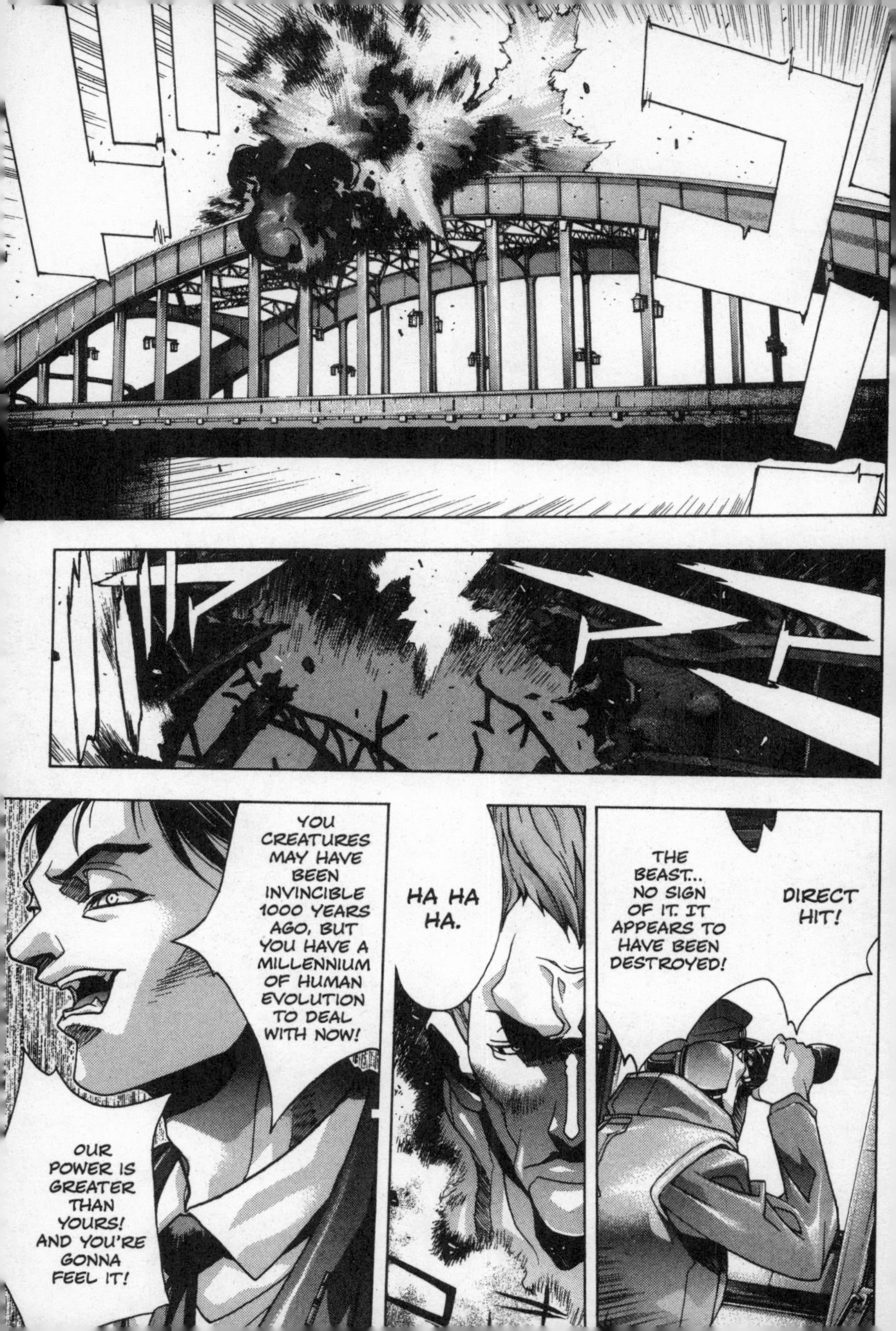
DIRECT HIT!
THE BEAST... NO SIGN OF IT. IT APPEARS TO HAVE BEEN DESTROYED!
HA HA HA.
YOU CREATURES MAY HAVE BEEN INVINCIBLE 1000 YEARS AGO, BUT YOU HAVE A MILLENNIUM OF HUMAN EVOLUTION TO DEAL WITH NOW!
OUR POWER IS GREATER THAN YOURS! AND YOU'RE GONNA FEEL IT!

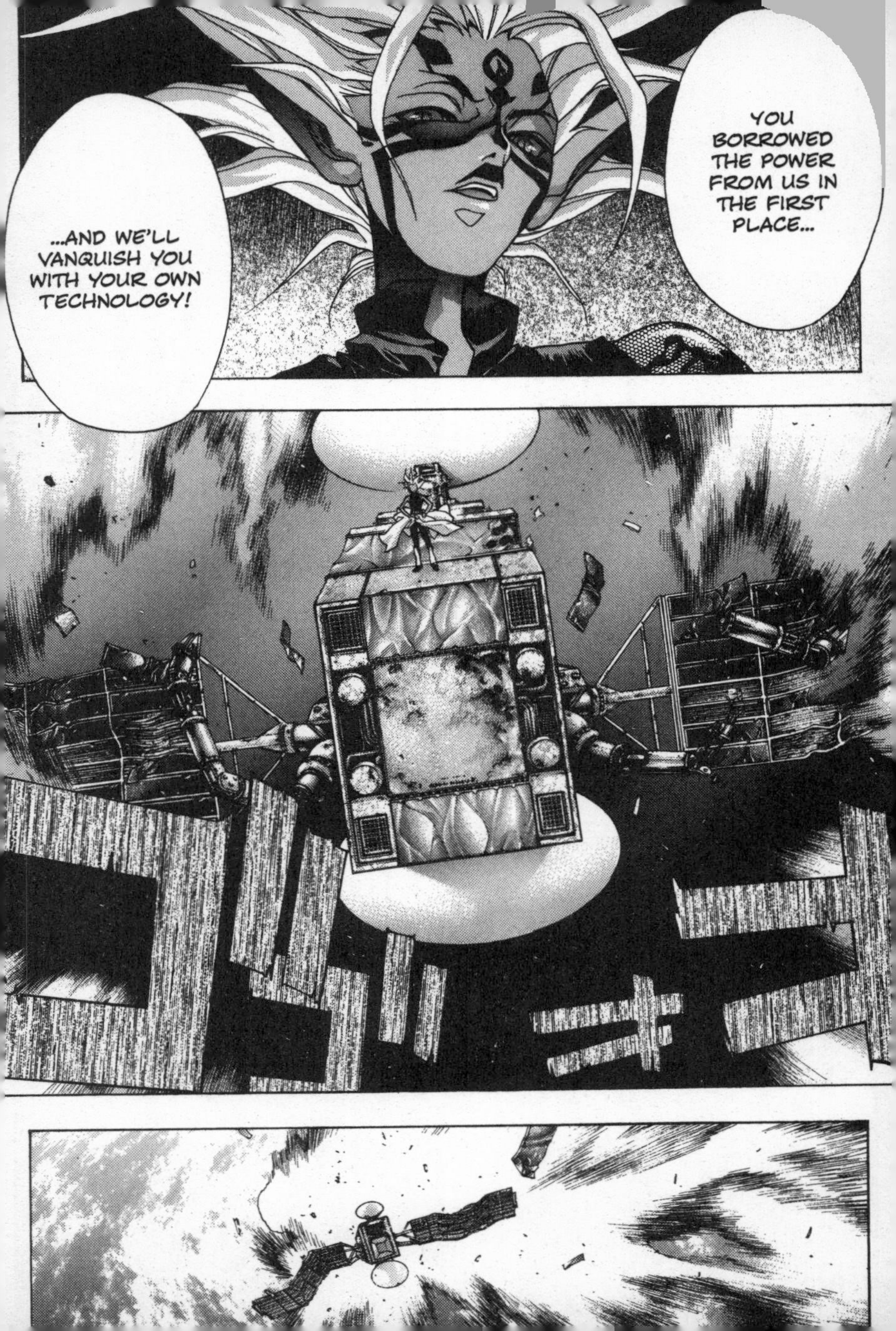
YOU BORROWED THE POWER FROM US IN THE FIRST PLACE...
...AND WE'LL VANQUISH YOU WITH YOUR OWN TECHNOLOGY!

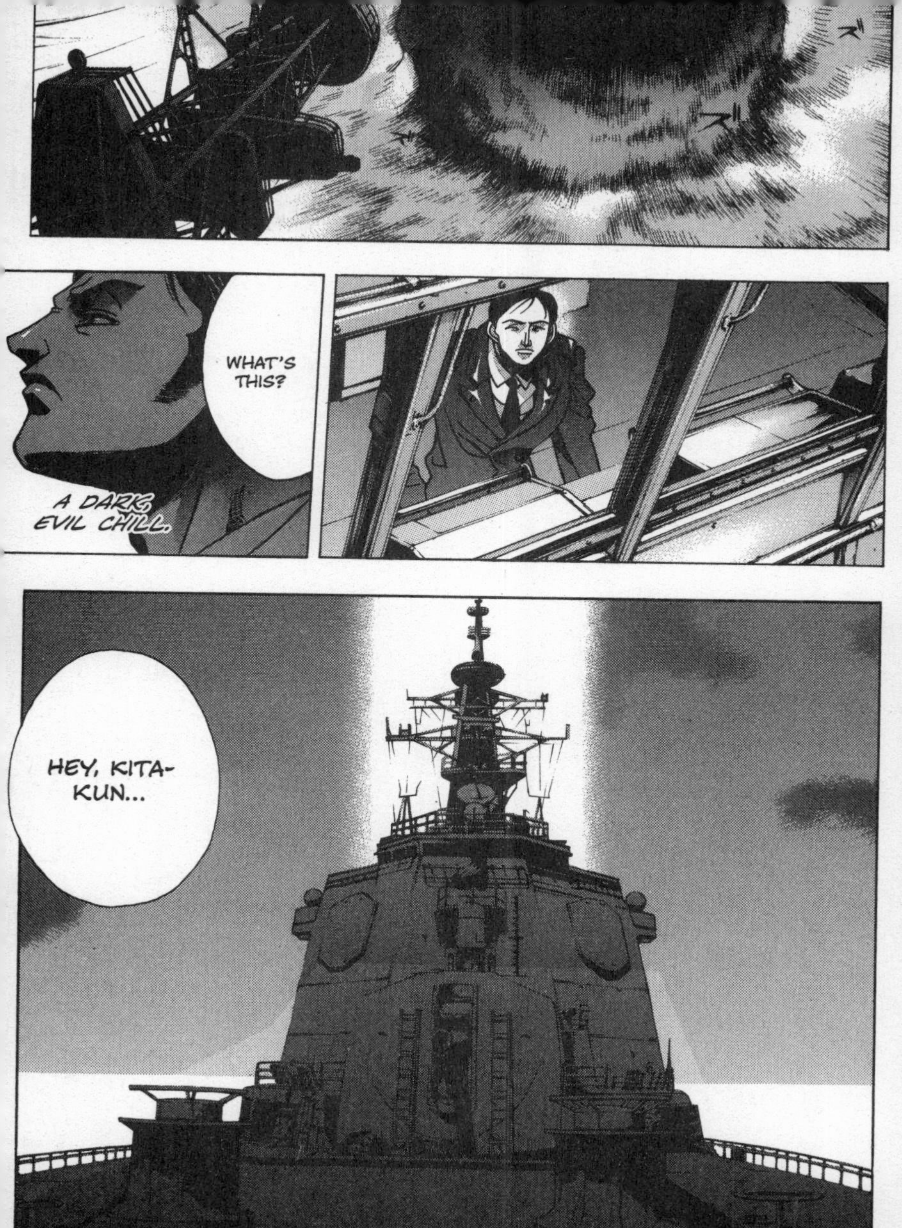
WHAT'S THIS?
A DARK, EVIL CHILL.
HEY, KITA-KUN...

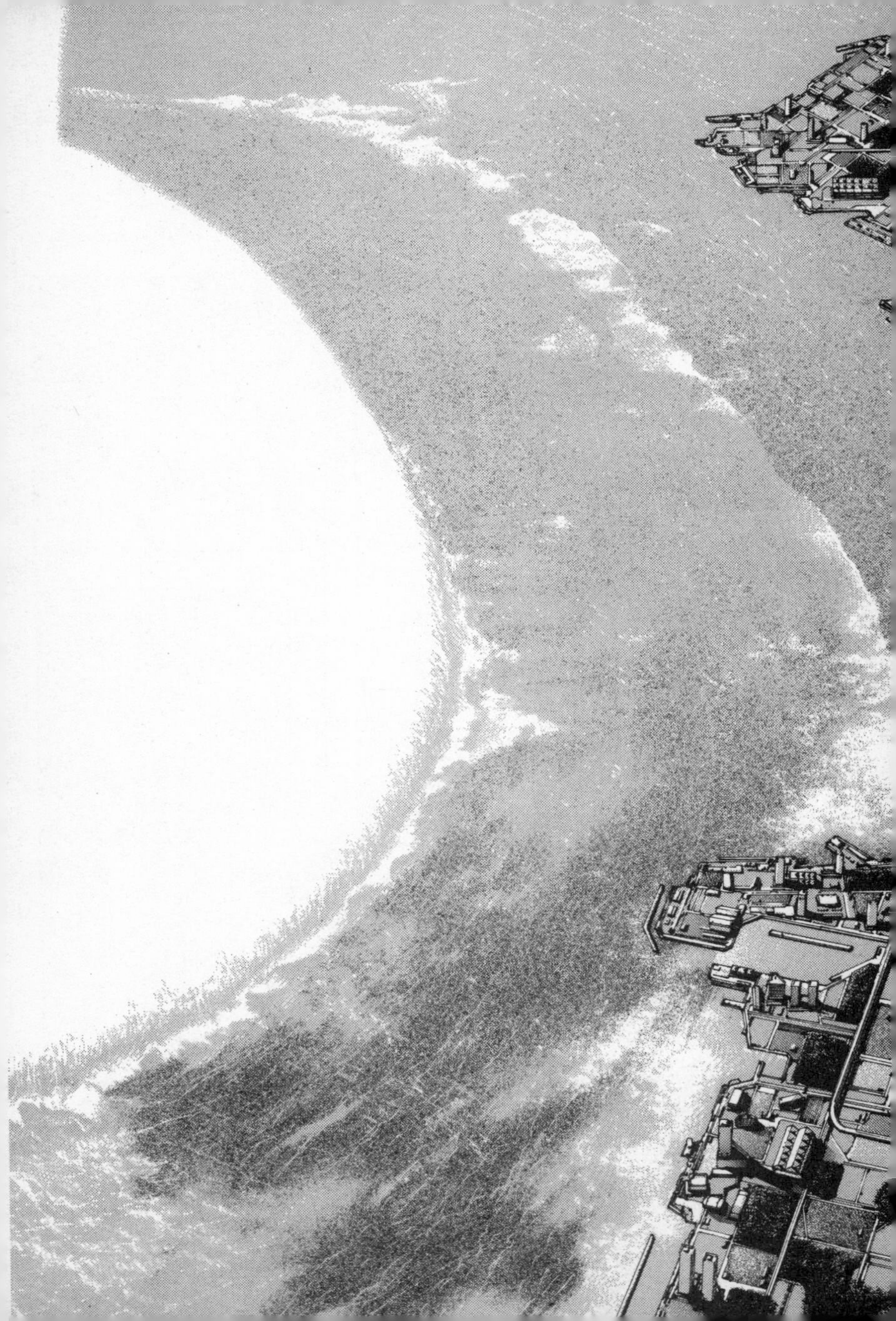

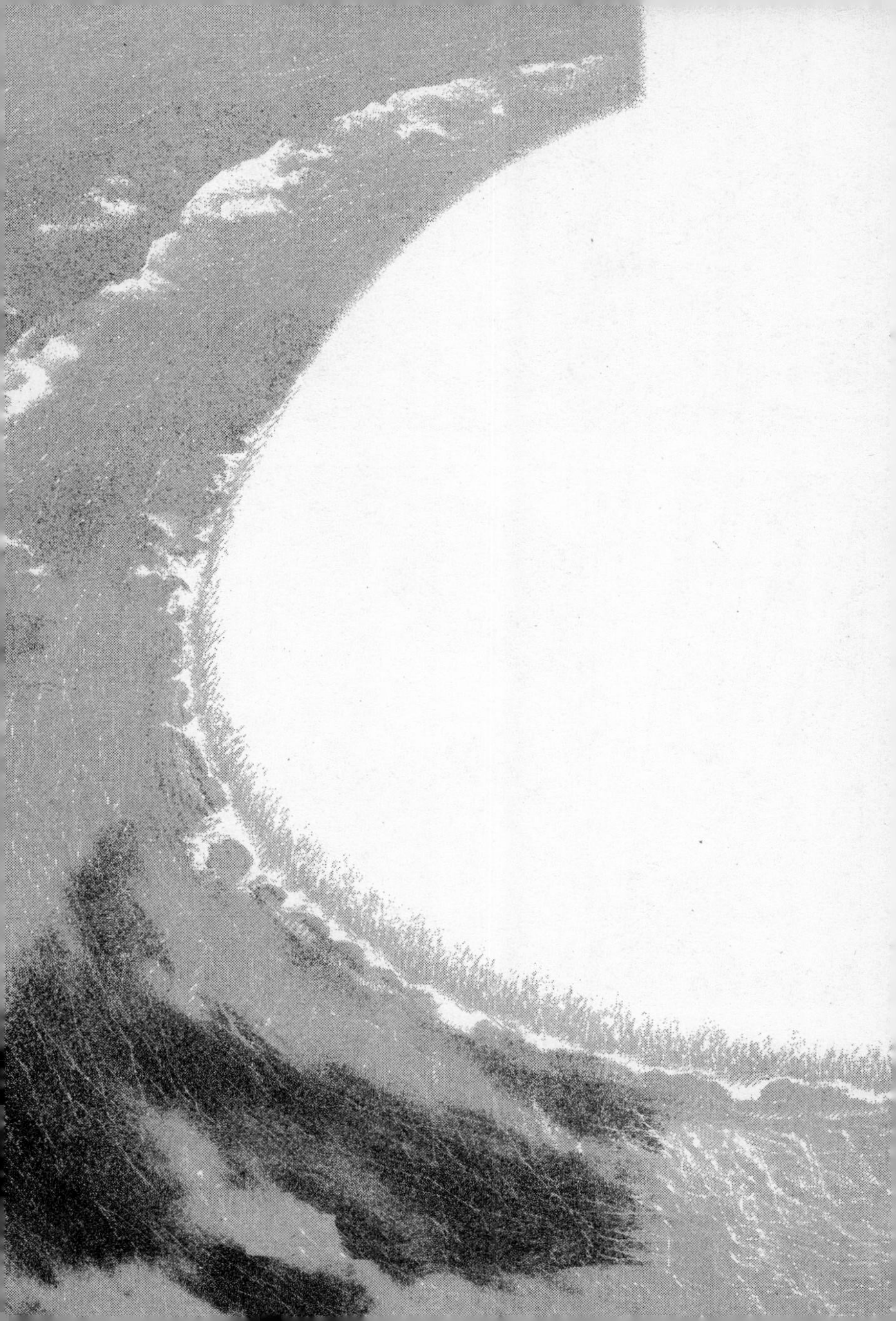

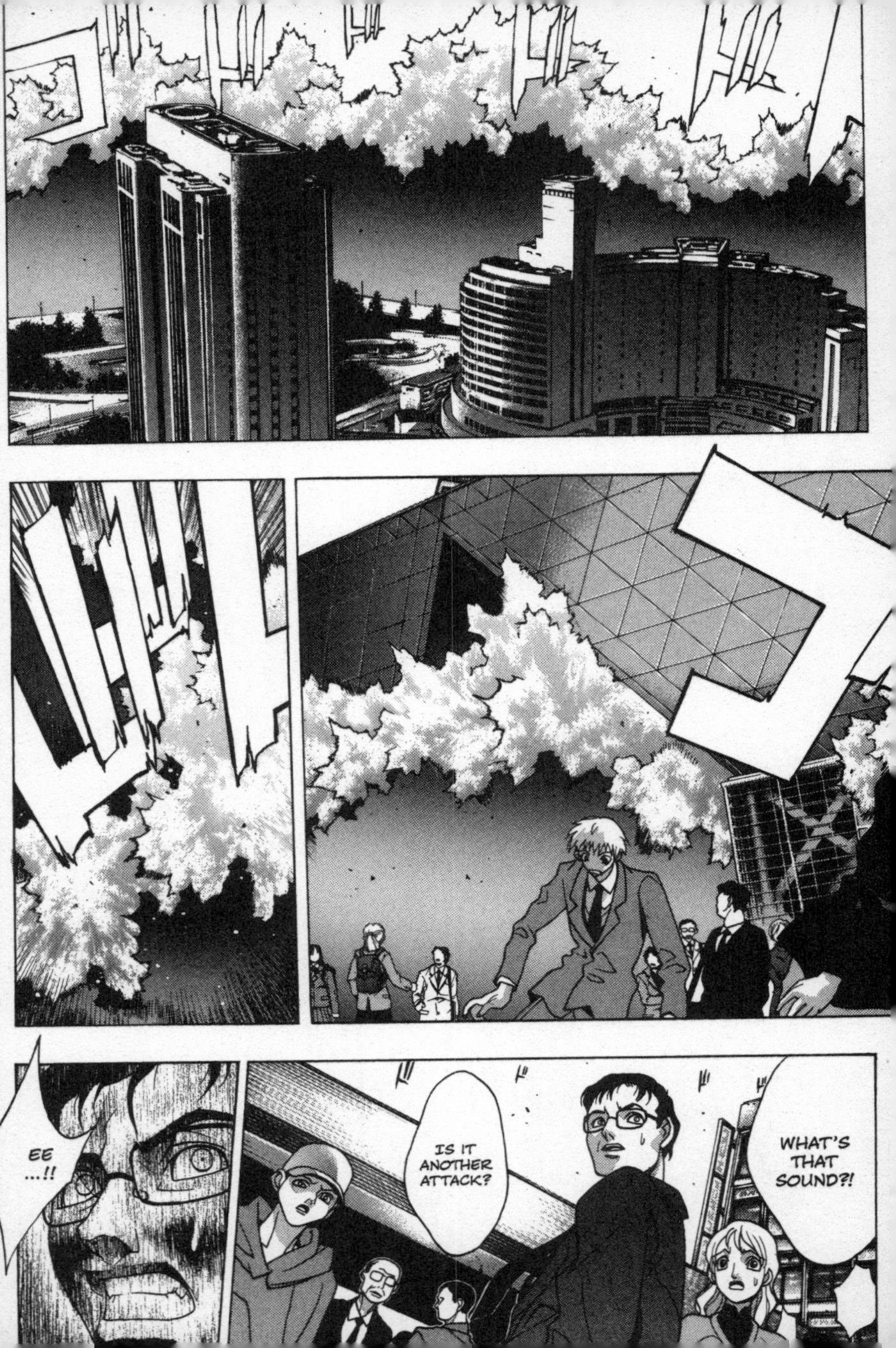
WHAT'S THAT SOUND?!
IS IT ANOTHER ATTACK?
EE ...!!

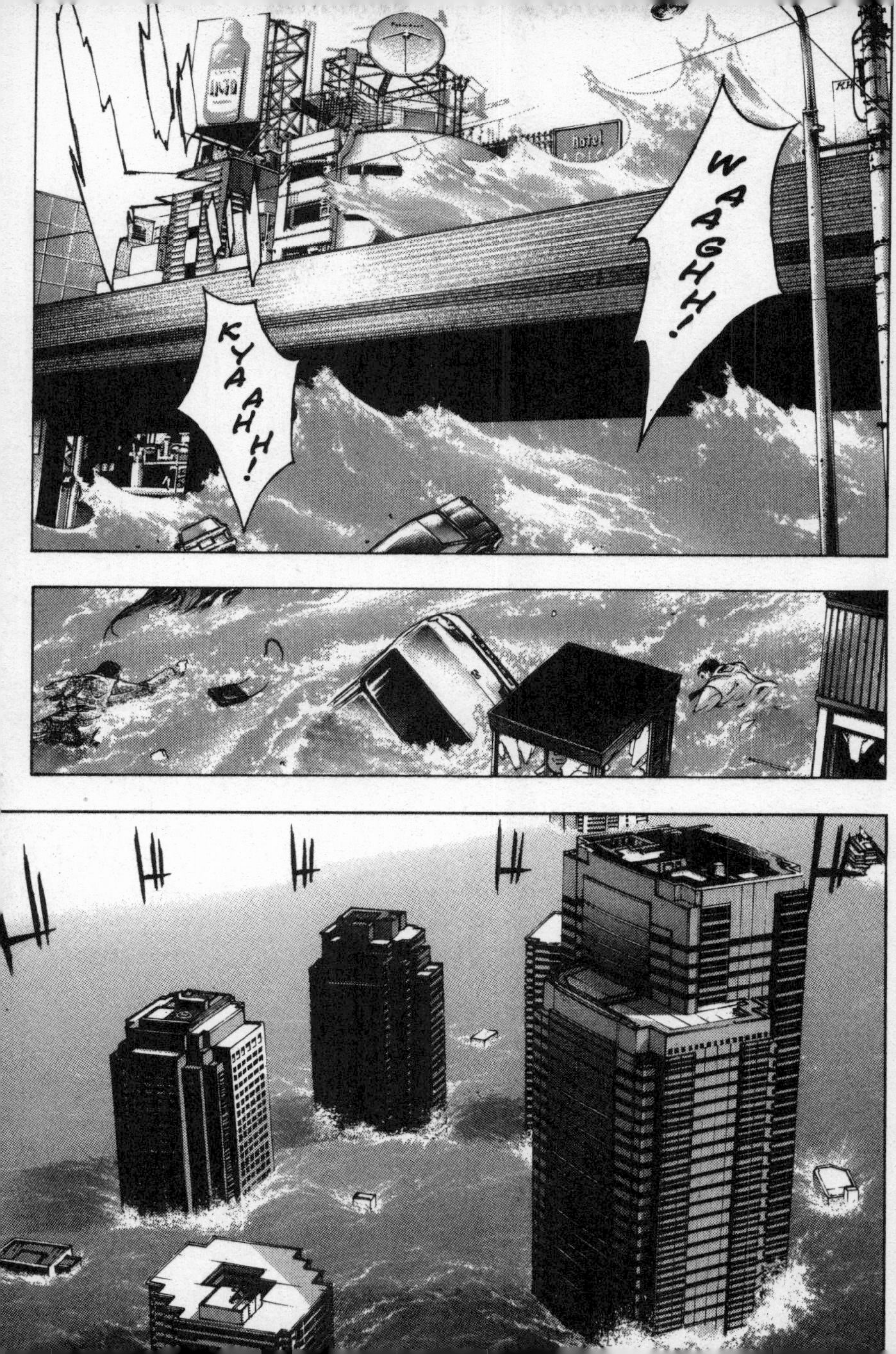
WAAGHH!
KYAAHH!

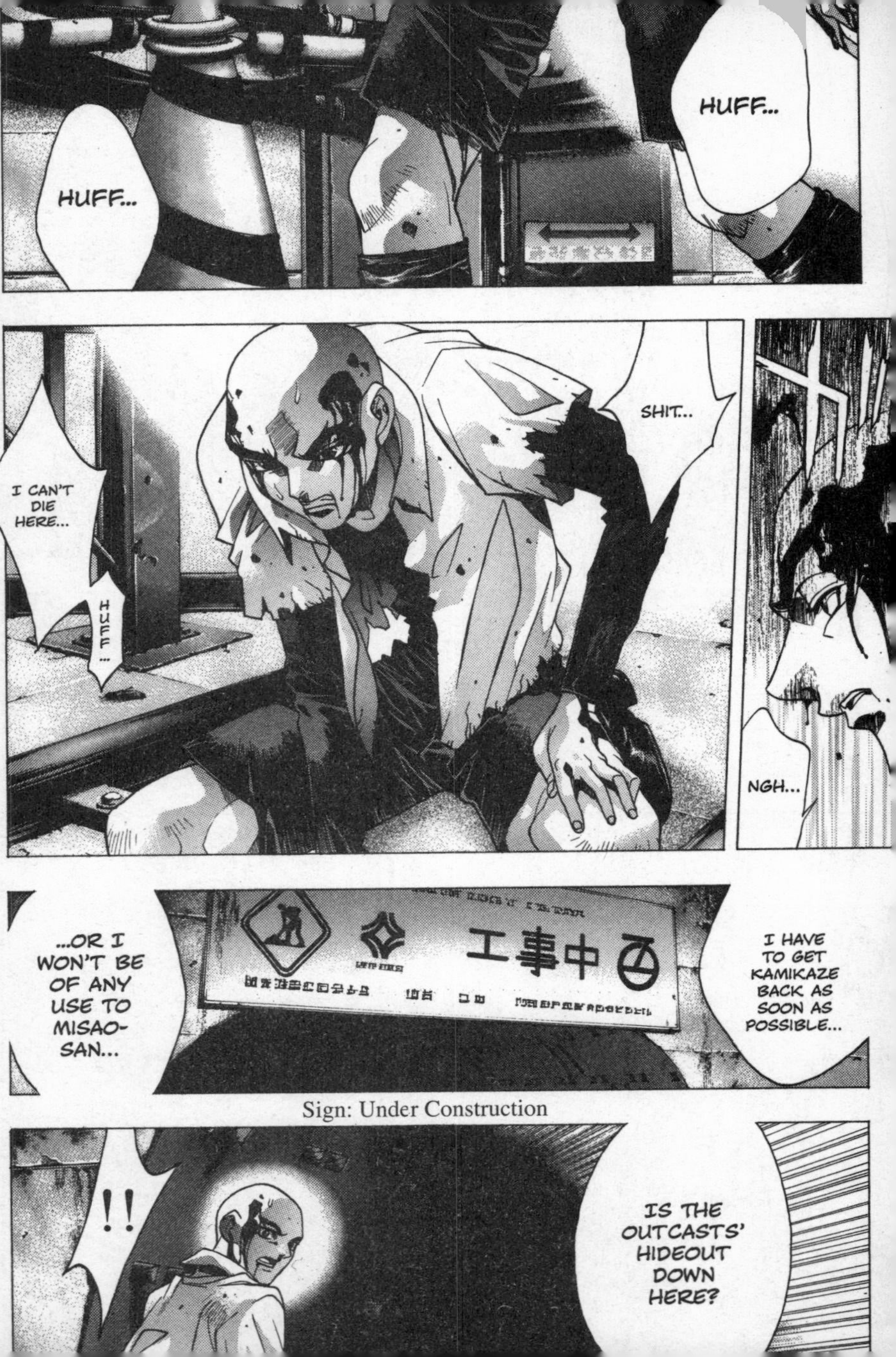
HUFF...
HUFF...
NGH...
SHIT...
I CAN'T DIE HERE...
HUFF HUFF...
I HAVE TO GET KAMIKAZE BACK AS SOON AS POSSIBLE...
...OR I WON'T BE OF ANY USE TO MISAO-SAN...
工事中
IS THE OUTCASTS' HIDEOUT DOWN HERE?
!!
Sign: Under Construction

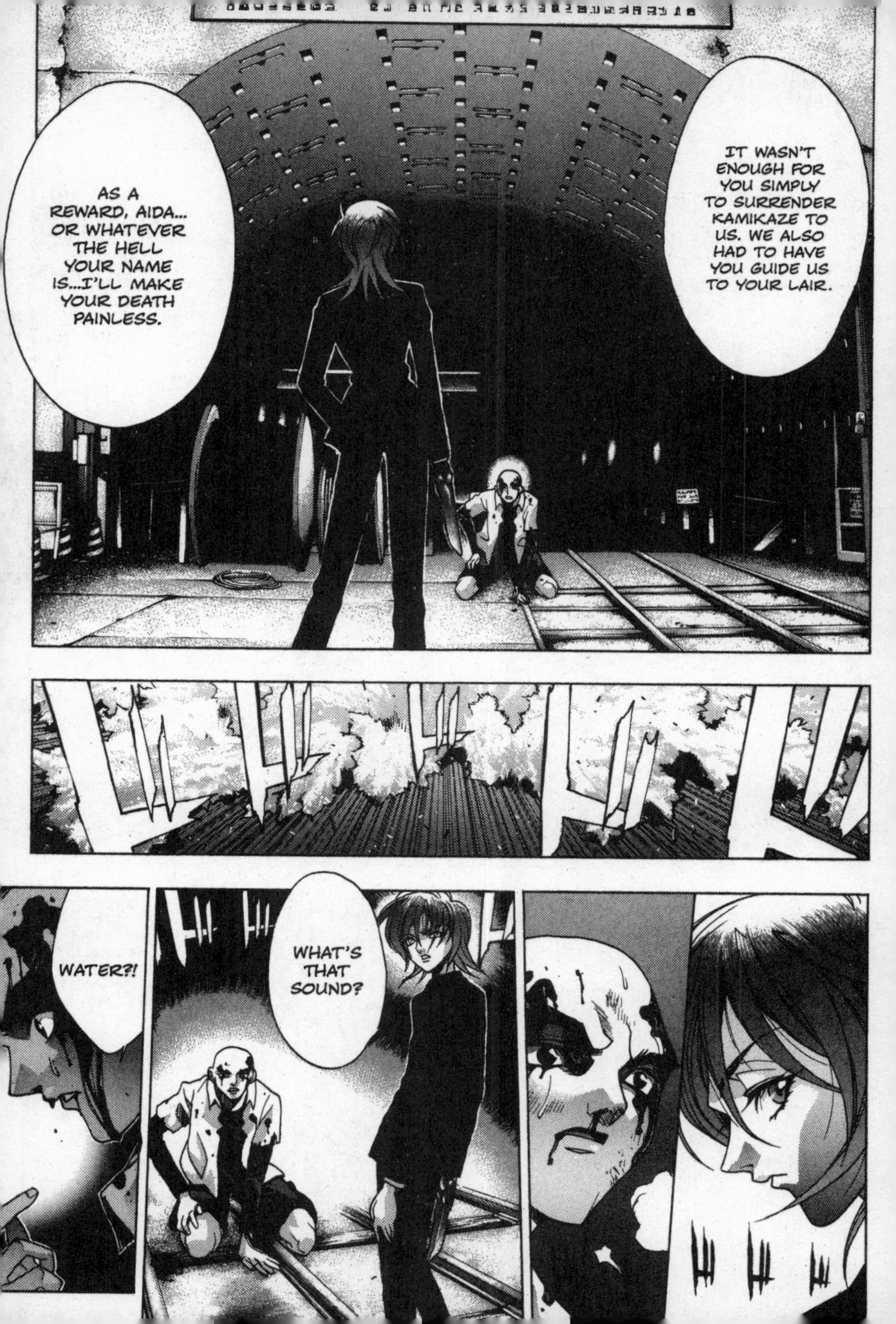
IT WASN'T ENOUGH FOR YOU SIMPLY TO SURRENDER KAMIKAZE TO US. WE ALSO HAD TO HAVE YOU GUIDE US TO YOUR LAIR.
AS A REWARD, AIDA... OR WHATEVER THE HELL YOUR NAME IS...I'LL MAKE YOUR DEATH PAINLESS.
WHAT'S THAT SOUND?
WATER?!

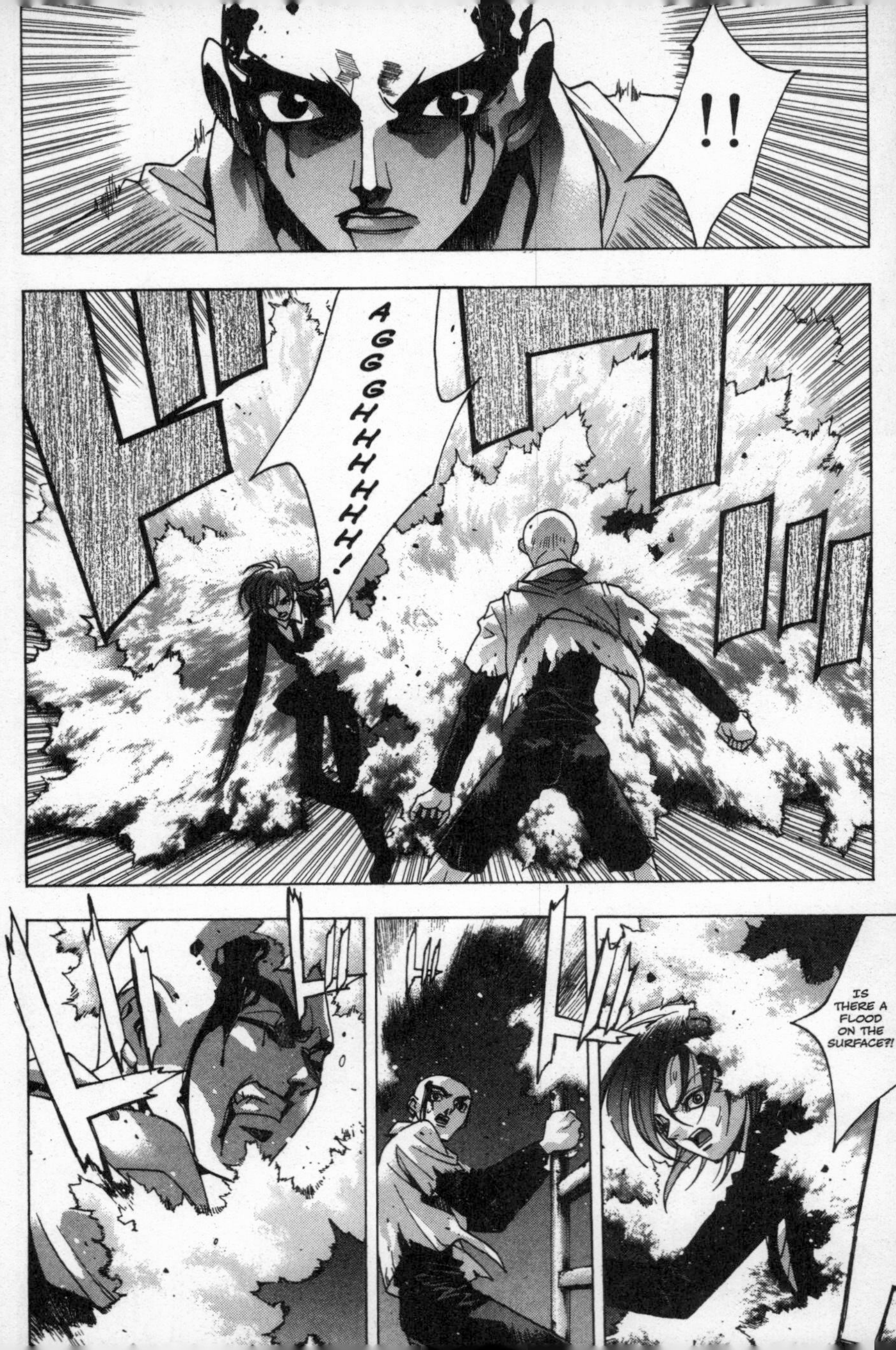
!!
AGGGHHHHHHH!
IS THERE A FLOOD ON THE SURFACE?!

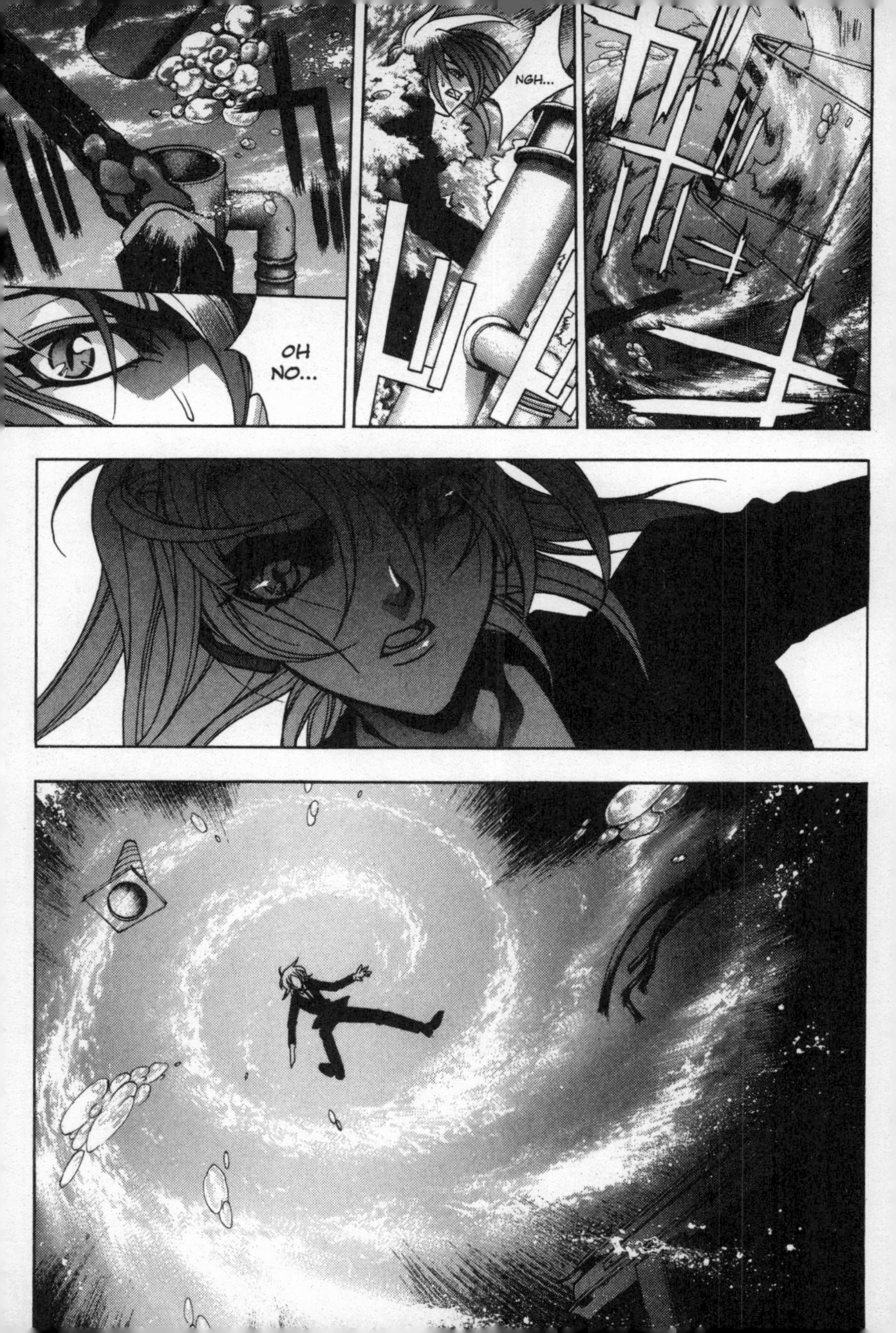
NGH...
OH NO...

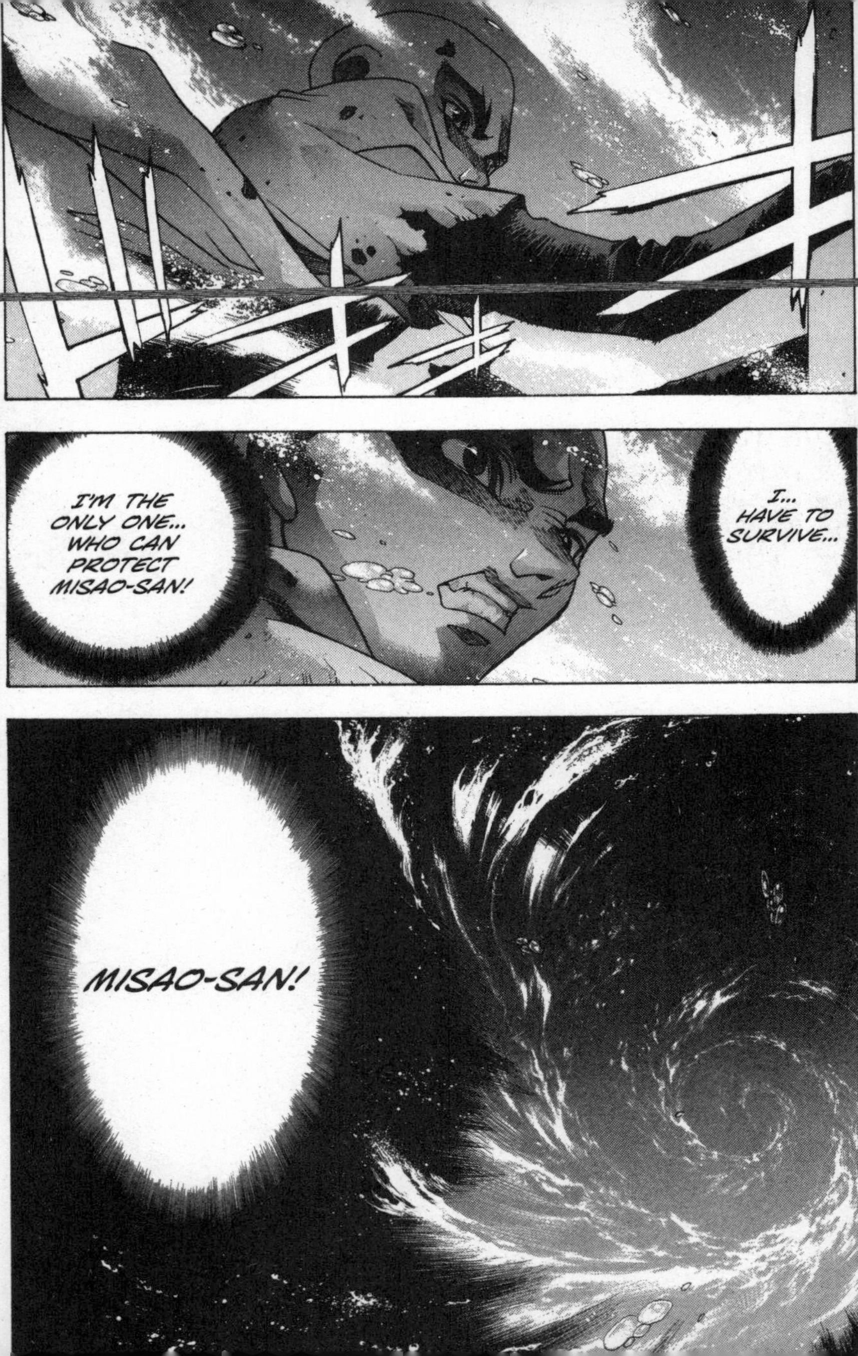
I... HAVE TO SURVIVE...
I'M THE ONLY ONE... WHO CAN PROTECT MISAO-SAN!
MISAO-SAN!

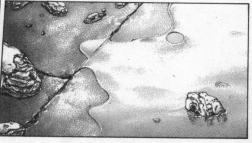

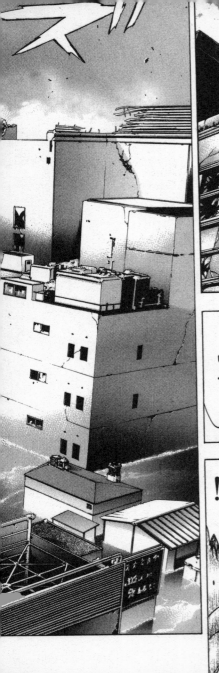

WHAT IS... THIS?

WE'VE ENDURED A GREAT CATAST- ROPHE, BENIGUMA- DONO.

A DISASTROUS TSUNAMI HAS LAID WASTE TO THE CITY.

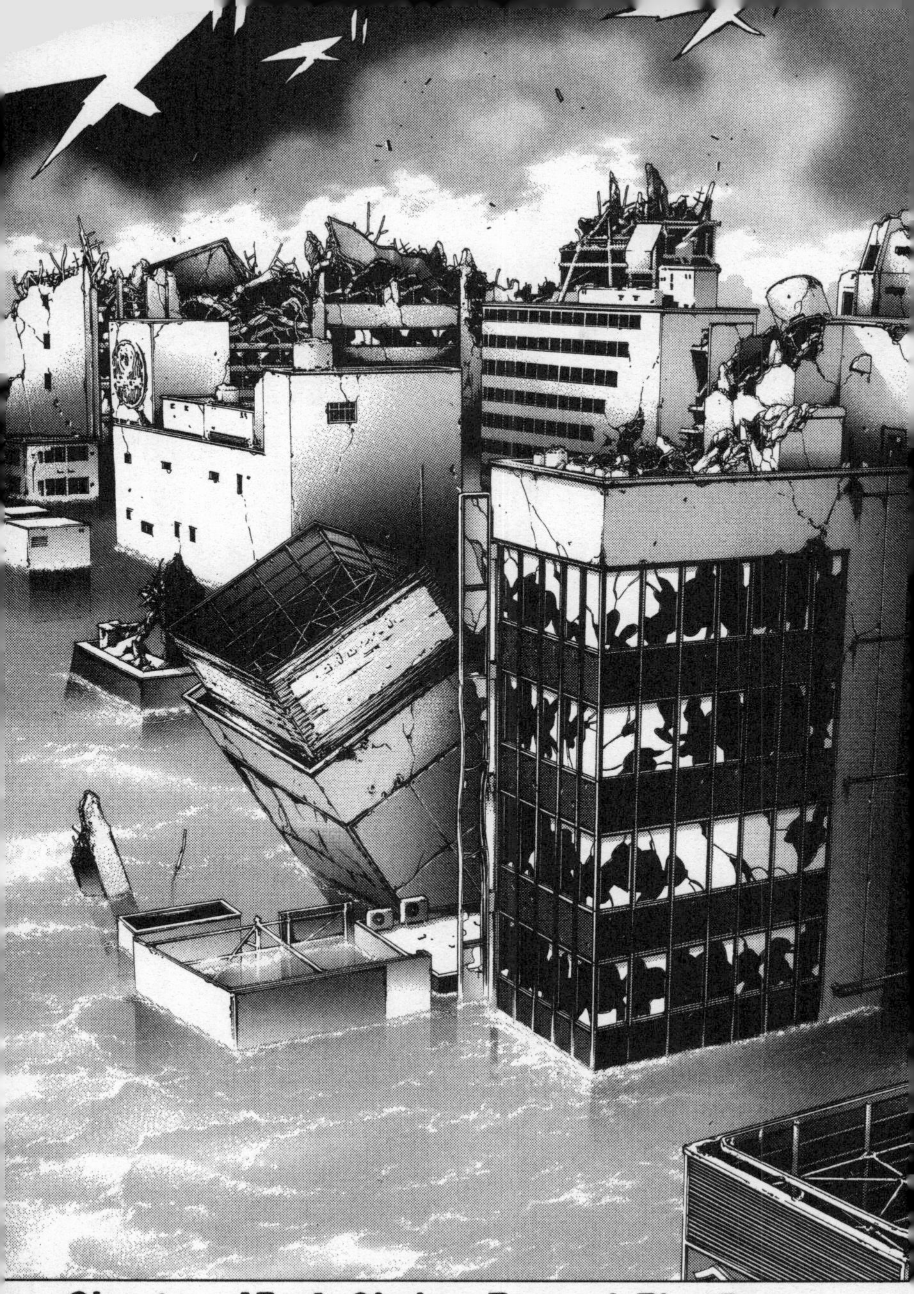

Chapter 45: A Choice Toward The Future

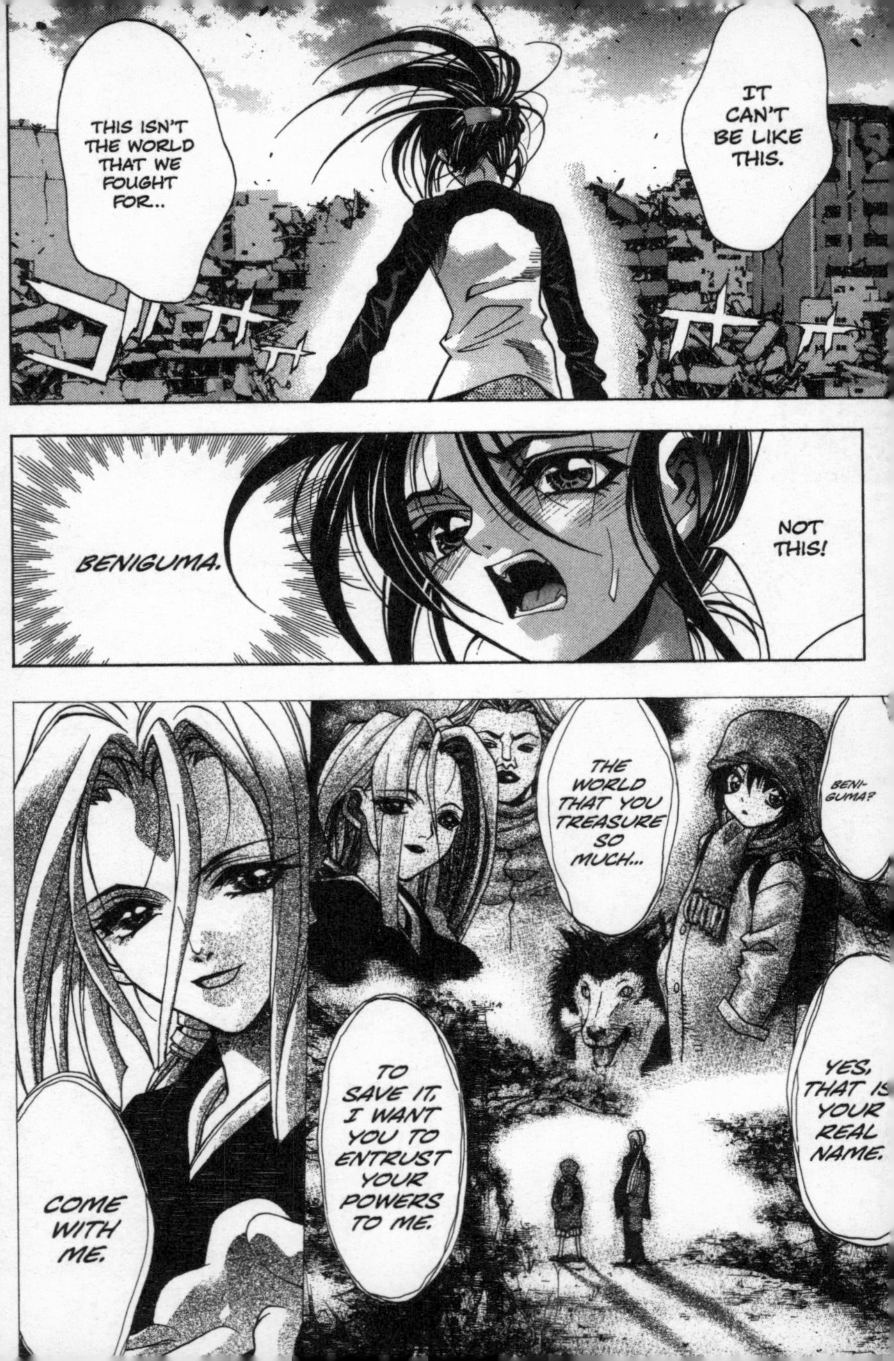
IT CAN'T BE LIKE THIS.
THIS ISN'T THE WORLD THAT WE FOUGHT FOR..
NOT THIS!
BENIGUMA.
BENI-GUMA?
THE WORLD THAT YOU TREASURE SO MUCH...
YES, THAT IS YOUR REAL NAME.
TO SAVE IT, I WANT YOU TO ENTRUST YOUR POWERS TO ME.
COME WITH ME.

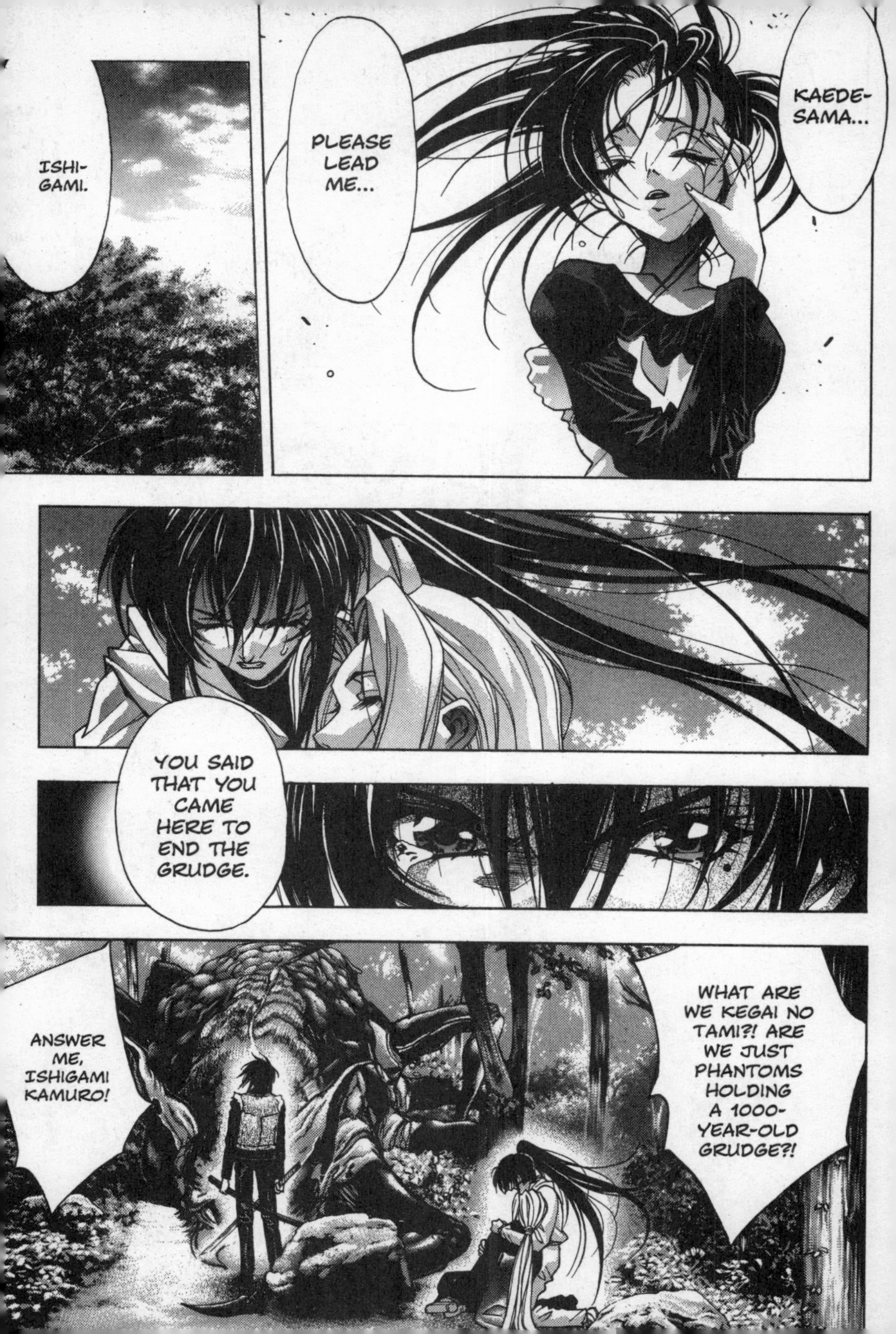
KAEDE-SAMA...
PLEASE LEAD ME...
ISHIGAMI.
YOU SAID THAT YOU CAME HERE TO END THE GRUDGE.
WHAT ARE WE KEGAI NO TAMI?! ARE WE JUST PHANTOMS HOLDING A 1000-YEAR-OLD GRUDGE?!
ANSWER ME, ISHIGAMI KAMURO!

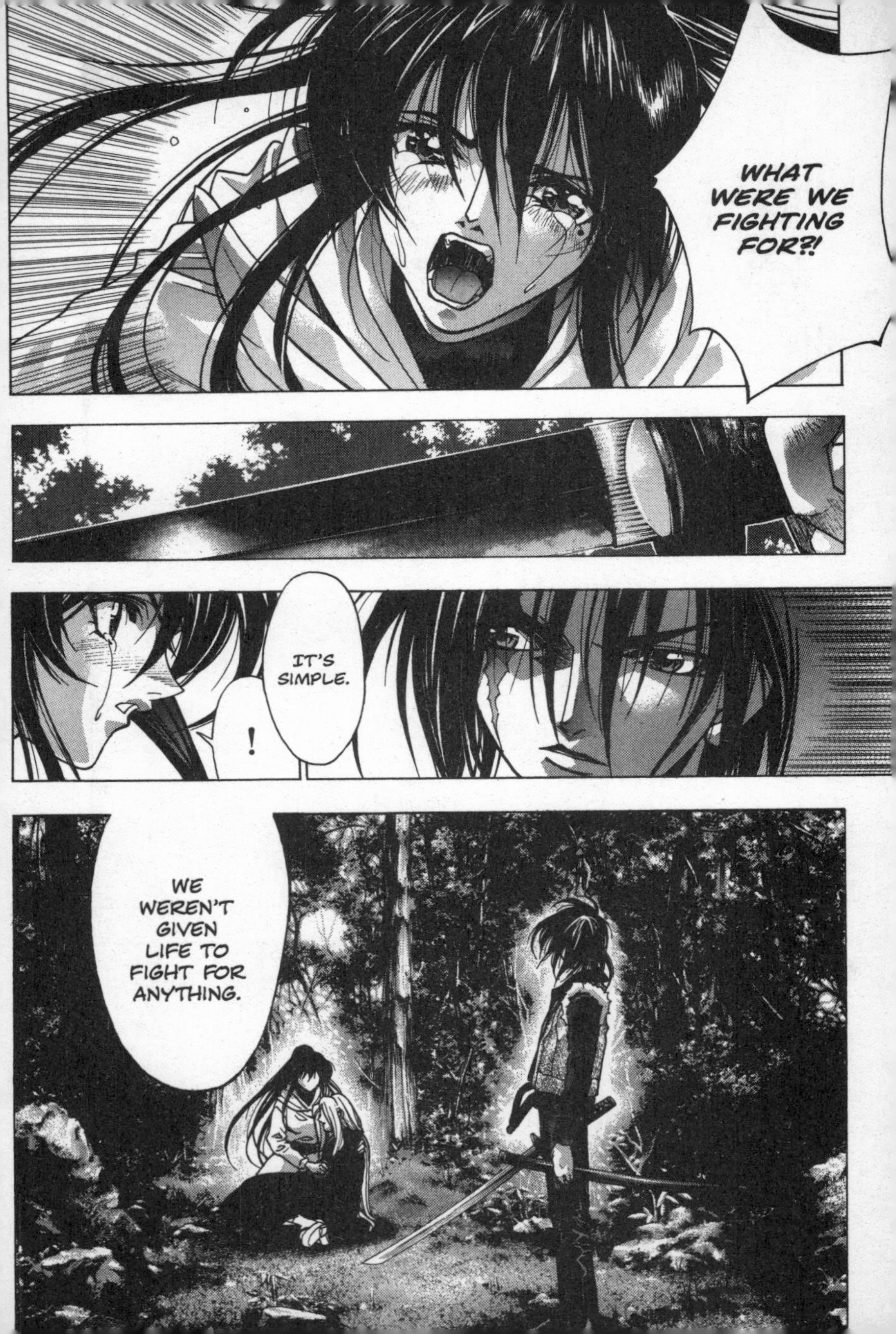
WHAT WERE WE FIGHTING FOR?!
IT'S SIMPLE.
!
WE WEREN'T GIVEN LIFE TO FIGHT FOR ANYTHING.

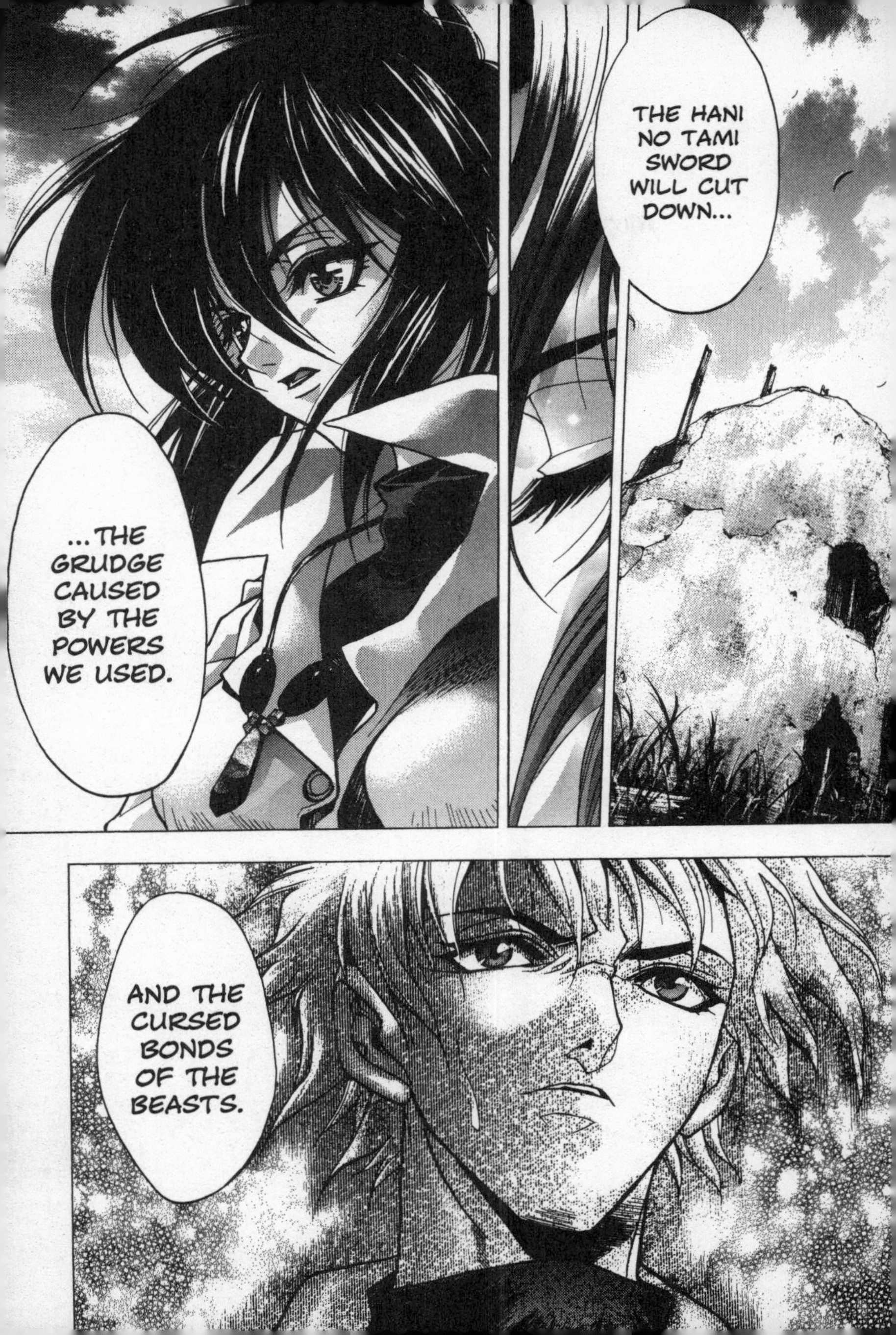
THE HANI NO TAMI SWORD WILL CUT DOWN...
...THE GRUDGE CAUSED BY THE POWERS WE USED.
AND THE CURSED BONDS OF THE BEASTS.

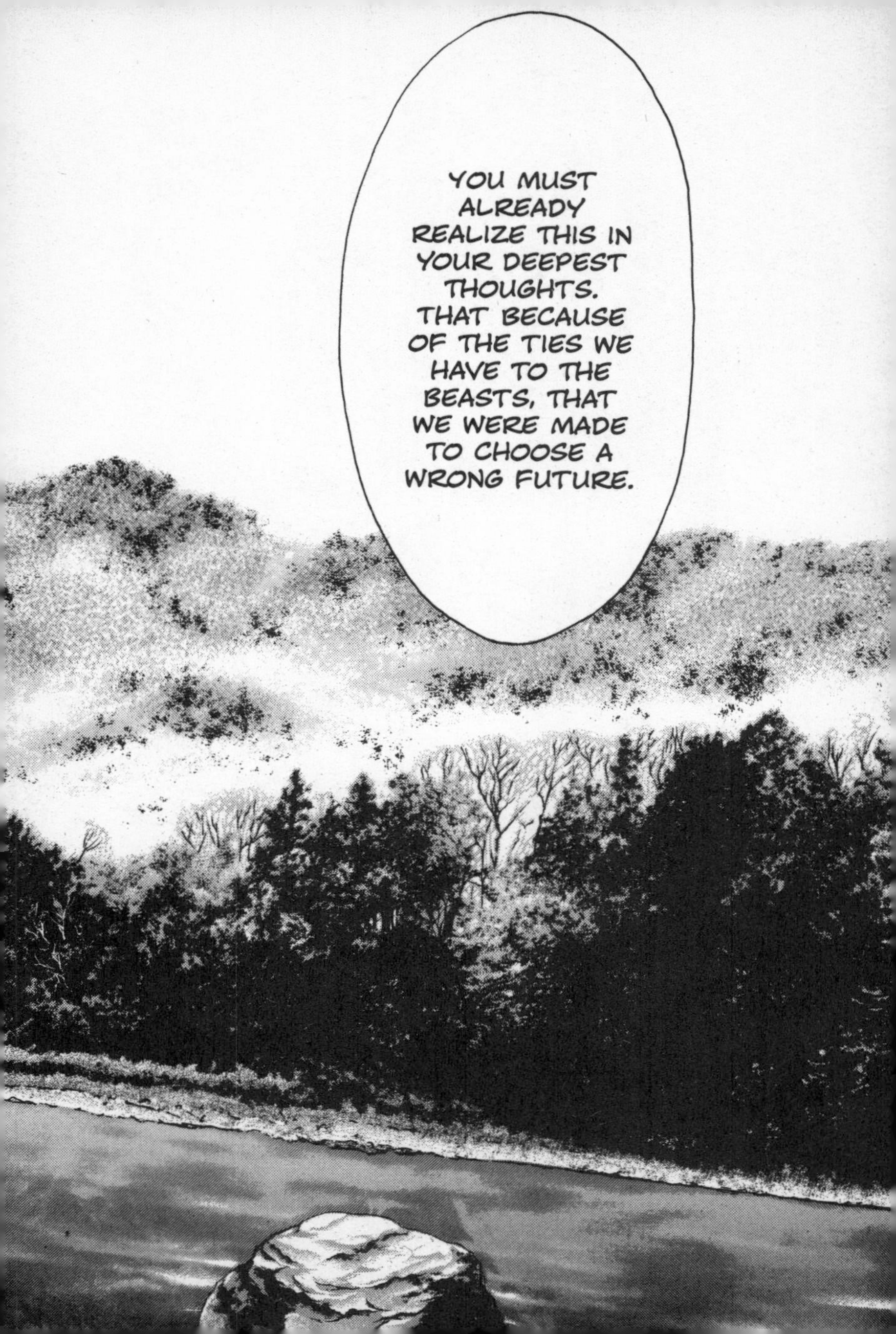
YOU MUST ALREADY REALIZE THIS IN YOUR DEEPEST THOUGHTS. THAT BECAUSE OF THE TIES WE HAVE TO THE BEASTS, THAT WE WERE MADE TO CHOOSE A WRONG FUTURE.

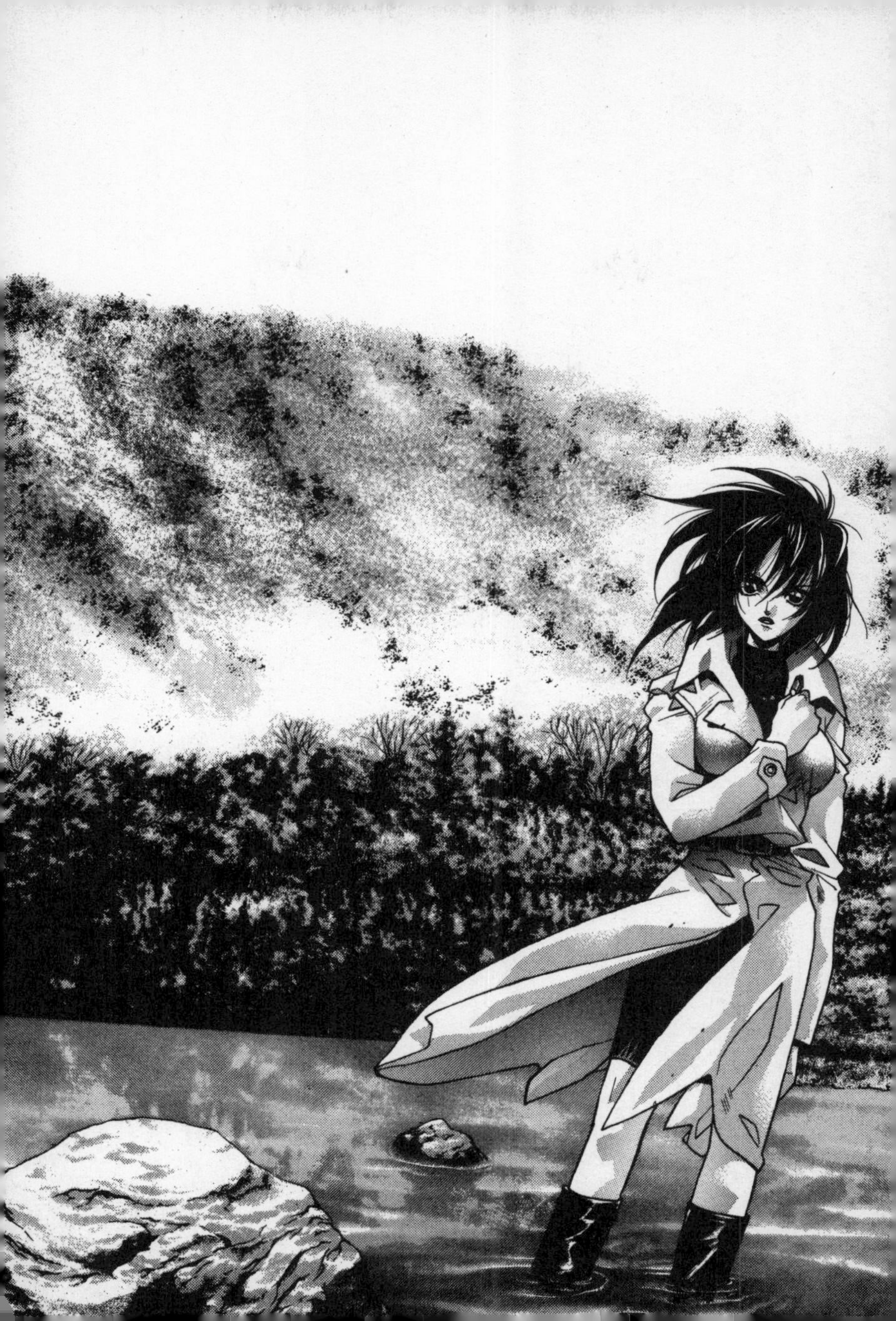

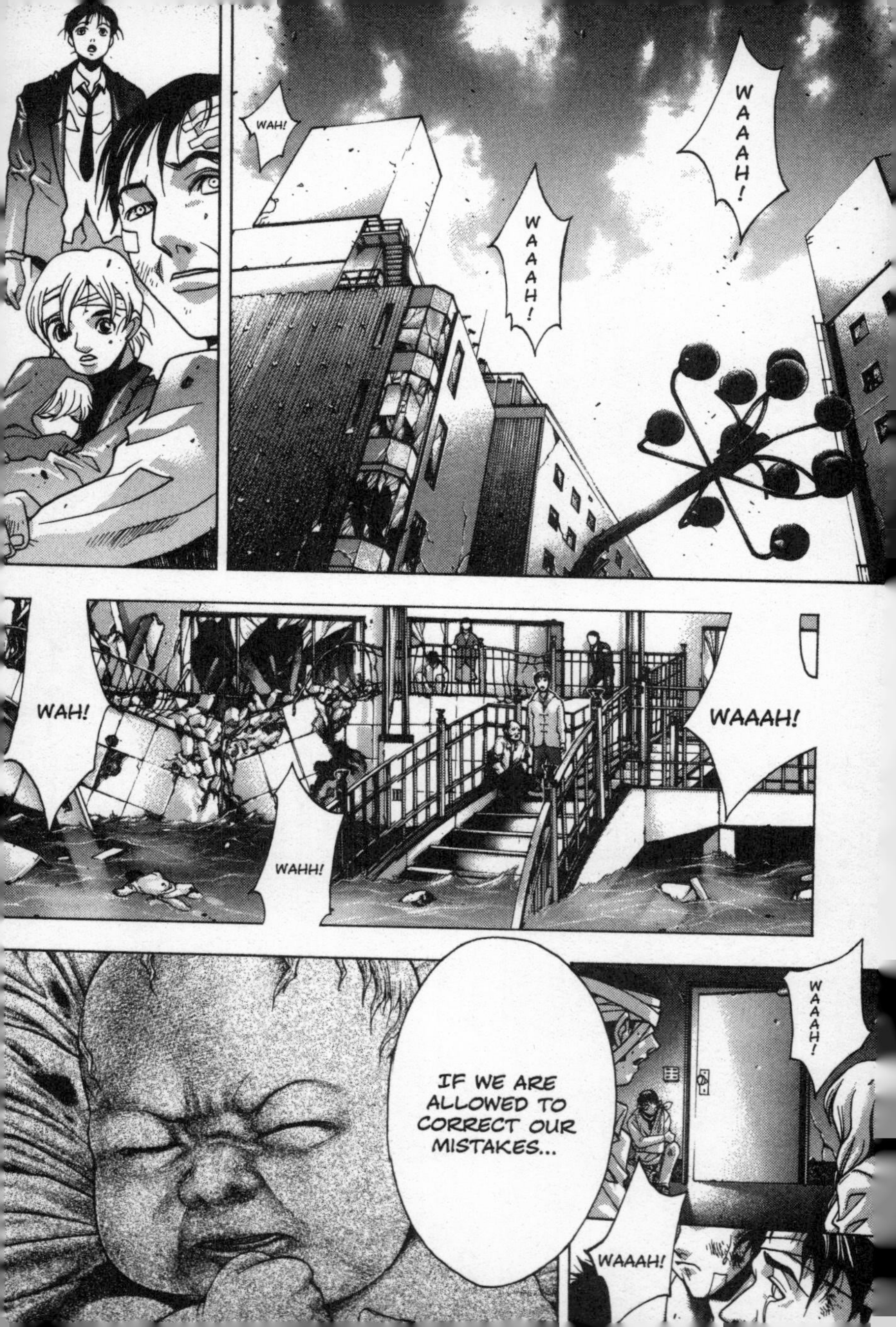
WAAAAH!
WAAAAH!
WAH!
WAAAH!
WAHH!
WAH!
WAAAAH!
WAAAH!
IF WE ARE ALLOWED TO CORRECT OUR MISTAKES...

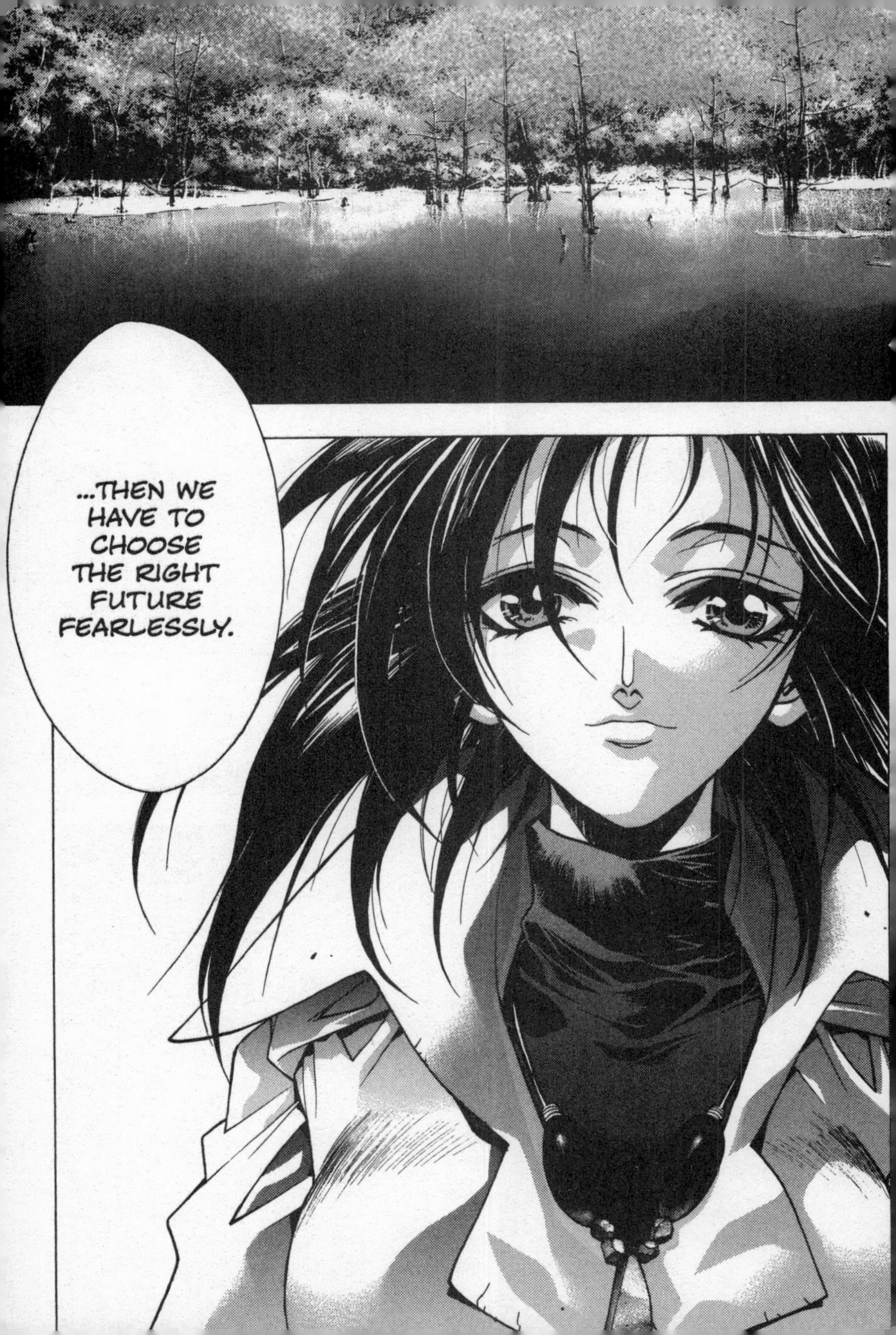
...THEN WE HAVE TO CHOOSE THE RIGHT FUTURE FEARLESSLY.

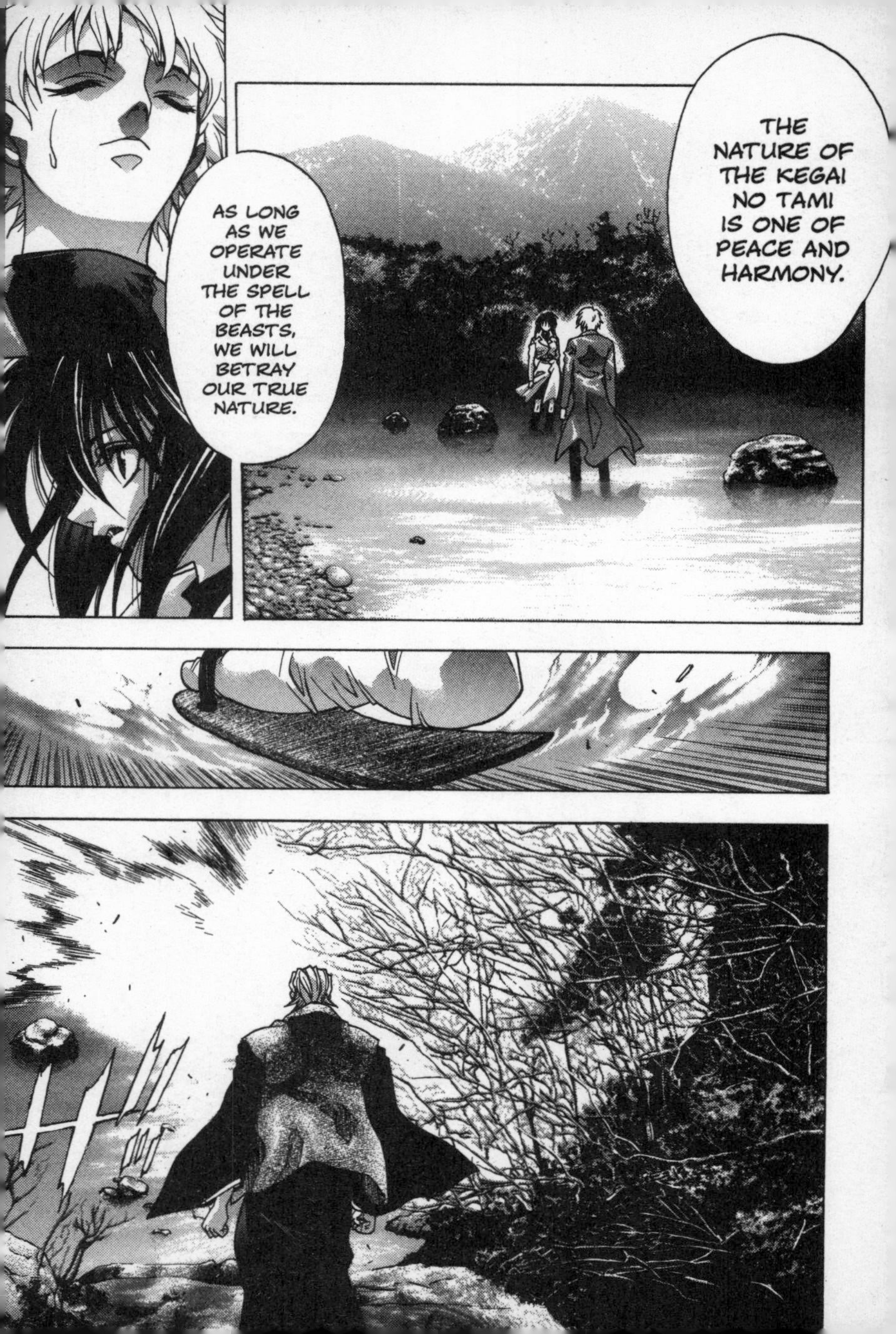
THE NATURE OF THE KEGAI NO TAMI IS ONE OF PEACE AND HARMONY.
AS LONG AS WE OPERATE UNDER THE SPELL OF THE BEASTS, WE WILL BETRAY OUR TRUE NATURE.

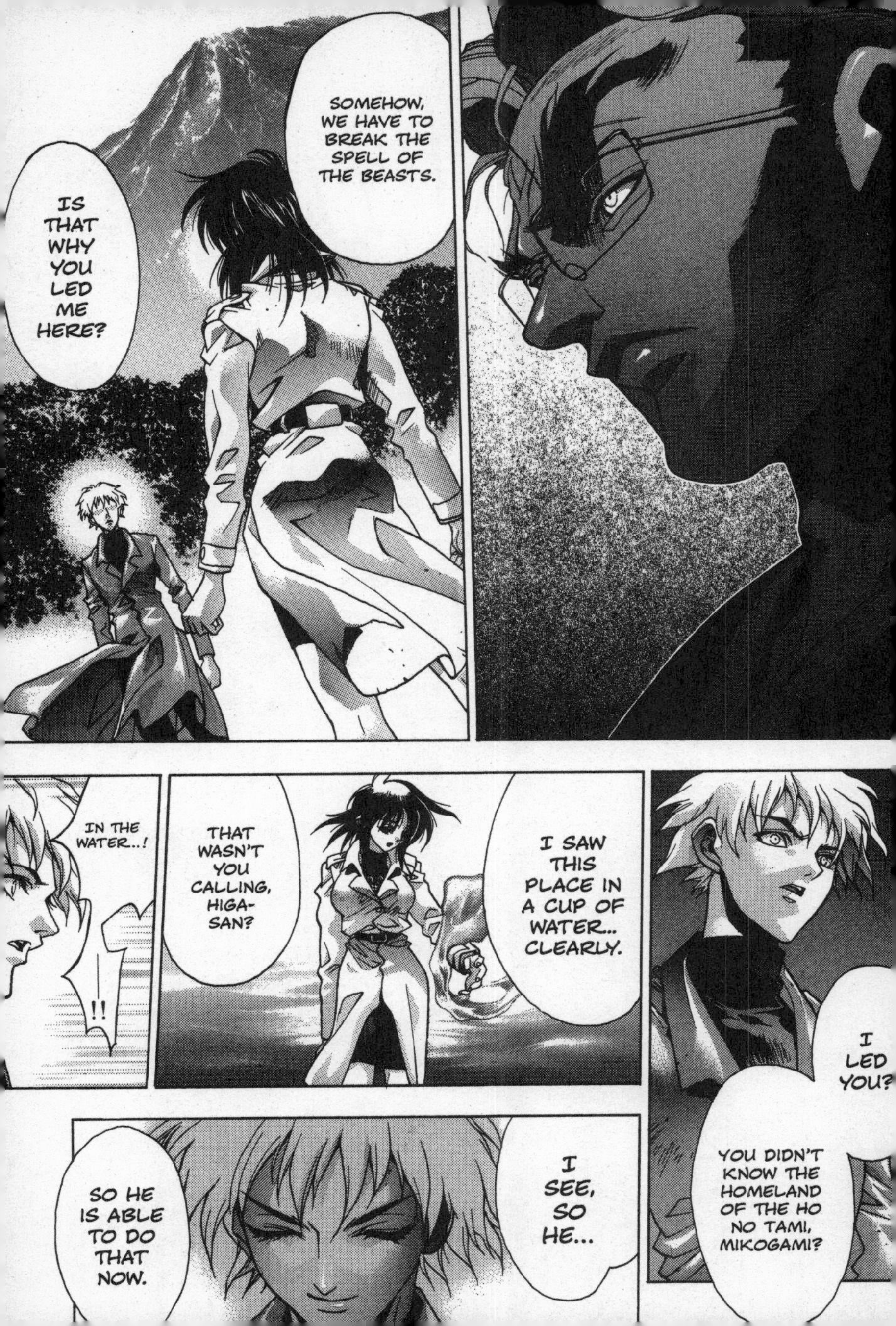
SOMEHOW, WE HAVE TO BREAK THE SPELL OF THE BEASTS.
IS THAT WHY YOU LED ME HERE?
I LED YOU?
YOU DIDN'T KNOW THE HOMELAND OF THE HO NO TAMI, MIKOGAMI?
I SAW THIS PLACE IN A CUP OF WATER.. CLEARLY.
THAT WASN'T YOU CALLING, HIGA-SAN?
IN THE WATER..!
!!
I SEE, SO HE...
SO HE IS ABLE TO DO THAT NOW.

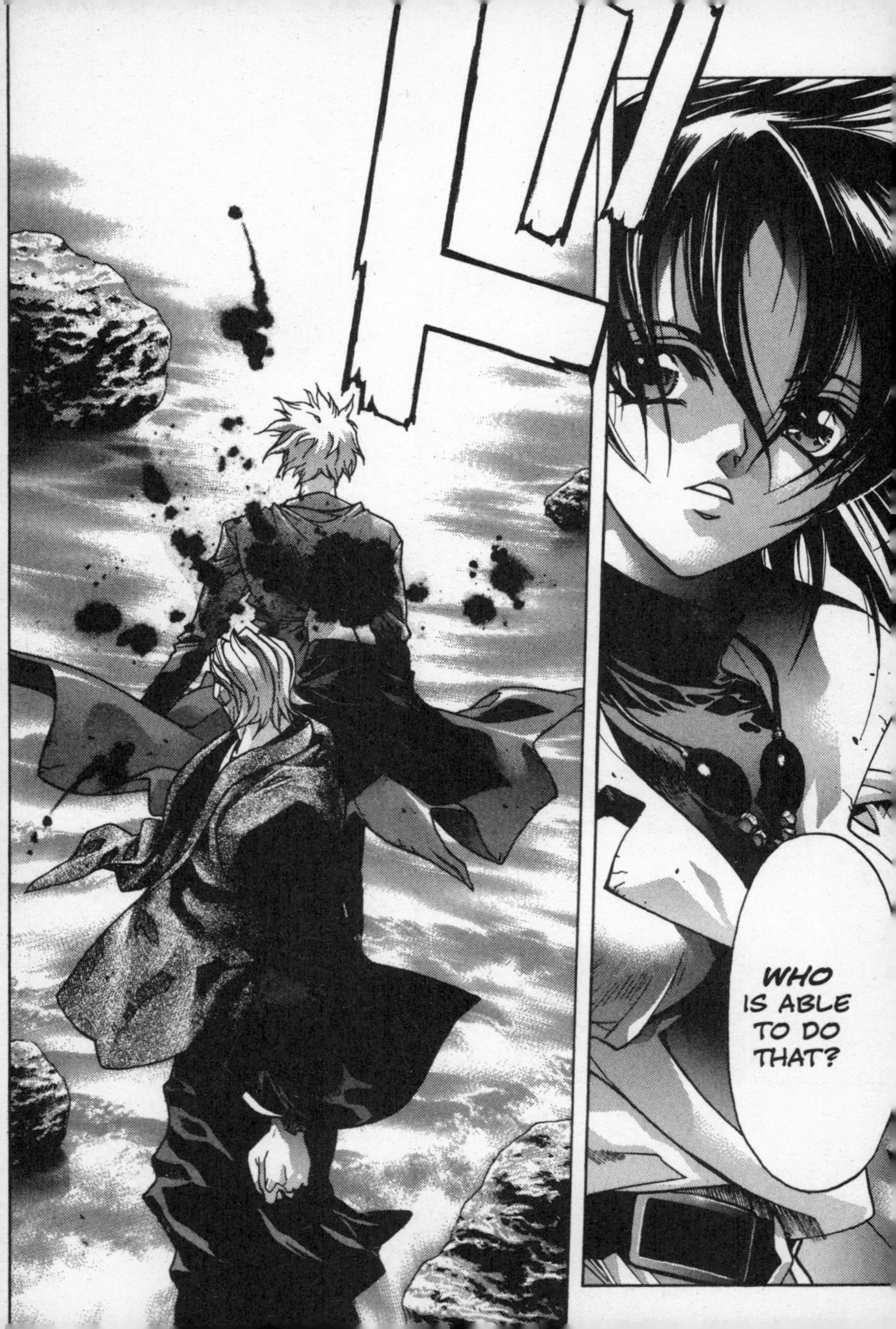
WHO IS ABLE TO DO THAT?

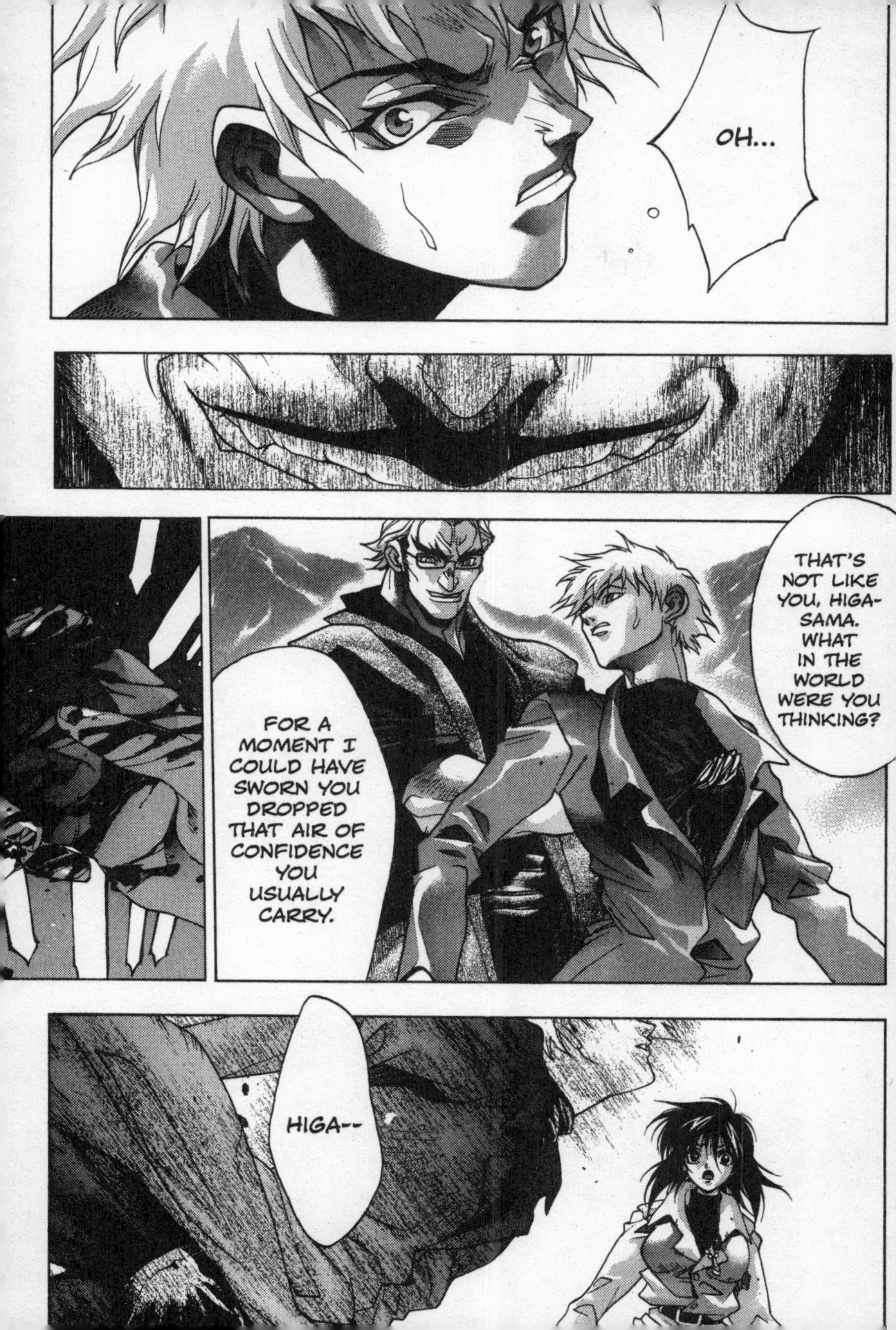
OH...
THAT'S NOT LIKE YOU, HIGA-SAMA. WHAT IN THE WORLD WERE YOU THINKING?
FOR A MOMENT I COULD HAVE SWORN YOU DROPPED THAT AIR OF CONFIDENCE YOU USUALLY CARRY.
HIGA--

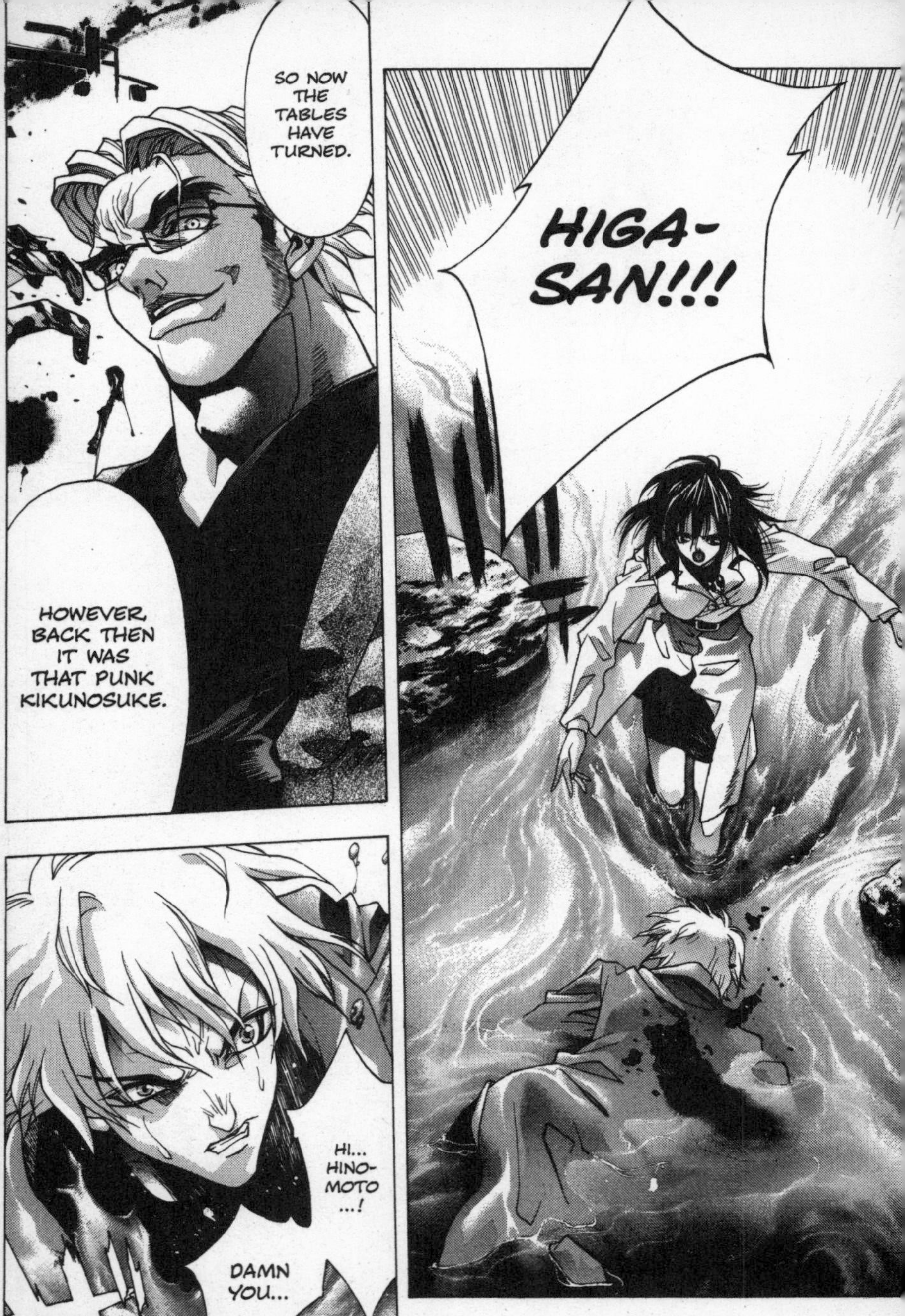
HIGA-SAN!!!
SO NOW THE TABLES HAVE TURNED.
HOWEVER BACK THEN IT WAS THAT PUNK KIKUNOSUKE.
HI... HINO-MOTO ...!
DAMN YOU...

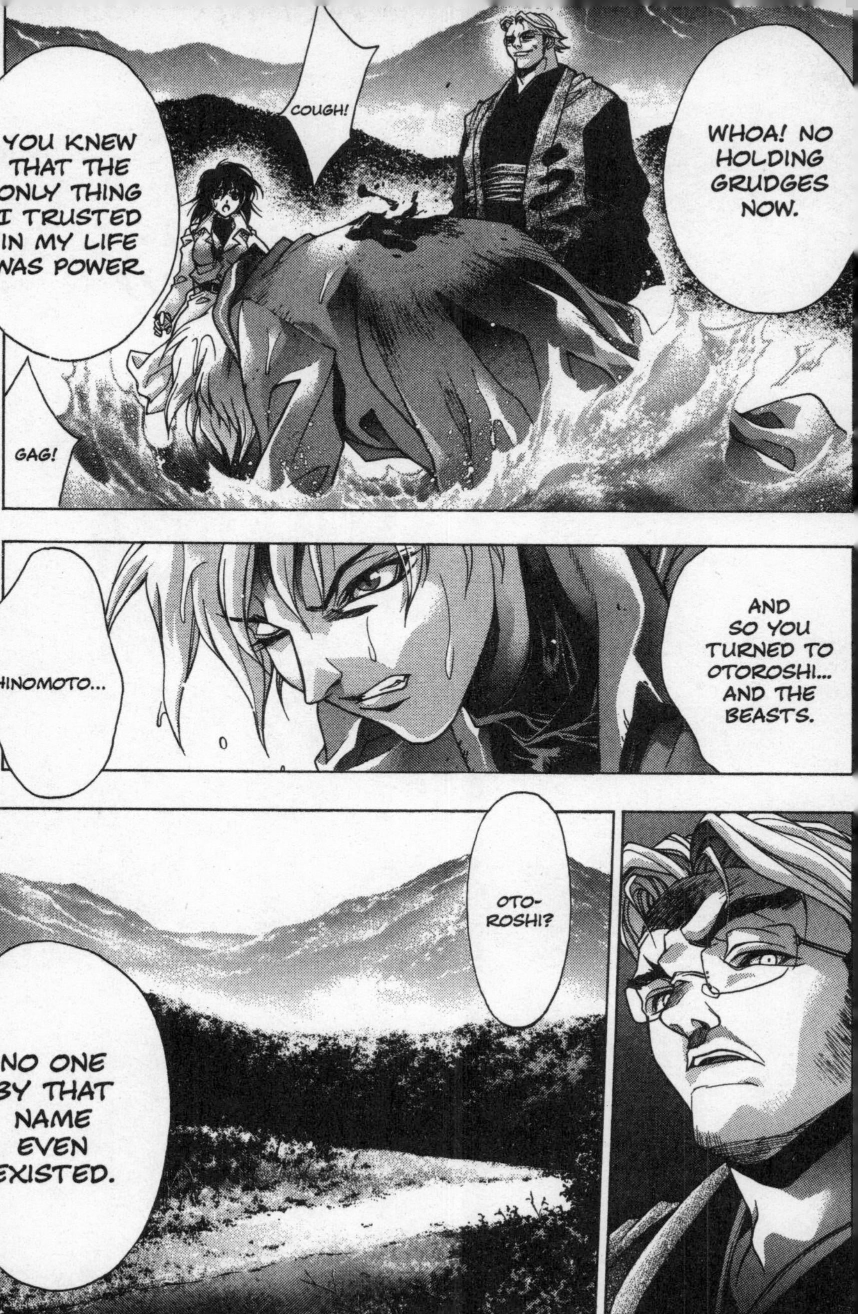
WHOA! NO HOLDING GRUDGES NOW.
COUGH!
YOU KNEW THAT THE ONLY THING I TRUSTED IN MY LIFE WAS POWER.
GAG!
AND SO YOU TURNED TO OTOROSHI... AND THE BEASTS.
HINOMOTO...
OTO-ROSHI?
NO ONE BY THAT NAME EVEN EXISTED.

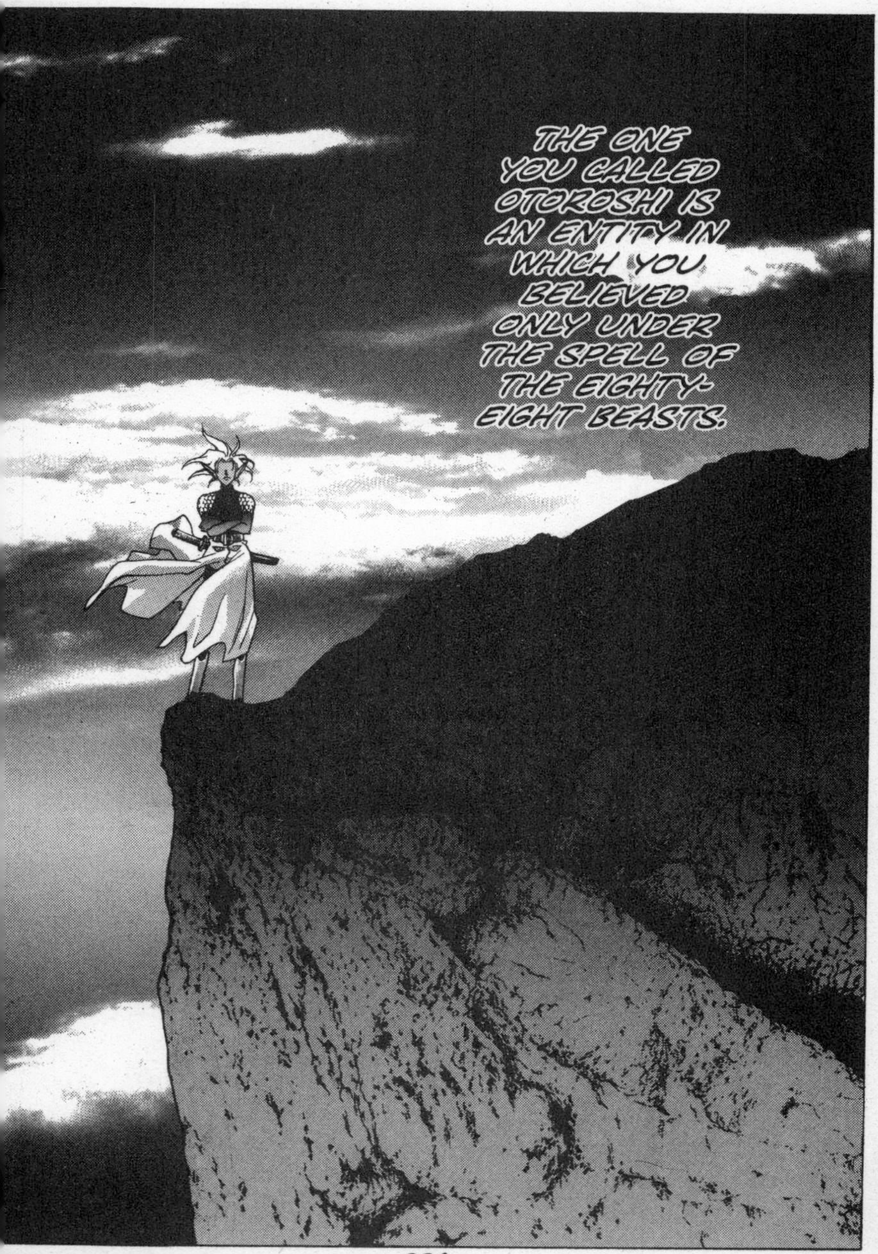
THE ONE YOU CALLED OTOROSHI IS AN ENTITY IN WHICH YOU BELIEVED ONLY UNDER THE SPELL OF THE EIGHTY-EIGHT BEASTS.

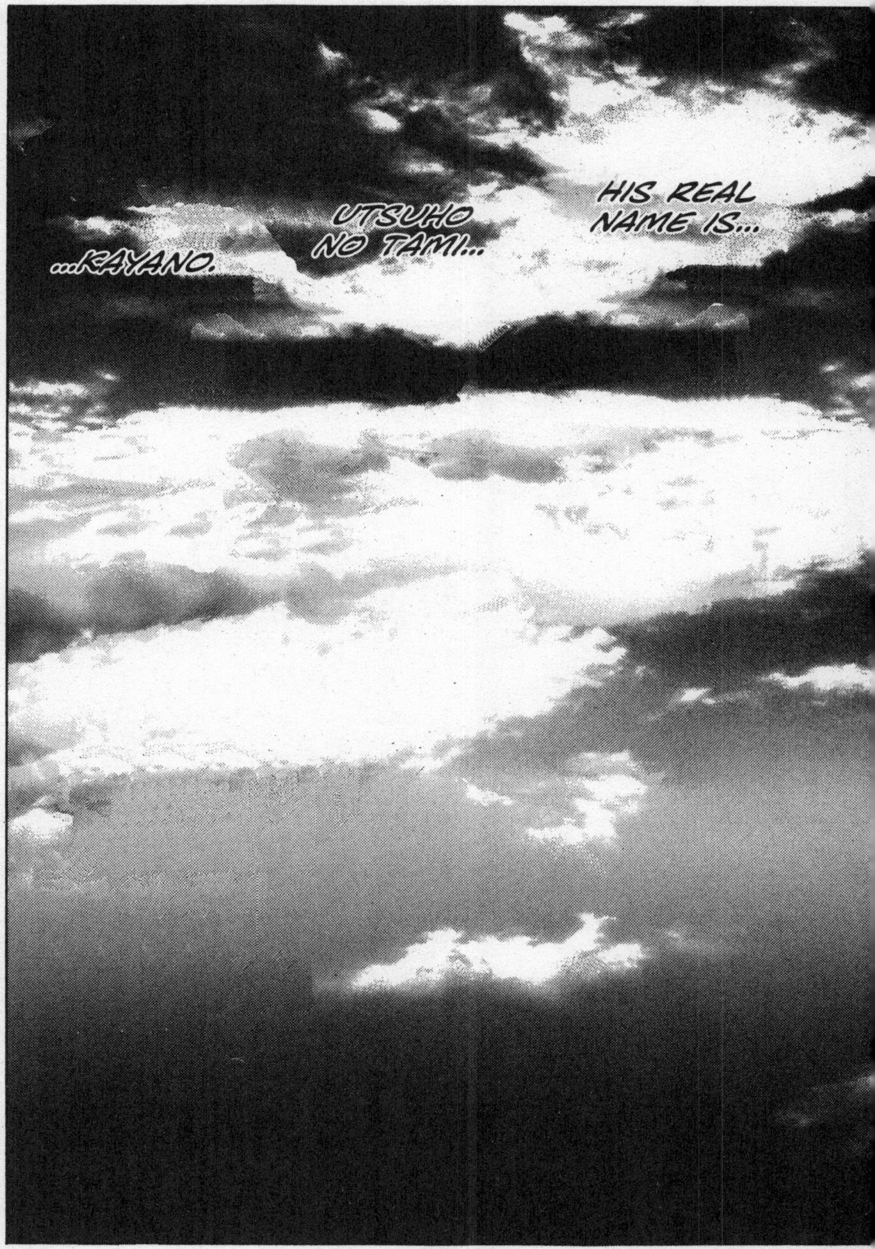
HIS REAL NAME IS...
UTSUHO NO TAMI...
...KAYANO.

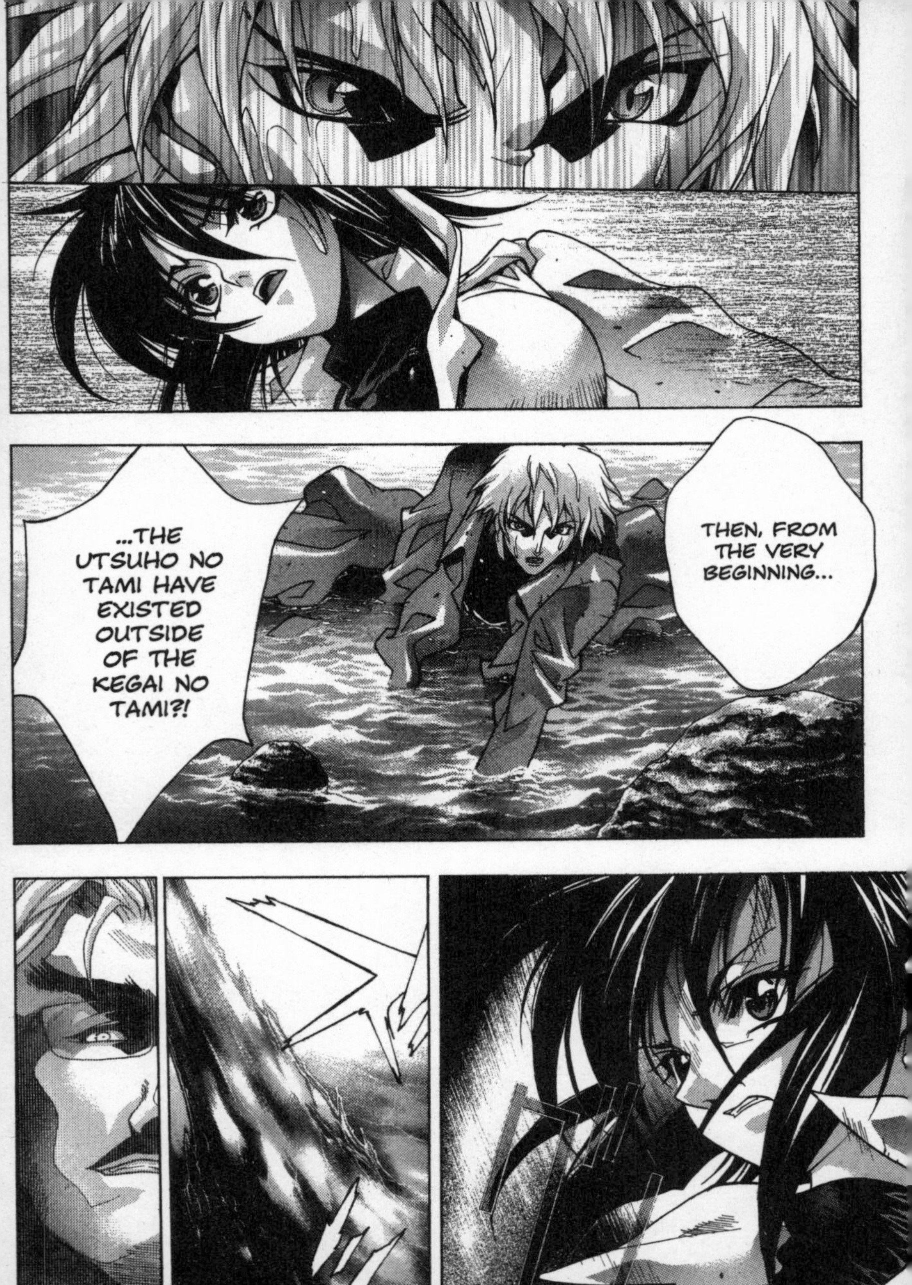
THEN, FROM THE VERY BEGINNING...
...THE UTSUHO NO TAMI HAVE EXISTED OUTSIDE OF THE KEGAI NO TAMI?!

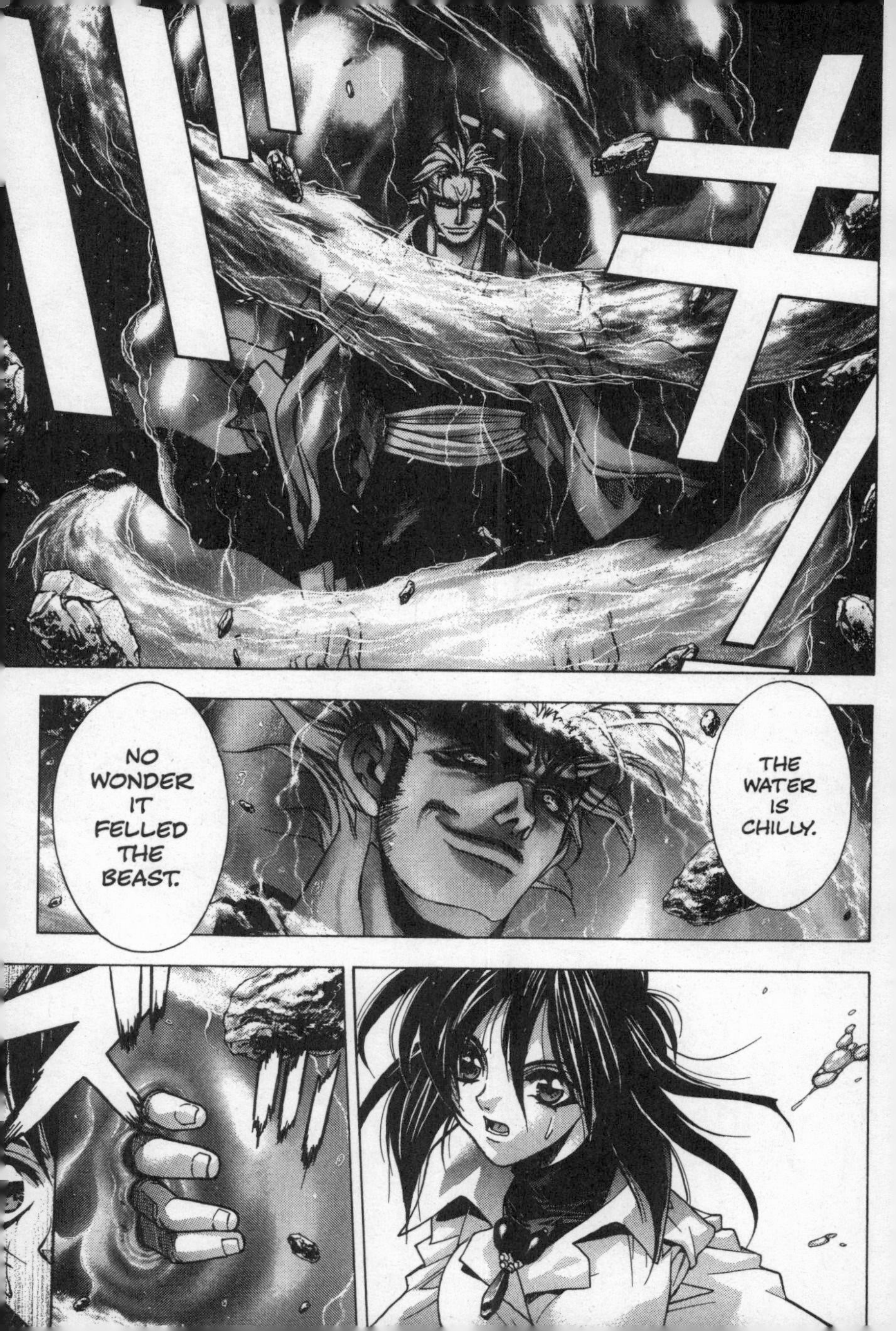
THE WATER IS CHILLY.
NO WONDER IT FELLED THE BEAST.

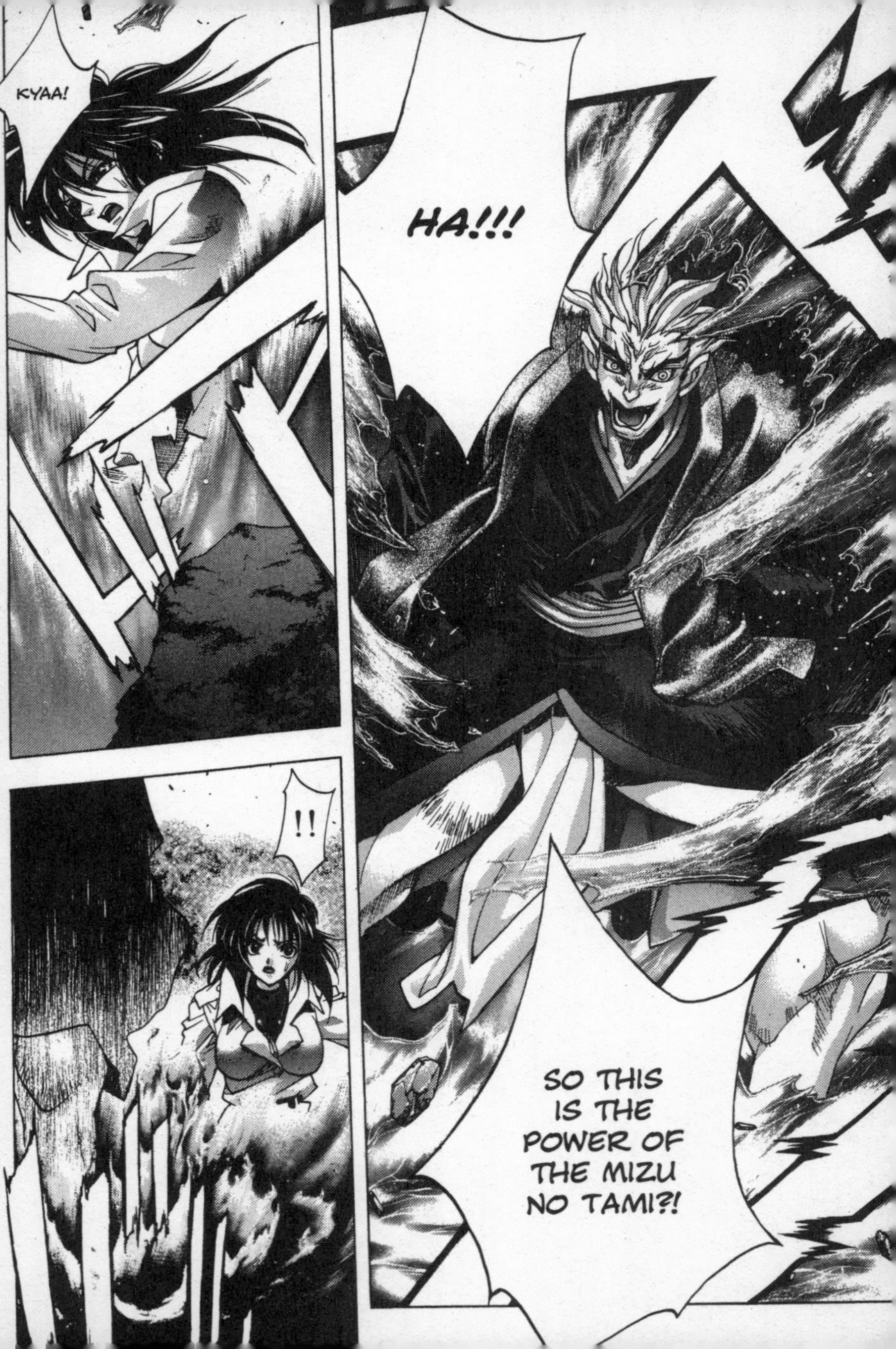
HA!!!
SO THIS IS THE POWER OF THE MIZU NO TAMI?!
KYAA!
!!

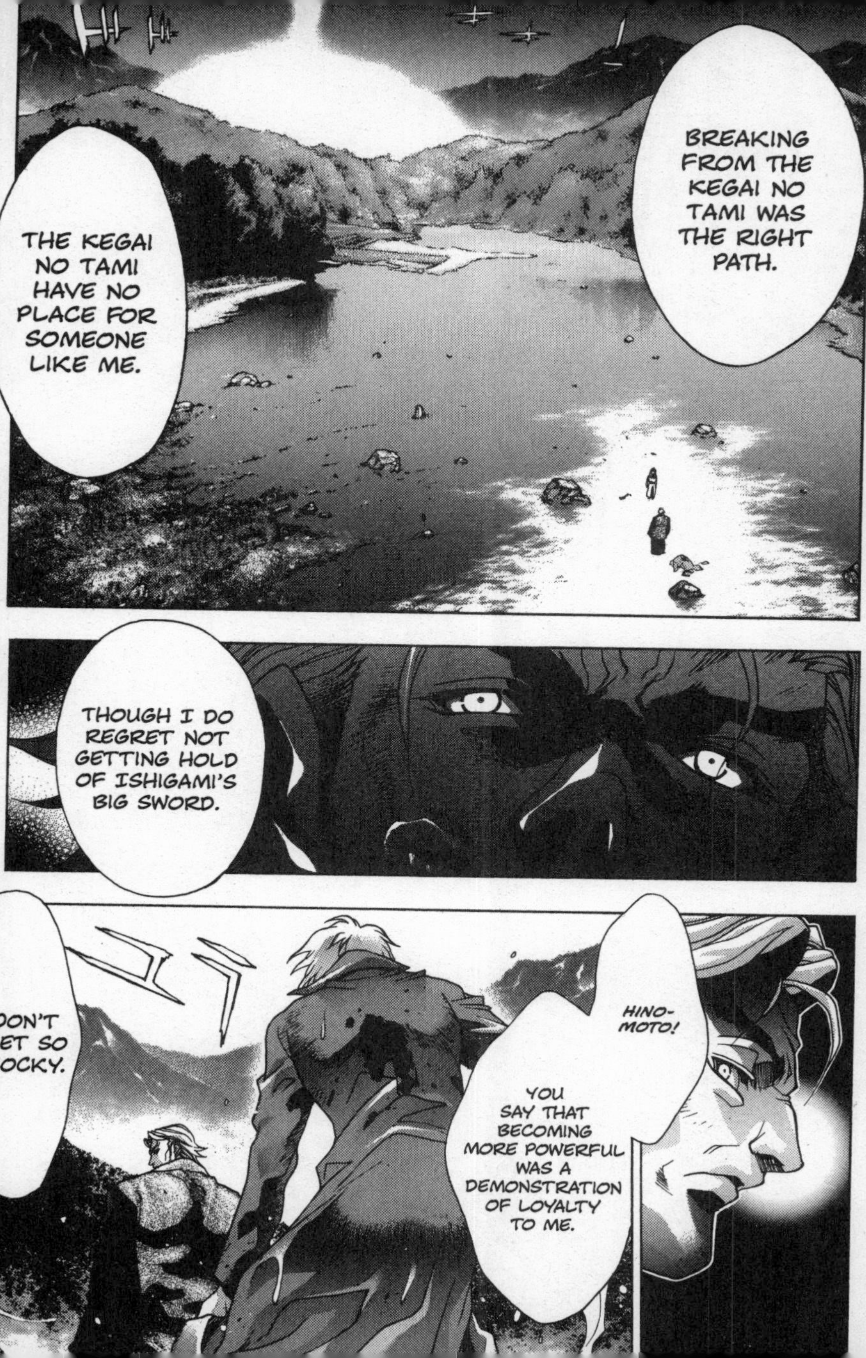
BREAKING FROM THE KEGAI NO TAMI WAS THE RIGHT PATH.
THE KEGAI NO TAMI HAVE NO PLACE FOR SOMEONE LIKE ME.
THOUGH I DO REGRET NOT GETTING HOLD OF ISHIGAMI'S BIG SWORD.
HINO-MOTO!
YOU SAY THAT BECOMING MORE POWERFUL WAS A DEMONSTRATION OF LOYALTY TO ME.
DON'T GET SO COCKY.

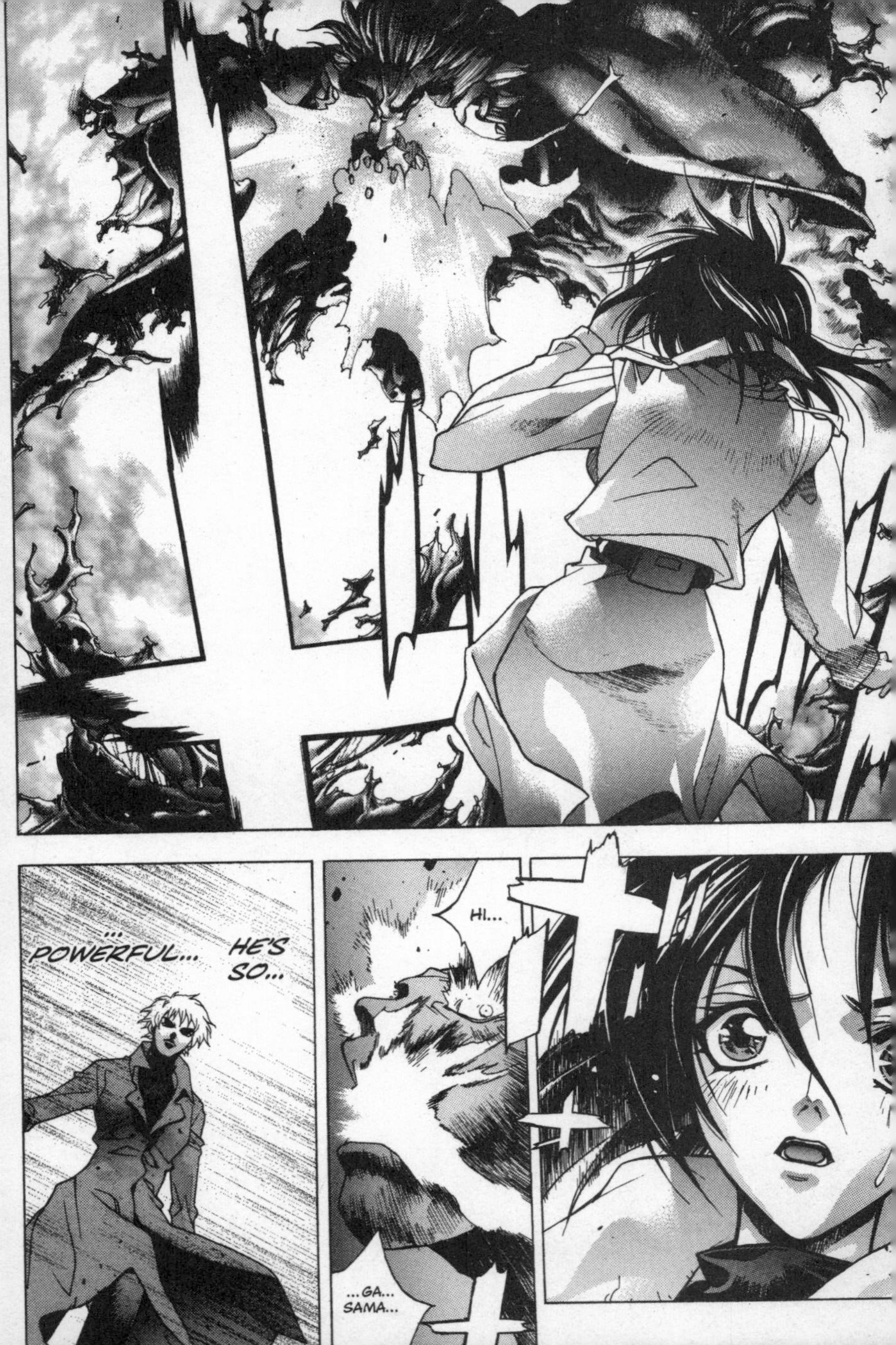
HI...
...GA... SAMA...
HE'S SO...
...POWERFUL...

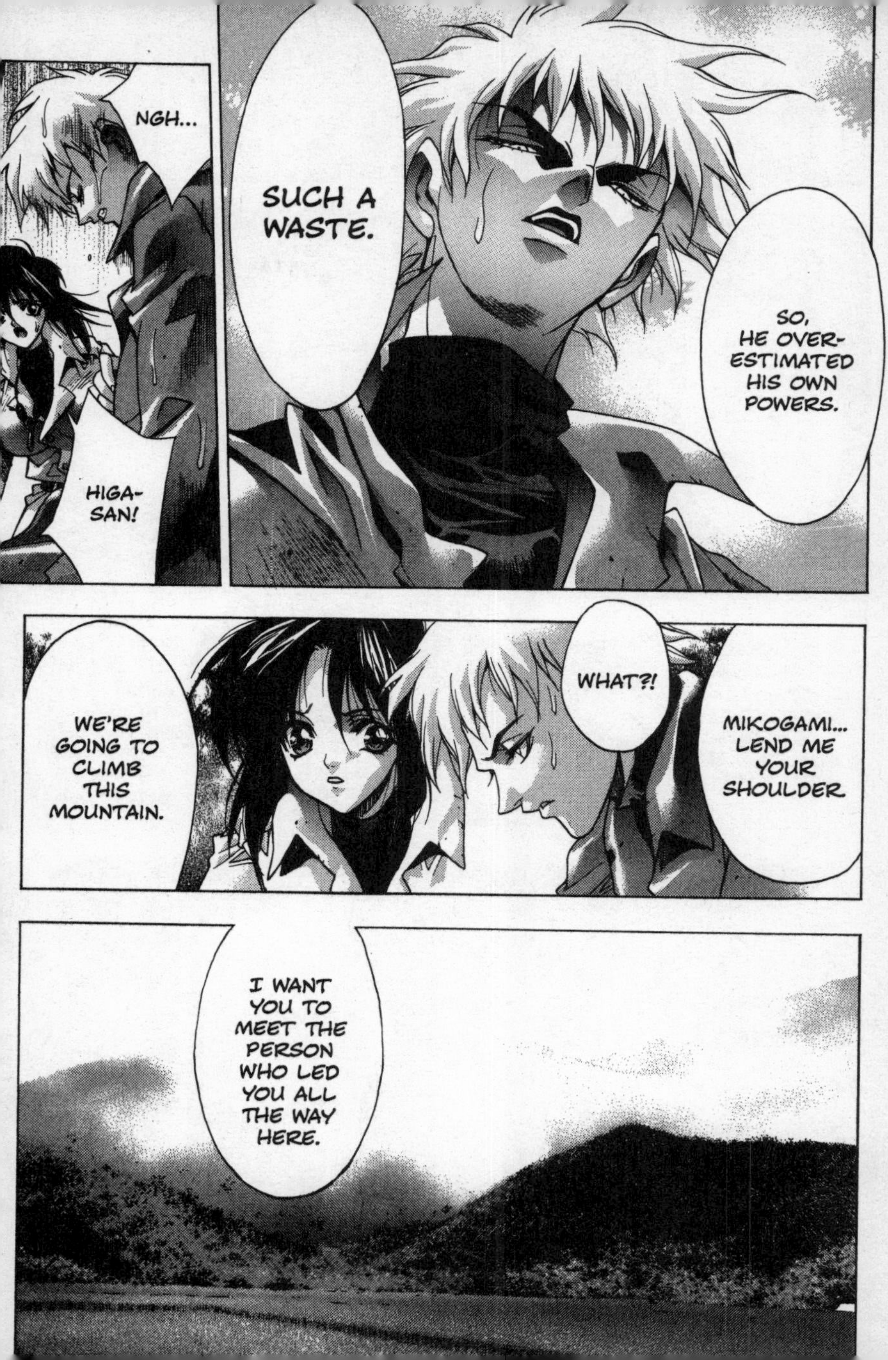
SO, HE OVER-ESTIMATED HIS OWN POWERS.
SUCH A WASTE.
NGH...
HIGA-SAN!
MIKOGAMI... LEND ME YOUR SHOULDER
WHAT?!
WE'RE GOING TO CLIMB THIS MOUNTAIN.
I WANT YOU TO MEET THE PERSON WHO LED YOU ALL THE WAY HERE.

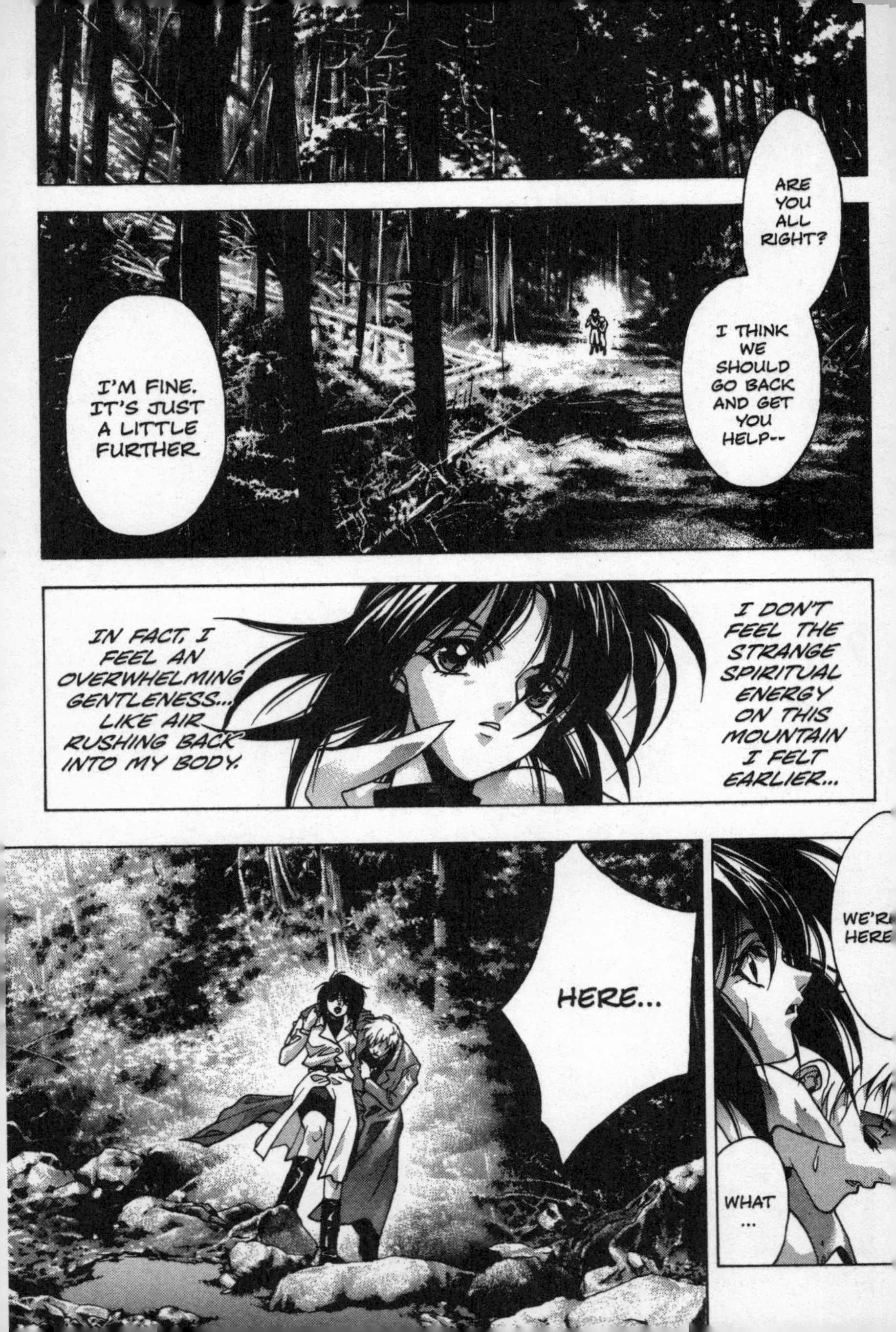
ARE YOU ALL RIGHT?
I THINK WE SHOULD GO BACK AND GET YOU HELP--
I'M FINE. IT'S JUST A LITTLE FURTHER
I DON'T FEEL THE STRANGE SPIRITUAL ENERGY ON THIS MOUNTAIN I FELT EARLIER...
IN FACT, I FEEL AN OVERWHELMING GENTLENESS... LIKE AIR RUSHING BACK INTO MY BODY.
WE'R HERE
WHAT ...
HERE...

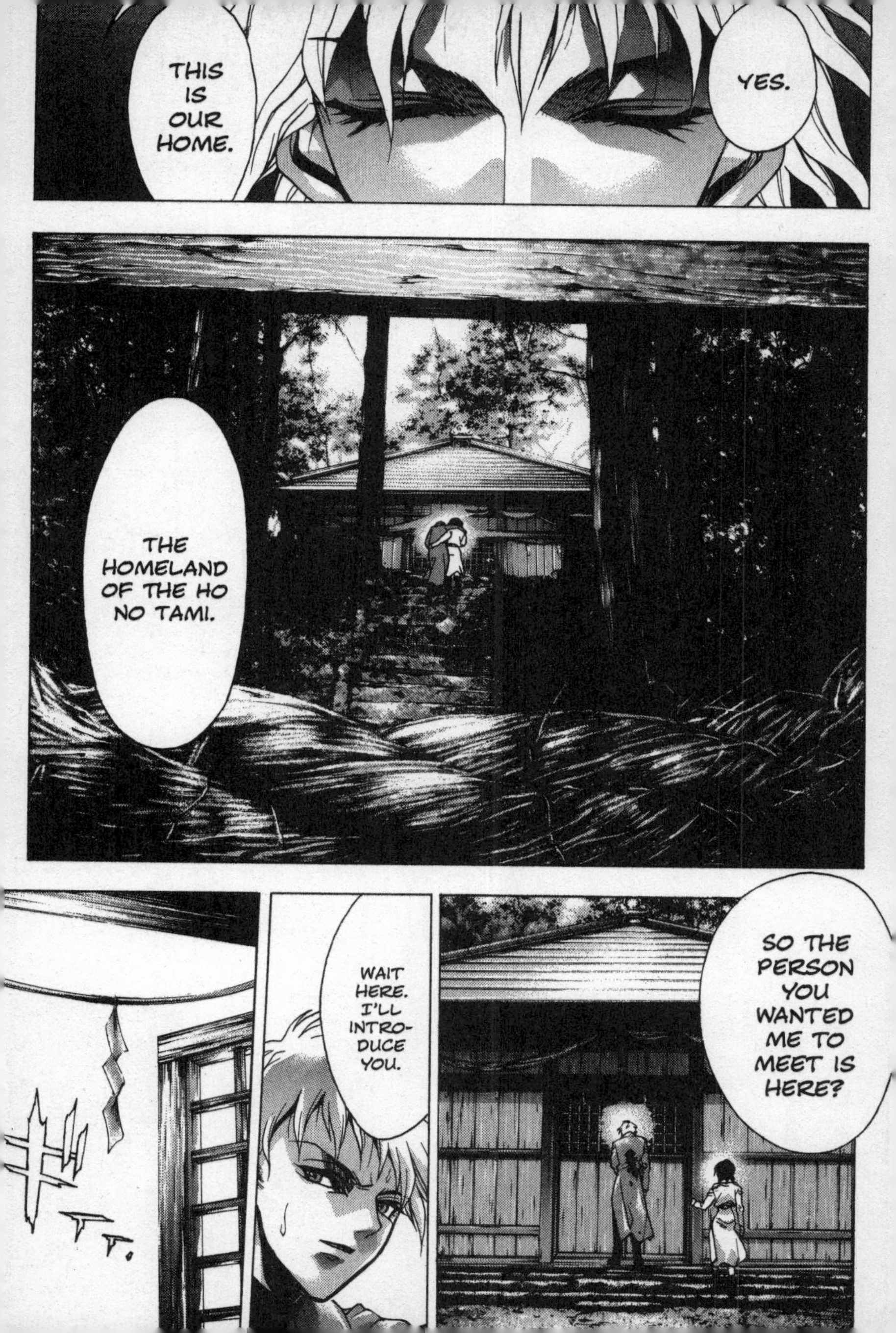
YES.
THIS IS OUR HOME.
THE HOMELAND OF THE HO NO TAMI.
SO THE PERSON YOU WANTED ME TO MEET IS HERE?
WAIT HERE. I'LL INTRO-DUCE YOU.

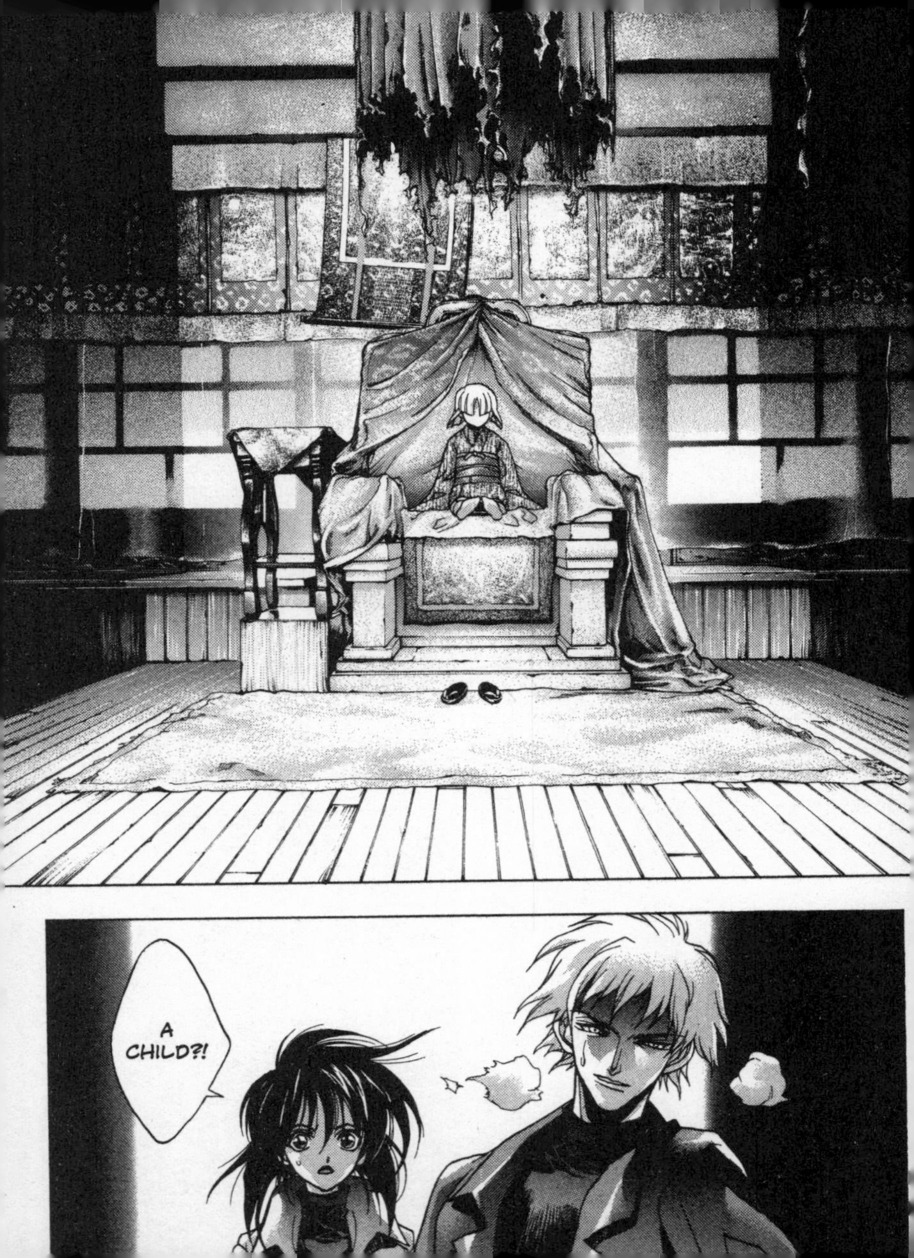
A CHILD?!

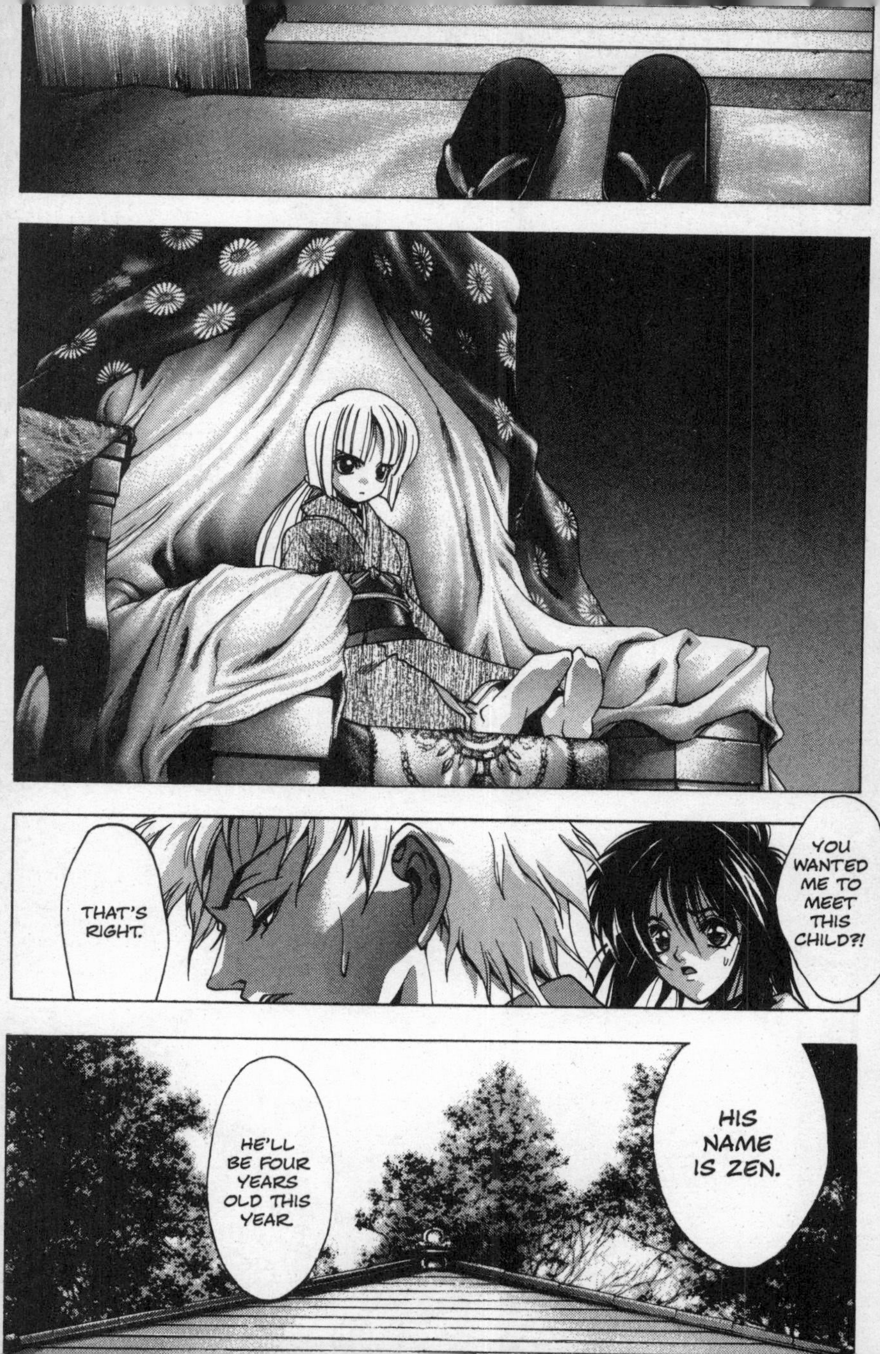
YOU WANTED ME TO MEET THIS CHILD?!
THAT'S RIGHT.
HIS NAME IS ZEN.
HE'LL BE FOUR YEARS OLD THIS YEAR

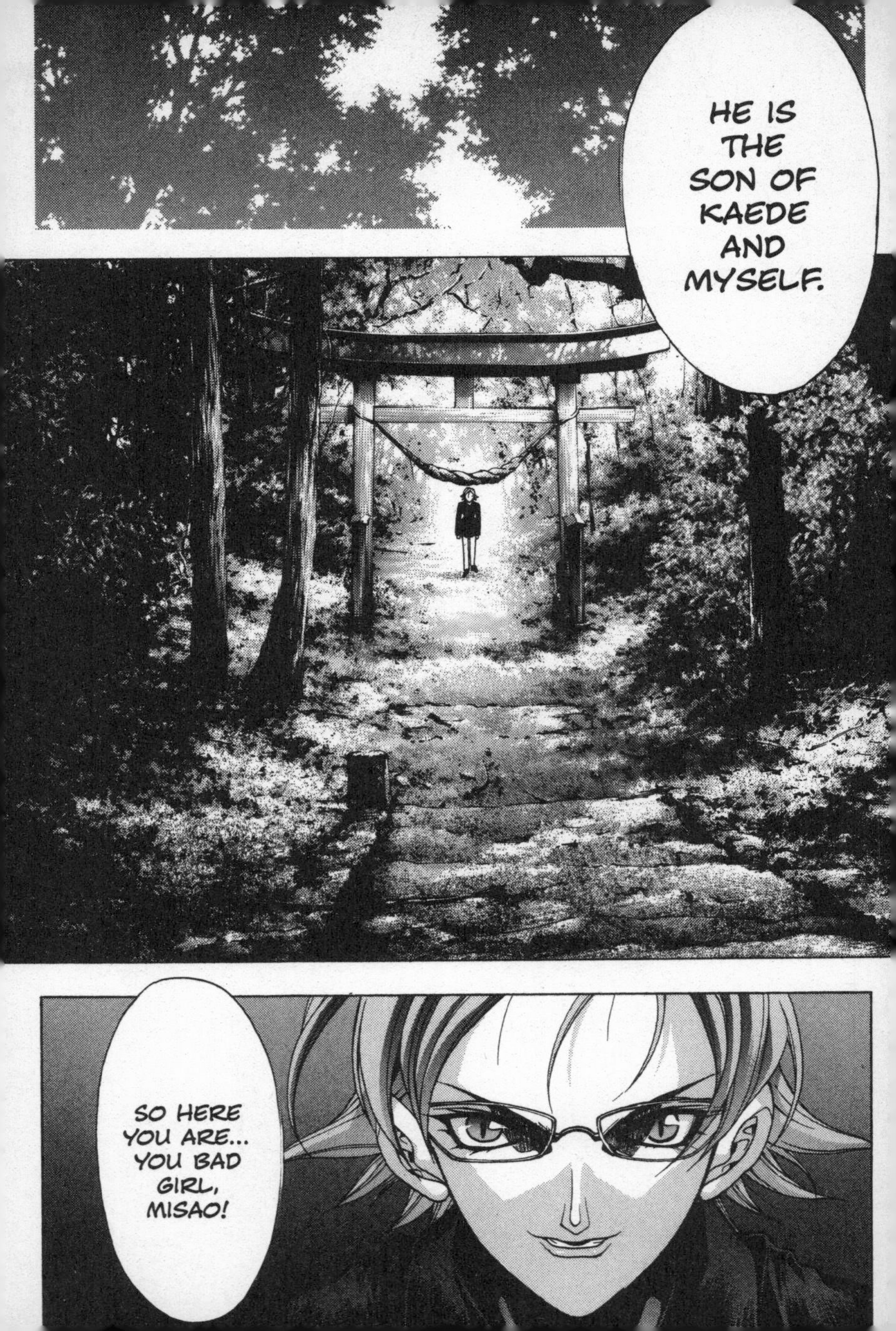
HE IS THE SON OF KAEDE AND MYSELF.
SO HERE YOU ARE... YOU BAD GIRL, MISAO!

To be continued in VOLUME **6**

In the next VOLUME of

KaMI·KaZE™

Keiko has been reborn as Princess Bishagatsuku, the daughter of Kayano, and great power within her has been awakened. Now a mighty enemy of Misao, Kamuro and Higa, Keiko still wears the face of a friend. Will this spell destruction for the heroic warriors? It all leads to a showdown in the homeland of the Mizu no Tami, where the last torii lies and where the final battle for humanity's salvation will take place. But how can our weary warriors expect to stave off the unstoppable Beasts?

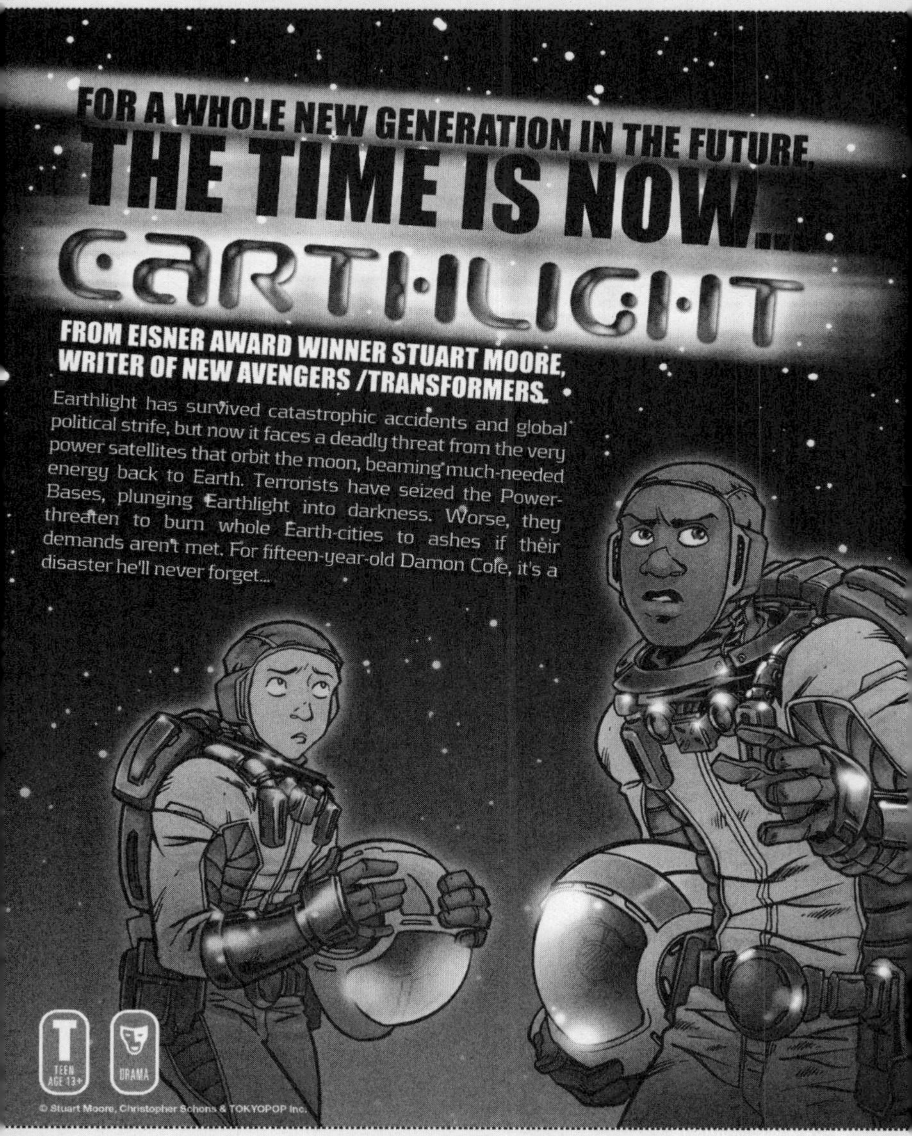
FOR A WHOLE NEW GENERATION IN THE FUTURE,
THE TIME IS NOW...
EARTHLIGHT
FROM EISNER AWARD WINNER STUART MOORE, WRITER OF NEW AVENGERS /TRANSFORMERS.
Earthlight has survived catastrophic accidents and global political strife, but now it faces a deadly threat from the very power satellites that orbit the moon, beaming much-needed energy back to Earth. Terrorists have seized the Power-Bases, plunging Earthlight into darkness. Worse, they threaten to burn whole Earth-cities to ashes if their demands aren't met. For fifteen-year-old Damon Cole, it's a disaster he'll never forget...
T TEEN AGE 13+
DRAMA
© Stuart Moore, Christopher Schons & TOKYOPOP Inc.

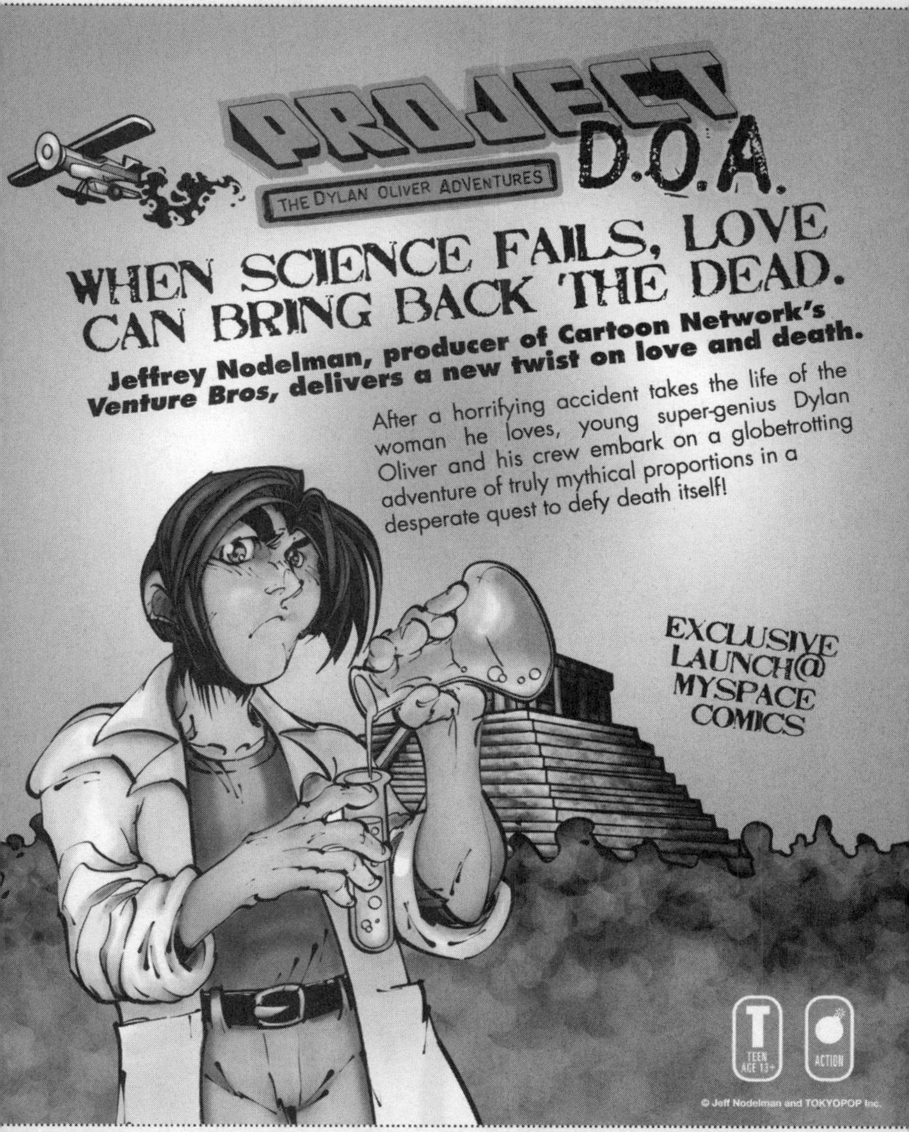
PROJECT D.O.A.
THE DYLAN OLIVER ADVENTURES
WHEN SCIENCE FAILS, LOVE CAN BRING BACK THE DEAD.
Jeffrey Nodelman, producer of Cartoon Network's Venture Bros, delivers a new twist on love and death.
After a horrifying accident takes the life of the woman he loves, young super-genius Dylan Oliver and his crew embark on a globetrotting adventure of truly mythical proportions in a desperate quest to defy death itself!
EXCLUSIVE LAUNCH@ MYSPACE COMICS
T TEEN AGE 13+
ACTION
© Jeff Nodelman and TOKYOPOP Inc.

STOP!

This is the back of the book.
You wouldn't want to spoil a great ending!

This book is printed "manga-style," in the authentic Japanese right-to-left format. Since none of the artwork has been flipped or altered, readers get to experience the story just as the creator intended. You've been asking for it, so TOKYOPOP® delivered: authentic, hot-off-the-press, and far more fun!

DIRECTIONS

If this is your first time reading manga-style, here's a quick guide to help you understand how it works.

It's easy... just start in the top right panel and follow the numbers. Have fun, and look for more 100% authentic manga from TOKYOPOP®!